Crescent

Camilla gulped hard, but she stopped crying as Anne's American optimism came to the fore and she promised them the futures they dearly wanted.

'Now you listen to me, Camilla. And you, too, Fatima and Leila. Nothing really bad is ever going to happen to us, do you hear me? Not to any of us. Not ever, not to *us*. I'm going to go to Boston and become a doctor and come back here and work in the American University Hospital, which just happens to be the best in the entire Middle East. I'll marry someone wonderful, and I'll be really happy. Leila's going to England to become a famous professor, and then she'll fall in love and marry somebody even richer and more famous than she is. And Fatima . . . why maybe Madame Kismet was a little bit right after all. Maybe Fatima's going to have a great love when she marries her cousin. As for you, Camilla, why, you're going to be as rich and famous as if you were the Queen of Lebanon. And you have Pierre, don't forget Pierre . . .'

As Camilla quietly started to cry again, Anne quickly veered away from the tragic present and conjured up a far brighter future. 'So! Anyway! Before long we'll all be back here together again. We'll all have terrific husbands and tons of kids, and we'll be so happy to live in Beirut, the most wonderful place in the whole world. And – yes, of course! – we'll be friends for alw

thing's going to be

would be.'

Also in Arrow by Laurie Devine

Nile
Saudi

Crescent

Laurie Devine

ARROW BOOKS

Arrow Books Limited
62-65 Chandos Place, London WC2N 4NW

An imprint of Century Hutchinson Limited

London Melbourne Sydney Auckland
Johannesburg and agencies throughout
the world

First published in Great Britain by André Deutsch
Limited 1988
Arrow edition 1989

Printed and bound in Great Britain by
Cox & Wyman Ltd, Reading

ISBN 0 09 951000 6

Nothing that is can pause or stay;
The moon will wax, the moon will wane,
The mist and cloud will turn to rain,
The rain to mist and cloud again,
Tomorrow be today.

Henry Wadsworth Longfellow

For Clair, Diane, Elaine and Monika,
and especially for Esther

Contents

Prologue	1
Waxing 1958-1961	49
Full Moon 1967-1976	381
Waning 1978-1982	691
Epilogue	847

Prologue

They were arm in arm and laughing, as always, as the four of them swept in from the blinding sun of the hot Beirut afternoon to the sudden gloom of the deserted nightclub foyer. Eyes unaccustomed to the dark, Anne groped forward until her white hand caught a fistful of the amber beads that curtained the entrance of the dark cave of the Crescent cabaret. As the red beads jangled and parted, all four of them stopped laughing and caught their breaths. The house lights were off, and on each of the tiny empty tables strewn around the gilded stage a candle glowed under a fluted red glass bulb. The air was stale with last night's cigarettes and heavy with the scent of fresh incense wafting from somewhere quite near, so that their quickening breaths grated on their throats. Backstage a reed pipe played and replayed the same undulating stanza of snake-charming music. Eerily the cut-out phosphorescent crescent moon that was the cabaret's symbol glowed in the dark above the stage.

None of them – not even Camilla – had ever seen her mother's nightclub like this before, and they weren't sure they wanted to be here now, when it was as menacing as the music in a movie just before something bad happens. Instinctively, with a touch of foreboding, they huddled close together. Anne took Fatima and Camilla by the hand as if she were ever ready to guide them through darkness and fear. Even Leila, always the boldest of the foursome, inched back towards the door and, as though by accident, edged so close that she brushed up against Camilla and Anne.

Suddenly a baby spotlight played on a red plush

corner banquette where a witchlike old gypsy sat huddled by herself. Fatima let out a frightened scream, and Leila was steeling herself to step forward and see what was going on when a musical laugh filled the room and all the lights came on.

'Surprise!' Nirvana, who was not only Camilla's mother but the darling of the Francophile Beirut jet set, danced on stage under the iridescent crescent moon and then hurled herself gracefully into Camilla's arms.

'Bébé!' She kissed her daughter on the lips and then, for good measure, an extravagantly Gallic three more times on both cheeks. Camilla, she was proud to see, looked like a girl should look – like a sex kitten starlet about to be cast in a Hollywood epic. Her long platinum hair tumbled over her rounded bare shoulders. The cleavage of her full, high breasts was displayed in daring *décolleté*, and the soufflé skirt of her flounced and flowered sapphire silk tea gown swirled fashionably out over her black patent spike heels. Perfect, almost perfect. Yet not quite. Nirvana pulled a compact from her pocket and dusted Camilla's shiny nose. She didn't have any rouge handy so she merely pinched her daughter's cheeks until they glowed with painful colour. Yes, now Camilla was perfect.

Nirvana craned her neck over Camilla's sweet fleshy shoulder so she could admire the reflection of her touching mother love in one of the smoky mirrors hinged to the wall. It was gratifying how everyone always insisted that she looked more like Camilla's sister than her mother. It was true, too. She was still as slim and lovely and in this kind light virtually as unwrinkled as dear Camilla. Nirvana all but blew a kiss at herself in the mirror. Scarlet was her colour. Despite what the dressmaker had said, these sequins and rhinestones and feathers had not been too much. She was on stage, after all. Her new act would be the talk of *la haute Beyrouth*. Briefly she considered adding another nest of feathers and some sprays of glitter to her peroxide blonde hair. And perhaps her skirt could be just *un centimètre* shorter?

Nirvana turned her attention to the three others who had been her daughter's constant companions ever since their first year at AUB. Everyone knew the American University of Beirut was by far the best and most famous school in the country. The contacts alone were almost worth the exorbitant tuition. As she gushed her breathless greetings in what one of Beirut's most avidly read gossip columnists had once called her 'enchanting patois' of French, Arabic and English, Nirvana kissed and hugged with gusto. Yet, squinting in the dim light, Nirvana was all the while critically appraising the clothes, coiffures, and most of all the soft glowing faces of these fresh young women whom she fervently hoped no one would ever guess were a generation younger than herself.

'Leila! *Chérie! Mon ange! Ma chou! Ma petite mignonne!*' Shrewdly, as Nirvana rattled off the endearments, she calculated, down to the piastre, how much the Palestinian Muslim girl must have paid for that tapered white linen sheath dress – Dior's 'New Look' – she would know those slinky lines anywhere – even if it was copied for a fraction of its original cost by a fleet-fingered Beirut dressmaker rather than ordered from a Rive Droite showroom. Leila was as canny about fashion as she was about everything else. This one was too smart for her own good. Too skinny, too. Even without that long-line girdle all of them dutifully struggled into these days, Leila could have modelled the new chemise dresses on a Parisian catwalk. She had no breasts, hips or *derrière*. Still, Nirvana had to admit the girl had elegance. Always her white gloves were immaculate, the seams of her silk stockings were straight, her black leather pumps were polished. This one never had a shiny nose. The hair, too, was new –

Nirvana spotted the tell-tale fireglow of henna in the curls. Pity the girl wasn't a Christian. With her style and class, Leila could have gone everywhere, done everything, even married almost as well as her own dear Camilla.

Not, she thought, that Leila's own connections weren't, in their Muslim way, impeccable. When Israel had still been Palestine, her family had run Haifa's thriving trade marts from a villa atop Mount Dan. Even now, despite what everyone euphemistically and politely called *al-nakba*, 'the disaster' that had befallen the Palestinians a decade ago, the Shahines were still filthy rich. It was rumoured that Leila's father could make or break a Lebanese prime minister, and Nirvana would kill to get an invitation to one of his extraordinarily *de bon ton* little dinner parties. So far, despite their daughters being in each other's pockets for so many years, Nirvana had only been invited to three of the family's gigantic and not-so-exclusive charity balls. The Shahines were too uppity for their own good. The way they carried on, you'd think God had given them Lebanon to make up for Palestine. This one, this Leila, didn't fool Nirvana for a minute. She was a cold little chit, never missing a trick with those too-bright black sloe eyes. Still, she and her kind were worth cultivating. One never knew whom or what one would need some dark day in the future. Perhaps the world would turn upside down, and Leila's family would sign her up for a long-term run in a cabaret atop the Jerusalem Hilton.

'Anne, my sweet darling! It has been – how you say? – too tall since I see you! No, too long! Let me look at you! So beautiful, always so beautiful!' And always, Nirvana added to herself, so terribly underdressed. The American favoured mannish beiges, navys, blacks, whites, greys, all of it always so boringly tailored. But her figure – even though she, like Leila, was too thin for the oriental voluptuary's taste – wasn't all that bad. At least she had curves where a man itched to feel them. Yet Nirvana could never understand why Anne didn't flaunt those long lithe pin-up legs. If she herself had legs like Anne's, she would wear short-shorts all the time. She would look so sensational that she would stop the traffic on al-Hamra, for a certainty they would put her picture in the paper and she would start a new fad.

Nirvana's eyes all but rolled at the thought. Too bad Anne's disaster of a New England Puritan mother wasn't capable of teaching the girl how to make the best of herself. Anne's Jewish father was a sweet old thing, a bit eccentric when he went on and on about those dusty piles of rubble left here by the ancient Romans, but after all it had a certain cachet in Levantine society to be the head of the archaeology department at AUB. The mother, however, had not a *soupçon* of taste, and after twenty-five years here she still couldn't speak comprehensible French much less Arabic. Nirvana couldn't stand it when, in that braying nasal whine of hers, she would always manage to imply that nothing in Beirut could ever measure up to her precious Boston. With a mother like that, no wonder Anne didn't know how to make the most of herself.

Nirvana would have liked to take this girl in hand, for Anne after all was her favourite. She had long been a good friend not only to Camilla but, more surprisingly, to Nirvana herself. What was it about this young American that made others trust her so? Nirvana remembered one occasion, when Anne had been staying the night; Camilla had gone to bed and she and Anne had sat up until the early hours talking like friends of exactly the same age. For once she had let her own façade slip and poured out tearful confidences about all the men who had done her wrong. She had even broken her cardinal rule and talked about Michel, her first husband and the love of her life, the Vichy French officer who had abandoned her and Camilla when the

Allies chased him and his kind out of Lebanon in 1941. Funny, how she hardly ever thought of Michel anymore. She had believed for so long that having him and then losing him were the only two facts that mattered in what she used to regard as her cracked and jagged life. But she had been young then, young like these girls, and too vulnerable.

For a fleeting second she thanked God that, even though the price be wrinkles, sags and varicose veins, she was young no longer.

When, later, she had wondered why she had chosen Anne for her confidante, she had decided that she liked the way the girl listened without interrupting or hurrying things along or attempting to steer the conversation around to herself. And then there were those sensitive brown eyes of hers that never seemed to judge, only forgive. Nirvana could hardly wait for Anne to go off to America to finish her training and then come back and stay here for ever as a fully-fledged doctor. She would trust this one with all that ailed her, although she would probably still dash off to those divine Swiss plastic surgeons now and then for a little nipping and tucking. In the meantime, however, she would have liked to take comb and scissors to Anne's unruly mess of thick black curly hair, and then dress her up in sex-pot high heels, clinging cashmere sweaters, and swishy taffeta skirts. Her heart-shaped face was pretty enough, but she badly needed to accent those extraordinary eyes with smouldering splashes of colour. She could use rouge, too, and glossy jungle red lipstick. Or maybe not. Maybe it was just as well that neither Anne nor anyone else ever outshone her own Camilla.

'Fatima! *Habibi! Ahlen wa sahlen . . .* ' As Nirvana's gaze fell on the last of the four, her easy patter almost faltered. She never did and never would understand what these other three lovely flowers of Lebanese society saw in this pitiful little Muslim Shia weed from the south. Despite the friendship of her betters, despite four years of exposure to Western styles and Western ways, Fatima still insisted on wearing that ghastly white scarf and those horrid rayon cabbage-rose print dresses in garish shades of magenta, orange and chartreuse. She was a peasant, this one. Yet as Fatima shyly smiled at Nirvana, the older woman felt a touch of envy. Even in those awful clothes, the girl was a knockout. *Y'Allah!* Oh God, her skin was fabulous. *Yaadra!* Oh Virgin Mary, she would do anything – pay any price, go anywhere – to have skin like that. With that skin and those big innocent doe eyes Nirvana herself could wrap any man in the world around her little finger or, more to the point, around her nearly firm thighs. Ah, well. Even without the skin, eyes and innocence of young Fatima, Nirvana reminded herself that she wasn't doing so badly after all, considering how she had begun. Long ago, so long ago that it almost seemed another life, back in her north Lebanese village she had quite rightly feared her father would kill her when he found her naked in the arms of one of his married friends. She had fled for her life from that suffocatingly conservative mountain eyrie down to Tripoli, where she had been forced to choose between the degradations of going to work as a maid or the glamour of gyrating as a belly dancer in one of the clubs down by the docks. After that, she had hardly looked back. Already she'd had three husbands and oodles of lovers, and she liked to think there were lots more to come. After all, the gypsy had promised her just that.

Remembering why she had invited her daughter and her friends to the cabaret, Nirvana gestured grandly to the old one hunched on the banquette. 'Darlings! This is Madame Kismet!' Her surprise, she said, as she guided the girls across the dance floor towards the old woman, was this exotic little fortune-teller she had found last week on a back street down by the port. She was thinking of using her in the club to circle the tables in the lulls between acts. She had thought that name up herself – it was perfect, no? She was going to try her out this afternoon on the girls, *lay la*, 'why not'? At a time like this, with all four of them about to graduate from the university and scatter to the four winds – Anne to America, Leila to England, Camilla to the heights of the Lebanese mountains, and Fatima back down to the wretched south – *especially* just a few days before '*ma petite fleur*' – she reached out and ran her fingers through Camilla's tousled hair – was about to marry that prince of Lebanese society, it would be great fun to have their fortunes told, '*n'est-ce pas?*' Nirvana rolled her eyes drolly as she whispered that the old woman had forecast more husbands for her, and then as she clapped her hands a boy scampered out from the kitchen with a brass tray covered with four small painted porcelain coffee cups. Nirvana blew a spray of theatrical kisses as she disappeared behind the scarlet stage curtain. '*Bonne chance!*'

'*Yaadra!* Holy Virgin, she has done it again.' Camilla thrust out her lower lip in the baby pout everyone said made her look more than ever like Brigitte Bardot. This was not the first time her notorious mother had mortified her. She would have liked to apologize to her friends for her mother's behaviour, but she was after all her mother's daughter and had been taught that a pretty woman never had to say she was sorry for anything except looking less than her best. Even so, though she would never admit her embarrassment in words, she couldn't stop herself from blushing. She felt her face go hot and remembered that her mother always said she was at her prettiest that way, her skin petal-soft and the colour of her flowery namesake. Her mother, her mother, would she ever manage to shake off her mother? Camilla felt that old familiar impulse to cut and run from this uncomfortable moment to another that would surely be better or at least more diverting. '*Yalla*, let's get out of here. I must have a drink.'

'Not so fast.' Anne had seen that tell-tale flush and guessed at the emotion that had caused it. Once, when the girls had all come to Anne's for what they imagined was an authentic American 'pyjama party' with Cokes and hamburgers and Hershey bars, Camilla had suddenly blurted out that she wished her mother had been anyone else – even one of the old beggarwomen who lurked in the alleyways selling matches – rather than the Levant's most scandalous *chanteuse*. Anne was not about to let her friend down today, or any day. She would do her best to save the situation, even if it meant having to put up with the rantings of this crazed old lady. 'I've never had my fortune told,' she announced, admitting to herself that, in a way, she wouldn't mind listening to what Madame Kismet had to say. In a matter of months she would be leaving hot Beirut for cold Boston, where she was finally going to achieve her heart's desire and study to be a doctor. Surely fledgling doctors were supposed to be sceptical of the supernatural. Yet she was curious about what the gypsy would see in her future – whether she would make it through medical school, whom she would marry, whether her life on the whole would be happy and full and rich. Just this once, she would indulge her impulse and take a peep at the future. Anne sank down on the banquette and caught Leila's eye.

The Palestinian nodded. 'I've never done this before, either.' She liked to think that she and Anne were the co-captains of their tight little quartet. So long as the two of them stuck together, Camilla and Fatima almost always fell into line. She took off her gloves, sat down next to Madame Kismet, and tapped a fresh Craven A cigarette from her monogrammed gold-plated case. As she fitted it into her ivory and bamboo cigarette holder and lit it with one careless wave of her Cartier lighter, she leaned confidently back and waited for the old biddie to confirm the promise of her own doubtlessly bright future.

'I don't know,' Fatima hedged. Nervously she tucked a stray lock of her lustrous black hair under the headscarf she still insisted on wearing even on the free-and-easy streets of Beirut. For the past four years Leila had waged an unsuccessful campaign to persuade her to fling off the repressive past and let her hair fall free on her shoulders. But Fatima came from a very religious family. She was a strict Shia Muslim, and she took pride in clinging stubbornly to the old Muslim ways. She felt that she had won a victory of sorts when Leila had given her this finely embroidered raw silk white scarf on her last birthday. Yet still, even now, Fatima's uncertain struggles to reconcile East and West continued.

Leila saw Fatima looking longingly at her packet of expensive foreign cigarettes, and so the Palestinian shook out a filter-tip, placed it between Fatima's lipstickless lips, and lit it with a flourish. As Fatima inhaled the smooth rich tobacco, she reminded herself that even some of the best women back in her conservative village smoked. Some puffed away the long evenings on *nargilehs*, water-pipes kept aglow by charcoal fires, and the others rolled their own from the small leather bags of tobacco that dangled from their waists. But even Fatima's simple pleasure in this single cigarette was tainted by ambivalence. None of the women and few of the men could afford the indulgence of Craven As. Soon she, too, would be back in the village rolling her own harsh lumpy cigarettes. Maybe it would have been better if she had never developed a taste for what she would soon have to give up.

Fatima fervently wished, as the expensive smoke swirled around her headscarfed head, that she were safe back inside her uncle's house in the teeming

Muslim Basta Shia quarter. She knew very well that she wasn't supposed to be in this godless nightclub, no matter that it was only the afternoon and no one was drinking forbidden alcohol yet or doing what she imagined were other unspeakable things to near-naked women. She had come along against her will, because Camilla teased her and Anne coaxed her and Leila bullied her. But she hoped to God that no one she knew from her village – especially her brothers! – ever found out that she had gone inside a Christian-owned nightclub. Her good name could be sullied for ever if anyone from her village found out. Those who had shaken their heads and prophesied doom when she won her scholarship and moved north to Beirut would say this was what came from breaking the old taboos. She would be remembered not only as the first but as the last girl from her village ever to go to university. If her brothers knew, they might write to her dear father where he worked far away in West Africa, and then . . . ? Her father might even change his mind and call off that marriage he had planned for her when she was just a little girl.

Fatima clenched her teeth so hard that she almost bit through the cigarette's filter. She wondered if it would be a great shame or a wondrous blessing if she didn't have to marry her cousin Ali. He had been nice enough as a youth – she remembered him as being a gentler soul than the other rough and tumble boys in their village. But she hadn't seen him for seven long years, not since he had gone off to immerse himself in religious study with the most learned Shia mullahs in Iran and Iraq. By now he might be fat or have one of those greasy Persian beards. What would it be like if, instead of marrying Ali when he returned to Lebanon this year or next, she could marry someone she truly loved – if she could have a romance like those she saw in the Rivoli and Empire cinemas with her friends?

She envied Camilla, whose love match with Pierre was just like those in the movies. On how many sultry afternoons and humid nights had she, Anne, Leila and Camilla sat around speculating about what it would be like to be loved and married? The other three always said they could never marry for anything but love. They always gave her a hard time when she admitted that she would probably end up marrying the cousin of her father's choice. Often they dared her to be brave and independent and set off – just as Anne and Leila sometimes dreamily said they were about to do – to find her one true love on her own.

Fatima sighed as she looked over at the fortune-teller. Madame Kismet hunched miserably at the table, rubbing her hands together as if her old bones were cold even on this hot early summer afternoon. The gypsy's face was furrowed with a lifetime of disappointments and defeats. If this tired old woman, who looked as beaten down by life as one of her ancient aunts, could give her some wise advice on how to live a good, clean, happy life – then she, too, would eagerly thrust out her hand. But Fatima believed that all the important answers to all the crucial questions lay not with this Madame Kismet but in the sacred words of the Koran. And now it seemed her friends were not content just to have dragged her inside this nightclub. Now they wanted her to go one step further and participate in something that she suspected was wrong. She would have to answer some day, before Allah, for all the free choices of her life. Fatima remembered how her Uncle Muhammad would always blink his eyes to demonstrate how short were these lives of trial and testing. Life was fleeting, but paradise would last an eternity. 'In the Holy Koran there is much about God knowing the future but nothing about His will being spelled out in coffee grounds. Maybe it's *haram*, "forbidden", to be superstitious and do as Nirvana says.'

'Oh, for God's sake, Fatima.' It annoyed Leila to see how slavishly Fatima insisted on carrying out the letter of the Koranic law. Sometimes it even made Leila feel a little guilty that she herself didn't do the same. Yet when it came to the pinch – for instance, when it was four-thirty in the morning and the muezzin call to dawn prayers was sounded – Leila hardly ever rolled out of bed and made her ablutions and bowed and salaamed to God. She wished, just once, she could believe that, over in her depressing slum, Fatima was having a lie-in as well. Leila could see no reason, now, in 1958, for a modern Arab woman to be a slave to so many outmoded conventions. Still, Fatima looked as if she was about to bolt out of the door. If she flounced off, the rest of them would undoubtedly follow, and she herself wouldn't get to hear the old gypsy reveal the gratifying details of her wonderful life to come. Accordingly, Leila tried to soothe Fatima's overactive religious conscience. 'There's not a thing in the Koran about gypsies and the future. Not one word. Remember, I could recite thirty-eight *surahs* of the Koran by the time I was eight. Only eight! I know the Koran! And even if there's not a single reference to anything as harmless as sitting down for a little entertainment like this – think of all the *surahs* about obeying your parents. Camilla's mother arranged this. Are you going to insist that Camilla fail to respect her mother's wishes?'

'Come on,' Anne coaxed. 'It'll be fun. And Leila's right. It's just a way to pass the time. It's not for real. She can't really see the future. None of us need believe what she says. It'll be like going to the movies.'

'Sit, Fatima, sit.' Because Leila was almost as fond of Fatima as she was of her toy poodle, she used the same tone of command she usually reserved for little Fifi. She meant that as a sincere compliment. Leila adored her dog, she let it sleep on her bed, she thought it was absurd that devout Muslims like Fatima considered even pampered pets like Fifi to be dirty and despicable. Yes, Fatima was as obedient and loyal and endearing and sometimes as dumb as a dog. Leila just wished she would stop being so damned good, and relax and live a little.

As Fatima fiddled uncertainly with her scarf, pulling it lower on her forehead with the instinct of an ostrich burrowing its head in the sand, Leila shifted tactics and exerted a little of her practised charm. She peppered Fatima with artful and totally unrelated Arabic compliments – she was like a flower, she said, like the moon, like the stars – until Fatima gave in and smiled back at her. Leila took satisfied sips of her coffee as Fatima perched doubtfully on the edge of her chair.

'*Mes amies*, you do not have to do this.' Camilla smiled tremulously. 'It could be *mal chance*.' Camilla was not ashamed of being superstitious. 'It is possible she will say to us something we do not want to hear. Something terrible – *un porte-guigne*, a jinx.'

What if – she added to herself, as she stole a look down at the flashing twenty-two carat diamond engagement ring she wore on her right hand – she would never be able to wear it even more proudly on her left hand, as a married woman does? Suppose Pierre wouldn't marry her after all? At the university she might not be as brilliant as Anne or Leila, but she wasn't stupid. She could tell, especially when she was thrown together with Pierre's catty sisters, that some of his family thought he was marrying beneath him. No matter how many times her mother told her to hold her head up high – '*Vous êtes française, bébé!* They're just Arabs, but your father *il était français!*' – still Camilla couldn't overcome the tawdry reality that her mother had once been a belly dancer. Pierre, however, was the only son of one of the most powerful Christian warlords in Lebanon. He could marry *anyone*. If he jilted her . . . Camilla's delicate stomach lurched.

She hadn't even told Anne that she had missed two periods, that her breasts were swollen and itchy, that she felt nauseous all the time. She wished now that she had never – *ever!* – given in to Pierre on the back seat of his Thunderbird convertible. She had been able to hold him off until they were officially engaged after Christmas, but after that . . . She would be ruined if Pierre at the last minute broke off their engagement. 'Forget this old woman. We can have instead some real fun. Drive up to the mountains. Have a swim in a *piscine*. Or maybe shop. *Mais oui*, yes, that is the best! We will go to the Souk al-Tawileh! I think, you know, all the time about my trousseau. It is possible that I do not have enough negligees. Yesterday – I forgot to tell you – I saw some very beautiful lounging pyjamas I must have. Red! *Décolleté!* Maybe—'

'By the way Pierre looks at you, you're not going to need *any* nightdresses, much less more of them.' Leila laughed and nudged Fatima, who primly chose to ignore the insinuation.

'No more shopping.' Anne was not about to waste another interminable afternoon watching Camilla try on every pretty article of clothing in Beirut.

'Why not?' Fatima was eager for almost any means to avoid the fortune-telling. Besides, she liked sitting in the ritzy shops watching Camilla pirouette in all those beautiful clothes.

'*Alors*, Fatima, we will go.' Camilla grabbed her purse.

'I'm staying.' Leila brought her tiny coffee cup to her lips with finality. 'I'm not afraid of a fortune-teller. Or the future.'

'Me neither.' Anne held up her cup. 'I think the way this works is that after we've drunk up, she flips over the cup and reads the grounds.'

Camilla shrugged, Fatima sighed, and the two of them gave in. Together they all silently sipped and swallowed and then waited for Madame Kismet to do what she had been paid to do.

The gypsy let them sit awhile, for she resented having been kept waiting all this time like a deaf and dumb servant. But then finally, when she had their full attention, she lifted her head and squinted at these four young women – each so very pretty, each so very privileged. She thought about her own daughters, old before their time, ruined by bad men and worse fates. In the end, for everyone, life was cruel. The gods delighted in making fools of men and women, and the devils were always on the lookout for smug souls – perhaps like these girls? – who tempted fate by believing that they were in control of their own destinies. So these four wanted to know about the future? She would not utter the sugar-coated platitudes about long lifelines, wedded bliss, and money in the bank. For once she would forget about enticing these four to pay up and come back again and bring other gullible customers with them. She did indeed – sometimes, when the conditions were right and she concentrated hard – have the gift of second sight. Like her mother before her and her eldest daughter after her, she had been born with what the gypsies call 'the veil over her face'. She would, just this once, tell them straight.

She seized Leila's cup, swiftly overturned it, and then peered down at the pattern the silty residue left on the bottom and sides of the cup. As usual, all she saw were the muddy remains of a small and bitter cup of coffee. She knitted her brows, shook her head, and lost patience with this tourist trade trick with the coffee grounds. She reached instead in her pocket and seized the egglike prism of crystal that had been her mother's, and her grandmother's before that – the devil only knew how many generations of women had held it and its powers in their hands. She grasped Leila's fingers in hers, and her dark eyes drilled deep into the crystal.

'A dove soars high in the sky. High, so high into the clouds,' she said in a thin quavering voice. 'I see it, yes, a white dove.' She let go of Leila's hands. 'What that means I think is power. A flight to great heights.'

'Power!' Leila laughed in triumph. 'Power . . . Allah!' As she swept her long mane of thick hennaed hair back from her glowing face, Leila's large calculating eyes were very bright. 'Palestine! Do you think she means Palestine?' Leila leaped to the wonderful conclusion that was always on the tip of her tongue. 'Peace! A dove means peace! We shall be able to go home, get our land back, the villa, everything!' Leila's shell of cool reserve cracked, and for once she was not the Leila they all knew but someone softer, even sweeter, a little girl before the bitterness soured not only her but her people. 'Yes, everything! Haifa! I was only six when we left, I only remember bits of it. The orange groves. My canopy bed. Our house at the top of the mountain. We could go home.' Leila sighed and, as she remembered the humiliations of twelve years of exile – even for the rich and the powerful, it was humiliating to have lost what is most dear – a little of the familiar hardness crept back in her voice. 'Power. She said "power". I wonder . . . Maybe she means Father will go back into politics in Palestine. That must be it, he'll be running the country. My country! Palestine! I can hardly believe it!'

'Palestine, always all you talk about is Palestine. As if in all the world there is nothing but your precious Palestine.' Fatima was still smarting at the way Leila had treated her. 'But she didn't say a word about Palestine. And she didn't say you would *get* your precious power, either.'

'Will you two stop it?' Anne gave the two Muslims an exasperated look. Why was it that the Arabs could never resist going for each other? Half the time Leila and Fatima fawned on each other, and the rest of the time they bickered like enemies. Anne was weary of refereeing their fights. '*Salaam*, please!'

'My palm!' Leila was already eagerly thrusting forth her hand, which was heavy with gold rings set with pearls, small diamonds, a ruby. 'Tell me exactly what you see there. Will we get Palestine back? And will I marry and have children and be happy?'

But the gypsy was still looking into her crystal. 'I see something – an arrow? a stone? – hit the dove. It falters, falls, bleeds.' She frowned. 'It is dead.'

'So much for your Palestine,' Fatima muttered.

Before Leila could pin her down about what all that meant, the gypsy laid aside her crystal with a sigh. She studied the Palestinian's carefully lacquered nails and turned over the smooth white hand that had never done a day's hard work. She narrowed her eyes. 'I see a big life.'

'A "big" life?' Leila scowled at Madame Kismet. 'You must mean "long".'

'I said exactly what I mean.' The gypsy considered, then rejected, telling the girl more. She didn't want to go too far with this reading. If she really let rip and the girls ended up in tears, Nirvana might not set her up in this cushy club. She looked down again at Leila's palm. 'Two – no, maybe three – husbands. Yes, and again I see the power. Much power but little happiness. More I cannot say.'

'My turn,' Anne said, before Leila used up all their fortune-telling time.

Madame Kismet stared hard at the crystal ball once again. She held on to Anne's hands so tightly that – as Anne swore to the others later – the American felt a tingle like an electric shock race from the gypsy's fingers to hers.

'I see . . . a two-headed man with the body of a snake.'

Anne recoiled and tried to pull her hands away from the gypsy's grasp. But the old one held on. 'Betrayal,' she continued, as she sagely nodded, 'yes, that's what I see for you.' She turned over both of Anne's hands and peered down at the palms for confirmation. 'Yes, just as I thought, betrayal. Once, twice, maybe always, betrayal.' But when she looked up and saw Anne's credulous brown eyes wide with disappointment, she took pity. This one, she thought, deserved better than she would get. It couldn't hurt to give this fresh young woman with the long curly hair some hope. Maybe, after all, she was mistaken about what she read in her palm. 'But I see at least one husband – perhaps another, I don't know. Your love line blurs, first it's deep, then I almost can't see it, then the lines run together. Ah, but yes, in the middle – here! – I see your love line again. And there are many young children, happiness of a sort later . . . maybe.'

Fatima had heard more than enough. The gypsy had implied that Leila wasn't going to live either very long or very happily, and poor Anne who had never done anything bad to anyone had some horrible snake lying in her path. Fatima tried to put her hands in her pocket, but Leila reached over and dragged them up on the table. As the gypsy closed her rough gnarled fingers around Fatima's, the girl shuddered.

Madame Kismet felt that tremor and looked up into Fatima's fawn-like eyes. Yes, finally here was a girl after her own heart. For the first time the old woman's face cracked into a smile, and she gave Fatima's hands a motherly squeeze. She was still smiling as she gazed into the crystal ball. 'I see writing. A word – I can't make it all out – but it begins with an "A", and then there's an "L" . . . and there's more, but it's cloudy. I see that, and I also see those clouds closing all around it – and I know what those clouds are, they mean a great love.'

'Ali! You must mean Ali!' Fatima smiled incredulously at the gypsy. 'How did you know my father says I will marry Ali?'

'I see what I see.' Madame Kismet smiled like a buddha. She was after all only human. She always warmed to a customer when it seemed that her reading had been exactly on the mark. She turned over Fatima's hand to see her palm. 'A happy marriage, many sons, yes, good fortune. I see troubles, too, but more than that I see a great love.'

'*Her?*' Leila glowered at the gypsy. 'You've got the wrong girl. She's going to marry her cousin.'

A little of the radiance died on Fatima's face. She lowered her eyes. '*Inshallah*,' she murmured. 'God willing.' But she said it woodenly, without hope.

'Me, Madame Kismet. Now me!' Camilla forgot not only her manners but also her reservations as she greedily took the gypsy's hands. She wanted to be told what she and her friends all knew, that she already had an even greater love.

The old woman stared for a long while deep into the crystal ball. She stared so long and so deeply that she seemed to have forgotten the four girls who waited for the oracle with bated breath. The gypsy shivered with a sudden chill, and she folded her hands around the prism as if she couldn't control her impulse to block out what she had seen there.

Her mind veered back to that other time in that other place. This was not the first time she had glimpsed a future like this in her crystal ball. In Germany in the late twenties, long before the war, when she'd had a similar job in that other cabaret, she had seen the blood and the gore in the ball just as she could see it now. Then she had had the good sense to get out before the madness started. She had led her family's gaily painted caravan back through her tribe's ancestral lands in the Balkans, but she hadn't been able to talk her sisters into continuing south through Greece and Turkey. Much later – long after she had settled here in this heavenly Levantine country – she had heard how her sisters perished in those Nazi death camps. After that she had resolved always to heed what her gift of the second sight revealed to her. But how could it be that Lebanon would one day, not too far in the future, turn from heaven into hell? She had thought she would be safe for ever here. This glorious Biblical 'land of milk and honey' was so easy to love. Its rivers and mountains and groves glimmered like paradise. Waterfalls cascaded through verdant glades. Bounteous fields rippled beyond every horizon. Pine forests crept down to the turquoise sea. Best of all, so many of the people who lived in this Eden were rich not only in material goods but also in laughter and contentment. She had been so enchanted by this blessed country where she had hoped to stay the rest of her days.

Madame Kismet shook her head. 'Enough today.' She was suddenly exhausted and depressed. As she had aged, the exercise of the second sight had begun to take too much out of her. Yet she supposed she would have to steel herself to look back in the dark depths of her crystal ball again, so she could be sure. It had seemed, she thought, that Lebanon's fall was still some way in the future. Surely she did not have to take flight just yet. But she was rattled, and she wanted to be alone to think this over. She swayed to her feet. 'I am tired.'

'You have to tell me what you see!' Camilla did not let go of the old one's bony hand.

'No, enough.' The gypsy disengaged her hand. 'Another time maybe.'

'*Dites-moi.*' Camilla dug in her purse and then slapped a fifty-pound note down on the table.

Madame Kismet gazed at the boss's daughter. 'As you like.' She flicked the Lebanese banknote up the sleeve of her dress and sat back down and looked grimly into the crystal ball. 'I see trees covered with white on a mountain—'

'The Cedars!' By now Camilla believed every word

that issued from Madame Kismet's lips. 'She must see the Cedars of Lebanon! The symbol of our country! You know what Pierre always says? "Lebanon without the Cedars is like a song without words!" He is a poet, my Pierre!'

'I see what I see.' This time the gypsy did not smile. 'I see the white trees change, and they are red. Blood. I see blood. On the trees, on the mountain, on everything. In the beginning and at the end, I see blood. Blood everywhere.'

'Blood!' As Camilla let out a peal of nervous laughter, Leila seized her friend's hand and held it out to the gypsy.

'And her palm?'

But the old woman had already shuffled away, she was on the far side of the dance floor, she was on the other side of the dark curtain. The amber beads jangled.

'Well,' Anne said finally, to break the hushed silence that had fallen over the foursome, 'I for one don't believe in fortune-tellers . . . ' She didn't say out loud that she had no wish to give the slightest credence to a prophecy that not only promised blood for Camilla but also cast the dark cloud of betrayal over her own bright future. She wished the gypsy hadn't told her about that two-headed snake. She exchanged a meaningful glance with Leila.

'Neither do I,' Leila said, just to stay on the good side of Anne. But her voice lacked conviction. Everyone knew that some gypsies could see the future. All things considered, she wouldn't mind it if Madame Kismet had predicted her own future right. She liked the idea of a 'big life' and a powerful future, even if she had to pay a price for it. She was willing to gamble very high stakes for power.

'*Malesh*, Camilla, never mind.' Fatima took Camilla's cold hands in her warm ones. Even though her fortune had surprised them all by its rosy romantic cast, Fatima still wished they had not tempted God and fate like this.

'We shouldn't have done this. I knew it.' Camilla was near to tears. 'Why didn't you all listen to me?'

Anne, too, regretted what had happened. The sooner they all forgot about it, the better. 'I think the show's over.' When Anne stood, the rest of them obediently got to their feet. 'It's early. Just after five. If we hurry up, we can still have tea and cakes at La Brioche. Or would you rather have Arabic sweets at Samedi? Some *kunnifeh*, perhaps?'

'La Brioche.' Leila linked her arm with Camilla's. 'My treat.'

Without another word, the four of them all but ran from the darkness into the light, from the sinister red shadows of the darkened cabaret towards the door that opened on the strong sunlight of the Beirut afternoon.

The guests sweltered side by side two Sundays later in a cedarwood pew on the bride's side of the Maronite parish church as they waited impatiently for Camilla to come down the aisle to marry Pierre, the heir apparent to one of the richest and most politically powerful Christian fiefdoms in Lebanon.

'Where the hell is she?' Leila's voice was louder than she'd intended.

'You must not use bad words in a church!' Fatima looked around as though one of these big beefy Christians would realize she didn't belong and throw her out before she'd seen the wedding. She had been worried sick that her family wouldn't let her come, but – *el-hamdulillah*, thank God! – her Uncle Muhammad had said there was no harm in witnessing her good friend's great day. Even though she was very conscious of being an outsider, Fatima was thrilled to be moving, if only for an afternoon, in such grand circles. Traffic on the tortuous, hairpin-bend mountain road that led north to Pierre's village had been bumper to bumper with chauffeur-driven Mercedes and Cadillac sedans. Inside, fine ladies had sat resplendent in their Parisian frocks beside their lordly husbands. As Leila's father's driver had tooted his horn and boldly overtaken each limousine, everyone had blown kisses to everyone else. Then, when they had snaked almost all the way to heaven, Fatima had caught her breath in wonder at her first glimpse of *le Château Croisé* – for significantly, Pierre's Francophile father had named his modern 'Crusader castle' in French instead of Arabic. This Nazrani fortress, complete with medieval turrets and even a moat, was perched at the crest of a cedar-covered mountain. In the village Fatima's sensation of stepping into a fairy tale had only increased as throngs of cheering, rosy-cheeked peasants had lined their path from castle to church. But now Leila was blasphemously breaking the spell. 'You can't swear in a church!'

'I can say whatever I want wherever I want. Besides, since when did you know or care about how to act in a church?'

'Knock it off, both of you,' Anne whispered. 'We don't want to embarrass Camilla.'

'No one else is being quiet,' Leila grumbled. 'We could be screaming blue murder, and no one would even notice.'

To herself Leila added that, instead of a solemn religious ceremony, Camilla's wedding was more like an overblown Cecil B. De Mille movie production. For the past hour, as this captive audience of six hundred sweating guests had fidgeted in their seats, the public address system had been booming out with a medley of Nirvana's greatest recorded hits – introduced with the idiotic patter of one of Radio Lebanon's most familiar voices. What kind of wedding had a paid disc-jockey in its party? She wouldn't be surprised to find Nirvana's albums on sale at a discount in the vestibule. The aisles were all but crawling with snap-happy photographers from *al-Hayat* and *La Revue du Liban* who didn't bother to lower their voices as they begged society matrons for just one more picture. Every woman had dressed for the occasion in her flamboyant silk, taffeta and chiffon couture best. Leila spotted dresses, gowns and ensembles from Balenciaga, Lanvin, Patou, Givenchy, Balmain, Cardin and – *bien sûr!* – Dior. Today there were no cheap copies here, only the genuine Parisian originals. Diamonds dripped from earlobes. Emeralds cascaded from necks. Rubies, pearls and a sultan's ransom in gold sparkled on fingers. Chanel No. 5 all but lay in clouds. But despite their finery, the congregation was anything but sedate. Here and there a guest was surreptitiously munching on sugared almonds – a good luck tradition at Lebanese weddings – and sucking on *raha*, that heavenly Lebanese candy which the tourists erroneously persisted in calling 'Turkish delight'. If Camilla delayed much longer, some of these fat old ladies would be bringing out the hampers of food that Leila suspected they had hidden under the pews. Everyone was gossiping, laughing and jumping up to take each other's photographs. As the wedding party milled around in front of the altar, the bridesmaids and ushers grinned and waved to their mothers. But even those gorgeous rainbow-hued Nina Ricci chiffon gowns couldn't hide the bridesmaids' dreadful pudding figures. But God knows, Leila thought, all this wasn't Camilla's fault. Left to her own devices, away from her mother and Pierre's family, Camilla had splendid – although sometimes just a wee bit too flashy – taste. Leila was certain the nice witty touch of those thousands of fragrant pink and white camellias banking the altar, attached to the pews, even hanging in baskets beside the windows was Camilla's idea. Thousands more petals had even been thickly spread the length of the aisle, so Camilla's path to the altar would be a carpet of her flowery namesake. But it was a real Christian foible, Leila thought, to take a basically good idea and then go over the top with it. The church reeked of those camellias! Still, Leila was certain that Camilla hadn't wanted her wedding party overrun by every marriage-able cousin from Pierre's vastly extensive family tree. It would have been bad enough if she had been forced to take three or four of them, but *sixteen* bridesmaids was going too far. Like so much else in this overdone Maronite extravaganza, the size of the wedding party was an exercise in bad taste.

Fatima reached in one of her voluminous pockets, rattled a paper bag, and then plucked at Leila's arm and offered her a fresh plump black date.

Leila popped it in her mouth and, as she spat the stone on the floor and held her hand out for another date, she seemed to forget her disdain for the other snacking guests.

'I have bananas, too. Bread. Tomatoes. And chicken.' Fatima was reaching down for the sack she had wedged under the kneeler. Her aunt had packed her a picnic lunch so she wouldn't have to eat any of that possibly unclean Christian food at this afternoon's reception.

'Don't you *dare* touch that chicken. Not *here*. This is a *church*.' But Anne, too, couldn't resist a handful of Fatima's dates. As the disc jockey announced what he called one of Nirvana's 'golden oldies', and the wedding guests began to tap their feet and sing along with the music, Anne couldn't help giggling. 'What we should really have is hot buttered popcorn.'

Fatima laughed when Anne laughed, although she really didn't get the joke. She hadn't understood much of what was happening inside the first Christian church she had ever entered. This church was so different from her mosques, which never had the slightest idolatrous hint of icons or statues. This church, however, was chockablock with ornate frescoes, gilded paintings, lifesize statues and – behind the altar, along the walls, everywhere! – graphic representations of Christ's death throes on the cross. When she had first come inside, she hadn't been able to tear her eyes away from that cross that towered above the altar. She, like all Muslims, revered this Jesus – in Arabic his name translated as 'Isa' – as one of the foremost prophets of God. But at her mosque Fatima had been taught that Isa was never crucified, that instead Allah took him up to heaven and let another die in his place. Fatima stared unhappily up at the suffering Christ on the cross. She found the Muslim theology less disturbing. From what she had read in the Koran, Isa sounded so loving and good. How could these Christians bear to sit in church each Sunday and watch him in agony on that cross?

Anne caught Fatima staring up at the altar with a look of open consternation on her face. As she followed Fatima's eyes to the crucifix, Anne wondered what could be bothering her friend. Churches, to Anne, were museums of art and architecture rather than personal and emotionally charged temples of worship. Neither of her parents had been especially religious, and so – the child of an uneasy mixed marriage – she had grown up neither a practising Christian nor a Jew. Still, as one who belonged nowhere but was a good guest everywhere, she found this three-hundred-year-old church very beautiful. Even though the afternoon light shone brightly through the stained glass windows that had lately been installed at what Camilla had bragged was an enormous cost, this church had that beguilingly mystical early Christian look and feel which she loved. Sunlight did not pierce all the dark shadows behind the tabernacle. Beseeching candles flickered before sad-eyed icons of suffering saints. A full-bosomed statue of the Virgin seemed more akin to Astarte fertility goddess amulets than to alabaster-skinned European Madonnas. A crypt under the altar held a medieval martyr's hoary bones. Anne reflected that here in the Middle East religion was more primitive – and in a way, perhaps more satisfying – than it ever seemed even in somewhere far more exquisite like Notre Dame cathedral in Paris. Sitting here, it must be easy to believe that two millennia ago their Christ had preached his gentle gospels not so far away, along the banks of the Galilee and the Jordan. Anne smiled to herself as she recalled how she had visited all the sacred Christian, Jewish and Muslim holy places in every remote corner of this dusty ancient world. She had spent the best summers of her life accompanying her father on archaeological jaunts throughout the Levant and Mesopotamia – 'the Fertile Crescent', as her father lovingly called their stamping ground.

'It's late, it's hot, and I'm hungry.' Leila was fishing in Fatima's sack for a banana. 'Maybe Camilla got cold feet. Could be that the whole thing's off.'

'She would never do that.' Fatima peeled a banana and passed it to Anne. 'Would she?'

Anne shook her head and polished off the banana. But Leila was right. Even though here in Lebanon everyone was always late and brides were expected to be the latest of the late, it was long past the time when Camilla should have appeared. Anne craned her neck back towards the door and then twisted in her seat so she could look up into the choir loft. Nirvana wasn't where she was supposed to be either. 'I bet the families are fighting again. Poor Camilla. Her mother and Pierre's father have been driving her crazy.'

Anne wished she could be back with the bride now. She would have liked to be beside her oldest friend to fuss with her veil, to adjust her train, to brush away the tears she was sure would be rolling down her cheeks. Camilla was such a weeper! She had been a dear sweet crybaby even back in kindergarten. She and Camilla had been bosom friends that far back and, even though in these last years Anne had often felt closer to Fatima and Leila, on this particular occasion fifteen years of affection, growing pains and shared confidences weighed wonderfully heavy. She wished, too, that she had been allowed to be one of the bridesmaids. Camilla had after all asked her first, on the very morning after Pierre popped the question. She had asked Leila and Fatima to be in her wedding party, too.

Anne smoothed down the skirt of her demure beige silk shirtwaist and adjusted her wide-brimmed apricot-coloured hat. She looked over in approval at Leila in that elegantly ravishing peacock blue Cardin sheath and Fatima in her really rather fetching long ruffled green dress. By rights the three of them should be the ones standing up by the communion rail decked out in those gossamer designer gowns. But Anne supposed lots of brides didn't get their way at their weddings. It wasn't only in Lebanon that the families took over and insisted that this younger sister and that distant cousin must take precedence over a mere unrelated friend – especially if the friend wasn't of the right religion. Theirs had always been an ecumenical foursome: a Maronite Christian, a Shia Muslim, a Sunni Muslim, and she herself, an American Jew. They used to joke that all they were missing was one of the Druze mountain girls, and then they could hold Lebanese cabinet meetings. They sometimes flattered themselves, too, about how international they were: a Palestinian, an American, a Lebanese, and Camilla was even half-French. Not that their differing religious and national identities had mattered much to any of them. Like everyone else in the generally tolerant and peaceful modern nation-state of Lebanon, they took pride in how they all mixed and mingled. Yet Anne thought it would have been better still if religion, family and nationality really didn't count at all. It would have been best of all if friendship and love were the only considerations. Then she, Fatima and Leila would have been able to stand up at that altar behind good old Camilla, the first of them to tie the knot. Anne reached in her new white satin purse for a handkerchief. She dabbed at her eyes.

Leila was surprised that self-possessed Anne was sniffling. It was a wedding, after all, not a funeral – although the carnival atmosphere made it seem more like a circus. Yet, even as Leila's eyes glinted with contemptuous amusement while she continued to catalogue the many ways in which she thought herself and her people superior to these vulgar Christians, she was nonetheless glad to be here. Camilla was one of her best friends, and she would have turned up for this wedding even if it weren't the social event of the season. She was pragmatic enough to realize, however, that it would do no harm to the pride and position of her own family for a Shahine to be an honoured guest at the wedding of a clan with the clout of the Nazranis.

Leila got out her cigarettes and was just about to light up when Anne told her in no uncertain terms that she would be thrown out of the church if she dared to smoke.

Leila shrugged. She would have loved to blow haloes of smoke in this church. But she put her cigarettes away and idly let her mind wander. As far back as she could remember, she had sat with the men in her family's tastefully appointed salon as they talked far into the night about the ways and means of winning back their birthright. She had always been her father's favourite child, and she had taken special delight when Baba complimented her that she thought like a man. And so, like a man, she had shouldered the burden of recovering lost Palestine – even though, at least for now, all that burden consisted of was words and more words. By the time she had reached puberty, she could spout the stirring sentiments about God and country as glibly as the rest of them. Early on she had understood all that it was necessary to understand. Zionism was the arch-evil. Israel and its American uncle were the devils. The way to recover the lost paradise that lay just south of the Litani was to make themselves, as the best of the Palestinians, even richer and more internationally indispensable than the Jews. To this exalted end, her father had not only diversified his portfolio of holdings on the New York and London stock markets but also deployed his family on the Middle East chessboard as though they were his own personal international Palestinian guerrilla band. Years ago her eldest brother had been dispatched to Kuwait, where he watched over the family's oil interests and took the pulse of the Gulf big money men. Another brother was managing editor of the most influential daily in Jordan. One sister was happily married to an Egyptian diplomat in Cairo, and another – less fortunate – had reluctantly but obediently wedded a distant cousin of the Saudi royal family in Riyadh. As the *pièce de résistance*, her baby brother was going to be sent this autumn to Harvard University, where Ramsey would be duly expected to learn slick American lessons about how to manipulate not only corporations but governments. Maybe, Leila reflected, she had been wrong in interpreting what Madame Kismet had seen in her crystal ball. Palestinian power could be a full generation away. One day it might not be her father but Ramsey who was prime minister of the free democratic state of Palestine. And what of herself? Even without a crystal ball, Leila doubted whether her father was about to leave her future entirely to the fates. Yet when she asked, all the old patriarch ever did was stroke her hair and say she shouldn't worry about such things while she was still little more than a child. In the meantime, until she went off to graduate school in England, Leila didn't have to be asked to do her best to shore up the family's connections here in Lebanon.

Leila crushed the remains of her cigarette under the stylishly pointed toe of one of her white spike heels.

Then, as she more thoughtfully looked over this assemblage of Nazranis, she saw not vulgar Maronite *parvenus* but a source of raw power that had to be respected, even courted, in the garish crazy patchwork of Lebanese politics. Here, what mattered most was a man's religion, and there were sixteen major sects who in the main lived in their own *quartiers*, ran their own schools, and elected their own politicians. When Lebanon had shaken off the French Mandate towards the end of the Second World War, even the national offices had been parcelled out to the various religions, so that the President was always a Maronite Christian and the Prime Minister a Sunni Muslim. Within each of these sects, the political permutations were increased by the presence of both leftist and right-wing parties and factions. One predominantly conservative Sunni Muslim political party wanted to merge the Lebanese state back into Greater Syria. Another left-wing Sunni movement looked to Nasser's Egypt with just as fervent a longing. Yet for better or worse, her father – like the best class of Palestinians who had fled north in '48 – had relocated his Middle East operations in Beirut, where he bought and sold their future on the Levantine Bourse. Beirut might be cosmopolitan – the Switzerland of the Middle East, the tour operators liked to call it – but Lebanon was still feudal. Power here was in the clutches of a handful of hereditary warlords called *zaims* who ran the country as ruthlessly as Mafia gangsters had controlled the Chicago underworld of the Roaring Twenties. Her father said all the *zaims* – no matter what religion they purported to follow – were cut-throats who would sell their own mothers for a caravan of hashish. Yet even her fastidious father had not disdained to make his own shrewd deals with virtually every one of these warlords, including the Christians who held the lion's share of Lebanese political and financial power. Still, her father always said, the Nazranis were the best of a bad Christian lot. Shaykh Georges might be a liar and a thief, but he was the biggest liar and the best thief in Lebanon. Besides, the Nazrani clan had been a potent force in Lebanon for hundreds of years. In their way, they were as aristocratic as the Shahines had been back in Palestine.

Leila looked down at the political button she had fixed to the bodice of her dress as though it were a priceless jewel. In less highly-charged times, she would doubtless have pinned on her stunning sapphire stickpin, but here and now she was far more proud of this cheap tin badge of a triumphantly grinning Gamal Abdul Nasser. Since the Egyptian president had defied the West and nationalized the Suez Canal two years ago, Nasser had become the darling of Arab nationalists throughout the Middle East. To Leila, Nasser represented the hope that all things – especially recovering Palestine – were suddenly possible in an Arab world united behind Nasser's victorious standard. Last winter Syria had blazed the way when it federated with Egypt in the United Arab Republic. Jordan, Iraq and even Lebanon could be next.

Leila ran a finger lovingly over Nasser's image. There was a long way to go before the Christian-dominated Lebanon became a bright star in the Muslim sky. Her father had told her precisely who were their friends and who were their enemies in the Christian camp. The Maronite sect, of course, overshadowed the Greek Orthodox, the Greek Catholics and the Armenians. Among the Maronite warlords, then, he much preferred Georges Nazrani to the others. The current president of Lebanon, he said, danced on strings held by his puppetmasters in Washington, London and Paris. In defiance of the rising tide of pro-Nasser Arab nationalism, the President had mortally offended Lebanese Muslims by making their country the only Middle East state to sign the Eisenhower Doctrine which invited the United States to send in troops wherever there was the possibility of a Communist threat. But the final outrage was that the President had lately launched a campaign to rewrite the Lebanese constitution to allow him a second term of office. Leila's father vowed that Lebanon's Muslims would rise up and fight to the death before they would give the President six more years to turn the country into a limp-wristed Western satellite. Nearly as bad as the current régime, in Leila's father's estimation, were another clan which had modelled their own private 'Phalange' army on the Hitler shock troops which the head of the family had admired on a visit to the Berlin Olympics in 1936.

It was anyone's guess which of these Maronite politicians would come out on top in next autumn's elections. The chances for a truly democratic vote were slim. In the last parliamentary election, the results had been so fraudulent that even the foremost chieftain of all the Druze had supposedly failed to win in his own mountain stronghold. Already this year deputies had been bribed with far more than the usual sums, and there were even rumours that some pro-Nazrani politicians in remote parts of the Bekaa were going to be kidnapped and held at gunpoint until after the elections. But frankly, her father had told her, it's in our best interest as Muslims if the Christians fight each other to a bloody standstill. So long as they keep having a go at each other, they'll never be united enough to turn on *us*.

Over the microphone there was a very loud and pre-emptive clearing of a throat, and Nirvana's husky bedroom voice began a provocative supper club rendition of 'Ave Maria'. All heads turned up towards the choir loft, where at the end of her number Nirvana – dazzlingly electric in purple sequined *décolleté* – took a theatrical bow and rained kisses down at them all.

Heels clicked on marble, and all heads swivelled towards the front of the church. The bishop swept up to the altar and stood waiting in regal purple robes which were almost as resplendent as Nirvana's. Then Pierre – princely in the trim dress white lieutenant's uniform he had earned in his stint at officers' training school – strode beside his brother towards his place at the centre of the communion rail. The guests on the groom's side of the church beamed at this *bon diable* who was, they all agreed, a chip off the old block. To one another they murmured approvingly that this singer's daughter was the luckiest girl in the Levant. Pierre might walk a bit on the wild side, but scandalously flaming youth was after all in the Nazrani blood. A few indiscretions – bar girls, drink, a little hashish – were only to be expected in a young man endowed with his genes and hormones. Pierre would settle down now and put all that excessive energy into following his father's orders.

Lebanon's most eligible bachelor turned his back on the altar, removed his sunglasses, and winked at his mother. Yet as he gazed at the door where, any second now, he would be able to glimpse his bride, Pierre for a moment seemed as nervous as any other bridegroom. He reached in his pocket for a monogrammed linen handkerchief and mopped the sweat from his swarthy face.

The organist finally struck up the wedding march, and the guests sighed in relief as they came to their feet.

Camilla remembered to follow her mother's stage directions, and paused under the arch in the doorway long enough for everyone in the church to turn round.

'Ah . . . ! *Al-arous!* The bride!' As one, the guests saluted the radiant bride glittering on the threshold. Children climbed up on the pews for a better look. Heads craned, flashbulbs popped, and matrons began to weep as they remembered a time when they, too, had felt the way Camilla looked.

'She looks like an angel,' Fatima breathed.

'She looks better than an angel,' Leila corrected. 'Allah created the angels, but – my dear! – that ivory satin is by Christian Dior.'

'She looks sensational.' Anne kept to herself the thought that she would rather Camilla had looked a little less sensational. She would never allow a breath of criticism about Camilla to pass her lips, but – even if it was trite – Anne liked to see brides decked out in all the old clichés of innocently billowing lace. Instead, Camilla's voluptuous curves were daringly packaged in a slithery, skin-hugging sheath. The neckline plunged low enough to show several tantalizing inches of cleavage, and the side seams of the skirt were slit thigh-high so the bride would be able to walk down the aisle. But at least her gossamer Alençon lace veil was traditional. Pierre's mother had insisted that Camilla bow to family custom and wear the heirloom veil that had graced every Nazrani bride for hundreds of years, maybe even – legend had it – back in the time of the Crusades. But even under that billowing veil, Camilla looked too provocative for a virgin bride. Anne didn't like the way the male guests were all but salivating over her friend's lusciously displayed curves. She wished Nirvana hadn't insisted on keeping Camilla's wedding dress a secret even from her best friends. Maybe the three of them might have been able to talk Camilla into wearing something a little more appropriate. Anne narrowed her eyes as she stared at her old friend framed so very dramatically in the doorway. What in the world was that extraordinary golden sparkle that seemed to envelop the bride from veiled head to slippered toe?

Leila was on the same wave-length. 'I heard', she whispered to Anne and Fatima, 'that last week old man Nazrani actually went down to the souk and had gold bars ground to dust. He must have sprinkled her with eighteen carat gold!'

'No!' Even here, where every week these careless

rich people must throw away more than her Uncle Muhammad earned in a lifetime, Fatima could not believe so extravagant a rumour.

Anne, too, was sceptical. 'It must just be glitter. Even the Nazranis wouldn't throw gold away like that.' Anne reconsidered. The Nazranis *were* big spenders. 'At least I don't *think* they would.'

Leila's sharp eyes had meanwhile focused on the very slight but discernible bulge in Camilla's stomach. They had always teased poor round Fatima that someday she would swell to the size of a blimp. Yet she, Anne and Camilla had always had exactly the same slim flat-bellied silhouette. Camilla was either pregnant or going to pot.

Camilla stood trembling a moment longer under the archway. As her mind skidded wildly, she concentrated on keeping her stomach sucked in. None of these veteran gossips must guess her three-month-old secret. Nothing must spoil this day of days. She wished this mob of people she didn't know or care about would melt away. She wanted to share all this only with those she loved. She would have liked to search the throng for Anne, Fatima and Leila. But she only had eyes for Pierre. She could see him standing at the far end of the aisle, waiting for her. She savoured that lovely prospect: Pierre was waiting a hundred feet away for her to marry him! She had an impulse to throw away her bouquet of camellias and not walk but run down the aisle to her beloved. Camilla smiled rapturously in the direction of the altar.

In that instant before she could put her best foot forward, however, an elegant white-haired, lion-like old man stepped from the shadows of the vestibule. Georges Nazrani took masterful possession of Camilla's right arm as he prepared to deliver the bride to his son.

'Shaykh Georges! Oh-ho!' Leila almost laughed out loud. 'What a cheek!'

'I thought Camilla said her Uncle Henri would do that,' Fatima said.

'Nirvana', Anne added, 'must be having a fit!'

From chancel to choir loft, the church rippled with scandalized delight. Everyone knew Nirvana's brother was supposed to be escorting the bride down the aisle. Yet there was Henri sitting rather sheepishly in the last pew on the bride's side. Leave it to Shaykh Georges to take over! And wasn't it a touch incestuous for the father of the groom to give the bride away? The church buzzed with speculation that this must be the reason for the long delay in the ceremony. Nirvana must have been none too pleased at having her brother shoved aside. Heads swivelled back up to the choir loft, where Nirvana seemed to have discarded her nightclub act and was indeed glowering down at Georges.

But as the organist began another chorus of the wedding march and a triumphant Shaykh Georges began leading Camilla down the red-carpeted aisle, even the most cynical of the guests forgot to be hard and brittle. What did it matter which old man tottered along beside the bride on those thousands of camellia petals scattered, so charmingly, the length of the aisle? Camilla truly was not only blushing but beautiful. Pierre really was eager and handsome. The radiance reflected on both their faces had to be love. As a collective sigh filled the church, even bankers and international wheeler-dealers turned into fuzzy-headed romantics. To hell with money, power, position; for this one heady moment all that counted was love. Everyone drank in how *he* looked at *her* and how *she* looked at *him*. By the time Camilla stood at the altar within hand-holding distance of Pierre, a rapt and reverent hush had fallen over the dewy-eyed crowd.

The bishop intoned the fine old Syriac words that would seal this couple together for ever as man and wife. Love and honour, harmony and devotion, compassion and forgiveness – the sweet words rained down like a blessing from on high. When the cleric asked the ritual questions, Pierre and Camilla gazed into each other's eyes and recited the cherished answers as if they were the first man and woman ever to promise each other a lifetime of such surely guaranteed bliss. Rings were slipped on fingers. The sign of the cross was inscribed in the air. Finally the bishop pronounced them man and wife.

But just then, as the bishop was ascending the sanctuary steps to begin celebrating the nuptial Mass, cries – which almost everyone assumed to be shouts of joy – drifted in from outside. Seconds later there was a commotion at the back of the church. The heavy wooden doors burst open. Running feet skidded on marble. Heavy metal clanked on stone.

Up by the altar, at the first screams from outside, while the wedding guests were still straining to see the cause of the uproar, Pierre's combat-trained reflexes were fast and true. In the instant before the first bullets could begin whistling towards them, he grabbed his bride around the waist and thrust her to safety behind the cover of the pulpit. As astonished guests still stared stupefied at this strange spectacle by the altar, the staccato rip of automatic gunfire reverberated the length of the church.

'Assassins! Assassins!' The cries of alarm from the Nazrani men outside were a few moments too late.

The gunmen let loose with repeated sprays of automatic fire as the terrified guests dived for cover under the pews. Fatima threw herself on top of Anne, and the two of them held on to one another for dear life. Leila was crouched by the aisle, cautiously angling her head in order to catch a glimpse of the gunmen. Five men whose heads – all but the eyes – were hooded in black balaclavas stood boldly in the centre aisle with their machine-guns aimed straight at the altar. They shot from their shoulders and then pivoted in a wide arc. Gunfire raked the altar, the pews, finally even the choir loft.

The bishop took a hit on the chest and was the first to fall. He staggered, cried out, and slid down the sanctuary steps where he lay unmoving in a pool of his own blood. An altar boy screamed and fell beside the bishop. Three others scuttled over to safety behind a statue of Saint Maron. As the deadly fusillade continued, all was pandemonium in the church. One bridesmaid screeched a horrible soprano cry of mourning over the body of another girl in blood-soaked couture who had been her sister. An usher was shouting for help at the communion rail. Blood ran in the aisle. Women shrieked, men cursed, children wailed, and up in the belfry someone began ringing the churchbells.

As the guests continued to cower in the pews, Fatima angled herself towards what she hoped was the direction of Mecca and began to pray out loud. Anne listened for a moment to the gentle rise and fall of the Arabic on Fatima's lips, and then very carefully she pulled herself up so she was crouched on the kneeler. All she could see was her row of guests huddled so close to the floor that they seemed to be trying to dig their bodies into the cement. But she could hear the whimpers of the wounded and the dying.

Leila meanwhile had turned her attention from the gunmen to a slow and steady shuffling sound coming towards her from a few feet away in the aisle. Georges Nazrani was sprawled just beyond her reach. He seemed to be wounded in the thigh or legs, because he was trying to use his arms to drag his deadweight legs inch by inch towards the cover of their pew. Leila's mind raced as she watched the one who was surely the target of this attack struggle for life before her eyes. It was less than four months before the national elections. One of Nazrani's rivals, she reasoned, must have sent out this death squad. How could anyone, she wondered, dare to try to assassinate Shaykh Georges? Perhaps, she thought, the gunmen had only been sent to make a show of violence and intimidate the Nazranis into withdrawing from the election. Surely, she decided, that must be the case. There would have been all hell to pay in every nook and cranny of Lebanon if Shaykh Georges was murdered at his son's wedding, in the sanctuary of his own parish church. There would, in fact, be all hell to pay in Lebanon even if the *shaykh* and his family escaped unscathed. Whoever had sent these gunmen was mad to raise the level of violence like this. Even in the remote Lebanese mountains, where bloodfeud vendettas could go on for generations, some taboos were never violated. It was unthinkable that assassins should shoot up a church, mowing women and children down like tin soldiers.

Leila risked another look down the aisle at the gunmen. They were still firing round after round, but there seemed little method to their madness. Instead of concentrating their fire on the wedding party, they were shooting wildly – almost gleefully – everywhere and anywhere. Stained glass windows shattered in jagged shards. Empty pews were blasted to smithereens. Statues toppled and fell. Though wasting much of their fire, the slaphappy assassins were still making steady progress. As they advanced down the red-carpeted aisle, Leila noticed, their boots trampled the delicate camellia petals under foot. Surely, before long, they would spot Shaykh Georges, and then they would crush him once and for all.

Leila watched one of the most powerful men in Lebanon crawl like a crab before her eyes. Yet his fierce eyes were without fear. She had to admire this old man who would die rather than plead for mercy. Shaykh Georges and her own adored father were perhaps two of a kind.

But now, as the Nazranis began firing back, the level of fighting escalated sharply.

Georges Nazrani finally dragged himself behind the corner of a pew and pulled out the pearl-handled revolver he always carried with him in his back pocket. As Fatima shrieked and Anne held her hands over her ears, Shaykh Georges shot back at his enemies. Other pistol-packing wedding guests, too, had finally found the presence of mind to join in the shooting. Caught in the crossfire between the pews, two of the assassins fell in their tracks. Finally an armed contingent of Nazranis raced into the church. All the guns seemed to go off at once. The two squads fought it out face to face at point-blank range until all five of the interlopers lay dead in the aisle.

For one time-stopping instant after the guns finally fell silent, all was absolutely quiet. But then the screaming began. The wounded moaned, and the relatives of the wounded shouted for help. But worst of all were the mourning shrieks of those who, when they finally dared to move from their hiding places, discovered that a mother or son or cousin had been lying dead beside them. Thirty-eight people – including not only the bishop and two bridesmaids but all five of the assassins – had been killed. But the targets of the attack – Georges Nazrani and his son Pierre – were very much alive.

Shaykh Georges had finally managed to pull himself up on both feet. Then, his face twisted with pain, he was in the centre aisle leaning on a pew. With a superhuman effort he supported the weight of his body on one arm as he raised his fist high in the air. 'Vengeance! Revenge! By Saint Maron, I promise they will pay for this!' His hoarse voice soared above all the other screams and screeches as he howled curses to the heavens.

Up beside the altar Camilla still lay stunned, face down, with her bridal bouquet crushed against her stomach. As she heard Pierre's father vowing that more blood must and would be spilled, she opened her eyes and looked down in shock at herself. The bishop had fallen not far from her, and his blood had spattered the altar. Her wedding gown was stained with the cleric's blood. She stared down at the red on the ivory, and remembered what the old gypsy had foreseen in her future. 'Blood', she whispered in horror, '*Yaadra*, O Virgin Mary, the blood . . . '

She reached out in blind and desperate need for Pierre – for her husband! – for the one whose presence of mind had saved both their lives. But Pierre was already beyond her grasp. The second the firing had stopped, he had leaped down from the altar and over the communion rail to be at the side of his father. Camilla concentrated on her body. Her shoulders, chest and legs ached from the way she had fallen as Pierre had flung her down behind the marble pulpit. But she didn't think she was wounded. She remembered the baby then, and in a panic brought her hands up to feel her belly. She sighed in relief as she touched the bouquet of camellias which had broken her fall. Thus reassured, she lifted her head and finally dared to look out at the carnage in the church. Bodies were sprawled in the pews and along the aisle. Frantic relatives were beseeching somebody – anybody! – to help. A society press photographer from *al-Hayat* who had once told Camilla that he longed to be a serious photo-journalist had seized his golden opportunity and was standing on a pew shooting film not only of everything that moved but of all those things which didn't. Blood was everywhere.

As she watched, a seething mob of outraged Nazrani clansmen swept the patriarch and his heir up on their shoulders. Shaykh Georges and Pierre were borne down the centre aisle, their supporters chanting aloud for revenge. As the men surged out of the door, only weeping women and crying children were left in the church. Camilla suddenly wanted her mother. She wanted to be a little girl again and hide her face in her mother's breasts and have Mama reassure her that everything would be all right. But as usual her mother was not there when Camilla needed her. Nirvana was still up in the choir loft shrieking hysterically. Camilla curled up like a child and started to cry.

She lay sobbing there for what seemed like a lifetime of moments before Anne was suddenly kneeling over her, asking her if she was hurt, holding her in her arms just as Camilla had wished her mother would. 'You're in a state of shock, don't worry, you'll come out of it soon, you're okay.' Fatima was there, too. 'You are alive, *Allah karim*,' Fatima was murmuring over and over, 'God is generous.' Anne and Fatima had their arms twined around her as they helped Camilla to her feet.

Leila meanwhile was still lost in thought as she stood at the communion rail. Belatedly she strode to the altar and dabbed the blood off Camilla's face with the hem of her bridal gown. 'You'll be all right,' she said absently, as she straightened the bridal veil and picked up the crushed bouquet of camellias.

Leila's eyes, however, were all this while brighter with calculation than with concern. As the three of them began leading the bride in a less than triumphant wedding procession back down the aisle, Leila could contain herself no longer. 'Do you know what this means? After what's happened here today, it might even come to civil war!'

'Oh, Leila.' Fatima's voice was shocked. 'Not now.'

Camilla stopped dead in her tracks and shook her head. 'Blood. It means blood. Madame Kismet said that. In the Crescent. You all remember. She saw blood for me. In the beginning and in the end, she saw blood for me. This is only the beginning, and look what has happened!' Camilla trembled as she stared down at the bloodstains that were drying brown on her ivory satin.

'I laughed then. Laughed!' She was not laughing as she crossed herself.

Anne shivered in the hot dark church. The stench of blood mingled with the smell of incense in the heavy flower-laden air. In such a place, at such a time, it was almost possible to believe in black magic. But then, with an effort of will and a burst of common sense, Anne banished all such weird fancies. 'And that's just what you should have done, laughed.' She told a tiny fib. 'I didn't believe a word the old hag said, not for a minute.'

'Yes, but she saw a two-headed snake for your future.' Leila tried to lighten their mood. 'Of course *you* wouldn't want to believe her.' She was the only one who laughed, and even her laughter had a hollow ring to it.

'I, also, did not believe what she said.' But Fatima's eyes were wide with fright as she looked at the faces of her friends.

'Nor I.' Leila smiled uncertainly.

'But the blood!' Hysteria was creeping into Camilla's voice. 'Blood everywhere, just as she said. Oh my God, what's going to become of me? Of us?'

Anne was not about to let them all be carried away by a wave of superstitious nonsense. It was bad enough that this wedding had turned into a funeral wake. Now they all had to put the horror of the tragedy behind them. This silly fortune-telling stuff had gone far enough. She must not let her friends – or herself – become afraid of their own shadows. 'Forget Madame Kismet. She's just a nightclub act, that's all. She doesn't know any more about the future than we do.'

'But the blood.' Camilla was crying now. 'She was right about the blood. She could be right about everything else, too.'

'Stop it right now!' Leila seized this golden opportunity to slap Camilla, just as she had seen actors do in the movies.

Camilla gulped hard, but she stopped crying as Anne's American optimism came to the fore and she promised them the futures they dearly wanted.

'Now you listen to me, Camilla. And you, too, Fatima and Leila. Nothing really bad is ever going to happen to us, do you hear me? Not to any of us. Not ever, not to *us*. I'm going to go to Boston and become a doctor and come back here and work in the American University Hospital, which just happens to be the best in the entire Middle East. I'll marry someone wonderful, and I'll be really happy. Leila's going to England to become a famous professor, and then she'll fall in love and marry somebody even richer and more famous than she is. And Fatima . . . why maybe Madame Kismet was a little bit right after all. Maybe Fatima's going to have a great love when she marries her cousin. As for you, Camilla, why, you're going to be as rich and famous as if you were the queen of Lebanon. And you have Pierre, don't forget Pierre – after all, he saved your life today. If it weren't for Pierre . . .'

As Camilla quietly started to cry again, Anne quickly veered away from the tragic present and conjured up a far brighter future. 'So! Anyway! Before long we'll all be back here together again. We'll all have terrific husbands and tons of kids, and we'll be so happy to live in Beirut, the most wonderful place in the whole world. And – yes, of course! – we'll be friends for always, and everything's going to be just as great as we always knew it would be.'

But the mourning shrieks of the bereaved women drowned out Anne's optimistic forecast of the best of all possible futures as the four of them paused in the aisle for another long moment. Then Camilla sighed and wiped her eyes.

'Really,' Anne repeated, 'everything's going to be wonderful!'

They made their way together, arm in arm, up the

aisle and out of the door, and up the path to the castle at the crest of the mountain.

But when the four of them were to look back on Camilla's wedding, it wasn't Anne's hopeful last words which stayed with them. Recalling this day when the bloodletting first began, they would remember the slightly rotting smell of dying camellias, and would hear the echo of a sound that was to haunt all the bad dreams and dark days of their lives. Leaving that church of doom the last thing they heard was a woman's high-pitched, heartsick shriek – a quavering, desperate, piercing sound of mourning for all life's losses. They were to remember that brokenhearted sound – and what it portended – not just for a few months or years, but for ever.

Waxing

1958-1961

Chapter 1

'It's hopeless!' Anne gave up and flopped down on a pile of lingerie spread over her bed. With a wave of her hand she indicated the overflowing trunks and suitcases piled on the floor. Now, in mid-July, her baggage was being shipped to Boston as freight, but she and her family wouldn't be flying to the States until the end of the summer. Her remaining six weeks in Beirut had seemed, until now, to be an eternity. But as she was folding her skirts and sweaters, it had begun to hit home that very soon she would have to leave Beirut – and her friends – behind.

'I mean,' Anne wailed, 'how can I pack for three whole years away from home?'

No answer was called for, and none was given. Fatima just looked up from where she was sitting crosslegged on the floor hemming the slinky black cocktail dress that they all agreed made Anne look like a Jewish Audrey Hepburn. She gave her friend a wide-eyed stricken look before she smoothed out the jet-beaded skirt and went back to her work. Camilla was sprawled out on the bed in a billowing Hawaiian print muu-muu, leafing slowly through French *Vogue*. From time to time, she would look up and make oracular pronouncements: 'French twists are out' . . . 'False eyelashes are in' . . . 'Lanvin's showing two clashing prints together. Imagine that!' Then she would yawn. She was well into her fourth month now and tired all the time, and as she glanced at the fashion pages her hand would snake out to the dish of pickled cucumber *torshee* Fatima had brought her from home. Leila was chain-smoking as she paced, panther-like in her trim black toreador pants and slick black halter top, from the bed to the window and back again, sometimes pausing to pull back the ruffled white curtains and stare intently, as though she expected to see something more than the garden, the beach, the sea. Anne's old Turkish-style house was in the throbbing centre of the city, just off the American university campus and almost overlooking the Corniche, on the appropriately named Rue Bliss. Her third-floor windows, which afforded an unparalleled view of the placid blue sea on one side and the snow-capped green mountains on the other, also let in the mad tooting, screeching and whooshing sounds of Beirut's free-for-all traffic.

It was one of those languid Beirut afternoons that they all loved. Maurice Chevalier was singing 'Thank Heaven for Little Girls' over and over on the record player. Outside, the surf was lapping on the beach. They could hear, not far away, the soprano shouts of children at play. Always these sleepy afternoons were their favourite time to stretch out and give themselves up to those heart-to-heart talks they so adored. They had assembled here for lunch hours ago, ostensibly to help Anne pack, but mostly just to be together. Yet today, even as they revelled in their old companionable ease, time was starting to press in on them. By summer's end none of them would be left in Beirut. Leila would be in England, Fatima back in her village, and Camilla cloistered in her father-in-law's mountaintop fortress. So today, since they hadn't wanted even Anne's family to intrude upon their intimacy, the cook had obligingly served their lunch on a big copper tray here in the bedroom. They had eaten on the floor, Arab-style, from communal dishes, teasing Camilla – who had finally admitted she was pregnant – that she would surely give birth to triplets the way she was eating. They had spent some of the best hours of their lives just like this – blurting out their innermost secrets, laughing away all the fears that sounded so silly once they had said them out loud, prattling on apparently about nothing but really about everything. As people tend to do when they're happy, they had taken what they had together for granted. Without thinking about it, they had somehow assumed this would go on for ever, that they would always be able to while away the hours in perfect companionship right here in the haven of Anne's lemon-yellow bedroom. Yet the open suitcases told another story.

'Sometimes', Anne said, in a voice so low it seemed she was talking to herself, 'I wish I weren't going at all.'

'Then don't go.' Fatima had thought long and hard about how to convince the one she always possessively thought of as her 'best' friend not to go a world away. She had talked all this over last week with her uncles, and now, before Anne locked up her suitcases, was the time to tender her offer. She took a deep breath and plunged ahead. 'Stay here. Become a nurse. Train at the American Hospital. Then come to my village in the south. We need a health centre. The nearest doctor is far away, over in Sidon. I could open a school, and you could open a clinic.' She smiled earnestly, aware that she had saved the best for last. 'My family will even build you a house.'

'Oh, Fatima!' Anne was touched, even flattered. She knew that, in a way, Fatima considered her stony white village at the top of an undulating southern hill to be the centre of the universe. She had visited Fatima's family down there, usually in the spring, when rippling fields of thigh-high wild flowers stretched serenely to the horizon. But never before had Fatima offered to take her in and make her part of that closed and sheltered world. She must have been nurturing this dream of the two of them healing and teaching her cousins and neighbours for a very long while. Gently Anne shook her head. 'I don't want to be a nurse. If I did, I might take you up on that. Someday I'd like to work in one of the villages, especially in the south. I'd really like to go where I'm needed. Where I can make a difference. I think it's terrible how the government doesn't pay any attention to the south. As far as I can see, there are hardly any good doctors down there. But that's what I want to be, a good doctor. I don't want just to be a nurse, handing out pills and bedpans. I want to be a *doctor*.' Reminding herself of that great ambition seemed to spur Anne on. She stood up, tossed back her black halo of hair, and gave the heaps of clothes she would be wearing in that hallowed new life a distracted look before she picked up an armful of blouses. 'It's only three years anyway. It's not for ever.'

Leila let the curtain fall from her hand as she turned away from one of the best sea views in Beirut and rounded on her friends. 'Jolly right.' She didn't want them all to go soppy. At this rate, they would be weeping and moaning through the best months of the whole summer. Beirut was magnificent in all seasons. But for the young, the rich and the lissom, the red-hot summers were the best of all. Leila loved to start out at dawn in her convertible, speeding up narrow winding mountain roads with her radio blasting rock and roll for a rhythmic hour. If she was lucky, at Faraya she could put on snow skis and whiz down the slopes *vite*. Then she would zip back to Beirut, slip on her bikini, and roast on Riviera Beach or water-ski in St George's Bay. By sunset she could be back at her father's villa in Aley sipping a cocktail on a breezy balcony with a view that seemed to stretch all the way to Spain. But this was their last summer together in Beirut . . . With the rounded toe of one of her flat black ballerina slippers, she pointed at the overflowing suitcase nearest her. 'If you want my opinion, you're absolutely mad to take all this junk with you.' Her tone of voice was sharper than she'd intended. It wasn't only her anxious watch at the window that was telling on her nerves. Those open suitcases were reminding her that she, too, would be packing very soon. She put the thought aside and tried to make her voice sound playful. 'It's not as if you're going to China or something. They have shops in America. I hear you can buy almost anything you want there. It's not London, of course. But it's hardly the Belgian Congo.'

'Junk?' Camilla leaned over and absently picked up a knife-pleated beige skirt, looked at the label, then tossed it back on a pile of clothes. 'Anne never wears junk. But Leila is right. Don't take all these old things.' Since the wedding she had, with great gusto, taken to the Nazrani habit of extravagance. 'Buy everything new in America.'

'You're the one who's rich now, not me.' Anne laughed. Since each of them contributed in a different way to the friendship, they had long ago left off being sensitive about money. Leila was not one for cloying sentiment, but she quietly picked up their bills at Chez Paul, La Brioche and Samedi, and gave them thoughtful and exquisitely expensive presents – a Hermès scarf, a phial of Joy perfume, a silver-handled Kent hairbrush – on their birthdays. Fatima had nothing to give but herself. She was the one who rarely missed a chance to drop a kind word or – as now – to hem a dress. Camilla had always been careless about money – flush one minute, broke the next – alternately borrowing cash, even from Fatima, and then splurging on some splendid silliness like salon pedicures for the whole group. Anne was usually short on cash but long on hospitality. Her father's middling income at the university meant that she had to make do on a tightly budgeted weekly allowance. Instead of treating her friends at the cinema or cafés, she usually – like today – turned her bedroom into their clubhouse. 'In Boston I'm just going to be a poor medical student.'

'Maybe you are the lucky one.' As Camilla turned the pages of *Vogue*, her hand trembled.

Fatima looked up from her hem and caught Anne's eye, and even Leila stopped pacing. This was not how a happy bride should be talking. Anne firmly shut and locked a suitcase and then sat down beside Camilla. 'Would you like to tell us what's wrong?'

'Nothing.' Camilla would not look up from her magazine. But she did not turn the page. She stared at a photograph of a long-limbed model in a narrow tweed Mainbocker suit. 'Everything.'

'*Malesh*, don't worry.' Fatima smiled knowingly over her sewing. 'It is only the baby. I think all the time you feel a little bit sick? You are always tired? And you feel everything more in your heart? One woman in my village always cries for all the nine months of every pregnancy. But then she is so happy once she has it. You will be, too.'

'*Peut-être*.' Camilla shot Fatima a hunted look. 'If it's a boy, that is. They will *all* think I am very wonderful if I make a son for the Nazranis.'

'Old Shaykh Georges', Leila said, 'will buy out all the gold souks in the Levant if you give him an heir.'

Camilla sighed as she twirled a lock of her platinum hair around her finger for a long moment before deciding to say more. Finally she closed her magazine. 'I did not tell you, *mes bien-aimées*, what it was like when they found out I am pregnant.'

'I bet Pierre's nasty mother and her sisters had plenty to say.' Leila let her gaze rest pointedly on her friend's ballooning stomach. Camilla was obviously more than three weeks pregnant. 'Listen, darling, since you brought this up, when *is* the baby due?'

'Who knows?' Camilla lifted her shoulders in an eloquent Gallic shrug. 'Perhaps it will even be a little bit premature.'

Even Fatima could not help smiling.

'Well, whenever the baby comes, and whether it's a girl or a boy, I'm sure Pierre and all his family will be delighted.' Anne said that matter-of-factly, as though there could be no doubt about it.

'Oh Anne! All your life you live with us and still you understand nothing!' There were huge milky tears forming in Camilla's big blue eyes. For Camilla was fortunate in being one of those rare women who cried beautifully. Her eyes turned bluer, her cheeks bloomed with rosy colour, and even her plump and pearly tears were perfect in their way. When Fatima handed her a tissue, she expertly blotted her tears so that her mascara would not smear. Finally, then, she told her friends about the scene a week ago at the château.

'Oh, Pierre, my Pierre, he was so very happy! I told him in the bedroom, you know, and he picked me up in his arms! He is so strong, you know, like bull!' Camilla's eyes were shining now, and not only with tears. 'He kissed me and kissed me, and before I could stop him he carried me down the stairs to tell all the family. They were all in the salon drinking coffee. He kept shouting, "*Moi! I did it*", that he made me pregnant on the night we were married. He did not care if that was exactly true or just a little bit of an exaggeration. His father, too, did not care about precisely when the baby began. The old man was crazy with joy. Georges grabbed a long gun from the wall and went outside and shot at the moon. Then all the men – Pierre, too – they get their guns and go outside to shoot. I am surprised that they did not shoot down the moon.' Camilla heaved a great sigh. 'But I was left in the salon with the mother and the sisters and the aunts. They begin then to ask – what was that word you said, Leila? My English, it gets worse. Always at the château we talk *français*. And Arabic to the maids. Ah, yes, I remember your word – nasty. Yes, they begin then to ask the nasty questions. They do not like me, you know. They never did. And I do not like them.' The tears were welling up again. 'Pierre's mother – the cow! – made me come up to her bedroom and kneel at a *prie-dieu* she has to the Virgin. She told me to pray for purity. And to pray that God would not punish me for what I did – by maybe giving me only girls, not boys. As if this was only my fault! It was Pierre who made me! Her son, not me!'

'How awful.' Anne clucked her tongue and shook her head. At times like this, she was very glad that her own reserved New England mother would never dream of carrying on like Camilla's in-laws. Most of the time she liked the warmth and excitement of the Arabs. It was good fun when they kissed and hugged and said and did the things she was too reserved to do. But she hated it when they became overheated and went off on these frighteningly melodramatic emotional binges.

But Fatima obviously had a very different reaction to Camilla's story. 'So, have you been praying?'

'Why don't *you* pray for Camilla?' Leila couldn't stand it when Fatima went pious on them. 'A perfect little Muslim like you surely has no sins of your own.'

Even though Leila's voice had been syrupy with sarcasm, Fatima took her at her word. 'Of course I will pray for Camilla. And, *inshallah*, for her son.' Gravely she smiled at Leila. 'I will pray for you, too.'

Hastily – before Leila could really blow up at Fatima – Anne turned their attention back to Camilla. 'So really, it's only your in-laws that are the problem?'

'*Oui et non*.' Camilla would not meet Anne's eyes. Evasively she re-opened *Vogue* and gazed longingly at an advertisement for an art correspondence course. She had always dreamed of some day turning her flair for drawing into a career as an internationally respected artist. Back at the château, she had filled out the coupon for this course. But she doubted if she would ever post it. She had chosen to be a wife and mother, not an artist.

Leila had decided to let Fatima – for now – get away with that crack about praying for her. But she perched on the window-ledge and beamed her full attention on Camilla. 'I think the real problem is Pierre. Mind you, from the first time I saw him, I thought he looked a bit of a brute. My father always says those Maronites are animals. Does he beat you?'

'Pierre? Oh, no.' Camilla blushed, and then she slyly smiled to herself and *Vogue*. Already, just after the wedding, she had let down her hair and told her three virgin friends just what 'it' was like. Pierre was passionate, but he could be tender, too. Sex was not their problem.

'If he doesn't beat you,' Leila relentlessly continued, 'then what is it that he does that makes you feel so bad?'

'I don't know, exactly,' Camilla whispered. Finally she looked up, and the truth burst out of her. '*C'est moi!* I am so disappointed! I wanted to marry him so much. I thought he was the most wonderful man in the world. All I wanted in the world was him, him, him.' She held up her hand and pointed to the blue veins on the inside of her wrist. 'I think to myself, all I am now is Pierre. I do not have the blood in my veins. I have Pierre. He is all through me. Pierre in my veins.' She sighed. 'But now I have him, and . . . I begin to feel – yes! – so empty.' Again the tears were running down her flushed cheeks. 'I am empty even with the baby here inside! He is not enough. Yes, it is wonderful when we are together, when he sits there only with me, when we are in the bed. Yes, *magnifique!* But I am so empty when he is not with me. And most of the time he is with the men. *Vraiment*, I think he should have married his father. Or his mother. I am sure he loves his mother more than me.'

Fatima sighed over her sewing. 'I have heard other women say this.'

'I haven't.' Anne looked doubtfully at Camilla. She and Pierre had seemed so in love. If, just three weeks after the wedding, Camilla was talking like this – then what was the point of getting married at all?

As she blew her nose lustily, Camilla began to relish her sympathetic audience. 'It is not what I thought it would be. He leaves me alone too much. I hate to be alone.' She sniffled. 'And I'm hardly ever even in Beirut! Because of all the fighting, the strike, and this miserable curfew, they keep me like a prisoner in that terrible château. I hate it there! I want to be here.'

It was the first time this afternoon that any of them had referred to the one matter that was uppermost in all their minds. They had preferred to focus their attention on the less dangerous ups and downs of their own lives rather than on the volatile fuse burning on the national powderkeg. In the momentous weeks since Camilla's wedding, Lebanon had been riven by what some were already calling a civil war. That fateful shootout in the Nazrani parish church had been only one spark in a country and a region that had already been long smouldering. A Lebanese journalist had been gunned down shortly afterwards in Beirut, and within days there had been violent demonstrations in Tripoli and a general strike in Beirut. The government had responded on 12 May by imposing a curfew from eight in the evening until five in the morning. Since then shops, cinemas, restaurants and nightclubs had all put up their shutters. But still the fighting had continued. Militant Muslims had erected wooden barricades in the Basta quarter, scattered explosions had gutted Muslim and Christian shops, and the President had requested the intervention of American troops. The opposition forces had won control of half the country, and the other half remained sharply divided. At the beginning of their revolt, the Muslims and their allies had simply demanded the resignation of the President and democratic elections. But, elated by their success in the field, they had then begun to call for broader reforms: a new national census that would reflect the probable fact that Muslims were now a majority of the population, a reform of the civil service to provide equal opportunities for those of all religions, and a restructuring of the governmental and economic power that would finally give the Muslims their fair share of anything and everything. Then, just yesterday, in a bloody coup in Baghdad, the pro-Western Iraqi monarchy had fallen to Arab nationalists. Anything now might happen. It was rumoured that the next to fall might be the shaky British-oriented monarchy in Jordan. Or red revolutionary banners might even triumph here in Lebanon. Beirut buzzed with the wild rumour that the Communists were about to take over.

'The only reason they let me come here today was they had room in the car to Beirut. Pierre and his father, they were making the trip to see a man here. They were very excited. This man will make for them a new deal for the guns.' Camilla said it casually, as though she were talking about shopping for a winter wardrobe.

'Guns?' Leila jumped on that shred of news as if it were meat and she were a starving animal. 'So Shaykh Georges hasn't had enough? Who's he going to this time – the Americans? The Syrians? Or is it true that he's doing some dirty deals with the Israelis?'

'How should I know?' Camilla's emotional storm had passed. She pulled out a compact, dabbed at her face, plumped up her hair, and then yawned as she reached for another pickle. Even though she thrived on tears and scenes, and it was divine to have poured her heart out to the girls, she could do with a siesta now.

With one of her characteristically lightning mood changes, Camilla cheerily changed the subject back to what she vaguely remembered them talking about before she had broken down. 'Too bad, Anne, you are not going to school in New York. I hope you will love this Boston. But New York is supposed to be *fantastique*.'

The thought of New York revived her. 'I would *love* to do Fifth Avenue. And the big stores. I have heard so very much about them.' She thought for a moment. When she tried, when she cared deeply about something – such as shopping – she had a highly retentive memory. 'There are three "Bs" – Bloomingdale's, Beindele's, Bergdorf's. And one called Six – no, Saks. Like sex, ha! There is also Gimbel's and Macy's, although I think they are for the poor people. And – I can't remember for sure – maybe Selfish's?'

Leila could not help laughing. 'You mean Selfridge's, and it's in London.' She, too, was a passionate shopper. A little later she would bully Camilla into telling all she knew about this intriguing Nazrani arms sale. But for now she could not resist her favourite roll call. 'As is Liberty's, Harrods, Harvey Nichols, and ye olde trusty Marks and Spencer's. London, here I come!'

'I wish you were not all going away.' Fatima bit off the cotton thread unhappily. Lovingly she folded Anne's beautiful black dress and, as she placed it just so in a suitcase, she looked as though she would have liked to pack herself in there as well. 'I wish you were all staying here with me.'

Leila reached down and, their differences almost forgotten, she fondly – and only a little painfully – pinched Fatima's cheek. 'We will return, *habibi*. We will return.' She lit one of her cigarettes for Fatima and another for herself before she coiled up next to Camilla on the bed. 'Strange, isn't it? Anne and I are both going to live in a Cambridge. But she will be with her rich aunt in America, and I will be in England.' Leila's dark eyes darkened even further as she considered how much duller – and how much lonelier – her life would be without Anne. She was attached to the other two, of course. Camilla was very amusing when she wasn't pouting, and Leila liked being seen at all the best places with someone else who made heads turn in envy. It was uncanny how, wherever Camilla went, men of all ages always jumped up to open doors for her. Leila was also more deeply drawn to Fatima and all she represented than she would ever let on to the others or even to herself. But gutsy, forthright, idealistic Anne was her favourite. She considered Anne to be almost her equal in everything. She didn't even mind that Anne's father was Jewish. Professor Rosen was not a Zionist, and neither – *el-hamdulillah!* – was Anne. In many ways, except for her own family, Anne was the only one in all the world whom she entirely trusted. 'I wish we could be in the same Cambridge.'

Anne nodded. She, too, could not resist this eleventh hour temptation to try to hang on to those she loved. 'Listen, why don't you change your mind and come to America? You got into Cambridge. I bet you could get into Harvard, too.'

'Sorry. It would be smashing to be with you, Anne. But it's far too late to change everything now. And, frankly, I don't know that I would if I could. You know how I've always wanted to go to university in England.' Leila's father kept an elegant Park Lane penthouse, and for at least two weeks of every Ramadan the whole far-flung family escaped the rigours of the Muslim fasting month by reuniting in the shadow of Hyde Park. Those happy annual fortnights had enticed Leila to spend four years of her adolescence boarding at a private school in Dorset, and she had emerged from that experience with an even more abiding love for all things British. She and the rest of the Shahines would, of course, never forgive England for turning Palestine over to the Zionists. But that major political point had not kept any of them from affecting rather posh English accents. 'But you won't be all alone in the wilds of America. My baby brother will be at Harvard. And I've given him express instructions to look out for you.'

Anne laughed at the idea of Ramsey, who was

a mere eighteen years old, looking out for her – a sophisticated lady of twenty-one. Still, it would be nice to have someone from Beirut there.

They all jumped when the bedroom door suddenly flew open. Anne's sixteen-year-old brother Ben stood there flushed and out of breath from running up the stairs three at a time. As Fatima scrambled in a panic to cover her hair, Ben blurted out his news. 'The Marines are here! It's on the radio! The Lebanese president has asked for them again, and this time Eisenhower's sending them. They're already landing on Khaldé Beach! Here in Beirut!'

'*Yaadra!* Holy Virgin!' Camilla crossed herself and began to cry again. 'I *told* Pierre we should spend the summer in Paris. I *begged* him at least to let *me* go.' She rocked herself back and forth, as if she were in a cradle, but she was not soothed. 'All this fighting! I can't stand it. The blood – *Yaadra!* – I remember that blood in the church.'

'There, there . . .' Anne put her arm around her. Over Camilla's head, she and Fatima exchanged worried looks. They had been concerned about Camilla ever since the wedding. Even though she had always been highly strung, Camilla had taken Madame Kismet's dire predictions altogether too much to heart. She had even dashed back to the Crescent for another reading from the old gypsy, and when she had discovered that the fortune-teller had packed her bags and left Lebanon – Nirvana thought she was going to New Zealand, of all places – Camilla had taken it into her head that she must flee to Paris. They hoped her obsession to cut and run was just some passing pregnant fancy.

'But that's absurd.' Leila gave Ben the dirty look she would have liked to give Eisenhower. 'They wouldn't dare! That's an act of war. The United States can't invade Lebanon.'

Ben backed into the hall. He had never liked his

sister's Palestinian friend. He, like his mother, was not especially fond of any of the Arabs, but above all he hated the arrogant ones like this Leila, who never bothered to hide the fact that she thought she was better than everyone else, even Americans. His eyes darted to the other girl who always wore that funny scarf. She looked scared to death. Yet when he had managed to catch a glimpse of her long rippling black hair a moment ago, he had been surprised how pretty she was without that ugly scarf pulled down on her forehead. Why would a girl who looked like she did not want to flaunt it? Wistfully, then, his gaze lingered on the beautiful one he often thought about when he lay in bed at night before he went to sleep. Camilla was crying again. She was always weeping like some sad, mistreated princess in a fairy tale. Ben wished he could single-handedly stop the fighting so she would call him a hero and stop crying and maybe kiss him. She would look up at him from under those long fluttering black lashes of hers and—

'Exactly what else did they say on the radio?' Anne's crisp voice cut into Ben's reverie.

With an effort he brought himself back to the here and now. 'The President of Lebanon asked for the Marines. He said we needed them to protect us all from the Communist menace.' Ben belatedly remembered the other bulletin. 'And the same thing's happened today in Jordan. The British have airlifted in their troops to make sure King Hussein can win out over the Reds.'

'Communists, my ass!' Leila cursed eloquently and elaborately in Arabic. 'Lebanon – and Jordan, too – have the weakest Communist parties in the Middle East. Lies, lies, I'm sick of these lies! Goddamned America! Goddamned Marines! They're not sending them in to protect anything but American power. *And* to prop up the Christians.'

Camilla raised her tear-stained face. Almost in spite

of herself, she had absorbed some new political lessons in these first weeks of her marriage. 'Lebanon is a Christian country.'

'Listen to the little Maronite.' Leila's eyes flashed as her sorely strained temper finally careered out of control. 'Let me give you a bit of advice, darling. Stick to things you know about like shopping and having a good cry. Leave politics to your betters.'

'Leila!' Fatima was used to being the object of Leila's slurs, but she wasn't going to stand for her hitting out at poor defenceless Camilla. 'How can you talk like this?'

'How can you not?' The Palestinian glared at the Shia. 'You're an Arab and a Muslim. Act like it! Stand up and fight for what you believe! All you and your kind ever do is pray and sigh and hope that Allah will give you paradise on earth. I have news for you. It's up to *us*, not to your precious Allah, to make this country into what it should be.'

'And what should Lebanon be?' Anne was tight-lipped. Even though she prided herself on her tolerance, Anne hadn't liked it one bit when – right here, in her own bedroom – Leila had cursed America and the Marines.

'Whatever the Lebanese want it to be. *The Lebanese!* Not the Americans, not the French, not the Syrians, not anybody else who wants to butt in and take what they can.' Leila's eyes were bright with conviction. 'Why – for once – can't we set up a Lebanese government for the Lebanese? If America would keep its goddamned hands off us, maybe we'd finally be able to set up a government here that did what the majority of the people wanted.'

'For a Palestinian, you have much to say about Lebanon.' When pushed too far, Fatima, too, could fight with words. 'In a house – or a country – most guests, I believe, are more polite than you.'

The colour drained from Leila's face, and for the first time that any of the others could remember, they saw tears spring to her eyes.

In the sudden uneasy silence that fell over the bedroom, they heard footsteps on the staircase. Anne's parents stood framed with Ben in the doorway.

'Glad to see you ladies are all right.' Anne's father adjusted his horn-rimmed glasses as he looked intently at his daughter and her friends. 'But perhaps I spoke too soon. I think the shooting war outside is virtually over. But from the looks on your faces, maybe there're still some fireworks going on in here.' Professor Joseph Rosen was short, stocky, bookish, and every bit the absent-minded professor when it came to trivia like time, appointments and remembering telephone numbers. But he took his responsibilities as a father seriously, and so he had taken the time to get to know and appreciate these girls who were like sisters to his daughter. He wanted to break his next bit of bad news to them gently. He ruffled his son's hair. 'Thanks for looking after the girls, Ben. Now, how about going downstairs? You two can keep tabs on what's on the radio while I say something to Anne.'

Ben was glad to have an excuse to be gone. He marched back down the stairs singing the US Marine anthem at the top of his lungs.

'I'm not going downstairs.' Martha Rosen's frightened green eyes surveyed her daughter's partially packed trunks and suitcases. 'I'm staying right here to make sure Anne gets busy and finishes what she's begun.' She couldn't help the fact that her high-pitched voice was querulous. The shooting had terrified her. She longed to sweep through Anne's room, toss her clothes and shoes into brown paper shopping bags, and throw her belongings into the back seat of the car. Then, this very afternoon, she wished she could flee like a refugee out to the airport and up into the sky, west to Boston, forever away from this alien place she had hated even before the shooting had begun. 'Up here all afternoon – the four of them! – and none of it sorted out.'

'Mother!' Anne loved her mother, but nevertheless she wanted to die when her mother embarrassed her like this. 'Not in front of *them*.' But Anne could not help guiltily beginning to fold skirts, sweaters, blouses.

Leila had already collected her bag and was making for the door. 'I really must be going.' She studiously ignored Anne's regrettable mother. Her own mother had died giving birth to Ramsey, and when she saw Anne's and Camilla's mothers carrying on as they did, she was almost glad that she didn't even remember her own. She preferred to forget all the vulnerable years when she had ached to have a real mother of her own. Leila gave Anne's father a bright social smile. 'By the sound of it, sir, you have something you want to talk over with your daughter.' But she couldn't resist giving Fatima an icy drop-dead look. 'And I certainly wouldn't want to overstay my welcome.'

'You are always welcome here, Leila. You know that.' Professor Rosen continued to block the doorway. 'And I really think you'd better stay a while longer. Perhaps even all night. I don't want any of you out today.'

'No, no. That is, I think, too much trouble.' Fatima longed to flee home. Her family would be so worried about her.

'You are *très gentil, monsieur*.' Camilla automatically batted her wet eyelashes at the professor.

Martha Rosen's eyes flicked from the shameless chit, who flirted with every man she met, back to her husband, whose old-fool eyes were a bit too bright as he smiled at the blonde bombshell who was decidedly young enough to be his daughter. But finally Martha took hold of herself. Apart from causing her endless grief by bringing her to live in Lebanon, Joe was a model husband. He had never done anything to make her doubt his fidelity. Still, she wished these girls would vanish and leave her family alone on this day of stress and uncertainty. 'Maybe Leila's right. Perhaps they should go home now. It's safe. The Marines are here now.'

'Shhh. There, now, Martha . . .' The professor put his arm around his wife. 'Besides, I think you girls will all want to take a little time to bury the hatchet on whatever it was you were fighting about when we came in. You see, I'm afraid I have some more bad news. Anne's mother and I were talking . . .' He paused. He wanted to say this just right, so he wouldn't alarm them. He didn't want Camilla turning on the waterworks again. 'With the Marines coming, and God knows what happening after that, we think we'd better move up our own schedule a bit.' He paused and looked expectantly at Anne.

'What do you mean by "a bit", Daddy?'

'Well, I was going to see to some business at home this fall anyway. And you know how your mother's been all summer, with the curfews and the demonstrations. She could use a vacation. And even though Ben's dying to stay here and cheer on the Marines, it won't hurt him, too, to get away from it all for a while. Besides, at this time of year—'

'Get to the point, Joe.' Sometimes she could not bear the way her husband beat around the bush.

He cleared his throat. 'We talked this all over, and to the best of our estimation, the troubles—'

'Tell them the truth, Joe. We're getting out when the getting's good. And if they have any sense, they'll do the same. It's not safe here. God knows it's bad now. But it's going to get worse.'

'That's just what Madame Kismet said.' Camilla nodded sagely.

This time Anne broke in. 'When are we leaving, Daddy?'

'Okay, okay.' The professor held up his hands. 'I've just called the airlines. We're on the waiting list for tomorrow's flight out. But frankly, considering the situation, I doubt if it's even worth going to the airport to stand by. We've got a confirmed booking for the day after tomorrow.'

'*Bad bokra?* You go away after tomorrow?' Fatima sounded as though she were talking about a sentence of death. She wrung her hands in despair.

Anne wailed as she looked at the partially packed suitcases and trunks scattered the width of her room. 'I can't possibly be ready by then.'

'That's the other thing. Your mother and I were just saying that, considering how long it takes to ship anything to the States, and the way the airlines charge for overweight baggage, and the chaos at the airport—'

'Pack two suitcases and leave the rest.' Anne's mother managed a smile. She knew she hadn't been at her best this summer. But she couldn't help it, the troubles in this miserable country had simply got the better of her. She would make it up to her family once they got back to civilization. 'I'll take you shopping in Boston, honey. You can buy whatever else you need right there. You'll want some new things anyway. Some real *American* clothes.'

'Didn't I say that before?' Camilla clapped her hands in approval. 'Yes! I wish I could come, too, and we could – how you say it? – spree together!' But then the import of Anne's father's message got through to Camilla. 'But *Yaadra!* That means you go away on Thursday! No, it is too soon!'

Leila gnawed on her lower lip as she dug in her bag for her cigarettes. If Anne went away on Thursday, that awful little argument they had just had would be their goodbye. She noticed, as she was lighting up, that Fatima was looking longingly at her Craven As, and for a moment she could not decide whether to offer her one.

Fatima had cut her to the core. She had never expected passive little Fatima to strike out and wound her so. As Leila inhaled deeply, the smoke seemed to soothe her jangled nerves. What with the shooting, the bloody Marines coming, that nasty little clash right here in the bedroom, and now Anne being told she was leaving . . . Leila inhaled again, and she could almost feel the smoke curling around her long aristocratic toes. What the hell! She herself, on not one but many occasions, had said far more insulting things to Fatima. She would surely do so again, and soon. She would not forget that snaky little Shia comment. 'Here.' Leila did not quite succeed in making herself smile graciously as she grudgingly extended the pack.

Professor Rosen had been watching the girls closely. 'In my country, I think they call that smoking a peace pipe.'

'Thank you very much.' As Fatima lit one of the cigarettes, she shifted her attention back to Leila. In her alarm at losing Anne, she had almost forgotten that she had finally said what she had always wanted to say to Leila. She did not regret her harsh words. There were many examples, in the Holy Koran, of how righteous anger was pleasing to Allah. It was long past the time when someone had to make Leila understand the consequences if she didn't learn to control her poisonous tongue. But there was also much in the Holy Koran about forgiveness, especially between one believer and another. Leila might not be the best Muslim in the world, but she still counted as a sister. 'I did not want to hurt you before,' she said. 'I hope – no, I pray – that I never have to say anything like that again, to you or to anyone.' Fatima smiled shyly. 'Especially to you, my dear sister.'

Leila had such a terribly constricting lump in her throat that she knew she couldn't possibly say a single word. So she did something better. She cast off her shell of British reserve and gave way to the Arab in herself. She put one hand on each of Fatima's shoulders and kissed her soundly on her left cheek, right cheek, then her left cheek again. She and Fatima beamed at each other – their bitter words for the moment entirely forgiven and forgotten.

'At least you two kissed and made up.' Anne was fighting very hard to hold on to her composure. She hated to cry in front of anyone, even her family and her very best friends. 'It would have been awful if you'd gone home mad. Since I guess today was our farewell lunch.'

'But this isn't goodbye.' Leila's voice was brisk.

'*Au revoir*, then.' Camilla was reaching for the tissues.

'Wrong again.' Leila was her old confident, bossy self. 'We shall all see you off at the airport. Your flight is at what time on Thursday?'

'Just after noon.' Professor Rosen gently shook his head. 'But I don't think you girls should count on coming to the airport. They said on the radio that everyone should stay home except for essential business.'

'Seeing Anne off *is* essential. Wild horses – and the entire United States Marines – couldn't keep us away.' Leila snapped her bag shut and slung it over her shoulder. Now that they had established that this wasn't goodbye, she was suddenly anxious to be gone. She wanted to get home to hear her father's version of what had gone so terribly wrong in Lebanon today. 'It is most kind of you, Professor Rosen, to offer us your hospitality tonight. But we really must be going. I have my car. I'll give Fatima and Camilla a lift.'

'I wouldn't hear of it. Why, if anything happened to you girls, I'd never be able to face your families. Kemal Shahine and Georges Nazrani would have me hung, drawn and quartered.'

'Let her drive if she wants, Joe. I'm sure Leila can take care of herself.'

'*Yalla! Emshee!*' Leila began the laborious process of shooing her friends towards the door and her waiting car. All of them had to kiss, hug, wipe away tears, and promise to telephone the next morning before they began to make their final and even more elaborate goodbyes outside by the car.

It was the better part of an hour before Camilla and Fatima finally wedged into Leila's red MG sports car, and they roared off into the darkening shadows of the Beirut twilight. By the time Leila turned east to Ashrafiya to drop off Camilla and then zoomed back west to leave Fatima in the Basta, the sun was already close to sinking in a flaming ball of fire into the purple sea.

Leila slammed shut her car door, ran inside her family's villa, and joined the wake her father was holding for Arab nationalism in the drawing room. Kemal Shahine's long-faced Muslim and Druze cronies from the Bourse, from Parliament and from the big landowning families of the south and the Bekaa had come together to console themselves on this dark day when the US Marines had landed in Beirut. Leila threw herself into her father's arms, and Kemal for a moment held his favourite child fiercely to his heart. She was dry-eyed thereafter and coldly composed as she circulated in the drawing room refilling the glasses, pouring orange juice for the practising Muslims and straight whisky for the rest. With the men, she raised her glass on high when her father proposed toasts to a free Lebanon, to a liberated Palestine, to a victorious Nasser, to the inevitable triumph of all their just causes. On the day that the 1958 Lebanese civil war had ended, the Muslims drank thirstily to the future.

Chapter 2

Anne was already half awake when the morning breeze carried the muezzin's call to dawn prayers over the rooftops and into the bedroom that had always been her refuge. Sleepily she let the beguiling drone of the Arabic chant wash over her. Day or night, awake or asleep, she loved the sound of the prayer calls. Sometimes at sunset she stood on the balcony of Fatima's flat in the Muslim quarter of the Basta and, with as much enjoyment as if it were a Bach violin partita, she listened to one muezzin after another, from every mosque on every other street corner, sing out the deep-throated news that now was the time to praise the Lord. Those prayer calls stirred her, in some mysterious but vastly satisfying way, to the very depths of her soul. When she was just a little girl, and had first asked her father what that sound was, she had felt very left out when he had explained that it was a spiritual signal not for her or for him, but for the Muslims. He had taken her, then, on one of their infrequent visits to Beirut's main Jewish synagogue. She had liked the sonorous Hebrew chanting, and had later asked her father why they didn't shout these prayers from the minarets, too. 'Not here,' her father had told her as he gazed southwards to the Jewish state in Israel. 'Later, when you're older, I'll explain all that to you.' But he never had, at least not to her satisfaction. For her father had never talked to her much about the religion, and the heritage, that he had turned his back upon when his family had pronounced him dead to them after he married a Christian. Yet then and there, at the age of six, Anne had decided to offer an ecumenical answer to the Muslim prayer calls. Even though she didn't know any Hebrew, forever after she had silently offered up a Judeo-Christian 'Amen' to the muezzins.

She was yawning and stretching when suddenly her eyes flew open.

Oh, no. Today was the day. Her suitcases were already packed and waiting downstairs. She, her parents and her brother were leaving for Boston. This was the last morning, for a very long while, that she would wake in Beirut.

Anne felt an impulse to throw the covers over her head and go back to sleep, in the vague hope that when she opened her eyes again it would be any other day except this wrenching one when she had to leave everything she loved behind. But she fought the desire to give in to those wayward run-for-cover emotions of her weaker self. She reminded herself that she must always think positive. She wanted to be a doctor more than anything else, and in order to learn to be the kind of doctor she wanted to be she had to go away. She would be on that twelve-thirty flight. Still, she was dreading the misery of today's goodbyes. Dear Fatima would make it harder by clinging too long, and Camilla of course would carry on until even the porters were weeping and moaning in sympathy.

Anne sighed as she stared dry-eyed at the yellow ceiling of her girlhood bedroom. It wasn't that she wouldn't feel bad enough today to cling like Fatima and cry like Camilla. Sometimes when people told her how cool and calm she was, she wanted to burst out with the vulnerable truth that inside she was quite the opposite. She didn't want to be a doctor because she liked starched uniforms and a sterilized life. She burned to cure life's wrongs and alleviate human suffering. Just because she kept her passions stoked deep inside her didn't mean the hot embers weren't all aglow. If she ever let herself go, she knew she could put even Camilla to shame. But Anne was determined not to let go, not today, not any day until she was sure that whatever – or whomever – she let herself go for was never going to betray her. Her thoughts turned darkly, and inevitably, to Madame Kismet and that horrible reptilian future she had forecast in her crystal ball. Of course the old gypsy couldn't really see the future. Yet it wouldn't hurt to be more cautious than ever if and when she finally met the man of her dreams.

Anne threw off the sheet and all such dark doubts. She bounded to the window, leaned on the ledge, and took an exhilarating breath of the fresh sea air as she drank in the silvery pink sight of Beirut at dawn. The city lay in a glorious crescent, in snug embrace between the sweeping blue sea and the rippling green mountains. Pale clusters of high-rise towers glinted starkly in the sky, taller than the cross-crowned Christian steeples, wider than the crescent-peaked Muslim domes. Lacy minarets stretched upwards like rockets poised on launch pads to heaven. Here in fashionable Ras Beirut – as in a travel poster – the turquoise water lapped in soft white surf on the sparkling golden sand. Along the seafront the ultra-modern buildings that prize-winning architects had engineered shimmered in steely whites, golds, greys. But this modern metropolis that the international bankers had built was only Beirut's face-lifted, expertly made-up façade that looked out yearningly to the Mediterranean and to the West that lay beyond. Anne turned her head away from the skyscraper sprawl that could have belonged to any of the world's modern capitals. As much as she loved the cosmopolitan excitements of modern Beirut – the smart shops, the luscious *pâtisseries*, the restaurants and the clubs which equalled anything in Paris – for her the heart of this city beat elsewhere. The Beirut she adored was a dirtier, yeastier and altogether more fascinating world that lay hidden in layers further inland and uphill beyond the clanging trolley lines. She leaned out of the window and looked up from the Rue Bliss towards the sun-bleached sienna colours of the old Arab quarters. Fretwork balconies of pastel-painted villas with red-tiled roofs leaned out over lanes wide enough only for donkey carts. Flowers sprouted in old petrol cans, clay pots and all along the walls of secret pocket-sized gardens. Already, only a few minutes after dawn, the streets were starting to throb with life. She fancied she could hear pedlars winding through the ancient lanes hawking fruits and vegetables. She could see yesterday's laundry flapping on balconies. Already women were airing the bedding, beating the dust from rugs, and lowering baskets to the hucksters in the streets. How she loved the rhythms of this city and this life!

Anne looked up at the sky, where the pinks and purples were giving way to the blues and the golds of what would surely be another brilliantly sunny Beirut day. Flocks of small dark birds fluttered by the steeples and the minarets. Over the water big white gulls swooped down in the waves, fishing for breakfast. It was hard, on such a morning, to dwell on anything other than the fullness of life.

Anne considered the possibility, then, that her farewells didn't have to be all tears and sadness. She firmly believed life was what you made of it. If she only tried hard enough – and she always did try very hard, at everything – there was no reason why she couldn't laugh instead of cry through the sweet richness of her last hours at home.

She heard a car roar around the corner in fourth gear, then an imperious horn blast, and finally her name sung out. Leila had pulled up her MG under Anne's window. Camilla was waving a bottle of champagne like a battle trophy, and Fatima was already hammering on the door. Anne grinned. Once again she and her friends were on the same wave-length. Tomorrow they might pine for lost friendship, but today they would celebrate every last moment. She slipped on a dressing gown and ran to greet her friends.

Breakfast on the balcony facing the sea was a festive affair, with everyone except Fatima and Ben sipping champagne to accompany their ripe red strawberries and their freshly baked croissants. The conversation was light-hearted. Even Anne's mother, who was usually such a wet blanket, joked and flirted with her husband as if she were a girl again. Neighbours began to drop in for coffee and *adieux*. Ladies from Anne's mother's card club called by with flowers and chocolates. Classmates the girls hadn't seen since graduation miraculously came flocking, and professors stopped by on their way to campus. Champagne corks popped, and the maid kept running from the kitchen with fresh jugs of coffee.

Suddenly it was past ten o'clock, time to dash to the airport. The men wouldn't hear of Professor Rosen lifting a single suitcase. One car was commandeered for the luggage, another for the professor and his family. The girls piled into the MG – Anne and Fatima sitting up top on the rumble seat, and Camilla wedging herself in next to Leila in the front. Leila hit the horn, revved the engine, and darted away at the head of their cavalcade.

The wind was in their hair, and all four of them were laughing as they whipped down the Corniche. But when they looped off on the airport road, Leila cursed as she hit the brakes. 'Allah! Another checkpoint.'

Anne shielded her eyes with her hands. At least twenty cars were stalled behind a bottleneck where a knot of uniformed men with guns seemed to be questioning every motorist. She had been so engrossed in her packing yesterday that she hadn't kept up with what had been happening to Beirut. 'What's that about?'

Leila angrily drummed her fingers on the steering wheel. 'The American Marines.' She did not trust herself to say anything more. She was in no mood for another fight with her friends.

'Yesterday, when they came, they made these road-blocks. At every one they have maybe one Lebanese soldier, the rest are American.' Fatima rattled off the sites of the Marine checkpoints. 'There is this one here by the airport and back at the port. Also on the roads to Damascus, Sidon and Tripoli. Everywhere important. But they did not come into our Basta. My uncle said they would not dare!' Yet Fatima, too, seemed nervous about triggering another argument on the way to the airport. '*Malesh*, never mind. My uncle says these soldiers only check papers. And look for guns.'

'The queue, it is moving fast, yes?' Camilla was as anxious as the others to keep the peace in this car. She turned to smile at Anne. 'Your Marines are very efficient – *très efficaces*.' No one replied. 'And handsome too.' Camilla was the only one who laughed. They sat in uneasy silence for a tense few minutes before Camilla dared to speak again. 'I do not think I like this. So many men with the guns! I do not like the guns.' She was shredding a tissue in her hands. 'Also I do not like to see the foreign soldiers on our streets like this. I ask you, is this New York or is it our Beirut?'

'Bravo!' Leila flashed a very small smile in the general direction of Camilla as she ground into gear and pulled up to take her turn with the Marines. With sullen hauteur Leila flashed her identity card and gunned her engine as the other girls showed their papers. When the Marine waved them on, she peeled away with a screech and left the soldiers standing in the cloud of dust she had done her best to raise.

Even though none of them ventured to say one word, pro or con, about the Marines in the few more minutes it took to get to the airport, the encounter had deflated their high spirits. Fatima took Anne's hand in hers as they zoomed up the palm-fringed boulevard to the terminal. Camilla turned around and stared soulfully back at her old friend. Anne's tanned face had gone shades whiter with the strain of the parting that was now so near.

When Leila double-parked smack in front of the entrance, Fatima scurried out to get the parcels she had stored in the boot. 'My mother sent these.' She opened a bag and pointed to a huge red plastic tub. 'Black olives from our village. She remembered how especially you like our *zeitoun*. She says you can eat one every day, and when they are finished you must come back home to us.' Fatima tried to laugh. 'Also then she said maybe you should sit down and eat them all at once here, and not go away at all.' She wiped her eyes as she peered down in the sacks. 'What else?' She fished out another huge container, this one full of home-made pickled vegetables. '*Torshee*.' In another bag was a plastic dish of parsley salad and one of raw seasoned lamb that had been pounded to a pulp. 'My sister Zainab made you *tabouli*, and Somaya sends *kibbe* for you and your family to eat on the airplane. My aunt made bread.' Fatima smiled through her tears. 'Also last night I baked for you your favourite pastries.'

Camilla was also scrabbling in the boot for food parcels that her family had sent down from the château. 'Leila, help me please. With the baby, this sack is too heavy.' But it was Fatima who lugged over the parcels as Camilla listed what was in them. 'Apples, Lebanese apples, the best in the world. From the Nazrani orchards. Also pomegranates. Dates. Prickly pears. And pistachios!'

Anne studiously avoided Leila's knowing eyes. Obviously Fatima and Camilla didn't realize that, unless she smuggled this food in illegally, she would never be able to import it through customs and into America.

'It seems you won't starve on your way to Boston.' Leila presented Anne with two exquisitely gift-wrapped and beribboned packages. 'Open these now, please.'

Anne sniffed the orchid Leila had twined around the ribbon, then slid off the wrappings on a box of elegant ivory parchment stationery with 'Dr Anne Rosen' engraved in gold at the top of every page. 'Oh, Leila! It's beautiful! But I'm not a doctor yet.' Anne lovingly traced the confident title with her finger. 'I hope I can really earn this.'

'Open the other one.' Leila's voice was gruff, as it always was when she was keeping a tight lid on her emotions. 'I had copies made for each of us, too.'

Leila had mounted, in an antique silver frame, a blown-up photograph of the four of them dancing down by the craggy Pigeons' Rocks on the seashore below Raouche. 'Ah,' she sighed. 'That day – that perfect day – last spring!' It had been hot and sunny, one of the first of a long season of such days, and they had caught spring fever. The four of them had cut French literature class and fled out into the sun, intoxicated with the sheer heady wonder of being young on such a glorious day. They had bought paper cones of salted chick peas from a cart as they ran into the wind down to the water, and then they had danced on the rocks in the sun. Leila had happened to have her camera with her, and so they had dragooned a passer-by to record this lyrical moment for posterity. The photograph caught the four of them for ever dancing for sheer joy. Fatima was curtseying prettily to Camilla, who was executing an exuberant can-can kick. Anne had her hands on her knees for a Charleston step, and next to her Leila was most definitely doing the Twist. The four of them had their heads inclined together, and mutual affection was visible in the way they were laughing and in the way not only their feet but even their eyes were dancing. 'I will treasure this always.'

But by now the rest of Anne's family and their baggage had arrived. Well-wishers were not supposed to accompany passengers past the foyer and into the chaos of the check-in hall, so their final goodbyes had to be made here. Fatima clung so tightly to Anne, and held on so long, that Leila threatened to prise her off. Camilla, who had been crying in a steady rain since they stopped at the airport, broke out into loud oriental lamentations as she and Anne kissed and hugged. Leila and Anne – in a way, they were two of a kind – fought off tears as they kissed cheeks and then held on to one another for dear life for a long moment more. 'We'll be up on the observation platform,' Leila promised, as Anne wiped her eyes and trailed sadly behind her family into the bowels of the airport.

A weary hour later, as she and her family climbed the steel stairway up to the silver plane, Anne looked over at the airport roof where miniature figures were jumping up and down and shouting goodbyes. She stood at the doorway, waving both arms above her, and then took a deep breath and stepped into the future.

The plane thundered down the runway and then caught the wind and dipped up into the sky. Anne eagerly looked out the window, but at first all she could see, on the dirty edges of the airport tarmac, were the surly sprawl of the Palestinian refugee camps. She glanced quickly away from Sabra and Shatilla and craned her neck for a last fond look at the better part of home: Beirut's wide palmy boulevards, its sandy golden beaches, its fancy old world hotels, its teeming picturesque quarters. From up here near the clouds, Beirut looked like a lovely white pearl nestled on the seashore inside a crenellated green mountain shell. Anne remembered countless star-drenched summer nights in villas up in those mountains, sitting on balconies watching Beirut wink off to sleep below her. The plane banked higher, and Anne tried to peer over the far side of these mountains, where the heart of a darker Lebanon throbbed to more primitive rhythms. But the villages hidden in their ancient valleys kept their secrets intact this afternoon, as on all afternoons. She could not see past these first mountain peaks, let alone over the next range of mountains to the flat arid deserts where huddled the inward-turning old caravan city of Damascus. Beyond the horizon to the south, too, past the snowy peak of Mount Hermon, lay the disputed homeland of Israel-Palestine and all its bitterly insoluble contradictions. Beirut was the gate to it all. These zesty, sun-burnt cities; these high mountains, and wide deserts, and deep plains; these overheated people: her Middle East, God, how she loved it, how she hated to leave it. She would not have a moment's real peace until she came back to it.

The jet turned wide in a crescent, heading west over the Mediterranean, and Anne looked down to bid a last goodbye to her home. Finally, then, as they circled over the sea, her father leaned over and broke into her reverie to point out what she either hadn't noticed before, or perhaps what she hadn't wanted to see. At anchor below in the not-so-tranqil sea, just far enough west to lie beyond the Lebanese horizon, was the gigantic American aircraft carrier that had carried the US Marines to the shores of Beirut. Just before the plane nosed into the clouds, that was her final disquieting image of home. While the city slept in the sun, hidden guns were trained on the coast. Beirut suddenly seemed as vulnerable as a pearl lying in an oyster with an opened shell.

Six weeks later Anne was being marched through Boston Common with her arms full of parcels, her mother on one side of her, her widowed Aunt Bert on the other. Anne lagged a bit behind, only half-listening to the two older women who were chattering like starlings on this, their long-postponed shopping expedition to buy what Aunt Bert decreed was a proper Bostonian winter wardrobe. Back in flamboyant Beirut, Anne's tailored taste had been regarded as too subdued. But here in Boston, Aunt Bert was always tsk-tsking that Anne's colours and styles were too flashy. No more taffeta, rayon and plush velvet, she had decreed. Here one wore cashmere, wool and linen. What had looked good on Bab Idris apparently just wouldn't do for Commonwealth Avenue.

'I don't know, Bert, maybe we shouldn't have bought the grey ones, too.' Martha Rosen was short, and as they hurried along she fell into her lifelong pattern of looking up to her older sister.

'Anne looks good in grey.' Bert was her usual oracle of good taste. 'Besides, grey's always good.'

Anne couldn't help smiling. Today, as on most days, Aunt Bert was dressed in her favourite dour shade of grey, this time a boxy gaberdine suit. Aunt Bert prided herself in her splendidly understated style that was the hallmark of Boston good taste. She had relieved the severity of her suit not only with her ever-present pearls but also with a soft white blouse whose lace collar had been made, at great trouble and expense, by hand in an Irish convent. Her rimless black felt hat helped to keep her short, blue-rinsed, salon-styled hair precisely in place. The heels of her sensible walking shoes clicked bossily as she walked, and she clutched her Nantucket-woven reed handbag and her imported Harrods' folding umbrella in her spotless white gloves. But even though Anne had always fondly regarded Aunt Bert as a real character, she was discovering what a formidable force she could be at close quarters. Aunt Bert had spent the best part of this morning at Bonwit Teller's and Peck & Peck trying to bully her into slightly more youthful versions of the matronly old Boston classics. Now they were off for another round, cutting through the park en route to the bargain-hunter's happy hunting ground of Filene's Basement.

'Joe will absolutely kill me when he gets the bills.' Martha, however, sounded less worried than gleeful as she ticked off their purchases. 'Beige, navy, brown *and* grey cashmere twinset sweaters. Four wool pleated skirts. Six broadcloth blouses with those Peter Pan collars you say all the young girls wear. That wonderful walking suit in Conan Doyle tweed. Not to mention that camel hair wrap stadium coat.'

'You let me worry about the bills.' Bert angled her neat snub nose the slightest degree higher into the air. In her estimation, it no longer mattered that she had never been as pretty as her sister Martha. What was more important now was that she was far richer than poor Martha. Bert could not help feeling secretly pleased, too, that the passing years had been kinder to her than to her sister. Martha's skin was taking on that tough leathery look from too many years in the Beirut sun. She had begun to put on weight a few years back, and by now she was built like a fire plug. Most important of all, anyone could tell from that constantly disappointed look in Martha's eyes that she was a woman discontented with her lot in life. Bert fancied, by way of contrast, that she herself had grown rather handsome in her late middle years. She was sixty-one years young, and she was looking forward to being an indomitable old lady one day in the not-so-distant future. She liked to think that she wasn't getting older, she was getting better. 'Besides, my dear, Anne has to wear something suitable to school. This is *Boston*.'

'You can say that again.' Martha Rosen looked as

though she might fling her saucy wide-rimmed black straw boater into the air for sheer joy.

Anne dropped further behind and, noticing how this made her even more out of step with her mother, she wondered wistfully if the two of them would ever manage to think and feel in harmony. Her mother had undergone a startling metamorphosis as soon as she touched down on American soil. Gone was the fretful old-looking woman who seemed too wilted to walk a block in the summer sun. Now that she was back home in Boston, she seemed to have cast off not only her all-encompassing sadness but also years of care and woe. Anne, on the contrary, had begun to act like what Aunt Bert called 'a dying duck'. From her lonely new perspective, she finally had an inkling of how her mother must have felt for the twenty-five homesick years of her exile in Beirut.

Anne shivered as she lengthened her stride to keep pace with her indefatigable elders. Compared to Beirut, the late summer afternoon was cold. The sun here was so thin. The air current was a chill wind, not a balmy breeze. If it was like this in September, how could she stand a bitter Boston winter?

Yet life here had started out well when she, her parents and her brother had gone off to Nantucket for a two-week holiday at Aunt Bert's grey clapboard summer cottage. Ben had made fast friends with a bunch of prep school boys at South Beach, and Anne had fondly observed her middle-aged parents falling in love all over again right before her eyes. She had enjoyed the splendid solitude, too, of wandering over the island on her bicycle and exploring the moors on foot. She loved Nantucket's old whaling-captains' houses, its cobblestone streets, and the dreamy sense it gave her of being caught up in a web woven long ago. One of the highlights of her family's vacations back in America had always been a fortnight out on Nantucket. This latest interlude on the island had been just another pleasant holiday.

But now that they were back to reality, across the river from Boston at Aunt Bert's house on Brattle Street, Anne had begun to pine for the happy uncertainties of Beirut and her friends. Life in Cambridge pinched and wobbled like those fashionable pointy toe spike heels she had bought at Bonwit Teller's the week she arrived. It would have been hard enough, she supposed, to adjust to the demands of an unfamiliar new world. But what had been impossible was dealing with her father and Aunt Bert's festering old feud. Bert had carped and picked at Joe during every stuffy family dinner at her spacious red-brick Federalist townhouse, and it hadn't been long before Anne's parents had begun acting as though their second honeymoon on Nantucket had never happened. The tension had even seemed to affect Ben, who had threatened to run away and lie about his age so he could join the Marines. Anne had done her best to patch up the family quarrels, but she had been relieved when her father finally had fled with Ben to New York and Chicago to visit old academic colleagues.

Even though there had been less strain in the house with the men gone, Anne hadn't liked being marooned here with her mother and aunt. She had never been crazy about coming to live under Aunt Bert's thumb. She was twenty-one: an adult. She had yearned to strike out and live her own independent life. But back on the Rue Bliss, as she and her parents had struggled to balance the overextended family budget, accepting her aunt's offer of free room and board had seemed an answer to all their prayers.

Now, however, she was beginning to regret that choice. When she had come here to visit as a little girl, she had hung on every one of her garrulous aunt's words. But Bert didn't seem to realize that she was a little girl no longer. Anne appreciated how generous her aunt was with her time and money, and she supposed she couldn't help being so domineering. Yet Anne hated seeing her mother fall so utterly under the spell of her older sister, and she was aghast at how Aunt Bert talked to her father. She had no taste for sipping oversweet sherry from Waterford crystal. She was bored making polite conversation with Aunt Bert's snobby friends who were so very much more aloof than everyone she had left behind in Beirut. These days, even when she woke up in the morning after ten hours' sleep, she was always tired. She supposed she would be happier once classes started next week. She would meet students her own age and finally have something to do other than feel at odds with an anxious world. She had high hopes, too, that she would feel better once Leila's brother Ramsey arrived in Cambridge this weekend. She longed to let down her hair and talk to someone who would instantly understand everything. Ramsey wasn't Leila, Camilla or Fatima, but at least he was a living link to that other world.

Anne juggled her packages so she could button up the jacket of her navy-blue suit. She would have to learn to adapt to this chill new Boston climate and quit trying to live in the warmth of the wonderful past. She reminded herself that she was here for the hallowed purpose of learning to be one of the best doctors in Beirut. If, along the way, she had to endure a little loneliness and a lot of alienation, then she would simply have to make the best of it. There was much to love in America, after all. The people – except, she thought, for Aunt Bert's friends – were as warm and hospitable in their way as the Arabs had been back home. She liked the way everyone bustled about with their efficient lists of things which were certain to be done on time and with every detail attended to. She admired American energy, drive and enthusiasm. It was high time, she thought, that she came to terms with her own country. She might very well choose to live out her life in Lebanon, but she was an American. She would learn as much about herself as her country in these next years in Boston.

She could not keep her heart from leaping for an instant, however, as she spotted an old man hawking the afternoon papers beneath spreading oaks whose leaves had not quite yet begun to yellow and wither. But she knew that, even if she ran up and breathlessly bought a copy, she would only be disappointed. There was hardly ever any news of Beirut in the Boston newspapers. Even the venerable *New York Times* only published the scantiest dispatches reporting what had happened in Lebanon after the Marines landed. Reading those few bald sentences only made her feel further away from home. She had to rely on letters not only to keep up with her friends but also to keep tabs on her adopted country.

Fatima wrote faithfully every week from her village in the south. Lebanon, she reported, had reverted almost to normal over the past month. Out in her remote hinterland, there were no Marine checkpoints. Life – as always – was hot, sunny and serene. Reading through the lines, however, Anne worried that Fatima must be finding it hard to readjust to a world that had hardly been touched by the twentieth century. Her villagers were more concerned with the price of this year's olive crop than with which Christian warlord occupied the presidential palace at Baabda.

Camilla had managed to dash off one weepy note from the château. Her husband and father-in-law were in foul humours, since Shaykh Georges hadn't won the presidential elections that had taken place soon after Anne left. To hear Camilla tell it, all the Nazrani men ever did these days was sulk, shoot small, harmless birds, and guzzle French brandy. The women amused themselves by taking up the hems in last year's dresses and persecuting Camilla until she burst into tears. Pierre had promised her a trip to Paris if his father won the election, but she despaired that that would now never happen. She swore she could hardly fit into any of her old clothes, and her baggy new maternity smocks were *affreux*. Anne should take her advice and never marry and get pregnant.

Leila was caught up in a last glittering round of farewell parties before she set off for England. It sounded as if every rich Muslim from Syria, Jordan and Egypt had flown in for a gala dance in her honour in the ballroom of the Saint Georges. Leila had worn a black Balenciaga gown and even had a diamond tiara in her hair. She wrote that she was being fêted at champagne breakfasts, midnight suppers, and cosy dinner parties for the *crème de la crème* of Beirut society. But somehow she had found the time to pen a witty account of how votes for the presidential election had been all but bought and sold on the Bourse. In polished prose, as clipped and impersonal as a journalist's, she had reported how the leading Christian politicians had cancelled one another out. A Western-backed general had broken the stalemate and won the presidency.

But, still, as avid as Anne was for any shreds of news from home, Lebanon's internecine rivalries had begun to retreat from the centre of her universe. Here and now as they veered off Boston Common towards Filene's, Anne cocked her head and listened as her mother and aunt dropped intriguing hints about what lay beneath the surface of affairs in their own family.

'No, Bert, I simply won't let you pay for Anne's clothes.'

'But it's my pleasure.'

'You're being more than generous as it is. Sometimes I just hate feeling like we're the poor relations.'

'Martha, Martha, you must never say that.' To herself Bert added that some things which everyone understood never had to be said out loud. Still, it was gratifying that her sister realized exactly how things stood in the family.

'But it's true. Why, we took over your house on Nantucket for the best weeks of the summer. We've imposed on you yet again here in Cambridge. And now Anne's going to be here with you for three whole years.'

'She can stay for ever if she wants.' Bert smiled magnanimously. Anne was her favourite, and only, niece. She admired her cool Junoesque beauty, and she warmed to the challenge of trying to subdue another strong and kindred spirit. Anne didn't know it yet, but she had drawn up the latest in a series of wills naming the girl as her heiress. 'Frankly, Martha, I've never really liked rattling around in that great big house on my own. I would have sold it long ago, but it was in Peter's family for ages.' Her house was situated in a line of old money mansions on a dignified tree-lined avenue just off cosmopolitan Harvard Square. 'And I suppose I'm used to Brattle Street.'

'Who couldn't get used to Brattle Street?' The longing in Martha's voice revealed that her world still tilted on a New England axis. But she and her husband and son were returning to Beirut very soon, just in time for AUB's fall semester.

'You know you're always welcome. You don't have to go back to that heathen country with him, you know.'

'Aunt Bert!' Anne would not stand for her home being slandered and her father being belittled in the same breath. 'I've told you before. Lebanon is not a heathen country. It's half Christian and half Muslim. No one worships trees and rocks there.' She took a deep breath. 'And of course Mother's going back with Dad. That's where we live.'

'Not anymore, darling. You live in Cambridge now.' Bert smiled benignly but decided not to say more in front of Anne about her old nemesis, that wretched Jewish professor who had spirited her beloved sister off halfway around the world. She had never approved of Joe Rosen. His family, after all, were impoverished garment-workers from the slums of New York City. Even though he did have a doctorate from Harvard, Bert would never forgive him for daring to marry above his station. She and Martha had grown up with the gentry just outside Boston, in Concord. Their father had been a widely respected doctor, and their grandfathers had been a preacher and a lawyer. All the women in the Wentworth family, up to and including Bert herself, had always been stalwarts in the Daughters of the American Revolution. To Bert's mind, the days of her sister's misalliance were inevitably numbered. There was always a stolen moment, every time her sister came home, when Bert took her aside to ask if she was ready to leave her husband yet. Last June Bert had even gone to see a divorce lawyer just so she would be armed with the exact letter of the law. But on this visit, as on all previous visits, Martha had flatly refused even to consider leaving her husband. She had married Joe for better or for worse, she said. The two of them had their ups and downs. But she loved Joe, and so she would shoulder her own personal cross and return with him again to the place she had always hated. Still, Bert remained convinced that some day her sister would cast aside her husband and come back home for good. She was willing to bide her time and wait for the inevitable.

'But back to Anne's wardrobe. I don't think, Martha, that even Joe can complain about the bills. Anne can't go around mother-naked. Why, she hardly brought more with her than the clothes on her back. You all looked like refugees when you got off that plane.'

'I felt like a refugee. I said to Joe, "When they have to send in the Marines, it's time for us to get out."'

Bert smiled again, as she was careful to do every

it wouldn't hurt to humour her mother and her aunt just this once.

But then, as the three of them stood at the railing overlooking the Lower Basement, Anne's misgivings melted and she couldn't help bursting into laughter. Below them a mob of well-dressed women, who at any other time and in any other place would be only the most proper of Bostonians, were scrimmaging around racks of fur coats. Two spry old dowagers were actually engaged in a tug of war over what appeared to be a perfectly matched ranch mink. Younger but no less determined women wrestled over the cheaper racoons. Particularly fierce battles were raging over the mink stoles and the fox jackets. Around the sidelines clusters of male onlookers were all but placing bets on the eventual triumph of their favourite shoppers. Anne could hardly wait to describe this marvellous scene in her next letters to her friends.

Bert had donned her silver-framed glasses and was expertly reconnoitring the terrain. 'Minks to the left, foxes to the right, racoons in the centre. I think there're still a few rather nice ones over there on the end of the rack. Behind the old girls with the minks.'

'Thank God we got here in time.' Martha was already gambolling down the stairs.

Anne hung back for another moment. But then she could not resist participating in this new life. It was about time that she forgave Boston for not being Beirut. She wasn't tempted by mink, and a floor-length fur coat would be overdoing it. But she wouldn't say no to a mid-calf silver fox. With a gusto she hadn't felt since she left Lebanon, she charged down the stairs at the heels of her mother and her aunt.

'You're sure I didn't tell you all about Leila's send-off the very moment I arrived? No? I can't imagine how I could have overlooked it.' Ramsey paused to swirl his glass of neat whisky and then sip it very nearly drop by drop. He always enjoyed milking the last possible moments from a good story. He liked to keep in practice, for his father always said a good politician had to be able to talk for ever about nothing. 'So there we all were, pulling up at the airport a full quarter of an hour after Leila's plane had been scheduled to leave.'

Anne was smiling over her rum and Coke at the dapper and ebullient young Palestinian whose posh English accent was precisely like Leila's. He was a miniature masculine version of Leila. He had the same sloe eyes, dark hair and slim build. If it weren't for his pencil stroke moustache and the fact that he was a good head shorter than his sister, they could have been twins. 'Yes?' she prompted. 'So what happened? Did she miss the flight?'

'No, they held it back for her.' Ramsey's even white teeth sparkled as he smiled at his sister's best friend. He genuinely liked Anne, as indeed he appeared to like almost everyone. That was another lesson his father had taught him. A good politician on the way up has to seem to like everyone. It is only when he's at the top that a successful politician can admit to being more particular. Since Ramsey was very definitely on the way up, he diligently practised his charm. Doing well at Harvard and here in America was only a rehearsal for what waited back in Lebanon and – please God! – in Palestine. He put himself out to be attentive to Anne, for Leila had commissioned him to regard this splendid brunette as one of his own sisters once they were both stranded on the shores of America. And so, often since he had arrived last month, he had taken her out for drinks. It was no hardship to squire around this smashing older woman and reminisce about the Beirut they had both hated to leave behind.

'As you might know, my father holds a fair amount of shares in MEA. He rang the chairman of the board before we left the villa. And you know how Middle East Airlines are. One more delayed flight hardly mattered. The plane was sitting at the far end of the runway when finally they let us all race through the departure lounge and out on the tarmac. There must have been at least twenty of us to see Leila off, and that's not counting the porters who were carrying her luggage. The MEA rep was in a panic to get that plane off the ground, and so he begged and pleaded with a squad of Marines to take Leila out on to the runway. They threw her baggage into a jeep, and off she went. She is quite possibly the only Palestinian to be escorted out of Beirut by the US Marines.' Ramsey laughed until he had to wipe his eyes. 'The Marines! And you know what Leila thinks of the Marines!'

'If I know Leila, she probably gave them *bak-sheesh*.' Anne laughed at the thought of her haughty friend insisting on giving the soldiers a tip. Yet here and now, she would give anything for an hour with Leila, even if she was in one of her difficult moods. 'God, I miss Beirut. Don't you?'

'But of course. It's dreadful being away from Baba and Leila, not to mention all the lads at school.'

'It's more than just the people, though, don't you think? I miss the life there. The sun. How free and easy everything was – is! – there.' Anne's voice was wistful. 'I even miss the pedlars calling out on the street at six in the morning. How mad I used to get when they woke me up! But now I'd do anything to hear some old man screeching out that his apples are the juiciest in the world, his tomatoes the ripest, his olives the saltiest. I'd even like to hear the knife-sharpener man begging housewives to bring out their scissors and knives.'

'Ah, yes,' Ramsey added. 'But you've forgotten the best cry of all – the muezzin. The days here don't have the right rhythm without the prayer calls.'

'I miss it all,' Anne admitted. 'From morning to night, I miss everything.'

'You dear old thing,' Ramsey said as he covered her hands sympathetically with his. 'You're homesick, aren't you?'

Anne nodded mutely, afraid that she might cry if she said more. After four months in America, Anne still ached for home. She had felt even more estranged from all she held dear when her parents and brother had returned to Beirut last month. Despite her resolve to fit in, life in Cambridge was lonely. Medical school was every bit as challenging and satisfying as she had hoped it would be, but so far she hadn't made any real friends among her fellow students. There were only a few other women enrolled, and on the whole the girls kept to themselves. She had whiled away a few Friday afternoons drinking with her male classmates. But after champagne cocktails in Beirut, Anne had no taste for watered-down rathskeller beer. The fellows in her classes were nice enough, but they seemed many years too young for her. Most nights she was content to stay in and study hard. After sitting down to a rather formal three-course dinner with Aunt Bert in the dining room, she often studied long past midnight before she brewed a restful cup of camomile tea and went to bed.

'I think', Ramsey announced, 'that what we need is another round.'

Still, Anne reflected as Ramsey went over to the bar, it was too solitary a life. Back in Beirut she had basked not only in the company of her women friends but also in the attentions of a string of engaging young men. Her classmates at the American University had been an urbane lot who hailed from some of the best families of the Middle East. She had briefly dated the son of an Egyptian pasha and the younger brother of a prominent Turkish general. She had attended her share of French, Italian and American embassy receptions on the arms of junior diplomatic attachés. And always, when she and her friends had breezed around Beirut visiting everyone's distant cousins, the salons had been chockablock with charming jet-set Arabs like Ramsey. None of these young men had meant much to Anne. She had never fallen in love like Camilla or even teased a series of possible fiancés like Leila. But she missed that wonderful electricity of flirting with a handsome man who might just end up being the love of her life.

Anne leaned back in the wooden booth and let her disinterested glance travel around the basement of this dark-panelled pseudo-English pub just off Harvard Square. Ramsey loved the place because it reminded him of pubs back in England. Leila's brother was a confirmed Anglophile. Maybe, Anne thought, that was the reason Ramsey was finding life here in New England such an easy fit. Yet she had been disappointed when Ramsey had left his Triumph two-seater back on campus and walked her down Brattle Street to this collegiate pub. She had given him a clue of what sort of evening she had expected when she had thrown on her silver fox instead of her camel-hair coat. But, for once, Ramsey hadn't taken the hint and whisked her off to the Ritz Bar. Instead they were ensconced here amid a crowd of boisterously callow undergraduates. She thought that too many of these effete Harvard types looked as if they would run the other way from anything other than a similarly overbred Radcliffe girl.

But then, jauntily leaning against the bar, she saw one a bit different from the rest. He was older, taller, manlier – he looked as rough and tough as a football player. Anne liked men who were bigger than she was. She had spent her college years in Beirut slouching down and wearing flat shoes so she wouldn't tower over diminutive Arabs and their Mediterranean cousins. This particular fellow's face wasn't bad, either. Even from here, she was drawn to the sensual set of his features: strong nose and chin, glinting eyes, a slightly cruel mouth. He looked like trouble, yet she couldn't take her eyes off him. A pity there weren't more men like him around here, or anywhere else. But the crowd shifted, and she lost sight of him.

She went back to watching Ramsey move from one knot of drinkers to another, hailing new acquaintances as though they were long-lost friends. Leila's brother had already entrenched himself as one of the most popular young blades in the freshmen class. She saw him clapping one young fellow aristocrat on the back and then inclining his head as he was evidently being introduced to an entire circle of them. Ramsey stood conversing longer than usual, and then turned and pointed in her direction.

Anne wished she could disappear into the woodwork. Tonight she wanted to recall sweet memories of Beirut. She didn't want to have to sit through Ramsey playing the politician with undergraduates whom she would – hopefully – never see again in her life.

She had second thoughts, however, as Ramsey headed their way with two fellows in his wake. One of them was short, pale and bespectacled. But she looked, and looked again, at the other one. Before she glanced away – for she didn't want him to catch her staring at him – she registered that the man who had caught her attention earlier was striding purposefully in her direction.

Anne tossed back her mane of long dark hair, pulled the collar of her silver fox coat up around the neck, and mentally thanked Aunt Bert for almost forcing her to buy the fur at Filene's Basement. She wanted to knock this gorgeous man off his feet.

'Anne, I've just met some chaps that you have ever so much in common with. After I told them all about you and pointed you out, nothing would do but a formal introduction.' Ramsey nodded at the forgettable one. 'Bill's in his final year at the Harvard Med School.' He inclined his head toward the other one. 'And Mike's already made it through that grind. He's an intern at Mass General.'

'You can't be a medical student.' Mike looked over her hair, body, coat.

'Can't I?' Anne suddenly wished she smoked cigarettes. She would have liked to fiddle with one just now so she didn't have to watch those smoky grey eyes so intently sizing her up.

'No. You're either a model.' Mike let an insinuating smile curl his lips. 'Or the mistress of a very rich man.'

'Perhaps Anne is very rich in her own right.' Ramsey set down the drinks and slid in next to her before Mike could claim that place. He had liked this older fellow well enough a moment ago, but now he wished he hadn't brought him to their booth. He did not at all care for the way Mike was looking at and talking to Anne. Ramsey felt a rush of brotherly concern and not a little jealousy at the way Anne was feasting her eyes on this over-sized American. He preferred having her undivided attention riveted entirely upon himself. 'For all you know, she could be an heiress.'

But Ramsey need not have worried about sharing Anne. As Bill sat down and started asking Anne a battery of earnest questions about how she liked medical school and what she eventually planned to specialize in, Mike's attention had shifted to a buxom blonde who had just bounced down the stairs from the first-floor restaurant. He smiled and waved to her and remained standing as he politely made his goodbyes. 'Always good to see you, Bill. Say hello to the other guys for me.' He took a step away from the table. 'Nice to meet you, Ramsey. And you, Miss Poor Little Rich Girl.'

Anne hid her disappointment with a cool, close-lipped

smile and a careless wave of her hand. If he wasn't interested in her, she wasn't going to reveal that she was interested in him. She pretended not to see Mike's eyes speculatively lingering on her a steamy instant longer, and instead turned her attention to the boring Bill and his even more boring questions. She was launching into a vivacious resumé of why she wanted to be a doctor as Mike turned his back and walked away from her.

But a moment later Anne was surreptitiously watching when Mike greeted the girl with the big breasts. He put his large hands on her small shoulders and kissed her soundly on the lips. Anne was surprised that someone like Mike would choose a girl in such a tight orlon sweater, with such obviously bleached blonde hair and daubed with pancake make-up. But Mike appeared not to care that he could do better as he put his arm possessively around the cheap-looking girl and ushered her towards the door.

Well, Anne thought, that's that. She sipped her rum and Coke and made desultory conversation with Ramsey and Bill.

But the next day, when she wrote to Leila in England and Fatima in Lebanon, she found herself describing every detail of her brief encounter with the one who got away. He was, she wrote, the most attractive man she had ever met. She had been drawn not only to how he looked but also to the way he had instinctively made her feel. As he had stalked towards her across that crowded room, she had felt a thrill course through her – a feeling both of attraction and repulsion at the predatory danger she sensed in this man.

Anne was surprised to find herself writing with such passion about a man she had barely even met. It wasn't at all like her to go on so. She was a little disturbed, too, to read what she had just written about him being dangerous and thrilling and yet at the same time – apparently – irresistible. Perhaps it was just as well that nothing had really happened between her and Mike. But, she wrote to her friends. if there were more handsome Americans like him lurking in the medical schools, hospital wards and cocktail bars of Boston, she might not be as lonesome here as she had feared.

Chapter 3

From where she reclined in the belly of the boat on a nest of Paisley cushions, Leila smiled languorously up at the fair, slim, ginger-haired chap who looked down adoringly at her as he poled their punt up the Cam. It was one of those rare and deceitful sunny afternoons when it seems it might never again rain in England. The blue sky was cloudless, and the sweet air so fresh that it felt more like late spring than early autumn. Across the wide lawns, gardeners bent to rake the golden leaves. Further afield, on the far side of the college spires and turrets, housewives crossed cobbled streets to stock up at the market. But all along the green banks of this grey river, time and work stood still. Students dozed and sprawled and sipped wine. Graceful willow boughs drooped into the current. The dappled light glimmered here and there as fleets of small low boats drifted from the shadows into the sun, down the slow winding river.

Leila stretched out her long legs and smiled her catlike smile of satisfaction. When she had dreamed from afar of coming here, she hadn't remembered the drizzle and the dampness and the irritating way the English whispered and tiptoed through life. What she had longed for was a succession of perfect English moments: dew on flowers, a silver teaset on a silver tray piled high with scones and strawberry jam and clotted cream, the celestial glow of sunset as she walked across Waterloo Bridge in the spring, and this – punting down the river in the Cambridge sun.

She trailed her hand in the water and revelled in the satisfaction of living out an old fantasy. Long ago, when she was just a little girl here on a Ramadan holiday, she remembered standing on the Bridge of Sighs with her father's arm around her, watching beautiful women in filmy dresses recline on pillows while handsome patrician fellows stood in the sterns piloting the way with long wooden poles. She had been captivated by that dreamy scene of lords and ladies floating down the River Cam like refugees washed up on the tide of a far more leisurely and romantic past. She had felt a surge of wild impatience to grow up and conquer worlds so much more thrilling than the schoolroom. She had wanted to be the loveliest lady with the most dashing man in the fastest boat on the river. And now she was living out her dream. It was too chilly for the pastel gossamer frocks she remembered from that day long ago, but she fancied she looked like a princess royal in her Liberty print shirtwaist with glitters of embossed Florentine gold at her neck, wrists and ears. Lazily she smiled up at Clive, who was so admirably, albeit unknowingly, playing galley slave to her Cleopatra, the part she had scripted for a decorative young aristocrat like him long ago.

But suddenly Leila pulled herself back from the banks of contentment and sharply willed herself to be tired of this tableau. She must not laze away her life on trivialities like happiness, comfort and Clive. She must keep in glaring three-dimensional focus that one thing which was important in life. Palestine had been lost, but Palestine must be regained. Seductive as it was to be here, this world was not her world, and it never would be. She was no longer seven years old, enchanted by the reverie of a lordly England that had essentially become extinct many moons ago. Until she and her people rewon what was theirs by right, it was a betrayal to revel in the rare pleasure of English sunshine, or anything else.

Always she must fight to keep herself perched on the nervous edge. Palestine, Palestine!

Leila sighed very softly to herself. It wasn't that she wouldn't, for reasons great and small, always love England. She adored Harrods, cream cakes, red double-decker buses, and those absurdly fussy little flowers and girlish ribbons and twee bits of lace the English stuck over everything. She was mad, too, about their woollens, and already she had bought an entire new wardrobe of cashmeres and tweeds. She approved not only of the class system but also of how even the brainwashed poor seemed meekly to accept their inferior station in life. Most of all she admired these cool resolute people who, like herself, did a jolly good job of covering up their weaker emotions and never wept except behind tightly closed doors. After the hysterical melodrama of Arab life, it was soothing to rest awhile – although perhaps not for ever – in a culture that varnished all the crude veins of emotion with artfully applied coats of civilized behaviour. Yet sometimes this controlled English detachment got on Leila's nerves. Just occasionally it would be marvellous if the English made slurping noises when they drank and lip-smacking sounds when they ate – anything to indicate that a vibrant, sinning, quivering human being lurked behind the careful masks. Occasionally she pitied these tight-lipped people for having irrevocably lost whatever *joie de vivre* they were born with. At other more exasperated and less generous times, she felt like jabbing a pin into them to make something happen. She had been in Cambridge for less than a month, but already she was restless and wondered if it had been a mistake to leave home for here. Every day in one way or another, she was growing more conscious of being a foreigner. It was lonely, being different from everyone else.

Leila lit a cigarette very quickly, before Clive could

overturn their boat by lunging to light it for her. Moodily she smoked and longed for home. Life here in this picturesque university village was far more insular than she had ever imagined it would be. She supposed she might have been happier if she were a rah-rah undergraduate, living in one of the colleges overlooking an ancient lawn, rushing off to class on a second-hand bicycle. But, instead, as a postgraduate doctoral candidate, she had to forge her own independent programme of solitary study. She was supposed to bury herself in the library for a few mole-like years of research and then eventually produce a brilliant thesis. Eye brows had been raised when she had complained that she missed the social give-and-take of AUB classes, where she had always made attention-getting points by asking sharp and pertinent questions. She was supposed to be above attending undergraduate lectures now. Every fortnight or so she met her tutor in his study, when the two of them discussed such abstruse problems as had cropped up in her library research. From time to time she was invited to teas and receptions, and every so often she had to show up in flowing academic robes for dinner at high table in college. But apart from that, official Cambridge left her strictly alone. In Beirut she had been one of the brightest stars in a stellar family, but here hardly anyone even knew she existed. She lived in solitary splendour not in college but in pricey Tudor digs on leafy Trumpington Street. For days at a time no one except Clive knocked on her door.

Leila was alarmed to feel self-pitying tears forming in her eyes. She resolutely blinked them away and took a last deep drag on her cigarette before throwing the stub in the river.

She reached in the pocket of her grey-toned Harris tweed jacket for the special treat she had been anticipating ever since she had collected her mail late this morning. The lonelier she became, the more she relied on her letters. She scrutinized every word from her father, brothers and sisters. She laughed over Camilla's descriptions of her bulging stomach and waxed nostalgic over the village scenes painted by Fatima. But it was Anne's rambling letters that always made her feel that she wasn't alone. Anne, too, was trying to make the best of a bad bargain far from home. Leila ripped open the letter with her long tapered bloodred-varnished fingernails and smoothed out the expensive parchment of the stationery she had given 'Dr Anne Rosen'.

She nodded her henna curls in approval of the cut-rate fox Anne had managed to snatch up at that fabulous sale. That old aunt seemed to be writing her a blank cheque, which was very good news indeed, since poor Anne must be terribly tired of being poor Anne. The aunt sounded as if she might be troublesome in the future, but in the meantime Leila made a mental note to advise her friend to play the old biddy like a silver-scaled fish. This Aunt Bert had to leave her money to someone, so why not Anne? She didn't want to have to be dependent on her own earning power and that of some feckless man all her life. Money was power, her father had taken great pains to impress upon her, and power was money. Her father had warned her never to dismiss this wisdom as a mere cliché.

Leila smiled as she read Anne's confirmation of how much time she was spending with Ramsey. Her brother rang her up here in Cambridge every Saturday afternoon for expensive sibling chats, and hearing his cheery voice was the best antidote she had found to homesickness. Leila wished she could fly over to Boston every week and join them for a night out on the town. But then, as she read further into Anne's letter, Leila frowned, narrowed her eyes, and reread the overwrought passages about Anne's encounter in the pub. How could commonsensical Anne sound so thrilled at the approach of a man she called 'dangerous' and 'predatory'?

Leila looked back up at her own man of the hour. No one and nothing – except perhaps a small and defenceless bird which found itself at the wrong end of a gun barrel during a hunting party weekend – could ever describe Clive as either dangerous or predatory. Many generations of iron-willed upper-class Englishwomen had admirably succeeded in breeding the brute out of their men, which most of the time suited Leila perfectly well. She did not think she yearned to be swept off her feet by an uncontrollable romantic passion. She seldom succumbed to sado-masochistic swoons at the thought of man the demanding master and she the willing slave. She did not in fact want a master of any sort, at any time. In the kind of marriage she intended to have one day, she would play the tune and her husband would dance. Of course she would do her best to strum the sweetest of all possible tunes, especially in public, for it wouldn't pay to outrage all the old conventions.

Leila lay her head back on the cushions, half-closed her eyes and let her mind wander down might-have-been paths. If she had been born a man instead of a woman, she was sure she would have been not only the leading Palestinian politician of her generation but also the most predatory man ever to stalk women on the open plains of the world. Predatory . . . what a wonderful word! It conjured up all sorts of images of herself stalking through cocktail parties, rejecting this one, pouncing on that one, feeding until she was sated, and then, when she felt the urge, prowling out on the hunt again for the conquest of another palpitating warm body. Leila sighed to herself. It was a great pity that she could never get away with being quite as aggressive as she sometimes thought she might like to be. What must it be like to be a man who could go anywhere, do anything, and never have to worry about stepping one foot too far off the beaten social path?

Leila lit another cigarette and stared up, unsmiling, at the disappointing figure of Clive who was no more than a pale shadow of ancestors who had once conquered the world. She had wondered fleetingly, when she had met him at a college reception soon after arriving last month, if he might be the one she would marry. He looked like a young prince, he had all the necessary social graces, and he was very well-connected among the minor nobility and major government circles. She had found it shockingly easy first to dazzle him and then – just as in a Victorian penny romance – to make him vow on bended knee that he loved her. But before long she had realized that it wasn't so much her as her race that he adored. Clive was one of those dreamy and sexually ambiguous Englishmen who all but slept with Lawrence of Arabia's shoes under his bed. He was so infatuated with the fantastical romance of the Arabs that he might have fallen in love with any Semite who turned up sipping sherry at his don's. She could imagine him getting as equally passionate about a boatboy from the marshy Euphrates or a belly dancer from the inundated Nile. He had been lusting after Arabs, from afar, for many years. He had read Arabic at Oxford and was up here at Cambridge now to study Arabic poetry. What this fragile blueblood should do with his life was remain in the rarefied atmosphere of an academic tower, perhaps satisfying his erotic and romantic yearnings every few years by flying off to Cairo or Casablanca for what he would doubtless like to think was no more than professional research. But his father was in the Foreign Office and expected Clive to join the club as well. In the first glow of their hand-holding promenades by the Cam, Leila had entertained the notion that it was the possibility of a match like this that had spurred her father to let her come here to study; it could hardly hurt the family to have her husband some day ensconced in Whitehall. Leila had, accordingly, shot down to Mayfair to sound out her father the next time he was in London. But Baba had only shaken his head gently and said that he didn't think she would be happy with a man who was not one of their own kind.

Leila yawned and stretched. That had essentially been the beginning of the end of Clive. If she had been as passionate about him as she was about Palestine, she might have risked fighting for her man. But it wasn't worth defying the one she loved most for an alternative as lukewarm as this Englishman. Though ceasing to take him seriously, however, she had continued to see Clive. She needed a presentable escort to squire her around, and Clive served as well as any of the others. But she had lost her appetite for him and all his brethren. Her father had as good as forbidden her a European marriage, so what was the point of beating the mulberry bushes for a man after her own heart?

Leila glanced sidelong up at Clive. She supposed she would have to give him his walking papers sometime soon. She could not continue to exploit his feelings for ever. He was a decent, true-blue, good doggie of a man, and she had in passing genuinely considered marrying him. But ever since her father had put Clive off limits, she had convinced herself that she didn't want him anyway. She had all but forgotten that first rush of enthusiasm at his devotion, his connections, his pale hair and skin. Lately it was an effort not to pick and carp and show her growing contempt. She was ashamed of herself when she lashed out at him for his lack of aggression, for the way he followed her about like her pet poodle back in Beirut, even for how he wiggled his hips as if he were wagging a tail as he walked. But she couldn't help it; Clive, now, was just one more reminder of something else she couldn't have. Losing Palestine had drained her dry. She had no tears left for whatever else might have been.

Her eyes smouldered in resentment as she looked up at this latest blow life had dealt her. How could she have toyed with the possibility of marriage to this man? She was sick to death of him. What made her seethe, above all, was Clive's insulting romanticism about her people. A kind of reverent awe would fill his voice when he asked naive questions about how the desert looked at sunrise or whether her family ate with their fingers as they sat crosslegged on the floor. When they had first spent a full day together, he had been breathless with impatience for her to pull a prayer rug out of her handbag and salaam towards Mecca. He had even asked her if she could ululate her tongue on the roof of her mouth in those womanly *zaghareit* joy-cries he had been reading about for years. But it hadn't taken her long to set him straight about what a modern and liberated Arab woman did and did not do. She had never seen a desert at sunrise and doubted if she ever would. There were no deserts in Lebanon, and back in Palestine – where, yes, there was sand – her family had lived in a luxurious mountain-top villa overlooking the Mediterranean. In Beirut or London, her family sat down to dinner on Chippendale chairs, their engraved cutlery was solid silver, and the servants sometimes even wore white gloves. She rarely prayed, and she had never learned to make quaint peasant sounds with her tongue. Still, she was touchy about the implications of his patronizing questions. If Clive – who loved the Arabs – thought they were noble savages, it erred her to think what everyone else in the West must think of her people.

Leila stared sourly at the effete youths who were reclining rather too artfully on the riverbank. They might look down on her people, but in her estimation these bloodless upper-class Englishmen would be none the worse for a bit of primitive fire and flash.

Her gaze softened slightly, however, as the boat drifted past a knot of twittering girls in billowing high-necked dresses. Leila had first admired these English roses from a wistful distance back at her Dorset boarding school, for it was only in Beirut with Anne, Camilla and Fatima that she had mastered the knack of friendship with other women. when she had first arrived back here, she had rung up a few of them and met them later for lunch or tea. But she found that she had even less in common with these girls now than she had had back in her days on the hockey field. All they talked about were society weddings and weekend jaunts to somebody's house in Yorkshire or Scotland. Their world was not her world. Yet, over the years her respect had only grown for these strawberries-and-cream English girls who looked so sweet but were made of sterner stuff indeed. They were strong as oxen, able to hump suitcases without sweating or panting. More to the point, they outclassed their men in courage, passion and resolve. What must it be like for these technicolour women to be married to these grey men? England, in her estimation, lacked both sun and men. Baba had been right. Englishmen weren't her sort.

Idly, as she floated with the current, Leila indulged herself in her favourite imaginings about what sort of man she would eventually marry. Even if she could have had him, she would have been bored to death with a husband like Clive. But neither could she endure being bullied by a brute like the one Anne had met in that pub. She had been turning this problem over in her mind since she was old enough to cast a cold eye on the compromises her sophisticated elders had struck back in Beirut. Passionate love affairs waxed and waned and were the talk of the town. The marriages that endured, however, were shrewdly negotiated family alliances.

She shivered slightly. It was hard, at the age of twenty-two, to write off romantic love. Of course she wanted a love match. She wanted – and she intended to get – everything.

But Clive, who had been avidly watching her every expression and movement, had noticed her tremble and was pulling off his jumper. 'Here, darling. I can't have you catching cold.'

She snuggled into his Shetland pullover and, for the moment, set aside her grudges against the hapless Clive. At least until someone better came along, this solicitous Englishman would do very nicely. It occurred to her, moreover, that from what she had heard, the Duke and Duchess of Windsor were a pair much like herself and Clive. The vaulting ambition of such a comparison cheered her immensely, and she smiled at her escort with genuine fondness. Too bad that Clive didn't really have a kingdom to give up for love of her. Rotten luck, too, that Queen Elizabeth's son was nearly a generation too young. She would have *killed* to be the first Palestinian Queen of England.

Yet even as Leila amused herself with the thought of being crowned at Westminster Abbey, she tucked away another small regret and large fear in one of the secret parts of herself. She had never felt more than fluttery infatuation for Clive or for any of the scores of young men who had squired her in Beirut. Maybe, she worried, she wasn't able to fall in love. She might have to spend her whole life alone like this, in the company of inferior men she didn't give a damn about. What was it that old gypsy in Beirut had forecast for her? 'Much power but little happiness' – that was it. Leila hugged herself in Clive's sweater and assured herself that she must and would seize a better destiny.

Leila ducked out of the black taxi into the driving London rain, sidestepped the splashing puddles on Cork Street, and – head up and eyes flashing – all but pranced over the threshold of the chic Mayfair gallery. After long soporific weeks of yawning library research up at Cambridge, she was parched for human contact. Everyone who was anyone in London's small and tightly knit Arab caucus was sure to be here for this gala invitation-only opening of a Palestinian artist's exhibition. Under her Burberry trench coat, she was dressed to kill in her new black velvet Chanel dinner suit with its white satin blouse, and a bosom full of Chanelesque chains and oversized beads. But her first glance at the crowd proved disappointing. Discreetly chattering knots of tweedy British guests stood shoulder to shoulder smoking cigarettes and sipping champagne from rented crystal, while above them on the walls blood-red canvases seemed drenched in passion and despair.

Leila scooped a glass of champagne from a waiter's silver tray and paused to give the paintings a dismissive glance before she threw herself into the social whirl. To her critical eye, these pictures were little more than crude splashes of violent colour. Floating like bloated carcasses amid the jarring bleeds of red, purple, orange and cobalt were disembodied faces from the refugee camps: old men with vacant eyes, young men with outraged eyes, women with furious Medusa eyes, and children with eyes that questioned why they had been born into a world that hurt so much. The canvases were not only primitive but childish in the extreme, and somehow disturbing, as if they might have been painted by an emotionally disturbed child. She had heard the artist was a grim nobody from the Gaza camps who had somehow wormed his way into the affections of a horse-faced British lord's rebel daughter. She had actually married her Palestinian and had not only paid for this exhibition but rounded up her old aristocratic chums to imbibe free drinks and pretend an evening's-worth of interest in revolutionary art. Leila let the icy champagne bubble on her tongue as she stared at the stark images on the walls. She hated to see her people portrayed as passive victims. The less said about those squalid camps the better. It was a pity that this so-called artist came from such unfortunate beginnings. But why, when he evidently now lived in a much more diverting milieu, did he insist on not only wallowing in but celebrating squalor? She curled her lip and turned her head away from those depressing images which had nothing to do with her own view of Palestine.

'*Habibi!*' The sprinkle of Arabs in the crowd had found one of their own, and Leila was suddenly engulfed in clutching arms. A visiting Egyptian singer crushed her to her heaving bosom. A dapper Jordanian entrepreneur touched his lips to Leila's fingertips. The wife of the Syrian ambassador kissed her coldly three times on her cheeks and then stood back and pursed her thin lips in envy of Leila's understated Chanel. The Syrian was overdressed in red satin, for even after three years in London she had not mastered the British penchant for dressing like frumpy schoolgirls. Students who were distant nephews and cousins of acquaintances from the best Beirut families brushed against her cheeks and told her she looked marvellous, smashing, sensational. One of her father's very junior business partners all but kissed her feet, and a Gulf *shaykh* – absurdly wearing a white robe and red-checked headscarf even here – beamed idiotically in her general direction. After the cool damp of English life, Leila basked in the happy heat of their welcome. She had missed the human warmth of home. She felt it beating against her skin as palpably as though she were laying naked in the tropical sun.

In racing torrents of excited Arabic, they exchanged

the latest gossip. Marriage, divorce, remarriage, another string of divorces, yet more marriages. This one was going bankrupt, that one was now worth a fortune. The Shah's sister had been spotted at a Swiss clinic, reportedly having her buttocks tucked. The better half of the Saudi royal family was in Boston to keep an ageing prince company during a fancy new heart operation. So-and-so's son had disgraced himself with gambling debts at Oxford. More alarmingly, somebody else's daughter was living in sin in Pimlico, with – God might forgive the slut, but her family never would! – a Jew. Leila had been away from this delicious palaver for far too long. For a blissful, acid-filled quarter of an hour, she let herself gorge on every trivial lash of their tongues.

But then, as the men began to whine about imaginary aches and pains and the women begun to purr about their latest greedy sprees in the Paris showrooms, Leila suddenly had her fill. She could not bear to go on for ever about nothing. Back home in her father's salon, the conversation was never so petty for so long. She missed the parry and thrust of real political debate. The Arab world was bursting with revolutionary ferment. Nasser was taking on the West and winning. The Iraqis had deposed their reactionary king. Anywhere and everywhere, Arab students were in the streets indulging in a new passion for bloodsports. At such a pregnant historical moment, was there nothing to discuss but sexual excess and plastic surgery?

Leila slipped away from the Arabs, took up a fresh glass of champagne, and skulked in her sophisticated Chanel on the fringes of the British crowd. But she knew none of them. Although they were never so rude as actually to turn their backs on her as she did her best to snake into their conversations, after another quarter of an hour of hanging about, she still knew none of them. It astonished her how deft they were at ever-so-politely excluding non-members of their class and club. She even admired the subtlety of their arrogance. She could most certainly learn a high-handed trick or two from these Brits.

Out of desperation, then, she detached herself from the crowd, shook a cigarette out of her pack, and gazed up at the wretched canvases.

Squat nicotine-stained fingers waved a cheap match with a sputtering flint in front of her face. She touched her cigarette to it, inhaled, and did not smile at the stocky youngish Arab with the overgrown crewcut, no tie, and a shiny polyester suit which was two sizes too big for him. He was not smiling either. He stared so intently into her face for so long that the match burned his fingers before he remembered to blow it out. 'So what do you think of our brother's work?'

'Brother's?' She pretended not to understand. She could use a little time to size up this bold one whose black eyes were as insolent and mocking as her own. So he was Palestinian. Probably from the camps. Possibly a friend of the artist. She blew smoke into his face.

'May I?' He took one of her cigarettes, lit it, and blew a deep breath of smoke back at her. He watched her struggle not to cough. 'But perhaps, Leila, I presume on what you evidently think are my betters. The great Shahines! Of course one of *you* would never admit to brotherhood with one of us!'

She bristled. 'You're very rude.'

'And you are a snob.'

'So why bother talking to me?'

'Because this was meant to happen.' His eyes which had been so scornful suddenly filled with longing, and he smiled.

He looked, she thought, really rather appealing when he smiled – like a homeless mongrel dog who might just be trained to act like a pedigree, if he were lucky enough to be taken up by the right master. She had thought he was ugly at first, but now she wasn't so sure. His blunt-featured face seemed clumsily chiselled from stubborn Jerusalem rock. It was nevertheless a fascinating face to watch for it – again, like Jerusalem rock, which changes colours as the sun shines and sets – changed so, from moment to moment, as a startling array of emotions flashed across it. Even though he did not deserve it, she smiled back.

He all but clicked his heels. 'Forgive my bad manners or not, as you like, that is how I am, no apologies, now or ever. I have no time to waste.' He took her arm in an iron grip and steered her into a corner. 'So, now, we begin. I am Hussein Ibrahim, and you and I are going to make a Palestinian revolution.'

She of course had to laugh in his face.

He narrowed his eyes. 'Never laugh at me again, or I will go away. You will lose me for ever if you dare to laugh at me again.'

She very nearly did, nervously or for spite. But she wanted to hear more, and so she forced the smile from her face. 'Go on. About this Palestinian revolution of yours.'

'Of ours, you mean.' He grinned. 'Yes, yes, of course I will continue. Good, I see that you don't waste time either.' He made a hissing sound as he sucked impatiently on his cigarette. 'Armed struggle is the answer. Not a negotiated settlement. No matter what the Americans, the British and even the Soviets say, the world will never give us back our land. Never! And maybe that is as it should be. We do not want charity. We will not beg and grovel for that which is ours. We will have to win our Palestine back with our own blood.'

'Maybe.' Her eyes for the first time rested on his, and she felt a current of understanding pass between them. Night after night in her father's parlour, she had passionately argued the same violent blueprint for the future. Yet she would never have guessed she had anything in common with this rough man in the vulgar suit. She glanced from him back across the room to the glittering pack of well-dressed Arabs who had bored her so. It was exhilarating to talk to someone who was not a fool. Yet she felt at a disadvantage. He knew too much about her, but she knew nothing about him. 'How did you know who I was?'

'It is my business to know everything about our people.' He shrugged. 'And of course everyone knows the Shahines. I heard about you from your professors at AUB, and I saw you sometimes in Beirut in the cafés on al-Hamra. I, too, was a *habitué* of the Horseshoe, but I didn't attract as much attention as you.' A smile curled his lips. 'Not yet, anyway. We are also in the same field, you know. I am doing a PhD here at the London School of Economics. But our paths, at least for now, diverge. You are a capitalist, and I am a Marxist.'

She raised her perfectly arched eyebrows. Yes, he had the manners and tailoring of a Communist. 'Pity,' she said, just as a Brit might as an exit line.

'Yes, it is a pity. But in time, with instruction, you will doubtless admit the error of your ways.'

She could not help smiling. After the vapours of lily-livered Clive, Hussein's raw vitality had a certain appeal.

'That is better. You should smile more. Most of the time you look like these British. Cold like ice, the lot of them. But you are an Arab. Never forget that.'

'I don't need you to tell me what I am.' She squashed her cigarette in an ashtray and prepared to dispose of this presumptuous little upstart just as neatly. 'In fact, I don't need you, or your kind, at all.' She squared her shoulders and was about to brush past him.

'Yes, yes, that is much better. Bravo! Those eyes, that hair, like fire. Yes, you are a Palestinian woman. And you have the possibility of some day being a great beauty.' Urgently, not so much to bar her way as to punctuate what he was saying, he reached out and touched her shoulder. 'Understand, Leila, that I will never try to win you with lies. I repeat, I will never lie to you. If that is what you want – glib lies from the bourgeoisie – then go join your oppressors over there, where they watch us.' He nodded towards the knot of Arabs who were, just as he said, avidly observing their *tête-à-tête*.

She stopped in mid-stride. All her life, everyone had plied her with outrageous compliments. Now this stranger had the temerity to insult her to her face. But she was intrigued enough to stand her ground. 'You're cheeky.'

'Thank you.' He preened as though that was a compliment, and then elaborated on what he had just started to say. 'I did not mean you are ugly. You know you are not. Real beauty, however, comes not just from the face and the body but from the heart, the soul, the mind. Perhaps very soon, if you are as smart as I think you are, yes, you will be the woman you were meant to be. With me.' He smiled again, this time fondly, and then looked up at the paintings on the walls. 'You have still not told me what you think of them.'

Airily she waved a manicured hand as she delivered a neat cocktail-party précis of the exhibition. 'They're all rubbish. Self-indulgent. Crude. Witless. Boringly depressing.'

'That is not very nice of you.'

'I'm not nice.'

'Nor am I.' He threw his half-finished cigarette down on the rug and ground it in with his heel. 'But I know more about art, life and struggle than you do.' He nodded towards the canvases. 'Gaza! The camps! The filth! The tears! The years of nothing! It is all up there, bleeding on those walls.' His voice, which had very nearly moaned with emotion, took on a bitter edge. 'You dare to call the pain of our people "boring"?'

She paled and looked away from his accusing eyes.

'You are no better than we are, you know.' He seemed to stare into her very soul, and then he snapped his fingers. 'Ah, yes! So now I understand! Yes, that is your fear, that if you admit we are all the same, then you will have to dirty your pretty white hands and descend from this world into that. But you still do not understand. That world, with all its miseries, is better than this one. And like it or not, your only chance of saving yourself – not our people, *yourself!* – is by coming down from your high and mighty villa into the camps where the real Palestine still lives.' His actions, then, belied the harshness of his words. He took her hands in his and slowly and tenderly kissed her palms and her fingertips.

Her hands tingled in his. She looked down at her smooth slim hands resting in his gnarled and stubby ones. They looked incongruous together. This man was unsuitable, and impossible. Everything about the two of them had to be wrong. So why then did all this feel so right?

'Let's get out of here,' he said.

Before she quite knew what had happened, he had retrieved her raincoat from an attendant and hustled her towards the door. She managed to blow a few quick kisses in the direction of the still raptly-watching Arabs, and then she and Hussein were out on the street, striding forward under a black umbrella in the London rain, talking fiercely about politics, revolution, philosophy, about all the great passions, even love.

Early one November morning, Leila stood in a red wool Jaeger suit outside the gate at Heathrow, impatiently waiting for her beloved brother to finish with his customs formalities and run into her arms. Ramsey by rights should still have been deep in his autumn term classes, but at their father's command he had ducked down to New York to wine and dine well-connected Shahine contacts at the United Nations. That, Leila fumed, meant they would only have this long weekend together, which was hardly long enough to share every detail of her new world. She wasn't certain, but she thought, if the conditions were perfect – if everything seemed casual and natural and not as important as she knew it actually might be – that she might want Ramsey to be the first member of her family to meet Hussein. But the entire Shahine clan had gathered in London for their Baba's birthday. With the inevitable sequence of dinners, parties, receptions, outings and marathon shopping expeditions squeezed into so few days, she worried that she wouldn't have the time or opportunity to carry out her plan.

'Ramsey!' She hesitated a second as the one she always thought of as her baby brother sauntered through the door. He looked less boy than man in his Brooks Brothers suit and topcoat. His shoulders were broader, and he even seemed taller. How could Ramsey have grown up in the short time they had been apart? But a moment later, when they were embracing, kissing and both talking at once, it was as though they had never endured those famished months of transatlantic separation. Smiling broadly, arms intertwined, they all but danced to the garage where Leila showed off the new Porsche their father had bought her for her birthday. On their exuberant lunge down the long road into London, Ramsey chattered as Leila broke the speed limit. Yes, Ramsey said, Anne was as smashing as ever, working too hard perhaps, and a bit at sea – 'aren't we all, really!' – in exile from Beirut. Harvard was just as he had expected it to be! He wasn't crazy about all of his classes, but the Americans were jolly good fun! Had Leila ever noticed how Americans always talked in exclamation marks! They laughed all the way to Hyde Park.

The family were already sipping sherry in the lush green damask shadows of the formal drawing room. Kemal Shahine rose majestically from the tapestry-covered baronial wing chair he had bought for a song from a bankrupt stately mansion in the Midlands. 'Son!' His tanned, wrinkled face was creased in welcome as he held out his arms to greet the young white hope of the family. Ramsey touched his bowed head reverently and kissed his father's hand for a patriarchal blessing, and then the two men were joyfully rocking in each other's arms. When they finally broke apart, the impatient sibling pack took over. Randa, the sister from Saudi – fatter and louder, by the look and sound of her – all but threw Ramsey over her shoulder and patted his back. Selma, the sister from Cairo, was roundly pregnant yet again, and Ramsey joked that he could hardly get close enough to kiss her chubby face. Muhammad, the eldest brother stationed in Jordan, who had once been more like a father than a brother to Ramsey, seemed still older and wiser; they clasped each other tightly and then kissed cheeks four times, six times, many times more. Ramsey vowed as he embraced Fatih, the brother from Kuwait, that he looked distinguished with those new sprinkles of silver in his ebony hair. As Ramsey continued to kiss his way through sisters, brothers, children, in-laws, cousins, Leila ducked into a bedroom to change from her red suit into a narrow bottle green velvet chemise that she had had her seamstress run up from a Dior design last summer in Beirut.

By the time she had rejoined them, Ramsey had a niece and nephew on each knee and was already presenting his father with the latest bulletin from New York. She only half-listened to Ramsey's unsurprising reports about the State Department, the Jewish lobby and the United Nations commission on Palestinian refugees. Always the news from New York was depressing, and she was in no mood today for melancholy. She poured herself a glass of sherry and perched on the arm of Baba's chair. Since she had met Hussein six weeks ago, she had been obsessed with how she could integrate him into this familial world she loved. But here and now Hussein's aura began to dim, and her priorities shifted. What was one man compared to all this? She put her arm around her father and basked in the happy perfection of the whole family reunited for the first time since last Ramadan.

The butler announced dinner, and at the table Kemal Shahine put sentiment above seniority and tucked Leila to his left and Ramsey to his right. Politics for the moment were put aside in favour of roast beef and Yorkshire pudding. As they ate, Kemal played the doting grandfather. He made the eyes of the youngest generation shine as he praised their progress at school, their prowess at sports, the sweetness of the girls, the boldness of the boys. He teased Randa, his daughter married to the distant cousin of the Saudi royal family, that she was wider than her eight-months-pregnant sister Selma. Was Randa going to give birth first? Randa blushed and admitted that she was three months pregnant. The Shahines raised their wineglasses and toasted their burgeoning numbers. Selma already had seven sons and two daughters, Randa had eight of her own, Muhammad had three sons and six daughters, and Fatih had five boys. They joked that Leila and Ramsey were ruining the family average. Selma said shyly that she wanted to name the new baby after her father if it were a boy. Already there were three other Kemals, as well as the inevitable clusters of Muhammads, Alis and

Abdullahs in this next generation. But Kemal beamed at the idea of another namesake, 'Why not?'

The mothers and the fathers launched into what Leila and Ramsey thought was an interminable discussion of the relative merits of boarding schools in England, France, Switzerland and Egypt. Of course, they all agreed, the children had to be fluent in English and French. But Fatih's oldest boys, who had been sent to the best international institute in the Alps, could hardly remember how to recite their prayers in Arabic. Perhaps, after all, it was best to keep the children rooted snugly in the Arab world until they were ready for the Sorbonne, Oxford or Yale. All heads turned towards the head of the table. What did Kemal think? The *paterfamilias* announced that some of the children could handle school in the West but that others would be better served closer to home. Sometime this week each of his sons and daughters should come to him, and together they would decide what was best for each child.

Muhammad struck his wineglass with a spoon to get their attention for his glad tidings. He had just bought a villa in Antibes, and of course the whole family would always be welcome. Fatih's eyes lit up. Ramadan, he said, was always a dreary time in the hot and humid Gulf. Why not send all the women, children and nannies to Muhammad's new villa? Everyone began talking, excitedly, at once. Ramadan fell in the spring this year, but why not stay on after it and spend the whole summer together? The men could fly over when business permitted. Kemal could bring his secretaries, his extra telephones, his telex machine, and run the family empire from a luxurious suite overlooking the Med. Leila could write her thesis as easily there as in England, and perhaps she could teach the children how to water-ski as well. By then Selma and Randa would have had their babies. Away from the pressure of family duties, Randa – who of course, along with the rest of them, would have to be fasting for Ramadan – could concentrate on dieting her way back to her girlish figure. Selma had such splendid taste that everyone always said she could be a professional decorator. She could help Muhammad's wife scour the Côte d'Azur for the villa's finishing touches. Most important of all, Kemal pronounced, was that all his grandchildren would be together. It was crucial that the cousins grow up as close as brothers and sisters. The Shahines had always stuck together, and so – generation after generation – it would always be. They drank a toast to next summer's rendezvous on the Riviera.

After that, as the butler brought in the English trifle and the treacle tart and, of course, the birthday cake from Harrods, Kemal first blew out the candles on his cake and then settled down to the heady silliness of light chatter. They badgered Ramsey to fill them in on all the latest rages in America: 'Perry Mason's' suspenseful detective series on the television, Peggy Lee's sultry 'Fever' on the hit parade, Doris Day's most recent enchanting bedroom romp in the movies. And, Leila asked, how about those blonde and long-legged American girls? Ramsey vowed they had it all wrong. Radcliffe women were no-nonsense bluestockings who couldn't hold a candle to his own dear Palestinian sisters. His eyes twinkled as he paid Leila back in kind. What was it he had heard about her upper-class British beau? Leila launched into a series of cruel though witty anecdotes about the pale young man she had most definitely left behind in Cambridge.

But inwardly she breathed a sigh of relief when the conversational ball moved on to her father and his new peaks of physical fitness at a Knightsbridge gymnasium. *El-hamdulillah*, that she hadn't blurted out her news about the real man in her life when she had met Ramsey at the airport. She could never have been so glib and callous if he had teased her about the confused jumble of emotions she felt about Hussein. She had seen him just three more times since that night they had ignited, crashed and burned at the Mayfair gallery. The next two Friday afternoons he had come up to Cambridge – principally, he said, to use the research facilities of her university library. A fortnight later she had rung him up when she was in London at her father's flat. On these three occasions, they had continued much as they had begun. They had walked in the rain, chain-smoked, talked revolution, and sparred to see which of them was going to hold the upper hand. Except for the four times he had kissed her, he had treated her more like a man than a woman. She wasn't sure whether she liked that or not.

His lips were hot, wide and probing; and he had not chosen to kiss her as often as she would have liked.

Leila studied the dear faces of her brothers and sisters laughing and talking over their birthday cake and English puddings. Her family, she was sure, would hate Hussein Ibrahim on sight. Her father, in particular, would detest not only his politics but also the way he walked, talked, lived and dreamed. What if some day she had to choose between Hussein and her family? She did not think she loved him yet, but someday soon – if matters continued as they had begun – she might. The way all the songs, movies and books portrayed it, romantic love burned brighter than all the other loves combined. Yet how could any single mortal come before these men and women of her own blood, this family which she loved without reservation? Leila was glad, as she settled down with the men over coffee and brandy in the drawing room, when the conversation finally turned back to politics. She might be all in a muddle about Hussein, but never about politics.

'Nasser', Kemal was saying with some exasperation, 'is still up to his old tricks,' playing his cat-and-mouse game with Palestinian nationalism. With one side of his mouth he had authorized border raids into Israel, and out of the other side he was vowing at international forums that keeping the peace was a pan-Arab goal.

Selma's husband Adel squirmed in his hot seat which was too close to the crackling open fire. As an Egyptian who worked in the Foreign Ministry in Cairo, he sometimes dreaded being dragooned into Shahine family reunions. 'Really,' he said, 'you must know that Abdul Nasser has committed his heart and mind to your cause.'

'It's his army we want,' Leila snapped.

Ramsey repeated the one word the Egyptian ambassador to the United Nations had told him: '*Sabraa*, my sister. Patience.'

Leila nearly exploded. 'Patience? That old fool Egyptian in New York still has nothing to say to us but "patience"? Okay, I understand that the Security Council is a hopeless cause. The Americans will veto anything and everything we want. But why doesn't he get the General Assembly to condemn Israel for its raids in Gaza? And whatever happened to the plan to get the UN to condemn Zionism as a racist dogma? Why don't our alleged friends in the General Assembly do something – anything – to help us? How long must we wait to get our country back?'

Kemal ran his fingers wearily through his thinning silver hair, which had been thick and black back in Haifa, before . . . he sighed. 'It seems, my dear, that we must wait a bit longer.'

Fatih chimed in about an interesting new development in Kuwait. A young Egyptian-trained engineer named Yasser Arafat was leading a new association of disaffected Palestinians in Kuwait city. It would probably come to nothing, but just to keep the family finger on every Palestinian pulse, Fatih had detached a junior engineer from one of the Shahine companies to join Arafat's Thursday night discussion group.

'I think I've heard of this fellow.' Adel was delighted to be off the firing range. 'He was active at Cairo University. Student things, mostly. A born troublemaker. We were watching him.'

'Yasser Arafat.' Kemal repeated the name so he would not forget it. 'Good. There are enough Palestinians working along the Gulf to bring the oil industry to its knees some day.'

'Now you're talking, Baba!' Leila drained her snifter of Courvoisier. 'We could sabotage the oil fields. Hold the Saudis to ransom.'

'What's got into you, Leila?' Kemal smiled indulgently, as though at the endearing antics of a wayward child. 'I send you to Cambridge, which I hardly thought of as a hotbed of revolution. And four months later you sound as if you've been learning to make bombs.'

As the men dutifully laughed, Leila decided to take care lest she reveal too much too soon in her father's house. Hers might always have been the most radical voice in the family, but until now she had not dared to be quite so outspoken. After a few encounters with Hussein, she was beginning to sound like Leila the Red.

She demurely refilled the men's drinks as Muhammad gave them the Palestinian perspective on political events in the frontline states of Lebanon, Syria and Jordan. The general who had restored order in Lebanon had his hands full trying to reform the civil service. But at least the fighting had stopped and the US Marines had packed up and gone. Syria was its usual economic mess, and in Jordan – after being pressured into expelling his British military advisers – King Hussein had dug in his heels and refused to listen to any more passionate Palestinian persuasions. Scurrilous rumours to the contrary, however, Muhammad sincerely doubted whether the King had allowed Israeli politicians to nip across the Allenby Bridge for secret meetings. It was only a few years ago, after all, that a Palestinian assassin had gunned down his reigning grandfather for negotiating with the Israelis. King Hussein didn't want to die the same traitor's death.

Leila smoked and listened. But although she did not butt in again, inside she burned with resentment. She had heard all this drivel before. The Arab leaders hedged and hesitated as the Palestinian people rotted in soul-destroying exile. She was sick to death of all these degrading compromises and this cowardly vacillation. Maybe Hussein Ibrahim was right. Armed struggle could be the only answer. She longed to stand up and fight for what she believed, not only here in this drawing room but on the battlefields of Palestine itself. But she kept her opinion to herself. This was clearly neither the time nor the place to go against her father. Yet some day . . .

She sat silent, charmingly curled up at their feet on a leather hassock, the very picture of submissive Arab woman. But inside subversive thoughts and revolutionary feelings had begun to take hold. She had had twenty-two years of love and trust with Baba and only four heady nights on the street with Hussein. And yet now, for the very first time in her life, she truly questioned her father's judgement. She stared into the fire, troubled that the day might come when she would have to choose between Hussein and her father.

Chapter 4

Fatima scooped up a dollop of the damp dough, rolled it back and forth between the palms of her hands into a seamless ball, and slapped it down on the clean piece of linoleum that served as her bread board. It was not yet dawn, and she yawned in the shadowy light cast by the single low wattage electric light bulb which dangled from the ceiling. But even though it was still too early for the sunrise prayers, it was not too early to smile, joke and gossip. The six women squatting down on the dirt floor in their heavy winter bathrobes and white polyester scarves and thick woolly socks chattered in a high-pitched melodic chorus as they transformed flour, yeast, salt, sugar and water into *khubz*. This work, like so many of the daily tasks in this south Lebanese village of Suker, from picking olives to washing clothes by the water tanks, was performed as if it were play, with the *élan* of one big happy family on an outing. The sisters, aunts and cousins who were baking bread together this morning had known one another all their lives. Their great-grandmothers had all been sisters. Their baby sons and daughters would one day marry. There were no secrets in this village, and not many silences either.

As the women bent over their bread, their teasing tongues worked as fast as their fleet fingers. Zainab confided that her husband was losing his hair. She had caught him moping in front of the mirror the night before. Yes, he had admitted, this was the reason he had taken to wearing a black and white *kuffiyeh* headscarf from early morning to late at night. What should poor Hamid do? Perhaps, her sister Somaya suggested, he should eat more meat, eh? Every white-scarved head nodded. More meat, when a family could afford it, always helped everything. But who, they all agreed, could afford more meat this winter? Ah, her sister said with a twinkle in her eyes, maybe what Hamid really needed was a new wife who didn't worry him so much! No, Zainab answered as she butted her sister with her hip, the solution is a wig! They broke out in merry peals of laughter at the thought of Muhammad trading in his *kuffiyeh* for a wig.

Yet even as Fatima laughed along with the others and her dancing fingers dipped and swayed and all but pirouetted through the dough, she let her mind wander up and away from the tactile rhythms of village life.

Dreamily she remembered that other world. In Beirut, she had never had to stumble up from her sleeping mat before the cock crowed, before the muezzin cried, before the cold winter dawn crept over the mountains. In Beirut, she never had to make her way in the dark down to the communal bakery to light the charcoal fires. In Beirut, the women of each family didn't have to take turns baking bread for the rest of the village. In Beirut, bread was something that even the poor could generally afford to buy in the shops. In Beirut—

'*Ya*, Fatima!' Zainab broke into her reverie. 'Our Fatima is dreaming again! Tell us what you're dreaming about, oh Fatima!'

Her sister Somaya answered for her. 'She's dreaming of her cousin Ali.'

Another cousin chimed in. 'And the house he'll build her on the hill behind his father's house.'

An aunt smiled fondly. 'And the sons, *inshallah*, she will give him.'

'Is that what you dream of, Fatima?'

Fatima laughed and blushed as if her mind really had been on the cousin they all seemed to assume she would marry one day not too far in the future. Then, as if she were overcome by the shy modesty that it was seemly for a maiden to feel at the mention of her intended she ducked her head so none of them could see her frown. As her marriage date had crept closer, she had begun to nurse more doubts about its inevitability. She had never agreed to marry Ali, and it was possible that she never would. The match had been mentioned since she was a girl, but there was no certainty that it would ever happen.

It wasn't, Fatima assured herself as she pummelled the dough, that she hated her cousin. She didn't have any feelings about Ali, one way or the other.

She hardly, she thought as she slapped the dough around on the block of linoleum, knew this long-lost cousin. It was possible that he was the model man that his mother, father, brothers and sister always insisted he was. It was even possible that someday she would want nothing more in life than to marry him. But before this loose talk of a wedding went any further, she wanted the time and freedom to decide for herself. She hadn't seen Ali since she was a little girl. He had been away in Iraq almost since she could remember.

Perhaps, she decided, as she gave the dough a good hard bashing, he would stay in Iraq for ever. It was Beirut she longed for, not her cousin Ali. She could remember every smell, shape and sound of those glamorous years in the city that she had begun to think of as her own. Before dawn prayers in Beirut each morning, instead of squatting down on her haunches to bake her own bread, her aunt would send one of her young sons out to buy fragrant loaves of flat pitta from the bakery on the corner. In Beirut, sometimes, too, on very special occasions – on one of the Eids or one of the Twelve Imams' birthdays or when cousins were visiting from the south or Syria or even faraway Africa – Abdul would be sent a neighbourhood away to buy crunchy, garlicky, open-faced meat pies from the Armenian shop at the far side of the Basta. In Beirut, life was so different from what it was here.

Fatima's mouth watered for delicious Beirut as she continued to work the dough back and forth and up and down into a pliant mass. She rolled the loaf into a sphere again and patted it out flat with light little slaps of her fingers. Absent-mindedly she smiled as her sisters and her neighbours laughed at some great joke one of them had just cracked. In Beirut sometimes, she remembered, on those happy mornings after she had spent the night at Anne's villa on the Rue Bliss, the maid would run out to a *pâtisserie* for fresh croissants and brioches which everyone swore were as good or even better than those in Paris. They would all breakfast out on the balcony overlooking the sea, sitting on rattan chairs under a turquoise-striped umbrella. They would pile those buttery foreign pastries high with imported English strawberry jam and sip strong French filter coffee as they discussed current events in America, Europe and the Middle East. Fatima for a moment tuned back into the chatter that was continuing around her in the village bakery. Someone's aunt was feeling poorly. Someone's uncle was looking for a wife for his cousin's son. Everyone enthusiastically agreed that this year's oranges were as sweet as honey. Somaya was undecided whether to make her new dress blue or grey. Um Nasser's milk was drying out long before the two-year weaning time decreed in the Holy Koran. As her sisters and aunts and cousins nattered on and on about everything and nothing, Fatima tried not to compare them unfavourably with those she had left behind in Beirut. Maybe her sisters weren't as brilliant as Leila or as beautiful as Camilla or as sensitive as Anne, but nonetheless they were her sisters and she loved them.

Artfully Fatima tossed the loaf up in the air, catching it on her open hand so that when it came down with a slap, the impact spread it thinner. Back it went into the air, higher, still higher; thinner, still thinner; wider, still wider. She sent it into spins and caught it on her open hand, then her forearm, finally up by her shoulder. She twirled it from arm to arm until it was nearly as light and thin as the air atop snow-capped Mount Hermon further down south by the Israeli border. For awhile she almost forgot about Beirut. This joyful juggling had always been her favourite part of baking bread. She liked the alchemy of making something warm and light from something cold and hard. When she was just a little girl watching her mother gaily tossing loaves almost to the roof, she had clapped her hands with pleasure and longed for the day when she would be old enough to perform this woman's magic art. She had made a mess of the cookhouse the morning her mother finally let her try it. She had dropped dough all over the dirt floor and even splattered it way up on the cement ceiling. But finally she had managed to get the hang of it. Her father had happened to be home on one of his rare visits from Africa, and so she had presented her first loaf of bread to Baba as if it were the greatest of golden treasures. She could still remember how he had said it melted in his mouth, and how he had put his fingers to his lips and blown a kiss to her on the wind.

Fatima tested the temperature of the rounded iron hump of the griddle with the tip of her finger and then, satisfied that it was just right, she edged the dough down her arm and finally tossed it on to the heat. In an instant it sizzled and bubbled. In a moment its edges crackled and curled. She peeled off the paper-thin layer of bread and flung it on top of the growing stack in the corner. Just so had she done this hundreds of times in the past. And just so, *inshallah*, would she do it exactly the same way thousands of times in the future.

It was strange, she thought, as she reached into the vat for another handful of dough, how intensely she both loved and hated the certainties of life in the village. How could the very same thing be both the best and the worst of life back home? She liked baking bread just as she liked so many of the other slow and patient rituals of this life. Usually she felt content, as she awoke each morning, to go through the gentle motions of another sweet day. It made her feel that all was right in the world when she rose and washed until she was clean and pure and ready for prayer. Then a deep serenity would come over her as she heeded the call of the muezzin and stretched out her prayer mat and whispered the ancient words that brought her nearer to Allah and all that was good in this world and the next. It was just so with many of the other daily rites, from airing out the sleeping mats to washing every grain of the rice. It made her feel snug inside always to know exactly what was required of her, and to be able to predict precisely how most days would begin and unfold and end. But at other, less felicitous times, she felt just the opposite. With the exception of prayer, which always centred her in the best of all possible places, sometimes the very thing that might have made her feel tranquil yesterday could make her edgy today. Sometimes, since returning to her mother's house last summer, she had even felt that she would suffocate if she had to live all her life like this. What was hardest to take was the way everyone always seemed to treat everything as inevitable. Life had always proceeded one way, and so, *inshallah*, it would continue. But in Beirut it had always seemed that all things were possible. If she were in Beirut – here, now, today – anything might happen. She yearned for Beirut's infinite possibilities.

She kneaded the dough, smiled at her sisters, joked with her aunts. Yet inside she seethed. Was this, she asked herself, all that her life was to be? Back in Beirut she had somehow expected more of it. Early on her father – may peace always be upon him! – must have sensed something special in her, for he had written from Africa that she alone among his daughters was to be sent to his brother's in Beirut to learn to read and write. He had been so pleased with the glowing reports his brother Muhammad sent him that later he had allowed her to go to university to study as a teacher. It was her father's great dream, and Fatima's, too, that one day she would return home to teach all the girls in Suker everything she had learned in Beirut. But so far that great dream had come to nothing. Despite the best wishes of the men and the best prayers of the women, there was still no school for the girls in her village. Fatima knew very well that what was wrong was simply the same old story. The Christian-dominated government in distant Beirut had never placed a high priority on education, health care, or even providing electricity or paving the roads in the impoverished villages of the Shia Muslim south. Three-quarters of the best land in the arid plateaux of the south's Jebel Amel was monopolized by clans of rich landowners who treated their poor tenant farmers as though they were serfs back in the European Dark Ages. These landowners sat in the National Chamber of Deputies, but they did little to assure the welfare of their sharecroppers. Now, as always, the Shia were Lebanon's forgotten people. And so, here in Suker, the little boys had to make do learning the Koran from the *shaykh* at the mosque. Only the smartest of the lads were sent off to the government school in a faraway valley. The illiteracy rate among the Shia was twice as high as among the Maronite Christians. A school for girls was still a luxury that Suker had not yet been able to afford. But someday maybe, if her people were richer, if the government were more caring, if her father were here to speak up for her . . . Enough, Fatima told herself sternly. Let Allah make those decisions. It is enough, this morning, that you make the bread.

Fatima laughed out loud as she tossed the bread in the air. It was sometimes a great relief to leave everything to Allah. She nudged the bread up and down her arms, then back up in the air, finally down on the sizzling griddle. She took satisfaction in peeling off a perfect layer of fragrant bread to add to the stack in the corner.

Her mood of elation held as she piled her arms high with bread and, flanked by her sisters, trudged back up the steep path. Near the crest of the high hill where their house perched, Fatima looked out over the humpy green fields that rippled all the way to the far mountains. The sun was just about to rise; she would have to hurry to pray before first light. Yet she lingered a moment longer. The sky was purple and pink and streaked with gold. The glowing dawn light caught the twining leaves on the twisting olive trees and made them shine like silver. She leaned over and took one deep, aromatic breath of the bread she carried like a baby in her arms. An Egyptian girl she had known in Beirut had told her once that her people called bread not *khubz* but *aish*, which was the word for 'life'. At the time Fatima had thought that quite odd. But now, inhaling the good life on this hill, it seemed that maybe the Egyptians had been right after all. How good this *aish* was, how perfect. As soon as she took this bread inside and performed her ablutions, she would bow and salaam to Allah with a lighter heart. She would thank Him for giving her this moment of peace here on this hill.

Once indoors she gave her mother the bread, scooted outside to perform her ablutions at the water tank, and then quickly laid out her prayer mat in the women's bedroom facing south towards Mecca. She was the last of her sisters and brothers to pray. As she salaamed, the others were already sitting down on the floor in a circle around the tin tray scooping up yoghurt, cheese, olives with handfuls of the newly baked bread. By the time she joined them, her brother Hassan had already finished eating and was slurping his sugary tea as he reached in his pocket for the letter he had forgotten to hand over yesterday.

Fatima brightened up, popped another plump olive into her mouth, and wiped her hands expectantly on the lap of her robe. Most of the mail that came to the house arrived with her name on it. Anne wrote often, Leila when it suited her, and Camilla sent the occasional postcard. But the long, thoughtful letters that came with the American stamps on the envelope were Fatima's favourites. Usually Anne wrote to her every fortnight, but this time the gap had stretched to six weeks. Fatima worried that Anne might be angry with her. Maybe she had gone too far when she had warned Anne in her last letter to be careful of men who lurked in American bars. Still, she didn't regret what she had written. She worried about Anne being alone in Boston, so far away from her parents and everyone else who loved her. She had advised her best friend to study hard, stay home with her aunt, and wait until she came back to Beirut to look for a good husband – somebody whom everybody knew and respected, a man who had the sort of character a woman needed in a husband. Fatima eagerly reached out for the envelope that surely must be Anne's answer.

But Hassan was shaking his head. 'It's for Ummie.'

'*Allah karim!* God is generous!' Fatima's mother, whom everyone called Um Ibrahim – the mother of her eldest son Ibrahim – took one look at the thin blue airmail envelope and the colourful red foreign stamps and then kissed the letter that had been in her husband's hands in Africa not so very long ago. Her wizened face, which was usually so sad and careworn, was suddenly transformed. She cast a radiant glance of longing at the massive shrine-like portrait of her husband that hung in a heavy gilt frame in a place of honour beneath the shelf that held the Holy Koran. As if it were yesterday instead of twenty-seven years ago, she could remember the exact day and hour, just before Abbas went off to join his uncle in Senegal for the first time, when that picture had been taken in a studio in Beirut. He had been so young and handsome then, so robust, and hot like the sun in midsummer. Before Africa had baked him brown and tough, his skin had been as pink and tender as a Syrian's. For the hundred thousandth time, Um Ibrahim wondered why it had been God's will that she and her husband, like so many of the men and wives of their blighted village, should live apart for so much of their lives. She could calculate the exact months and years of Abbas's visits by the birthdays of the sons and daughters he had fathered each happy time he came home with gifts of textiles and tales of adventures. Their three oldest sons were with him now, too, in Senegal. Allah had willed that she endure most of a lifetime without her husband and three of her beloved sons. If only their village were more fruitful, if only they could own their own plot of land instead of sharecropping it for the landowner who lived like a pasha in Beirut, if only life were less difficult . . . As she thrust the letter at Fatima, Um Ibrahim's knobby arthritic hands trembled with anticipation. 'Read it out loud! What does he say!'

Fatima slipped her finger inside the back flap, removed the single translucent sheet of stationery, and let out an excited whoop. 'He's coming! Baba is coming to see us!' She scanned the final lines of the brief message. 'And I think he arrives today!'

The room was pandemonium. Um Ibrahim was kissed and hugged by all her sons and daughters at once, and then in turns. The girls let out high, trilling *zaghareit* cries of joy. The boys thumped each other on their backs. Finally, then, the brothers and sisters swung into action and scattered to begin preparing for the great visit. The youngest daughter, Amina, was sent to tell the aunts. The youngest son, Mohsen, ran out to the lookout facing the Sidon road so he would be the first to spot his father coming. Zainab took stock of the bedding, for tonight the house would be chockablock with overnight guests coming from afar to pay their respects. Somaya ran up to the storeroom on the roof to begin listing what they would need to buy at the market. Little Abbas set out to buy a sheep they would slaughter for the occasion. Hassan went off to the mosque to spread the glad tidings among the men of the village.

Fatima was about to speed off to her father's oldest sister to make sure Khadiga would bake her famous rosewater cake, when she took one look at Um Ibrahim and realized that the shock of the news had obviously been too much for her mother. 'Sit a moment, Ummie.' Tenderly Fatima led her over to the bed in the corner. As she sat with her arm around her mother, Fatima reflected on one of life's ironies. Only a few minutes ago in the bakery she had despaired that there were never any surprises here in her predictable village. She had felt so sorry for herself as she had longed for the infinite possibilities of Beirut. But Allah was merciful and compassionate, and He always had a glorious trick or two to teach even those with a fancy Beirut education. 'There, there . . .' Fatima patted her mother's back.

Um Ibrahim leaned on her daughter's strong young shoulder and sighed as she gazed misty-eyed up at her wedding photograph that hung on the wall next to the portrait of her husband. She had known all her life that she was destined for her cousin Abbas. She had adored him even when they were children and he had protected her from harm in the hit-and-run games that the little ones play. As she raptly remembered the joy of their wedding day, the years seemed to drop away and it was easy to imagine her as the plump and hopeful young girl who solemnly stared down from the photograph on the wall. In that portrait she was stiffly sitting on a straight chair, and Muhammad stood by her side with his hand possessively on her shoulder. As Um Ibrahim stared up at the dear image of how they once were, she could almost feel his hand burning through her wedding dress as it had done on that day of days.

Um Ibrahim sighed under her breath. She had not seen her beloved husband for six long years, not since the summer before Amina was born. What would he think of his wife now? She looked down in distress at the frayed dark blue dressing gown that hung in folds over her skinny body. Under her white headscarf, her hair was grey and stringy. She lifted her gnarled hands to her face and felt how withered her skin was .'I am old now,' she whispered as if to herself. 'I have become old.' When had that happened, exactly? Had it come on her suddenly like a deadly fever, or bit by bit, like a fatal wasting disease, on every lonely night of these long years of waiting? She hid her face in her hands and wept in the sudden despairing fear that she would disappoint him as she was now.

But then, with a massive effort of will, Um Ibrahim shook off her panic and wiped her eyes. What was she doing, crying over lost youth like some silly rich lady whose worth rested only on what she looked like instead of what she *was*? She was a good Muslim woman, and she had always been a loyal wife to her man and a devoted mother to her children. She had earned every one of her wrinkles and sags in the service of her family, and so she should be proud – not ashamed! – of the marks she carried from this labour of love.

Besides, she told herself tartly as she glanced back at the portrait taken of her husband long ago, Abbas couldn't have been getting any younger in the intervening years, either. The last time she had seen him, his hair had been thinning and his paunch had been thickening. He was still a fine figure of a man, but he was no longer the young lion she had married. And what, after all, did it matter? Old or young, the two of them were pledged before Allah to be man and wife for ever. Theirs was not a childish love dependent only on supple skin and languishing looks. He had been her husband for thirty-four years, since she was fourteen years old. She had given him six sons and four daughters. He was not coming home expecting to be greeted by a dancing girl with a jewel in her navel.

Still, she reflected, there was no harm in presenting her very best front to her husband. God willing, she could look forward not only to many contented years but also to a multitude of satisfying nights. Her children, Allah's blessings be upon them, were taking the preparations for their father's visit into their own capable hands. Before he came she had time to wash her hair, rub her body with the jasmine oil Abbas had always loved, and encase herself in the long green silk dress she had sewn herself from the fabric he had given her on his last visit. She would not greet him with the others out in the blinding sun, where he would instantly see what the years had wrought. She would wait for him here in the shadows, like the maiden she had once been in this very room on their wedding night. She might be old, but the thought of being with him made her feel almost young again. Abbas, she was about to be with her Abbas!

And yet, even as Um Ibrahim was about to jump up and begin her *grande toilette*, she was assailed by the doubts that had become a habit after so many years of disappointment. Maybe, she fretted out loud to Fatima, she wasn't going to see him today. Perhaps her daughter had read the words of his letter wrong.

Fatima obediently smoothed the paper out again and read it aloud to her mother. Patiently she assured Ummie that there was no mistake. Baba's ship should have docked in Beirut on 5 December, which was yesterday. He would reach Suker on 6 December, which was today. '*El-hamdulillah!*' her mother cried over and over again. 'Thank God, thank God, thank God.' Then, with the eagerness of a young bride, Um Ibrahim went to prepare for her beloved.

The big black Mercedes taxi purred over the crest of the hill just after noon, when even the winter sun was warm and welcoming.

'Baba! He comes!' Ten-year-old Mohsen jumped up and down for joy. He waved his arms at the taxi, and then cupped his hands so that his voice would carry all the way back to their house. 'I can see him! Baba!'

In the back seat, wedged by the open window next to his three strapping sons and among his parcels and cases, Muhammad reared back his massive white-haired head and let out an answering bellow. 'I return! I am home!'

By the time the taxi pulled up in front of the house Muhammad had built long ago with his own hands, most of the village was waiting. They surged around the cab before the doors were even open. 'Baba! Abbas! *Ahlen was ahlen*. Welcome!' The women made high-pitched trilling noises with clicks of their tongue, and the men pushed up so tightly against the doors that at first no one could get out of the taxi. But then the door jerked open, and at once Abbas's great bulk was engulfed in a sea of arms, hands, lips. 'Son!' In the press of well-wishers little Abbas bent as best he could to kiss Baba's hand, but instead the father exuberantly swept his namesake into his arms. They kissed four times, six times, eight times, back and forth on their cheeks. Then it was Hassan's turn. 'My boy! My son! *Ya*, Hassan!' When they were still embracing, a small but determined hand plucked at his father's back. 'Don't forget me! Mohsen? Did you forget about me, father?' At once Abbas wheeled and peered down at the thin little boy who was nearly twitching with excitement. 'Forget you? Forget my heart, my blood, my soul, my little Mohsen?' He picked the glowing boy up in his arms as easily as though the child were still an infant and gave him great smacking kisses on his cheeks. Just then the crowd realized that Abbas had not returned home from Africa alone. 'God be praised! Ibrahim! Ali! Hussein!' The family had not been all together like this for many years. Even among the men, there wasn't a dry eye as brother embraced brother, uncle kissed nephew, cousin hugged cousin. Next Abbas's own brothers pressed insistently forward in the crowd. '*Ya habibi!*' The older generation, who were also called confusingly by the most popular Shia names of Muhammad, Ali, Hussein, Hassan, Abbas, Mohsen and Ibrahim, passed their long-lost brother from one to the other, kissing, hugging, exclaiming over how wonderful he looked.

'What about us?' The women in the back could not endure another minute of waiting. Embarrassed at how they had monopolized Abbas, the brothers stepped aside so the sisters could take their turn. Zainab and Somaya flew at once into their father's arms and peppered his cheeks, lips and forehead with kisses. 'My flowers! My jewels!' Abbas beamed at the young women who had been mere girls the last time he saw them.

'Baba!' Fatima threw her arms around her father's neck and hugged him with six years' worth of longing. 'Ah! My treasure!' Abbas gazed rapturously down into the eyes of his favourite daughter. But then, as her father held her in his arms for a lingering moment, Fatima was startled by what he whispered in her ear. '*Inshallah mnaakulum mlabbas khutubtak!* We look forward, God willing, to eating sugared almonds at your engagement!' But this was neither the time nor the place for Fatima to ask him if he meant what she thought he meant by that.

Already her father had released her and was looking around expectantly for the one he had only seen in pictures. 'The baby? Where's the baby?' A blushing Amina hesitantly stepped forward. 'You mean me, Baba?' '*El-hamdulillah!* Can this be my Amina? I was looking for a baby, and instead God has given me an angel?' Amina's small face was one big smile as, for the first time in her life, she was swept up in her father's wide arms. Proudly, then, Zainab and Somaya presented their babies. Abbas cradled his grandchildren in his arms for the first time ever. He had to wipe his eyes when he finally handed them back to their mothers.

After Abbas's sisters had duly kissed him and his cousins had embraced him and even the neighbours had welcomed him with the sweetest of words, he finally managed to extricate himself from all those who had succeeded in holding him back from the one he had crossed a continent to see. 'Where is she?' he muttered impatiently under his breath as he ran up the steps to the house two at a time.

She was waiting for him just inside the front door, in the cool shadows of the room where they had first been alone together as man and wife. She had wrapped her hair with a soft white scarf and cloaked her body in a rippling green gown. She had ringed her flashing dark eyes with kohl and pinched her cheeks until she seemed to glow with a girl's rosy ripeness. God and the filtered light were kind to her. Abbas caught his breath and saw what he wanted to see. The years receded. To his fond eyes, his wife, the only woman he had ever loved, was more beautiful now than when they had married. Without a word he took her in his arms and held her tight, revelling simply in the wonder of touching her. But then she lifted up her head, and he kissed her lips like a lover, again and again. They laughed out loud, then, and embraced like the lifelong friends they had always been. They were still kissing cheeks and laughing and hugging when their sons and daughters could control themselves no longer and burst into the house.

'Surprise, Mother!' Ibrahim sang out in his husky baritone.

'We're here, Mother!' Hussein beamed at her.

'We all came back!' Ali joined his brothers' chorus. 'We're all here!'

Um Ibrahim reeled and might have fallen if her husband hadn't been holding her so tightly in his arms. Her mouth dropped open, and she stared in shock at the three sons she had not seen since they went off to toil by their father's side in Africa. Ibrahim had been gone ten years and Hussein nearly as long. After his last visit six years ago, Abbas had taken Ali back to help in the string of general stores he owned along the Senegalese coast.

'My boys . . .' Um Ibrahim's voice quavered. 'Oh,

my sons . . .' Without even being conscious of moving, she was suddenly in her sons' arms. Zainab and Somaya burst into tears, and everyone was kissing and hugging yet again. The room was packed with all but one of the living branches of the family tree.

The one who was missing sat alone on the crest of the hill behind the house. Fatima brooded as she looked far away, past the undulating fields to the mountains on the horizon. Of course she was thrilled to see her father and brothers again. But why had Baba spoiled the homecoming by whispering that fearful news in her ear? '*We look forward to eating sugared almonds at your engagement.*' She had been able to shrug off her aunts' chattering assumptions about her impending marriage, but she could not so easily dismiss her father's chilling words. She had always believed that Baba knew more than anyone about everything. All her life, even when he was far away in Africa, pleasing him had been almost as important to her as pleasing Allah. If her father insisted that she marry Ali, how could she refuse?

Thoughtfully Fatima began rolling herself a cigarette as she turned her father's references to sugared almonds – the customary good-luck favour at Lebanese betrothals and marriages – over in her mind. Baba had not mentioned Ali by name. Yet clearly he assumed she would be getting married during the month or so that he would be home. So far as she knew, however, Ali wasn't expected back in the village for many months, perhaps even a year or two. Either Ali was coming home sooner than she had realized, or her father had another arranged marriage in mind.

She spread a little tobacco out on the white paper, expertly rolled it into a cigarette, and sealed it tight with spit. As she struck a match and inhaled, a pang shot through her. She didn't especially want to marry Ali, but at least she was accustomed to that possibility. What would she do if her father insisted she marry some other cousin? Quickly she ran through the roster of available relatives of her generation. Just as quickly she rejected each of them in turn. None but Ali had her education. None but Ali was exactly old enough, and suitable enough, and – in a way – good enough. She had never much fancied the idea of marrying Ali, but who else was there?

As she smoked, Fatima shaded her eyes against the midday sun and looked longingly out at the far horizon. The world beyond was wider than her family. What if she – like her Beirut friends – could follow her heart and scour the world for her perfect match? How wonderful it would be to fall in love of her own free will and be able to marry the man that she alone believed had been made for her! Anne, Leila and Camilla were so lucky.

Fatima stamped out her cigarette and dusted off the back of her robe. She tried to look gladder than she felt as she dragged her feet back inside the house to join her one big happy family.

Her father had his arm around her the next morning as the two of them walked the long way through the olive orchards up towards the graveyard by the mosque where Baba's father and mother and all the other departed members of the family were buried just as they had lived, side by side.

For once Fatima and her father were alone. Everyone else in the family had scattered for work and chores. On any other morning, Fatima would be helping her mother and sisters peel vegetables or wash floors. On any other morning, having her father to herself, safe and snug in the circle of his arm, would have been one of Fatima's dreams come true. But at breakfast, when Baba had asked her if she wanted to come with him as he paid his respects at the cemetery, she had almost choked on a piece of bread She had thought he would wait longer before breaking the bad news to her.

Fatima was silent as she trudged by her father's side. What had to be said, *inshallah*, would be said.

'In Africa the mornings are never like this. Never so fresh.' The dew was still wet on the high grass, and a chill wind whipped through the valley and across their path. Abbas inhaled deep breaths of the air he loved. 'It is always so hot there. Damp. Heavy. And the smells! Everything smells rotten. A man cannot even breathe. If you go outside and stand and listen, you can almost hear the jungle creeping closer, green inch by green inch. I have to hire boys to keep cutting it back, or maybe it would come in the windows at night and choke us in our beds.' His dark eyes were haunted as he remembered that, and too many other fears, that he had struggled to live with in the lonely years of his African exile. 'It is not for me. Some of the other foreigners, even some of the Lebanese who went out there when I did, call it home now. They marry local women, start second families, forget the old ways. But not me. A day never passes when I do not wish I were back here, right here, in this village. I remember every tree, every hill, every face.'

'We wish you were here all the time, too.' Fatima was beginning to hope that she had been wrong at breakfast. Maybe Baba just wanted to spend time with her because he had missed her in those choking years in damp Africa. 'This morning that's what I prayed for, that you would stay here and never go back there.'

'Child, child . . .' Abbas tightened his grip on her shoulders. 'You must know how it is. There is no work here. The land is too old and tired to feed so many of us. And do not forget that the government tells us that it is not really our land. Even though our family has lived here for ever, even though the father of the father of my father planted these olive groves, the law says this land belongs to another.' There was bitterness in every line of his wrinkled face as he looked out over the beautiful stony hills that would never quite be his. 'The owners would refuse to sell this land to us even if we had the money to buy it. And how could I raise all ten of you on what the big bosses would pay me for picking their olives?'

'In Beirut they say it won't be like that for ever.' Fatima had never cared for politics, but she was proud that for once her father was talking to her like a man. She was eager to respond in kind, and so she fell back on what she had heard the few times she had tagged along with Leila to hot-headed Nasserist rallies at the university. She had liked those stirring speeches more than she had thought she would. It had been intoxicating to join the excited throng and feel at one with the great Arab nation. 'They say that one day there will be land reform. Free schools for everyone. Hospitals everywhere. And justice, Baba. They say that one day the Arabs will win back Palestine, and we'll all finally be free of our oppressors.'

'They talk a lot of rot in Beirut. They always did, and they always will. But I never thought I'd hear my own daughter talking like a Communist. Or like a Palestinian. I did not send you to Beirut to learn to be a revolutionary. I sent you there to be a teacher.'

Fatima bit her lip and wished she were down on her hands and knees scrubbing the bedroom floor. 'Yes, Baba.'

Her meekness reassured him, and so he continued on in a gentler vein. 'No, *habibi*, the way to make things better is not by changing the government or fighting wars or even screaming in the streets. The way to do it is by working hard, saving your money, and putting up with things you hate so that those who come after you will not have to. That is the Lebanese way. I had to go away and stay away so that you could all have a chance at a better life. And someday it will all be worth it. *Inshallah*, someday all of what we have endured will be worth it.'

'*Inshallah*,' Fatima dutifully echoed.

Abbas's face cracked into a wide, proud smile as he beamed down at his daughter. 'When I look at you, Fatima, I think, *el-hamdulillah*, already it is worth it! You are a teacher! My daughter is a teacher!' His broad chest seemed to expand even further. 'And you are only the beginning. Your mother tells me all of you are clever. She claims you got your brains from her! Ha! So little Abbas will be next, eh? I am told he did very well at the government school in Nabatiya. Next year I want him to go to Beirut, like you. He will be an engineer. Hassan is good with numbers. Maybe he can be an accountant and keep track of all our money. As for little Mohsen, why someday he might even be a doctor! I will be the father of a doctor, a teacher, an engineer and an accountant!' He laughed out loud as he pounded his chest with his free hand, but then the smile died on his lips as he remembered the less favoured lives of his older children. 'I wish I could have done the same for all my boys and girls. But I had to take your three big brothers to Africa, so we could send enough money home to help the rest of you. Allah knows it is hard enough there for an old man like me, but for them . . .' He shook his head. 'I remember what it was like to be young there.' He paused and then, judging that the time was right, began to work towards the point of this conversation. 'That is why I brought my boys home. It's time all three of them had wives. We can have four happy weddings! I bought a whole case of sugared Jordan almonds at the best confectioner's shop in Beirut. I will marry you all off while I am here, and then they can stay in the village for a year or two to start their families. I will make do alone for a while in Africa.'

With a sinking heart, Fatima seized on that one telling word he had, seemingly casually, dropped into his speech. 'Four weddings, Baba?'

'Last night I already talked to my brother Hassan. Ibrahim can marry his second daughter, Sarah. I wrote a long time ago to my brother Muhammad in Beirut. Hussein will marry his daughter, Elham. And your brother Ali will marry your cousin Amina. But you know all this. None of this was ever a secret. As for the fourth marriage . . .'

'Yes?'

He stopped, turned, and put one of his large hands on each of her shoulders as he looked deeply into her eyes. 'You know I only want what is best for you. Always, everything I have ever done, has been for the good of every one of you. For the family as a whole, and for each of you in turn. Is that not so, Fatima?'

'It is so, Baba.' But she cast her eyes down and, even though he pressed hard on her shoulders, she would not look up at him.

'You know I love all my sons and all my daughters. But I think that you also know that maybe I love you in a very special way because . . . I don't know why because. You were always different from the other girls. Cleverer. Braver. God gave you special gifts, Fatima, and so I bowed to Allah's will and tried to give you a special life. Even though many of my brothers thought I was crazy, I sent you to Beirut to get a better education. I could have sent one of the older boys in your place instead of taking him back to Africa with me. But no, you were the first to go to college in Beirut. I did that for you, Fatima. And so now I want you to do something for me.'

'Baba, I—'

'Let me finish. I saw your face yesterday when I could not wait to whisper what I thought was the good news in your ear. You have always been the same, you never could hide your feelings. What is wrong? I thought you would be thrilled to marry Ali next week instead of next year.'

'Ali?' Shyly she raised her eyes and glanced timidly at her father.

'Of course Ali.' Abbas looked bewildered as he studied his daughter's face. 'You have always known it would be Ali.' He let out a great booming laugh. 'So that was all it was? You were afraid I wanted you to marry someone else?'

'Yes and no.' She did not quite have the courage yet to tell him that she wanted to pick her own husband, that she wanted to marry for love instead of family solidarity, that at the very least she wanted to wait and get to know Ali better before she committed herself to him for ever. Miserably she talked around what she wanted to say. 'You didn't mention his name yesterday. And I didn't know he'd be coming back to the village so soon. I thought he'd still be in Iraq.'

'Iran. He is in Iran now. Studying with the mullahs in the holy city of Qom. Ali is a very learned young man. He'll be a *shaykh* when he comes back to the village next year. You will see, it will be a great honour to be the wife of such a man.'

'Next year? But you just said I'd be marrying him next week.'

'We live in the modern age, Fatima. You are a modern woman, I should not have to remind you of that.' Abbas smiled. 'If God wills it and you yourself agree, next week you will marry your cousin Ali on the telephone.'

'*On the telephone?*'

'Yes, why not? You have never heard of this? Last year one of the Lebanese I know in Africa married a girl from his village back here, just like that. For, you see, as with you and Ali, it is not always possible for a man and woman to be in the same place when it is the right time to marry. So a mullah can marry them on the telephone. Or it can be done by proxy. But I think the telephone is better. More personal.'

'Is this a joke, Baba?'

'I would never joke about something I consider essential to your happiness.'

'But why the rush? Why can't I wait until he's here?'

'For the same reason that I want my three sons to marry while I'm here. You are my children. I am fifty-nine years old, and I will not live for ever.' He looked ahead on the hill, where the graveyard waited. 'This could be my last visit home. Before I go back to Africa, I want to see you all settled.' Abbas wasn't above applying a little blackmail to get his way. 'God knows, it is little enough to ask. I have had to miss too much of your lives as it is.' He sensed that he would have to prod Fatima into speaking her mind. 'What are you really saying, daughter? Is it the telephone you object to, or Ali himself?'

She gulped and equivocated. 'It's not that I don't *want* to marry him. Someday *inshallah*, maybe I will. Or maybe not, I don't know.' Finally, earnestly, she blurted it out. '*I* want to choose, Baba. *Me!* Not you or Mother or Uncle Muhammad. When and if I marry, I want to marry for love.'

He seemed to take her declaration better than she had expected. 'And so you will, Fatima.' Indulgently he smiled. 'Everyone in our family marries for love. We all love each other. I loved your mother from the time that she was a little girl, and she says she always loved me, too. If it's love you want, you are in the right family.'

'Oh, Baba!' Hopelessly she tried to marshal the arguments that had sounded so unassailable in Anne's bedroom. 'Not that kind of love,' she said lamely. Part of her wanted to rebel and vow that she would never marry her cousin, and another part of her wanted just as passionately to do anything and everything her beloved father ever asked of her. She hated feeling tongue-tied and confused like this. 'Real love. Romantic love. Like in the movies.'

'I see.' He pursed his lips and said in a low voice, as if to himself, 'I send a good Muslim girl to Beirut to learn to be a teacher, and she comes home talking like a Communist and wanting to turn her life into a Hollywood movie.'

Without another word he led her inside the cemetery, and in silence they approached the corner where their ancestors lay. Muhammad reached out his hand to touch the long greyish stone slab that covered his father's grave. Tears filled his eyes, and he moved his lips in a blessing. Then he moved a few steps away to his mother's grave and prayed again. He wiped his eyes and laid his hands, one by one, on the graves of an elder brother, his grandfathers and grandmothers, five uncles, three aunts, many cousins.

When he had finished, he turned to Fatima. 'Real love is here, daughter. Not in your movies, but here in these graves. In this village. In your family.' His eyes were very sad. 'I will not force you to marry your cousin Ali, even though I believe he is the best man for you. I believe, in fact, that he is the best man not only in our whole family but in our whole village. When it is time for me to take my place here in this graveyard, I would rest easier to think I had left you in Ali's hands.' He sighed. 'But, as you know, it is contrary to the words of the Holy Koran and the example of the life of the Prophet Muhammad to force a Muslim woman to marry against her will. You tell me you want to choose your own husband. So be it. That is your right. You may marry Ali or not, as you like. But understand that you will disappoint me if you refuse this marriage.' He looked deeply into her eyes, and when she opened her mouth as if to answer, he put his finger over her mouth. 'Enough now, daughter. We have said enough.

Now I think it is time for you to go home and help your mother, while I go to the mosque and read the Koran and talk with the men. I am old, and I am your father. At least let me have the last word.'

Fatima bowed her head and turned away and began the long and thoughtful walk back home.

A fortnight later Fatima's father stood shouting into the telephone receiver in the post office in Nabatiya, as he struggled to make himself heard on the faint line that stretched from this south Lebanese market town hundreds of miles across the Fertile Crescent: through Syria, over Jordan, down the length of Iraq, all the way to the holy Shia Muslim city of Qom in distant Iran.

'Ali? *Enta Ali?*'

Abbas was certain that somewhere near the other end of this line, Ali waited to marry Fatima. Days ago he had talked to Ali on this very telephone and settled the time and date of the official call that would connect the two of them for ever. But of course nothing was proceeding quite according to plan today. Even though the Nabatiya postmaster had promised to book the call to Iran for one o'clock this afternoon, Fatima and most of the men in her family had been waiting in the post office for the past three hours. The connection buzzed, echoed, faltered, but then Abbas heard the whisper of another voice at the end of the line. But he couldn't understand what was being said in that thick Farsi accent.

'Ali? *Enta Ali?*' Finally he realized that the faint voice would be more fluent in Farsi than in Arabic, and so he passed the receiver to the mullah who could converse in the Persian language. After expensive seconds of what sounded like polite social patter, the mullah nodded and handed the telephone back to Abbas.

There was a pause, and then a more intelligible voice

came on the line. 'Ali!' Abbas's face lit up with relief. A great collective sigh ran through the assembled men who were jammed into the post office.

Sitting woodenly in a straight chair in a corner, Fatima went a shade paler. She cocked her head to listen to her father. He was smiling and saying 'yes' to everything. In a moment, Fatima dully reminded herself, she would stand and walk over to the telephone and say the same thing. She steeled herself to do what her father and everyone else in the family wanted her to do. These last two fraught weeks, she had talked to her mother, her sisters, her brothers and – again and again – to her father. Without exception, all of them had begged her to agree to this match. Miserably she had paced the olive groves alone, praying and hoping that Allah would give her a sign of what she should do. She had longed for the comfort of being able to talk all this over with Anne or even Leila or Camilla. Finally, then, when no one and nothing had come to her rescue, she had given in and bowed to the family consensus. But now it would take all her resources simply to go through with it. She could not allow herself, at this stage, to reconsider. It was too late now to choose another path, to flee to Beirut, to live the life of a free and modern woman.

'Fatima!'

She got to her feet and jerkily walked over to her father and held out her hand to take the telephone and talk to Ali. But instead it was the mullah who was holding the receiver, asking Ali if he agreed to marry Fatima and maintain her as his wife. Satisfied with Ali's answer, the mullah asked Abbas if he agreed to the marriage. Then he asked Fatima the same simple question. '*Nam*,' she said weakly, 'yes.'

Abbas grabbed the telephone. '*Ya Ali, khelas!* It is finished, Ali!' Finally he passed the receiver to Fatima. 'Say something to your husband.'

She could hardly hear the whisper of the voice at

the other end of the line. Try as she might, she could not associate that faint crackling voice with the cousin she had not seen for eight years. But yes, she said, she was fine, her mother was fine, everyone was fine. She said she was happy to hear that Ali was fine. Yes, she too was looking forward to seeing her husband when he finally returned home to Lebanon.

She was relieved when Ali's father took the telephone and let loose with a string of endearments, questions, answers. Then it was a brother's turn, the mullah had more to say, her father smiled and laughed into the telephone.

A cousin was passing round a box of sugared almonds. '*Inshallah bithannou*,' the men all chorused. 'May their lives be happy, God willing!'

Fatima walked back to the straight chair and patiently munched sugared almonds until they were finished on the telephone and ready to take her back to the village.

Chapter 5

Camilla opened her eyes to pitch dark and did not know where she was. Groggily, she thought she might be sleeping over at Anne's on the Rue Bliss, or waking in the tarty teenage room her mother had let her plaster with magazine pictures of movie stars. Sharply, as fresher and sadder memories began seeping back to her, she wished she were all the way back in her childhood cot next to Mama.

She sighed as she let the warm safe past slide away. She was married now. She was married, and something was nightmare wrong. She was sweating though it was cold. It was never this cold at home.

As her eyes got used to the faint light that filtered in the window from the streetlamp below, she could make out the shape of a Louis Seize gilded chair, the shadow of an ormolu and ebony Empire wardrobe, the shine of an ornate baroque mirror on the wall. Paris, they were in Paris. They were paying a fortune for their suite of rooms on one of the best streets in the best *quartiers*, but still, all winter long, it had been freezing in this underheated apartment.

She reached out and groped beside her for Pierre. But she was alone in her cold marriage bed. Again he wasn't here. She remembered the rest of what was wrong, how he left her alone so much, what he said to her when he came back, how much it all hurt.

She tried to turn over on her side to see the opalescent Lalique glass clock on the bedside table. But as she went to roll over, the swollen clumsy mound that was her stomach got in the way. She groaned and glowered at the beamed ceiling. In this ninth month, she was as helpless as a turtle on its back. No wonder he never wanted to look at her, much less touch her, anymore. He was right, she was *une vache bouffie*. A bloated cow he wished he had never married.

I wish I had never married him either.

She clapped her hand to her mouth as though she had spoken that bad, black thought aloud. She must never think an unnatural thing like that again. She loved Pierre, and she always would. He was handsome, charming, virile – everything she had always dreamed a husband should be. She was lucky to have a husband like Pierre. They were just going through a difficult patch. It was probably her fault. Just as he said, she was hysterical and made too many demands on him. Just because she felt so horrible all the time was no excuse for the way she screeched at her beloved husband. He was right, she carried on like a low-class shopkeeper's wife. Or like her mother. She hadn't been able to stop crying that first time he had accused her of acting exactly like her mother. He had been forced to hit her to help her stop crying. She had resolved, the first time he had hit her, never to do anything to provoke him like that again. She would be so sweet and loving that he would never dream of leaving her side, much less of slapping her around the bedroom. It was her own fault that she had failed again, and again after that, and he had been forced to strike out at her. She was a failure as a wife, and that was the only test that mattered for a woman. A pain shot sharply through her belly, and she screamed. 'Pierre!'

A door banged open. A maid shouted. Running feet pattered. '*Chérie!*' It wasn't her husband but her mother who came to the rescue.

Nirvana tenderly blotted the sweat from her daughter's face with the long purple chiffon scarf that had been twined around her neck. It was three o'clock in the morning, and she had just come home. She hadn't yet wiped off her thick stage make-up and was still dressed in the spangled costume she had worn for her final numbers at the cabaret off the Champs Elysées. In her sequins and plumes, her eyes ringed like a racoon's, she hardly looked like the image of anxious mother love. But as she crooned to Camilla to calm down, that it was only the baby coming, time fell away; the two of them reverted to nursing mother and suckling child. Perhaps in the past, Nirvana admitted, she and Camilla had not always seen eye to eye. She had never been the most orthodox of mothers, and sometimes she had regarded her daughter as more of a burden than a joy. But as Nirvana held her daughter fiercely to her, she thanked God that this time she had followed her maternal instincts and come running when her *bébé* needed her most. She would have made an average of three thousand and twenty-seven more Lebanese pounds each week back at her own cabaret in Beirut. And she was sure that in her absence her *maître d'* and cashier were robbing her blind. But not for an instant did she regret having jumped at the opportunity of taking this cut-rate run at the Rive Droite club. At Orly airport, she had taken one shrewd look at Camilla's wan face before brushing aside Pierre's objections and ensconcing herself in their guest bedroom. As the maid skidded into the room in her nightgown, Nirvana hissed at her to call the doctor.

Camilla clutched her stomach as another pain knifed through her. It hurt worse than when she had cracked her head open on a cement floor as a little girl. Worse than the skiing accident when she had broken her arm. Worse, far worse, than anything ever before. Camilla's blue eyes widened in terror. '*J'en creverai!*' she screamed. 'I will die! The baby, he will kill me!' She broke out in loud keening shrieks. 'Pierre? *Où est Pierre?*'

'Where indeed!' Nirvana silently cursed her son-in-law, his mother, his father, both his sisters, and every wretched ancestor whose genes had contributed to the *bâtard* Pierre had turned out to be. It had been a dreadful mistake for the newlyweds to come to Paris. Back at home, constrained by his family, Pierre would never have dared to do as he had done here. Yet who would have guessed that putting Pierre in such close proximity to the Parisian fleshpots was the worst possible blow that could have been delivered to their fragile young marriage? Last autumn, Pierre's idea of averting a family scandal by whiling away the winter in France had seemed an inspiration. For by then Camilla had finally told him that she had been nearly three months pregnant on their wedding day. The baby was due not in April but in January. From that moment on, even though Camilla had not realized it at the time, the honeymoon had been over. But she had been entranced by Pierre's plan to dally in Paris until after the baby was born. She had imagined that they would have visiting Egyptian film stars for friends, that she could buy to her heart's content in the couture showrooms, that she might even set up her easel and paint by the Seine. Accordingly, they had flown off to France in early autumn for what they said was some pre-Christmas shopping. Once here, however, they had rung home with the story that Camilla had developed complications in her pregnancy. The doctors had advised her not to risk the return journey home. Their plan was to linger here in Paris as long as they could after the baby was born. Eventually, back in Beirut, they would lie about the infant's birthday and maybe even try to pass the baby off as premature.

All this, Nirvana thought with some resentment as she crooned and stroked her daughter's matted blonde hair back from her temples, because Pierre and Camilla had simply jumped the gun a little bit. In any other family no one would much care when a baby had been conceived. They had been engaged to be married of their own free will long before she was pregnant, and the entire clan longed for an heir to carry on the family name. It was absurd to quibble over the exact second when the sperm had hit the egg. But the Nazranis were not a normal family. In Lebanon they gave themselves royal airs, and so they were acting as if the genesis and birth of this baby were a sacredly anointed matter of state. Nirvana supposed that if it had only been up to him, Pierre's father would probably have just winked and overlooked an early birth. But even though Shaykh Georges might rule his patch of Lebanon, it was his wife who ruled the roost. Pierre, like the rest of the Nazranis, was intimidated by his mother. Even in the summer he had worried when she had voiced suspicions that Camilla was more pregnant than she had any right to be. She would never forgive them, he had fretted, if the baby's birthdate proved they had been sleeping together before the wedding. Camilla said he had quivered like a naughty schoolboy as he had desperately tried to figure out how to outwit his sainted mother.

Nirvana glared at the antique silver-framed photograph of Pierre still resting smugly in the place of honour on Camilla's bedside table. Now that she loathed Pierre, she could see so clearly in the weakness of his chin, and the swagger of his stance, what she had only sensed when he first came sniffing around her daughter. She should have disposed of this nasty young pup the first time he had thrown her those steamy, heavy-lidded looks behind Camilla's back. It would have been child's play to lure him between her own rustling silk sheets. God knows he wouldn't have been the first of Camilla's objectionable boyfriends whom she had so deliciously deflected. It was a pity that her daughter had never quite understood that she was only eliminating those rutting young men for her own good. Camilla had even accused her once of stealing her boyfriends just for spite, because Camilla was young and she was getting old.

Nirvana could not resist glancing over in the gilded mirror. She wasn't so old. Thank God she still wasn't really showing her age. She had hardly a bag under her eyes, there wasn't a hint of flab under her upper arms, and her slim thighs rippled almost like those of a girl half her age. Yet she wished her judgement were as good as her muscle tone. Back in Beirut, she should have heeded the signs of the storms that were sure to come with Pierre. Even under his mother's thumb, he had never been an angel. There had been plenty of rumours about his gambling at the Casino du Liban, his drinking at the Kit Kat Club, and his wenching in the brothels of the Rue Ahmed Chaoqui. It was said, too, that he smoked only the best grades of hashish from his father's Bekaa Valley plantations. Still, Nirvana reflected, none of this behaviour had been all that alarming; she herself had been known to kick up her heels and take an occasional puff of the weed. Yet now Nirvana bitterly regretted that she had ever let him touch her *bébé*. Somewhere deep inside, in her gut or maybe even in her womb, she had always known that Pierre was a creature of darkness. But he had been a scion of one of the 'best' families in Lebanon. Everyone had said Pierre Nazrani was the catch of the season. And so she had swallowed her misgivings.

'Pierre!' Camilla cried and melodramatically rolled her eyes as another contraction ripped through her. Now, near the convulsive end of a miserable pregnancy, she was losing consciousness of everything but her physical pain. Other women endured morning sickness, but she had suffered nausea and exhaustion at every vile hour of the day and night. Ironically, during these last sodden months in Paris, the story they had concocted for Pierre's family had turned out to be true after all. There had been no couture shopping sprees and no intimate receptions with the *crème de la crème* of Parisian society. Camilla hadn't even been able to nip over to England to visit Leila and buy out Harrods. For, exactly as they had said when they had telephoned the Château Croisé, she had been confined to bed these last two months with her legs swollen to twice their size. Now the baby was two weeks overdue, and she had thought she would die from the waiting. But that had been before these wrenching labour pains had begun. She couldn't stand pain like this. She writhed and doubled over as she felt another jagged spasm coming, and then she screamed. 'I want Pierre!'

'He's coming, he's coming.' Nirvana lied to keep her daughter calm. Why she still wanted him at all was the first question Nirvana planned to ask, once she finally delivered the baby and was herself again. She hadn't brought Camilla into the world to be the passive victim of a dissolute man. But – perversely – the more Pierre mistreated her, the more compulsively she seemed to love him.

Nirvana suppressed a sigh. She was afraid that

it was her daughter's bad fortune to be yet another woman caught up in a passion that could – if she weren't very careful – one day destroy her. From her own disastrous first marriage, Nirvana remembered how that sort of love could scar and maím, how addictive its ups and downs could be, how nothing could rival its searing hurts and thrills. Obviously, even though Camilla could work herself into a fury at Pierre, she was still obsessed with him. Yet Nirvana wanted to believe that somehow, some day, Camilla would be able to crawl out of this pit she was digging for herself. A love like that didn't necessarily have to blight a woman's life. Once, when she herself had been as young and foolish as Camilla, she too had eagerly abandoned her pride and everything else for a man who treated her like *zift*, like the pavement he walked upon. Yet, even now, twenty years later, if she could find him, she would probably let him walk all over her again. She had loved Michel far more than any of the multitude of his successors. She would have done – in fact, she had done – anything and everything for him. But he had left her anyway. The only reason it had ended was that Michel had gone away and never come back. Afterwards she had even shamelessly followed him here to France to beg him to give her another chance. But he had eluded her in the end even more successfully than he had in the beginning. Yet – perhaps – not altogether.

Nirvana possessively stroked their daughter's fair blonde hair back from her milky white skin. Camilla was so like her father. She had his delicate bones, his colouring, his effervescent charm. But she had some of her father's faults as well. Like him, she always tried to run away from her problems. She was weak, this daughter, and Camilla was going to need all the strength a woman could muster to cope with her bully of a husband and his overbearing family. Yet perhaps Camilla was not as frail as she feared. Camilla was *her* daughter, too. After Michel had left her, she had discovered an artesian well of strength that would never run dry. Somewhere in Camilla, under all that fluff and all those tears, was a shrewd peasant woman who would do whatever had to be done to survive. In the end her daughter might flourish and triumph. She was, after all, starting out with advantages other than good genes from her mother's side of the family. Camilla wasn't poor, and she wasn't alone. She would always have her mother to help her.

Nirvana let out a heartfelt sigh of regret. She supposed she herself had to take some of the blame for Camilla's character flaws. She had always spoiled her only child. She had never been able to resist giving in when Camilla cried to get her own way. She had always been such a doting mother that it outraged her when Camilla accused her of neglect, and being too possessive, and – unkindest cut of all – of being jealous. But she had only wanted her daughter to love her, and not to leave her. She had never wanted her *bébé* to repeat her own mistakes with men. And now, after all her sacrifices and dreams, here lay Camilla – suffering like a sick animal.

As her daughter broke into another bout of hysterical weeping, Nirvana wished she could strangle her son-in-law for going off and leaving her alone when she needed him most. Like so many of his kind, Pierre seemed to view women as either virgins or whores. And Camilla had fallen off the pedestal once he had discovered when the baby was really due. It wasn't until days after she had flown to the rescue in Paris that Camilla had finally broken down and told her mother the whole sorry story of how Pierre had reacted to her little secret. How he had blamed her for not taking precautions. How he had carried on as though she had been the seducer and he the reluctant virgin. How he had then admitted that he was worried about what his mother would say when the baby arrived wicked months early. How finally he had seized and gnawed upon far more terrible notions. Camilla had given in to him, so maybe she had also given in to others. Her baby might not be his baby. His blushing bride was her mother's daughter.

Nirvana reached over and slammed Pierre's photograph face down on the table. She would never forgive him for implying that the very mention of her was the ultimate insult. It was true that she had been implicated in a tasty scandal or two in her time. And, she tartly added to herself as she looked back into the mirror and tucked a wayward spit-curl into place, her time was still far from over. But she had never in her life consciously set out to hurt another human being. Until her divorces were final, she had been faithful to every one of her husbands. It was her own business what she did in those rollicking months when she was between spouses. If she had made mistakes along the way, they were only due to her innate – perhaps legendary – generosity of flesh and spirit. Besides, who was Pierre to be casting stones?

'Mama, it hurts.' This time the contraction made Camilla scream as the tears coursed down her cheeks. 'Why didn't you tell me it would hurt this much, Mama?'

Nirvana wiped away her daughter's tears. Why, she wondered, didn't every mother tell every daughter how much everything was going to hurt? She supposed no mother wanted to believe her little girl might be destined to repeat the same old womanly mistake of loving the wrong man at the wrong time. But, Nirvana thought, let other mothers worry about their daughters. She had her hands full with her own. For no sooner had they leased this lavish penthouse apartment near the Avenue Foch than Pierre had begun ducking out alone at night. In the beginning, when he was still coming home drunk at midnight, he had told them he was visiting a friend just in from Beirut or an old family chum who worked on the

Bourse. But only a few weeks later, when he had begun staying out all night, he had stopped making excuses altogether. Nirvana's gossipy show business cronies had reported spotting Pierre with showgirls at the Lido, the Crazy Horse and the Folies Bergère. Sometimes, after he had been gone for days at a time, Nirvana had heard rumours that he had been seen at the casinos in Monte Carlo and Cannes. All this had been bad enough. But more outrageous still had been the bills that had begun arriving at their apartment for perfume, lingerie and flowers that Pierre had most certainly never given to his wife. Nirvana remembered sitting with them at the dinner table the first time Camilla had let fly with a flood of recriminations. Instead of backing away from a fight, Pierre had curled his lip and gone on the attack. A man, he had said, had to take his pleasures somewhere when all his wife did was cry and nag and when Camilla had inevitably burst into tears, he had warned her to stop or he would hit her. Until then it hadn't dawned on Nirvana that Pierre was beating her daughter. When she had flown to Camilla's defence, Pierre had actually raised his hand to strike his mother-in-law. After he had finally stormed out that night, Nirvana had bolted the front door behind him. If it had been up to her, she would never have let him in again. But three days later Camilla had welcomed him back with open arms,and for a very short while the two of them had billed and cooed like lovebirds in a gilded cage.

The doorbell sounded, and Camilla's eyes leaped with hope. 'Pierre! I knew he'd come!'

But it was only the doctor. This matter-of-fact French specialist had infuriated Camilla last week when he had observed that her histrionics were complicating an otherwise fairly normal pregnancy. Later she had raged to her mother that they must find another physician who was more to her liking, someone *sympathique*, like their family doctor back in Beirut. Old Dr Yusef had always indulged Camilla like a favourite niece who could do no wrong. Yet now the very entrance of this doctor seemed to work wonders on Camilla. She stopped sobbing, sat up, and studied the physician's face intently after he had pulled up the sheet to give her a brief preliminary examination. She was relieved that he did not seem at all alarmed. She resented, however, that he even looked bored. He was acting as if the excruciating pain of trying to squeeze a large baby through a narrow passage in her delicate body were the most natural thing in the world.

'My *bébé*!' Nirvana wrung her hands. Up to now, because Camilla needed her, she had managed to keep her own emotions under control. But now that Camilla showed signs of having pulled herself together, it was Nirvana who seemed on the verge of collapse. '*Bébé, bébé!* What has he done to you, *bébé!* Doctor! Tell me the truth! Will she live?'

'She is not sick, madame. Your daughter is a strong and healthy young woman. She is not dying. She is only having a baby.' The doctor shook his head as he washed his hands in a basin on the dresser. The old girl in the feathers was carrying on as if her daughter was at death's door. Apparently hysterics ran in this family. Or perhaps all Arabs were like this? He wondered briefly what the husband was like. As often as he had been summoned to this pampered woman's bedside – and he had lost count of the times, at all hours of the day and night – the husband had never been here. Perhaps there was no husband. That could account for whatever was wrong in this household. 'So far I can see no complications.'

'But the pain, doctor. I don't think my daughter can stand the pain.'

As if on cue, Camilla was shaken by another contraction and screamed blue murder.

'She must,' the doctor said matter-of-factly. 'She

is going to have a baby.' He yawned as he consulted his watch. Three forty-five. The baby most probably wouldn't arrive until the afternoon, or perhaps even the evening. It was going to be a long and trying ordeal, sequestered with this overwrought pair of women.

Two mornings later a radiant Camilla sat propped up in bed like an empress receiving the homage of the world. Around her were banked baskets of pink and white camellias. Gift-wrapped boxes of chocolates were strewn about the ivory silk sheets. Lifesize stuffed animals all but cavorted on the floor. All this – flowers, candy, toys – were her mother's offerings to the infant son Camilla rocked in the crook of her arm.

'Yes, yes, a boy!' From necessity as well as for joy, Camilla was shouting into the telephone receiver she cradled in her other hand. The connection to Boston was faint and full of echoes. 'Oh, Anne, he is so very beautiful, my Tomas, to hold him, to kiss him, never have I felt like this!' She could not resist leaning over to kiss her baby's dear wrinkled face. She beamed as she listened to Anne's congratulations, and then answered the inevitable questions about the delivery. 'No, it wasn't so bad, not really.' Camilla's eyes rolled at her mother sitting in the chair of honour beside her bed. She would never forget how dear Mama had stayed right here by her side for all of it. Yet, oddly, already Camilla was beginning to forget the length and breadth of her pain. '*Pardon?* No, not so long. Fourteen hours.'

Camilla was so intent on Anne's far-away voice that she failed to hear not only the front door opening but also the heavy footfall in the hallway. Nirvana, however, had heard it. She looked up and glowered at the enemy.

Cold sober but very hung over, Pierre stood blinking in the doorway. He was wrung out from five tequila-soaked days in the bed of an insatiable black-skinned stripper from Alabama. He had always wondered if what they said about black sexual prowess was a myth, and now he knew. Never again would he gorge on dark meat. He felt like a sick old man. That Mexican fire-water had taken its toll as well. He had hardly had the stamina to make his way home. As he had let himself in the apartment door, he had hoped that for once his wife would be out somewhere with her mother. All he had wanted to do was crawl into bed and sleep off that binge. And so, at his first bloodshot glance around the bedroom, all that registered was the blinding sunshine and the high-pitched sounds of his wife.

Still bent over the telephone, Camilla let out a riff of her flutey laughter. '*Vraiment!* Four kilos! He is a big one, my boy!' Again, as she listened to Anne, Camilla kissed her sleeping baby's nose, forehead and lips. 'Leila? No, not yet. I wanted to tell you first. Next I will ring her. Maybe she will come to see my angel, yes?'

Nirvana sat back in her ringside seat and waited for Pierre to get his come-uppance. For, in the first flush of triumph after her labour, Camilla had become a tigress committed to defending her cub at any cost. Fiercely she had vowed that Pierre was never going to lay his abusive hands on this baby. She had said she would never forgive him for not being with her for the birth. Never again, she had promised, would she let that devil touch her. Pierre could divorce her or not, as he liked. If he couldn't manage to bend the rules of the Maronite church to get them a divorce, they would simply live apart. Nirvana couldn't hide her bittersweet smile of mother-in-law satisfaction as she waited for the fireworks to begin.

Pierre was meanwhile rubbing his eyes as he leaned against the open door. The room was different some-how. But his head was so foggy that he could not quite grasp what was different about it. He still could not take in the baby in her arms or her mother by her side, much less the banks of flowers and zoo of stuffed animals. But suddenly one sight came into focus, and he stared at *her*.

When he had left his wife this last time, just as he had left her so many times in these last sour months, Camilla had been crying again. She had always cried more than most but back in Beirut she used to look so sweet and helpless when she wept that it had been a pleasure to be the saviour who came to her rescue. But there had been nothing pretty about her crying fits here in Paris. When she carried on as she did, she had made him feel so angry – and so guilty – that he had been unable to stop himself from lashing out at her. What man wanted to be near a wife whose hair hung in limp strands, who lay slumped like a slattern in an old nightgown, whose face was bleary from all that weeping, whose body had bloated into a misshapen mess? It was better, really, when he felt his black rage against her mounting, to storm out of the door and not come back until he had cooled off and was what he liked to think of as himself again.

But here, suddenly, when he had least expected it, that shrew he had so resented was gone. The girl of his dreams had come back to him.

Pierre gazed in wonder at the one he would always adore. The bad times fell away as if they had never happened. As if a man could really fall in love at first sight, and as if this were his first glimpse of Camilla, he fell in love with her all over again. Her exquisite face glowed as she laughed that intoxicating laugh of hers. He hadn't heard her laugh like that for so long. He felt the corners of his mouth turning up as if her laughter was contagious. How could he have forgotten how beautiful Camilla was? Her mane of platinum hair was draped over the mound of lace-edged pillows behind her head. In that fluffy pale pink negligée, she looked like a cotton candy confection, or like the spun sugar dollies the Muslims sold at street stalls for their Prophet's birthday. But not exactly. That filmy nightgown was cut enticingly low over the swell of her breasts. Tired as he was, his groin tightened. Just as it always used to before her unfortunate pregnancy, the mere sight of her made him want her.

He had already taken one excited step forward when he saw her lean over and kiss the baby. The baby! She had had his *baby!* He stopped where he stood, but his smile broadened as he feasted his eyes on the bundle in her arms. His wife was holding his baby. She was more than beautiful. She was holy. To him, as she held his baby, she became the Madonna.

Just then she glanced up from the telephone. As she saw that look of adoration on his face, she caught her breath and dropped the telephone. For the space of a long and sorcerous moment, she forgot what she had promised her mother she would say to him. She lost sight of the fact that he hadn't been here when she needed him, that he had missed her labour and delivery, that his son was two days old before he had even caught a glimpse of him. She even forgot about the baby in her arms. Nothing else mattered except that he had come back. It was always like this when first she caught sight of him even after their bitterest fights. Always his sheer physical presence overwhelmed every other thought and feeling. 'Pierre!' Her mind was a crazy jumble of silly *el-hamdulillahs*. She thanked God that she looked her best this morning, that a beautician from the salon just down the boulevard had come in to wash and set her curls, that the maid had scented her bath water with the heavy musk oil Pierre loved, that Mama had given her this new negligée along with all these flowers that made their room into a lovers' bower. And over and over again in her mind, like a catchy hit tune played incessantly on the radio, she thanked God that Pierre was finally here! But as she went to open her arms to him in welcome, the baby woke with a start and began to cry. She looked down almost in surprise at this evidence of their love, and in triumph she held out their son to him. 'It's a boy!'

'Camilla!' Nirvana's voice was a shrill warning, but her daughter didn't seem to hear it.

For Pierre was already on the bed. He had his arms around Camilla, and she was hugging him back. They were kissing each other, and then kissing the baby. Pierre was babbling incoherent endearments. Beautiful happy teardrops were rolling down Camilla's cheeks. The baby was gurgling, smiling, laughing. The three of them were a tableau of tender domestic bliss.

Nirvana sat helplessly watching her daughter make another mistake. How could she take him back without even a second's hesitation? But then, as she saw the radiance on Camilla's face, Nirvana sighed and remembered how it had been with her and Michel. In the long and lonely years since she had lost him, she had tried to forget how wonderful it had once been to have him. Instead, it had helped her keep her sanity to focus on how much he had hurt her, on what a bounder he had been, even on how much better off she was without him. But, watching Camilla aglow in Pierre's embrace, she remembered that she had never been happier than when she had had Michel's arms around her. Yes, *comme ça*, it had been just like this with her and that one she had loved and lost. It was perhaps expecting too much – at least this early on, when the two of them could still look as they were looking just now – for Camilla to give up this rapture for something as abstract as self-respect. These two, she supposed, would simply play out their love until there was no love left. Here and now, Camilla might indeed be as happy as she looked. But, with Pierre the way he was, Nirvana doubted if her daughter would remain happy for long. Yet who was she to begrudge Camilla this moment? Nirvana shrugged off her misgivings and tried to look on the brightly materialistic side. Why should the Nazrani money and social position slip through Camilla's fingers? Pierre probably wasn't much worse than any other man Camilla was likely to love, but he was most assuredly richer. She picked up the receiver and told Anne that her daughter would have to call her back. Then she sighed under her breath and slipped out of the room so the young ones could be alone.

Long after Nirvana had gone, Camilla and Pierre continued to kiss, hug and murmur endearments. Still their eyes flashed with love and longing. Tomas was a lovely name, yes, they had been wise to choose it months ago. They laughed when Tomas opened his eyes and seemed to answer to his name. Still they praised the baby from his fingers to his toes. He was such a perfect baby. This was such a perfect morning.

'He is beautiful, no?' Camilla was stroking the baby's cheek.

'Like you.' Pierre kissed the tip of Camilla's nose and then did the same to his son. As Tomas reached out a tiny hand towards his father, Pierre laughed and kissed those sweet fingers. He leaned closer, then, and studied the face of his son. It was hard to tell from that fuzz on his head, but it seemed the boy was going to have Camilla's fair hair. He had heard that all babies had blue eyes like this one, but it was hard to imagine eyes so exactly like Camilla's in depth and shape and colour ever turning dark like his own. From his forehead to his mouth to his chin, his tiny face was just like Camilla's. 'He looks exactly like you.'

'You think so?' Camilla tossed her hair back from her face and fondly agreed. 'But he has your nose, I think.'

Pierre squinted at the baby. 'No, his nose turns up like yours. A Nazrani nose is always arched.'

'And very big.' She reached up, tweaked her husband's beaky Lebanese nose, and laughed.

But Pierre didn't laugh with her. Instead his eyes were uncertain as he continued to study the baby. 'I thought my son would look more like a Nazrani. Even if he didn't look like me, you'd think he would look a bit like my father. Or even my mother. My sisters' girls look just like my mother's side of the family.'

'But he is just a wee one, eh? Give him time.' Camilla did not feel like laughing, but she forced a laugh so she wouldn't sound as irritated as she was beginning to feel. If they continued in this vein, they would soon be fighting again. But he'd just come back. He'd only just seen the baby. Surely it was too early for everything to begin to unravel.

But as the baby stopped smiling and began wailing, even Tomas seemed to sense a change in the mood. Gingerly Camilla touched his nappy, and she wrinkled her nose when she felt the damp. She buzzed for the nursemaid, spread a blanket out on the bed away from the two of them, and set the baby aside. Pierre drew back to the edge of the bed and lit a cigarette. As they silently waited and the baby howled, Camilla picked up a silver mirror and began to brush her hair with hard quick strokes.

When her head was turned away and he thought she couldn't see him, she angled her mirror and caught that tell-tale look crossing his face. As he gazed down at the shrieking baby, Pierre's brows were knit together and his eyes were full of doubt. She knew him so well that she could read his mind: *Is it mine?*

She stopped in midstroke with her brush at the nape of her neck. How dare he doubt that this was his son? How could he still suspect that she had ever been with any man but him? In that heady instant when she had seen him in the doorway, it had seemed that she had forgotten and forgiven all the ways in which he and their marriage had gone wrong. But just as quickly as this golden interlude had begun, it was suddenly over. All her old anger came flooding back, this time swelled by a new wave of fury. She might love this impossible man. But she hated him, too, for doubting her, for betraying her, for hurting her. She couldn't stop the tears from welling up in her eyes and spilling down her cheeks.

Still Pierre's eyes were locked on the baby. Was it his or was it not? It certainly did not look like a son of his should look, but he supposed all the same that Tomas was his. If only he had never started to doubt his wife! He was certain that he had been her first man. He had felt the tearing and seen the blood that first night on the back seat of his Thunderbird. But a woman as passionate and sexy as she was could have done the same with others later. She could have had her pick of all the men in Beirut. Even when she had been coming down the aisle to marry him, he had seen them looking her over. His mother had warned him that he could never trust a woman who looked and acted like Camilla. Blood, his mother had reminded him, always showed in the end. Nirvana was notorious all over Lebanon. Was he absolutely certain, his mother had purred, that he wanted to marry this cabaret singer's daughter? At the time he had thought so. He had been so besotted with Camilla that he had even risked his mother's wrath to make her his wife. It was only later, after he had found out about the baby coming too soon, that he had begun to have second thoughts.

The cigarette smoke curled around Pierre's head. He was so confused about all this. But of one thing he had been certain: his wife must at all costs not be the centre of a scandal. If anyone in Beirut knew that Camilla had given birth six months after being married in white, they would count back on their fingers and assume that theirs had been a shotgun wedding. They might even make jokes about the rival warlord knowing what was up when he sent in those gunmen. Always after that, there would be sly innuendoes about Camilla's virtue. There might even be insinuations that he hadn't been the first to plough that fertile field. He had been maddened at the thought of such speculation about his wife. He was a Nazrani. He could not allow himself – or what belonged to him – to be made into a laughing-stock. And so, to protect her, and his own, reputation, he had brought them both to Paris. But Camilla had never even tried to understand the sacrifices he was making so that people shouldn't think she was just like her mother. He hadn't spent these cold and rainy months in Paris for the fun of it. Beirut was the best fun in all the world. He missed his old chums, his family, the showgirls at the Casino du Liban. He hated the way these haughty Parisians made fun of his Lebanese accent. And sometimes, because it was her fault that they were here, he even hated Camilla. In a way it was almost better when he hit her with his fists instead of with those poisonous words that rolled unbidden off his tongue. Pierre bowed his throbbing head and held it in his shaking hands.

Camilla was meanwhile still secretly crying. Yet she knew he would yell at her if he caught her weeping again, and so surreptitiously she reached over and took a tissue from the box on her bedside table. As she wiped her eyes, she studied her husband's reflection in the mirror. Even now, when he was crumpled over in an attitude of despair, she was still physically drawn to him. He was the handsomest man she had ever seen. She loved the hardness of his body, the feel of the hair on his chest brushing against her bare breasts, how he felt when he was grinding inside her. But she didn't like much about her husband other than the look and feel of him. She loved him, but she didn't like him.

Silently she dabbed at her streaming eyes. Nothing in married life was as she had dreamed it would be.

But perhaps it was like this for every married couple. And maybe, now, with the baby, everything would be better. Her first thought when she had gazed at Tomas was that he was their love child. All was not right between the two of them now, and maybe it would never be right again. But once their love had been a kind of perfection. She would treasure their love child as the living proof of a better time and place. It wasn't much to live on, but it would have to be enough. She blew her nose very softly.

But not softly enough. Pierre looked up and rubbed his bloodshot eyes. 'What, again?' As he saw not only the tears but also the reproach return to her eyes, the anger that he had thought he would never again feel for this woman coursed through him once more. He did not have to ask her what she blamed him for this time. So he hadn't been here for the birth? So what? Lots of men weren't around when their wives dropped their babies. But somehow – the way women always do – she had managed to make him feel guilty. When she cried, she always turned everything upside down and made it all seem his fault. But she was the one who had gone and got pregnant too soon.

When, not more than a minute later, the nursemaid finally rushed through the bedroom door with a string of excuses for why she was late, Camilla was sobbing hard and Pierre was towering above her with his hand raised to strike. Over it all the baby cried.

Pierre turned, saw the nursemaid, and lamely put his hand in his pocket. Theirs might not be a marriage made in heaven, but there was no divorce in the Maronite church. Camilla was his wife now and for ever.

In weary silence, Camilla and Pierre watched the girl pick up the child.

Chapter 6

Anne stood in the medical textbook section of the Harvard Coop, dithering over whether to splurge and buy a brilliantly illustrated reference tome on the muscles and bones of the human body. On the one hand the book wasn't on the required list for her spring term anatomy class. Yet having it at Aunt Bert's would spare her time-wasting trips to the library. The deciding factor, however, was that the book cost more than she could afford. Although it was only April, she had already run through most of the spending money her father had said she would have to make last until September. Everything cost more here than they had estimated back in Beirut. Even though she wasn't extravagant, the money still didn't stretch as far as they had hoped. She could, of course, always write a cheque for the book. As always, Aunt Bert would be only too happy to cover a thirty-five dollar draft for this book, or for any other small or large indulgences she craved in the cosmetics department of Bonwit Teller's or the dress salons at Peck & Peck. Aunt Bert always urged her to buy, buy, buy; constantly she tempted her to spend, spend, spend. Yet eight months under her aunt's thumb had reinforced Anne's wariness about running up bills in Bert's name. It simply wasn't worth feeling like the poor relation just to possess a silk shantung Oli Cassini dress, a red leather Gucci handbag, or even this splendid medical textbook. Moreover, Aunt Bert always exacted a tit-for-tat bit of gossip for every bill she settled. She believed a silk Hermès entitled her to ask intimate questions about that young man Anne had gone out with last Saturday. A fox hat to match her fox coat bought the right to grill Anne about how her parents *really* got along back in Beirut. Always Bert probed and prodded for ways and means to increase her control not only of Anne but of everyone else in the family. And so instinctively, to keep her at bay, Anne had learned not to confide her heart's desires to her aunt. She even did her best to keep her social life away from such meddling. Except for Ramsey, who had charmed her aunt as he charmed everyone else here, she shied away from inviting her casual dates and acquaintances over to the Brattle Street house.

As Anne was reluctantly about to reshelve the tome on muscles and bones, she felt eyes upon her.

'Hi, gorgeous.'

She looked up, and there finally was the fellow who had sent her pulse racing in the pub last autumn, smiling down at her cockily just as he had six months ago. And, as before, his sheer physical presence hit her like a high wind whipping around a skyscraper. She would like to have stared at him so she could discover what it was about him – his eyes, his smile, his very size – that affected her as it did.

Instead she frowned as though she couldn't place him and then looked back at the row of books as if captivated by their long-winding titles. After she had first spotted Mike last autumn, she had been certain that sooner or later she would run into him again. She was surprised, however, that it had taken this long for their small Boston medical student world to narrow once again to just the two of them. Yet it would never do to fall all over this man who had so casually walked in and out of her life so many months ago. In the tantalizing glance that she had just allowed herself of him, she had decided he was even more attractive than she remembered. But he was just as brash as before, too. Her name wasn't 'gorgeous'. Coolly she ignored him as she went about her business of replacing the textbook on the shelf.

'That's a good book you had there. But don't waste

your money on it. I'll lend you mine.'

As if he had not spoken, she marched a good way down the aisle and then pretended to stare with great fascination at a row of volumes immediately ahead.

He followed her, leaned against the bookcase, and then grinned. 'So when did you change your mind and decide to be a vet?'

'I beg your pardon?' She looked up as though she had never seen him before.

He pointed to the 'Veterinary Medicine' sign at the top of the bookcase, laughed, and stuck out his hand. 'Mike Spagnolli. We met at the Hapenny last fall. You were with that little foreign guy, the one with the phony English accent. And your name is . . . let's see . . . it was something ordinary. Linda? No. Not Carol, either. Nancy?'

'Anne. Anne Rosen.' Once again he had put her off-balance. She had remembered his name, but he had forgotten hers. And she didn't like the way he had spoken disparagingly of Ramsey, who was a very special fellow from a very special family, as being 'little' and 'foreign' and having a 'phony' British accent – although she had to admit that all those words did describe Leila's brother. What's more, she didn't like her name not being remembered because it was 'something ordinary'. So what if her parents hadn't been inventive enough to call her Amanda or Claudia? His name, after all, was just as commonplace as hers. Yet even though his words and manner put her off, still his great, looming presence kept her rooted to the spot. Limply she shook his proffered hand, and then she put that hand which had touched his into her pocket.

'I'm hopeless on names. But I could never forget a face like yours, Annie. Can I call you that? Back in second grade, I was in love with a girl named Annie who sat at the desk in front of me. She was a pretty little thing, too. But by now she's probably fat and has eighteen kids, or else she's running a pizza joint in Revere. You want a pizza?'

'I prefer to be called Anne.' He talked so fast, in that slurred and slangy American way she still couldn't get used to, that it took her a moment to catch up and realize that he had just breezily asked her out. Apparently he moved as fast as he talked. If he was asking her to go out for a pizza, he *must* like her. And vaguely he had just implied that she was pretty. All in all, she might possibly forgive him for the venial sin of not remembering her name. She allowed herself a very slight smile – what Leila always used to call her 'ice cube' smile – as she looked up at him. She didn't expect to face that same slow and insinuating smile he had turned on her when they had met last autumn in the bar.

'I prefer Annie.' He stared down at her, and she stared back. Neither of them were smiling any longer. Both of them were worlds away, together and yet still very much apart. In that look, however, there was acknowledgement that something was beginning, and something else, too – a cautious measuring of the powers each had to inflict the ultimate pleasure or the maximum pain. For what that look most contained was raw sexual passion, a current that ran deeper than affection and lashed wilder than mere love. Without a word or a touch, what was to be between them grew from this one thunderbolt look. They stood like that, staring, for another sultry moment.

He was the first to try to recover. 'Jesus,' he finally muttered. 'What are you doing to me?' Boldly he reached out and flexed his hand in front of her face as though he wanted to grab and keep for himself whatever it was that had just passed between them. But finally he came out of the trance. 'C'mon, Annie.' He reached down, jauntily took her arm, and began steering her towards the escalator. 'I think I just lost my appetite, but I'll buy you a beer.'

He sat across from her at a formica table in a back corner of Cronin's, a bleak but popular student hangout just off Harvard Square. She sipped weak beer as though she had suddenly developed an unquenchable thirst for it and listened raptly as he told her all about himself. His father, as his surname implied, was Italian – 'a real wop', he said – an immigrant from Naples who worked hard all his life as a shoemaker in the North End. 'Pop died when I was in high school. Cancer.' His mother was East Boston Irish, and after she had buried her husband she went back to waiting tables to help support her nine young children. 'She was a wonderful woman.' Mike's fair Irish eyes darkened. 'But then, about five years ago, she had a stroke. Poor Mom! She never really recovered.' He drained his glass and signalled the waitress for another. 'She died last year.'

As she listened to him talking about how hard it had been for a boy from the wrong end of town to become a doctor, she revised her first impression of him. There were good reasons for his being such a rough diamond. While she had been water-skiing in Beirut Harbour, he had been growing up as a tough guy on the mean streets of the North End. She reminded herself she should be listening to what he was saying with a critical ear. Now was the time carefully to consider whether she wanted to be even superficially involved with someone like him. Aunt Bert, Camilla or Leila would say that she was slumming even to sit here listening to this shoemaker's son go on and on about himself. Yet she ignored the voice of caution in her head and instead followed her heart. Her eyes lingered on his broad athlete's shoulders when he told her he had gone to Penn State on a football scholarship.

'I was always a big, dumb jock,' he said.

'Surely not dumb,' she cut in to reassure him. 'Nobody dumb gets into Harvard Med.' The only reason she was enrolled at Boston University was that Harvard had turned her down. In a shivery way that she wasn't altogether proud of, the possibility that he might be her intellectual superior thrilled her. Whenever Camilla and Fatima used to maintain that a woman must always be able to look up to her man, she had always wryly replied that her problem was that she was usually not only smarter but taller than most of the fellows. And yet here she was, feeling glad that Mike was at least six foot three and had been accepted by a school that had rejected her. What was crazy, too, was that even though she had always looked down on athletes as having more brawn than brains, she now found herself enthusing like a cheerleader when he told her how he had played on a semi-pro team in Chicago for three years after college to help earn his medical school tuition. She liked him even better when he said that most of his savings had gone to help his younger brothers and sisters go to college. With family responsibilities, it had taken him five years instead of the usual three to get through school. Her tongue clucked in sympathy when he said he had been forced to take time off in the middle to work on construction labour gangs and even as a bouncer at a club in Kenmore Square. She smiled when he confided that it was only now, when he was just about to turn thirty, that success seemed finally within his grasp.

'Annie, when I got this internship at Mass General, for the first time I really believed I was going to make it as a doctor. A doctor! And not just any doctor. A doctor who graduated from the best medical school in the world! And who was going to do his residency at the best hospital in the world!'

She liked how his eyes glowed when he talked about his work. She liked how modest he was about how far he had come on his own steam. All in all, in every way that truly mattered, Mike was a much finer man than she had imagined he would be. His manners were a bit dicey, but she liked his values, his courage and his perseverance. And there was also the matter of how this exemplary man made her feel when his grey eyes pierced into hers.

Anne was just starting to tell him about herself when Mike looked down at his watch, whistled, and slapped money for the beers and a tip down on the table. 'Got to run, Annie. I'm on duty in twenty minutes.' He leaped to his feet and looked distracted. But just as he seemed about to dash for the door, he grinned down at her. 'Say, I almost forgot about that book you seemed to talk yourself out of in the Coop. I got it second-hand for ten bucks at one of the stalls up on Mass Ave. I'll bring it to you here, tomorrow, same time, same place. Same damn watered-down beer.' She was already nodding her head when he amended his proposal. 'Oh, no, Christ, not tomorrow. I have to work tomorrow, too. And Sunday and Monday all day. But Tuesday. Here Tuesday at . . . let's say . . . nine o'clock.' Before she even had a chance to agree, he sprinted towards the door.

She gazed at the remains of the foam that coated the lip of her glass and wondered why he had left her feeling as flat as the dregs of her beer. When they had exchanged that one heady look back in the bookstore, she had almost hoped that this fine young animal of a man was about to sweep her up and away to someplace marvellous. Instead, as if she were nothing more than an old football pal, he had brought her down to a grimy joint to drink diluted beer and listen to the story of his life.

She stared with a pang of longing at the rough wooden chair opposite her where, only a moment ago, Mike had been sitting. Until this afternoon, she had always hated Cronin's glaring fluorescent lights, its blaring jukebox, and the seedy students who congregated here for long afternoons that stretched into the small hours of the morning. Yet, as long as he had been here to share it with her, even this cheap keg beer had madc her feel higher than the best bottle of imported French champagne. But now that he was gone, so, too, were the illusions he had conjured up. This raucous bar was as shabby as it had always been, and this encounter which had seemed to promise so much had left her feeling cheated. She had been truly engrossed in everything he had been so eager to tell her about himself, but why hadn't he made the time to listen to her own history? She was annoyed, too, at how he had taken it for granted that she would want to see him again. And it hurt her pride how he had shunted their next date from one time to another before settling on one of the least glamorous nights of the week. She was worth Saturday night.

Anne gathered up her purse, her raincoat and her thoughts. Her instincts must have been way off this afternoon. There was no reason to be over the moon about this Mike. Perhaps she had been studying too hard these last months in preparation for her exams. But she must be far more tired than she had thought, to imagine so much from that one stray look.

She suppressed a renegade little sigh of regret. But maybe it was just as well that she and Mike would probably come to nothing. Even though he was attractive, bright and every bit as committed to his work as she was to hers, Mike's personal style was not quite up to cosmopolitan Beirut standards. Once she finished medical school, she planned to go back to Lebanon. But Mike was deeply rooted in Boston. She asked herself, therefore, why she was letting herself feel so disappointed that this casual drink with an unsuitable man in a student bar wasn't going to lead to the love affair of her life? She shouldn't have let him think she would meet him here again. On the strict schedule she had set for herself, Tuesday was one of her marathon study nights. If she called him at the hospital, perhaps she could beg off their date.

'Annie?' Suddenly he was towering above her, looking

down at her with that same insinuating smile on his lips. 'You won't let me down, will you, Annie?'

As she stared back up at him, again that current passed between them. She forgot all about her resolution not to see him again. She would be here Tuesday at nine o'clock, or anytime or anywhere else that he wanted. Yet she retained enough of her icy self-control to smile what she hoped was a pleasantly social smile. 'Yes, of course, I'll be here.'

He grinned and sped off again in the direction of the Harvard Square subway.

He kissed her for the first time that next Tuesday night, after they had been drinking for a few hours at the same back table at Cronin's. He kissed her only once under a streetlight on Mt Auburn Street, and it was a great bruising kiss that went on and on until she was dizzy. He let her go then, gave her a light little comradely slap on the buttocks, and turned her around in the direction of Brattle Street.

'See you here Sunday night at nine,' he called back as he loped off towards the subway.

She found it harder to concentrate on her studying the rest of that week as she waited for Sunday finally to come.

'Of course I'd like to see more of you.' His grey eyes were earnest and, she thought, full of love as, three weeks and a dozen kisses later, he looked her straight in the eye under the stark bright lights of the inevitable Cronin's. 'But you, of all people, Annie, should understand about my schedule. You're not some silly little secretary. You're going to be a doctor yourself. You know the score. I shouldn't have to keep reminding you what a grind this life is. Med school's hard enough, but it's nothing like being an intern. I'm on call at all times. Sometimes I have to work double shifts. It's tough. Tougher in some ways than being in training for a big game.' He laughed. 'Yeah, the Mass General Playoffs.'

'But you must get a whole day off sometime.' She hated to hear herself all but begging him to give her more time, more attention and more kisses than he had so far been able or willing to supply. Yet, now that she had finally plucked up her courage and begun this conversation which she had been rehearsing all week, she was determined to speak her mind. It was driving her crazy just to meet him at Cronin's and then kiss him under the Cambridge streetlights. 'It's not like this for all the interns. I've asked around at school. Other interns see their girls more than you see me.'

'I'm not just any other intern,' he snapped. 'I want to be the best.'

'Yes, yes.' Hastily she stroked his hands that would one day perform life-saving surgery. 'It's just that we never seem to be able to be alone.'

He gave her that smouldering look that killed her. 'It doesn't have to be this way.'

She bit her lip and stared down at her beer so that she could avoid having to say 'no' again. The third time they had met at Cronin's, he had pulled a key out of his pocket, plopped it down on the table, and suggested that they adjourn to a friend's apartment in the Fenway. 'Where we can really be alone,' he had whispered as he gave her that stare of his, for his friend was on duty all night long. Of course she had refused. A nice girl would never venture alone to an empty apartment with her boyfriend. But this time Anne wasn't only worried about her reputation. Always before when she had let her beaux kiss her, she had remained coolly in control of their hands and her heart. But when Mike's arms were around her and his lips touched hers, the last thing she wanted to tell him was to stop. She didn't trust herself to be alone with Mike at his friend's place. Nor, here and now, did she like how he was once again letting her know in no uncertain terms exactly what it was that he wanted from her.

She picked up the nearly empty beer glass in the palms of her hand and sloshed it round and round as though it were fine cognac that should be warmed to body temperature before being sipped, swallowed and enjoyed. Still, as she took a little dallying sip of the beer, she refused to look up at him. She resented the fact that he couldn't think of anywhere else to take her other than Cronin's and somebody's borrowed bedroom. Other men with not much more time and money than Mike managed to take their girls out to dinner, strolled the city with them on long walks, and attended concerts and films and dances. But with her and Mike, it was always the same. First they spent two hours of intense conversation at Cronin's, with much touching of hands and leaning together of heads. It was wonderful talk for the most part, for they seemed to share exactly the same feelings about becoming doctors. Nonetheless, it was too limiting always to be in the same place at the same table over the same weak beer. And, because of what always came after, their conversations had the teasing air of a prelude. Night after night, she was every bit as impatient as he to get out of Cronin's. Sometimes, oblivious of passers-by, he would sweep her up in his arms and frantically kiss her on the crowded sidewalk right in front of the bar. After a few moments they would stagger a little way down the street, soldered together with his arm around her shoulder and her arm around his waist, until he found a lamppost that caught his fancy. He would lean against it then and take her back in his arms and kiss her slower and deeper with his tongue inside her mouth. After what felt like a long while, he would say it was time for him to get back to the hospital. She would always begin to come to her senses then, as she hastily brushed her hair and peered into a hand-mirror under the streetlamp to repair her make-up. She, Anne Rosen, the ice queen of her sophisticated Beirut set, would feel like a bit of a tart as she walked the three blocks to the Brattle Street mansion alone.

She took another sip of beer and still avoided Mike's smouldering eyes. She watched his hands impatiently beating time on the table to the hard driving beat of the Elvis Presley hit blasting from the jukebox. She wished those hands were on her right now. Instead of circling for a fight, she wished the two of them were kissing with their eyes open wide and sparking with desire. Before Mike, she had chastely fluttered her eyes shut for every casual goodnight kiss. But she had learned to like staring back into his open eyes while his magic lips did whatever they wanted to hers. Just thinking about his kisses made her almost forget all her reservations about the way he treated her. As always, she was so conscious of the nearness of him that she could hardly concentrate on anything but the seductive inches that kept his skin from hers.

Anne drained the dregs of the beer and finally succeeded in recapturing her lost train of thought.

How he treated her was degrading. She was tired of making her way home alone every night after she had seen him. Yet at first she had been relieved that he had never even offered to see her to her door. She hadn't wanted to risk her aunt being rude to him, and she hadn't wanted to face the inevitable inquisition about his family and prospects. But now, even though she was sure her aunt would never approve of him, she wished that she had insisted on bringing him home and making him a part of her normal life. She would have liked to have him over for dinner and then sink down with him on one of the drawing room sofas and kiss him until long after midnight. But Mike stubbornly refused to set foot inside her aunt's house. Anne sorely regretted those funny-at-the-time stories she had told him about how domineering and pretentious Bert could be. Every time she invited him home with her now, he dug in his heels and said that the one thing he couldn't stand was snobs. She supposed that, Boston being Boston, a brash Italian like Mike must have been put back in what the Yankees would consider 'his place' far too many times over the years. Perhaps it was asking too much for Mike to be patronized by the likes of Aunt Bert. Every time she realized how vulnerable Mike truly was, her heart went out to him. As always, she had to forgive him anything and everything.

Out of the corner of her eye, she saw him, in that gesture she had grown to hate, looking down at his watch.

'Gotta go.'

She looked right at him, and felt something like a shiver run through her. Why was she resisting this devastating man? Unless she gave in, he might go away and find someone else who didn't cause him so much frustration. Any other girl might jump at the invitation to visit his Fenway love nest. Maybe she had been too demanding tonight. Perhaps he was angry with her. This could be the last time she would ever see him. 'I thought you weren't on duty again until midnight.'

'It's nearly eleven. C'mon.' Without waiting to see if she would follow, he turned and made for the door.

Her whole face brightened as though she had been given a life-saving reprieve. At least tonight she had not, after all, gone too far. He was still as eager as she was for their kisses. And tonight he had left the bar even earlier than usual, so they would have nearly an entire moaning hour alone under the streetlamp.

She was right behind him as he opened the door.

On the sidewalk, he stood staring down at her for an

excruciatingly steamy moment. When finally he pulled her to him, her lips were as devouring as his.

'I daresay the Mahler this afternoon was jolly good. But in many ways his Eighth Symphony which I heard in London last summer at the Proms was vastly superior.' Ramsey paused, sipped his tea, and continued in his elongated English vowels and his clipped English consonants. 'Mind you, some of it could be the setting. Your Symphony Hall here is fine in its way. Charming, really. But the Albert Hall has that *je ne sais quoi* . . .' Even his French had an Oxbridge accent.

As he held out his teacup, Anne absently raised her aunt's museum-quality Paul Revere silver teapot and topped the Spode 'Victorian Violets' bone china cup off with more Earl Grey. Vaguely she smiled at Ramsey, her aunt, and the two other old women gathered around the Brattle Street drawing room. Finally, having performed the socially acceptable minimum at her aunt's tea party, she went back to dreaming, worrying and fantasizing about Mike.

Bert shot her niece a very pointed look. What had gotten into the girl these days? Anne had lost weight and even had bluish circles under her eyes. Medical school must be too much for her. But when Anne did not pick up her cue to continue with the tea-pouring ritual, Bert herself solicitously added the precise amount of milk and sugar that she knew by now this Palestinian, along with devoted Anglophiles scattered the world over, affected to like. With her own pampered hands she buttered him another scone and piled it high with strawberry jam.

'You are very kind, Auntie Bert.' Ramsey all but rolled his eyes as he took a delicate bite. 'Marvellous scones! If we only had some clotted cream, I would swear we had somehow managed to nip over to Devon!'

Bert and the other two old dowagers who had been

friends for most of their lives smiled vaguely as they sipped their tea.

'Dear Devon,' Bert said. She wondered if she might be able to get some of that mysterious English cream – 'clotted', he had called it, like blood – on special order from Cardullo's. Or maybe she could get a recipe in an English cookbook and tell the cook to whip up a batch for them. It would be a real coup if she could serve it to Ramsey and the girls at her next get-together. Lilly and Emma, of course, always came for tea after the Boston Symphony's Friday afternoon concerts. But perhaps she could entice Ramsey here again if she could produce some of that English cream he seemed to think so delicious.

'Actually,' Ramsey continued, rolling out that one word into four splendidly British syllables, 'I am hoping to get down to Devon this summer, when I pop over to see Leila on the way home to Beirut for my hols.' He looked expectantly at Anne, for this was the first time he had mentioned his new plan to visit both Leila and Lebanon. By now she should be eagerly peppering him with envious questions about visiting the people and places they both loved. But Anne seemed not to have heard his great news. It had been just the same at the concert, when she had seemed lost in another world that had nothing to do with the heavenly music coming from the orchestra. Anne looked, he thought, paler than her usual robust self. Either she was coming down with flu, or Leila was right in her hunch that Anne was in love. Ramsey longed to hear all the juicy details but it was too early to make some excuse to get Anne away to himself. He bided his time and made conversation with the old girls. 'And I expect we'll take in a Prom or two in London.'

'I went to the Proms once.' Lilly patted her blue-rinsed curls with satisfaction. Usually it was Bert who had gone everywhere and done everything first.

'How very splendid, Mrs Beaumont.' Ramsey smiled in encouragement. 'What was on the programme?'

She wrinkled her brow and then shook her head. 'My mind's a blank. Something classical, I guess.' Her voice became more definite. 'But what I do remember is giving Harry a piece of my mind after it. It was just before he passed away, when we were in London on our last theatre trip. One of our guides – a nice young man, some kind of foreigner, like you, Ramsey – told us we wouldn't really know England until we knew the Proms. But we couldn't get real tickets – it had been sold out for ages, apparently – so we had to stand down on the floor the whole time. My feet were killing me, so we left at the intermission. If that's the real England, no wonder my ancestors came over on the *Mayflower*.'

'Now you're talking, Lilly!' Emma was sick and tired of all this British nonsense. She, too, had a season ticket to the Symphony, a box at the ballet, shopped the Filene's Basement sales, and wrote earnest letters to many different editors when something riled her. But unlike her other two friends sipping what they called a 'civilized spot of tea', she was drinking strong black American coffee. She was not of the opinion that anything in England was automatically better than what they had here in New England. In fact, she was inclined to believe that Boston was the centre of the earth, if not the universe. She had been born on Beacon Hill, and moving just across the river to Brattle Street when she got married had been enough travel in her lifetime. 'If those concerts are as popular as all that, you'd think they would have the sense to hold them somewhere bigger – say, outside by the river, like ours at the Hatch Shell.' She considered writing that advice in a letter to the editor of *The Times*. She had had letters published in the *New York Times* before, but never the London version.

'But, my dear, the Proms are an old British tradition.' Bert had been to London on three separate occasions, and so she felt entitled to smile as though she were the repository of all knowledge and appreciation of the best in Britain. 'The dear Proms! The dear Albert Hall!' She was not about to admit that she had never been to either the Proms or the Albert Hall, and that she had never actually wanted to, either. Just because she never missed a Friday concert at the Boston Symphony didn't mean that she liked classical music. She was tone deaf and hard of hearing, besides. 'Isn't that so, Ramsey?'

'Quite, Auntie Bert.' Ramsey hoped that was the right answer to whatever the old lady was asking, for he had been paying more attention to Anne's puzzling behaviour than to the birdlike twittering of the widows. Obviously, even though he faithfully rang Anne every few days, he was out of touch with whatever – or whoever – had wrought such a change in her. What with examinations approaching and all the splendid rites of Harvard in the spring, lately he hadn't been seeing her as often as he should. Last weekend's hectoring transatlantic telephone call from Leila had taken him by surprise and even hurt his feelings a little. Who, Leila had demanded, was this glorified football player Anne had been cryptically mentioning in her recent letters? He had been forced to admit that, even though she had written to Leila about this new man, she had never mentioned him in any of their own conversations. He had thought that Anne told him everything, yet it seemed she hadn't trusted him as her confidant. This had worried Ramsey in professional as well as personal terms. His father had always said it was important for a budding politician to worm his way into the heart and mind of everyone who mattered. Gossip, his father had said, sometimes weighed heavier than issues of high state. He had accordingly advised Ramsey to master the techniques of intimacy with his friends. So it was that this afternoon Ramsey had passed up a diverting sherry party for that concert and this tea. But so far he hadn't managed to have a single moment alone with the object of the exercise. He saw Anne angling her wrist so as to glance surreptitiously at her watch. She was obviously preparing to bolt upstairs at the first opportunity. If he couldn't succeed in arranging a *tête-à-tête* with her, this interminable afternoon with the old girls would have been a waste.

Anne set her teacup on the table with finality. 'Well, it's after five. Time, I'm afraid, for me to hit the books.' She stood up and sighed as though she regretted the lateness of the hour. Yet she longed at last to be able to make her way upstairs and abandon herself to an elaborate technicolour daydream starring Mike. With a massive effort of will, she was still able to concentrate on her studies. She never missed a class, and she spent long hours yawning over her lessons. But, as soon as she shut her textbooks, she thought of nothing but him. She had hardly heard a note at that concert or a word at this tea.

'Right you are, Anne.' Ramsey, too, got to his feet. 'I'm very much afraid that I shall have to be going as well. Duty calls! Our budding young physician here is not the only one with examinations coming up.'

'Must you, Ramsey?' Bert pouted. 'I thought we might have a hand of bridge.'

'Another time, Auntie Bertie.' He came very close to clicking his heels as he made hasty but effusive farewells to the triumvirate of widows. Before Anne could flee up the stairs, however, he firmly took hold of her arm. 'You *are* going to walk me to my car, aren't you, darling? Leila rang the other day with some smashing news I simply must tell you about.'

'Leila . . .' This time Anne, who used to beg him to repeat every word of his conversations with his sister, sounded as though she hardly remembered her old friend.

Outside on the street, Ramsey leaned against the door

of his Triumph sports car, folded his arms, and judged that – much as he hated to be so crudely direct – he had better get down to brass tacks before Anne disappeared back inside the house. 'Leila thinks you're in love.'

'Does she?' Anne smiled a cryptic smile and refused to meet his eyes.

'Are you?' he countered.

'Maybe.' She felt as shy about admitting the truth to Ramsey as she was to declare it to Mike. Of course she was in love, but it was too early to tell anyone – even *him* – how she felt. There was time for that, and for everything else, in the lifetime that surely the two of them were going to share.

'Tell me about him.'

Coyly but firmly, she shook her head. She wanted to keep Mike all to herself. And, a little, she didn't think Ramsey would approve.

'At least you can tell me his name.' Ramsey's curiosity was increasing by leaps and bounds. 'You told Leila he was a football player. What sort of chap is he? Do I know him?'

But Anne still wasn't talking. Instead she laughed as she kissed him a comradely few times on the cheeks. 'Don't worry, Ramsey, everything's wonderful. Just wonderful! As soon as there's something to tell, you'll be the first to know.' She waved goodbye before she escaped back inside the house, up the stairs, and into her room. She shut the door firmly behind her.

Mike, she thought. His name was Mike Spagnolli, and she loved him!

With an immense sigh of relief, she threw herself full-length down on the bed. Finally she could stop pretending an interest in Mahler and scones.

She stared at the ceiling. It was getting more difficult to say goodbye every time they parted. It was getting harder to think about anything but him. She had not been able to stop her lustful wonderings about exactly what it would be like if some day she threw caution aside and went off with him to that hideaway in the Fenway. All day and all night – on the bus over the river to school, as she walked to classes, as she made conversation with Aunt Bert, as she lay sleepless on this hard single bed – she imagined every carnal detail. How it would feel to kiss lying down on a bed like this instead of standing up against a lamppost . . . How it would feel to have his hands next to her skin instead of outside her blouse. Sometimes she would spin out her daydreams for libidinous hours. Her dreams at night were even more exciting. When she woke up in the small hours of the morning after one of these erotic dreams, she would try to reconstruct every detail of what he had done and how it had felt. Yet even though her nights and days were a sexual blur, somehow she had managed to restrain herself with Mike. She might feel like screaming if he did no more than kiss her under 'their' streetlight, but she had never given him a clue that she was beginning to doubt whether their stalemate could continue much longer. If they did not soon get married, she would either have to break it off with him or give him what he – and she – wanted without the blessing of marriage.

Anne threw cold water over her face in the bathroom. No matter how he made her feel in his arms, she could not and would not sleep with him until they were married. She would never change her mind about that.

She walked slowly back to her room and picked up the medical textbook he had loaned her weeks ago. Tenderly she ran her fingers over its cover. She did love him, and she was certain he felt the same way. Yet even though he was thirty years old and surely ripe for marriage, so far he had never mentioned that possibility to her. She might have to maintain her sexual siege for years. Steadfastly she had refused even to discuss the possibility of slipping off to the Fenway with him. Yet perhaps, she thought, he knew she was beginning to want it as much as he did. For as they sat and talked over the weak beer that she had now started to like, Mike would casually play with that shiny silver key to his friend's apartment. He would throw it up in the air and catch it, toss it teasingly back and forth from hand to hand, and then fondle it with his fingers. She would watch him toy with that key as if she were mesmerized. Just standing here in her bedroom, thinking about that key, Anne felt almost hypnotized with desire.

But not quite. She switched on the light, pulled out her chair, sat down, and cracked open her books.

Chapter 7

'As much as we want it now, as much as we would have liked to have it yesterday and even before that, we – and the Palestinian masses – are not yet ready for revolution.' Hussein paced back and forth and sucked in hard on the end of his hand-rolled cigarette as the political argument in his cramped London bedsitter wound on towards midnight. 'Read your Marx. Study your Lenin. A revolution takes education, organization, agitation. First we must reform ourselves. Then we educate the masses. And finally – when the historical moment is ripe – we will be ready to strike.' His black eyes evaded Leila's sceptical glare and focused instead on the bright young faces of the others he was intent on forging into a London University cell. 'If we follow our hearts, if we pick up our guns and start the armed struggle prematurely, our enemies will wipe us out before we are strong enough to win.' He wagged his nicotine-stained index finger to silence the impatient cries of the quartet of lean young Palestinians sitting across from him on the mattress which he had strewn on the floor for extra seating. 'Quiet, please, comrades! Listen! Do not make the mistake of underestimating the Zionists and the imperialists. And do not forget our other enemy, maybe our enemy number one – the corrupt and decadent Arab bourgeois leadership.' His gaze lingered pointedly on Leila. 'Unless we are smart, and unless we are patient, we will never win back *our* Palestine.' He touched his heart as his Arabic rhetoric soared to a climax. 'A Palestine that is worth not only dying for but living for. Palestine, our mother, our father, our womb!'

As the other Arabs predictably erupted into an excited babble, Hussein lit another cigarette from his stub and leaned against the cluttered table that served as his desk.

'Patience? Even *you*, the great Hussein Ibrahim – the one they say will someday be Palestine's Lenin – even *you* tell us we must be patient?' Jamal pounded one closed fist upon the other. 'Enough patience! We have been too patient already. We must fight, and fight now!'

'Bombs in Tel Aviv!' Muhammad jabbed his cigarette out on the scarred wooden floor. 'Night raids from Gaza!'

Ibrahim had caught the fever. 'Palestine will rise. In every camp, Palestine will rise.'

'Our deeds', Abbas added, 'will live for ever in the hearts and minds of the entire Arab nation.'

'What as? Martyrs?' Leila's eyes met Hussein's, and a rare current of understanding passed between them. In the long, volatile months that they had been keeping company, often they couldn't agree on anything more fundamental than their passion for Palestine and each other. Yet mostly these two obsessions consumed the rest of their differences. With an effort she tore her gaze away from the man she loved to those she loathed.

'Lads, lads . . .' Intentionally, she spoke not in Hussein's colloquial Arabic but in the posh and patronizing English accents of Oxbridge. She could not be bothered to hide her contempt for this riff-raff whom Hussein seemed to think were the future of Palestine. She knew it antagonized them to see her dressed as she was, in a snaky little black dress that – even though it wasn't couture, since she never wore her good clothes when she came to these meetings – still probably cost more than most of them lived on for months. But except for Hussein, whom she thought was a superior individual born by mistake into an inferior class, she liked to accentuate the gulf between herself and these wretched students who had somehow clawed their way up and out of the squalid refugee camps. Besides, she was sick of being cooped up for so long in this seedy bedsit with these shabby boys. She was only down from Cambridge for the weekend and had assumed, after making a quick appearance at a Holland Park cocktail party on her father's arm, that she and Hussein at the very least could take in a French art film before settling down to the political wrangles they both adored. But if Hussein insisted on throwing her together with her inferiors, he would have to suffer the consequences. She would not hold her tongue for Hussein, or any man. 'Stop wasting everyone's time for once, boasting like small boys about what you're going to do to the Zionists tomorrow and after tomorrow. We don't need hotheads. We need workers.'

'Comrade Leila speaks like a true sister toiling for the revolution.' Hussein's tone was laced with irony. Leila was still, of all of them in this room, the furthest from party membership. Since they had first met, Hussein had been fighting an exhilarating but losing battle to make a Communist out of her. She, all that time, had struggled just as relentlessly to turn him into a full-blooded capitalist. Yet he was addicted to this exciting woman from that other world he so despised. On any other night he would have been delighted to parry and thrust with Leila. But when she had arrived unannounced on his doorstep, these four ripe firebrands had already been ensconced on his mattress. Tonight, as always, Hussein was prepared to sacrifice the personal for the political; his revolution would always come before his woman. He couldn't allow Leila to insult his potential recruits and risk their not only flouncing out of his door but also wriggling for ever out of the web he had been skilfully weaving for them over the past weeks and months. He shot Leila an exasperated look that pleaded for her silence, and then he made his voice conciliatory as he turned his attention back to the men. 'You must know that I share your impatience. I, too, am tired of too much talk. I, too, would rather fight. And I promise you, the time for the gun is not so very far in the future. But first—'

'Hussein . . .' Leila leaned back in her wooden folding chair and very elegantly and very slowly crossed her long shapely legs that gleamed provocatively in the best French silk stockings money could buy. She had been sitting on this hard cheap chair for three hours, and she was in no mood to let even Hussein insult her family and class. That crack he had made about the Arab bourgeoisie rankled. She was proud, not ashamed, of her father's life and work. When she was sure that every eye was upon her, or at least upon her legs, she continued with what she was determined to say. 'Let's go back to what you said before about enemy number one being not the Zionists but what you called our "decadent" and "corrupt" Arab leaders. You must be mad if you think our own leaders are worse than the Zionists.'

If Hussein had been a less self-controlled man, he would have sighed. He and Leila had covered this ground over and over again. She always allowed family loyalty to take precedence over reason, and he very much doubted if he would be able to change her mind tonight. Out of the corner of his eye he saw the other students begin to fidget and whisper among themselves.

He might lose them if he allowed Leila to continue to dominate the stage. Unsophisticated boys like this were always far more susceptible to heart-thumping exhortations about blood and honour than to ideological hair-splitting about the failures of Arab leadership. Yet he could hardly gag Leila. He was not a Stalinist. He bowed to the inevitable and joined the argument. 'Of course the most obvious enemy are the Zionists who have taken our country and the imperialists who have aided and abetted them. But what good will it do us if we exchange one set of oppressors for another? What we must—'

'There you go again,' Leila cut in, 'with your name-calling. First you say our leaders are corrupt and decadent. Now you call them oppressors. I want facts, not slanders.'

'Do you?' He was no longer amused. If she wanted a real fight, he would take off the velvet gloves and give her one. 'Fact: all over the Arab world, the leaders are corrupt and decadent. Fact: a tiny percentage of the population controls almost all the land. Fact: the peasants work the landowners' fields like medieval serfs, barely managing to stay alive. Fact: health care is almost non-existent. Fact: education is reserved for the wealthy. Fact: the masses are intentionally kept as ignorant as they are poor. Fact: while all this is going on, the corrupt and decadent – yes, Leila Shahine, daughter of Kemal Shahine – the corrupt and decadent Arab upper class live like kings and queens, with their champagne and their sports cars and their Paris frocks.' He paused so that they could all look once again at Leila's dress. When he continued, his voice was softer, more persuasive and less accusing. 'Leila, *ya habibi*, our own so-called Palestinian leaders were asleep when the Zionists stole our country. They are still asleep. Yet now, not only in Palestine but all over the Arab world, the people are awakening. We are working for revolution not only in Palestine but in Lebanon, Jordan, Syria, Iraq, along the Gulf and in Egypt, where even our brother Abdul Nasser sometimes deviates from the straight path. And everywhere, all over the Arab world, it will be the people – the vanguard of the masses – who will triumph in the end. The people will lead us towards our goal, a free and democratic Palestine.'

'I see.' She cocked a well-plucked eyebrow and patted the strands of her hennaed hair which she had coaxed into a sleek French twist. 'And these masses – these people you have just told us are so poor and sick and illiterate – how are they going to lead you onward and upward to your great victories?'

He smiled. Even though she was a reactionary, her mind was as sharp as his own. Someday he was sure she would finally come over to the side of the angels, and then she would be his perfect mate. 'I told you before. First education and organization, then agitation, and finally revolution. As I said, we and the masses of the people are not yet ready for revolution.'

But Jamal, who had no manners and little natural charm, was tired of the attention his mentor was lavishing on this brash fascist girl. 'What I am ready for is coffee.' He looked insolently at Leila, and then – in an age-old masterful gesture of man to woman – he curtly inclined his head towards the electric kettle on the table. Finally he proceeded to add insult to injury by addressing himself not to her but to Hussein. 'Can you tell your woman to make the coffee?'

She leaned forward to lash out at this impertinence, but Hussein was quicker on the draw. He smoothly cut in with his own rebuke. 'She is not your slave, Jamal.' His eyes met Leila's, and in that look was a year's worth of respect and affection. 'Nor is she mine.' He glanced down at his watch and considered, but then reluctantly rejected, elaborating on the non-exploitative way a good socialist brother was supposed to treat a Palestinian sister. The revolution that he had in mind must root out all oppressions, including that of Arab men over Arab women. But that, and all other lectures, he decided, would have to wait for another night. Without Leila's distracting and disruptive presence, he would be freer to take up his unfinished business with these raw young soldiers of the revolution.

Hussein yawned as though tired, and then made a point of turning on the kettle himself and measuring out the instant coffee into the cracked cups. He hadn't planned to bring matters to a head between Leila and himself just yet. But tonight may as well be the night. It was a fine midsummer evening. There was a lucky crescent moon. And for once it wasn't raining. There would be more than enough opportunity, as he walked her the long way back to her father's Mayfair apartment, to say what had to be said. Surely all this would not take her by surprise. Leila must know the choice that lay before them. They had not been playing at love for the past year. Although Leila had her frivolous side, her essential character was as serious as his. He was confident of her answer. Their future as a couple was as inevitable as the triumph of the revolution.

But as Hussein poured the water into the cups, he fumbled and spilled some on a stack of important papers. Then he mixed up the coffees, forgetting who wanted milk and who liked extra sugar. Finally, as he burnt his tongue gulping the scorching coffee, he was forced to admit to himself that he was nervous about tonight's confrontation. Hussein dearly wished that love were as simple as politics. What a relief it would be merely to have to fight a war to win her. In his year-long courtship of Leila, however, Hussein had learned some hard lessons in finesse. She, perhaps even more than most skittish women, was maddeningly unpredictable. Even though she insisted on being treated with all the prerogatives of a man, when it suited her she also claimed the traditional privileges of a woman. He couldn't simply lay out a cut-and-dried proposition and then negotiate hard to get what he wanted. Tonight she would demand soft words, sighs, romance and nothing less than the pledge of his entire heart and soul. She would drive a hard bargain, but he believed that in the end she would be worth it. Someday, once she discarded those selfish bourgeois habits of hers, she would be the epitome of a strong and committed Palestinian revolutionary. Tonight he must be ruthless and do whatever he had to do to win her for ever.

So it was that an hour later, after he had suggested that they take a bus from his bedsitter near Victoria station down to the Embankment, Hussein held her hand as they strolled like the most conventional of lovers in the moonlight by the river. It was a soft late July night, and below them the wide sluggish Thames glittered in the reflected fairy lights from the bridges. Big Ben tolled the half hour, and behind them in the Houses of Parliament the midnight oil burned. As they walked from the shadows into the pools of dreamy light cast by the ornate Victorian streetlamps along the Embankment, they talked for once not of politics but of trivialities. Every time he said something witty, a coquettish little trill of laughter would escape her lips.

Why, she fleetingly wondered, as he knotted his fingers more tightly around hers, wasn't it like this more often between them? Why did they insist on making themselves so miserable fighting losing battles with sour words when this world of sweet contentment was surely always within their grasp?

For it seemed that Hussein, too, as he concentrated on nothing more momentous than insinuating himself precious inches closer to her, had left his political persona behind in the bedsitter. He had planned to manipulate her tonight by creating a seductive mood of romance, but by luck fate had bewitched the two of them with the real thing. He, who usually burned with overheated intensity, for once laughed along with her at everything and nothing. For the space of a few blissful moments he, too, forgot about Palestine and all the other hurts of the world and was as happy as any other man in love.

As they walked and talked and flirted in the moonlight, more intoxicating than the warm breeze, the rippling water and the sickle moon was their heady feeling of being young and invincible. That night by the river, with the rest of their lives stretching before them, it seemed impossible that their futures could be anything but golden.

It was this optimism that finally spurred him to ask the question on the tip of his tongue. He leaned against the balustrade, held her in the crook of his arms, and for a long shy moment looked lovingly into her dark eyes.

'Enough of these games, Leila. Enough of this talk. As you know, I love you. And as you say, you love me.' He decided he was being too brusque. He reminded himself that this wasn't a political manifesto. But what should he say next? When he had thought about how to make his proposal, he had assumed that at the crucial moment the right words would come to him as they always did. Yet he had never before asked a woman to marry him. He fell silent for a nervous moment. Finally he simply said her name. 'Leila, Leila . . .' Tenderly he touched his lips to the soft skin at the corner of her eyes.

For once she stood very still and waited, with the patience of the eternal woman, for him to say what any other man would have said long months ago. Clive had gone down on bended knee to her after only a few dates. Back in Beirut, the arrival of fresh proposals had been as predictable as the phases of the moon. Yet tonight, as she waited for Hussein finally to ask her to marry him, she trembled with anticipation.

'So! Leila! So what then must be done?' Old habits die hard, and he could feel a blast of rhetoric about to escape his lips. He reminded himself to try to make what he was about to say sound like a proposal instead of a non-negotiable demand. But then he shrugged and simply poured out what was in his mind and heart. 'I want you for ever, Leila. You, no woman but you! What perfection we will be! I want you beside me, always and everywhere. In the same bed, up on the same rostrum, part of the same struggle.' He forgot his resolve to be soft with her, and his fingers dug insistently into her shoulders. 'Commit, Leila! Commit, tonight, here and now, not only to me but to the revolution! Say it! Promise you'll commit!'

She sagged in his arms, and her eyes were black pools of disappointment. She had thought he was about to ask her to marry him, and instead he was mouthing the same old political platitudes. 'I've told you before I'm not joining the Communist Party.'

It was his turn to be bewildered. 'What are you talking about? I ask you to be my wife and you answer about the party?'

'Your wife?' Her heart leaped. She had thought that was a witless cliché, that a heart was stationary in a chest, but now she could feel hers all but dancing a conga inside her. Hussein wanted her, for ever, as his wife.

'Of course my wife. That's what I said, didn't I?' He tried to remember his exact words, but then he gave up and simply laughed in relief that she, too, was smiling.

It seemed to him that she was about to agree to marry him, and so he was emboldened enough to press ahead earnestly with the rest of what he had planned to say. 'For a long time I was dead set against this. Marriage is a bourgeois institution, and some Marxists live together instead.' Hopefully he watched her face for signs of encouragement that they might live together like the best of comrades instead of marrying like the bourgeoisie. Several times already he had sounded her out about free love. But now, as then, her face was forbidding. Leila's Western sophistication was sometimes only skin deep. When it came down to the old sexual taboos, she was a true daughter of Abraham.

Hussein beat a hasty retreat to his proposal of marriage. 'Of course some very good Communists do get married.' His eyes began to glow. 'Actually, I think I like the idea of marrying you.' He began to wax enthusiastic. 'Think of it, Leila! You and me! No one and nothing will be able to resist us! There is nothing we cannot do together!' As always when he was excited, he began to pace. He strode in and out of the pools of light on the Embankment. 'We will finish up our studies here in England and then go back to begin our life's work. We will start in the camps, in Gaza I think, yes, Gaza is the best. You can organize the women while I work with the men. Together we can help those suffering in the camps to liberate themselves. And then, when the historical moment is ripe, we will all liberate Palestine! Comrades, Leila! Ours will be a true marriage not only of bodies but of minds, hearts, souls!'

But as she stood alone in the shadows, she was no longer smiling. Why had Hussein ruined one of the happiest moments of her life? A second ago she would have sworn she was willing to follow this man anywhere, but that was before he had been specific about the grim path he intended to tread. Warily she narrowed her eyes as he ranted on about those wretched camps of his. 'Gaza?' She spat out the word. 'Why would *I* want to live in that bloody hole?'

He stopped in mid-stride, turned on his heel, and

stared at her frozen face. Belatedly he remembered his resolve to be ruthless tonight and win his woman with not thorns but roses. He felt like butting his head up against an iron lamp-post. How could he have forgotten that she was Leila Shahine, a pampered princess who had lived all her life in luxurious villas? She wasn't an impressionable and deeply committed young comrade from the camps. He should have carefully plotted out a winning strategy tonight and then stuck to it exactly. Later, when she was already in too deep to get out, it would have been easier to coax her into sharing a life ennobled by revolutionary sacrifice.

But then Hussein took a deep breath and plunged ahead on the uncompromising course he had already set. He would not trick this woman into wedding himself and his life of struggle. He had too much respect for her – and for himself – to sink to that level. She would have to love him with her eyes wide open. If she chose him and what he offered, she would have to do it of her own free will.

He walked back over to her, put one of his hands gently on each of her cheeks, and spoke so quietly that she had to incline her head even closer to hear him. 'I want us in the refugee camps because that is where the struggle is, where our people are, where we should be. We are gifted, you and I, and with our gifts of intelligence and courage and strength of character also come responsibilities. We must help our people where they need us most. We were born for that, you and I. And that, my love, is why we must go to Gaza.' With his right hand he smoothed back a single vulnerable red curl that had escaped her fierce French twist and fallen into her eyes. 'I want to marry you, Leila. You know I love you, and that I am not one of your rich silly fools who make a game of courtship. I am offering you a good, honest life. As my wife, my comrade, my lover and my friend.'

She stared back, very nearly mesmerized, into his eyes. Always, even when she didn't agree with what he was actually saying, the passion of his words stirred her being. Allah, she loved this man! Her heart was in her mouth and almost cried out that of course she would share everything he had to offer.

But then, as she remembered whom and what else she also loved, she swallowed hard and her heart sank achingly back into her breast. She turned away from her lover and stared down at the murky depths of the old river. As much as she sometimes wished it were so, she and Hussein were not alone in a world of passion and romance. She loved her family and her friends, and – even if it wasn't very noble of her – she also loved every expensive possession in her privileged world. Of all these loves – with the possible but by no means certain exception of her love for Hussein – the currents of her love for her father ran in the deepest and swiftest channels. She paled as she remembered that Sunday lunch last spring at the Savoy when she had finally introduced Hussein to her father. Even when they had first shaken hands like prizefighters, these two men whom she adored had already recognized one another as the enemy. That first encounter, despite Leila's frantic efforts, had been such a disaster that she had taken care never to bring the two of them together again. Baba was not going to welcome Hussein into the family with open arms.

Her eyes were troubled as she finally turned back to the man she loved. 'I will have to think this over.' She reached up and her voice caught as she traced the premature lines already etched on Hussein's drawn cheeks and around his burning eyes. He worked too hard, dreamed too greatly, compromised too little. Lesser men were hollowed out and then puffed up with fluff and nonsense. But she remembered thinking, that first time she met him, that Hussein was hewn from hard Jerusalem stone. In one of those moments of clarity when stark truth lay bare, suddenly she was sure that she would never find a better man than Hussein. 'Oh, sweetheart!' For the second time in these last moments, as she gazed up at him, she almost forgot all her doubts about their separate worlds. She wished she could marry him this instant, and that the two of them could right all the wrongs of the world at the snap of their fingers. She even wished that there were no Palestinian holy grail to live and die for, and that they were simply a man and woman who wanted to marry and raise a family and live a quietly commonplace life. But then she forced herself back to reality. 'I will give you my answer as soon as I can.'

'By all means. Take your time.' Hussein was disappointed, but not altogether surprised, that she hadn't immediately promised to be his wife. Victories that were worth anything were always dearly won. 'If you like, we will go hand in hand to your father. Remember, *habibi*, that we are in this together. If you want me, and if you are willing to commit not only to me but to everything I stand for, then you have me for ever.' They kissed and then rocked in each other's arms for a silent moment.

When finally they broke apart, Hussein put his arm snugly around her as they turned round and began walking back along the Embankment towards Westminster and Mayfair. 'But don't take *too* long making up your mind, eh? Maybe I will get cold feet.' He laughed, even though he wasn't joking. 'You know, I didn't decide on this overnight. Frankly, I was not sure you had the stuff of a revolutionary.'

As he had hoped, her combative spirit revived. Leila detached herself from his grip and stood blocking his path with her hands on her hips. 'What makes you think I wouldn't be good at whatever I set myself to, even your revolution?'

'Ah, *habibi!*' He took her back in his arms and

kissed her exuberantly on the lips. 'Now I am sure. Now I am very sure indeed.'

When he held her like this, when he kissed her like this, she was sure, too.

But Leila was not so sure of herself, or anything else, a week later as she knocked hesitantly at the door of her father's study in the Mayfair apartment. All week she had agonized over what to do, and finally on impulse she had dashed down from Cambridge with a desperate compromise she wanted to try out first on the one she trusted most. If her father agreed, she would use all her wiles to get Hussein to fall in with her plan. 'Baba?' She opened the door and peeked inside, where her father sat on the sofa with a thick book on his lap.

'Yes?' Kemal Shahine frowned at the interruption until he saw who it was. 'Ah, yes, Leila! What a lovely surprise.' Yet he looked down at the open book for another fleeting instant before he carefully marked his place and came to greet her with his face wreathed in welcome. She bent respectfully to kiss his hand, but instead he kissed her warmly on the forehead and then, sensing that something was amiss, he studied her anxious face. He had spent the last months at his son's villa in the South of France and so – except for paying her extravagant department store bills – he had not been keeping close tabs on his daughter. 'First,' he said briskly as he rang for one of the servants, 'I think we'll have a nice cup of tea. And then I want to hear all about what's making my girl look so worried.'

Leila nodded and ran her fingers despairingly through her tousled hair as she threw herself down on the sofa. She was dressed as she knew her father liked to see her, in a conservative navy Chanel suit. She lit a cigarette and, as she drew an ashtray towards her on the coffee table, her eyes fell on the book her father had set aside.

'The Koran, Baba?' Her eyebrows arched. 'But you're not religious. Since when did you start reading the Koran?'

'I've never stopped. Your grandfather and I used to sit down together with it every Friday afternoon when I was a little boy. Long before I ever went to school, that's how I learned to read, with his finger tracing every curve of every letter.' As he joined her on the sofa, Kemal fondly gazed at the old Koran that had been in the family for generations. 'It comforts me. Reading the Koran by my father's side used to be the high point of my week. It still is now.' He gave her a grave look of fatherly concern. 'You might try it yourself, child. You're looking troubled.'

'Yes.' Just this once she, who despised all pious talk, would have been grateful to stave off her moment of truth with a long-winded discourse on the disparate commentaries of the Koran. But she prided herself on being her father's daughter, and taking a grip on herself she plunged ahead. 'It's about Hussein. You know, the one you met at the Savoy? Hussein Ibrahim? From Gaza? I met him last autumn at—'

'I remember him.' Kemal glowered at the memory of that tense Sunday lunch. 'And I know everything about him, and his kind.'

She had hoped that at least they would begin this discussion on a more positive note. Bravely she continued, although with a fainter heart. 'We love each other.' She looked her father dead in the eye, and her voice grew stronger. 'We really do.' She let out a long intake of breath. 'He's asked me to marry him.'

'Has he?' Kemal avoided his daughter's pleading eyes and fussed with his pipe as he paused to consider this painful development. He twisted a cleaner through the stem, tapped out the bowl, and examined every sleek ebony centimetre for shreds of tobacco and ash. He had not expected this. He had trusted Leila absolutely. And so he had thought it couldn't hurt to let the girl enjoy at least the illusion of freedom, flitting here and there in England as if she were truly as free as the Western young women of her generation. She was his favourite, and he supposed he had always spoiled her. But this man she had set her heart upon wasn't a box of chocolates or a new dress. After Kemal had made it very clear at the Savoy that he did not approve of a Communist courting his daughter, he had assumed she had finished with him. Until now, Leila had never gone against his wishes. He could not allow her to do so now on something that mattered as much as this. His daughter's marriage was another bargaining chip that could and would further the family's interests. Once she had picked up her impressive degree from Cambridge, he had always expected that – like the rest of his children – she would marry the mate of his choice. He had already come to a tacit agreement with his old friend Mustafa el-Kuttab, who was one of Lebanon's richest landowners and leading Sunni Muslim politicians. Within five years – ten years at the most – Leila's intended would almost certainly be Prime Minister. It was out of the question that she could be allowed to throw herself away on Hussein Ibrahim.

Kemal refilled the bowl with tobacco, packed it down, lit it, and sucked in to get the smoke coursing up the stem. He reproached himself for not nipping this affair in the bud, before Leila lost her head and heart. He didn't doubt that she loved this fellow. He had made discreet inquiries about Hussein Ibrahim, and everything he had heard reinforced Kemal's first impression. Leila's young man undoubtedly had a brilliant mind and could be one of the next generation's most charismatic leaders. If Hussein weren't such a committed Communist, perhaps he might even overlook his humble origins and consider him as a son-in-law. But Hussein was Red to the core. He was a revolutionary and a fanatic, and

Kemal could never take such a viper to the bosom of his family. Again he cursed himself for letting this matter go so far. Obviously he shouldn't have allowed Leila to stay here in England while he went off to France with the rest of the family. He had always tried so hard to protect his daughter from the slightest of life's hurts, and now here she was facing one of the worst. Yet Kemal was convinced that, compared to courting certain disaster with Hussein, her distress in owning up to reality here and now was a necessary evil. But he wished it wasn't so. He had never wanted to hurt the one he had always thought of as his treasure. How, then, could he gently let her know what had to be?

He puffed on his pipe, exhaled in a sigh, and then simply looked over at Leila and sadly shook his head.

'No, wait, Baba! You don't understand! Let me explain.' Eagerly Leila set out to persuade her father of what, after a vacillating week of second thoughts, she had finally convinced herself was right. 'I don't want to marry Hussein the way he is now. You think I want to go off with him to Gaza and live out my life in a succession of foul refugee camps, without running water and electricity and with fleas and cockroaches and rats?' She wrinkled her nose as though even here she could smell the stench of Gaza. But then, as she realized how outraged Hussein would be to hear her dismiss his precious camps that way, she hastily backtracked. 'It's not that I don't sympathize with those poor people who have to live in those wretched camps. I feel sorry for them, I really do. And I'll be the first one to cheer once we get our country back and they can return to their homes. It's just that I don't see why *I* have to share their misery as a mark of my good faith.'

'Jolly good.' Kemal nodded his approval as he puffed on his pipe. 'I'm glad to see you haven't lost *all* your common sense.'

She ignored the insinuation and continued with

what she had decided to say. 'But I love Hussein, Baba, really I do.' Her voice throbbed not only with conviction but resolve. 'And I want to marry him.' She was accustomed to getting what she wanted, and she wanted this man with every fibre of her body. She wanted him badly enough to cut a deal with him and her father to get him. 'Look,' she wheedled, 'forget his background and his politics and look at his potential. He has the best mind of anyone I know. He can go anywhere, do anything.' Her eyes shone as she proposed that she be able to have her cake and eat it, too. 'I don't want to share Hussein's life, but why can't he share mine? If you'd welcome him into the family, I know he'd fit in before very long. We know everyone who matters. You could get him a good job. You could take him to Savile Row to your tailor and get him some decent clothes. He'd have to watch his manners a little, I suppose, but I would help him with that. It would work, Baba, I just know it would work! And I'd be so happy! So very happy!' She repeated what to her was the essential fact. 'I *want* him.'

'Just because you want him doesn't mean you're going to get him.' Again Kemal shook his head. 'It will never work. A man like that . . .' He puffed and frowned. 'He's just not our sort.'

'Not our sort?' Leila's black eyes snapped at her father. 'What's that supposed to mean?' But she knew. She had always known that Hussein Ibrahim was not their sort.

'A man like Hussein', her father said gently, with some kindness and much truth, 'could never be happy among people like us. As I think you know very well, a revolutionary like Hussein is as much the family's enemy as the Zionists'. If he and his kind ever come to power in our country, then God help all of us. We're the first people they would put up against the wall and shoot. Make no mistake, your precious Hussein would sign my death warrant. Yours, too, if it came to that. He's a fanatic.' Again, very sadly, Kemal shook his head. 'Leila, Leila, surely you can see that this match will never work. Maybe these differences wouldn't matter so much if politics weren't so important to all of us. But we are what we are. I could never accept Hussein. And if you're honest, I'm sure you'd admit that he feels the same way about me as I feel about him.'

She looked away from her father and lit another cigarette and sagged against the arm of the sofa. Only last week Hussein had said virtually the same thing. 'But I want him, Baba.' Her girlish voice was petulant. 'He's the one I want.'

'I know, *habibi*. I know.' There was not only sympathy but finality in his voice. He sensed that he had almost won this battle for his daughter's heart, mind and future. 'And I'm sorry.'

As the maid brought in tea and scones, Leila suddenly began shivering. 'It's cold in here. It's meant to be July, but still it's so cold.'

Leila poured the tea as the maid laid out the logs in the fireplace. After she'd lit the fire and left them alone again, Kemal closed in for the kill.

'Suppose, Leila, just for the sake of argument, that it were possible to do as you suggest. Suppose I agreed to accept Hussein, and we were able to transform him into one of us. Suppose, too, that Hussein went along with this unlikely scheme. What then? Has it occurred to you that the Hussein Ibrahim you would have then – well-dressed, suave, working perhaps in Middle East Airlines management – would be very different from the man you fell in love with this year? It's possible, you know, that in the process you might have killed off the essence of your man. Could you love the man you'd be left with? Would you want to? No, I'm afraid, my child, that you cannot have it both ways. If you want your revolutionary, you'll have to take all the suffering and the deprivations that go along with him.' Kemal let her think that over a moment before he went on. 'I know *I* could never choose a life like that. But perhaps that's what you want after all. You're young. Maybe all that dirt and squalor wouldn't bother you so much.'

She sipped her tea, stared at the fire, and wondered if – even for Hussein – she would ever be able to endure Gaza or any of the refugee camps that encircled Beirut in what everyone aptly called the 'belt of misery'.

Kemal gave her a little while longer to ponder the variegated miseries of refugee camp life, and then insidiously he spread forth the other alternative. 'But it doesn't have to be like that, darling. If you are wise enough to be guided by your loving father, by this time next year you could be married to the next Prime Minister of Lebanon.' He paused for dramatic effect. 'Mustafa el-Kuttab has told me he would like to marry you.'

'Mustafa el-Kuttab?' Leila almost stuttered as she repeated the name. This was the first she had heard of such a match.

'He'll be Prime Minister before long,' Kemal repeated, as though she hadn't taken in that essential fact the first time he had said it. 'And you know, of course, that you would never want for a thing, married to Mustafa, what with those thousands of hectares of prime farmland in the Bekaa and those factories along the coast and that real estate in Beirut itself. Everyone knows how generous Mustafa is. I'm sure he will build you a marvellous villa on the highest hill overlooking the city. You could have a salon that's the talk of Beirut. And of course, when he's Prime Minister, you would be one of the most powerful Palestinians in Lebanon. I don't have to tell you how important all this could be to the family. For the present, until we can return to Palestine, Beirut is our home away from home.' Kemal rubbed his hands together. 'It would be a brilliant match. Absolutely brilliant.'

Leila frowned. Of course she knew Mustafa el-Kuttab as well as she knew her old uncles. His wife had died just last year, and everyone always agreed that it was a tragedy she had given him no children. But in his description of the man just now, her father had left out one crucial fact. 'He's old, Baba – fifty at least.'

Her father smiled beatifically. 'For that much power, what're a few extra years?'

She almost smiled back. But then she remembered Hussein, and she looked away in alarm from her father's devilish temptations. Power, the gypsy had foretold power for her.

But as Leila stared into the fire, the realization of how her father was trying to manipulate her filled her with silent rage. Baba didn't care about her, or her happiness. All she was to him was another body to be bartered on the Middle East marriage markets. But this time her father had made a serious miscalculation. She wasn't some silly little girl to be bought off with promises of houses and parties. Hussein was the best man she would ever find, and she was going to marry him. Despite the predictions of that swarthy gypsy back in Beirut, she was going to grasp at her chance for real love.

Fiercely she stubbed out her cigarette in the ashtray, and then turned to her father to inform him that this time his machinations had not produced the desired effect. But instead, as she stared mutely at her father, tears filled her eyes. Still she loved her Baba. Even now she could not bear to open a breach between them. Without saying another word she simply turned her back on her father and ran out of the door of his study.

She felt better when, out on the street, she breathed in the fresh cool London air. Her father's study had reeked like a Middle Eastern bazaar at closing time, although –

she told herself furiously – what was putrid in his Mayfair apartment was not over-ripe mangoes but bad faith and rotten compromises. But she promised herself, as she revved up the engine of her Porsche and sped off towards Hussein's bedsitter, that she was done with her father's sorry compromises. Hussein had been so right. Her father's generation of tired and corrupt gentry did not represent the vanguard of the future. She could see it all so clearly now. Yes, finally she understood everything. In a few minutes she would throw herself in her lover's arms and commit not only to him but to his revolution. They would get married without delay, maybe even this week here in a London registry office. Her father had misjudged not only her but her future.

Later, when she looked back on this day, she was to decide that her life might have taken an entirely different course if Hussein had been at home that afternoon. But although she rang his doorbell again and again and even sat for a while like an urchin on his doorstep, Hussein was not there to sweep her into his arms and off into a different world.

She waited until it was dark and she could wait no longer. And then, in a deflated but perhaps more thoughtful mood, she drove alone all the way back up to Cambridge.

Two days passed before she finally received Hussein's hastily scrawled note telling her that he had been summoned to Rome for two weeks of political meetings. A fortnight, she thought with despair, up here alone with my thoughts. That night she drank most of a bottle of sherry to blot them out.

But of course they were lying in wait for her the next dull and rainy English morning. She stared at her bedroom ceiling and admitted that her father had been right about her, and Hussein, and Mustafa, and everything.

She cried into her pillow for a while on that dark

morning. She wept because even though she loved Hussein, she knew that she was going to lose him. She cried too, for herself, because she knew she would never be the same now that she had chosen coldness over heat, reason over passion, comfort over sacrifice. For the first time in her life, she was aware of her own limits. She wept because she wasn't as brave as she needed to be.

But then she wiped her eyes and washed her face and applied a soothing medicated mask to take away the redness and swelling. No one must ever guess that Leila Shahine had been crying her eyes out all morning.

After that she carefully applied her make-up and studied her face in a magnifying mirror to make sure that all her flaws and defects were not visible to the naked eye. Before going out shopping, then, she sat down and wrote two dry little notes – one to Hussein, and another to her father – telling them of her decision. But on second thoughts, she slipped the letter to her father back in her desk drawer. She would let Baba squirm awhile. Maybe she would even hold out until he upped the stakes. Instead of a few new Parisian frocks, she would ask for a portfolio of blue-chip stocks.

Then she slid the letter to Hussein into a post box and went out shopping. For herself she bought two new dresses, snakeskin high heels and four cashmere pullovers in the season's freshest colours. For her nieces and nephews she bought an assortment of heathery Fair Isle British jumpers. For her sisters in Egypt and Saudi, she bought some miracle-working new face creams. For Ramsey she bought a silver flask which she left for engraving at the jeweller's. She might have bought more if she had been loose in the metropolis of London rather than merely the town of Cambridge.

All that shopping passed the time. She was tired when finally she came home and cooked dinner. She took a hot bath, put on her beige satin pyjamas, and went early to bed.

She did not dream of anything that she remembered.

Chapter 8

Anne sat waiting for him in a bar again. He was late; always he was late. Every time she sat like this waiting for him, she promised herself this was absolutely the last time she would go through with it again. As soon as he rushed in the door with those same old excuses about too much work and too little time, she would tell him in no uncertain terms that her time was just as valuable as his. She would not allow him to continue to treat her like this. The next time he told her he would meet her at seven o'clock, she would give him at most ten minutes' grace, and then she would leave. She checked her watch. Never again would she sit fuming like this for forty-three minutes, and still counting. This time he would be *more* than forty-three minutes late. She would, she decided, give him exactly seventeen more minutes, and then she would leave.

She looked around in disgust at the hole-in-the-corner workingman's bar on Cambridge Street, across the river in Boston, a stone's throw from Massachusetts General Hospital. She used to think Cronin's was scraping the bottom of the barrel, but that was before Mike had introduced her to Paddy's. Sad ageing men sat propped up on stools the length of the dusty bar watching a wrestling match on television, and at the table next to hers a hard-faced blonde haggled with a mean-looking man over money. In the back a morose old codger drank rye and ginger as he pumped nickels into the jukebox that – in glaring competition with the wrestling on the television – played 'Old Cape Cod' over and over again. Oblivious to all the racket, a couple necked in the corner. That's the next step, Anne thought. She and Mike had not yet quite resorted to pawing each other at Paddy's. She considered the possibility that the forlorn atmosphere of this place might not get to her if she were sitting here laughing with Leila and Camilla. The three of them might even think it was a lark to while away an afternoon in a world as different as this. But she was not slumming at Paddy's; what really bothered her was that, in a way, she belonged here. She had come here so often in the past three months that she was almost as much of a regular as the fellow who played Patty Paige on the jukebox.

'Hey sweetheart, ya want another?' The bartender peered over her way.

Anne shook her head and shrank further down in her chair. She kept her eyes fixed on the glass of draught beer that she had hardly touched. She had learned weeks ago that it wasn't wise to catch the eye of any of the drunks up on the stools, for then they might come over and bother her and there could be a scene. The only reason she had ever agreed to set foot inside this depressing place was that it was so handy for Mike. Just as soon as he went off shift, he could run across the street to meet her here. He was able to be with her at least fifteen or twenty minutes sooner if she met him here instead of three stops down the subway line at Cronin's in Harvard Square. Mostly she thought it was worth braving the hazards of Paddy's just to increase their precious time together. These days they were seeing each other more often, sometimes three or four times a week, even though on occasions it was only for a single hurried hour. Sometimes now, in late August, there was only time to snatch a fleeting kiss out on the sidewalk before he ran back to his shift on the wards.

Anne took a sip of her beer. Despite everything – despite never having enough time and money to have a normal relationship, despite never getting around to meeting each other's friends and family, despite having to kiss and run at street corners, despite how *late* he nearly always was – she had never been as emotionally alive as she had been since she had fallen in love with Mike. When she was with him, when he talked with her or kissed her or simply sat across a barroom table from her, she left her workaday life behind and went up and away with him to a supercharged world where everything – cold beer on her tongue, his gliding fingers on her thigh, even that inane wailing song on the jukebox – vibrated with more intensity than she had ever imagined possible. It was only when he wasn't with her, when she was waiting for him like this or when not being with him made her so nervous that she felt like bursting into tears, that she wondered if anyone or anything could possibly be worth all the pain he caused her. How could it be, she often wondered, that everything – both good and bad – which revolved around Mike always fell into the extremes of best or worst? She had never laughed or cried harder than when she was with or without this man. Yet, all in all, the bliss he gave her was worth every second of the suffering he caused her, and more. In what she regarded now as the long grey years of her life before she had met him, she had always kept her emotions on a tight leash. She was off the leash now, running free, running wild. Or almost.

Anne reached in her handbag and took out one of the white monogrammed linen and lace handkerchiefs Aunt Bert had bought her. It was so hot in this airless bar that she could feel her hair sticking damply to the back of her neck. She mopped the sweat from her forehead, temples and neck. The dog days of summer in Boston affected her more than she ever remembered the hottest weeks of August bothering her back in Beirut. Back home the humidity was far greater and the temperature climbed much higher than here, but in Lebanon there had always been time for dips in the swimming pools and afternoons lolling down on the beaches. And, when a heatwave had settled on Beirut, they always escaped to somebody's hideaway villa up in the mountains. But here in Boston, summer was all concrete, and congestion, and workloads that were every bit as heavy as they had been during the January snowstorms.

Anne got out her pocket mirror, repaired her lipstick, powdered her nose, and used her comb to fluff her hair out over the collar of her white linen dress. When finally she couldn't think of any other fussy ways of passing the time, she went back to staring down at her beer and worrying about the choice she was going to have to make very soon about the two of them.

For she had not been altogether honest with herself a moment ago when she compared summers in Beirut with summers here. Mike could make a winter in the Arctic seem steamy. She almost broke into a sweat even thinking about him touching her as he did.

Yet still she steadfastly refused to sleep with him. Her lifetime's habit of tight self-control died hard. Even now, on those honeysuckle summer nights when she wanted him more and more, she had so far been able to succeed in making a last disciplined stand against this new wildness in herself. She still managed to hold the line, insisting that she would not do any more with him now than when he had first begun kissing her four months ago under the nightlights of Mt Auburn Street. Yet of course it was getting harder and harder to stop where they had first begun.

Once, in the first hot flush of a June summer's night, he had steered her from Cronin's down to the banks of the Charles, and he had taken off his blue pinstriped seersucker jacket and gallantly spread it out for her on the ground a few feet from the rippling water. That night she had been as eager as he, at first, to lie with their arms intertwined atop the long soft grass. She had been very tempted to let herself go, right there on the banks of the river. But then his kisses had turned too urgent, his hands too probing, his thighs too insistent. She hadn't wanted it to be like this the first time for the two of them – so cheap like this – with other couples grappling not more than ten feet away. And so she had wriggled away, jumped up, and refused to see him for five whole days, until he promised he would never again try to make her do what she didn't want to do, at least not down by the river.

He had restrained himself for weeks after that, until the night when he had led her away from the light of a streetlamp into a deserted alley. He had put his arms around her and leaned her against a brick wall and kissed her so ferociously that she hardly had breath to cry out 'No!' when he swiftly reached up under her dress and pulled her knickers down around her knees. There was one fierce second, as he was fumbling with his trousers, and as she felt the hot night air on her bare stomach and thighs, when she wanted nothing more out of life than for him finally to plunge inside her and finish what they had started too many weeks ago. But she came to her senses and lunged away from him just in time. If her reflexes hadn't been even faster than his that night, he would have taken her then and there.

Afterwards, it was only after he had promised that he would never try to pull anything like that again that she had agreed to go on seeing him. Mike had been very contrite about what had almost happened in that alleyway. He had said he didn't know what had gotten into him, except that he had wanted her more than he had ever wanted any other woman. At the time, looking up into his soulful eyes, listening to his earnest explanations, she had even been a little flattered at the passion she had roused in him. It was only later that night, after she was home alone in bed, that she realized that he still hadn't said he loved her. He had said only that he had never wanted any woman more than her. Yet she was as sure that he loved her as she was that she loved him. Still, she wished he would tell her so. She had considered, then rejected, making her declaration first. All this frustrated waiting might make her grind her teeth in bed at night, but she was going to hold out until she got what she wanted. He would be the first to tell her that he loved her, and then he would ask her to marry him, and then maybe – just maybe – she would sleep with him after they were properly engaged.

And yet all her good resolutions could not make her forget that night up against the brick wall in Cambridge. Sometimes in the early hours of the morning when she couldn't sleep, she could almost feel that hot air on her naked thighs; and more often than not, she wished she had surrendered to the impulse of that torrid moment. Just thinking about it, sitting here waiting for him at Paddy's, she could feel her secret juices softly flowing.

Anne crossed her legs. Enough of *that*, she thought.

She looked at her watch. He was an hour and five minutes late. She recrossed her legs and decided to give him just a little while longer.

Anne drummed her fingers on the table in that impatient gesture she had picked up from Mike. Idly she entertained the thought that perhaps she had made a mistake when she decided to accelerate her time in medical school by enrolling in the summer sessions. With things as they were between Mike and herself, a three-month cooling off period over the summer recess might have been the best thing for both of them. He might appreciate her more if she went away for a while. By the time she returned, he might go right down on bended knee and beg her to marry him. She indulged herself, for a long and satisfying moment, by imagining exactly the words he would use to convince her to be his wife. She savoured the thought that she would not agree at once. She would let him wait for her answer, just as he always seemed to make her wait for everything. In

June, while he was stewing here in Boston, she could have winged off to London with Ramsey to see Leila. Perhaps they could have even talked her into setting aside her thesis for a while and flying on to Beirut for a real homecoming.

Anne, for one dreamy moment, left the down-at-heel realities of Paddy's far behind as she imagined how she would have heaved a great happy sigh of relief to be back home in Beirut, enfolded in the bosom of that splendid golden city by that balmy blue sea. She would have regained the twelve pounds she had lost this year in Boston by eating *tabouli* and *kibbe* and *baklawa*. She would have lost her medical school pallor by soaking up that healing Mediterranean sun down at Saint Simon Beach. There would have been picnics in the mountains, barbecues by poolsides, receptions at embassies, dances at private clubs. She would have made her way up north to spend at least a week at Camilla's château in the mountains, cooing over her baby and trying to help her old friend sort out whatever had gone so wrong in her marriage with Pierre. Then she would have turned south for a fortnight or more luxuriating in the peace of Fatima's village, sharing confidences about her own romance with Mike and Fatima's odd long-distance marriage to Ali. It would have been so very wonderful to while away the summer back in Lebanon.

Suddenly, sharply, Anne was so homesick that she felt like bursting into tears. Often lately, since she and Mike had begun to wear on each other's frayed nerves, she had felt like bolting home to hide. Sometimes she could hardly bear to look at that photograph of her and her friends dancing down by the sea. She longed for those lost days of innocence. In a way she missed Beirut even more now than in her first lonely weeks last fall. Sometimes even something as simple as listening to one of Nirvana's records or even biting into a black olive would set her off into a sentimental bout of nostalgia.

These green pimento-stuffed olives that she bought in Boston, she would gripe to Aunt Bert, were vastly inferior to the *zeitoun* back in Beirut. Boston olives weren't juicy enough and salty enough. Lebanese olives were the best in the world. But there were no real *zeitoun* to be had in Boston. Months ago she had finished all of Fatima's olives which she had managed to smuggle past customs last year.

Anne tossed her dark hair back from her pallid face, took a determined drink of her beer, and told herself sternly that there was no point in indulging in frustrated fantasies about Beirut. She could not afford to go home this summer, and that was that. She had agreed with her father long before she came here to medical school that she would not be able to duck home for visits. In spite of Aunt Bert's elaborate house and Aunt Bert's expensive gifts, she was in America on a shoestring. She would simply have to endure this separation from the people and the places that she missed so much. After all, she would be seeing her parents and her brother this Christmas when they came to Boston for the holidays. But she wouldn't be able to get back to Lebanon for two more years, until she finished medical school and could – she hoped – serve out her internship at the American University Hospital in Beirut. That was the plan. Long ago she had carefully figured out exactly what she wanted from life, and until lately she had – step by careful step – achieved her goals.

Anne moodily pushed her glass of beer round in circles on the tabletop. The problem was that Mike was making hash of all her plans. It was possible – but not, if she were honest with herself, altogether probable – that she might be able to talk him into returning to Beirut with her, and that they could one day set up a joint practice and live happily ever after on Rue Bliss. But with Mike as rooted in Boston as she was in Beirut, she doubted if he would ever be able to consider Lebanon his home. It could be that someday she might have to choose between the man she adored and the city she loved. It made her heartsick even to think of having to live for the rest of her life anywhere but in Beirut.

She drained her beer and pushed it to the far end of the table. Sooner or later she would have to face the problem she was avoiding, and it had nothing to do with where she and Mike would spend their married life. They might never get married. They might not even continue seeing one another. Matters had been coming to a head between the two of them over the past tense weeks. Any day now he was going to give her the ultimatum she dreaded: either she would sleep with him, or he would call it quits. Either way, she might lose him. All her woman's instincts warned her not to give in until he was absolutely committed to her. But sometimes every fibre of her being wanted just the opposite. It was getting more painful to kiss for a half hour than not to touch each other at all. What would she do when finally he made her choose?

Anne signalled to the bartender for another beer, walked over to the bar to retrieve it, and paid what she owed. After she took her first sip of the brew, she glanced around the bar again, fiddled with her hair, and smoothed her skirt down over her thighs. When finally she had no choice but to be alone with her thoughts again, she continued to shy away from the problem at hand. Instead, she fretted over the very peripheral issue that she and Mike didn't even have access to a car. Their relationship wouldn't be so tense, she believed, if they could go on normal dates like a normal couple. But they couldn't even drive up to one of the North Shore beaches on a warm summer's night like this. She very much regretted that Ramsey was away all summer. If he had been around, she could have borrowed his sportscar for an occasional night out with Mike. She missed Ramsey. She would have liked to ask him for advice on how to handle Mike. She wished now that she had confided in him last spring, when he had cornered her outside Aunt Bert's after the tea party. It might have made her feel better to talk all this over with somebody she trusted. She and Mike could not continue forever marking time, grabbing each other under streetlamps like randy sixteen-year-olds.

As she stared out towards the street, a hulking shadow fell across the doorway. 'Mike!' She waved so he could pick her out of the crowd, and at once he began striding her way, waving to the regulars on the stools, the bartender, the old guy still crouched by the jukebox. Always when she caught sight of him moving towards her, her whole body responded. It had been like that even the first time, when he had moved towards her like a predator on the prowl back in the Hapenny pub nearly a year ago. He had stalked her then, and he was stalking her now. A primitive thrill coursed through her. She froze like a deer sighting a hunter. But she had no desire to flee from the danger she sensed in his nearness. She liked his aura of danger. In a way she was addicted to it, and to him. With every step he took closer to her, the memory of how aggravated she had been waiting for him dimmed and finally died. By the time he was finally beside her, and had bent over and kissed her hard on the lips, she was radiant.

But he didn't sit down. 'C'mon, gorgeous. Let's get out of here.'

She didn't have to be told twice. Anywhere – out on the street, down by the river, trudging up and down Beacon Hill – was better than Paddy's. Usually he was so tired when he first came in that he simply sank down on a chair and drank and chatted for a while until he was ready to take her outside and commence the kissing. But tonight he was in such an ebullient mood that he whistled on their way out of the bar.

When he gave her a far more lingering kiss out on Cambridge Street, she noticed that he had freshly shaved and liberally slapped on the Old Spice. After he went off shift, he must have ducked back to that little cubicle of his in the interns' residence and showered and shaved. That must be why he was so late.

She had to sprint by his side to keep up with his athletic stride down Charles Street. They were halfway across the Public Gardens before she had caught her breath enough to ask where they were going in such a rush.

'It's a surprise.' He threw her a dazzling smile and put his arm possessively around her as they raced down the garden path. 'Tonight's our four-month anniversary. Exactly four months ago tonight, I kissed you for the first time on the street outside Cronin's.'

'Really?' She was always touched at these proofs of how romantic he really was. She, who thought of him constantly, had not even remembered the exact date when they had met again by chance in the Coop last spring. She reproached herself for not giving him credit for being so thoughtful. He must be taking them to dinner to celebrate their 'anniversary'. As they crossed the Public Gardens and headed for the Arlington Street subway station, she chattered happily to him about her summer courses. As they caught a Green Line trolley going towards Brookline, he explained all about a mysterious infectious disease he had correctly diagnosed this morning as they made the rounds of patients on the big wards. As they clambered off the trolley, they were deeply engrossed in a discussion about the relative merits of working with patients in an urban hospital or devoting themselves to a life of medical research in an institution attached to a university. He had led her down two streets and was skirting a marshy parkland before she looked around and realized where they were.

'The Fenway? Mike, what are we doing in the Fenway?'

'I told you. It's a surprise. For our anniversary.'

She kept walking, but only with a supreme effort was she able to control her sudden suspicions. It was just possible that he was going to head over Symphony Road and take a shortcut to some little out-of-the-way French bistro or an Italian trattoria known only to Boston natives. But it was far more likely, she seethed, that he had brought her here for another purpose entirely. His friend's apartment was just ahead on Park Drive.

'Here we are.' Mike turned into the circular driveway of one of the formerly grand but now dilapidated apartment houses that was part of the student ghetto ranged along the Fenway. He pulled that familiar silver key from his pocket.

'Oh, no.' Like the donkeys she had seen in Fatima's village, Anne stopped in her tracks and refused to move one step further. She was furious that he had tricked her like this. It used to be that she hardly ever lost her temper, but these days she didn't seem to be able to stop herself from exploding. 'I told you before, Michael Patrick Spagnolli, that I will never – *repeat, never!* – go up there alone with you unless we are, at the very least, engaged to be married.'

'Now, honey . . .' He put his arms around her and tried to pull her to him. 'Nothing will happen up there. I promise.' His voice was husky. 'C'mon, Annie.' He kissed her neck. 'You want to.' He was whispering, and then blowing, in her ear. 'I know you do.'

Part of her was wild to do just as he said, but the rest of her was so angry that she wanted to knee him in the groin, scratch out his eyes, cut his sneaking heart out of his body. If he had a heart! She fought her way out of his arms. 'I will not!' She glared and stood her ground a good three steps away.

'Then this is it.' His thin lips had shrunk to a cruel slashing line. 'It's been four months, Annie. I'm not some little boy. I'm a grown man, thirty years old. You've got me so beside myself that half the time I can't eat or sleep, much less work the way I'm supposed to. Do you think we can go on for ever like this?'

'No.' Her anger was ebbing, and now she simply felt tired and very depressed. Just as she had understood for some time that it must come to this, so she had known not only how she must answer but what finally would be the result. And yet she desperately bargained against the inevitability of what would surely come next. 'We could get married. It would be different if we said we were going to get married.'

His eyes were hooded. 'You know I can't support a wife until I'm a real doctor. It would be different if you had a job, if you were a secretary or something. Then maybe we could get married.'

For one treacherous moment she was about to promise to drop out of school and take a job in a typing pool – anything to be with him. But she came to her senses just in time. As much as she wanted him, she could never give up her dream of being a doctor. She shook her head. 'I have two more years of med school.'

'Then that's it, then.' He looked deeply into her eyes, and for a moment it seemed he was about to say more. Instead he bit his lip. 'I'm sorry, Annie.'

'So am I.' She concentrated all her strength on holding back the tears. She would not break down and cry, not here. If she was going to lose him, she would do so with her dignity intact. She would not beg him please not to leave her.

'So.' He studied her face intently, not so much as though it were a mystery he was trying to unravel but a formula he were trying to commit to memory.

The finality of that look terrified her. He was looking at her as if he didn't think he would ever see her again.

'I guess there's nothing more to say,' he said.

'I guess not.' Her throat was so dry that she croaked out those words. She left unsaid all the torrents of words, promises, pleas that she longed to pour out to him. There was nothing she could say that would break their impasse. In a way, he was right. There was nothing more to say.

He let out a small sigh of regret. 'Except one thing, maybe. I was going to tell you this upstairs, when . . . Well, you can imagine when. I love you, Annie. I've loved you for four months. And now, just when I'm losing you, finally I tell you.'

It took all of her resolve and control not to answer, fervently, that she loved him too, and then let him sweep her in that door and up those stairs and into the bed that both of them wanted. But she couldn't, and wouldn't, give herself away so cheaply, in a sordid hour of borrowed time in a friend's seedy apartment. Perhaps she couldn't stop her eyes from lingering lovingly on his face, his lips, his everything. But she could bite her tongue to keep it from betraying her. Instead of telling him that she loved him, she merely nodded. 'Take care of yourself, Mike.' She turned her back on him. Quickly then, as if she were late for a class, she headed back the way they had come.

Her face was white and she was trembling as she hailed a taxi on Park Drive.

In vain she waited for him to telephone her that first week after they split up. She only cried herself to sleep once, on the night it all happened. But after that she studied hard every evening, she spent more time than usual with her aunt, she went up to Maine over the weekend to visit a distant cousin who ran an inn along the coast. She congratulated herself on how very well she was surviving. She told herself that if she could just manage to hang tough for a little while longer, surely he would give in first and promise to marry her. He would find it impossible to live without her. He had admitted he loved her. He must be suffering just as much as she was from this separation. Yet every time she lunged to answer the phone and it wasn't him, all that was good and strong and hopeful inside her died a little bit.

The second week she weakened and almost broke down and called him, just to see how he was. She was desolate without him. Some mornings she could hardly make herself crawl out of bed and face another day that didn't have him in it. One afternoon she cut class and sat weeping in the dark at a movie that the critics all dismissed as sentimental claptrap. Then one night she gave in to temptation. She had dialled five digits before she finally was able to pull herself together and slam the receiver back on the cradle.

It was three weeks and four days after she had walked away from him that she finally gave up and called him back into her life. She knew she shouldn't do it, but she was in a place far beyond shoulds. She had to be with him. She would do anything to be with him. Yet she hated herself as she rang up and had him paged at the hospital. Her voice was vacant of all emotion as she tersely told him she had to see him that very night at Cronin's. Her last great hope was that, as soon as he heard her on the line, he would blurt out how sorry he was and how right she had been that night on the Fenway. But instead Mike sounded businesslike as he informed her that he was on the swing shift tonight and couldn't possibly get over to Cambridge. She lost what little pride she had left, then, when she begged, in a very small voice, 'Please.' She waited in misery for an agonizingly long moment while he hesitated. But then he finally said he thought he could manage a stolen half hour at Paddy's. Even though she swallowed hard, that strangling lump was still in her throat as she agreed to meet him there at ten o'clock.

For once, he was waiting for her at a back table when she came in the door. She felt old and tired and utterly defeated as she dragged her feet the length of the bar, towards the man she had to have at any price. He took one look at what was written all over her face and then leaped to his feet and went to take her triumphantly in his arms. But she was not yet up to embracing. She shrank away from his touch and instead slid down into a chair and stared at him without smiling. 'Okay,' she said. 'You win.'

Her only condition was that, at least for the first time, she would not go to that vile apartment in the Fenway. Instead they would spend a long weekend together at Aunt Bert's house on Nantucket. 'It will be', she said, with a new note of bitterness in her voice, 'a sort of honeymoon without the marriage ceremony.'

He seized her hands in his. 'Of course, sweetheart. Anything you want. We'll go this Friday. I'll pull out all the stops and get off duty somehow.' He bent closer so that his head was next to hers. 'It's been hell without you.' He whispered. 'I love you so much.'

Steadily she looked him straight in the eye. She had learned a few home truths in these last wrenching weeks. 'Not as much as I love you.'

'Don't say that, honey.' His hands were warm and reassuring. 'I'll make it up to you, I promise.'

Very faintly she smiled. She had every intention that he should make all of this up to her. She had desperately wanted to wait at least until they were engaged before she slept with him. She had been willing to endure all the frustration in the world until everything was perfect and they were committed to a lifetime together. But he had made mincemeat of her good intentions. It was his fault that now everything was different between the two of them. She had wanted them always to be one hundred per cent honest and trusting with each other. She had never intended to play the same sort of manipulative games with him that she had observed too many other men and women sadly playing. But he had given her no other choice. She had lost this round, fair and square; but she was a good loser. The game, she knew, was far from over. She would make him love her so much that he would be begging to marry her, if not this coming weekend then at least before the year was out. The way to his heart lay right between her legs.

He leaned even closer to her, and she did not resist when he kissed her on the lips. Until now she had never let him do so at Paddy's, but this time she went further and snaked her tongue inside his mouth.

'Jesus,' he breathed, when she was the first to pull away. She sat just out of his reach and rallied her strength and managed to turn her sultriest smile on him. She felt colder and harder now – but far less like a victim – than when she had slunk to his table. She had decided exactly what she must do before she had called him at the hospital, and she was confident that she could do it. If it was sex he wanted more than anything, then she would serve him up the best sex he had ever had. From now on, she was altogether off the leash. She would match him kiss for kiss, and more. She hadn't wanted to do this before they were married. But now that she had agreed to do it, she would do it like a champ. She was playing to win.

Just before sunset that Friday they stood on the deck of the ferry, huddled together against the chill September wind. The fog had lifted enough for them to see the sky turn mauve and gold as the sun hovered in an orangy blur above the purple horizon. His arm was around her, and she leaned her head on his shoulder as the boat churned through the choppy water towards Nantucket Island. It was cold on deck, but they were warm with love. From time to time during the three-hour ferry ride from Wood's Hole, he would lean down to kiss her very tenderly or to wrap her thick wool shawl more securely around her neck and shoulders, and she would look adoringly up at him and cuddle a few millimetres closer to his legs, chest, shoulders.

'It's magic, isn't it?' she whispered.

'You're magic,' he answered, as he held her even closer.

'No, no.' She laughed and tried to explain. 'I mean the ferry. The boat ride. Just getting to Nantucket is like going to Never-Never Land or Oz or some other wonderful place that's detached from all the troubles of the real world. You know that "Twilight Zone" show on TV? When I see it, I always think of Nantucket. The trip out's almost always foggy like this, so it's like travelling into another dimension. I always feel that I'm leaving my real life behind and stepping off the end of the earth.'

'This is real, honey,' he growled. He leaned down and tasted her lips, cheeks, and the soft skin at her temples. 'I'm very real.'

'Yes,' she murmured. She stood on tiptoe and kissed him back. Despite her bitter feelings of defeat on the night she had agreed to do as he wished, these last four days had been some of the happiest of her life. He had been more loving than she had ever dreamed possible. At least three times every single day, he had rung her up to say he loved her. The day before yesterday he had sent roses to her at Aunt Bert's, and last night he had splashed out and taken her for martinis in the Ritz Bar. He had even arrived at the Trailways bus station this afternoon on time with another bouquet of red roses for her and two magnums of champagne packed on ice in a plastic cooler. In a way she wished she could spin out the lush promise of these sweetly innocent days, or at least postpone having to do what she had said she would do for days or weeks or months. She had assumed at first that giving in to him like this would be not only a defeat but an ordeal, and that she would have to be the world's greatest actress to go through with it. But now, as she revelled in his sudden shower of loving proofs, she was beginning to wonder why she hadn't agreed to such bliss sooner. Of course she was nervous about tonight. But she was determined not to be swamped by misgivings. At the crucial moment, she would shut her eyes and grit her teeth and pretend to like it a lot.

'There it is!' She pointed to the faint shape of land just ahead. 'Nantucket! I love it here. After Beirut, it's my favourite place in all the world.'

'Not me, baby.' He slackened his hold on her and narrowed his eyes as he looked at the coastline of one of the most fashionable islands off the East Coast. He didn't like it when she let him know that she had done things and gone places that were notched above his reach. 'Nantucket was always too rich for my blood. The closest I've ever come was a rented cottage on the Cape. Before Pop died, we came down to Centerville sometimes. But what's the difference anyway? It's all the same ocean.'

'Centerville's very nice,' she said lamely, even though she knew it was overcrowded and very common and nothing like Nantucket. She reproached herself for making him feel inferior. With Aunt Bert always subtly reminding her that she was a poor relation, she knew how that could hurt. Besides, she didn't want any dark shadows falling on what should be the most perfect weekend of her life. Again she angled herself as close to him as she could.

He seemed just as eager as she was to forget their differences. 'I think Nantucket's going to be my favourite place in all the world, too, about a minute and a half after we get inside your aunt's house.' He grinned wolfishly down at her and then held her tight again and kissed her on the lips for what must have been a long while. For when they finally broke apart as the landing horn was sounded, the sun had set and the boat was about to dock.

Below decks, trucks and cars roared to life in clouds of noxious fumes, and a crowd of foot passengers huddled by the gangway so they could eagerly stampede ashore the second the sailors had tied the final knots. Mike's arm was still securely around her as they tramped down the pier and into the sleepy town with its cobblestone streets, its grey clapboard houses, and its aura of stepping back two hundred years in time to the heyday of the New England whaling industry. The fog was rolling in from the sea, so that it seemed the streets and hedges and houses were swirling in clouds. 'You were right,' he said. 'It's just like you said it was.' They stopped at a corner store – and, she whispered hopefully, 'just like a real married couple' – they bought everything they would need to cook breakfast. She pointed out the quaint town landmarks – the bank, the inn, a rambling cottage everyone swore was haunted – until finally they rounded a curving lane and unlatched Aunt Bert's white picket fence. But inside the vine-covered grey shingle cottage that had been built for a sea captain more than two centuries ago, nothing happened when Anne flipped a light switch. 'Damn,' she muttered. 'They promised to turn it on for the weekend.' In the dusky light that crept in from the open front door, the summer house was ghostly. Sheets were draped over sofas and chairs. The shutters were bolted firmly shut. Even the cold air felt old and stale. But it was better when Mike lit a candle and Anne flung open the shutters. He took the sheeting off the furniture while she hunted around until she found the gas lamps in a cupboard. Mike carefully poured in the kerosene and lit all three of them with a flourish, 'That's better.'

She smiled uncertainly, suddenly conscious not only that she was alone with him in this house but also that the reason they had come all the way out here was to go to bed together. She wished, for a moment, that she had not insisted on such a premeditated surrender. If she had given in one night down by the river or even in that seedy alley, she might have been able to justify her conduct as losing her head in a torrid moment. Coming here like this was so cold-blooded. Even though he was the one who had insisted she had to do this to keep him, she had agreed of her own free will.

She fled to the kitchen carrying the sack of groceries and the picnic lunch she had packed back in Cambridge. Aunt Bert thought she had come out with two of the women from medical school. She wished that were the truth. But Mike was right behind her with one of the glowing kerosene lamps. She turned on the gas stove, waved a match experimentally above a burner, and was glad to see that at least they would be able to cook. 'Hungry?' she asked brightly.

He set the lamp down on the sink. In the flickering light he towered over her as he took her in his arms and kissed her long and hard. 'Only for you,' he murmured. 'Where's the bedroom?'

Doom was in her tread as she led him up the narrow crooked stairs to the second floor. The master bedroom was all in shadows even when he set a kerosene lamp down on a dresser. The two of them stared at the double bed with its hand-worked lace canopy hanging grandly above it. He put down their overnight bags, dug in the plastic cooler for one of the magnums of champagne, and went back downstairs for glasses. By the time he returned, she had put clean sheets on the bed and disappeared down the hall into the bathroom. He popped the cork, poured two foaming glasses, and unbuttoned his shirt. As he waited for her, he turned down the kerosene lamp and lit nests of long tapering white candles on either side of the bed.

A long while later she finally stood hesitant in the bedroom doorway, her face as white as the low-cut slinky white satin nightgown she had bought the day before on Newbury Street.

He was standing naked at the window watching the fog drift in from the sea. He turned to face her. 'You look beautiful.'

She could never have summoned the nerve to tell him that he looked beautiful, too. But he did. In the shimmering pool of light where he stood near the bed, at first she dared only to look at his shoulders and chest. His skin was a warm gold colour, and curly black hair covered his chest, and lower. Mike's athlete's body looked so big and strong and powerful. But for art book photographs of Renaissance sculptures and the impersonal figures studied in med school, she had never seen a man naked like this. Her eyes travelled slowly from his broad shoulders and massive chest down to his tapered waist, then more quickly past his slim hips and his muscled thighs. She blushed and averted her eyes. Then her curiosity was stronger than her embarrassment. In the candlelight she stared at all of him.

He seemed amused as he smiled a slow smile and let her look him over. He sipped his champagne as nonchalantly as though he were fully dressed and sitting in a sidewalk café. 'I poured you a glass over on the dresser.'

Gratefully she put both her hands around the glass and drank it all at one gulp.

'Help yourself.' He was still smiling and still standing at the opposite end of the bedroom by the window. 'There's more in the cooler.'

She poured another glass, sipped it, and studied the label as though there were nothing more on her mind than the vineyards of Champagne. She polished off the rest of that glass and poured herself a third. She felt better now, a little light-headed but not quite so terrified.

He flicked on a portable radio he had brought from home and fiddled with the dial until he found some slow music. 'Shall we dance?'

'Sure.' Bravely she walked towards him with what she hoped was the sophisticated slither of a woman of the world. But her eyes were wide with terror when he came forward and took her in his naked arms. She shuddered with fear and delight as, for the first time ever, she felt his bare skin against hers. It was cold in this room but his skin was hot.

'Relax,' he said. 'We've got all the time in the world. I won't do anything until you're ready.' He lowered his voice until it was just above a whisper. 'Until you want it as much as I do.' He held her very close and bent her body expertly to his as they swayed and dipped on the sloping wooden floor of her aunt's bedroom.

She was so nervous at first that she stumbled and couldn't follow his smooth strong lead. But then when he simply danced her here and there and didn't seem about to throw her down on the bed and rape her, she relaxed a little. By the time the third song came on the radio, she was liquid in his arms. He hummed the words in her ear, and she leaned her head on his chest. He held her closer and slid both his arms around her back. When finally he leaned down and kissed her on the lips, she sighed a heartfelt 'yes' and gave herself over to the most swooning kiss she'd ever had. On and on that kiss went, his tongue was in her mouth, hers was in his, then he was kissing her neck and blowing in her ear. His arms roamed over her shoulders and her waist. He cupped his hands around her buttocks and pressed her hard against him. Through the thin stuff of her nightgown, she could feel him hard against her. She gasped and broke away, frightened again.

'I have to go to the bathroom,' she called back to him as she fled down the hall.

When she returned, he had turned off the radio, set the cooler beside the bed, and poured two fresh glasses of champagne which were waiting on the bedside table.

'Sorry.' She was ashamed of herself. She had wanted to be a tigress with him so that he would love her for ever, and instead she was acting like a silly girl.

He smiled reassuringly and patted the bed beside him. She felt very vulnerable as she perched at the far end of the bed and took a tentative sip of the champagne.

'Annie, you really do act like a virgin.'

'But I am a virgin. I told you that.' She flared for a moment, hurt that he should doubt her. But then it occurred to her that maybe he wouldn't want to be the first one to do it to her. It would be mortifying to come this far and then have him be the one to call it off. 'I'm sorry,' she said miserably. She took a deep breath. 'But don't worry. It's okay, I promise. I wanted to wait until we were married, but since it's you anyway, it doesn't really matter. I mean, this is like a honeymoon, isn't it?'

He was in the shadows and she couldn't see the look on his face. But his voice was strange – almost strangled – and there were timbres of pain in it. 'God, I love you, Annie. Whatever happens, I want you to remember that. I really do love you.'

She ignored his implied warning and instead focused on the desperation she had heard in the voice of the man she loved. She set aside her own fear and her own needs. In a burst of generosity, she longed only to comfort him. 'I love you, too.' Suddenly she wanted to give him everything and anything. Tonight she had planned to act as she imagined a passionate woman would behave. But the impulse that overwhelmed her now was genuine. Nothing in all the world mattered but giving him everything he wanted from her. His happiness was her happiness. His desire was her desire. 'Now,' she said. 'Kiss me now.'

He took the champagne glass from her hand and set it on the floor, and then he took her in his arms and kissed her sweetly at first, then harder, longer, deeper. He bent her back on the bed, and she felt his weight on her. He was kissing her neck, her shoulders; he pulled down the thin straps of her nightgown and ran his hands over her breasts. She moaned as he touched her nipples with the tips of his fingers and then kissed her breasts and teased her nipples with his tongue. He rolled over so she was on top of him and her breasts hung down. He caressed them slowly with his hands and his lips. She was lost in a blur of sensation. His hands, his lips, his tongue were everywhere.

'Let yourself go,' he whispered as she felt the satin hem of her nightgown sliding up her thighs and beyond her breasts and over her head. She was finally naked in his arms. 'Just let yourself go.'

He started kissing her lips all over again, and then her breasts, and then her stomach. His hands were on her thighs and higher, and she heard herself make strange soft little animal cries of delight when he stroked her between her legs for many sweet urgent moments.

She had never felt like this before. Her arms and legs were heavy with desire. Her legs were spread wide and slack, and she could not have pressed them back together even if she had wanted to.

His long rippling body lay full-length over her,

and his lips, when he kissed her again, bruised hers. She kept her eyes open and stared straight into his, as that wanton kiss of desire went on and on. She matched him stare for stare as he kneaded her breasts harder and rougher this time. Their bodies were slick with sweat.

When again his hands probed between her legs, she shut her eyes and gasped. She was wet as his fingers pleasured her. She hardly noticed that something was different a second later, when there was a new pressure between her legs. All she felt at first was him stretched over her again, his thighs atop hers, his chest grinding into her breasts, his lips ravenous on hers.

But then she felt him creeping further and further inside her until he couldn't move any deeper. She was just starting to tense up when suddenly he pushed harder, and he was all the way inside her. She tried to pull away, but he wouldn't let her. He squirmed further inside; he filled her all the way up. She was just getting used to him being in there and trying to decide whether she liked it or not, when all of a sudden he growled and started to move their bodies in a rhythm that cut so deep she could almost hear it beating in her heart. She cried out and hung on to him in a spasm of delight. But then the savage rhythm of it all took her over, and she started to push back. Suddenly the two of them melted together, panting, as he frantically kissed her lips, her cheeks, her eyes. Faster he pumped, harder, until finally he cried out and was still. He heaved a great sigh, then, and opened his eyes and smiled down at her. 'I love you very much,' he whispered as he tenderly stroked her damp hair back from her sweaty face.

'Mmmm,' she purred lazily as he rolled off her and lay on his back with his arms around her. She cuddled close to him with her head on his chest. How could she ever have been so afraid of how it would hurt and how degraded it would make her feel? For a long while, as he caressed her hair and murmured sweet nothings, she simply marvelled at the wonder of it all. Truly, they had made love. She would never – ever! – regret this. The poets were right to rhapsodize about it so. Camilla had been right, too: *C'est merveilleux!* The tension that had been building between them over these last quarrelsome months had drained away, and they lay blissfully at peace in each other's arms. She had, she decided, gotten it all wrong before. She had nothing to fear from Mike. He had surrendered to her in this bed just as much as she had surrendered to him. There were no losers on this sheet, only winners. Gently she snuggled even closer to her perfect lover.

'That was very good, you know,' he said a few moments later, as matter-of-factly as though he was a coach commending his star player. 'Usually it's not that good the first time, especially with a virgin.' He patted her on her shoulder. 'You're a helluva woman.'

She frowned in his arms. Exactly how many women – virgins and non-virgins – was he comparing her to? But then she shrugged off her suspicions and told herself not to be so jealous. He was thirty years old. Of course other women had been unable to resist him. She should thank them, really, for giving him the opportunity to learn to be such a good lover. What did it matter how many women had come before her, so long as he was going to be with her from now on? Instead of fabricating problems for herself, she should concentrate on pleasing her man. If she was the sexiest woman he had ever had, he would marry her and never dream of turning to someone else.

Anne rolled out of his arms, reached over to the table, and poured them a single fresh glass of champagne. She bent over and held it to his lips, and then took a long thirsty drink of it herself. In the candlelight she smiled down at him. She was very conscious that she was naked, and that her legs were spread invitingly open. His eyes were lingering on her breasts, thighs, buttocks. She watched him swell hard again.

'Get back here where you belong.' Impatiently he opened his arms.

She laughed, throatily, and did as she was told.

Chapter 9

Fatima leaned over her niece's white-scarfed head and watched the little seven-year-old use the blunt pencil to trace the sweeping curves of her name with a flourish. 'Very good, Zahra, yes, just like that.' Zahra beamed radiantly up at her educated aunt, who smiled back at the one who was not only her most faithful but also her most gifted pupil. Her older sisters could hardly write their own names, but already Zahra could read aloud whole passages from the Koran.

God knows, Fatima thought as she moved on to the rest of her relatives who had assembled this morning – for here in the village, almost everyone was at least a cousin – that each of them had the best intentions of coming to school every morning. When her father, before he returned to West Africa, had talked the men in the mosque into setting up a literacy class for girls in this abandoned shed, almost everyone had been enthusiastic. Most of the villagers – the men even more than the women – were dazzled at the possibility of someday being able to boast that their daughters could read the Holy Koran. No one could publicly disagree that it was commendable for a girl to be learned as well as pious, industrious and of a sunny disposition. But, day after day, pressing family responsibilities always seemed to take precedence over education. On Monday a mother might need help with the laundry, on Tuesday a little brother might have fallen ill and need nursing, on Thursday the olives might be ripe for the picking, and on

Saturday the whole family might be off to the market in Nabatiya. Some mornings when Fatima rushed in from her own family chores, eager little Zahra was the only girl sitting crosslegged on the worn reed mat.

But today, *el-hamdulillah*, the small hut which dear Baba had talked the village elders into converting into a classroom was crowded with seven would-be scholars who had not yet altogether mastered the alphabet. The mostly perplexed little girls sighed as they bent their heads, identically covered in modest white polyester, over the cheap lined paper. Fatima moved a few feet away where her ten-year-old cousin Amina was almost in tears as she failed to make her pencil repeat the graceful Arabic strokes and loops. 'I am so stupid!' she wailed, and then she did start to cry. 'I will never learn. My brother Musa is right. I should stay home and cook the food and mind the babies. I am too stupid for anything else.'

Fatima wished she could throttle that ignorant bully of a brother. 'There, there. *Inshallah*, it will just take a little time and practice to get it right, that's all.' As she put her arm around Amina's shaking shoulders, Fatima thought acidly that it had always been Musa who was the stupid one in that branch of the family. He had sat at the feet of the *shaykh* in *kuttab* school for at least five winters, yet still he could neither read nor write. Fatima made a mental reservation to take her dear cousin Musa aside at the earliest opportunity and remind him that it was his Islamic duty to treat his little sister with respect. Yet, Fatima thought, she would have to take care not to offend Musa, or anyone else. Her humble classroom had a fragile foothold in the village, and so she always had to tread carefully, persuading rather than demanding. When she needed books and paper, she had to beg for them sweetly at the mosque. When she went to a family to find out why a little girl hadn't been to school in weeks, she had to sit and drink tea for more than an hour before she could gently bring the conversation around to the truant daughter. Constantly she had to defer to anyone and everyone so as not to be criticized for setting a bad example of womanly virtue. For even though Fatima had been born and raised here, many of the more conservative elders still regarded her with suspicion because she had spent too many years off in scandalous Beirut. In a way, not only the school but also Fatima herself was an experiment. If she made one false move – if she spoke up once too often or was observed by some malicious tattletale acting in any other way that was considered unseemly for a woman – the entire concept of educating girls could be in jeopardy. It would be bad enough if her school was closed almost before it had really opened, but even worse was that little girls like Zahra might never have the opportunity to follow Fatima to university. For despite what the men had said to her father's face when he proposed this school, Musa wasn't the only male in the village who harboured doubts about taking the girls away from the home and into the classroom. She had to be constantly on her guard against antagonizing those who thought the old ways were best.

Fatima sat down and cupped her hand around Amina's. 'See, like this.' Painstakingly she guided the girl's pencil across the page until her name stared back at them from the paper. 'Now, try it yourself.' Amina gave her a stricken look, but then, excruciatingly slowly, she bore down on the pencil until, after a fashion, she had produced the desired result. 'Exactly right!' Fatima hugged her young cousin. 'See, you're not stupid.' As warm and anxious to please as a puppy, Amina threw herself in her teacher's arms and kissed her on her cheeks.

Just so, with hugs and kisses all round, Fatima passed through the ranks of little girls, encouraging this one, correcting that one, until finally each of them had been able to reproduce her own name. She went down again to the front of the room beside the large blackboard she had wangled from the mosque. 'Now let's practise some words we all know. First, of course, Allah—'

Outside on the street there was a loud screech of brakes, a series of hoots on a car horn and an answering chorus of excited masculine shouts. The entire village jolted to attention, for everyone knew the sound of the service taxi pulling in from Sidon. Someone from the outside world must have arrived, and so this slow sleepy morning had been transformed into a date to be remembered. Men looked up from their ploughs to see who it could be. Women stopped chopping their vegetables and sent their sons for the news. Packs of eager children raced down to the square in front of the mosque. In Fatima's classroom, even diligent Zahra couldn't help craning her neck towards the window. 'Now, girls!' Fatima clapped her hands. 'Our lessons are not finished. Attention, now!'

But there was a loud pounding on the door. 'Fatima!' Her sister Zainab – pregnant again, but still the village's fleetest gossip – burst in and leaned against the wall, panting until she could get her breath back. 'He's here! He's come!'

Fatima frowned at the interruption. Her mother and sisters knew not to disturb her class unless something extraordinary had happened. But surely her father couldn't have returned after less than a year back in Africa. 'Who?'

'Your husband!' Zainab gasped out the words as though they would set her sister swooning off into rapture.

Instead Fatima paled at the blackboard. Since their long-distance marriage ceremony nearly a year ago, Ali had written her six pleasant but formal little letters that had been vague about when she might expect him home.

And so she had been lulled into believing that this marital day of reckoning was many months – perhaps even years – away. Ali had gone off to study with the mullahs in Iran and Iraq nearly nine years ago, and sometimes she had prayed that his religious studies would stretch until Judgement Day. In the meantime, however, she had begun to enjoy her new status as a married lady. With Ali away, she had most of the privileges and none of the upheavals of marriage. Instead of having to move into a small house of their own or a spare bedroom at Ali's parents' house, she had been able to stay in the snug family nest of her early childhood. She had continued sleeping in her accustomed place beside her sisters on the mat in the girls' bedroom, and all day long in the hive of her mother's house her family had buzzed in and out the door that was never locked. Yet, far more than a fancy degree from the American University of Beirut, marriage had instantly conferred respectable adult status upon her. At family gatherings she sat talking with the women instead of the girls, and her mother and her aunts had begun treating her as though she were one of their own generation. She didn't doubt, moreover, that some of the villagers sent their daughters to her school only because they were reassured by her being the wife of a *shaykh*-in-the-making. All the women in the family had pitched in to sew her trousseau. Lovingly she had stitched her own beautiful white silk wedding dress from a pattern she had bought in the souk at Sidon. Her mother, her sisters and her aunts had fashioned her a wardrobe suitable for the *shaykh*'s wife: a black silk dress, a tailored black suit, a black coat for winter, a black jacket for spring and autumn, and an armful of pretty rainbow-hued long dresses suitable for receiving well-wishers in the first months of her married life. As the seasons had changed and still Ali had not arrived, the women had artfully begun working intricate needlework designs into the bedsheets, dinner-cloths and towels that would last her a lifetime. Even more wonderful in its way was the magnificent carved walnut bridal chest her brother Muhammad had bought her up in the Shouf Mountains where famed Druze craftsmen made these wedding chests their speciality. For the first time, as she had tied her embroidered linens in white ribbons and laid them into her Druze chest, she had felt truly like *el-arous*, the bride. But now she would have to pay the price for those perquisites. Like it or not, her life would now revolve around her stranger of a husband. They would eat together and – dear God! – they would sleep together. She would have to move out of her mother's house and start a new life with this husband she had not chosen for herself.

Fatima seemed to forget not only her husband but also her students as she stared off into space. How and when was it, she wondered, that she had finally submerged herself in this life back in Suker? Her old friends from what she now thought of as the glory days back in Beirut still, of course, kept in touch. Camilla posted her fat packets of adorable baby pictures from her fancy château in the northern Lebanese mountains, and even Leila sent her the occasional scrawled postcard from London. But Fatima never knew how to respond to the troubling letters Anne wrote about her boyfriend. She wasn't sure exactly what was happening between this Mike and Anne, but it seemed to her that Anne might be straying too far from what the Muslims always called 'the straight path'. She wished Anne had never gone off to Boston. She – like Fatima herself – should have stayed at home in the bosom of her family, where she would be protected from life's dangers. Yet even though Fatima continued to pray for Anne and the others, sometimes when she looked at that photograph of the four of them at Raouche, her years in Beirut seemed like a splendid fiction she had read long ago in a much-loved book. But real life was here in her village. As her longings for the halcyon days in Beirut had grown dimmer, she could sometimes almost swear that she had never lived anywhere but in Suker. The village was as much a part of her as her bones, hair and lungs. She, and it, were indivisible.

Fatima sighed and, reluctantly putting down her chalk, returned to the matter at hand. The husband she hadn't chosen was waiting for her outside.

Again Fatima sighed. What did she want with a husband? Long ago she had come to the conclusion that here in Suker being a mother usually brought a woman greater happiness than being a wife. Even from a little girl, she had noticed that, in the marriages of her aunts and older cousins, most of the women's love seemed centred more satisfyingly on their children than on their husbands. There were exceptions, of course. Newlyweds tended to make calves' eyes at each other until the first baby came, and more than one hot-blooded Suker wife seemed to eat passion for breakfast, lunch and dinner. But here in the village the sort of romantic love Fatima had mooned over in the Beirut cinemas was rare. Although her own mother was still very much in love with her father, more often cousin married cousin and simply made do with the mate Allah had decreed. In general wives endured their husbands and adored their children. What were men, after all – the ageing village women always said knowingly when their husbands were out of earshot – but overgrown boys who had to be coddled, pampered and tolerated? Fatima supposed she wasn't so different from her sisters. Even though she had wanted *more*, she, too, would learn to make do with a shell of a marriage. And she supposed her fate could have been worse. She remembered Ali as a kind and thoughtful cousin, and since their marriage every member of the family had made it his or her business to take her aside and repeat some touching little story about Ali's generosity, humour, patience and compassion. If she had to have a husband, this family saint certainly wasn't any worse than any of the alternatives. But she hadn't wanted a husband; she had wanted a school.

Fatima gave the classroom that meant so much to her a frantic look, as though hunting for a corner to hide in. She was sick at the thought of having to live with this man she hardly knew. Despite how well-matched everyone in the family seemed to think they were, what if she and Ali didn't get on? There might be scenes and recriminations, and the entire family would inevitably join in and try to save the union. Fatima remembered the village scandal of one of her father's distant aunts who had long ago gone against all womanly tradition by trying – for no good reason, everyone said – to divorce one of her father's more distantly related uncles. Forever afterward, even though her exasperated husband had finally given her the freedom she wanted, that aunt had been unable to live down her reputation as a troublemaker. Suddenly, wistfully, Fatima wished that stubborn old aunt was still alive so she could sit at her feet and take lessons in independence. For it had just come to her as a revelation that her aunt might after all have had very sound reasons for doing as she had done. Fatima wondered, when it came down to it, if she herself would be brave enough to insist on divorce.

But then, even as she searched her classroom desperately for reassurance that she was capable of such daring, an even more anxious fear coursed through her. What if Ali forbade her to continue with her school? He would have to be an exceptional man indeed to approve of his wife working outside the home. When Baba had provided her with this classroom, she had understood without being told that this was her reward for bowing to his wishes and agreeing to the marriage. Yet now that Ali was back, it was possible that she would be expected to put away her toy school and get down to the real business of married life.

Her eyes were sad as she bid a kind of farewell to each of these little girls whose days of learning in this classroom might be numbered. Even if Ali let her go on teaching, she worried that it might never be the same for her and these girls. She would have heavier responsibilities making a home for her husband and, *inshallah*, she might very soon be pregnant. Some mornings Zahra might wait in vain for her in this classroom.

Fatima looked at the window, and beyond, where the sun beat down in the bright blue sky. She longed to skip out and slam the door for ever on all these insoluble problems. She imagined herself striding through the fields, over the highest hills, down to the coast, and then up to Beirut where she would be free to live a fulfilling life according to her own wishes rather than her family's. She dreamed not of fast cars and drop-dead frocks and lazy afternoons roasting on a sunbed beside a swimming pool. Instead, what joy it would be, she thought with longing, to be the headmistress of a school where all the little girls had the latest books, pencils with sharp points, and freshly pressed navy-blue uniforms. Sometimes if she shut her eyes and wished very hard, she could almost smell the sharp cleanliness of those starched uniforms and almost see the classrooms full of bright-faced girls like Zahra. What would it be like to live a life that brimmed with such satisfactions?

Fatima smoothed down her headscarf, wrapped a shawl around her shoulders, and then – with a dreadful welling up of despair in her chest – she prepared herself to go and meet the man whom she would probably have to live out her life with here in Suker. She might dream of divorce and freedom, but she lived in the real world where even a reluctant wife hastened to greet her husband with every outward appearance of gladness. 'Class dismissed.'

Arm in arm, flanked by Zainab and Zahra, Fatima allowed herself to be led out of the classroom towards the pandemonium where the taxi had pulled up in front of the mosque. For by now the entire village had heard of the return of their native son. Men, women and children had abandoned whatever they were doing to rush here and welcome home the village boy who had reportedly covered himself in glory in the Shia heartlands of Iran and Iraq. People were shouting, laughing, crying. The men surged forward towards the hugging and kissing heart of the throng, where Ali himself was being passed from the eager embrace of his brothers to his father. One strapping young man stood on the roof of the taxi passing down suitcases and cartons to his cronies. The women let out excited little *zaghareit* cries of joy even as they modestly hung back on the fringes of the crowd. Children darted here and there, from mother and father to uncle and aunt, as everyone joked and yelled and waved.

As Fatima allowed herself to be drawn closer, the ranks of women drew aside to make way for the wife of the *shaykh*. She stood on tiptoe and searched the faces in the crowd for that new one who, from now on, would anchor her world. Most of the men were bare-headed or had chequered scarves wound around their heads to ward off the cold and the sun. But at last Fatima managed to pick out an immaculate white turban and flowing brown robes. Zainab, too, had spotted Ali locked in the embrace of his weeping father, and she shouted as she pointed the austere stranger out to her sister.

Fatima caught her breath as Ali turned. Despite her misgivings, she was so excited by her first glimpse of him that she could hardly take in whether he was tall or broad or handsome. She stared intently at this mysterious husband, until gradually Ali's features became less of a blur. She took in the dark slash of moustache and the smudge of black beard which covered his chin. Instead of the round-faced cousin she remembered from her childhood, he had become as foreign and glamorous as if he had just stepped out of an exquisite Persian miniature. Whatever had happened in Iran and Iraq had worked a transformation upon him. He was ascetically thin. Unlike his apple-cheeked brothers here in the village, Ali now had one of those mournful oriental faces whose plaintive liquid eyes and hollowed cheeks seemed the image of suffering. His was an achingly sensitive face. He looked to be the sort of man to whom total strangers confide their heart's desires. Yet Fatima checked her impulse to trust herself to this man with the dark soulful eyes. She reminded herself that even though she hadn't really wanted to marry him, she was most probably stuck with him for good. She resented this marriage, and she resented this husband.

As she continued warily to gaze at him, Ali seemed to feel the intensity of her stare. He turned his head and frowned back at the pretty young woman who was being perhaps too bold for her own good. But then he bent to whisper in his father's ear, and at the answer Ali's sad face was transformed by a smile. As Fatima watched him try to make his way through the crowd towards her, she was struck by how beatific that luminous smile of his was. No one could ever say that Ali was as handsome as a film star. His face was too angular, his eyes were too gentle, he didn't have even a fraction of Camilla's husband's masterful good looks. But Fatima fancied, as her husband inched towards her, that it was not a mere man but goodness itself that was heading her way.

Fatima blushed and pulled her scarf down low, as though hiding her face was hiding her feelings. She was shy, suddenly, that in another moment Ali would greet her with all the village watching. Until now, to her, this arranged marriage and this unwanted husband had been an abstraction foisted on her by her father. She had never expected that Ali would be as he was, and – she finally admitted to herself – that she would feel so drawn to him. The enormity of starting a new life at the side of such a man made her tremble, and not just with fear. But she did not want to make a public show of their first meeting. Before they struck the tone of whatever was to be between them, she longed to go off by herself and sort out her welter of conflicting emotions. She also wanted to get out a mirror and try to see herself as Ali must be seeing her. Her mother and sisters always told her she was pretty, but that might be just because they already loved her.

And so Fatima turned and bolted back to her mother's house.

Fondly, as one, the whole village laughed at the shyness of the blushing bride. If Fatima had plotted how best to win the approval of every man and woman in Suker, she couldn't have found a better strategy than to flee home to mother at the approach of her bridegroom. Old women sagely nodded their heads and said that – even with modern education and all these modern ways – it had always been so, and so it always would remain. Married men smiled to themselves as they remembered a time when they, too, wished they could have run home to their mothers rather than face the trials of married life. Young wives nudged each other and launched into reminiscences about how bashful they had been the first time their husbands saw them without their headscarves. Even the conservative old Hajji, who never had anything good to say about Fatima's fledgling school for girls, grinned and pronounced that Ali's wife wasn't so bad after all.

And at the head of the crowd, with the young village blades slapping him on the back and urging him to go up and claim what was rightfully his from his bride, Ali stood bemused.

Thoughtfully, as he watched his wife scurry up the hill to her mother's, Ali fingered his beard. When he had bowed to family pressure last year and married this cousin, against all logic he had somehow expected her still to be the sweetly solemn child he remembered liking when he was a boy. Little Fatima had been different – brighter, more serious, certainly more sensitive – than the other boisterous members of the family's younger generation. Even then he had been glad that his father and uncles had marked her out, God willing, as the one he would some day marry. Unbeknown to Fatima, it was Ali himself who had convinced her father to depart from the usual village practice by sending her off to school in Beirut. For Ali had sensed in her the potential to be far more than a good wife who shared his bed, mothered his children, and kept his house. With the right education and guidance, precocious little Fatima might someday grow up to be his lifetime partner. Hand in hand they could work together for the greater glory of Allah and the peace and prosperity of their people.

Yet now, as Ali watched her retreating back disappear into the shadows of her mother's house, he wondered if he had perhaps lingered too long about his hallowed business in Najaf, Kerbala and Qom. It might be endearing to see her blush and hide, but it was worrying as well. Had he alienated this woman whose first response to him was to run away as fast as she could? Already he might have gambled and lost not only his opportunity for a marriage made in heaven but even his chance for a placid and contented marriage like those of his brothers and cousins. He was troubled that he had seen fear and rebellion in the naked play of emotions on Fatima's open face. This bride of his was no longer a simple village girl who would automatically adore whatever husband Allah and her father had decided was best for her. Somewhere along the line, along with those delectable female curves which even her loose long dress couldn't altogether hide, Fatima had developed a mind of her own.

Ali heard his bride slam shut the door, and then fancied he could even hear her shoot the bolt into place against him. Obviously he had his work cut out for him with this woman. Even before undertaking all the other daunting tasks he had ahead of him in the village – working in harmony with the senior mullah at the mosque, making a place for himself in the local religious hierarchy, tending to a multitude of neglected family relationships – he would have to set about the mystifying business of courting his own wife. Again Ali remembered that look of fear on her face. He had never, he fretted, wanted his wife to be afraid of him. He would have to take care to proceed very slowly with this skittish young cousin he had married on the telephone. He would try to win her slowly and tenderly, so that when, *inshallah*, he had her, it would – please God! – be for ever.

Ali was still watching her house a moment later, when he could have sworn he saw her face at the window, staring down at him just as intently as he was staring up at her. His face cracked into an eager smile, and – even though it might only have been wishful thinking on his part – he thought he saw an answering smile curve her lips before hastily she shuttered the window and shut him out. With a growing feeling of elation, Ali considered the possibility that matters between himself and his bride might after all proceed at a faster pace than he had thought. Perhaps he had been mistaken about her reasons for running away from him. What, after all, did he know about women? The only ones he had ever kissed were his mother, his sisters and his aunts. He was as much a virgin in these matters as she was. Hastily he amended that last thought. He was as much a virgin as he sincerely hoped she was.

Ali stood smiling very broadly for another moment,

and then he gave his father the sort of ardent embrace he hoped he might soon be sharing with his wife.

'*Allahu akbar . . . Ash hado an la ilaha il-lallah . . . Ash hado anna Mohammadar rasoolullah . . . Ash hado anna ameeral momeneena alian walee ullah . . . Hayya alas salah. Hayya alas salah.*'

The sonorous rise and fall of the muezzin's call to the noon prayers echoed in a blast of amplified static from the loudspeaker atop the village mosque. First things first, Ali told himself. He banished profane thoughts of romance as he hurried off to the mosque with the rest of the men. They performed their ablutions, and then bowed and knelt and salaamed with one voice as they gave thanks to Allah for bringing one of their own home again.

But when it came to the place where a worshipper could add his special intentions, Ali whispered only one word: 'Fatima.'

Shyly that night they exchanged the first words of their married life.

When hesitantly – after much procrastination – Fatima edged into the room, the entire extended family was already seated crosslegged in a circle around the welcome home feast spread out upon the floor. Ali was in the place of honour next to the largest platter of roasted lamb, and he was laughing and joking with the cousins and aunts and uncles he hadn't seen in many years. The womenfolk had prepared the favourite Lebanese dishes which they supposed Ali had not tasted in the long years of his exile: *mashee* stuffed vegetables, *dolma* stuffed vineleaves, two kinds of kebab, *kraish mlhshieh* stuffed sheep's stomach, and of course *tabouli, kibbe* and black *zeitoun* olives. He seemed, however, more interested in his family than the food. Everyone was talking and laughing at once.

But the merry hubbub was instantly hushed by the sight of silent Fatima standing with her head bowed almost to her chest. Miserably she wrung her hands and wished she were anywhere but here. All afternoon, as she had worked with the women in the kitchen preparing this feast, her embarrassment had grown. As she had sat on the floor pounding the raw lamb into a paste with a mallet for *kibbe*, her sisters had unmercifully teased her about how wise her husband was, how gracious, how manly. As she had washed a mountain of parsley and then set about the exacting work of chopping it into minuscule pieces for *tabouli*, she had overheard her aunts' stage whispers about exactly how it had first been with themselves and their husbands. In her heart Fatima understood that her sisters and her aunts were only trying to help, for the time-honoured way that the villagers disposed of fears was to laugh or pray them away. But this time their technique had backfired.

Fatima was so abashed that she stood with her headscarf pulled so low that it nearly covered her eyes. The older children nudged each other knowingly, and the men did their best to hide their most indulgent smiles. But this time the women made sure that not even the giddiest teenager giggled. Her aunts had finally lost their appetite for teasing. They frowned and fell silent and fussed with their own scarves, as they remembered a time when they, too, had stood in Fatima's vulnerable position.

Finally Zainab put her arm around her for support, and Fatima's mother hugged her for courage. 'I wish your father were here,' Um Ibrahim fretted, mostly to herself. 'But my husband is never here when I need him.'

The tableau continued. In a graceful swirl of well-tailored brown robes, Ali rose and smiled gravely at his bride. '*Salaam aleykum.*'

'*Aleykum es-salaam.*' Automatically she repeated the

proper Muslim response to his greeting. She felt a little better that his voice was accented exactly like everyone else's in the village and not at all foreign or intimidating. But still she did not dare to look him in the face.

'So,' he said.

'So,' she repeated.

They stood there, each staring blindly at the other's bare feet, as the children could no longer repress their giggles.

Even as he desperately wondered what to say next, he wished she would look up so that he could see her face. Out by the mosque this afternoon, even before he had known who she was, he had thought she was pretty. Like so many of the village girls, her face radiated innocence. But he had only caught a glimpse of her then. Now he wanted a good long look at this woman who, *inshallah*, was going to be his wife.

As though she could read his thoughts, and in a way shared them, she raised her head very slightly and darted an anxious glance his way.

'Ah!' he said. She had glowing fair skin, flashing dark eyes, and when she blushed – as now – her cheeks were the colour of Lebanese apples. All that he saw in just one precious instant, for then he could not stop himself from shyly averting his eyes. His own cheeks felt hot. He was very much afraid that he was blushing.

His silence emboldened Fatima. She raised her eyes so she could study the austere contours of his extraordinary face. But when she saw that he was blushing an even brighter pink than herself, she couldn't help smiling. A man wasn't supposed to go red at the sight of his woman. Despite her own nervousness, the absurdity of it made her laugh.

Startled, he looked over at his laughing wife. He was mortified that this woman should first run away from him, and next be laughing at him. But then it struck him what a picture he must make, here in his stately robes, blushing like . . . well, like a bride. Sheepishly he smiled.

Fatima's face lit up. Yes, now she remembered her cousin Ali. He had always been so kind and considerate but a bit awkward in social situations. He had been endearing then, and he still was. All the same, it was funny to see a man blushing. As Fatima threw back her head and laughed from her belly, her scarf slipped back to the crown of her head. Ali stared in wonder at this wife who was so very beautiful. He laughed, too, but for joy.

A moment later, as the family laughed with the blushing young couple, Ali shyly guided Fatima over to the place of honour beside him. For the rest of that evening, they sat side by side eating, talking and laughing with gusto. For as soon as they had shared that first laugh, it had been easier to forget that they were nervous newlyweds and remember instead that they were long-lost cousins. They reminisced about incidents from the childhood they had shared. They gossiped about what had happened to the neighbours' children. They laughed at old family jokes. They even delighted the assembled family by reddening on cue as they were teased about what a picture they had made at first blush.

Only once in that first evening did Ali directly touch on their future as man and wife rather than their past as cousins. He pitched his voice so low that only she could hear him as he suggested that they follow the old custom and live apart until he had found and furnished a home of their own. 'That means', he whispered, 'that we will have, *inshallah*, a month or six weeks or even two months to get to know each other better before we . . .' Ali blushed again and lowered his eyes and could not say more.

Fatima modestly looked away as she let out an

audible sigh of relief. He would have been technically within his rights if he had insisted on consummating the marriage tonight. Thank God for his sensitivity, she prayed silently to herself. *El-hamdulillah!* She nodded eagerly when Ali, in another intimate aside, proposed that they stage a proper marriage feast before they moved in together. She had felt so cheated last year when she had married this man in a blur of static on the long distance telephone. She would feel well and truly married only after she had worn her beautiful white dress, bathed in musky oils, and been fêted by all the village. She had feared she might have nothing, but now it seemed that in the end she might have everything. From under her lowered lashes, she dared to glance up at her husband. Would his kisses be as sweet as his talk?

She was not to find out that night.

For as the two of them stood at the door to say goodnight, he kept his distance from her. Even when his brothers hooted that he must at least kiss his bride goodbye, Ali only blushed and edged down the path towards his father's.

Still, sometimes a look can burn more than a kiss.

Fatima was still framed in the doorway, watching Ali's retreating back, when he turned and gave her such a look of passionate longing that she shivered.

That night, as she helped wash up the dishes, she was impervious to the teasing of her sisters. Serenely she smiled as they giggled over how Ali had blushed, how she had wrung her hands, how he had fled away into the night without even kissing her on the cheek. She treasured that final look he had given her as though it were the world's most precious secret.

Fatima was still smiling as she finally stretched out on her mattress. As she lay in the dark, snug with one sister to the left of her and another to the right, she prepared for sleep as she always did, by counting out the Muslim rosary on the joints of her fingers. For long ago, when the Holy Prophet still lived in Mecca, after his favourite daughter Fatima had wearily asked him for a servant to help her with her household tasks, Muhammad instead had given her this prayer to lighten her burden: thirty-four *Allahu akbars*, thirty-three *subhanallahs*, thirty-three *el-hamdulillahs* – 'God is great, all worship to God, all thanks to God.' This was the same paean good Muslims the world over ticked off on their prayer beads as they sat in coffee-houses, commuted on buses, and rested in mosques. Every night, since she was just a little girl, Fatima had lulled herself to sleep by repeating her namesake's prayer.

And just so, on this night of nights, silently, gratefully and with a quiet heart, Fatima praised God before she turned over and fell into a deeply contented sleep.

High-pitched girlish laughter and hushed feminine ohs and ahs filled the sitting room six weeks later as the guests began to arrive at Fatima's mother's house for the women's half of the wedding reception.

Zainab was at the door enthusiastically welcoming those who had come from near and far. Every baby was kissed, every toddler was petted, every child was hugged and told it was big and beautiful and exceptional in all possible ways. As Zainab helped the mothers out of their black *abaya* outer cloaks, she gushed over the gloriously colourful dresses each aunt and cousin had put on for the party. For in Suker it was only on special occasions like this that the women laid aside their dour cocoons of navy and grey and black and instead burst out like gaudy butterflies in turquoise and purple and scarlet.

'Anaya! *Ya habibi!*' Zainab fervently kissed her cousin who had married a family connection in a village three hills and two valleys to the east. Anaya was twenty-two years old and because she was, *el-hamdulillah*, pregnant with her sixth child, she hadn't been able to make the journey home as often as she would have liked.

Before Anaya could be seized upon and passed from one eager embrace to another, she flung off her headscarf and let her brightly hennaed reddish-black tresses cascade down her back. Tonight all the women were free to let down their hair. In their own homes, because Muslim modesty required that they cover up only when they were around non-family men, women were technically not obliged to wear headscarves. But here in Lebanon, because there was such constant visiting from friends and neighbours in every open house, it was the Shia custom for women to keep their white scarves on from dawn to bedtime. Tonight, however, was an exception. Men were barred from the ladies' celebration, and so every hair on every woman's head had been washed and brushed until it glowed.

As Zainab ushered another young woman in the door, she pretended not to recognize her with those bright smears of cosmetics on her face. 'Yes? You have come for the party? Are you a friend of our bride?'

'But Zainab!' The teenager couldn't understand why her cousin was blocking her way. 'It's me, Halima! You know me. You see me every day.'

Zainab studied the anxious, upturned face as though still perplexed, but then she let out a squeal of recognition. 'Can this beautiful flower truly be our little Halima?'

The women guffawed at Zainab's good-natured teasing. But it was true that, dressed in bright colours, with their hair loose and cosmetics applied with a heavy hand, they all looked quite different tonight. Every face vibrated, like Halima's, with unaccustomed splashes of colour. A good village woman could, of course, slap on the make-up to her heart's content whenever she wanted to dazzle her husband behind the closed doors of their house. Except for segregated parties like this, however, no woman who valued her reputation went outside sporting so much as a shine of lipstick. But since the men were holding their own private wedding celebration at Ali's father's house tonight, the women had been free to pile on the kohl, eyeshadow, rouge and lipstick. Accordingly, they had rushed through their chores early in the afternoon so they could spend deliciously giggly hours primping in front of mirrors. Dusty boxes stashed deep inside trunks had been rooted out, and the squat pots and wandlike brushes that had tarted up generations of village women had been passed around and exclaimed upon and shared. There had been much surreptitious prancing from house to house, as women bartered flicks of iridescent gold eyeshadow for slides of thick black kohl. Happily the generations had settled down, then, to manufacture beauty of a certain sort. More often than not, however, as so often happens with women, amid the peals of laughter and the peaks of vanity, mothers and daughters and sisters and cousins had found themselves settling down to heart-to-hearts about love and men and marriage.

So it was that after such a satisfying afternoon, every guest – whether young or old, pretty or plain – sashayed into Fatima's house with the *élan* of Parisian models on a Rive Droite catwalk. Tonight they believed that each and every one of them was beautiful. They told one another they were far lovelier than the rich painted ladies some of them had seen on the boulevards of Beirut. They assured each other that if they wanted to, if it weren't that they were good Muslim women who would never display themselves for the titillation of men who weren't their husbands, they could show those shameless city women a thing or two. Suker girls – they all agreed – were the prettiest in all Lebanon, and everyone knew that Lebanese girls were the prettiest in all the world. Sisters stared in wonder at cousins who –

it was now revealed through the wonders of cosmetics – had startlingly beautiful dark eyes. Somaya looked like a film star, and Miriam looked like a famous singer.

But as soon as they came into the sitting room, they all sighed and caught their breaths. *El-arous* was the undisputed star of this show. The bride sat like a queen on a sort of makeshift elevated throne at the centre of the party.

Fatima looked like a queen as well. When she had set her heart on a Western-style wedding gown, her family had agreed that it would do no harm to depart from the old traditions. More and more village girls were choosing white gowns and veils rather than the customary vivid-hued flouncy dresses of the past. Some very prosperous families even went off to the capital to buy ready-made wedding gowns in the fancy shops around Bab Idris. Instead, Fatima had spent much of the last year sewing this dress from a pattern that was much like the gown the angelic blonde model wore in the glossy fashion magazine Anne had sent her from America. The white silk dress had a billowy full skirt, puffy long sleeves, a magnificent stand-up collar, and even a sweeping train.

Fatima tried to remember to act like a queen as well. She was supposed to follow the bridal custom by sitting in her place of honour as stiff and mute as a painted china doll on a shelf. But when she spotted a long-lost cousin who had come all the way down from Beirut, Fatima was so excited that she couldn't help waving. A favourite aunt who had finally succeeded in giving birth to a son after presenting her husband with eight daughters, deserved – after all – a proper kiss and hug and many congratulations. And when Fatima overheard one mother telling her little girl that yes, someday she, too, could be queen for a day like this, sentimental tears made the bride's eyes glisten.

As Um Ibrahim reached over and carefully blotted Fatima's tears with an embroidered handkerchief that had been in the family for generations, Fatima whispered, 'Do you remember, Ummie, when you said the same thing to me?' At that, her mother was overcome with emotion and started to cry. Fatima held Um Ibrahim and, as if it were yesterday instead of a good fifteen years ago, she remembered another wedding when she had gaped in wonder at a village girl transformed for a night into a fairy-tale princess. Someday, her mother had promised, on the happiest day of your life, you, too, will be as beautiful.

Fleetingly, as Fatima used the linen handkerchief to wipe away her mother's tears, she allowed herself to wonder if this really was the happiest day of her life. Of course she liked dressing up and feeling beautiful and pretending she was a princess. But she was afraid of what must surely come after. She sighed. It had been the same when Ali had first started walking with her in the olive groves. It had seemed odd and somehow dangerous to walk about like that, since in the village a man and a woman were never supposed to be alone. But, after all, she had tried to reassure herself, even though they were not yet living together they were legally and religiously married. It couldn't be dangerous to be alone with her husband. Yet the intimacy of merely walking beside him had frightened her. How, then, she wondered, could she endure what surely had to happen tonight? After Ali came to carry her off to their fine new house, she and he would finally be left utterly alone to do what married people were expected to do. Would she like it, or not? Would it feel wonderful, or would it hurt? *He would see her naked body, and she would see his.* She had a sudden desire to leap off her dais, scoot out of the door, and search for a cloistered spot where she could spend the rest of her life only in the company of women.

Instead she stayed where she was and forced her lips to smile as one of her mother's third cousins from the next village came over to show off her latest grandchild. But as Fatima cooed over the infant, she felt the hard fear that was knotted inside her begin to melt. Radiantly she smiled as she held the child in her arms. If Allah were kind to her, by this time next year she could have a baby of her own. For, walking and talking with Ali these last weeks, she had sometimes been overcome by tender feelings for her husband. More and more she had become convinced that there was a rightness to this marriage. She had written just those words to Anne last week, hoping that her old friend would come to her senses and start looking for a man like Ali. For everything that everyone had told her about him was true. Ali was gentle, kind and compassionate. Ali was patient. Ali was witty, and Ali was wise. She loved even his name. Imam Ali – peace be upon him! – had been the devoted husband of the Holy Prophet's favourite daughter. Sometimes she fancied that it was a special blessing from Allah that the two of them had inherited those beloved names. Ali and Fatima! In her classroom during one of those quiet moments when she set her students to work practising their writing, she had caught herself tracing their names in fancy scripts in the margins beside her lesson plans: 'Ali and Fatima'. Day after day, too, she had found herself proudly repeating Ali's exact words to her mother and sisters, and she had never been able to understand why they always smiled so indulgently at her and chucked her under the chin as if she was an adorable baby. It wasn't, she had insisted hotly in the first weeks of Ali's courtship, that she was falling in love with her husband. Anyone – themselves included – would have been entranced by Ali's honeyed words. She repeated his charming story of how, one sultry afternoon on the dusty plains of Iraq, the sweetest breeze had suddenly sprung up, the old *shaykhs* said, from nowhere. But Ali had sniffed the fragrant air and knowingly shaken his head. 'That wind comes from my Lebanon,' he had said as he had blown a homesick kiss to the land he had never stopped missing. Yet Zainab and Somaya had merely rolled their eyes as she enthused about how Ali had gone everywhere that it was necessary to go and done everything that it was desirable to do. He had made his pilgrimage to Mecca and prayed for all their souls as he circled the Kaaba. He had spent one holy Ramadan in Qom, and on the *Leilat al-Qadr*, the 'Night of Power', he had stayed up all night long salaaming to Allah. He had actually lived for three years in the shadow of Imam Ali's glorious tomb in Najaf. And each of the nine years that he had been away, he had spent the month of Muharram mourning dear Imam Hussein at Kerbala. He had moved her to tears as he told her how he had wept for their lost hero on Ashura. Shyly he had suggested then that, *inshallah*, they might name their first son 'Muhammad', another one 'Ali', a third 'Hussein'.

As Fatima sat in her bridal gown holding her cousin's baby, she thought what bliss it would be to have Ali's baby. Lately she had found herself getting dreamy-eyed every time she rocked her sister Somaya's infant in her arms. To achieve that supreme joy for herself, she would be willing to endure anything – even if she lost her nerve tonight and kept her eyes tight shut through the most mortifying parts of it.

Yet she considered the possibility, as the baby gurgled in her arms, that all of *that* might not be as bad as some of her married cousins had led her to believe. In these last weeks when she and Ali had walked together in the olive groves and she had sat listening to him read the Koran to her at her mother's house, increasingly she had found her attention wandering. Ali had such a seductive voice as he chanted the Koran. His lovely eyes glowed as he told her how he had felt when he prayed in Kerbala.

Could it be, she sometimes wondered, that this man was seducing her with the Koran and memories of mosques? As their courtship had progressed, she had found herself wishing Ali would talk to her less and touch her more. He had seen her every day for two weeks before he had ventured to kiss her for the first time on the lips. But since then he had slowly but surely grown bolder. His kisses under the olive trees had been sweeter than *baklawa*. And the way he had looked at her sometimes! But even more erotic than his kisses and his looks was how she had felt the first time she had taken her scarf off for him, when for once they were alone at her mother's house. That night he had at first been content with kissing her, but then he had begged her to show him her hair. At first she had coquettishly refused, for in a way a woman without her veil was stripped naked. But her mother and sisters and the mirror had always told her that her hair was her best feature. Every night for years she had brushed it for hundreds of strokes. Just as Ali had caught her in his spell by telling her about Kerbala, she had longed to weave a web of her own by showing him her hair. And, after all, she had reminded herself, he was her husband. He had every right to see her hair. Gracefully, then, she had finally allowed herself to be persuaded to take off her scarf. She remembered how her hands had trembled as she untied the knot under her chin, and how he had gazed adoringly at her, and what he had said: 'Ah, God is good to me.' He had reached over then and reverently kissed great handfuls of her hair and buried his face in it. As she had held him in her arms with his head on her breast, she had burned for her man.

Her cousin's baby started to cry, and, with a start, Fatima returned to the here and now. As she handed the baby back to its grandmother, she told herself that she had a lifetime to moon over Ali's every word and touch. But just now she meant to revel in her once-in-a-lifetime party. Yet another little girl was looking up at her in awe, and yet another mother was promising that one day she, too, would be this beautiful. Somebody's aunt was gushing that she had never seen a lovelier gown, and another cousin wanted to hear the story behind her veil.

Fatima lovingly fingered the priceless lace that fell in graceful folds below her shoulders. As splendid as her dress was, this exquisite ivory lace veil – the very one that Camilla had worn on her own wedding day – was the *pièce de résistance*. Her old friend had once told her that the veil had been in the Nazrani family for hundreds of years, and that some even said a French knight had brought the lace with him during the Crusades. But Fatima treasured this veil not so much as a relic from Europe's distant history but as the crown of her own glorious adolescence. For just as soon as she and Ali had set the date for this celebration, Fatima had sent a warm invitation to Camilla. Anne was still off in America and Leila in England. And so, from a desire to connect all her circles, Fatima had begged Camilla to come to her party. But along with her weepy regrets – she was very pregnant again, *peut-être* with twins this time, she wrote, fat as *une truie*, a sow, with ugly varicose veins, and, *hélas*, unable to travel – Camilla had also sent down her wedding present and the loan of this bridal veil. The eight crystal wineglasses had not been nearly as well-received as the veil, for not even the men in the family ever broke the Koranic rule and touched alcohol. They had even asked Ali if it was *halal* to drink water from a glass that had been made for forbidden wine. The lace veil, however, was the sensation of the wedding.

Fatima smiled as she overheard her sister Somaya proudly repeating the history of the borrowed veil to a cousin. No one much cared that the veil was six hundred years old. Everyone who could afford it liked to buy shining new things rather than recycle yellowed hand-me-downs. But one and all were impressed at this incontrovertible evidence of Fatima's connection to the rich and famous of the wider world. Some had heard tell of the Nazranis, and they whispered knowingly to the others that Fatima's friend had married into the richest Christian clan in northern Lebanon. But they were even more fascinated by Camilla's mother. Everyone had heard Nirvana sing on the radio, and more than one regretted that the great *chanteuse* herself wasn't here to make Fatima's wedding a village legend.

But all such chatter was hushed when the three musicians who had been hired from Sidon for the occasion finally struck up their opening notes. They had to hit their drums and blow their horns extra loud because – with their prying men's eyes – they were stationed out in the kitchen. If the musicians had set up in the sitting room, the women would have had to cover their hair, slip on their cloaks, and lower their eyes. Worst of all, none of them would have been able to dance.

But now, at the first tootle of the flute and the next beat of the drum, Fatima's sister Somaya stood and began shaking her hips and beckoning to her friends. From one end of the room to the other, she was joined by her dancing sisters and cousins. Grandmothers showed toddlers how to shimmy to the music. Willowy girls bumped and grinded to the ancient rhythm in their blood. Pregnant ladies almost lost their balance as they wiggled and wobbled to a sobbing old Arab love song. While ancient crones with ruined legs slapped their palms on old tin tambourines, their younger sisters whooped it up to music that had reverberated from the heart of these unchanging villages for most of forever.

All the while Fatima sat on the dais, watching and waiting for her moment to come. The music was rising to a crescendo when she stood up, carefully took off her veil, and shook out her black curls that tumbled below her waist.

At this signal the women broke out into high trilling *zaghareit* cries and made room for the bride at the centre of their bobbing throng. Fatima danced with her mother, with her sisters, with her youngest cousins. She held newborn infants in her arms and waltzed them off in a little lullaby of a dance. She put her arm around old widows and danced their cares away. When finally she had danced with all these women she loved, for a moment she seemed to collapse.

Fatima knelt panting alone, in the centre of the room, until every eye was upon her. And then, as though the unseen musicians had a second sense, the happy-go-lucky tempo of their music changed and began to throb with a pulsebeat of repressed passion.

Fatima knelt motionless for another instant, and then she slowly bowed her head and began to shake her long mane of hair like a pendulum in time to the music. The women settled down on the floor and began a rhythmic clapping. As the beat swelled stronger, she swayed and – still kneeling – began to toss her hair from side to side. Faster came the beat. Wilder tossed her hair. She swirled her body from side to side, at one with the sensual frenzy of the music. The women leaned forward, eyes agleam, and urged her on. 'Yes!' they cried. 'Oh, yes!' For sometimes it happened that a bride caught the primitive old fever just like this. Mostly the women were all tame now, but once long ago they had reigned in indomitable splendour. Even now there were passing moments like this, when history fell away and they were all stirred by the dim memory of a time before men had become their masters. Fatima had never moved her body quite like this before, and she never would again. But here, now, for one transcendent moment, the music took her over and it was as though she had become the reincarnation of some eternal woman's spirit that still lurked in the groves atop these ancient Levantine mountains. For long ago – before Ibrahim, before Christ, before Muhammad – the female fertility goddess Astarte had been worshipped here. Like Astarte, Fatima danced with pagan abandon. Tonight she would have her first man! Tonight there would be sweat, and fire, and blood! She thrust her pelvis as triumphantly as the insatiable Astarte.

But after so many millennia of male supremacy, the spirit of that time long lost had become too frail and ephemeral. As the melody grew harsh and heavy and then began to moan more with pain than pleasure, the rampant power of Astarte seemed to falter and then dissolve, vanquished, into thin air. Fatima, too, began to respond to the sickening oppression of the music. She drooped as wearily as though she carried the weight of thousands of years of female subjugation. As the music whined into the deepest octaves, Fatima sank lower and lower until she slithered like a serpent on the floor. Her body hissed from side to side, ticking off women's woes. Wombs that were too empty and wombs that were too full. No children or too many. Spinsterhood and polygamy. Barrenness and divorce. Men who betrayed them and men who beat them. Husbands and fathers. Brothers and sons.

At last, then, as the music began to crawl back up the scale from the universal depths of women's shared tragedies, Fatima – still tossing her hair back and forth, back and forth – started to inch up from the floor. Until now, as she had danced out everywoman's glorious past and painful present, her movements had been sure and confident. But now, as for the first time she began to act out her own individual rite of passage, every nervous flick of her body became uncertain. She jerked from side to side like a puppet on a string. Soon her husband would come to claim her from the women. Tonight she would be a maiden no longer. She shivered from side to side. Gradually, however, in time to the music, her pendulum swings became more fluid as she used her body to wave a sad farewell to youth. Finally, as the tempo and melody swelled with hope, Fatima, too, seemed to take heart. Childhood was over, but womanhood was beginning. All was not lost. Something – maybe everything? – was about to be won. When finally she threw back her head and knelt motionless as a statue, there was an expectancy about her, and a waiting.

All the women clapped.

But suddenly an insistent knocking at the door shattered this intense mood of female communion.

'Wait! Not yet!' The sixty or so women who were packed into the sitting room squealed and searched in a panic for the scarves and cloaks they had merrily tossed aside at the door. But now Ali and his menfolk were about to burst in, and the women had to be respectably covered. As old and young pawed through piles of identical clothing frantically trying to find their own scarves and cloaks, Fatima brushed out her hair, threw on her veil and climbed back on to her dais. Meanwhile, all around her, the women's confusion continued. Black *abayas* were hastily draped over technicolour dresses. Rippling tresses were subdued by thick white scarves. Yet even now, though they were modestly covered, the women's faces continued to glow with excitement.

After more insistent male knocking, and more giggly female procrastination, Ali finally swept into the sitting room in the company of his father and brothers, Fatima's brothers, and his cousin who owned the most expensive camera in the village. Conscious of the effect they were making, the brothers and cousins joked and preened and postured.

But Ali had eyes only for his bride. He took a long step towards winning her for ever as he stood, resplendent in his best brown cloak and white turban, gazing up at her in a sort of reverent rapture. The women tittered and hid their mouths as he asked his cousin to take a picture of her, sitting just so, like the queen of his heart. He looked as though he might have liked to say more, but just then Zainab brought in the cakes, Um Ibrahim began pouring out the tea, and Somaya began passing around the sugared Jordan almonds that assured good luck for every bride and groom. '*Inshallah btithannou*,' they all chorused. 'May your life be happy, God willing.'

As the women sipped and munched, the long-drawn-out business of recording the party began. The photographer ordered Ali to sit up beside Fatima – shyly he smiled and even more shyly she blushed as he took her hand – and then one by one every guest was photographed flanking the bride and the groom. Ali and Fatima smiled continuously for the camera, until finally the marathon picture session was over and it was time to go off on their own.

Without further ado, Ali linked arms with Fatima. Their brothers and sisters all but swept them off their feet and out of the door where a fine Arabian horse waited to carry Fatima down the path to the house Ali had renovated for his bride. As was the custom, the men had decorated the saddle with silver beads and silk cushions. The bridle was a riot of red, purple and green ribbons. Ali swung her up in the saddle, and the bridal procession proceeded. The men were in the lead, laughing, shouting and exuberantly shooting off their rifles as the Arabs always do to celebrate a great event. The women danced behind, laughing and joking, and at the end of the rollicking parade the musicians played a wedding march. Fatima was still laughing at one of her brother's catcalls when she approached the threshold of her married life.

Her mother-in-law – dear Aunt Zahra! – was just inside to welcome her to wifehood. Already the old woman had burned a tray of incense to ensure that the house would always be fragrant, pure and happy. And she had fastened a cake of yeast above the door so that Fatima and Ali's life would be as abundant and overflowing as yeast makes bread.

Her friends showered the bride with rice, flowers and the essence of orange blossoms.

But then Ali, who until now had been so shy with her, suddenly showed a more masterful side that took her breath away.

Before any of the brothers or cousins could launch into another series of pranks, he led his wife over the threshold and kissed his mother goodbye. Finally he shut the door firmly on the outside world, lit a lantern that shed a radiant light like that in his eyes, and turned to her to begin their new life together.

She wasn't frightened at all as he took her in his arms and kissed her. For Fatima was one of the lucky ones who was about to get her reward for following all the religious rules and village traditions. Her family and her religion had always told her that this was how it was supposed to be. And so, for her, as her husband for the first time lay beside her, never had anything felt so right, and so good.

As the night wore on, it felt even better.

Chapter 10

Mike let himself into their borrowed Fenway apartment so stealthily that out in the kitchen she didn't even hear his key in the lock. He set the wine bottle and the pizza box down on the hall table and tiptoed up behind her. Anne very nearly screamed when she felt arms around her waist and lips at her neck, and for one frightened instant she raised the knife she was cutting salad with and almost wheeled around to confront the intruder. But then he whispered in her ear, 'Surprise!' She dropped the knife and turned and threw her arms around his neck. 'You're early!' She kissed him deep and long, the way she knew he liked it, writhing her body against his, until he groaned and staggered back against the refrigerator. 'Christ, kid, you learn fast.'

'Not so fast. It's been exactly', she paused and only had to think a second, 'two months and three days since that first night on Nantucket. That's sixty-four happy days.' She gave him a sidelong glance and another of those kisses he loved. 'And nights.' He tried to pin her down against the kitchen cabinets, but she was too quick for him. He had taught her not only how to kiss but how to tease. She grinned as she sashayed out of his reach and back to her cutting board.

'Come here,' he growled. As always when he wanted her, his eyelids drooped half-shut and his body took on a predatory crouch. His eyes travelled in slow, hot appreciation up and down the boldly accentuated curves of her thighs, buttocks and breasts. At least when she came to meet him, she had stopped wearing those colourless upper-class twinsets and baggy pleated skirts he had always loathed. He took possessive pride in having transformed her from an ice princess into his very own erotic vision. She was dressed now exactly as he had told her he liked to see her, in rickety red high heel shoes and tight black toreador pants and a thin scarlet sweater that clung to the points of her heavily padded brassière. She had come a long way in these past torrid months. He savoured how he had led her every delicious step of that way, bit by bit, touch by touch, unlocking every last one of her inhibitions. She was altogether his now.

And yet, at least this time, she did not come when he called her. 'Not now, sweetheart.' She turned her back on him and picked up where she had left off with her salad.

Impatiently he watched her toss the shallots into a

wooden bowl with the lettuce and the cucumbers and then wash off the tomatoes and begin slicing them. He hadn't dashed across the city at rush hour, packed in the sweaty crush of a trolleycar, to come here to watch her cut up vegetables. He wanted to touch her all over. 'I said to come here.'

'Sure,' she said absently, without even looking up, as she concentrated on mixing exactly the right proportions of olive oil and wine vinegar for the dressing. 'In a minute.' These days she was surer not only of herself but of him. Since Nantucket, he had finally begun to treat her the way a man was supposed to treat a woman. He never kept her waiting anymore. He made seeing her his top priority, and he had stopped making excuses about how they had to fit their lovelife around his rigid hospital schedule. Two or three times a week they met here at his friend's apartment, and he slavishly telephoned her at least once every day they spent apart. It no longer bothered her that they never went out, that they spent most of their time together in bed, and that she still hadn't let even Ramsey really get to know him. There was plenty of time for all that in the future. But for now, here in this snug one-bedroom world of theirs, she was happier than she had ever been in her life. Mike was ardent, tender and devoted – everything she had always dreamed the man she loved would be. He was going to make her a wonderful husband. She was sure, too, that she was going to make him a wonderful wife. With a bit of practice, she was even going to be able to work wonders in the kitchen. She stated the obvious. 'I'm cooking.'

'*You?*' He frowned. 'You can't cook.'

She waved towards the tomato sauce bubbling on the stove, the parmesan cheese freshly grated into a bowl, the vegetables she was cutting for the salad. She had memorized the spaghetti recipe from a cookbook last night so it would look as though she was making this dish not for the first time but the hundredth. 'All I have to do is cook the paste, and – presto! – spaghetti just like Mama used to make.'

'I see.' He went out to the hallway, fetched his bottle of Chianti, and decided this was not the most diplomatic moment to surprise her with the pizza he had bought them. He uncorked the wine and took a swig from the bottle before he poured their glasses. 'You're getting awfully domestic.'

The way he said it, it sounded like a criticism. But she chose to ignore that as she put the salted water on to boil and stirred the sauce. These days she knew more about handling men in general and him in particular. Another kiss or two, an hour or so in bed, and he would be lapping up her spaghetti or anything else she chose to serve him. Meanwhile, she was not about to provoke an argument. 'Want a taste?' She offered him a spoonful.

He licked a tiny bit and made a face. 'It needs more oregano. A little more salt. And a lot more garlic.' Thoughtfully he swallowed the rest of the spoonful. 'I suppose it's edible.' He drank his whole glass of wine at one gulp, as though he were washing down bad-tasting medicine. 'But it's not at all like my mother used to make. Mom's spaghetti sauce was terrific. You'll never be able to make spaghetti like hers.'

'Oh.' She had thought it tasted just fine, but obligingly she sprinkled in more oregano and salt and minced four more cloves of garlic and added them to the sauce. 'Now try it.'

'Naw.' He put his arms around her and let his hands roam all over her body before he untied her apron. 'If you want to play house with me, little girl, why not get right down to the fun part?' He turned off the gas burners, grabbed the glasses and the wine, and steered her out of the kitchen. 'I bought us a pizza for later.'

'Pizza?' Anne glared at the flat white box that they passed in the hallway on the way to the bedroom. 'But what about what I cooked?' Wisely, she bit her tongue just as she was about to tell him how much trouble she had gone to for his spaghetti. As he would be sure to tell her, it had been her idea, not his, to cut her bacteriology class to shop for the food. Fair was fair, she reminded herself. It wasn't his fault that, long before she had understood everything she was supposed to about the chemistry of blood, she had shut her books and run out of the library to come here and cook. She had hoped that he would be delighted by the surprise she had waiting for him in the kitchen. He was Italian, and so, she had reasoned, what better way to get him to start thinking of her in practical terms as his wife-to-be than by serving him up perfect spaghetti? But obviously she should have stuck to pleasing him in the way that always worked.

'We'll leave your spaghetti in the kitchen for Fred.' They were always trying to think of small ways to please Mike's obliging friend who paid the rent and usually occupied this apartment. 'Fred will eat anything.'

Anne decided to let that remark pass, and she followed him down the hall without another word of protest. They would spend the evening exactly as they spent every other night together, in bed. She might have just lost her gamble in the kitchen, but she didn't intend to lose this next hand in the bedroom.

Yet even as they got down to it, her mind was still on that unfinished business in the kitchen. Perhaps, she thought, as Mike unhooked her bra, it had been a tactical blunder to try to use spaghetti as a means of impressing him with her culinary abilities. The next time, she decided, as he began kissing her breasts, she might try something non-Italian like, say, chili. As he pulled down her knickers, she considered serving something all-American like pot roast with mashed potatoes and apple pie. Or perhaps, she thought, more imaginatively as he left her alone for a moment while he took off his own clothes, she could, since all was fair in love and war, even get Aunt Bert's cook to make her one of her special lemon meringue pies which she could try to pass off as her own.

But finally, as his naked flesh touched hers, she forgot all about future plans for the kitchen and abandoned herself to the here and now in the bedroom. The touch of him shut off her mind as if he were flicking out a light. In that electric darkness, the whole world shrank to their bed.

He stood tantalizing inches away from her, then took her in his arms and stared fiercely into her eyes. She met him stare for stare, for she was used to him now and had stopped pretending to be shy. She knew what he liked and what she liked, too. Among other things, they liked to drag it out for as long and as high as they could, and then still longer and higher.

He kissed her deep and hard, and then kissed her even deeper and harder. He kissed her as if he was starving and her lips were the only food on earth. He devoured her lips and then her neck. He made her squirm in his arms. He bent her back until her knees and all the rest of her gave way, and she fell on to the bed. She gasped and arched her back and waited . . .

But all that happened was that he laughed a low hoarse laugh. 'So I have your undivided attention now, do I?'

He loomed above her for an infinitely long moment, not touching her, just looking her over and letting the tension build until she ached for him as much as she could see that he wanted her. When finally she couldn't stand it a second longer and reached for him, he snaked away from her on the sheets and paid her back for making him wait in the kitchen. 'Not just yet, sweetheart.'

She was fully roused now, and so she glared at him. If she could have laid hands on him, she didn't know whether she would kiss him or strike him, or maybe both. Sometimes she hated him more than she loved him, or at least as passionately. She would scream soon if she couldn't get to him. He liked it when she screamed, and when she sank her teeth into his flesh.

He came closer to her and wrestled against her for one hot clinging moment, but then he pinned both her hands above her head on the pillow. At first when he held her in place like that, it was to keep her at arm's length away from him as he did what he liked with her. He touched only the very tips of her nipples first with the smooth edge of his fingernails and then with his tongue until she shuddered and shut her eyes. 'What is it you want, baby?' His voice was husky.

She opened her eyes and stared up at him as though she had never seen him before. This time she couldn't, or wouldn't, tell him she wanted him. She was tired of his teasing, and a little bit scared of how much it excited her for him to be holding her down – sort of, but not really, she told herself – against her will. 'That's enough,' she said and tried to smile and wriggle out of his grasp. But she couldn't move. She started to panic. He was holding her down. She couldn't get away from him. He was bigger than she was. He could hurt her if he wanted to. Suddenly she didn't like this game anymore. He had finally gone too far. She tried to recoil from him then, but he held her taut against the pillow.

'Higher, baby,' he whispered. His eyes glittered in the semi-darkness of the room as he studied the tremble of her body. 'Trust me. I'm about to take you higher.'

Dimly, as though she were very far away and not spread out right in front of him, she heard his voice. She didn't trust him – not at all! – but he knew her body better than she knew it herself. Her flesh belonged to him. Even though the rest of her wanted to get away from this man who was making her feel things she didn't want to feel, her nipples seemed to have developed a will of their own. He tongued them to sharp fierce points.

Frantically she twisted on the bed, trying to get away

from him. Yet there was no escape. Still he slid his tongue around the points of her nipples. He bit them, he sucked them, he took his time and dragged it out for as long as he could, and then even longer. She quivered then, and sighed, and stopped struggling as something seemed almost to break inside her.

'Yes,' he said, as she began writhing with a new movement on the bed. 'Yes, that's it.' He raised his head from her breasts and his lips smiled at her while she begged him for more with her eyes. 'Tell me what you want. Tell me!'

'You, you . . .' Her voice was low and deep and seemed to come not from her throat but from the deepest and hottest recesses of her body. 'I want you.'

Finally, without any more warning, he arched high above and came down hard inside her. 'Yes!' she cried out and opened her eyes and all but hissed at him as she twisted her long legs around his buttocks. Her body jerked in convulsions, and he held on to her as she came even before he was ready.

She would have liked it to be over there and then and to snuggle up and fall asleep close to him, but he had only just begun. He moved inside her – slow and deep, slower and deeper – until she picked up his rhythm. He reached down and tenderly smoothed back damp tendrils of her hair from her face. 'I love you,' he said.

After a while he rolled her over and she rubbed herself the length of him. She was on top and they both were laughing as they played at love. She leaned low enough for him to put her breasts in his mouth, one after the other.

Again, suddenly, their mood shifted, and they were sweating instead of laughing as she rode him harder and harder, faster and faster. Finally then, with one great heaving thrust and sigh, he came and was still.

Afterwards, as they lay exhausted in each other's

arms, she was drifting off and almost asleep when she heard him say, in a faraway voice, 'This just gets better and better.' She thought he might want her again, so she yawned and ran her fingers down his chest and lower than his stomach.

But he closed his hand over her dancing fingers. 'No, sweetheart, that's enough.' He rolled over on his side and smiled as he stroked her hair back from where it had tumbled over her face. 'You've come a long way, you know. I can hardly believe you're the same cool little virgin I met last year in the pub.' He shook his head. 'You're some woman now. Tonight, when I was holding you down . . . phew!'

She blushed and was too embarrassed to look him in the eye. When she was lost in the sexual thraldom in which he held her, there was nothing she would not do for him. But now that it was over, and they had left that magical blurry world behind, her old inhibitions were back again. She wrapped a sheet modestly around herself.

He laughed. 'One moment you're a tiger, and the next minute you blush. You're perfect. Absolutely perfect.' His eyes were very bright. 'I wish, Annie, I . . .' He almost said something, then he hesitated and frowned.

'Yes?' She was alert now and altogether awake. She sensed that he might be on the brink of saying something important. Closely she studied his face. Just a second ago she had thought she had seen the shine of tears in his eyes.

'Nothing.' Absently he fished inside her sheet and pulled out one of her full breasts.

'Tell me.' She ignored his roving hands. But even as she pressed him to say whatever he had almost said, she decided she must have been mistaken about his eyes. Why would he be moved to tears?

He watched her one nipple get hard and then played with the other until it, too, was hard and taut. 'What a body,' he said to himself. 'I can't keep my hands off her body.'

'Mike?' She inched slightly behind his reach, for she knew how volatile their flesh was. If she let him touch her much longer, they would be off and running again. Usually she was eager for more loving, but this time she was on the scent of something even more heady. 'What did you almost say before?'

'Nothing.' He reached for her breasts again, but she rolled over on her stomach.

'Mike! Say it! Say whatever you were about to say.'

'How do you know it wasn't goodbye?'

She laughed as though she had not heard the warning in his little light joke. Nothing was going to stop her from nagging him until he told her what she wanted to hear. 'Tell me what you *really* were going to say.'

Reluctantly, then, his eyes locked on to hers, and it seemed to her that there was not only longing but also great sadness in his eyes. He shook his head and seemed about to say what was on the tip of his tongue. But then he shook his head again as though arguing with himself. Finally he seemed to come to a decision. He took a deep breath, and when he spoke his voice was gruff. 'I want to marry you, Annie.'

She took a sharp intake of breath. 'You do?'

'I do.' Now that he had finally said it, other words, promises, dreams that he had long repressed seemed to tumble out of his mouth. 'I want to marry you. I want you to be the mother of my children. I want to build you a house, our house, and live with you for ever and never stop touching you. I want to go to bed with you every night and wake up beside you every morning. That's the truth, Annie. That's the God's honest truth.' He took a deep breath and looked adoringly at her. Usually he tended to be critical about everything except her body, but now the compliments gushed out in a rush. 'God, you're the most wonderful woman I've ever met. You're beautiful, so beautiful. You could be a movie star, you're so beautiful. And you're smart, I never can get over just how smart you are. Second year med school, and already you know more than half the interns on my floor. But what kills me is how classy you are. The classiest girl who's ever looked at me. I'm always asking myself what someone like you could ever see in somebody like me. You're the best thing that's ever happened to me, Anne Rosen.' He nodded as though agreeing with himself, and then he looked earnestly into her eyes. 'Will you marry me, Annie?'

'Yes!' She laughed. 'Oh, yes, yes, yes!' She threw herself back in his arms and showered him with kisses.

'And Annie?' He drew away, grinned down at her, and made one final admission. 'Your tomato sauce was almost as good as my mother's.'

They both laughed, and he kissed her again, and they rocked happily in each other's arms.

But then, even as they continued laughing and kissing and hugging, everything began to change for Anne as the realities of her great victory began to sink in. The rest of the world, which she had been holding at bay ever since she fell in love with Mike, suddenly began to tilt back sharply into focus.

Now that they were engaged, she realized as she absently let her fiancé kiss her, everything was different. Mike would have to meet everyone now. First she would bring Ramsey around, and then she would have him over to Aunt Bert's for dinner. Her parents would be arriving next month for Christmas. They could have the engagement party then, and maybe get married in the spring. June weddings were a cliché, so why not get married in May?

Thoughtfully she stared over his shoulder at the wilted rosebud wallpaper in Fred's bedroom. She longed to spring out of bed and begin making lists of all the wonderful things she had to do between now and May.

She had been weaving such intricate dreams about this for so long that she knew exactly how she wanted everything to be. She would be through with her spring classes by then, and surely Mike could get some time off from the hospital. He didn't have much family left, so she didn't think he would mind having the wedding back in Beirut. It would be a relatively small affair, very tasteful, maybe with just champagne and wedding cake. They could have the ceremony outside in their garden at the Rue Bliss. She would insist that Fatima, Camilla and Leila were her bridesmaids. Somehow she would work around the fact that everyone, including Mike and herself, belonged to different religions. God, she hoped he wouldn't expect her to turn Catholic! She skidded away from that alarming possibility and returned to the great day itself. The bridesmaids would all wear lilac, perhaps long dresses cut along empire lines. They could all wear flowers in their hair. And as for the bridal gown itself, Anne had already ferreted out her mother's wedding dress folded in tissue paper in an old trunk in Aunt Bert's attic. Her seamstress in Beirut could nip it in here and tuck it in there, and perhaps update it with a few modern touches. Of course she would wear white, even though she was not quite entitled to it anymore. But at least she wasn't pregnant. Thank God the two of them were more careful than Camilla and Pierre had been. That first weekend they had been reckless, but since then she had been using a diaphragm. She kept it in there most of the time.

As Mike's hands began to roam more insistently over her body, Anne's thoughts became more scattered. Camilla had been such a beautiful bride. Anne remembered her coming down the aisle and standing up by the altar. Oddly, she could almost hear those shots being fired and see Camilla screaming about the blood. With a small but insistent shiver of fear, she remembered something else then, Madame Kismet and that silly fortune-telling back at the Crescent. Well, she might have been right about the blood in Camilla's future, but the old gypsy had been wrong about her own fate. She wasn't going to be betrayed. Not her. Never her.

'What's wrong, honey?' Mike had stopped kissing her and was quizzically studying her face.

'Nothing.' She banished that silly quiver of fear. She, and he, were the masters of their own destiny. They were in love, they were engaged to be married, and they were going to live happily ever after. She threw her arms around Mike and gave her full attention to making him the happiest man on earth. 'Everything's right!'

Just before midnight two nights after New Year's Eve, Anne squinted at her watch in the dim but elegant silvery light of the Merry-Go-Round nightclub at the Copley Plaza. 'I'm sure he's coming,' she assured her parents, her aunt and Ramsey. Her brother Ben had been invited along, too, but instead he had gone off to the movies in Harvard Square. Yet she wasn't sure, as she looked around the nearly empty club, that Mike was going to take this very last chance to meet her mother and father. All through the holiday season, it had been one ruined plan after another every time she had tried to get Mike and her parents together.

'I'd hate to have to leave tomorrow without getting a look at this fellow,' Anne's father said. They were flying down to New York in the afternoon so they could catch the night flight to Beirut. But for Anne's sake, he tried to keep the impatience out of his voice. 'It's not every day we get introduced to the man our only daughter says she's going to marry, is it, Martha?'

'Then he'd better hurry up,' Anne's mother snapped. She was tired of waiting for someone who, it seemed to her, was deliberately avoiding them. She had already talked the situation over in private with her sister, and she didn't like what Bert had said about this Italian boyfriend. It sounded as if Anne would be making a dreadful mistake in marrying this fellow. She herself had chosen a man whom her family had considered her social inferior, and she did not regret that decision. Yet, considering what both she and Joe had gone through to be together, she would have liked Anne to tread an easier path.

'I think it's a crime,' Bert fumed, 'making us sit here and wait like this. Mind you, he did the same thing when finally – after begging off I don't know how many invitations to tea and lunch and supper – he showed up in the middle of one of my dinner parties. By the time he got there, the rest of us were already eating dessert. I don't mind telling you, I had a fit about it.' Her thin lips narrowed to an even thinner line as she caught her sister's eye. 'We were brought up to believe that it is unpardonably rude to make a habit of being late.'

'But the night is young, Auntie Bert.' Ramsey, who was determined not to let Anne down in her hour of need, signalled the waiter to bring them another bottle of champagne. 'I dare say Mike would be here now if he could,' he continued very smoothly, as though he and Mike were the best of pals instead of virtual strangers. Except for a rushed drink or two at Cambridge bars, he had hardly met this elusive fellow who was supposed to marry Anne in a matter of months. Yet he was embarrassed for Anne, and so he made excuses for her man. 'Perhaps there's an emergency at the hospital. An accident. A fire. Or it could be that one of the other doctors fell ill . . .'

Anne's father shook his head. 'There can't be an emergency there every night.' He looked at his watch and whistled. 'Look, honey, much as I want to meet your young man, I agree with your mother and – for once – your aunt. This really is a bit much. It's late, we're all tired, and we have to face the fact that he's not showing up.'

'Oh, Daddy.' She gave Ramsey a grateful look as the waiter arrived with another bottle of champagne, popped the cork with a flourish, and poured them all frothy glasses. She seized the extra time this ritual gave her to go over it all again for her doubting family. 'He wanted to spend Christmas with us. Really he did! He really wanted to have the chance to meet you all and get to know you before the wedding. But first he had to work those double shifts, and then he had to go to his sister's in Buffalo to help take care of his nieces and nephews while her husband was away on business and she was in the hospital having the new baby. But he called, you know. He called every day. I passed the phone to you lots of times. And he sounded nice, didn't he? You even said how nice he sounded.' Her anxious eyes trailed back to the nightclub door. 'I'm sure he'll be along any minute. I know he'd hate to have you leave tomorrow without seeing you. But of course he'll see you in Beirut. In May. For the wedding.'

'Of course he will, darling!' But Ramsey didn't think he could endure sitting at this nervous little gathering with Anne and her family for one moment longer. 'Shall I ring the hospital and see what's wrong?'

Just then Anne pointed. 'There he is!' She shot across the floor, threw her arms around him, whispered in his ear, and then triumphantly returned with her fiancé in tow. Her face was radiant. 'Mother, Daddy . . .' She paused dramatically, savouring this proud moment. In his best pinstriped suit, her lover was so tall and handsome and serious-looking that surely her parents would adore him at first sight. 'This is Mike!'

'Professor Rosen,' he said, as he shook hands firmly with her father, 'it's a very great pleasure, sir!' Then he took both of her mother's hands warmly in his. 'And you, Mrs Rosen. Yes, I see where Annie gets her looks.'

Mike nodded his head warily to Anne's plain-speaking aunt, who had made no secret of what she thought of the likes of him. Then he slapped Ramsey on his back as though they were in the locker room at half time of the big game. As he sat down, he pulled his chair touchingly close to Anne's. 'Sorry I'm so late. There was quite some accident – a multiple fatality – on Storrow Drive, and I had to go down and help them out in Emergency. We're on short staff this week anyway, for the holidays.'

'Didn't I tell you it was something like that?' Ramsey beamed as he called for another bottle of champagne, and the waiter poured Mike's glass and topped up everyone else's. 'To the happy couple,' Ramsey toasted. Everyone except the glowering Bert drank and smiled.

As Mike went out of his way to be charming, the tension at the table finally began to evaporate. Mike was so courtly to Anne's mother that soon she was all but batting her eyelashes at him. He went a long way towards winning over Anne's father when, in a respectful man-to-man undertone, he said they would have to talk over his prospects at a more suitable time and place. Mike apologized profusely for not having been able to spend more time with them during their visit, and he promised to make that up to them when he brought Anne back to Beirut in the spring for the wedding. As Mike and Anne held hands, the whole family debated the relative merits of setting the date for the second or third Saturday in May. So Anne would have more time to prepare for the wedding after her spring examinations, they finally agreed on the twenty-fourth. Anne confided that they weren't sure whether they would economize on the honeymoon by borrowing someone's villa in the Lebanese mountains or splash out on a cruise to the Greek islands. Until he finished his residency and got a paid staff position somewhere, Mike said, they would have to live on a shoestring.

When the band struck up an old Glenn Miller favourite, Mike led Anne's mother out on the floor. As Anne danced nearby with her father, she couldn't help trying to eavesdrop on her mother and her fiancé who were laughing and talking like old friends. She had just plucked up courage to ask her father what he thought of the man she was going to marry, when the band swung into another number and Mike cut in. Without a backward glance at her father, Anne glided away in her lover's arms.

Anne's parents watched the two young people gaze adoringly into each other's eyes as Mike spun Anne expertly around the dance floor. They moved with fluid grace and in perfect harmony, as if they were not two people but one.

'They make quite a couple,' Martha said. 'She told me he was handsome. But I had no idea he'd be . . . like he is.'

'If I didn't know better,' her husband teased, 'I'd say you fancied that young man yourself.'

'Joe!' She laughed. But as she watched the young couple who were visibly so very much in love, she felt suddenly old. It didn't feel so long ago that her husband had first looked at her the way Mike was gazing at Anne. But it was more than twenty years now since the two of them had fallen desperately in love. She envied Anne not her lover but her youth. 'Oh, Joe, do you remember when it was like that for *us*?'

Absently, as he continued sorting out his first impressions of Anne's boyfriend, he kissed his wife on the cheek. 'How could I forget?' But he was more intent on his present responsibility as father of the bride rather than his past role as the eager bridegroom. He narrowed his eyes as he danced his wife around the floor. 'I like him, Martha,' he pronounced finally. 'Yes,' he repeated more firmly as he banished his last reservations, 'I like him very much.' He elaborated. 'I don't mind telling you that I was beginning to have my doubts about him. But he seems like a nice fellow after all. He's serious, responsible, and he must be at the top of his field or he wouldn't have an internship at Mass General. But what really matters is that he's crazy about our little girl. It's eased my mind that we did get to meet him. Poor guy, being a doctor over the holidays can't be the easiest thing.' He was silent for a moment as they dipped and swayed and twirled around the dance floor. 'Wouldn't it be great if Anne talks him into practising back in Beirut? What's the old cliché? We wouldn't be losing a daughter. We'd be gaining another son.' The two of them laughed.

Meanwhile, while Ramsey was off settling the check, Bert seethed alone at their table. She couldn't decide which misguided member of her family infuriated her the most. There was no reasoning with Anne, of course, while she was so starry-eyed. But she was incensed with her giddy middle-aged sister for succumbing to that Italian fortune-hunter's swarthy charms.

Sourly Bert sipped the dregs of her champagne as she watched Martha and Joe laugh and prance about on the dance floor like a couple half their age. She supposed it was expecting too much for Martha to see through Anne's young man. After all these years, her sister still refused to see through her low-born Jewish husband. One of the most regrettable chapters in her family's history would be repeating itself if Anne – just like her mother – married beneath her.

Bert's attention shifted to her old enemy. Tonight even Joe had disappointed her. Yet she had hoped that, just this once, the two of them might have worked together to sabotage this *mésalliance*. Anne still had the potential – despite the handicap of her Jewish father – to make a dazzling marriage someday. Because of Joe, she might never be able to marry into Boston's foremost families. The Cabots and the Lodges would look down their noses at a Rosen. But Anne had the Wentworth blood, too. If she played her cards right, her niece could still end up living in a red-brick Georgian townhouse on Louisburg Square.

Bert's eyes flicked, with distaste, over to the interloper who was holding her niece far too close to him. How could she let someone like that touch her? He looked like a gangster. His family was probably in the Mafia. Anne had told her that his mother had been Irish. What a combination! Even before she had met him, she had disliked the way he sounded on the telephone. As she watched him lean over and kiss Anne passionately on the lips right in front of everyone, she came to a snap decision. First thing Monday morning, she would set a private investigator on to Anne's boyfriend.

She was so pleased with her plan that, when Ramsey returned to the table, she even graciously allowed him to lead her a turn or two around the dance floor.

Bert put on her reading glasses and flipped open the private investigator's four-page report. She read silently and, except for one sharp intake of breath at the beginning of the document, she did not react until she had finished the whole thing. Then she took off her glasses, shut them away in their case, and clicked shut her purse. 'You're sure about this?' she asked the man she had hired two weeks ago to investigate Michael Patrick Spagnolli. When he nodded, tersely she told him to send the bill to her Brattle Street address. Without another word, she walked very slowly out of the office as she wondered how she was going to break this news to her niece.

She still wasn't sure how to do it after dinner, when she and Anne were sitting in front of the crackling fireplace in the parlour. Bert poured them both stiff tots of brandy. As she drank hers, she almost wished she had never hired that investigator. Anne would have found out the truth some time. Why did she have to be the one who did the dirty work? Bert sighed. She seldom postponed even the most difficult of tasks, yet this afternoon she had caught herself hoping that Anne wouldn't come home for dinner tonight. Nevertheless, here they both were. Try as she might, she had not been able to think of a kind way to deliver such a blow. Yet someone had to tell her. Bert steeled herself to begin. 'Drink your brandy, child. I'm afraid you're going to need it. I have some very bad news for you.'

'Yes?' Anne looked dreamily up from the fire, where she had just been debating the relative delights of honeymooning on a Greek island or a Lebanese mountaintop.

'It's about your young man.' Bert put down her brandy snifter and leaned over and picked up the typed report she had waiting on a mahogany side-table. 'As you know, I had some very serious reservations about the sort of fellow he was.' She held up her hand to forestall Anne from speaking. 'Wait. Hear me out. I had my . . . suspicions. And so, thinking only of your best interests, I made some discreet inquiries through a firm recommended very highly by my lawyer. A private investigator on State Street. I got this report back today.'

'You had my fiancé *investigated*?' There were two angry red blotches on Anne's pale cheeks. 'How dare you?' She stood up as though she was about to storm out of the parlour. 'I won't listen to this. In fact, I won't even stay under your roof another moment. You—'

'He's married, Anne. He's married, and he has three children. He's been married for eight years. He lives in Medford with his wife, his two little girls, and his little boy.' She paused to let all that sink in, and then she repeated the most important bulletin. 'Mike is married.'

'What! That can't be! You're making that all up because you don't want me to marry him!'

'I wish that's all it were, child. I wish none of this were true.' Bert held the report out to her niece. 'But it's all here. Names, dates, places. If you don't believe me, sit down and read this.'

Anne sank back down, opened the report, and – after giving her aunt one terrible stricken look – she bowed her head and read the four typewritten pages without stopping. Then she drained her brandy in one gulp and stared at the fire for a long speechless moment. Finally she shook her head, and oblivious of her aunt's presence, took the report and walked over to the telephone in the hall. First she called the hospital, where Mike had told her he was on duty tonight. But even though she had him paged, he was not there. It occurred to her that it was very rare for her to be calling him. He always called her every day, sometimes two or three times.

Anne chewed her lip, and then flipped open the private investigator's report. She found the reference to what was supposed to be Mike's home telephone number in Medford. Slowly she dialled it. A little girl answered. Anne's voice caught as she asked to speak to her Daddy. Instead, after a pause, a woman came on the other end of the line. 'Yes?'

From somewhere – she never knew where – Anne found not only her voice but her poise and a renewed confidence that all of this had to be a terrible misunderstanding. Obviously this wasn't Mike's home telephone number. That hadn't been his daughter, and this wasn't his wife. There had to be a reasonable explanation to all of this. 'Anne Rosen speaking. I'm trying to reach a Mister Michael Spagnolli.'

'Is this the hospital? Is there an emergency?'

'No, no, nothing like that.' Even while Anne's voice was polite and reassuring, deep inside her a terrible scream was building. This woman hadn't said it was the wrong number. She seemed to know who Mike was. The Mike this woman knew bore some resemblance to her own fiancé. 'Mike Spagnolli,' she repeated dumbly. 'I'm trying to reach Mike Spagnolli.'

'He's not here. He took his son to the Celtics game.'

'Oh, my God!' Anne gasped. 'His son! He has a son!' But then, again, she rejected the impossible. 'There must be some mistake. I'm trying to reach Mike Spagnolli. That's spelled S, P, A, G, N, O, L, L, I.'

'You've got the right number.' The woman's voice became suspicious. 'What did you say your name was?'

'Rosen. Anne Rosen.' She caught herself before she spelled her own name. Then she froze with the receiver in her hand for a long blank moment before finally she put it back on the cradle.

'Anne? Are you all right, child?'

She didn't answer her aunt. Like a sleepwalker, she very slowly, step by step, walked past Bert and up the stairs to her room. She locked the door behind her and lay down on her bed for what might have been a long time before she finally started to cry.

She lost all track of time, as she lay under a blanket, shaking on her bed. But before long she heard the doorbell downstairs, and then the murmur of well-bred voices. She cocked an ear and thought she could make out Ramsey's British accent.

They called her, but she did not come. Her aunt knocked on her door, but still she stayed where she was.

She didn't want to talk to Ramsey, or anyone else, except maybe *him*. She wasn't crying any more, although she had started the oddest sort of shivering. Her room was very warm, and yet she was trembling as though she were freezing. Part of her mind registered the fact that she was evidencing classic symptoms of shock. She tried to monitor how she felt so that she could call on her own experience when she dealt with patients in this same condition. But other than that, she hardly thought of anything at all. It would hurt too much to think. She was almost but not quite blank, as she lay waiting for whatever was to come next.

Surely something had to come next?

Surely everything wasn't all over?

After a while the telephone began ringing, and for a second her heart leaped with the hope that it was *him* calling with some explanation that would make everything all right again. But no one summoned her to the phone.

It wasn't until sometime later that dimly she heard the doorbell again, and then angry voices – Ramsey, Aunt Bert and a familiar deep voice – shouting in the hallway.

Him. He had come.

She stumbled to her feet, opened the door, and stood looking down at the three of them arguing at the foot of the stairs.

Short and slight though he was, Ramsey was blocking Mike's way more successfully than a three-hundred-pound tackle on the forty-yard line. 'Get out of this house and Anne's life.'

Anne had never heard Ramsey use this rasp of a voice. She frowned. How could he talk to Mike like that?

'If we were back in Beirut,' Ramsey continued in an even more threatening tone, 'I would have you killed for this. I might even have killed you myself. It would have been my very great pleasure to have slit your throat from ear to ear and then to have thrown your body into the bay. But as we're evidently not in a civilized country, as we are in a place where a man like you is allowed to go scot-free after breaking a young girl's heart and very possibly ruining her life, all I can do is throw you out of this house and warn you never to come back again.'

'You and who else?' Mike had just taken one menacing step closer to Ramsey when all of a sudden he saw her standing at the top of the stairs. Her hair was in wild disarray, and her eyes were vacant. 'Annie! My God, Annie, I came as soon as I got the message.' He pushed Ramsey aside so he could get to her.

But Bert was spry for her age. She beat him to the stairs and stood between him and Anne. 'You take one more step inside my house, and I'll have you arrested. Ramsey! Call the police!'

The Palestinian was already dialling the number when Anne began lurching down the stairs. Even though she leaned like an invalid on the banister for support, her quivering voice sounded determined as she told Ramsey to put down the phone. 'Leave us alone, please.' Ramsey protested and Bert scowled, but finally they gave in and agreed. 'We'll be waiting', Bert told her, 'right out here in the hall if you need us.' With a look of triumph, Mike shut the parlour door firmly in their faces.

Anne walked like an old woman over to the leather armchairs that were still drawn up in front of the fire. Had it only been after dinner this evening – two or three hours, at most – that she had sat here, whole and complete, with her aunt? She sat down in her aunt's chair. She did not, ever, want to sit in that other chair again. 'Well?' she said. She had not yet looked him in the face.

He threw himself down in that other chair and ran his hands in despair through his hair. 'Annie, Annie, what can I say?'

'Say none of it's true,' she suggested.

'Okay, it's not true.' Desperately he wished that were so. He had never wanted it to come to this. Even now he was so accustomed to living a lie that he almost believed the words he heard himself saying. But his wife had started screaming at him as soon as he came home from the game with his son. He knew not only about Anne's call to his home but also – from what Bert had just told him in the hallway – that her aunt had hired a private investigator to report on his other life. The jig was most definitely up, yet he still could not face up to the truth. 'Your aunt never liked me. You know she didn't like me because I'm Italian. She wanted to break us up, that's all. She had no business hiring that guy to write those lies about me.' When she said nothing, he took heart and went on. 'Lies, nothing but lies. It's all lies. How could that all be true?'

'Your wife said you took your son to the Celtics game.'

He moistened his lips with his tongue. 'Who are you going to believe, Annie, her or me? That private investigator or me? Trust me!'

'I did. Oh, I did.'

Mike stared deeply into her eyes, and his voice throbbed with passion. 'You know me, Annie. You love me. You know you do. And I love you!' He was on safer ground now. He was finally telling the truth, and so it was easier to be utterly convincing. 'Nantucket! Remember Nantucket!' His voice was rich with love as he laughed. 'Oh, that was wonderful, wasn't it, Annie? That was one of the happiest nights of my life. Of your life, too, I think.' As though he were bending over a photograph album, remembering a splendid holiday, he conjured up the other times he would never forget. 'How we used to kiss under the streetlamps on Mt Auburn Street. What a woman you were! And our apartment in the Fenway. How you made me spaghetti on the night I asked you to marry me! Remember that, Annie! Remember!'

That numbness that had enveloped her body ever since she talked to Mike's wife began to lift, and every one of his words pierced her like nails driven right into her skin. Mt Auburn Street! Nantucket! The apartment in the Fenway! The night he had asked her to marry him!

Anne started to breathe heavily and with effort.

Every time she took air into her lungs, her chest hurt where her heart beat too fast. Strange, she thought. She knew her anatomy. There was no connection between her lungs and her heart.

She tried to control her breathing and slow down her racing heart as she steeled herself to ask him what she must. She would not believe it unless she heard it from his own lips. She forced the hardest words she would ever speak out of her mouth. 'Are you married?'

'Married? What's married?' He looked wildly around the room, as though for escape. 'In a way, I'm married to you, yes to you. If love were all that mattered, you'd be my wife. Not *her*. You see, we had to get married. She was pregnant. We were very young. And Catholic, of course. She was a devout Catholic, so she wouldn't get an abortion. I never loved her. I met her in a bar in Revere. She wasn't important, like you. She was just some girl I knew. It was a mistake. The worst mistake I ever made.'

Still she couldn't quite let herself believe it. Still she needed more proof than the private investigator's report and the damning words from Mike's own mouth. 'Pictures? You have pictures?' She shuddered but went on. 'Of your children?'

He was so desperately anxious to please her that he pulled out his wallet and extracted a colour snapshot. 'Here.' He actually sounded proud as he handed her the photograph. 'That's my oldest girl, Maria, there on the left. Little Mikey's in the middle. And Patty's on the right.'

She held the photograph in her hand and stared. They were pretty children, so sweet and vulnerable, and all of them looked just like Mike. *Our children would have looked just like these.* But then she lost her grip on the photograph, and everything else, and the picture fluttered out of her fingers as she doubled over and retched on her aunt's fine purplish Persian carpet.

When she had finished, she took a tissue and carefully wiped her mouth before she finally looked him in the face. The enormity of how he had betrayed not only her but everything that was decent in life smote her. 'How could you?' There was not so much anger as curiosity in her almost lifeless tone of voice. If she only could understand that one thing – how he, or anyone else, could do such a thing – she thought she might be all right in the end. 'How could you ask me to marry you when you already had a wife?' She paused. 'A wife and three children. How could you ask me to marry you? How could you let me set a date for the wedding? How could you meet my parents? How could you do all that, Mike?'

He reached his hands in supplication across the divide that now separated them. 'I didn't mean to, honey. I didn't mean to do anything bad. I love you, you know that, you know I love you.'

He tried to take her hands in his, but she pulled her hands away. 'Don't touch me. I don't want you, or anyone else, ever to touch me again. Never. Never again.'

She stared at this man whom she had loved, whom – despite everything – she still loved. Of all the men in the world, how could she have chosen to love this one? What a terrible enigma the human heart was! And how untrustworthy. She could not trust her own heart. But she could trust Madame Kismet, who had gotten it so right. Mike was indeed a two-headed man with the body of a snake. And her life was cancerous with betrayal. Of course Mike had betrayed her. But perhaps even worse was how she had betrayed herself. Her judgement had been all wrong. How could she have trusted this man who had betrayed her so? *Malesh*, she told herself, never mind. She would have the rest of her life to puzzle over these questions. But never again, she promised herself, would she let something like this happen to her. If she couldn't trust herself to choose a good man to love, then she would love no one at all.

She hardly even heard Mike crying for her to come back as she walked out of the room and up the stairs and beyond the reach of him and his kind.

Chapter 11

Camilla wobbled down the narrow lanes of the souk in her pinching high heels, killing time until the chauffeur picked her up in the Place des Martyrs and whisked her home. She had been shopping since morning, and the balls of her feet burned as though she were treading on hot coals instead of the broken pavement of the Bourg. All around her swirled the street life of Beirut, in this quintessential Arab quarter of spice stalls, men's coffee-houses, and shops where anything and everything was available for a price. Haughtily she side-stepped a heap of donkey dung and wondered why she had ordered the driver to pick her up here instead of waiting for him in the air-conditioned comfort of the Saint Georges Hotel. But the shopping fever had still been upon her, and she could not have given up and stopped even if she had been forced to buy herself a cane and limp these last painful steps. 'Boys,' she scolded as she turned her head. 'Quickly now!' She waited for the Arab urchins she had hired to carry her parcels to catch up with her. Leave them out of her sight for an instant, and they might disappear to their wretched slums with her treasures. When they staggered up beside her, she made a great show of counting the shopping bags and boxes to make sure none of them were missing.

She was off again, then, leading her own personal caravan through the souk. With her head held high, she marched past the purveyors of cheap tin pots and gaudy rayon fabrics, the hawkers of shoddy tourist souvenirs and genuine fake Phoenician artifacts. Garish polyester dresses waved in the wind on wire hangers outside cut-rate clothing stalls. Plastic bangles dangled on sticks. Fattening honey-drenched sweets baked in the heat. Falafel bubbled in vats of fat. Oranges, carrots and bananas were being squeezed into juice. There was nothing good enough for her here. She longed to heave herself down in one of these rickety coffee-house wooden chairs next to the toothless old men sucking on their *nargilehs*. But she was a Nazrani and a lady, and it would never do for her to tarry in such surroundings. She wished they were a few thousand miles east in the real Orient and she could commandeer a rickshaw. Slavery, she decided, had been a most civilized institution. She would love to have four strapping Nubians carry her through this bazaar in a sedan chair.

Onward she trod, out of the dark yeasty lanes of the souk and into the hot sun near the central bus station. Service taxis revved their engines and shouted their destinations: 'Damascus! Amman! Homs!' Peasant women in long black robes and peasant men in baggy trousers and turbans shouldered boxes as they plodded past the taxis and into the helter-skelter turmoil of the bus station. She heard the babble of Arabic, French, English, Armenian and Turkish. Christians and Muslims, Kurds and Druze, Syrians and Palestinians, Americans and French jostled for space on the crowded pavements. Horns honked. Brakes screeched.

Martyrs' Square, with its monumental memorials to the sixteen Arab patriots who had been hanged here by the Turks during the First World War, was paralyzed by a traffic jam. Every horn sounded. Every car radio blared. Every driver shouted. But ahead Camilla spotted one of the family's shiny black Mercedes limousines double-parked beside a donkey-cart.

'*Le château*,' she commanded as she threw herself down in the back seat. '*Vite!*' As the driver relieved the boys of her packages and handed them their *baksheesh* coins, she shut her eyes and collapsed on the upholstered leather seat. She must be mad, she thought, to undertake the three-hour drive back to the Château Croisé on a whim like this.

As the chauffeur swung out into the traffic and thrust his way through the square, she wondered what had possessed her to follow her impulse like this and surprise Pierre by speeding back home from Beirut a night earlier than she was expected? For a long while now – since Paris, she supposed – their marriage had been so stormy that they might well have been divorced if that had been allowed by the Maronite church. Yet here she was, rushing back home to him as eagerly as a bride. Except in bed, where perversely their marriage was as bullish as ever, they generally kept their distance from one another. But this afternoon, as she had sauntered down the Beirut boulevards with her mother, sentimental memories of their courting days not so long ago had crept up on her. She and Pierre used to meet in the Horseshoe café, take tea at Chez Paul, eat grilled fish at Bahr, and dance the fevered nights away at the Caves du Roy. Tears of nostalgia had filled her eyes when she passed a cinema, where he used to kiss her in the passionate dark of the movie matinées. She had grown accustomed, in these last maternal years, to missing her babies far more than her husband if she was away from her family for even for a short while. But now she longed, too, for the Pierre she had once adored. She had decided, then and there, amid the bustle of al-Hamra, that she must try harder with her husband. Even though Pierre most certainly had his imperfections – he was a compulsive gambler, a womanizer, and too often he was foggy with hashish – nevertheless, whatever he did, she would always love him.

The Mercedes broke free of the Beirut traffic and

coursed northwards on the coastal road past Phoenician temples, Roman aqueducts and Maronite towns. They whizzed beyond the Nahr al-Kelb where Lebanon's many conquerors – the Babylonians, the Egyptians, the Assyrians, the Greeks, the Romans, the French, and even the British – had etched their names for posterity on the sheer Dog River rock gorge. But she didn't even bother to turn her head and look out of the window, for she had never much cared for the march of man's military history. She paid more attention, however, as, near Byblos, she saw the turning for the Cave of Adonis at Afqa. She had always adored the legend of Aphrodite and Adonis, the world's most perfect lovers. Long ago, the story goes, this fabled pair had used a cave in these lush mountains as their love nest. But jealous Ares, the god of war, had sent a wild boar to kill Adonis, and it was said that even now – every spring, when the winter rains wash the red Lebanese soil down to the sea – the river still runs with the blood of the slain lover. She and Pierre had once made love *al fresco* in a glade near that Temple of Love. Perhaps, Camilla thought dreamily, they would do so again. She never could love another man as she loved Pierre. She remembered telling Anne and the others once, when they were first married, that she had not blood but Pierre in her veins. She still felt that. She always would. Yet, even as Camilla allowed herself to be swept away by the illusions of romance, she was not quite the ingénue she once had been. Paris had left its cynical marks on her. Pierre was in her blood, she added to herself, like an incurable disease.

Camilla tapped the glass and haughtily commanded the chauffeur to take it more slowly if he wanted to keep his job. She was smug in the certainty that she finally had the clout to hire and fire the servants at will. Three years ago, when she and Pierre first were married, even the maids seemed to treat her with hauteur. But now that she was the mother of three Nazrani sons, her position as the matriarch of a new generation was assured. She might be the daughter of a belly dancer, but she was the mother of what the Nazranis thought were little princes.

Smugly Camilla patted her newly teased and heavily hair-sprayed bouffant coiffure, which Jacqueline Kennedy-style was *le dernier cri* in all the foreign magazines. Life might have its troubles, but it had its triumphs as well. After the spiteful way Pierre's mother had treated her when she was first married, Camilla revelled in her new status. Old lady Nazrani still snubbed her when she thought she could get away with it, but nowadays she couldn't get away with it very often. For Shaykh Georges thought that the young woman who had presented him with three grandsons deserved to be all but worshipped as the family's new patron saint. He had even had a portrait painted of her holding Tomas, which he had entitled '*La Madone des Camélias*' and hung over the fireplace in the parlour. When he went a step further and ordered candles to be lit and flowers banked beneath the portrait, Camilla thought he was coming close to sacrilege. Any further and her father-in-law would be saying Mass there to his new household gods.

Camilla angled her head to admire her hair-do in the driver's mirror. Perhaps, she fretted, she shouldn't have let the beautician talk her into cutting her old tousled Brigitte Bardot mane. Pierre always said he had taken a fancy to her because she looked like his favourite French film star. Still, he liked her to look chic, and this coiffure had come from Beirut's most expensive salon. Even if he hated the style, he would be impressed that it had cost him more than a hundred lira. Always he encouraged her to spend as much as she wanted to keep up with the latest fashions. She often heard him boasting to his friends about exactly what she spent on her dresses, shoes and furs. Sometimes she was tempted to come to a party with price tags prominently displayed all over her body. In Lebanon, everything – even a wife and a marriage – had a shrewdly negotiated price.

Unhappily Camilla eyed the boxes and shopping bags scattered over the back seat. In a way, she thought, she was as much a whore as the prostitutes who plied the streets down by the port. So what if Pierre wouldn't bat an eyelash at the price of everything she had snapped up in Beirut's most exclusive shops today? Did it matter that she could jet off to Paris to buy her clothes whenever she wanted, and that she partied with film stars and millionaires? As she had told her mother over lunch today down by the sea at Yeldezlar, all the Nazrani money hadn't bought her contentment.

Camilla simmered in the back seat as she remembered her mother's answer. The Christian *zaim* warlords ran Lebanon, and she should thank her lucky stars that she had married into one of the most powerful clans. Shaykh Georges was bending the truth only a little when he bragged that his patch of Lebanon was his own private feudal empire and that he was as rich as a medieval European king. 'Grow up, *bébé*,' her mother had advised. 'No one is happy. But not everyone is so rich.'

Anxiously Camilla fiddled with her hair in the mirror, trying, without success, to work her fingers through the gluey confection. Maybe, she thought gloomily, her coiffure – along with most everything else today – had turned out to be a disaster. Tomorrow she would force a comb through it, give it a good wash, and try to repair the damage.

As they headed off the coastal highway on the winding mountain road that would eventually take them to the château, the driver picked up speed.

'*Lentement!*' she screamed as the Mercedes screeched around the rim of a precipice on two wheels. Just in case this imbecile didn't understand French, she added the same command in Arabic, '*Shwayyah!*' If she somehow succeeded – superstitiously she made a perfunctory little sign of the cross – in returning home in one piece, she would make very sure that this village lout never again sat in the driver's seat of any of the Nazrani limousines. She wished, as the daredevil chauffeur kept his foot on the accelerator, that she had never told this maniac to get her home to the Château Croisé *vite*. She let out a moan of terror as he gunned the engine in order to execute the next series of hairpin bends at top speed.

As the Mercedes lurched round a corner, she dug in her spike heels to brace herself, but slid all the way over to the window. There, hunched in the corner, she gave up trying to avoid the issue that was most on her mind. Of course she regretted how everything had deteriorated between Pierre and herself. And, yes, she hated being trapped for life in the Nazrani web. But nobody and nothing could upset her like her mother. Even now that she was grown up and had her own babies, she still could not shake off the feeling that her life would never be right until she had made things better between her mother and herself. Sometimes – as in Paris – they got along passionately well. But for the most part they fought. How could it be, Camilla wondered, that even now, when she acknowledged how important her mother was to her, she had once again today allowed everything with Nirvana to go wrong?

As she sat brooding in the growing dusk, Camilla wished she hadn't tempted fate by going down to Beirut to be with her this morning. She would have been better off cooped up at home with the children. Yet she had desperately needed a break. She hadn't been off the mountain for months. If it had been up to her, she would have zipped down to Beirut at least once a week even during the final months of her pregnancy. But Shaykh Georges had been worried that something might happen to the precious twins the doctor had sworn she was carrying, and so he had all but put her under house arrest until she had given birth to Guy and Emile two months ago. Even now, although her three boys were well taken care of in a nursery that was as well staffed and equipped as a small hospital, Camilla felt guilty for leaving their side for a day. Her mother-in-law had, of course, seized this opportunity to let her know that she had never entrusted Pierre to the care of any hands but her own. Camilla reminded herself, however, that there was no reason why she had to be tied to her babies like some poor milkcow of a village woman. She had breastfed her darling Tomas for more than one blissful year, until her milk had dried up when she became pregnant with the twins. How she had wept when she lost that sensuously nurturing connection to her firstborn! Tomas, her love child, was the emotional centre of her world. She loved the twins, too, but not so intensely. Tomas had been conceived in a time of hope and ecstasy, but the twins had begun long after the honeymoon was over. She had resented being pregnant again so soon after Tomas was born. As she had waddled heavily through the last months of her pregnancy, she had dreaded the burden of breastfeeding two babies at once. And so Shaykh Georges, with his flair for the dramatic, had imported – at great cost, he always boasted – a pair of buxom French *nourrices* from Provence to provide truly Gallic mother's milk for his grandsons.

She stopped trying to run her fingers through her hair and abandoned her equally futile efforts to get the driver to slow down. Instead, wedged snugly against the window, she finally managed to focus on what exactly had gone wrong between Nirvana and herself today.

Camilla smiled wistfully as she remembered how very happy she had been to see her mother at first. Everything had started out well enough in the morning sun, over coffee and croissants on Nirvana's balcony overlooking the sea. Mama, for once, had been lavish in her approval of how slim she looked. With the help of a girdle, Nirvana pronounced, her daughter might just be able to squeeze into this season's slithery silhouettes. As usual, she said, opening a well-thumbed copy of this month's *Vogue*, the designers think we are built like small men. Nevertheless, the two of them had oohed and aahed over a black Balmain *suit-fatale* and a delicious pink chiffon evening dress by Balenciaga. As they had drooled over a black halter top matched with a white silk organza skirt, Nirvana had suggested they buy the fabric here in Beirut and have their seamstress run up a copy for a fraction of the original cost. Camilla, who had been starving herself and bending and stretching and Chubby-Checker-twisting to vigorous American rock and roll ever since the twins were born, had been thrilled that her mother thought she looked good enough for couture. And so, as she helped herself to another croissant, she had confided that this time she had despaired of ever being able to tighten up her tummy. After Tomas had been born, her skin had definitely retained more elasticity. But Guy and Emile, she complained had made her sag and droop like some old village woman who had been ploughed and reaped for too many seasons. Nirvana had been *très sympathique*. She had recommended that they shop for one of those torturous boned girdles, and then she had even helpfully jumped up and put a record on the stereo and demonstrated how some of her old belly-dancer shimmies could help rewin that muscle tone.

Again Camilla smiled fondly as she remembered what a good time they had over breakfast. How she and her mother had laughed and talked, plotting with the precision of generals at war just what they were going to look for in which shops. All had started off well, with earrings, at the new shopping sensation in Beirut, the marvellous three-storey department store, the Grand Magasin Byblos near the Bourg. Camilla had bought herself a pair of cultured pearls the size of marbles, and – never to be outdone – Nirvana had bought a spectacular pair of two-inch-long rhinestone earrings *and* gypsy hoop baubles that were exactly like those shown in *Vogue*. From there they had proceeded to silk scarves in the new 'light-struck' pastel colours – each chose half a dozen – and then they settled down to some serious shopping for summer dresses cut in the new princess line. But they had dithered in the changing rooms and put off their final choices until after lunch.

They had had such fun together this morning. Camilla treasured those rare times when she and her mother were in harmony as some of the most satisfying moments of her life. For as she had grown older and wiser, Camilla had come to believe that men came and went and were, on the whole, disappointing. But mothers endured for ever. Now that she was a mother herself and could compare the purity of her love for her sons to the equivocations of her love for her husband, she had begun to value her own mother more. At its best, maternal love had a perfection to which marital love could never aspire. A man and a woman could never be as content together as a mother and a baby. She would never forget what a tigress Nirvana had been when she had flown to her rescue in Paris. If Mama hadn't been there, she would have been all alone when she gave birth to Tomas. Again Camilla asked herself why, if she thought so much of her mother, they so often ended up squabbling as they did. How and why had it happened that in her own life both maternal and marital love had ended up in bickering and disappointment? Was every love destined to go sour?

Camilla sighed. There was no good reason why she and her mother shouldn't have had a wonderful time together today. Usually the two of them loved nothing better than to shop, and to stop for a gossipy lunch at one of the smarter restaurants, and then shop again, ending up with drinks on a balcony with a view of the bay. They had been invited out to a lavish dinner tonight and then to a reception at the French embassy which would have spun out deliciously until the wee hours of the morning.

If her mother had behaved, Camilla thought resentfully, she would now be drinking champagne and collecting diplomatic compliments, instead of risking her life on this madcap race over the mountains. She had set out from the château just after dawn this morning bright-eyed and eager for a two-day shopping spree in the capital. Again Camilla began to seethe as she remembered what had touched off their quarrel. In the course of the day Mama had settled into that particularly impossible mood of hers, the one Camilla hated above all the others, when she pretended that she and her daughter were friends of exactly the same age. She couldn't stand it when her mother refused to act like a mother, which was almost always. Camilla had always wanted a mother with nothing more remarkable about her than a wide lap and an understanding heart. As far back as she could remember, she had wished her mother was more renowned for the spices she pounded into her *kibbe* than for the spicy details of her personal life. The last thing she had wanted, today or any other day, was to be the repository of her mother's girlish confessions. But as usual, it had hardly mattered what Camilla wanted. Her mother had insisted on rolling her eyes and dropping her voice and telling all.

This time, it seemed, Mama had set her heart on marrying a handsome Greek named Andreas, who was not only the son of a millionaire shipping magnate but also a scandalous twenty-two years younger than she was. Camilla had glowered at the photographs her mother proudly showed her of Andreas bulging manfully in his bathing suit. Her mother, she thought, had finally gone beyond all reasonable bounds. This Andreas would be her fourth husband, which was a few too many even for libertine Beirut. And so, after she had downed her third martini, Camilla had forgotten her best intentions to keep her mouth tactfully shut. She had not been at all kind when her mother had pouted and carried on like an outraged virgin because Andreas was acting as though he didn't want to marry her. Tartly she had told her mother she might have had better luck if she had stuck to her own generation and gone after Andreas's father. One word had inevitably led to another, and there, out in the lavish open-air restaurant where anyone rich enough to afford Yeldezlar's celebrated *mezze* had assuredly heard them, they had ended up shrieking at each other like peasants at a village well. The upshot was that her mother had flounced off to her Crescent cabaret, and Camilla had been left alone to trail despondently through the gaudy lengths of her favourite Souk al-Tawileh, across the Souk Ayes, even all around Bab Idris. As she killed time buying bits and pieces, too dispirited to return to the major shopping they had left unfinished this morning, she had come to the unpleasant realization that unless she gritted her teeth and patched things up with her mother, she was left with nowhere to stay tonight but a hotel or the home of another prying relative. It was then that she had decided she missed Pierre so much that she couldn't bear to spend even one night away from him.

Camilla frowned at the gift-wrapped packages stacked beside her on seat and floor. There were more in the boot, and a few bigger ones up with the driver in front. Even so, though she had doggedly worked her way through toy stores and baby boutiques, nothing she had bought after her quarrel with her mother had made her feel that intoxicating rush of possession that usually made shopping one of the greatest pleasures of her life. Most of what she had bought in the late afternoon was for the children.

It was getting late, well after sunset now, and in the back seat of the Mercedes Camilla yawned as her mind drifted here and there. After her fight with Mama, she had endured an excruciatingly aggravating hour trying on bikinis in front of a pitiless three-way mirror. Even with all her diet and exercise, she obviously could not be caught dead on the beach this year. Still, Camilla reminded herself, it was only March. If she took drastic measures, maybe she could still get her perfectly flat stomach back before summer. Suddenly she thought of massage. If she had had this inspiration a few hours ago, she could have hired one of the best *masseuses* in Beirut to come and stay at the château and work out on her every day. Maybe she and the girl could even have become friends. Surely life on the mountain wouldn't be so lonely if she had at least one friend. Tomas and the babies were wonderful, but she missed the companionship of Anne, Leila and even Fatima. It was funny how things changed over time. She used to dote on Anne and could never find much to say to Fatima. But now that she and Fatima were the only ones of their foursome to be married – and especially now that Fatima had written to say that she was pregnant – she had more in common with her than with Anne. She felt so sorry for Anne nursing that broken heart in Boston. When Leila had rung her up from England to tell her all about it, Camilla had at first been speechless. She hadn't minded, really, that she had heard the bad news second-hand from Leila. Apparently Anne had come close to having a nervous breakdown, and so she hadn't written the painful truth to any of them. If it hadn't been for Leila's brother, they would all still be in the dark. But Ramsey had been so upset by the incident and so worried about Anne that he had telephoned Leila straightaway with all the dreadful details. Leila, then, had promptly rung up Anne to see if there was anything she could do to help. As soon as she put down the phone to America, she had booked a call through to Lebanon. Leila and Camilla had clucked their tongues and shaken their heads and nattered on for nearly an hour. It was no wonder, they had agreed, that Anne was depressed. Leila had said she sounded distant, very restrained, and not at all like the sparkling friend they had all known and loved.

As the Mercedes finally purred along a relatively straight and flat stretch of the road, Camilla sank back in her seat, smoothed out her skirt, and sedately crossed her legs. She thanked the Virgin and St Maron that she was safely married and the mother of three blooming boys. Marriage was not what it was cracked up to be, but at least she had succeeded in snaring a man, a home and a secure future. Even with all his dissipations, Pierre was a veritable prince compared to that Mike. Poor Anne! Camilla hated to think it, and would never have allowed herself to say it but Anne should have been more careful. It wasn't as though she hadn't been warned. As though it were yesterday, Camilla could hear Madame Kismet telling Anne that she saw a two-headed man with the body of a snake in her future. Mike, *exactement!* Anyone but Anne would have paid more attention to the old gypsy. But Anne had thought she was too bright to pay heed to the babblings of an old witch. It was only superstitious little fools like me, Camilla thought, who had believed every word the fortune-teller had said.

She knew it was wicked, but as she patted her bouffant hair-do back into place, Camilla even felt a bit complacent about how her destiny was shaping out next to Anne's. Of course she adored Anne. They had been best friends even when they were little girls. Yet Camilla had to admit that sometimes she had been a tiny bit jealous of Anne always being the brightest in their classes, the best at every sport, the most outstanding in every way. And yet, as fate would have it, for a girl who was supposedly so clever, Anne had been very stupid about men. Mama always said that Americans were the most gullible race in the world, and Jews the most arrogant.

She must have dozed off, for night had darkly fallen as the Mercedes began once again to assault the steep mountains in the final approach to the Château Croisé. A pity that they hadn't set off earlier, she thought as she peered out of the window into the void. The cedar groves that dotted these lush green mountains provided the most spectacular vistas in the whole of scenic Lebanon. Even now, as they twisted up and up the mountain road, the full moon burst brightly out from the cover of the clouds to illuminate the ancient trees, the winking lights of the nestling villages, and the jagged peaks on the horizon. The moonlight cast such dreamy shadows that Camilla was tempted to tell the driver to pull over so she could get out her sketch pad and try to capture this moment. *Yaadra*, she was eager to start drawing and painting again! On impulse late this afternoon she had stopped in an artist's supply shop to stock up on pads, canvas, brushes, paints, charcoal and even watercolours. Ever since the twins had been born, after three artistically dry years in which she had never once wanted to pick up brush or chalk, she had found herself itching to return to the drawing board. Even if Pierre and his mother laughed at her behind her back, she meant to start painting and sketching again. Perhaps some fine spring morning this week, she would tell the nannies and the nurses to pack up her sons and off they'd go for an artistic picnic out in the mountain meadows. Her babies were like cherubs now, and she yearned to capture their innocence on canvas. Before she had liked the passion of siren-bright acrylics, but now she had a yen for the soft maternal washes of watercolour.

The packs of piedogs gave chase and howled a fearful welcome as the Mercedes wound through the narrow walled lanes that led up through the village towards the château. At the heavy wrought iron gate, the guard held his machine-gun at the ready as he flashed a torch in the driver's eyes. Bandits roamed these lawless mountains, so even the chauffeur carried a pistol. But when the guard recognized Camilla, he lowered his gun and gave her a respectful salute.

Just as the chauffeur was about to sound the horn to alert the staff, Camilla sharply ordered him to be quiet: '*Tais-toi!*' Although it was only ten o'clock, the house was almost dark. Pierre and the men had gone out hunting even before she had left this morning. They had planned to while away the afternoon as guests of a distant cousin at a remote manor house over by the Syrian border. They must have been exhausted by the time they had made it back to the château. She could see their bedroom lights were off. Pierre must already be in bed. Yet she hoped that he wasn't *too* tired. She was seized by a mischievous urge, just this once, to surprise her husband by creeping into his bed and waking him with kisses in the most delicious places. She would turn over a new leaf in their marriage. Maybe tonight they would even start a new baby. She wanted a little girl.

She flung open the limousine door herself and put her finger to her lips to shush the startled maid who had come running as soon as she put her key in the front door lock. She didn't even wait for her packages to be carried inside as, with the air of an impish child playing a wonderful prank, she kicked off her high heels and held them in her hands as she stealthily tiptoed up the staircase towards their bedroom. Soundlessly she opened the door, slipped inside, and crept over to the bed. She had already unzipped her dress and was about to wiggle out of it when the moon came out from behind a bank of clouds and illuminated her marriage bed.

Camilla stared down in shock at the three dark heads and the three pink bodies.

Pierre and the two wet nurses were all sleeping in her bed.

She blinked and rubbed her eyes, but, still, there the three of them were in her bed.

She narrowed her eyes and put her hands on her hips and stared until this sordid tableau was branded indelibly upon her heart. Pierre had his head blissfully cushioned in the watermelon breasts of one *nourrice* while his hands were snugly in possession of the swollen pink nipples of the other. She could see every fleshy centimetre of them, for all three were stark naked. Their bodies were as intertwined as a litter of sleeping puppies, although there was nothing innocent about the position of one girl's splayed thighs, and Pierre's groin, and the other one's buttocks. The beautiful silk sheets which she herself had painstakingly embroidered with her and Pierre's initials lay in a tangled heap at the foot of the bed. She felt like gathering up those sheets and ripping them to shreds with her bare teeth. *Bâtard! Diable! Cochon!* Camilla very nearly let out an outraged animal howl as she glowered at her wretch of a husband. Leave it to greedy Pierre to bed them both at once! Silently she cursed him in French, in Arabic, even in broken English. How long, she wondered, had this been going on behind her back? She wouldn't put it past her husband to have taken the wet nurses to bed even while she was racked with the pain of giving birth to his sons.

She stood there for another unblinking moment, memorizing every searing curve and hollow of it so that its injustice would be with her for as long as she lived. An open whisky bottle leaned drunkenly on the bedside table, and the air was dense with the sweetish aroma of hashish. Clothes were flung here and there on the floor. In the moonlight their bodies shone as though they had been slick with sweat not so long ago. She even fancied she could see a trickle of semen on one of the girl's thighs. They were animals! They hadn't even bothered to wash themselves after rutting in her bed. She would have this bloody mattress burned, the sheets shredded, even the cedar headboard sawn into splinters. Never – ever! – would she forgive her husband for betraying her with his sons' wet nurses in her very own bed.

Camilla opened her mouth to let out a ferocious howl of rage that would have woken up not only the whole household but the entire village. She would screech so long and loud that the echo of her outrage might be heard by Fatima far away in the south.

But instead, as her eyes burned with sudden and bitter inspiration, Camilla grimly bit her mouth shut. *Why not*, she thought, as she weighed the diabolical plan that had just crossed her mind. *Why not? She could pull it off. And the bastard deserved it.*

She reflected, as her drilling eyes memorized the exact position of her husband's every finger on the wet nurse's breasts, that not so long ago it wouldn't have occurred to her that this could be turned to her own advantage. Before everything began to unravel between herself and Pierre in Paris, she would simply have dissolved into tears behind their shut bedroom door. She would have cried until her eyes ached, and Pierre would have hung his head and promised never to do anything so naughty again. She would even have believed him as he lied. Camilla suppressed a wistful sigh for those old days. It seemed now that she had lost for ever the innocent capacity to forgive and trust and begin again. Yet maybe, still, it wasn't too late for the two of them. Maybe . . .

Fiercely she told herself not to be so stupid.

Cruelly she tormented herself by observing that Pierre looked happier sleeping in the arms of these French tarts than he ever did when his head lay next to hers. Her heart turned to stone as she studied his smile of contentment. Bastard! She could feel the softness at her core jell, and then harden still further, until the point of her heart could have scratched her bitter story on the Hope diamond.

She shut her eyes and squeezed them tight so that no tell-tale tears should roll down her cold cheeks. She reminded herself that her mother had always boasted that they hailed from a long line of feisty women, and that they were both survivors. She was surprised that she drew strength from this, for always before she had wanted to be pretty and helpless rather than bold and tough. But then was then, and now was now. Life rolled along, and the strong adapted. She would do what she had to do. Pierre had assigned her the role of the wronged wife, and she would play it to the hilt.

Yet, before launching into her premeditated action, she stopped long enough to consider whether what she had in mind was what Leila, in her la-de-dah British accent, would call 'going over the top'. Of course it was *un peu exagéré*. But, as she coolly reminded herself, the Nazranis were not stiff-upper-lip English aristocrats. The whole lot of them carried on like caricatures from an Italian opera. She remembered old lady Nazrani standing over her like an avenging angel as she forced her to kneel at her *prie-dieu* and pray for purity. She recalled how Shaykh Georges had raised his fist in the church on her wedding day and vowed that he would make a river of blood flow in revenge for that sacrilege. No one in this family could ever resist a scene. The more melodramatic, the better they all seemed to like it. So just this once, she would act like a Nazrani.

A final sizzling look down at Pierre sandwiched between his girls galvanized her into zipping up her dress, picking up her shoes, and setting about the business of exploiting her husband's betrayal.

She made hardly a sound as she slipped out of

the door and down the hallway to the nursery. Gently she kissed Tomas awake. 'Mama!' He threw himself in her arms. As she held him nestled trustingly against her, for a moment her resolution faltered. Should she drag him into this? What if he never forgot it? But then, she assured herself, a two-year-old couldn't possibly understand what he was about to see tonight. Everyone said Tomas was precocious for his age, that he had learned to walk and talk earlier than other boys. But he was still only two years old. He would forget whatever happened tonight. She whispered in his ear that she wanted him to be brave and help protect Mama from a very bad man. Tomas squared his shoulders like a little soldier when she put him down, slipped on her shoes, and scooped the twins up in her arms. A moment later he marched right behind her as she clicked her heels resolutely down the corridor to her father-in-law's bedroom in the far wing of the château.

Here, she decided, there was no need for stealth. Pierre could never hear her this far away from his bedroom. She couldn't pound on the door with a baby in each arm, and so she kicked it. She pretended the wooden door was Pierre, and so she was able to kick it hard enough to wake the dead. 'Papa! Papa! Help! It's Camilla! Papa!' She encouraged Tomas to hit his fist against the door. '*Grand-père!*'

The twins were awake and howling for their one o'clock feed when finally Shaykh Georges threw open the door. With his long flowing white hair standing out from his skull in disarray, he looked like a fierce old lion who nonetheless was still the head of the pride. For even though he was half asleep, he was ready for action with his pearl-handled pistol in one hand.

'Justice!' Camilla howled. 'I demand justice! For my sons, for myself! Justice!' A volley of acid words shot out of her. 'Your son has dishonoured me, you, all the family! Pierre takes his whores into my own bed! Now, here, in the château, two of them! My babies' nurses!' As Tomas's face crumpled and he joined the chorus of the crying twins, Camilla had to raise her voice even louder. 'I swear to you, *beau-père*, as the Virgin is my witness, either you defend us or I take my sons from this brothel here and now!' Her voice caught in a sob. 'We leave tonight and we will never return! *Jamais!*' As though she really were the Lady of the Camellias, she demanded that the *shaykh* safeguard their holy family.

'What? . . .' Georges yawned and scratched his chest with the butt of his pistol. He never woke without a struggle, and so he had still not been able to grasp much more than that his screeching daughter-in-law and the howling babies were making his head pound. 'Quiet down,' he mumbled in his gravelly rasp of a voice as he put his arm around Tomas in an effort to calm his favourite grandson.

'Quiet down?' Camilla's voice shrieked out of control. 'That is your answer? I find Pierre in my bed with the two nurses, and you tell me to quieten down? Okay – *tant pis!* – so we leave. Tomas! Come with Mama! We go to Beirut!' As soon as she was sure Tomas was tagging along behind her, her heels beat a furious staccato as she sailed down the hallway towards the main staircase.

'No, Camilla, wait!' Shaykh Georges hared off behind her and scooped Tomas up in his arms. 'Wait! No, don't go!'

She turned to confront him. 'Then I demand justice,' she repeated. 'You must protect me and my sons.'

The *shaykh* was altogether awake now. He stared long and hard at the daughter-in-law whom he had always dismissed as a decorative and docile brood mare. But now the furious eyes of a scheming woman matched him stare for stare. 'Hmmm.' He began to consider the startling possibility that, from now on,

Camilla might prove a force to be reckoned with in the precious kingdom of his family. His always hoarse voice dropped a register lower, into a threatening rattle of a whisper. 'You say you caught him with the nurses?' When she nodded, his eyes narrowed as he weighed his grandsons in the balance against his son. Of course Camilla was bluffing. He – and she – knew that she could never get away with kidnapping his grandsons. Yet she was bold enough to play her high card. 'Beirut, eh? You would try to take the babies away?' When again she nodded, he decided that either he had misjudged her before or she had grown up overnight. His son's wife was every inch the cunning peasant as she stood planted before him with a baby on each hip. He could see that, like all peasants, she was intent on driving a hard bargain. Doubtless she had inherited this talent from that shrew of a mother of hers. Still, Shaykh Georges reflected, by giving him three grandsons, Camilla had kept her part of the bargain. If he had to pay her back now, tit for tat, then perhaps that was only fair. He might not even hold this against her. From time to time it strengthened the Nazrani line to have transfusions of fiery peasant blood like hers. And Camilla showed promise. He liked her far better when she acted like this than when she wept enough to make the colours in the sofa cushions run. In time, with the proper tutelage, his son's wife might even learn to act like a born Nazrani. As for that son of his . . . It seemed the *shaykh* had come to a decision as he cocked the pistol he still held in his free hand. '*Eh bien*, show me.'

Shaykh Georges was swearing a litany of father-to-son curses under his breath as he swept down the long corridor towards that other bedroom with a vengeful Camilla in his wake. By then others in the family had been wakened by the row. Pierre's mother was throwing a shawl around her shoulders and running after her husband and daughter-in-law. Pyjama-clad husbands were speculating on what new outrage had been committed against the family. Wives with unbound hair for once publicly loose on their shoulders staggered out into the hallway and whispered that something must be wrong with the children. Sleepily sisters, brothers, guests joined the procession and followed the head of the clan on his passage through the darkened house. Still, above every other sound, Tomas and the twins continued to cry.

Georges flung open his son's bedroom door so that it banged like a shot against the wall. As he flicked on the light switch, he aimed at the ceiling and pulled the trigger. He fired a volley of warning shots into the air.

Camilla was right behind him. As though on the stage of the Paris Opera, she screeched at her errant husband. '*Voilà!*'

Pierre sat straight up in bed, flanked by the naked nurses. '*Ya Mar Sharbel*,' he muttered as his mouth fell open. 'Oh, God, help me.' The girls squealed as they dived for the cover of the sheet at the foot of the bed.

Shaykh Georges shook his head in disgust. His sharp eyes took in every detail of this debauch: the brassières and knickers strewn on the floor between the door and the bed, the empty liquor bottles, the jiggling flesh of the girls he had hired to give mother's milk to his grandsons. 'This is the last straw,' he muttered to himself. He, too, had always taken his carnal pleasures without remorse, but even adultery had its code. He had never sullied his own nest, and never would. He curled his lip at his son. 'Here, in the house. In front of the whole family. In front of your own *sons*.' At that, Georges suddenly became aware that Tomas was still in his arms. The little boy was staring in horror at his father and the nurses who fed his brothers. Georges hastily jammed his gun into his pyjama pocket and clamped his free hand across the boy's face so he should not see more than he already had.

Meanwhile the rest of the family and a clutch of Syrian house guests had crowded into the bedroom before they realized what was at the centre of this midnight drama. As one, they gasped and stared. Pierre's mother crossed herself, bowed her head, and struck her breast for the shame of it. Pierre's sister Marie might have fainted if her husband hadn't caught her, and his other sister Yvette started to weep. One cousin smirked, and another nudged his wife and might have laughed if she hadn't glared back at him. The Syrians all this while were staring in fascination at the gigantic bare pink breasts of the nurses, who were still fighting over the one tangled sheet. Yet no one made a move to leave.

As all these judging eyes drilled into him, Pierre sat in a stupor. But finally he lifted his head and, as he searched the faces of the crowd, the extent of this débâcle began to sink in. His father was here, and – God save him! – his mother. All his family and some of his friends had caught him in the act. Miserably, Pierre's eyes finally fell on his wife. 'You,' he said, 'oh no, not you, too. You're supposed to be in Beirut.' Then his eyes flashed. 'You did this. You brought them here.'

Camilla took a few menacing steps closer to the bed. 'You'll pay for this,' she hissed very low, so that only he could hear. Their eyes locked in combat, and a look that burned not only with hate but – oddly – with a perverse pulse of sexual excitement passed between them. If at this instant they had been alone, they might have rolled panting and growling on the floor. As they punched and finally, ferociously, came together, they might have succeeded in clawing their way beyond the wall of guilt and anger. Even if they bruised each other physically, there would have been no lasting scars.

But they were not alone, and the aftermath of Camilla's drama would go far deeper than sexual titillation.

Tomas had finally wriggled out of his grandfather's grasp and was clinging to his mother's skirts as he screamed. 'Mama! Mama! What is Papa doing, Mama?' She took one look at her son's face and forgot about Pierre. She hunched down on the floor so Tomas could crawl on to her crowded lap. As she rocked her babies and murmured soothing words to her two-year-old, Camilla was the picture of all the family virtues Pierre had betrayed.

But the bedroom was still in pandemonium, and so Georges let rip with three more warning shots at the ceiling. 'Out! All of you! The show is over! Out! *Tous!*' As the spectators reluctantly milled out of the door, he waved the gun towards the squealing *nourrices*. 'You two, *allez!* Feed the babies, and then out of this house. *Maintenant!*' They screamed, and in their panic to get away from this madman they ran naked into the crowded corridor. Georges ran his hand through Tomas's tousled hair and, as he gave Camilla's shoulder a reassuring pat, he told her to take his grandsons back to the nursery. 'I'll take care of Pierre,' he said grimly.

Obediently she moved towards the door, but she was so caught up in the sweetness of her revenge that she could not resist standing in the shadows of the hallway as Georges gave his son the tongue-lashing of his life. She did not see her firstborn's anguished face as he stood clutching her skirt, listening to his grandfather's terrible words to his father.

A little while later, as Camilla finally crept down

the corridor to the nursery, her eyes gleamed with satisfaction. From now on, things were going to be different in this family.

She was so intent on exacting the last shred of vengeance, however, that it wasn't until she had personally hounded the wet nurses out of the door – and belatedly checked with the nannies to make sure the twins would take bottles – that she turned her attention at last to her firstborn.

As she tucked Tomas back in his bed, the little boy was still shaking uncontrollably. 'I hate him,' Tomas sobbed. 'I hate Papa. He is bad! He hurts me and you, and I hate him!'

She was about to agree that she hated Pierre, too. But she bit her tongue. She didn't hate her husband, not altogether. Come what may, he and she were tied together for life. She could never be as passionate about any other man as she was about Pierre. She – and he – would neither forget nor forgive the role each of them had played tonight. But instead of ending it between them, what had happened tonight had only tangled them more tightly together. Yes, he was in her blood.

'I hate him, Mama! Hate him!'

As Camilla looked down in dismay at her son's suffering eyes that seemed suddenly like those of a desperate old man, she hastily focused her attention on the one she loved without reservation. Of course, she crooned, he didn't hate his Papa, this was no more than a bad dream, he would soon forget all about what had happened tonight.

'No, I hate him! I will always hate him! You'll see! I won't forget!'

Camilla wondered then, as she crawled into his bed and held him close to her until finally his trembling stopped and he slept, if her revenge might have been bought at too dear a price.

It was only a week or so later, as Camilla sat dreamily in a meadow sketching Tomas at play with the twins, that out of the corner of her eye she saw the flash of metal on the path from the road. As it worked its way closer to her, she made out the bandoliers crossed on a gunman's chest and recognized one of her father-in-law's bodyguards. Hastily she drew in a line here and rounded off a curve there, trying to finish off her drawing before Shaykh Georges's emissary arrived with his message from on high. Yet her concentration was ruined. What did the old man want from her now! Last week putting herself under his protection had seemed a glorious inspiration. But she had begun to fear, now that the old *shaykh* was showering so much of his demanding attention upon her, that being the apple of his eye could be as much of a curse as a blessing. As she gripped her charcoal, her hand shook in that nervous tremble that had begun to afflict her since the other night. She swore softly under her breath. Her promising sketch was ruined.

She gave her drawing a last yearning look but told herself she could have another attempt tomorrow. A few more sketches, and she would be ready to start working in watercolours.

But for now, she flipped her pad shut. Her father-in-law's message – whatever it was – would have to take precedence over her doodling. She had done her best to keep her wits about her since the night of Pierre's disgrace. Even if Shaykh Georges often unnerved her, she was determined to continue on the perilous new course she had set herself. In general she was pleased with her performance. When her hands shook with fear, she put them in her pockets or – better still – she clenched them. When she could feel the familiar impulse to burst into tears welling up inside her, she controlled herself until she was safely alone behind a locked door. Besides, her rising status in the family had brought its compensations. She had relished putting Pierre's bossy sisters back in their rightful places, and she had taken infinite pleasure in letting Pierre's mother know that never again would she dance to the old lady's tune.

Camilla busied herself with putting away her sketch-book, replacing her charcoal in its box, and rearranging her art supplies in the fitted Italian leather satchel she had bought as an afterthought in the final moments of her last shopping spree in Beirut.

As she snapped shut the case, she wished it had been as easy to deal with Pierre as with the rest of his family. Only a few nights after the explosion, by randy mutual consent they had gone back to sharing the same bedroom. But even though they had scaled new erotic heights, they had also mined new depths. Pierre, not surprisingly, had been furious at her betrayal. He had taunted her about the wet nurses and said he wouldn't have taken them to bed if she had been enough to satisfy all his needs. But this time she had lashed back with her own cruel words about his not being the husband he should be. Yet, try as she might, she hadn't been able to beat Pierre at his own brutish game. She was never so vulnerable as when the laws of God and man – and her own ravenous sexuality – required that she lay open to him, naked in the marriage bed. Night after night he would reduce her to tears, and she would flee to the bathroom to cry. She would sit there for a long while, weeping until she used up all the toilet tissue. Then she would begin acting out the last exhausted steps of their old dreary ritual, washing off her burning face with hot water, staring at her blurry eyes and swollen cheeks, wishing – *Yaadra!* – that she were dead. When finally she would creep back out, she would find Pierre slumped in a sullen daze of whisky and hashish. *Plus ça change*, she would think as she crawled back into bed beside him, *plus c'est la même chose*.

Camilla put all that behind her as she ran over

and swooped Tomas up in her arms. Joyfully she swung him round and round until they both were dizzy with laughter. Ardently she kissed his rosy face. Wildly he clung to her. He had, she thought with alarm, been clinging to her far too much since that scene last week in her bedroom. He hated to let her out of his sight. Most nights he begged her to sleep in his own bed instead of hers. And one morning, just before dawn, she had awakened to find him mutely standing on the floor beside her bed, staring balefully at her and Pierre. Yet now, as then, Camilla shrugged off her misgivings. Even though he still shied away from his father, Tomas had never once referred to that midnight ugliness. Surely he would forget all about it in a few weeks or months. Her little boy would get over this, just as he was getting over the pain of his teeth forcing their way through his gums. In the meantime, however, she spoiled him even more than was her wont. She let him eat as much carrot *halwah* as he wanted, she dropped whatever she was doing as soon as he cried for her, and she cuddled him close to her whenever she saw his face contorted by that anxious look that made him seem like an elderly baby.

By the time the bodyguard got close enough to tell her that the big boss wanted to see her up in his cedar grove, Camilla was sitting in the soft high grass with Tomas snug in her lap. She hesitated when he pleaded, 'Don't go, Mama.' It was nearly lunchtime, and they had been about to unpack their picnic hamper here in the meadow. She was tempted to tell the messenger that whatever the old man wanted would have to wait until the afternoon. But nobody ever kept Shaykh Georges waiting. She gave all three of her boys a few reassuring kisses, promised Tomas a bigger and better picnic tomorrow, and disregarded his wails as she handed him over to the new nursemaids who had hastily been hired in Beirut. She turned and blew Tomas a kiss as she followed the bodyguard on the hard climb back up the rocky trail to the grove near the summit of the mountain.

When she finally caught sight of Shaykh Georges, he was splayed out in the brilliant late morning sun like the king of the lizards.

It was just like her imperious father-in-law, she thought, as she panted the final steps towards his famous cedar grove, to insist on holding court way up here. Perversely, the *shaykh* had never allowed the engineers to carve a road up to his eyrie. Since he had been born and bred in these mountains and boasted that he could still scale them without losing his breath, he gleefully insisted on imposing his sense of fitness on everyone else. Fat Levantine cabinet ministers, lean and hungry corporate officials from America, and even explosive German and Swiss arms dealers had to puff all the way up here if they wanted to do business with the Nazranis. Camilla had even heard that it took three of the family's strongest men a sweaty day's work just to carry his precious cedar chair up to his Olympian haunt, and then back down again so it would be ready for him once more in the salon of the château. But Shaykh Georges maintained that the thronelike effect was well worth their effort, and, as she drank in the awesome setting for the first time, Camilla had to agree that he was right. From here, high in the Lebanese mountains, on a clear day like this, Georges could look out on a lush kingdom of green peaks and valleys which undulated all the way down to the sea, just beyond the horizon. He had positioned himself in the sun, at the very head of the cedar grove, with the rippling green trees spread out and bowing in the wind before him as if they were his minions. He had even had a flagpole sunk into the rich black loamy earth beside him, so that the red and green Lebanese flag, emblazoned with one of these selfsame cedars, fluttered above him. Shaykh Georges was fond of pointing out that his chair, his forest and his flag were all of a piece.

Yet here, Camilla thought, where her father-in-law played king at the top of his mountain, radiant nature outshone all his pretensions. The beauty of these mountains, valleys and trees diminished anything merely human. Some said these ancient cedars had been young when other groves on nearby mountains had been felled to build King Solomon's temple in Jerusalem. Camilla reached out and touched their sharp dry needles and breathed in their rich resinous scent. Nazrani legend had it that the heart of the Lebanon lay alive and beating here in this very cedar grove. For a fragrant moment, she believed that.

Then, as she set about finishing her laborious climb, she shifted her attention back to her father-in-law. Dozing in his great carved cedarwood chair, Shaykh Georges looked less the monarch than a tired old man who could never get quite warm enough because he already felt the chill of his grave. It was so hot this morning that she had been perspiring even when sketching down in the meadow. But Shaykh Georges had a heavy wool shawl tucked around his hunched shoulders. His skin was as tough and pitted as a camel's hide, his manelike white hair was thinning, and even his bones seemed to have shrunk since she had married Pierre. Awake, the *shaykh* had so much vitality that it would have been as silly to think of him as old as it would have been to question the age of the wind or the sun. But asleep, he showed his age. She calculated, as she fidgeted before him, that he must be well past sixty. To her, he seemed as hoary as his cedar grove.

The *shaykh*'s eyelids twitched up a fraction and his lips cracked open in what passed for a smile. He rasped out a greeting to her and barked out a string of orders to the waiting servants. 'A chair! Coffee!'

As she settled as best she could in a low wooden

chair and raised her tiny cup of Arab coffee to her lips, Shaykh Georges lit a cigarette and began to wax expansive. 'These hills, my hills, and these trees, my trees, they are *magnifiques*, no? Forever my family have sat just here, the masters of all they could see. We are the heirs of the Phoenicians and the Crusaders, and it is our destiny – and God's will – that we continue to do so.'

Camilla beamed a saccharine smile at the Maronite Christian *zaim*. She was not about to contradict him on his slanted version of Lebanese history, or anything else. He, as well as she, must know that the Nazrani ancestors were neither the ancient Phoenician traders who had lived along the Levantine littoral nor the Crusaders who had succeeded in wresting control of much of the Levant in the twelfth and thirteenth centuries. His forbears, instead, had belonged to a Christian sect named after a fifth-century saint called Maron. Centred originally along the Orontes river in northern Syria, the Maronites migrated to northern Lebanon and to the coastal cities of Batron and Jubail in the eighth century. When the Crusaders landed, the Maronites had fought under their Christian standards and against the largely Muslim population. They had even cast off their status as an obscure Eastern Christian sect and joined the Church of Rome. Much later, in the fifteenth century, the Maronites had been forced by Muslim persecutions to retreat to these remote and inaccessible Lebanese mountains. Here they had stayed, prospered and triumphed.

'Why', Shaykh Georges continued, 'will our Muslim brothers refuse to understand that we have made this country what it is? Our money, our brains, our blood are the heart and soul of Lebanon! We are like these cedars! Strong! Invincible! And, like them, we will always endure, no matter how many enemies try to cut us down!' The *shaykh* glowered at the thought of so many enemies. 'Lebanon is a Christian island in a Muslim sea. They hate us for that. We try to love them – we are Christians, *n'est-ce pas?* – but still they would like to kill every one of us if they could. Remember the massacres of 1860!' The *shaykh*'s gravelly voice swelled with injury. 'Those treacherous Druze killed more than twelve thousand of our people. Four thousand more starved to death. One hundred thousand were driven from their homes. Here, in our own country!' Shaykh Georges's eyes took on a hunted look. 'It could happen again, you know. They have not forgotten. Nor have we. If it were not for Mother France, what would have become of us?'

'*Inna faransa immanahanuna.*' Camilla took her cue to murmur the sentiment she had learned to recite like a catechism in her Maronite primary school. 'Truly, France is our benevolent mother.'

'*Exactement!* Good! I see you understand! It is maybe good that my son has a wife who went to the university. *Peut-être* I made a mistake with my Marie and my Yvette. But my wife said no daughters of hers would learn too much for their own good. And you know how we all must listen to her, ha! I am the king, but she is the empress!' Shaykh Georges let out a rattling sound that passed for a laugh. 'But tell me,' he resumed, 'you with your fine AUB education, what is the lesson we must never forget from that terrible massacre of our people in 1860?'

'We must never trust the Muslims,' Camilla dutifully answered, while mentally asking the forgiveness of Leila and Fatima.

'*Bon!* But what else?'

Camilla shrugged prettily. 'You are so much wiser than I am, *beau-père*. You tell me.'

'I told you already,' he snapped impatiently. 'Mother France, that's the lesson. France sent her troops to protect us. And they forced the Muslims to let us be kings in our own country. Which we still are!' Shaykh Georges smiled radiantly. But then he seemed to tire of his historical ramble. He glared at the servants. 'You! All of you! I wish to talk in private to the wife of my son. Leave us be!' When they were alone, Georges cleared his throat. 'In the salon, always somebody listens. My wife, the servants, those spying Syrians Pierre is always bringing home – all have very big ears. What we must discuss is, shall we say, *délicat*. Here only the cedars can spy on us. You see, *chérie*, it is time we talked about your marriage.'

She paled and took such a gulp at her coffee that she burnt her tongue and swallowed a mouthful of bitter grounds. She was not prepared for another round of cat and mouse with this old master of intrigue. The last thing she wanted was a *tête-à-tête* with him about the mysteries of her marriage.

'You are *triste*,' he purred helpfully. 'And I cannot have my daughter-in-law *triste*. Come, tell me everything.'

'Oh,' she said, as desperately she racked her brain for a means to tell him nothing in the most charming of ways. 'I'm not so sad. I have Tomas and the twins. And I've started drawing again. That's what I was doing this morning. Sketching my sons.' At a loss for anything else to say, she fell back on flattery. 'They're beautiful, your grandsons. Everyone says, *beau-père*, that they look just like you.'

He smiled his crocodile smile. 'Ah yes, your little hobby. All of us need *divertissement*.' One of his eyelids drooped shut and then sprang open again. 'I myself have hobbies. And so, it seems, does your husband.'

She decided she had been mistaken when she thought she had seen him wink at her. He was not only an old man but her husband's father. Again she appealed to his vanity. 'And I'm a Nazrani now. Nazranis are never *tristes*.'

'No?' He was no longer smiling as he fixed his tigerish eyes upon her. 'No more lies, eh? And no more flattery. I did not bring you up here to listen to you tell me what you think I want to hear. *Tu comprends?*' As she nodded and pressed her shaking hands into her pockets, he lit a Gauloise and inhaled it with great sucking noises. 'I am waiting', he finally said as he threw the stub down to the ground and stamped on it, 'to hear what you aim to do about your marriage.'

Camilla shrugged, hoping to disarm the old man with this helpless gesture that she had long ago perfected in front of her mirror. Even if her father-in-law spent all afternoon alternately trying to bully and cajole her, she was still not going to be tricked into confidences she would one day regret. He was a cobra, and she couldn't have a heart-to-heart with someone she sensed was poised to strike at her. Crocodile, lion, tiger, cobra? Yes, this predatory old man made her feel like a cornered beast. She had heard that animals could smell fear on a human being, and she wondered if Georges had that same gift of scent. Even though her hidden hands still shook, she thanked the Virgin that at least her voice was steady. 'You tell me.'

'*Eh bien, chérie*,' he said very softly. 'And so I will.' Briefly his knowing old eyes studied her, and he saw her shiver. He was not sorry that he had intimidated her again. Camilla had been riding a bit too high since Pierre's disgrace. Still, even though he had once again shown her that he and only he was boss, nevertheless he had given her the chance to speak her mind. It was not his problem that she had not chosen to use it to her advantage.

He lit another cigarette and seemed content to do the talking as he sipped his coffee. '*La vue ici*, it is *parfaite*, no?' He was all charm as he smiled, a little sadly. 'I wish I could say the same for my son. Pierre, Pierre, what will I do with that boy? Always he was a wild one. I thought, when he was younger, that he would grow out of it. That soon he would show that, after all, he is his father's son. But no, he gets worse. He's a weak one, my boy. It must be his mother's blood. *Oui, c'est ça.*' Almost to himself, he added the observation that sometimes greatness skipped a generation. 'Perhaps it will be different with Tomas and the twins. Yes! Maybe!' Then, as he leaned closer to Camilla, his voice became even more confidential. 'But, my dear, what are we to do? We are stuck with Pierre, you and I. Forever, he is my son and your husband. I can't disown him, and you can't divorce him.' He snapped his fingers. '*Tant pis!* But all is not lost!' He fixed his stare benignly upon her. 'I know they say I drive a hard bargain. They say I am like the Armenians, *hein?* But I am not unreasonable, and I am not a cheat. You have done well, giving the clan three healthy boys. Perhaps one day there will be more. But now, maybe you need a rest. I think you can relax and take some . . . liberties.'

Uncertainly she smiled and backed away from the old man's hot breath. Yet in a way those strange hypnotic yellowish eyes of his fascinated her. She had what she thought was an odd and unrelated thought. Until this moment, she had always assumed that young girls took up with old men just for the money. But now she understood that raw power could be almost as attractive as palpitating youth. Her lips were dry, and so she wet them with the tip of her tongue.

'Yes.' Jealously he watched her tongue retreat between her parted lips. 'I don't mind telling you, that I had my doubts when Pierre first said he wanted to marry a belly dancer's daughter. But, after the other night, I have no doubts. You were *formidable!* What fire! What passion! We are two of a kind, you and I.'

He could not, she thought with growing horror, mean what she thought he meant.

'Yes,' he murmured, 'oh yes.' He smiled with amusement as he saw her cringe away from him. 'You're a coy one,' he observed. Deliberately and this time unmistakably, he winked. 'No one will be the wiser if you begin to take some discreet pleasures of your own.'

Her hands were clammy, and she was sweating. She wanted to jump up and run away as fast and far as she could, but she was so shocked that she seemed to have lost her powers of speech and motion.

Briskly, then, as though tidying up the loose ends in a business contract, he qualified his offer. 'This is not carte blanche. Do not – ever! – dally at home. Not in Beirut, and certainly not here. Nowhere in Lebanon.' The *shaykh*'s face darkened. 'I will never forgive my son for breaking that one cardinal rule. Nothing at home, I told him. Never in the château. Was that so much to ask?' Fiercely he ground out his cigarette, and then shook off his ill humour as he returned to the matter at hand. Like a tour guide recommending the best spots for a quick lunch, he gave his daughter-in-law a few helpful tips about where to take her pleasures. 'It's not Paris, I know, but Cyprus is *très convenable*. You can hop over there after breakfast and be back in Beirut in time for dinner.' He smiled fondly, as though he were remembering a seductive rendezvous on Cyprus. 'They call it the island of Aphrodite, *n'est-ce pas*?' He laughed. Or, he said, if she didn't fancy Cyprus, she could venture further afield to Cairo, Athens, Rome or Paris, anywhere she liked. Just so long as she was discreet and didn't try to pass off as Nazranis any children that came from such liaisons, no one would blink an eyelash. As an afterthought, he passed on the information that neat, safe abortions could always be had in Sweden. But, under no circumstances, he ordered, was she ever to try to get an abortion here in Beirut. 'Understood?'

Camilla was still staring wide-eyed at him, and so

Shaykh Georges calculated that she must understand even more than he had implied. He smiled in triumph as he put his withered hand on her slim thigh. 'I', he whispered, 'have my own little love nest in Larnaca.'

For one more awful second, Camilla sat aghast. Then she jumped up, backed away, and burst into tears as his mocking laughter followed her down the mountain.

It was late that same afternoon when Camilla charged into the Crescent cabaret just as Nirvana was on stage rehearsing a new act. 'Mama! You have to help me, Mama!' Oblivious to the band, the stage hands and the waiters, she ran onstage and threw herself into her mother's arms. She was frantic from her mad dash down from the Château Croisé. All the way to Beirut, casting anxious looks out of the back window to make sure Georges hadn't sent someone chasing after her, she had urged the chauffeur to drive faster. She held tight to her mother and, with a rush of fresh tears, felt finally safe. She had already forgotten about the fight they had had just last week. As she cried on Nirvana's shoulder, she was certain her Mama would help her escape from the decadent clutches of the Nazranis.

But Nirvana had neither forgiven nor forgotten their tiff. 'You look terrible,' she said, as she examined her daughter's tear-stained face. 'You've got to stop this crying, *bébé*, or you will look like an old woman by the time you are thirty. As you always tell me, youth doesn't last for ever.'

'Mama! You must help me! I want a divorce! Those Nazranis, they are animals!'

In this intriguing emergency, Nirvana decided that she would have to let bygones be bygones. She sent the band off for a break, led Camilla over to the bar, and poured them both stiff brandies. 'Now dry your eyes, *chérie*, drink up, and start from the beginning. Tell Mama everything that's wrong.'

'It was awful.'

But it was only after she was well into her second drink that Camilla began to tell her story. Nirvana's eyes narrowed into furious slits as Camilla described catching Pierre in bed with the wet nurses. But she laughed and almost broke into applause when she heard how Camilla had led Shaykh Georges and the rest of the household in to witness Pierre's disgrace. She refilled their glasses and clinked hers triumphantly to Camilla's when her daughter related how she had taken old lady Nazrani down a peg or two. But when Camilla told her what Georges had said to her today up in the cedar grove, Nirvana merely put her glass back down on the bar and stared off thoughtfully into space.

'And then he laughed, Mama! As I was running away, I could hear him laughing.'

'Perhaps he had been joking. If I went to bed with every man who put his hand on my thigh – *aiee!*' She slapped her thigh in amusement at the very thought. 'Maybe, *bébé*, that is the best thing, to treat it as a joke.'

Camilla shook her head and started to cry again. 'They are animals! And I will never go back up there to live with them on that awful mountain! *Jamais!*' She wiped her eyes. 'You have to help me get a divorce.'

Wearily Nirvana shook her head. 'You know that there is no divorce in the Maronite church.'

Camilla had thought this over on the ride down from the château. 'So I'll be Greek Orthodox. Convert, like *you* did. You used to be a Maronite. But you've had three divorces, Mama.'

Nirvana sighed. 'It was different for me.' She gave her shoulders a hopeless little Gallic shrug. 'After your father left, what else could I do? It seemed I had lost him for ever, and yet the church wouldn't give me a divorce.' Her tone grew defensive. 'Anyway, I'm not so religious. And what's the big difference, anyway? Maronite or Greek Orthodox, they're both Christian. It's not as if I'd turned Muslim.'

'*Exactement!* I knew you'd agree!' For the first time since she had arrived, Camilla smiled. 'So tell me, first how do I change to the Greek church? And then how long until I get my divorce?'

Nirvana shook her head. 'You don't,' she said gently. 'You cannot, *bébé*. The Nazranis would never agree. You know that. You must know that.'

As she poured them fresh drinks, Nirvana set about the delicate business of sharing a few home truths with her daughter. 'You must understand, *chérie*, that the Nazranis are different from you and me. Shaykh Georges is powerful. And, as I think you know very well now, he is ruthless.' Camilla might have been able to get her marriage annulled before she had Tomas, but such a thing was impossible now that she was the mother of a new generation of Nazranis. The legitimacy of the boys could never be called into question. Today, when he had said she was stuck with Pierre for ever, Georges had only been stating the truth.

Nirvana leaned over and brushed Camilla's hair back from her face. 'You must open your big blue eyes, *bébé*. You are not a little girl anymore. But do not despair. All is not lost.' Her voice filled with longing. 'You are still so young. So very fresh! You can have anyone. Anyone you want!' She snapped her fingers. 'I think that, once you give yourself a little time to think all this over, you might not be so hard on Shaykh Georges . . .' Nirvana's voice trailed off wistfully. She herself had always considered him a fine figure of a man, and *très viril*. If it hadn't been for that crone of a wife of his, she herself might have made a play for the *shaykh* ages ago. She still might someday. Reluctantly Nirvana turned her mind from that delicious thought back to the matter at hand. 'He may have only been trying to do you *une petite faveur*, today, you know. He has given you your liberty. And, believe me, *chérie*, that is a gift that you should treasure. You can have it all – marriage, money, and a bit of *l'amour* on the side.' She downed the remainder of her drink and then nodded sagely at her daughter. 'My advice is to take old man Nazrani at his word.' Of course, she added quickly when she saw the look on Camilla's face, she was not suggesting that her daughter dabble in incest. But Nirvana could not resist smiling wickedly. 'That is, not unless you fancy him . . .?'

'*Jamais!*' Camilla resolutely set her chin. '*Jamais!*'

'Never say never, darling. A woman is always entitled to change her mind.' Nirvana emptied what was left of the brandy into their glasses. 'Don't worry, you'll come round. Maybe not to Shaykh Georges. But there are lots of other fish in the sea.'

And so it was that, when Nirvana and Camilla flew off to Cyprus a fortnight later for a little holiday, the mother and daughter idled in the sun with a Danish water-ski instructor and a Greek god of a fisherman. By the time they returned to Lebanon, Camilla had shed what was left of her innocence.

Chapter 12

'Anne! Camilla! Fatima!'

Long months later, Leila was the last of them to arrive at their reunion in Anne's lemon-yellow bedroom on the Rue Bliss. Her timing, as she brandished a bottle of chilled Tattinger Comte de Champagne above her head, was as professional as that of an Equity actress. In her dazzlingly slender white Honan silk Chanel suit set off by gold buttons and a thick gold chain, she paused on the threshold just long enough for them to take in how she had changed for the better in the three years they had been apart. Her hair was bobbed shorter and teased out in a Jackie Kennedy-style bouffant topped by a white pillbox hat. 'Hello, you old darlings!'

Camilla tossed her mane of heavy blonde hair back from her carefully made-up face and wished she had pulled out all the stops and worn her heart-stopping geometric pink and red Pucci silk dress, instead of this little sleeveless black crêpe sheath her dressmaker had copied from a Marc Bohan photograph in a Paris magazine. She reproached herself for not remembering how competitive Leila was about fashion, and everything else. Camilla's eyes narrowed as she sized up the changes in her old Palestinian friend. Leila looked thinner, richer, but her colour-blind beautician must have left the henna on her now-orangy hair a good hour too long. Smugly Camilla patted her own coiffure, glad that she had let it grow out of that insipid American bouffant that Leila had taken up a year too late.

All this posturing and primping was lost on Fatima, who was engrossed in the laborious business of heaving herself up to greet Leila with proper kisses, hugs and kind words. Radiantly pregnant with her third baby in two years of marriage, Fatima was twice the size she used to be. Yet still, even with her clumsy figure and that old white polyester headscarf, Fatima's round sunburned face shone as luminous as a full harvest moon.

Leila, however, had eyes only for Anne. She had already talked to the others since she came home at the beginning of the summer to prepare for her wedding. But Anne had flown in from the States only yesterday. She opened her arms wide and swept the American into her embrace. 'It's been too long,' she murmured rapturously, as she clung to the one she still fondly regarded as her best friend. 'Now let me see how you *are*.' Leila expectantly stepped back, but her smile was stillborn. Anne was wearing thick-rimmed glasses and had strained her once-glorious hair severely back in a spinsterish bun. Worse, her face was pale and drawn, there were dark circles under her eyes, and her clothes looked like cast-offs bought by the pound in a jumble sale. 'Bloody hell,' she blurted out, 'it's been as bad as that, has it?'

Anne bit her lip and, as she shrank away from Leila, she wished she had not risked more rejection by coming home. So far, despite her wistful expectations, the first few wooden moments of this long-awaited reunion had only made her feel more depressed. True, until just now, the others hadn't said or done anything to hurt her. Dear Fatima would have been glad to see her even if she had come home with a shaved head, and Camilla had been too busy talking about herself to notice that anything was amiss. But in that honest and unguarded instant when Leila had looked her over and found her wanting, Anne had seen herself as others must see her. She had just enough pride left to be mortified that her old friends, who had known her before the nightmare began, should witness what she had become. She should have answered Leila's wedding invitation with heartfelt regrets and a splendid gift. It was a mistake to have come home. She had known that even at the airport, when her mother had burst into tears and said she hardly recognized her. Her father had acted as if she were an invalid, holding her tight and telling her not to worry, that she was home now, and that everything would be all right. But everything was not all right. Everything had been all wrong for more than a year, since . . .

Inside Anne there was a sensation of sinking lower and lower, back down into that pit where she had lived since Mike had done what he had done. No, she should not have come home. She should have stayed on ice, in exile in Boston. As soon as Leila's wedding was over next week, she would have to fly back to

New England and accept that prestigious internship she had been offered at Mass General. Mike wasn't there anymore. She had heard that he and his family had moved to Buffalo. She could have been safe at Mass General. She had been a sentimental fool to come home again and try to pick up where she had left off with her family and friends. Yet she had dreamed that, without her having to say a word, her old friends would have understood how things were with her, that she was in disguise – wearing what she thought of as her protective camouflage against all the predatory men in the world. But now that they had failed her and she had failed them, she was humiliated that she had allowed them to see her like this. She should have realized that not even her old friends could love her as she was now. Another illusion lost, she thought; another betrayal, this time of friendship. Soon they would all be making excuses and slipping out of the door. In a way, however, she almost wished they *would* leave, and right now. If any of them said one more critical word to her, she would burst into tears, and then she would lose the last tatters of her self-respect.

Instead, Fatima loyally leapt to the defence of *her* best friend who obviously, now that her heart had been broken by that devil back in America, needed her more than ever. 'Leila! Enough!' As if Anne were one of her beloved babies, she had an impulse to scoop her friend up in her arms and hold her tight and protect her against all the wrongs of the world. Poor Anne, to have had to endure such hurt and shame! Of course she should never have let that man touch her until they were married. That was wrong, yes, *very* wrong. But Anne had been lonely, far from home, and bewitched by too many Hollywood lies about what love was supposed to be. Still, Fatima was disappointed that a woman as good as she knew Anne to be could have fallen prey to such temptation. Anne's tragedy only proved how necessary all the old rules were to protect over-generous women from the cruelties of uncaring men. What had happened to Anne could have befallen any woman rash enough to follow her heart instead of the laws of God and society. More and more, when she saw the suffering caused by broken romances, Fatima was convinced that an arranged match like hers was the wisest solution to the riddle of how to form men and women – so different, really, that they seemed not of the same species – into durable families. She glared at Leila as though she were the one responsible for this situation. 'Leave Anne alone.'

The Palestinian bristled at the Shia. As if it were yesterday, she suddenly remembered how Fatima had once cut her to the core by reminding her that she and her people did not belong in Lebanon. She recalled, too, with growing irritation, how sanctimonious Fatima had always been, and how she still seemed to delight in trying to make the rest of the world feel guilty about anything and everything. Well, this time it wasn't going to work. The years in London, and her own bitter decisions there, had left her colder and harder. She hadn't said anything so terrible just now. 'Mind your own business, dearie.'

Drolly Camilla rolled her eyes. In the old days it had always been Anne who had kept the peace between the two bickering Muslims. But now Camilla smoothly stepped into the breach. 'Girls, girls!' She, too, was remembering the many boring occasions when Leila and Fatima had snapped at one another for hours. She hoped they weren't in for another marathon session, complete with contradictory quotations from the Koran. Instead she was eager to begin sharing her delicious discoveries of *l'amour*. Since the four of them had scattered to the winds, she had never found anyone to take their place. So often, after her marriage had begun to sour, she had longed for the solace of being together just like this. Yet everything was not as it once was. Fatima had turned into a contented milkcow, Leila had the lacquered gloss of a *mannequin*, and Anne had the hopeless air of a refugee.

As one expert in covering up the tell-tale traces of tears, Camilla studied the pink-veined whites of Anne's eyes, her puffy cheeks, and the nearly oriental narrowness of her eyes. Anne wasn't as pretty as she used to be. But in her sadly sensitive face, there was still the glimmer of something – was it character, wisdom, goodness, or just a trick of the light? – that might one day develop into true beauty. Obviously Anne, too, had come to know sorrow. Maybe later, when the two of them lunched together, she might confide the bald truth about what a mistake it had been to marry Pierre. But she was not about to be candid in front of Leila, who would probably spread her secret all over Beirut. Better to make a brittle joke of her own unhappiness. Everyone liked her better when she laughed, and so she seldom cried in public anymore. Her racy new *spécialité* was witty woman-of-the-world anecdotes that illustrated how sophisticated she had become. If she were *très amusante*, her friends might even slap their sides with laughter when she told them about finding Pierre in bed with the nurses. *Quel scandale!* Fatima would blush and blush! Then perhaps she would proceed with the rest of her repertoire about the first lover she had taken in Cyprus and the subsequent ones she had dallied with in Paris and Sardinia. But if Leila and Fatima were allowed to continue carping at each other, the four of them would never get down to sharing the juice of their lives. 'Three years we do not see our Anne, always only the letters and maybe sometimes the telephone. And so finally again we are together, and what happens?' It was clear the Palestinian was still the troublemaker, and so judiciously Camilla apportioned blame where it was due. 'Again, Leila, you begin with the bad words, just as before.'

Camilla and Fatima were picking on her again. But the only way Leila could defend herself was by hurting Anne's feelings even more than she already had. Anyone with eyes could see that Anne was a disaster, yet apparently they were supposed to pretend that nothing was wrong. For now, however, it was best to make hasty amends. 'Sorry, darlings. I was just concerned, that's all.'

As she studied Anne's pallid face, Leila reproached herself for not zooming over to Boston on a mercy mission as soon as Ramsey had told her about the disastrous business with that married man. Yet she had stayed put in England, doing no more and no less than what her father had sent her there to do: studying a little, socializing a lot. Even though she had not worked as hard as she might have at Cambridge, she had finished her thesis on Arab socialism and persuaded the dons to award her that coveted doctorate last month. What was even more important for her family in the long run, however, was that she had strengthened the Shahine connections by cultivating every Arab and Arabist who counted in London's cosmopolitan worlds of university, diplomacy, business and government. Yet she should have made the time to rush to her best friend's side when she needed her.

Leila hid a sigh of deep discontent by lighting a cigarette. She supposed that what others accused her of was true, that she was selfish. Still, she thought, as she inhaled all the way down to her toes, these last few cynical years had not been a bed of roses for her, either. After she had renounced Hussein, she had come to the conclusion that it wasn't only the weather in England – but life itself – that was grey and mean. This marriage she was about to begin with the old man her father had picked out for her was hardly a love match. Mustafa el-Kuttab was a hairy old spider, and her flesh crept when he so much as touched her hand. Nevertheless, she had smiled bravely and worn an exquisite creation from Maison Dior when Mustafa had flown in for the engagement party in the Dorchester ballroom. If the black of her strapless gown had made a rebellious statement about how she viewed this cold alliance, then so be it. But for the sake of her family and her people, she was determined to make him a stunning wife and a splendid hostess. She would trade loathsome kisses for luscious power, and in time she herself might even become a political force to be reckoned with in Lebanon. She was not going to allow herself to be dragged down by regrets. She had made her bed, and she was going to get the maximum benefits from lying in it. When she found herself yearning for Hussein and what she had lost with their love, she very determinedly turned her mind to other more pressing matters: places she had to go, people she had to charm, Palestine that had to be rewon. She would not brood over lost love. She was one of life's winners, never a loser. Yet sometimes, in a certain mood, she had only to glimpse a dark crewcut and a dirty mackintosh, or hear someone hiss as he sucked on a cigarette, or read a brooding poem by Mahmoud Darwish, and she was left desolate with loss. Hussein, oh Hussein! Sometimes – although she never actually did this – she felt like beating her chest in an ecstasy of grief, just as Fatima's Shias did every year on Ashura. Oddly enough, that was exactly what they chanted in honour of the hero they had lost long ago: 'Hussein, *ya*, Hussein!' But even though she – like Anne – had loved and lost, she – unlike Anne – had pulled herself together.

With a certain smugness, Leila smoothed her suit jacket down over her slim hips. Yet she hadn't meant to hurt Anne, who had after all come all the way from America for her wedding. She hadn't even wanted to start a new cycle of insults with Fatima. She had wanted this reunion, and everything else connected with her wedding, to be perfect. When she had looked fondly back on her halcyon university years in Beirut, she had remembered being closer to these girls than she was to her own sisters-by-blood. She decided to make another stab at getting back into everyone's good books. She reached over and removed Anne's glasses before the American could stop her. 'There! Now we can see that face we've all missed so much! That's *much* better.' She snapped her fingers. 'Contact lenses, darling! We'll go shopping for them tomorrow.' She eyed Anne critically. 'Now, if you'd just fluff out your hair a bit, add some good gold earrings, and maybe belt in that dress tight, to show off your figure – you've lost weight, I see! – then your new look could really be quite something. Still just a bit too casual, perhaps, but after all you *are* American. You'd look quite the California girl.'

'I think she looks wonderful just the way she is.' Fatima truly did believe that Anne looked dignified in her glasses, with her hair strained back away from her face. Without cosmetics, Anne's inner beauty was even more evident. Fatima bestowed the ultimate compliment on the one she loved like a sister. 'Anne is like a Shia, really. Yes! If she would just go one more step and cover her hair, she would look like a woman in my village. She is just a little bit tired, that is all.'

'The lag of the jets,' Camilla tactfully agreed. Frowning at Anne's baggy colourless dress, she nonethelesss gave her *chère amie* the benefit of the doubt. 'Maybe I saw that *robe* in *Vogue?* The sack dress, it is coming back?'

Anne shrugged and, as though she were seeing it for the first time, she looked down at what she had thrown on today. 'Oh, *this*. I got it on sale at Filene's Basement. It's really comfortable, you know.' Uncertainly she smiled. Despite her fears, her old friends hadn't walked out on her, at least not yet. And each, in her own well-meaning way, had tried to be supportive. How she had missed them! No matter what her passport said, her home was here among these people she knew as well as her own broken heart. For old time's sake, Anne made a final effort to be as they must remember her. 'You look terrific, Leila. As if you have the world by the tail.' For an instant, as she smiled at her friend, Anne summoned up her old champagne sparkle. 'You'll be such a beautiful bride.' But at the thought of love and marriage, Anne fell flat again. Her voice caught. 'I've missed you. How I've missed you.' She looked over at Fatima and Camilla. 'All of you. Maybe if you'd been there, if I'd had someone to talk to when Mike . . .' Anne sighed and wiped away a tear.

For one incredulous moment, they stared as the one who used to be the keystone of their foursome crumpled down on her bed. Helplessly they watched as Anne covered her face with her hands and cried with great wrenching sobs.

'The man who did that to her was a devil.' Fatima clenched and unclenched her fists. 'He was *al-shaytan* himself!' As she raged, there was a fierceness that her friends had never seen in Fatima before, a foreshadowing of a woman who, when roused, would some day be as implacable as an avenging angel. 'But take heart, Anne! On the Day of Judgement, he will have to answer for what he did to you. Allah is all-knowing, and even though He is merciful, He will punish those who transgress.'

'Bloody right!' For once, Leila was in complete accord with Fatima. She, too, seemed to relish the image of the man who had wronged Anne burning for ever in hell. She would have liked to cast him down there herself. 'But come now, darling,' she coaxed. 'It's been more than a year since that happened. Stiff upper lip.'

'You can't cry.' Camilla dug in her purse until she found a lacy linen handkerchief to give to Anne. 'I'm the one that's supposed to cry.' Instead she smiled.

When Anne, however, did not so much as look up but only cried the harder, the other three exchanged worried glances. Should they tiptoe out and leave Anne to her private grief?

Instead, something wonderful happened. As they crowded down on the bed beside Anne and put their arms around her, their knowing women's eyes met. Their old intimacy, which so far had eluded them today, was suddenly back for the taking. Leila and Camilla abandoned their pretence that everything was right in their compromised worlds. Fatima, too, stopped trying to judge these others whose lives contradicted all that she had been taught was right. For despite their differences of religion, class and culture, the lives of women were a great leveller. Life was hard, yes, hard and cruel. Nothing was the way everyone had told them it would be. Love hurt, and men seldom did what they should. A current of understanding coursed between them and wordlessly, as women sometimes can do, they drew strength and resolve from how they cared for each other.

Anne wiped her eyes on the sleeve of her dress. 'Sorry, gang.' Camilla handed over her dainty lace handkerchief, and Anne obligingly blew her nose into it. 'You don't know what it means to me to be with you, and here I am, carrying on. I'll ruin our reunion.'

'Actually, I think you've just saved it.' Leila grinned. 'It would take more than a few tears to ruin what we have.' As she lit another cigarette, she made an impulsive decision. To hell, for once, with weighing every word as though she were being quoted in a newspaper interview. Soon enough, Allah knows, most of her life with old man Mustafa would be a lie. She had intended to lay it on thick today about how ecstatic she was about her gown, her wedding, her future. She had hoped that, if she convinced them, she might even convince herself that she was happy. But these women were her friends, and she would trust them with the sad truth of what a mess she was making of her life. 'Besides, I don't know about Fatima and Camilla – at least not yet – but I've had a pretty bloody awful time of it in England, too.'

'You have?' Camilla looked astonished, and a little pleased. Maybe, after all, she would tell them exactly how it was with herself and Pierre.

As Fatima's hand crept out for Leila's cigarette pack, she let out a deep sigh that all of them heard. She never, ever complained to anyone about anything. But she had a sneaking suspicion, as she lit a Craven A, that she was about to let loose the dam of her discontents.

Even Anne smiled as they all eagerly leaned forward. The words spilled out in a rush, yet each of them took care to listen to the others.

Even when it came to the baring of souls, Leila of course insisted on going first. 'Anne is not the only one who fell in love with the wrong man. You will not believe this, but mine was *poor* and a *Communist!* Baba absolutely *hated* him.'

'Mustafa el-Kuttab is a Communist?' Camilla was aghast. 'But everyone says he'll be Prime Minister someday.'

'No, no. Not *him*.' Leila's contemptuous tone said all that it was necessary to say about the ageing Mustafa. 'Someone else.' She smiled mysteriously, but then she hesitated before she decided to trust them with her secret. 'His name was Hussein Ibrahim, and he was absolutely brilliant. Everyone says that one day he'll be known as Palestine's Lenin.' Her eyes flashed with pride. It was wonderful to say her love's name out loud, and to boast about him. 'Allah, we were over the moon about each other. He begged me to marry him. Begged me! And for a while I thought I might.' Leila's shoulders sagged, and as her grieving eyes met Anne's, a new bond was forged between old friends. 'But then I talked it over with my father. Baba was dead set against him –

it was his idea, you know, that I marry Mustafa. And so I broke it off with Hussein.'

'You still love him,' Anne said softly. It was a statement, not a question.

'Oh yes,' Leila admitted.

Fatima leaned closer and dropped her voice nearly to a whisper as she asked what for her was the crucial question. 'Yes, but did you . . . you know . . . *do anything* with him?'

Leila shook her head. 'A few kisses, that's all.' She looked Fatima straight in the eye, and they did not have to say aloud what they were both thinking. When it came to the point, they shared the same traditional values. Both had married as their fathers wished, and both would be virgins on their wedding night.

Fatima put her arm around Leila, and for a moment the two of them looked like true sisters as they smoked companionably with their heads together. 'Perhaps your father knew best,' Fatima said, to console her old friend. But the worried look on her face showed that she was not quite convinced of it. It had after all been different for her and Ali. She had not been in love with someone else when she had given in and married him. What was more, as she had begun to understand the ins and outs of a marriage, she had become aware what *baraka* it was – what a rare blessing from Allah – that she and Ali had fallen so passionately in love. Most of the arranged marriages in her village worked in their way, but few were as happy as hers. Some men beat their wives, and others – still more cruelly, Fatima thought – hardly bothered to acknowledge their existence. She understood now, too, that even a marriage based on shared values and mutual enchantment had its impossible seasons. Her heart ached for Leila, and the shell of a marriage that seemed to be her destiny.

'You really think so?' Leila, for once, allowed herself to sound uncertain.

'*Inshallah*,' Fatima said. 'I will pray that it is so.'

Camilla cut in briskly before the two Muslims could get too sickeningly pious. 'Maybe it was your *bonne chance*, Leila, to get away from that Hussein.' Camilla turned up her pretty nose at the thought of a Communist. '*I* married for love, and what did I get?' She thrust out her palms to show they were empty. '*Rien du tout!*'

'Pierre? Nothing? Can this be possible?' Fatima wrinkled her forehead. 'I remember at AUB, when he used to pick you up in his sports car. How he would kiss you, just there, in front of everyone! I never saw two people in love like you and Pierre. I used to wish it could be like that for me some day. You were like movie stars.'

'*Ah, oui.*' As though she were too weary to shrug her shoulders, Camilla made do with lifting and then dropping her eyebrows. 'But the honeymoon has been over for a long time. And *vraiment*, as far as I am concerned, the marriage, *c'est fini* as well.' Her face was not so pretty as she hissed, 'Pierre and his whores, and his whisky, and his gambling, and his hashish! Even when I was pregnant the first time, with my darling Tomas, already he goes here, there, everywhere with his other women. All I did in Paris was cry, yes, just like you do now, Anne, *chérie*. Then, here at home, the final blow!' Camilla had told the story of the wet nurses so often that her delivery was usually as ironical and detached as that of a professional *comédienne*. Now, however, as she repeated the sorry tale yet again, her voice was thick with emotion. She wept as she came to the end of it. 'In my own bed! He brought my babies' two wet nurses into my own bed! Two of them at once! I caught them at it! Imagine!'

Leila barely managed to stop herself from tartly observing what very big beds they must have up at the château. In her mind's eye, she could see it just as it must have happened: Pierre and the girls, Shaykh Georges firing his pearl-handled revolver, and Camilla crying a river of tears. 'So what did you do?'

'I got even.' There was nothing of the mewling sex kitten about Camilla as she grimly told her friends how she had led her father-in-law and the rest of the family into the bedroom to catch her husband *en flagrant délit.*

'Wonderful!' Leila was much more admiring of this formidable woman than of the crybaby she had known at university.

'*Merci.*' Camilla lowered her voice, even though no one but her dear friends were within earshot. 'But there are compensations, you know.' She giggled. 'The first one was a water-skiing instructor from Denmark, very tall and blond, like an angel. I met him on Cyprus. He was the best, really. The others . . .' Camilla pouted. 'Like Pierre, they are nothing to me.'

'You don't say?' Leila was intrigued. The thought had crossed her mind that someday she might, very discreetly, kiss her traditional values goodbye and go the same adulterous route.

'Lovers,' Anne said. Despite herself, she shuddered.

Fatima's eyes were still round with shock when Leila turned to her. 'And what about you, *habibi?* What's it like, married to your cousin, stuck back in that horrid village?'

Fatima was at a loss for words. Compared to her friends, she was a happy woman leading a contented life. But she knew it would never do to say so after the others had confided their sensational tales of woe. Yet her cares were so different from theirs that for a moment she simply smoked as she collected her thoughts. 'Well, we are poor, you know,' she began. 'Very poor. There is no work for the men in the south anymore, and this makes for much trouble. Some of the men go away to work in Beirut or even South America and Africa, like my father and brothers. But sometimes the money they send home doesn't come in time, or at all. You might not believe it, because of how big I am now in my seventh month, but there is not always enough for us to eat. Sometimes the children die. Even those who live have so much sickness. My sister's three babies died last year, one after the other. And in the rains and the cold of his first winter, I thought my Muhammad would never live to see the spring. But God was merciful. He's a big boy now, my Muhammad. Allah be praised!'

'I didn't know how it was with you.' Camilla impulsively put her hand over Fatima's and squeezed. She was a mother herself, and she was appalled at the thought of anyone she knew having to worry about her baby's survival because it was cold, hungry or sick. So far as she understood it, things like this happened in outlandish places like Africa or Asia, or under harsh régimes as in Russia. It was news to her that anyone suffered like this in a rich and modern country like Lebanon. 'Why did you not tell me? I would have helped. Sent money, food, blankets – anything!'

'I am not a beggarwoman,' Fatima said with the hauteur of one who, though she had been born poor and expected to remain so all her life, would always cherish her pride.

'I'll talk to Mustafa,' Leila promised. 'When he's Prime Minister, I'll make sure your village is put to rights.'

Fatima shook her head. 'It is not only my family and my village that suffers. It is the same with all the Shia. Not just in the south but in the Bekaa Valley, too. Always it has been like this for my people. Everywhere in the Islamic world, we have less than our Sunni brothers. As my husband says, what we need is not charity from one friend to another, but a government that does more than take our taxes and then forget we exist.' A hopeless sigh escaped her lips. 'Ali says this is God's will. That we will have our reward in Paradise, *inshallah*. But I cannot help it! I get so angry when the children are hungry!'

Anne shook her head. 'So it's still the same down there, is it? How about the schools and medical care?'

'What schools? What medical care?' Bitter new lines were etched on Fatima's face. 'For a while I tried to make my own little school for the girls. Some of them came in the mornings to learn to read and write. One or two succeeded. But then Ali returned, and we began our married life. I got pregnant, and it was harder for me to go every day. After Muhammad arrived, I was needed more at home than in my little school for the girls.' Her eyes grew sad. 'That was my dream, you know, to teach all the women, not just the little girls but the old women, too. I wanted them all to be able to read the Koran. But I failed.'

'You didn't fail,' Anne warmly assured her. She was moved by Fatima's battles against ignorance and disease and a little ashamed of herself for brooding so long and hard over the injustices of her own fate. 'It might take longer than you thought, but you'll get there. I know you will.' Her face glowed with admiration. 'I think you're very brave.'

Jealously Leila watched Anne and Fatima exchange shy smiles. A little mouse like Fatima brave? If she thought she could have got away with it, she would have snatched her cigarette from Fatima's lips and crushed it into Anne's cheap imitation Persian carpet. Instead she set about showing up Fatima for what she was. 'And what about that husband of yours? I suppose you let him treat you like a slave.'

'No, it is not like that with us at all. Ali is a good man.' Fatima's face brightened as she remembered how good, and in how many different ways. Now she understood that what the others wanted was not so much the story of her life but the story of her love, she felt enough at home with them to oblige. She was truly in a woman's world in this bedroom, and so she took off her headscarf and let down her hair. 'You know I did not want to marry him? I told my father, "No, no, no." But in the end, like Leila, I did as I was told. How I cried when I got home after agreeing to marry him! They made me do it on the telephone, without even seeing him. But then when he came back from Iran, we fell in love. I was so surprised! Ali and I in love! Just as Madame Kismet said!' She laughed. 'I think now that we have all been in love, no? Yes! And I think, too, for all of us, to be in love must feel the same. Ah! How he would look at me! Just to be near him was bliss! Is there anything more wonderful on this earth? Paradise must be like that, eh?'

'Only in the beginning.' Camilla was not smiling. 'After a few years, it is more like hell.'

'For me it was good for only a few months.' Anne seemed once more on the verge of tears.

Fatima hastily continued. 'But everything began to change when the babies came, one right after the other.' She patted her swollen belly. 'With this one, I will have three of them, and the oldest not yet two years old.' She sighed. 'It is hard, so many children, so fast. I am big, no? Even when I am not pregnant, I am big.' She looked longingly at Leila, so slim and elegant in her Chanel. 'Sometimes I feel so old,' she whispered. 'But I am twenty-four years old, the same as you.' She shook her head. 'I should not be saying all this. I tell myself that it is wicked for me to complain, that I am blessed by Allah with a good husband and two beautiful sons.' A single tear trickled down Fatima's cheek. 'But sometimes I ask myself, "Is this all there is? One man, many babies, endless work?" And now that Ali is used to me, he takes me for granted. He is so busy at the mosque, and I am so busy with the babies, that it seems there is never time just for the two of us to be together. Sometimes I miss him so much. Love? Is this how love feels? Is this all there is?'

Anne put her arm around Fatima, and Camilla passed the Shia another handkerchief from the stack she kept ready in her purse.

Now that she was satisfied that Fatima was having as miserable a time as the rest of them, Leila was once again all smiles. Belatedly she remembered her bottle of champagne. 'I say it's time for a drink.'

While Leila peeled off the foil wrapping, twisted off the wires and popped the cork, Anne and Camilla raced downstairs for the glasses. When they returned carrying not only the glasses but a tray of tea and cakes, Leila was trying to bully Fatima into setting aside her old-fashioned religious scruples just this once. 'It's only wine,' she wheedled. 'You eat grapes and raisins. This is the same thing.' She poured four foamy glasses.

'Now a toast,' Camilla said.

'To Leila, Mustafa, and her wedding!' Anne raised her glass.

'May God bless you with many children and a good life.' Fatima followed the custom and lifted her glass.

'*L'amour! Toujours l'amour!*' Camilla laughed.

'No! We can't drink just to my wedding or to love. Let's drink to something that lasts.' Exuberantly Leila raised her glass way above her head. 'Here's to us! And to eternal friendship!'

They clinked their glasses, laughed, and even Fatima allowed a little of the forbidden alcohol to touch her lips. But as the others drained their glasses, discreetly Fatima used Camilla's handkerchief to wipe away the champagne. She passed her brimming glass to Anne, and Camilla and Leila giggled as they set about finishing off the bottle between them. Anne poured the tea, Fatima passed around the cakes, and the girls draped themselves out on the bed and the floor.

When they all were settled in, the four of them opened their mouths and began talking at exactly the same time.

'Hussein . . .'

'Pierre . . .'

'Ali . . .'

'Mike . . .'

They laughed and, as she bit into a honey cake, Anne said she really didn't understand why they all cared about men so much.

'*Exactement*,' Camilla agreed. 'They are not worth it, the devils.'

'Why can't they be more like us?' Leila asked.

'In my village, too,' Fatima shyly admitted, 'always the women say these same things.'

So it was that the four of them polished off the cream cakes as they resumed the delicious business of making up for lost time.

Leila dipped and swayed and glided in glorious swirling circles around the palatial ballroom of the Saint Georges as the orchestra played the schmaltzy waltz that her father had commissioned from a Viennese composer specially for her wedding. As she danced in her husband's arms with her head flung back and eyes flashing, she heard the murmurs from the thousand or so friends and enemies who had come to see and be seen at what Beirut's most jaded society columnist was calling 'this year's wedding of the century'. Yes, she wanted to call out, this exquisite ivory lace and *duchesse* satin gown was designed just for me by Yves Saint Laurent. More to the point, that's right, it did cost sixteen thousand dollars. Her wedding presents had been equally lavish. Besides giving her a portfolio of stocks at her engagement party, her father – who was taking up permanent residence in London – had settled his villa in Aley on her as part of her dowry. One of the hotel's more commodious reception rooms had been pressed into service to display the treasure trove of her other gifts: gold-plated china, silver teasets, an Aubusson carpet. Leila had joked cynically to Anne just the other day that it would not be entirely out of keeping with the increasingly vulgar spirit of the occasion for her to wear price tags plastered all over her: so much for the dress, so much more for the rest of her trousseau, and a grand total of such-and-such for her fair tanned body. *Stop it*, she told herself sharply. No regrets, especially not here where I belong, dancing in the spotlight. This was my choice. I said I would marry Mustafa, and I have, dear God I have.

Leila's lips smiled, but her eyes were cold as she stared at her husband of only a few hours. Mustafa el-Kuttab was fifty-six years old, and he looked it, with his bald pate and big bullish body. He had kinky hair, a bulging paunch, and he always wore black-rimmed glasses with lenses as thick as the bottom of Coke bottles. Still, besides being as rich as a Gulf oil *shaykh* and everybody's favourite candidate for the next Prime Minister, he was a kind man. He had been a model husband to his first wife who had died a few years back, and he served on the boards of seven Beirut charities. Even so, Leila's stomach lurched, and in her mouth was a sour aftertaste like vomit. It had been bad enough at the mosque this afternoon when she had recited the few words that bound her to this old man. But worse was to follow. Soon, too soon – in just a few hours – this rich, powerful and reputedly kind man would lie naked on top of her and make her bleed into wifedom. Try as she might to tell herself that this was as it should be, that Baba would never have married her off to anyone who would treat her as less than a queen, she longed to disappear out of the door and never come back. She had heard that, after collecting his doctorate, Hussein had returned to Gaza. She supposed she could find him there now. If she ran away before Mustafa had touched her, a divorce would be easy to arrange. Instead, she missed not a beat as she danced to the rhythm of the waltz like a baroque figure on a rococo music box.

'They say that music was written just for her,' Camilla breathed enviously to Anne from where they stood with their heads together on the edge of the dance floor. Fresh from a shopping spree in Paris, Camilla had pulled out all the stops and come in the latest sensation from Dior: a long and lavish mauve beaded blouse over a ballooning white *peau de soie* floor-length skirt. Yet even though she was accustomed to being very rich now and buying whatever struck her fancy, neither she nor anyone else she had ever known had had the wit to dream of buying a song. As usual, Leila and her snooty Palestinian family were the first off the mark in Beirut.

'Yes, that was a nice touch,' Anne agreed, even though she thought this trite little waltz was about as original as the cereal jingles that played incessantly on American television. 'Your veil looks wonderful, too.' Camilla had insisted that, just as she had loaned Fatima the Nazrani bridal veil for her wedding, Leila must also honour their friendship by wearing the heirloom. Anne looked at her watch. Would this reception never end? It was two o'clock in the morning, and the dancing had just begun. Still to come were the fireworks out over the bay and what was inaccurately described as the 'midnight supper'. Unhappily Anne faced the fact that this ordeal would last long past dawn, when the inevitable champagne breakfast would be served. She would have to smile and laugh and pretend that she was enjoying herself for three or four more hours. She longed to race home, throw off this absurd ball gown Camilla and Leila had insisted she wear, and then soak her aching feet in the bathtub. Camilla had spotted the photograph of this opulent Balmain strapless off-white satin gown in the latest *Vogue* and fallen in love with the way the glorious blue satin stole was wrapped around the bodice. Leila had promptly commissioned her dressmaker to run up a copy. When she had put it on for the first time at home on the Rue Bliss, Anne had hardly recognized her glamorous new self. But now she had had enough of this Cinderella masquerade. She hated weddings. This was the first she had dared attend for more than a year, since *that*, and *him*.

As Anne gnawed her lower lip and watched the bride and groom, she told herself she should have realized that a wedding would re-open her wound. But she was determined not to let her bad humour show. She would never say out loud what she thought about the grossness of those eight groaning buffet tables scattered around the public rooms of Beirut's most fashionable hotel, the troupe of plump Egyptian dancing girls who had snaked their way down the grand staircase with candles like wreaths of fire in their hair, and the costly Damascene inlaid mother-of-pearl cedar boxes filled with good-luck almonds that were being handed out to every guest as a memento. She looked up at the unctuous master of ceremonies on the ballroom stage who had signalled for drum rolls as he read out the congratulatory telegrams from Arab heads of state, millionaires and film stars. Leila and her family usually made such an exaggerated point of their understated British style. But when put to the ultimate test of a wedding, they had been unable to resist Arab tinsel and glitz. Anne's mind turned to what she herself might have chosen for her own wedding day. She would have been content to wear a tailored beige suit and have wedding cake and a few bottles of white wine with a handful of close friends gathered in somebody's garden. No, she would have been happy with two hired witnesses in front of a justice of the peace. *To marry him!* What would her life have been like if she could have married *him?* Always what might have been ate away at her. They were to have been married a year ago last May. By now she might have been pregnant with their first baby.

'This is the most expensive wedding I've ever been to,' Camilla was saying. She wished Leila had let the grand total slip when they had shared that wonderfully gossipy reunion at Anne's last week. Just this morning, as she and her mother had sat drinking orange juice and champagne on Nirvana's balcony, they had been unable to resist putting pen to paper and trying to work out exactly how much Leila's wedding must be costing old man Shahine. All the public rooms of this, Beirut's grandest hotel, had been taken over for the reception, and Nirvana calculated that the entertainment alone must have cost more than fifty thousand dollars. Leila's father had hired New York's most fashionable society dance band and installed it here in the grand ballroom. In one of the smoky cafés just off the main foyer a celebrated French *chanteuse* was singing that Edith Piaf song that had taken Paris by storm: '*Non, je ne regrette rien*'. Out by the swimming pool Egypt's most popular belly dancer was gyrating to a sixteen-piece oriental band. As the *pièce de résistance*, a Los Angeles disc jockey had turned the hotel's nightclub into a twist-and-shout disco. Camilla couldn't help contrasting this tidal wave of a wedding to the relatively small reception that had been planned for hers up at the Château Croisé. Even if her nuptials hadn't been turned into a bloodbath by those terrible assassins, Leila's wedding would still have been infinitely superior to her own. It irked Camilla that once again Leila had outdone her, and so she couldn't keep the catty purr from her voice. 'Mama says Mustafa will make her a wonderful husband, a man that old, with so much experience.'

But Anne was hardly listening, and so Camilla babbled on, mostly to herself, about how much this one's evening gown had cost and whether that one's jewels were genuine or paste.

As Anne took a reflective sip of champagne, she felt another wave of culture shock beat over her. She supposed that, even though mostly she loved being back home, she still wasn't altogether used to the grand swagger and flash of this life. Either Beirut had gotten more vulgar in the boomtown years that she had been away, or New England had affected her taste buds. Earlier this evening she had wandered round the public rooms, where political and financial bosses had all but set up shop in a makeshift *Bourse du soir*. Usually the sects didn't mix socially, but everyone who counted had deemed it politically necessary to celebrate the wedding of the Prime-Minister-to-be. The Christians – Maronites, Greek Orthodox, Greek Catholics and Armenians – held forth in one crowded salon, Sunni Muslims lounged in another, and the Druze chieftains had dragooned a strategic corner for themselves by the main ballroom. Even the clergy had established their own bailiwicks. The bishops had their heads together out by the swimming pool. Stout Sunni *shaykhs* had anchored themselves beside the main buffet table. And Anne had spotted Fatima's husband sitting sedately in his flowing brown robes and his neat white turban amidst a nest of Shia mullahs in a quiet little parlour. Everywhere powerful *zaim* warlords, ageing priests and merchant princes graciously inclined their heads as lean young men who wanted something kissed their hands and begged for jobs, money, wives. At its worst, Beirut was a big-hearted tart of a port city where everything but honour was for sale at a shrewdly negotiated price. Here conspicuous consumption reigned supreme, and the rich routinely wore themselves out with their fevered self-indulgence. Anne supposed her eye was still not accustomed to all these baubles and beads, these scarlets and purples, these gold stiletto high heels and these diamond earrings that dangled down to bare shoulders drenched in fifty-dollars-an-ounce Joy. Yet just the other night, when she and her father had sat down for a heart-to-heart about her future, she had confided that she was home to stay. She would turn down Mass General and accept the internship she had just been offered at the American University Hospital. Beirut might be Miami-Beach-on-the-Med, yet she could not help loving the sheer childlike exuberance of it all. If anything could pull her out of her depression, Beirut could. And there was something else as well. She could not bear to return to what she sometimes thought of as the scene of the crime. Boston was haunted by too many bad memories.

The dance floor by now was filling up. Anne watched Camilla laughing as she was swept away in the arms of a tall and tanned man who was not her husband. Pierre, who had last been seen out by the pool with a diplomat's wife, had long since disappeared from the party. Either he had escaped to one of the upstairs suites for a stolen hour or so, or he had nipped off with his high roller friends to the Casino du Liban. Anne watched Leila and Camilla being waltzed about by men they did not love. As for herself, the music of *l'amour* had come to a crashing halt back in Boston. She wouldn't and couldn't dance without music. Yet now, as always, she was lonely. She looked up at the balcony that jutted out over the main ballroom, which a conservative contingent of more traditional Muslim ladies had commandeered as their harem for a night. She waved as she spotted Fatima sitting amidst her sisters on a gilt chair by the inlaid brass railing, wistful bystanders to this forbidden glamour. Anne supposed she might go sit out the rest of this party in that safe woman's world.

'So there you are!' Before she could escape, Anne was accosted by her father who had an elegant young man in his wake. 'Someone here I've been wanting to introduce you to, honey. This is Charles Jenkins. From the history department. He came out from Boston the year you went back.'

Another candidate. Woodenly Anne smiled. Ever since she had arrived back home, her friends and relatives had been scouring the hills and valleys for eligible young men to distract her from what everyone had been told was her broken heart. They meant well, she knew, and yet she wished they would leave her in solitary peace. She couldn't bear to have a man's insinuating eyes upon her now. When a man looked at her as *he* used to, she felt like running in the opposite direction.

Yet this one was different from the others. He scarcely touched her fingers as he shook her hand.

She relaxed just a little. He was hardly looking at her at all, and she liked that. She raised her eyes from his long-fingered hand. He was tall, slender and very fair – not at all, she noted with satisfaction, her type. In his white-tie finery, he looked as if he should be dancing behind Fred and Ginger in an MGM musical. To humour her father, she accepted Charles's offer of a dance. She was pleased that she could hardly feel the pressure of his hand on her waist. The fingers that barely touched hers were dry and cool, and their bodies were remote. As he waltzed her deftly round the dance floor, they talked shyly about the wedding, about Boston, about Beirut. Before Ramsey cut in and whirled her off, Charles had even succeeded in making her laugh with amusing little quips about his first efforts to fit into Levantine society.

But she forgot not only Charles but also her broken heart as Ramsey swept her away in giddy circles, crooning under his breath like an Arabian Bing Crosby. When the band struck up a tango, Ramsey snatched a rose from a nearby table and gripped it rakishly in his teeth.

Long before the dance was over, Anne had collapsed into gales of laughter. She had almost forgotten how good it could feel to laugh like this. She adored the zest of Beirut! She and Ramsey giggled their way through three more glasses of champagne and were just about to sneak down to the disco for some real cha-cha-cha dancing when suddenly everyone was cheering. Nirvana had wrested the microphone away from the American band leader. As she belted out old Lebanese favourites, everyone began to join in. A fusillade of champagne corks popped, and a drum roll and excited shouts announced that the fireworks were about to begin.

Anne and Ramsey stood arm in arm by the moon-drenched bay where some said that Saint George had once slain the legendary dragon. They oohed and aahed like happy children as the skies were bombarded with bursts of fire and flash to celebrate Leila's marriage. Red rockets streaked up to the heavens, went dark, and then exploded into glorious starry diamond shards that rained down on the splendour that was Beirut. Like strobe lights flickering on a dance floor, the fireworks froze for an instant fleeting images of aching perfection: the hovering green mountains, the restless black sea, the fragrant white city.

For a second Anne was blissfully happy. As she caught her breath in wonder, she vowed never to forget Beirut as it had been revealed to her in these staccato flashes that illuminated the city she loved. For now, for tonight, and maybe for ever, she thanked God that she was back home in the one paradise that could never be lost.

Full Moon

1967-1977

Chapter 13

Splayed out naked, sweating, on her reed sunbed, Leila tried to bake away her anxieties in the hot healing sun. Here, in her favourite nook in the well-manicured villa grounds on the far side of the swimming pool, the Prime Minister's wife could sometimes succeed in keeping the frustrating demands of vicarious power at bay. Even today, when everything that mattered was at risk, the relentless June sun succeeded in working its wonders. She could feel the tension seeping out of her as she heaved a deep breath.

She was just about to drift off to sleep when Camilla, on the sun-lounge beside her, noisily sighed, smacked her palm at a fly, and then sounded another of her siren shrieks pitched just low enough so that the solicitous maids wouldn't come running to interrupt them. '*Zut! Yaadra! Quel désastre!*'

Leila's bloodshot eyes shot open, and she did not try to hide her irritation. 'Now what?'

'These wretched insects! Always they want me! They are like all the men!' Camilla let out a peal of laughter and poured herself a fresh glass of white wine from the bottle in the cooler. She was dying to reveal the fabulous bit of gossip that had made her come running over to her friend's today, but knew that she still did not have Leila's undivided attention. Instead she set her tongue wagging on another topic that was equally near and dear to her heart. 'Did I tell you about Pierre's sister's shopping trip to Paris?'

Leila groaned, shut her eyes again, and turned over on her stomach.

'You will ruin your skin,' Camilla scolded as she

automatically reached for the sunblock and massaged it into her face. 'Here, at least let me put this on.' As she worked the cream into her friend's back, she wondered anew at how Leila and a few other daring spirits could bow to the new rage for topless sunbathing and all-over tans. She herself would never sacrifice her skin-deep proof that she had been born as white as any European. She was covered head to toe in a hooded white cotton kaftan she had bought last month in Crete. '*Eh bien*, that should do it.' Camilla tucked her long teased mane of streaked blonde hair back under her hood. The sun was bad for her hair, too. After so many years of bleaching, her once-silky hair was ultra-sensitive to the sun. Finally she settled back on her lounger and began talking nineteen to the dozen. 'Marie says it's all boutiques! Courrèges is the toast of Paris!' She raised her glass, drank it down, and poured herself another. 'Everyone's mad about those little white uniform dresses with the long white schoolgirl socks! *Boutiques, boutiques, toutes les boutiques!* Saint Laurent has opened one called Rive Gauche, Lanvin and Sonia Rykiel have their own, and even Cardin is supposed to have one by the end of the year. Except for ball gowns, when a woman simply cannot do without Dior or Givenchy or Balenciaga, no one – absolutely no one – goes to the couture showrooms anymore. I know you're still loyal to poor old Coco, *chérie*, but Marie says those braid suits of hers are quite *passé*.'

Despite herself, that heresy provoked Leila into opening one eye. 'Chanel could never be *passé*.' She shut her eye again. 'Marie's *passé*.'

Camilla's lips curled up in agreement. The fashions most certainly had changed in these free-and-easy 'sixties, but the realities of marriage and her in-laws had remained the same. Pierre still drank and chased women, and she still drank and allowed almost any man who chased her outside Lebanon to have her. Nine turbulent years of marriage had also hardly sweetened her feelings for Pierre's family, except for Shaykh Georges, who still believed that the mother of his grandsons could do no wrong. 'My sister-in-law is a cow. No, an elephant. Those legs! *Grosses!* She looks', Camilla added with satisfaction, 'like a fool in her short white Courrèges.' She stretched her own shapely legs up in the air, studied them critically for a moment, and thanked God that she was only a firm-thighed thirty, although she was sure that she looked much younger. She pointed a good six inches above her knees. 'Up to here! The new skirts are *comme ça*. Can you believe it! Out! Out! I must throw everything in my wardrobe out! I must buy everything new.' Her voice dropped to a conspiratorial purr. 'But I don't think we should take Marie's word for it, *hein?* I say we should go and see for ourselves, just you and me.' Her voice dropped an octave still lower, to a sultry whisper. 'Who knows what we might pick up in Paris?'

'At a time like this, how can you go on with such nonsense?' Leila kept her eyes, and teeth, clenched shut. She and Camilla had been squabbling like sisters for years. Even on their best days, when Leila's nerves weren't stretched taut by the threat of war, there was always a low point when she wondered why she wasted her valuable time on a silly fool like Camilla. Yet, at the same time, they were a perfectly matched pair, both groomed to a high gloss, each queen of her own buzzing hive. On any other languid Sunday, Leila was likely to find Camilla's bright childlike chatter as soothing as sunshine. The two of them amiably frittered away many an idle afternoon just like this, sipping chilled white wine out by the pool while the nannies minded their children.

'Why not?' Camilla pouted as she lovingly massaged a new coating of suntan lotion into her skin. She reproached herself for not having guessed that, with the mounting hysteria about what seemed to be certain war with Israel, her Palestinian friend would be in a nervous state today. But she hadn't wanted to stay at home, either. She had longed to put on her new black Balenciaga copy and dash up to the Casino du Liban to take in once again that fabulous review, *Mais Oui*, that had been packing everyone in for years. Down at their Beirut townhouse in the fashionable Christian enclave of Ashrafiyeh, Pierre, his father, and even most of the women had hovered in an edgy pack around the radios, shushing her up every time the martial music stopped for one of those wretched bulletins about Israeli shipping being denied access through the Straits of Tiran, armies being put on alert, and diplomats jetting from Washington and Moscow to Cairo and Tel Aviv. This current crisis had been dragging on for nearly a month, and by now it was all very tiresome. 'Listen, *chérie*, it's not my fault, what's happening. The Egyptians this, the Jews that. Never do they shut their mouths. The radio, the television, the newspapers. You all have a fever, with your big words about your little war. Pierre and his father talk of nothing else.'

Leila propped herself up on her elbows, so that the dark hard tips of her thin pointy breasts hung free. What interested her most was whether, when it came down to it, the Lebanese Christians would fight shoulder to shoulder with their Muslim brothers for the liberation of Palestine. 'So tell me, what exactly do they say?'

Camilla shrugged. 'What don't they say? One day this, the next day that. You know how the men are. They talk, they get excited, they grab their guns and run outside and shoot at the sky. Like small boys! Never do they grow up!' She rolled her eyes drolly. 'My big man with his little gun' – here she laughed wickedly – 'says he wants to fight to the death "for ze honour and ze glory of ze flag". To hear him talk about the lost honour of the great Arab nation, you would think he was Gamal Abdul Nasser. Always before he said he hated Nasser, but now he says he's the new Saladin. He says now, too, that he does not like the Americans so much, or the British. Only France – the great motherland – is still in his good books.' She wrinkled her brow as she tried to remember what else she had overheard. 'Sometimes Shaykh Georges agrees with him, and he shouts that this time we will beat the Israelis once and for all. He likes to say, too, that the Americans had better keep their hands off, unless they want to get their fingers burned. But at other times I hear Shaykh Georges saying something different. That it is not so good for our people – for us Christians, I mean – if the Jews are thrown out of the Middle East. He says then maybe the Muslims will decide to throw us out, too.' She laughed, a bit nervously. 'I think that's silly, don't you?' Without waiting for an answer, Camilla rushed ahead. 'But I tell you, darling, war, peace, what does it matter to me? Or to you? Soon enough it will be all over.' Camilla snapped her fingers. 'And everything will be the same as it's always been.'

Leila's eyes took on a glittering shine, as she lay her head back down and glared implacably at her blood-red patio tiles. What was the use of trying to educate a political idiot like Camilla? She had a certain peasant cunning, but she exerted it only in her small domestic and materialistic world. How could she make Camilla understand that soon nothing would ever be the same? The coming war was going to right everything that was wrong in her world. In a matter of hours, days or weeks, the Arabs were going to regain Palestine, and she could go home.

As she lit a cigarette, Leila switched off from her friend and reached over for the transistor radio on the table. It was 3 June 1967, and if there was any news, she wanted to hear it. She fiddled the knob from station to station, catching snatches of military music here, Koranic readings there, and always, everywhere, fiercely impassioned words about the war that was about to be won. After six months of mounting Middle East tension, the Arab and Israeli armies were finally poised for a fight to the death. Two weeks ago President Nasser had ordered a United Nations buffer force out of Sinai, and then announced the closure of the Gulf of Aqaba to Israeli shipping. Israel had responded by mobilizing its armed forces and warning that any interference with its sea traffic would be considered an act of war. Since then diplomats had been chasing peace from capital to capital. The Americans and the Soviets had traded threats and counter-threats of what each would do if the other interfered. The US Sixth Fleet was on red alert in the Mediterranean, and Soviet warships were steaming through the Bosphorus. From the coffee-shops of the Middle East to the private meeting rooms of the United Nations, there was anxious talk of the possibility of nuclear war. Meanwhile, inexorably, the Arab and Israeli armies had moved into battle positions. Israel had appointed arch-hawk Moshe Dayan as Defence Minister, and Egypt and Jordan had signed a mutual defence pact. All that was left in doubt was who would strike first.

Leila honed in, through the static, on a Lebanese politician hoarsely boasting that in two nights, three nights, four nights at most, he would be drinking coffee *mazboot* in a café in Tel Aviv. She leaned back, smiled, and told herself that inviting that politician and others like him to last night's marathon session here in her villa had been well worth the sacrifice of a good night's sleep. She had been up past dawn, as a cabal of Lebanon's top power-brokers huddled here in the Prime Minister's dining room trying to reach a consensus about their exact course of action if and when the hostilities began. As she had personally poured their drinks and served their food, she had done her best – with an insinuating word here, a lifted eyebrow there – to nudge and even goad her husband's tired old cronies into acting for once like proud warriors and honourable men. For as long as she could remember, she had waited, schemed, even prayed for this day when Palestine, finally, should be once again within their grasp. Now all the Arabs had to do was reach out and victory would be theirs. Their armies would sweep across from Egypt, down from Syria and Lebanon, and over from Jordan and Iraq. This time even these mercenary Lebanese who cared about nothing more than lining their own bulging pockets would surely be unable to resist running with the pack and joining in on the kill, for everyone knew that the Arabs were about to exact a bloodprice for their humiliating defeats in the 1948 and 1956 wars. Soon Palestine's beloved orange groves, palm trees and stony ridges would be back in Arab hands, where they belonged. The kibbutzim would lie in ruins. Arab legions would march through Tel Aviv. The blue and white Star of David flag would flutter only on soldiers' graves. A nineteen-year-old blot on Arab honour would finally be washed away, and for ever, blood bleaching out blood. Yesterday on the radio, one especially hot-headed Palestinian had been so intoxicated by the war fever that he had promised that very soon the Jews would be driven into the sea!

Leila sucked in on her cigarette with a hard hiss, fiercely, as Hussein used to do back in London in what sometimes seemed like a lifetime ago. She took last night's vote in her own drawing room as a personal triumph. When the chips were down, she had delivered what her family and her cause had expected. Lebanon's army wasn't as big as Egypt's or as ferocious as Iraq's or as well-armed as Syria's, but nonetheless its token force would be sent to fight on the side of the angels. When the time came, even the Christian-dominated Parliament would fall into Nasser's camp.

Yet as Camilla nattered on about skirt lengths, Leila simmered in the heat. Sometimes she wondered whether last night's political victory, and others exactly like it, were worth her sacrificing the hottest years of her youth on a man old enough to be her father. For six years she had lain in a marriage bed that was, at least for her, loveless. She had given old Mustafa two sons and one daughter, and she had never by word or deed let him or anyone except her girlhood friends know that all this time she had yearned for the love she had left behind. She still saw Hussein sometimes in the tightly incestuous Palestinian circles of Beirut. Yet she had kept her part of the marital bargain, and her husband had kept his. When, two years after her wedding, Mustafa had been elected Prime Minister, he had done his best to espouse the Palestinian cause. Even so, she sometimes found it hard to bear the sham of her marriage. She had wanted so much more . . .

'Ummie!' Leila's daughter Miriam threw her wet squirming body on top of her mother. 'I can swim, Ummie!' The five-year-old's dark sloe eyes were as lively as her mother's. 'Swim! I jumped in the deep end and swam the whole way!'

'Bravo, Mimi!' As though she were drowning and this beloved daughter were her life preserver, Leila hugged the living proof that her marriage had after all not been a total loss. Everyone said Miriam looked and acted exactly as she had when she was a little girl. Of course, Leila thought with a stab of guilt as she looked over Miriam's shoulder and saw that her small sons were also heading this way, she loved her boys, too. They were good lads, and their birth had guaranteed that Mustafa would always adore her. But it was only Leila's feelings for Miriam that cut as deep and true as her passion for Palestine. Her sons took after their cautious father, but her daughter was a true Shahine, a daredevil who swaggered on the playground beside much bigger boys like Camilla's eight-year-old son Tomas.

'I was watching her,' another piping child's voice assured them. As usual, wherever Miriam was, Tomas was not far behind. 'I would have saved Mimi if she needed me.' While the mothers fondly smiled at this latest example of puppy love, the boy and girl shyly exchanged a look of total trust.

'That's my good boy, Tomas.' But there was only time for Camilla to blow her favourite son a kiss before the rest of the children and their keepers swarmed down upon them with the news that their barbecue lunch was ready out by the pool. When her younger twin sons plopped down beside her on the lounger, dripping wet, Camilla shrank away. 'Careful you don't get my hair wet, darlings.' Holding them at arm's length, she patted their cheeks. 'Now run along, you know Mama's on a diet and never eats lunch.' She made a shooing gesture with her hands, so that she and Leila could get back to their *tête-à-tête*.

'That's right, off you go.' Leila wrapped herself in a towelling robe, gave her own small sons perfunctory hugs, and swung her long tanned legs down to the red tiles of the patio. She was about to do what she had been longing to do all afternoon. She would rather, single-handedly, have attacked and vanquished the entire Zionist state, but she would make do instead with this errant nursemaid. With relish, she rounded on the nanny she had hired from a pricy and supposedly exclusive agency on her last trip to London. 'And exactly where were you, miss, when my daughter was jumping into the deep end of the pool?'

'With your sons, madam.' The young woman flushed and stammered, as she always did when Leila found fault with her. 'In the paddling pool.' She wrung her hands and wished she were back home in south London. 'One second Mimi was right there with the others, and a moment later I heard a splash and there she was in the big pool with Tomas shouting as if he was at a football match. They're a pair, those two. They won't listen, either of them. We've got our hands full, me and Suzanne,' she added as she cast a despairing look at Camilla's nanny, 'keeping track of the two of them.'

'Need I remind you, that is exactly what you get paid to do.' Leila was about to let loose the full force of her temper, but the nanny was already on the verge of tears. In another moment the girl might lose total control of herself, perhaps decide to walk out, and then Leila herself would be stuck policing the children this afternoon. 'If this happens again,' she contented herself with saying, 'you'll be on the next plane back to England.' She nodded in curt dismissal and tossed back a full glass of wine as she waited for the intruders to be gone.

When finally she and Camilla were left in blessed silence, Leila shook her head in exasperation. 'I don't know which is more trouble, the servants or the children. I can't tell you the lengths I went to so that the children would have a proper English nanny. At the very least, I thought she'd make sure they picked up the right accent before going off to boarding school.' Leila poured the dregs of the wine into her glass. 'How was I to know she'd be so *common*? She'll have the children talking as if they'd been brought up in some horrid London slum.' She polished off the rest of the wine. 'I've half a mind to fire her here and now, and make bloody sure that she never gets a job like this again. Mimi could have drowned!'

Camilla nodded and made soothing noises as she uncorked another bottle and poured them both another glass. Now that Leila was – thank God! – back to normal, terrorizing the servants rather than turning on her faithful old friend, she decided to reward her by sharing the delicious news. 'I saw Anne last night.'

'Anne . . .' Leila seemed eager to set her eternal servant problems aside as she slid out of her robe and threw herself down again on her sun-bed. Absently she perched her Ray-Bans on the bridge of her nose. 'That reminds me, I had a message that she rang twice yesterday. But I haven't had a chance to call her back. I haven't seen Anne for ages. Every time I invite her over, she's always working.' Leila's voice swelled with injury. She didn't like to be turned down by anyone, ever. 'You'd think she was the only doctor at the hospital.' She lit a cigarette and was curious enough to forgive Anne just this once. 'So how is she?'

Smugly Camilla smiled as she buttered her face with more sunblock lotion. 'You'll never guess.'

'That's right, darling. I never would, and I never will. You know I detest guessing games. If you have some news about Anne, then be a good girl and tell me straightaway.'

Camilla knew that warning tone. Hastily she toed the line. 'It's Charles!' she said, as though that one telling name revealed all.

Leila opened her eyes wide and stared blankly at the sun through her expensive polarized lenses. It was a moment before she could remember who it was that Camilla was talking about. '*That* American? The professor at AUB? The one who teaches history?' When Camilla nodded, Leila wrinkled her brow. Of course she had met that tallish fair-haired chap who had been escorting Anne here and there, on and off, for almost as long as she herself had been married to Mustafa. In fact, now that she thought about it, Anne had met the fellow at her wedding. He wasn't a bad sort, she supposed, although she'd formed no strong impression one way or the other. Yet vaguely she remembered hearing something about him not so long ago. She couldn't recall exactly what it was, only that it was something juicy. 'What about him?'

'Anne is going to marry him!'

'No!' Leila flipped her sunglasses up on to the top of

her head and stared in shock at Camilla. 'Anne marrying *him?*'

'That's right!' Vigorously Camilla nodded her head. 'I, too, did not believe it at first. *Vraiment*, I did not think Anne would ever get married, not after what happened to her in America. But she has fooled us all, no?' Camilla chattered on. 'Already they have set the date. Now, did she say this autumn or in the spring? You know, I don't remember? The sun, it fries my brain!' As Leila glowered, Camilla laughed. 'Ah, yes, now I remember. They will marry in March. They wanted to do it sooner, she said, but Charles will be back in Washington to teach this summer for six months. So it will be something of a long engagement. The wedding will be at Anne's house. *Très intime*. Just family. And us, of course.'

There was not much that would have driven an impending war to regain Palestine from the forefront of Leila's mind, but for a moment the thought of Anne getting married did just that. 'Fancy Anne marrying somebody so . . . ordinary.' She shook her head, and not only in wonderment. 'I do wish she'd talked this over with me first. This Charles, I suppose he's all right, but . . . I hate to say this . . . he doesn't seem quite special enough for someone like Anne. I do hope she knows what she's doing.' As another thought occurred to her, Leila's frown spread to her eyes and forehead. 'She told you first.'

Camilla's smile was so wide it exposed not only all her teeth but her gums. 'After all,' she purred, 'don't forget, Anne and I were friends when we were just little girls. You didn't meet Anne until years later, when we were all at AUB. When it comes to something like getting married, a woman wants to talk to her oldest . . . and best . . . friend.'

'Indeed.' Leila put her sunglasses back on and stubbed out her cigarette. She unclenched her teeth just long enough to sip her wine. But then she brightened. 'The phone messages! Anne rang me yesterday. Actually, she tried to tell me first, but I was busy.'

Camilla turned spiteful. 'Don't fool yourself, *chérie*. Our dear Anne did not tell either of us first. She ran all the way down south to tell Fatima. You see, Charles asked her to marry him more than a week ago. Imagine that, a whole week, and she did not tell us! Like you, at first Anne had her doubts about what to do. But instead of picking up the telephone and asking us, here in Beirut, for our advice, she went down to that wretched village to talk it all over with Fatima.'

'*Fatima!*' Leila was scornful. 'Why her?'

Camilla shrugged. 'Who knows? To hear Anne talk, she is always down there, delivering babies and taking care of this one and that one. I think maybe she spends as much time there as she does in her real job in the hospital. You know how always she talks on and on and on – boring, really, sometimes even dear Anne can be boring when she talks about how terrible it is, how poor the people are in the south, and how the government should build roads and schools and health centres.' Camilla rolled her eyes. 'Why she wants to spend so much time in that village, I don't know. *C'est très primitif!*' By now the wine had gone to her head, and she was feeling giddy enough not to mind her words. 'You know I *adore* Fatima. So sweet, really. But she lets that husband of hers treat her like an animal. She looks older than my mother! And do you know, Anne says she's pregnant again. *Yaadra!* That will make eight – or is it nine? – children. Those Muslims! As Pierre always says, they're like animals.'

For a moment Leila lay stiff and silent on the sun-lounge, at a loss for words. So that was what Camilla and her fancy Christian in-laws said behind the closed doors of their château! They thought even Muslims as

Western, sophisticated and secular as herself were animals? She tucked this insulting revelation away to be dealt with another time, when it would perhaps not be so necessary for the Lebanese to be united in a common front against the Zionists. Still, she could hardly let a comment like this pass without correction. When she finally found her voice, her tone was deadly. 'Be careful, darling. Must I remind you that dear Fatima is not just Muslim, she's *Shia*. But I'm Sunni. I am hardly an animal with a litter like Fatima's. I have three children. Just like you.'

'*Bien sûr*,' Camilla hastily agreed. 'I wasn't implying—'

'See that you don't,' Leila cut in smoothly, to close off this particular discussion before Camilla could make it worse. She forced her tone of voice to be pleasantly social again. 'Eight children! Can you imagine what her body must look like even when she's not pregnant? Fatima always did run to fat, but by now she must be nearly as wide as she is high. How any woman could let herself go like that, I don't know.'

As the two of them sipped their wine, by unspoken mutual consent they defused the conversation with a few minutes of aimless chitchat about diet, exercise and a fabulous new Swedish masseuse who had begun to work out of the Saint Georges. But it was when their talk turned to the new South African tennis pro at the Sporting Club that Leila suddenly remembered what it was she had heard about Anne's fiancé. When she was out on the terrace of the Sporting Club having a drink after her last match, her friend Mona, whose husband was high up in the intelligence-gathering Deuxième Bureau, had let the titbit slip. Even though no one could overhear them, Leila dropped her voice to an urgent whisper. 'You won't believe what I've heard! You mustn't tell a soul!'

'Of course not.' Camilla all but smacked her lips in anticipation.

'This Charles Jenkins . . . I hear he's CIA!'

'No!' Camilla's eyes widened with delight. She had leaned forward on her sun-bed and was just about to sink her teeth into this scandalously exciting revelation when the yawning silence was shattered by a blaring car horn in the villa's driveway. Doors slammed, excited voices called out, and they could hear footsteps running their way.

'War! This is it! It must be war!' Leila forgot all about Anne and her husband-to-be as she lunged for the radio, twiddled with the knobs, and turned up the volume when she found a BBC announcer delivering the news in lovingly rounded Oxbridge vowels. But she frowned and shook her head. On this indolent Sunday afternoon, the possibility of war was seemingly at an ebb. The only news was that Jewish soldiers who had been in battle readiness all along the Sinai front for the past two weeks had been given weekend passes and been spotted sunning themselves on the beaches near Tel Aviv. Disappointed, she turned down the volume and looked over as a wide figure in white bustled towards them across the lawn from the driveway.

'Camilla! Camilla! *C'est moi*, Marie!'

From their sun-lounges the two young slim women cruelly sized up Camilla's stout, forty-two-year-old sister-in-law. Marie was the mother of four nearly-grown children, and yet, incongruously, she was wearing a sleeveless tight white minidress, white kneesocks, and a yellow and white polka-dot bow in her hair.

'See, I told you,' Camilla muttered low, for her husband's sister was almost within earshot. 'That's her new Courrèges. She is like an elephant, no?'

'Or a white rhino,' Leila smirked. She seized this first opportunity to pay Camilla back the first of many instalments for that crack about Muslims being animals.

'Sometimes you Christians, darling, have absolutely no taste.'

'Oh, Camilla!' Marie was out of breath, audibly panting and visibly sweating. 'Quick, get the children!' She cupped her hand and screeched in the direction of the swimming pool. 'Tomas! Guy! Emile!' Frantically she turned back to Camilla. 'We're all going up to the château! *Maintenant! Vite!* Papa wants us all up there by sundown.'

'The château? Whatever *are* you talking about? It's only June. We never go up to the château for the summer until July.' Languidly Camilla poured her a glass of wine. 'Do have a drink, *chérie*, and calm down.'

Marie accepted the wine, took a greedy gulp of it, and plumped herself down beside Camilla on the lounger. Urgently she gripped her sister-in-law's arm. 'Please, for once, don't be difficult. Do as I say! Get the boys! Papa says you must not, under any circumstances, bring his grandsons back to Beirut. If anything were to happen to those boys, I don't know what he'd do. You're all to get in the car with me and go right to the château. Now! Quick!'

'What's the rush?' Leila smiled encouragingly, as though to a demented child.

'Haven't you heard?' Marie's pale eyes were afraid. 'There was an explosion this afternoon at a warehouse down by the waterfront. No one knows who did it, but everyone says it must have been the Israelis or the Palestinians. Papa says it could be either of them, trying to make trouble . . .' Her voice trailed off, as she remembered Leila. 'Beirut's too dangerous,' she blurted out. 'Papa says that with everyone all whipped up about the war, anything could happen. Bombs anywhere, everywhere. There could be mobs in the streets.' She downed the last of her wine. 'They could even turn on us.'

Camilla cursed under her breath but, without waiting to hear more, she bowed to the inevitable. She began collecting her things and shouted instructions for the nanny to put the children in the car.

Meanwhile, however, Leila was pouring Marie another glass of wine and urging her to be brave and stay put. 'Really,' she was saying, in a voice that sounded sympathetic, 'I think you'll be safe in Beirut. Don't you?'

'They say the gypsies are leaving. They say the gypsies left Beirut in the night. That they were seen travelling north in caravans. Maybe they know something we don't know. You know the gypsies can see the future.' Marie shuddered, and then she couldn't help repeating the worst fear of them all. 'What if we lose? What if the Jews come to Beirut and kill us all?'

'Israelis? *Here?*' Leila laughed. 'That, my dear, I can assure you, will never happen.' Again she laughed. 'Haven't you heard? We're going to drive them into the sea.' Lazily she waved to the children and blew kisses to Camilla and Marie as they retreated across the lawn. 'Bloody cowards,' she muttered to herself as the car screeched out of the driveway and joined the stream of traffic climbing high up into the mountains, to Christian and Druze strongholds as stoutly fortified as medieval castles.

In a little while it would be time to shower, slip into something cool and elegant – perhaps her sensational Dior jungle print hostess gown, which would nicely complement the deepening bronze colour she had picked up this afternoon – and then greet the journalists, diplomats and politicians she had invited over tonight for a pre-war victory celebration. Meanwhile, however, she tuned the radio into a station playing stirring martial music, uncorked a fresh bottle of wine and confidently settled back to savour the victory that was surely about to be theirs.

The next morning, the telephone on the bedside table rang and rang and rang before Leila blearily groped for the cradle. Her last guests had stayed until four, and then she and Mustafa had finished off a bottle of Courvoisier out on the balcony. Her head ached as she held the telephone up to her ear.

'Have you heard?' Even on the crackling long distance telephone line from London, her father's voice, in excited Arabic, shouted out at her.

'What time is it?' Leila mumbled. She squinted at her alarm clock. It was still early, eight o'clock.

'Leila! Wake up! It's war!' Kemal Shahine collected himself and reverted to his more customary English. 'The war has begun!'

'No!' Leila was wide-awake now. 'Ha! At last!' She laughed. 'So what's happened so far? Tell me exactly! Don't leave a thing out!'

'Love to, darling, but I don't know much yet, just that we're bombing Tel Aviv.'

'Bombing Tel Aviv!'

'That's right. Bombing it off the map. No more Tel Aviv! It will be our Jaffa again. And our Palestine!' Kemal's voice, usually so dry and cultivated, was boyish and throbbing with emotion. 'But apart from that, I don't know much more. I've been on the phone to Cairo, Amman, Damascus. They say Radio Cairo is calling it a holy war. And I think . . . hold on, now, yes, someone's just called in on the other line to say they can hear gunfire in Jerusalem. God – and King Hussein – are with us!' Leila's father's voice became more urgent. 'Listen, put your husband on the line. Mustafa must engineer a special session of Parliament and get his army moving. I know they haven't been mobilized yet, but it would be a pity if they missed out on the fun. This is it, *habibi*, the war to win it all back.'

'Mustafa! Wake up! Good news!' Leila was laughing

in triumph as she passed the telephone to the Lebanese Prime Minister, who was just waking up to this wonderful morning of war.

Three nights later, Camilla sat marooned with her dour-faced in-laws in the château's main salon, as the entire assembled Nazrani clan kept an anxious vigil on the progress of the war. For, at the first electrifying radio reports, distant cousins from the fertile fields of the Bekaa Valley, the mountain fastness of the Shouf, and even the bazaars and workshops of Beirut and Tripoli had grabbed their guns, packed up their wives and children, and made their way to the *shaykh*'s fortress. When danger threatened, the tribe was mother, father, life itself.

From where she fidgeted in her white baby-doll minidress, picking without much interest at a needlepoint tapestry she had begun years ago, Camilla observed uncles, aunts, brothers, sisters and cousins munching sunflower seeds, slurping tamarind juice, and cheering on the advancing Arab armies. At any other time, Nazrani women lounged on Louis Seize sofas beside Nazrani men. But in a formal war council like this, the old ways held sway. The men took the upholstered furniture in the centre of the room, near the blasting radios, while the women fluttered in the corners, shushing the children and making sure the servants kept their lords and masters happy with fresh bottles of arak, carafes of juice and jugs of coffee.

Camilla studied their faces as they ate, drank, argued. When they were thrown together like this, the family resemblance was startling. One and all, from Shaykh Georges down to the smallest baby, had distinctive, high sloping foreheads, elongated skulls and hair that perched uncertainly on the pointy crowns of their heads. The Nazranis took pride in their physiognomy, citing the similar images on old Phoenician coins as proof positive that they and only they were the true descendants of the ancient Lebanese merchants who had once bought and sold the world, and even invented the alphabet. But now, eyeing them with distaste, as the outsider she would always be, Camilla thought disparagingly that they looked like a race of bullet-heads.

Shaykh Georges sat ensconced in his massive carved cedarwood chair in the centre of the room with a tableful of radios placed directly in front of him. When one radio crackled, he would point towards it. Pierre, who sat at his feet in the dress uniform of a Lebanese army captain, would instantly lunge forward to hone in on the news bulletin. For a moment all the palaver would cease, everyone would lean forward to listen, and then when the news was pronounced they would take their cue from Georges and either nod sagely or sadly shake their heads.

Three days, Camilla raged to herself. For three days and three nights she had been isolated here at the château with this tribe who were following the progress of the war with as much enthusiasm as if it were a soccer match. She was sick of this family, and she was sick of this war. As far as she could tell, none of them had the foggiest idea of what was actually happening on the battlefields, only a few hours' drive away, just south of the border. Ever since the first reports of the war had galvanized the clan into such cloying togetherness, Shaykh Georges and his kinsmen had been trying without much success to piece together an accurate picture of the fighting. Reports from Arab sources were sketchy, conflicting and longer on emotion than on facts. Even the most strident accounts from the Muslim stations agreed that one Lebanese fighter plane had been lost over Galilee in the first day of the war. But since then, strangely, there had been no news about the expected deployment of the small but supposedly determined Lebanese army. This morning Pierre, who had self-importantly donned his old military uniform at the first news of fighting, had lost patience and rung his commanding officer and been told that he and the rest of the reserve battalions should sit tight until they got the call to serve. Meanwhile, the radios blared with news of splendid Arab victories. On the western front the Egyptian tank corps was covering itself with glory in fiery battles up and down the passes and peaks of the Sinai. On the eastern front, King Hussein's Arab legions were triumphing in house-to-house fighting in Jerusalem, and it was even reported that very soon the Zionist state would be cut in two by an irresistible Arab pincer movement coming over from Jordan and up from Egypt. For three days now, too, the combined air forces of Egypt, Jordan, Syria and Iraq had been pummelling Israeli cities in heavy bombing raids. Oddly, however, in the face of this crushing Arab *blitzkrieg*, the Zionist state had shown no signs of suing for peace.

A radio squawked static, Shaykh Georges pointed, and Pierre tuned it in. The hushed throng listened to the voice of President Nasser on Radio Cairo blaming America and Britain for a combined air assault in the early hours of the war. Over the airwaves, Nasser's voice swelled with injury. The crippling blow was already being avenged. America, Britain and its lackey Zionist state would rue Monday morning's treacherous surprise attack on Egyptian airfields.

'What surprise attack?' Shaykh Georges growled. 'Nasser's talking nonsense.'

'What's going on?' Pierre added.

As the tribesmen shook their heads and anxiously crunched their sunflower seeds, Georges seized the radio, fiddled with the dial, and finally found the BBC World Service. In dead silence the family listened to unbelievable bulletins. Jerusalem had fallen to the Jews. The West Bank was at risk. After horrific desert tank battles, the Israelis had pushed through the Sinai and were at the banks of Suez. They were all but knocking at the gates of Egypt. Britain and America were denying that their bombers had joined Monday morning's surprise Israeli air attack that had destroyed the Egyptian air force on the ground.

'Imperialist lies,' a young cousin called out hotly.

Another cousin grabbed his gun, aimed at the offending radio, and had to be persuaded by his brother to hold his fire.

As the room erupted into pandemonium, bordering on panic, Pierre's mother fell to her knees and crossed herself. '*Ya Rab*,' she prayed loudly, 'O Lord, give us a sign that this is not so.'

A white faced Pierre, meanwhile had turned to a less divine authority. 'Can that be right, Papa? Can we be losing?'

'Maybe not,' Shaykh Georges muttered. 'Maybe not.' Grimly he lit a Davidoff cigar, smoked in silence for a moment, and then pronounced his opinion. 'Whoever wins, we will win. We are Nazranis first, Christians second, Lebanese third . . . and Arabs last.' He let the tribe digest that catechism. 'And remember, my sons.' He paused significantly. 'After Saturday, comes Sunday.'

The men furrowed their brows, the women narrowed their eyes, and after a moment the quickest wits among them finally made sense of the *shayah*'s Delphic-like riddle. Those who understood the patriarch's cryptic words explained them to those who didn't. The Jewish Sabbath fell on Saturday, they explained, while the Christian day of worship of course came on Sunday. What Shaykh Georges meant was that if the Muslims had been able to annihilate the Jews, next on their list might be the equally vulnerable Middle Eastern Christians. From one end of the salon to the other, the Nazranis switched sides with a sigh. With something akin to smugness, then, these Maronite Christians leaned forward in their seats so as not to miss any thrilling details of what was suddenly beginning to appear to be their own great surrogate victory against the Muslims.

The next afternoon, on day four of what everyone was only just beginning to admit was a disastrous Arab defeat, Leila came storming into her husband's office. For once, she seemed oblivious of what she was wearing. Her blue minidress was badly wrinkled, there was a run in her tights, and she hadn't even bothered to put on costume jewellery or make-up. Without the slightest pretence of wifely manners, she pounded his desk in fury. 'Do something! Don't just sit there! You're the Prime Minister! For once, do something!'

On the other side of the desk, Mustafa sighed and helplessly shrugged. He had known, as soon as he had been told that the commander of the Lebanese army was refusing to sacrifice his troops to a losing cause, that his wife would hold him personally responsible. He had thought that she would wait until he got home to reproach him, but once again he had underestimated the lengths she would go to assert herself and her cause. 'What can we do? They won't fight.'

'What do you mean, they won't fight! You're the bloody government! Make them!'

Mustafa lowered his gaze from those outraged Palestinian eyes. He was ashamed and embarrassed to have to admit this to the mother of his sons. 'The commander refuses,' he whispered.

'But that's mutiny! Shoot the bastard! If none of you has the guts to do it, give me a gun, and I'll shoot him myself!'

'Be reasonable, darling. You can't line up the entire army and shoot them one by one.'

'Can't you?' She curled her lip at the husband she had never wanted. 'You're telling me that our boys are dying down there, giving the last drop of their blood for Palestine – *Our land! Our land, Mustafa! For Palestine!* – and the Lebanese army refuses to help! How can this be!'

'I'm sorry.' Mustafa shook his head. 'But what can I do? The Parliament ordered the army to fight. The President of the Lebanese Republic ordered them to fight. But the general refused to lead the army south of the border.' He hated to say what had to be said next, and so his words were slow and reluctant. 'My dear, we have to face some very unpleasant facts. I tell you frankly that there are many here in Lebanon – Christians, mostly, though some of them I have to admit are Muslim – who agree with the general's mutiny. They say the Arabs have already lost Sinai and the West Bank. That the Israelis may even try to seize the Golan. If our army crosses the border, the Zionists could use that as a pretext to invade us. You know they've always wanted to use the Litani river for their irrigation projects, and they'd like to have our farmland south of the Litani, too. If we fight, we could lose our own land.'

'And honour? What about losing Lebanese honour? The way she felt now, there was no mercy left in her. She spat, contemptuously, in the general direction of the impotent Lebanese Prime Minister. 'There is no honour in Lebanon.'

'Ummie! Ummie! Planes!'

Fatima's two eldest daughters and two youngest sons burst into the kitchen where their mother squatted on the floor pounding raw meat to a pulp for *kibbe*.

Little Muhssin was wild with excitement. 'Come look, Ummie!' He grabbed at his mother's hands to try to stop her from working. He wanted her to come outside to help them play at their heady new game of war.

'Will they hurt us?' Six-year-old Zainab was terrified.

'Will they go boom-boom here?' Her five-year-old sister Salma had listened too much to the excited talk of the big boys.

'We will not let them,' small Ibrahim boasted.

'*Inshallah*, God willing, we'll be safe.' Both to reassure them and to see for herself what was happening, Fatima leaned on her daughters as she laboriously got to her feet. She was eight months pregnant, and her swollen legs were mined with varicose veins.

She stood with her children clinging to her skirts on the front doorstep of her house that baked in the sun atop Suker's highest hill. From here she looked down at the old sepia-coloured mosque in the heart of the village, where so many men had come today for Friday prayers that they overflowed out of the doors into the dusty main square. She could hear her husband's deep inspiring voice, from the loudspeakers hitched up to the roof of the mosque, exhorting the faithful not to despair, instead to trust in Allah once again to have pity on His people the Arabs. Fatima's face darkened with sorrow. It was terrible what they were hearing about the war, how the decimated Egyptian army was wandering all but naked in the Sinai, how West Bank refugees were fleeing for their lives across the Jordan, how the beleaguered Syrian army was fighting a last stand to hold the strategic heights of the Golan. But those small temporal defeats were as nothing to the great calamity that even now, two days after she had first heard the terrible news, made Fatima clench her fist and beat her breast again and again, harder and harder. Jerusalem! They had lost *Qoods*, dear *Qoods! Jerusalem!* The third most holy site in Islam had fallen to the Jews. Al-Aqsa Mosque and the Dome of the Rock were under Zionist control. The sacred rock that still held the imprint of the Holy Prophet's foot after he had ascended into heaven now belonged to the enemy.

She bowed her head and prayed silently, for a fervent moment, for a miracle. *Qoods* must be rewon!

'Ummie! Look! Listen! Here they come again!'

Fatima shaded her eyes against the sun and squinted south, to where her children pointed. At first she could hear nothing but the distant reverberation of the big booming guns fighting for every bloody inch of the Golan. But then she saw flashes of silver and heard the dull menacing echo of approaching engines, a sound that, even though she had never heard it before, filled her with terror. She held her arms wider, and her children huddled closer as the flock of Israeli fighter-bombers streaked north in a wide arc almost directly overhead.

'Watch, Ummie, watch us!' Muhssin ran out of his mother's reach, raised his arms, and pantomimed firing at the Israeli jet.

'Me, too!' Ibrahim stood shoulder to shoulder by his brother. 'For *Qoods!*' he shouted in his childish voice.

'Allah help us,' Fatima prayed under her breath as she stood in the doorway with her daughters, watching the aeroplanes turn east towards the Syrian supply lines. 'Stop the fighting. Save the boys.'

On the sixth and final day of the war, Anne wearily pushed open the door of the Beirut hospital's staff lounge and stood staring with bloodshot eyes at the man who waited for her. With only a few snatched catnaps, she had been in surgery for nearly twenty-four hours, since Friday afternoon, when the overflow of Syrian casualties from the fierce fighting on the Golan had been shunted here from Damascus.

'You look beat,' Charles said as he took her in his arms and patted the back of her white operating smock lightly, as a father might to an ailing infant. 'My poor baby.'

'It's terrible in there, just terrible.' Anne shut her eyes and let herself, for a moment, lean listlessly in the comforting circle of her fiancé's arms. In her five years as a surgeon on the staff of the American University Hospital, she had struggled to save the lives of mothers and babies in touch-and-go Caesarean births, done her best to cut out malignant cancers, and even performed delicate heart surgery. She had thought not only that she had long ago become accustomed to death but also that she had stopped taking the waste of human lives personally. But that was before she had faced these mangled young men from the war front. By the time they had been wheeled into the operating room, many of them had lost so much blood – and hope – that it had been too late to save them. How many had died under her knife since yesterday? Never would she forget their cries, their wounds, their waste. When she was training to be a surgeon back in Boston, she had never imagined herself a combat doctor helplessly watching boys bleed and die for causes they probably didn't even understand. She hoped to God this horrible violence would end soon, and life in Beirut would go back to normal. 'So many have died,' she said. She would always remember one soldier's beseeching dark Arab eyes, so full of fear, just before the light died inside him and his eyes glassed over. He couldn't have been more than fifteen or sixteen, even though the Syrians supposedly didn't draft boys so young into their army. 'They're only children. A lot younger than us, Charles. To die so young, and for what? It's such a terrible waste.'

'I know, honey, I know.' Charles pulled back and smiled reassuringly down at her. 'But hang on, the worst is past. I rushed here as soon as I heard the news. Syria and Israel have agreed to a cease-fire. The war's over.'

'Over?' She didn't know whether to cheer or cry. She wanted nothing more than for this war, and all wars, to be over for ever, and yet . . . Her feelings about this particular war were so mixed. She had lived most of her life among the Arabs, and she never wished to live anywhere else. But those bloodthirsty rantings before the war on the Arab radio stations and in the Arab press had chilled the Jew in her. One vulnerable night she and her father had talked out their fears and their torn loyalties. As Jews, how could they exist in this world that hurled such vile curses at their brethren south of the border? Until now, they had felt at home among these Muslims. But would there be a knife in the back for them here someday? True, Lebanon's Jewish community had been protected by a Christian militia during this war. The Phalange had cordoned off the Jewish neighbourhood of Wadi Abu Jamil, so that no one could avenge the Arab defeat upon the local Jewish population. Yet still Anne and her father had been heartsick at the hateful rhetoric directed not only at the Israelis but at all Jews. They had felt estranged not only from the Zionist state – to which, until now, they had felt no emotional pull – but also from the Arab nation. Whichever side won, Anne and her father had agreed, the two of them would feel like losers. Yet even before she had gone on her marathon duty call yesterday afternoon, the news reports had all been pointing to stunning Zionist gains on all three of the war fronts. Now that she was no longer worried about a massacre of Israel's civilian population, her Arab sympathies had once again come to the fore. 'Can it really be all over so soon?'

Charles was more enthusiastic. 'You bet. It took the Israelis just six days to roll through the Sinai, capture Jerusalem and the West Bank, and take the Golan Heights.' His voice was admiring. 'It's incredible, really, what they've done, and against such overwhelming odds. I heard one commentator on the Voice of America calling it a modern David and Goliath story.

'Is that what they're saying on the Voice of America?' She studied his pale, angular face as coolly as though she had never seen him before. Since she had finally agreed to marry him last week, her family and friends had enthused that he was good-looking enough to be in the movies or at least on the television. Yet, even though his was a nice face and he was a nice man, she had never thought his looks compelling. Mike had been taller, darker, and she had never seen the likes of his bedroom eyes. Even after all this time, though over the worst pain of losing him, she still measured every man against his memory. She had yet to find one who could stir her as he had. Again, now, as so often in the past week, she wondered if it would be a mistake to marry Charles. With Charles there was wit and friendship instead of fire and passion. Yet perhaps that was what she wanted now. Fire and passion had burned too deeply. She could not risk being manhandled again. She was especially grateful that he had not yet frightened her with too many sexual demands. After everything she had told him about Mike, she supposed he was simply giving her the time and space she needed. Charles was, above all, sensitive and caring. Still, as she listened to him rave on about the great Israeli victory, she wondered if she ever could be truly intimate with this man.

But Charles was so intent on sharing what he had heard on the radio and from other sources today that he entirely missed the edge to her voice and the questioning in her eyes. 'The other news is that Nasser's not resigning after all.'

'No?' Anne smiled as though that were a ray of hope. She took pride in leaving politics to the politicians. To her mind, most of them were rank opportunists. Yet back in her university days, she had sometimes given in to Leila's impassioned proselytizing and pinned a Nasser badge on her sweater. She still thought him the best of that rum lot of Arab leaders. She had been sorry yesterday, when she had heard on the radio on her way to the hospital that he had taken full responsibility for the Arab defeat and resigned from public life.

Charles shook his head. 'Apparently more than a million Egyptians took to the streets to beg him not to quit. They poured out of the slums, crying for Nasser not to leave them.' Again he shook his head. 'So he changed his mind and said he'd stay. From what I hear, the Egyptians love him more than ever. Arabs! Who can understand them?'

Not you, she thought, never you. How could she make a man who had no fire in his soul understand how it felt to burn with heat? Nasser had lost land, pride and honour, yet still – and always – he was and would be the beloved one. For the Arabs to allow him to slink away from public life in defeat, would truly have been the end of a dream. How could it be that Charles, who taught contemporary history, had failed to grasp these fundamental truths? She considered the disturbing possibility that, in the long run, she might not be able to rely on him to comprehend anything else that mattered in this world of theirs.

She looked into the light clear eyes of the man she was pledged to marry, and again she doubted her decision. As if it were yesterday, she could hear that old gypsy in the Crescent cabaret warning her about betrayal. Funny, she thought, that she should remember that again now, seven years after Mike had betrayed her. Of course she and her old friends had long ago agreed that Madame Kismet had seen Mike in her crystal ball. But all that was over and done with. A man like Charles could hardly betray her. From nowhere, a thought crossed her mind: this one is not what he appears to be, either. But she dismissed the premonition out of hand. She was just overtired and perhaps a little bit cross with Charles for not understanding the Arabs' depression at their crushing defeat in the war. But her own personal history was not going to repeat itself with Charles. He was not Mike. He would never betray her.

'A penny for your thoughts,' he said.

'Nothing.' She consulted her watch and swore. 'I'd better get back to work.'

'Don't you think you've done enough? The war's over.'

She kissed him lightly on the lips and then moved towards the door. 'Maybe so.' She turned and smiled enigmatically. She, after all, knew the Arabs better than he did. The last shot had most definitely not been fired over Israel-Palestine. 'Or maybe not.'

He had missed the point. 'Look, I'll come back tonight, around nine, and we'll go and get some dinner. You're working too hard.'

She shook her head. 'Sorry. There's something else I really have to do tonight, if and when I ever go off duty.' At the door she explained. 'You know, it's an Arab custom that when someone dies, all the family and friends have to make a courtesy call to the house to pay their respects.'

'Sure. We have wakes at home, too.'

'That's what I have to do tonight. I have to go to Leila's to pay my respects. Maybe you don't quite understand this, Charles, but tonight all the Arabs are in mourning.'

Chapter 14

One afternoon the next spring, Anne's aunt leaned on her cane as she gamely led the party of foreigners up the steep steps to the Temple of Jupiter at Baalbek. Anne and her father were just behind her, Charles and his parents came next, and Martha lagged behind with her arm around her visiting son Ben. 'Magnificent,' Bert admitted as she stared up at the six tall red granite columns that surpassed anything she had ever seen in Boston. Long ago she had vowed that she would never set foot in Lebanon, but even she had been lured here with the others for Anne's wedding tomorrow. 'And you say, Joe, that the Romans built all this?' For once her tone of voice was civil as she addressed her brother-in-law, who was finally making his archaeology career useful.

'The Emperor Antoninus Pius broke ground for this Temple of Jupiter in 138 AD, but it took three hundred more years to complete it. Once there were fifty-four of these columns, each of them sixty-three feet tall.' Baalbek, in his eyes, was nothing less than the cradle of civilization. His life's work was here, and he couldn't have been prouder of this acropolis if he had built it himself. He made a sweeping gesture that included not only these ruins but its idyllic setting nestled under the cedar-covered mountains and above the fertile red plains of the Bekaa Valley. 'Imagine what it must have been like then, when the colour of these wall paintings was as bright as billboards, and the priests and priestesses went about their sacred tasks just here where we're standing!' Knowingly he pointed beyond the sacred pool. 'The oracle was over there. Emperors – like Trajan in 116 AD – came all the way here from Rome to consult it.'

'An oracle?' Anne was intrigued at what the soothsayer would have said about her marriage. But then, remembering what she had heard that other time in the Crescent, she hastily decided it was just as well that no remnant of that ancient oracle remained. 'We'll go to the Temple of Astarte next, Aunt Bert. You'll love it.' As she helped the old woman on the broken stone path, Anne's mind was awhirl with all the last-minute wedding details she should be attending to in Beirut. But Aunt Bert had insisted on seeing Baalbek. She would only be in Lebanon long enough for the wedding, and so obligingly the two families had endured the two-and-a-half hour drive up to one of the Levant's most famous antiquities. Charles's parents had flown in from Florida a week ago, and Ben – on leave from his Vietnam tour of duty with the US Marines – had come home just yesterday. Her little brother looked quite the man in his lieutenant's uniform.

'Hey, Anne!' he called out. 'The Temple of Love's next. That should be right up your alley.'

She laughed along with the others, and she and Charles exchanged fond glances. He really was a dear, she told herself. Their marriage was going to work. But as her footsteps echoed in the Temple of Astarte, where ages ago passion had reigned supreme, she reflected that it was not with Charles as it had once been with Mike. It saddened her that, on the eve of her wedding, the most she could look forward to was a marriage that would 'work'. What of pleasure, desire and heart-thumping delight?

Inside the Temple of Love, even Bert caught her breath. 'This is really something.' She stared up at the dazzling portico ceiling decorated by delicate arabesques of fauns and cupids, and she shook her head in wonder at the symmetry, grace and glory of it all. The temple was so well preserved that it seemed the priestesses had left only yesterday. 'I had no idea there was anything like this here.'

'There is evidence', Joe recited, 'that Baalbek was a place of the gods even three and a half thousand years ago. Supposedly Abraham lived here in the Bekaa, Noah was buried near here, and Solomon gave Baalbek to Sheba as a love token. Some say human sacrifices to Baal were offered here in pagan times. Most certainly there were orgiastic rituals to Astarte, whom the Greeks called "Aphrodite" and the Romans "Venus". Then centuries later, after the Romans built their Heliopolis here, it was converted into a Christian basilica. Muslim prayers have been offered here as well.'

'From what I've seen and *heard*,' Bert said tartly, 'those Muslims pray everywhere, and at the most ungodly times. Those prayer calls of theirs woke me up last night.'

'That's the whole point of them,' Anne told her. 'Too bad it's not August. Some of the world's greatest artists perform right here in this temple at the Baalbek Festival. The New York Philharmonic's been here, and the Comédie Française. Everyone from Ella Fitzgerald to Dame Margot Fonteyn and Rudolph Nureyev. There's even a *son et lumière* at night.'

'Is that so?' Bert sank down on an ancient stone and mopped her brow. 'It's hot. I'm not used to this heat.'

'Joe!' Martha's voice was peremptory. 'Ben's just told me he's going to make a career of the Marines. Come over here this minute and talk some sense into him!'

'Excuse me, ladies.' Joe hastened to his wife's side.

Anne consulted her watch. 'We'd better be getting back. We've got a wedding tomorrow, remember? And everyone's coming over to the house tonight for drinks.'

'But we've only just got here.' Bert drank in the view of the Bekaa and pointed at the range of mountains to the east. 'Syria's just over there, isn't it?'

'The border's fifty miles away.'

'I would like to have seen Damascus,' Bert mused. 'Seems a shame to come this far and miss it. Maybe I'll stay on a little longer. There's more to see here than I thought.'

'You can stay as long as you like. Mother would be thrilled.'

'I'll think about it.' Bert patted the stone beside her. 'But come here a moment, child. I want to talk to you.'

Anne did as she was told.

For a while, as they watched Charles energetically leading his parents around the site and Joe and Martha earnestly huddled with Ben, Bert was silent. Then she cleared her throat. 'I have something to tell you. I was going to wait until tonight at the party, but now's as good a time as any.' She paused dramatically. 'I've made you my heir, Anne. Drawn up a new will and left everything – lock, stock and barrel – to you. When I go, you'll get it all.'

'Aunt Bert! But that's a long way off. You're in perfect health.'

'So the doctors say. But everyone goes sometime. My mother was ninety-three when she died, my aunt was eighty-eight, and my grandmother was eighty-two. You come from strong stock. But even the women in our family eventually have to give up and go.'

Anne grinned fondly at her indomitable aunt. Yet she was touched at the news of the bequest. 'I assume this new will of yours is a wedding present.'

'No, I've brought you my Paul Revere silver tea service for that. Had to pay overweight on my baggage to bring it out.' Intently she studied Anne's face. 'But my will's another matter, just between me and you. I wanted you to know that you'll be a woman of independent means. In case that makes any difference to whether you decide to go ahead with this wedding.'

'Why would you say something like that?'

'Call it a hunch.' Sitting on this ancient rock, the old woman looked like a mythical crone who, with one foot in the grave, was as intimate with the mysteries of what would come next as she was with what had passed before. 'This Charles. He's nice enough. Comes from a good family. And he's American to the core. I always worried about you taking up with some Arab out here. But is he the one for you?' She shook her head. 'You don't look as happy as a bride should look. I don't think you've ever gotten over that other one.'

Anne's face closed, and she stood and brushed the fine dust from her skirt. 'It's late. We should be getting back.'

Bert's bony hand caught at Anne's arm. 'Think about what I said, child. I'm only concerned with your welfare. I don't want to see you get your heart broken again.'

Anne stared into her aunt's old eyes. Madame Kismet had warned her not of one but of many betrayals. But she wasn't superstitious, and so she shook off her misgivings. 'Dad! Mother! Charles! Let's get a move on. I'm getting married in the morning!'

It was long past midnight when Anne and Charles stood at the door of the Rosen villa on the Rue Bliss, enmeshed in the long drawn out ritual of saying goodnight to their guests.

Leila was noisily kissing Anne again and again, hugging her, and then exuberantly kissing her again, as though they wouldn't be seeing each other for many years instead of the few hours when they all would return here for the wedding. Reluctantly she passed the bride-to-be on to Ramsey and his young Palestinian wife, Aisha, who kissed and hugged and jabbered happy sentiments.

Tonight all three of the Shahines were almost delirious with joy, and not just because Anne was finally getting married. After nearly a year of moping about, beating their breasts in bitter despair at the crushing Arab defeat in the Six Day War, they had just heard electrifying news from Jordan. A small band of poorly-equipped Palestinian guerrillas had, against all odds, held off a detachment of regular Israeli soldiers who were trying to raid the Jordanian village of Karamah. In the end the

Israelis had killed the guerrillas and levelled the village. But as far as the Shahines were concerned, those young Palestinians had been martyred for something worth more than the price of their own lives. This single defiant act was not enough to avenge Arab honour, but for the first time in many months honour had at least been resurrected. A new era, in which Palestinians would fight their own battles, might just have begun. Leila, Ramsey and Aisha kept kissing and hugging Anne, and then kissing and hugging each other, until a weeping Camilla butted in and clutched Anne tightly to her.

Then, just as Anne and Camilla were singing another chorus lamenting that Fatima had missed tonight's get-together and wouldn't be up from the south with her family until morning, the Lebanese limousines purred up the driveway to the door. Chauffeurs leaped out and opened passenger doors with royal flourishes. The Prime Minister ushered Leila into their Rolls, Ramsey settled Aisha in their Cadillac, and Camilla – who had come alone tonight, and this time hadn't even bothered to offer lame excuses for her absent husband – was whisked away in the back seat of her Mercedes.

While all this was going on, Charles was making a final farewell fuss over his family. Were they sure they didn't want him to escort them back to the Phoenicia? Could they manage the taxi on their own? And the hotel, were they certain it was okay? Instead of squeezing them in at his apartment or here at Anne's house, he had thought they would be more comfortable in a five-star hotel.

Anne joined the knot of her in-laws-to-be: his surprisingly young-looking parents, his bachelor elder brother who was a Wall Street lawyer, his glossy sister and her genteel husband who had arrived yesterday from California. Ben and her own parents were doing their best to make the newcomers feel at home. Yes, everyone agreed, Beirut was beautiful, Charles and Anne were a great pair, the weather tomorrow would be glorious. After more pleasantries, a few tentative pecks that hardly touched Anne's cheeks, and much firm handshaking, Charles paid a taxi-driver to take his family on the short jaunt down the Corniche to their rooms at the Phoenicia.

Meanwhile, back in the villa, Bert awaited them in the parlour. Ben yawned, pleaded jet lag, and escaped off to bed. But Charles, Anne and her parents sank down on the sofas.

'Now,' Bert said, as she cleared her throat and rehearsed who was going where after the wedding. The newlyweds, of course, would be flying to Paris and then taking the train down to the Riviera, where they had the use of Leila's brother's villa in Antibes for their honeymoon. But Bert, it seemed, had changed her mind about flying back to Boston tomorrow. As soon as they saw Anne and Charles off at the airport, she proposed that the rest of them – including, she added graciously, Anne's new in-laws, if they liked – set out to 'do' the Levant. She had drawn up an itinerary after they returned from Baalbek this afternoon. She clicked open her handbag and produced the list she had prepared of everything the guidebooks deemed worthy of her attention. She wanted to see the Cedars of Lebanon, the Crusader castles scattered here and there, and then go into the mountains to what was left of – here she had to squint at her spidery handwriting – 'the Beit al-Din palace of Emir Bashir the Second'. She nodded regally in the direction of her brother-in-law. 'I assume that since Joe teaches anthropology at that local school, we need look no further for a tour guide.'

'Archaeology,' Joe corrected. He and Bert exchanged looks that longed to kill.

'He's a professor of archaeology,' Martha said. She wet her lips with her tongue, nervous – as always – at having to correct her sister. 'You know very well, Bert, that he teaches at the American University, which is the best in the Middle East. And that he's an expert on the ancient world. He's written scholarly books! You know that.'

Anne surreptitiously rolled her eyes Charles's way. But her fiancé didn't appear to be listening. As though he had suddenly developed an overwhelming passion for Middle Eastern antiquities, he was staring across the room at her father's collection of Hittite vases, Phoenician glass and Assyrian cooking implements.

Anne cast a concerned look at her bridegroom. Now that she thought about it, these last few days he had seemed edgy and preoccupied. But having finally caught his eye and given him a nice wifely reassuring smile, she dismissed a quiver of foreboding. He must just have a case of wedding nerves. If she hadn't been so busy herself with what had turned out to be the endlessly complicated business of having the reception at the house, she, too, might have had second thoughts about giving in and getting married to this man who most assuredly wasn't the love of her life. It had, after all, taken Charles six years of lunches, dinners and pleasant drives up in the mountains before he had finally been able to convince her that they should, as he had not-so-romantically put it, 'face life together as a team'. During those years she hadn't met anyone else she liked more than Charles and after she had agreed to marry him last year, she had come to terms with the bargain they had struck. As she took care to assure herself nearly every day, Charles was witty, kind and sensitive. She could do far worse than settling for a calm life with this steady mate. And mostly, except when she couldn't sleep at night, she believed that. Yet Bert's warning at Baalbek had gotten under her skin. *Should* she marry Charles?

Anne's father, meanwhile, was smiling almost genially at his old sparring partner. He had, after all, spent most of his adult life in the Arab world, where the host-to-guest responsibilities were very nearly sacred. And he had told himself that the eve of his daughter's wedding was neither the time nor the place to try to even up old scores with his wife's sister. 'Of course, Bert,' he said gallantly, 'I'd be delighted to show you around.' This was not a lie. Always before he had enjoyed escorting friends and relatives once-over-lightly through the world he loved. Mostly, he knew, they would want to take quick looks at whatever wonders the guidebooks recommended and then spend the bulk of their time lunching in scenic spots and shopping in the souks for embroidered robes, inlaid wood boxes and solid gold jewellery.

But Bert was still methodically working through her list. 'After Lebanon, then Syria,' she said. 'Damascus, of course. And Palmyra. Then it's just a hop, skip and a jump over to Jordan. This Jerash seems worth a detour. And from what I've heard, I don't want to miss Petra.' She smiled condescendingly at her sister. 'It's a lost city in a deep valley. We'll all go down by donkey.'

Anne jumped in to bring her aunt back to reality. 'Sorry, but I'm afraid Syria's not such a good idea. Since the last war, Americans aren't welcome there.'

'Me?' Bert snorted. 'Even an old lady like me?'

'Even Joe couldn't get in the last time he tried,' Martha explained. 'They wouldn't let him in at the border. They kept him waiting there for hours. They even threatened to arrest him as a Zionist spy.'

Bert looked alarmed until a thought occurred to her. 'That must have been because you're a Jew. But I'm Episcopalian.'

Patiently Joe shook his head. 'It's because we're Americans. Since the Six Day War, there's been quite a backlash against us all over the Middle East.' He shrugged philosophically and opened his hands as though to show that a non-observant Jew like himself harboured no grudge against the Syrians or anyone else in the Arab world. 'You have to understand, they blame us not only for Israel's winning the last three wars but for its very existence. They say that if it weren't for our massive financial support, and the arms and other military equipment we keep pouring into it, there never would have been a Zionist state.'

Bert glared at her sister. 'I really think you could have warned me about all this before I came out here.' Yet it was only an instant later that Bert had second thoughts. She was made of stern Yankee stuff and was not about to allow herself to be so easily intimidated. 'I think you must be trying to pull my leg, Joe. Nobody's said anything bad to me since I got here. Those friends of Anne's who were here tonight, why, no one could be more charming. I myself have known Ramsey, of course, for years, and he's a perfect gentleman.' She rounded on her old adversary. 'If you didn't want to bother taking me to Syria and Jordan, Joe, why not just say so, instead of trying to scare me like you did?'

Anne cut in quickly. 'Daddy's right, it wouldn't be wise for you to go to Syria just now, even if they did let you in. But you're safe here. In Beirut, everyone knows that foreigners are absolutely safe. But, as Charles is always saying, Lebanon's a very different kettle of fish from the rest of the Arab world.' She looked expectantly at her fiancé. As a history professor, Charles usually liked nothing better than to expound his pet theory that the Lebanon was the only solid and secure liberal democratic state in the Arab world. He was fond of saying that the Lebanon was a beachhead of Western culture in a sea of Arab extremism. But tonight Charles did not even appear to have heard her. Moodily he stared off into space.

It was Anne's mother who stepped in to salvage the situation by brightly suggesting that Bert finish her journey with a trip to Greece.

'Greece!' Bert beamed. 'I've always wanted to go there. They call Boston "the Athens of America", you know.' She snapped down the point on her pen again and demanded that Joe, this instant, tell her everything she must see in Greece.

This time, however, Martha stood up to her sister. 'Please, not now. It's late, and tomorrow's the big day. We all need our beauty sleep.' Bert clucked and protested, but she was as tired as the others. Only a few moments later, the older generation disappeared upstairs.

'Whew!' Anne reached up and unpinned her long hair that had been fastened up in a bun for what felt like centuries. 'She's incredible, isn't she? Aunt Bert never changes.' She let her hair fall free below her shoulders and then ran her hands through it. 'What a day.'

She slouched further down into the sofa, stretched out her long legs, and put her feet up on an Arabian leather pouffe. For a moment she looked down, almost in surprise, at the very short skirt of her *espresso*-brown minidress and her slim legs encased in what Leila and Camilla had sworn to her were very fashionable white patterned tights. Her friends had been nagging her for years, ever since she crept back to Beirut after Mike and Boston, to stop dressing like a spinster and let herself be pretty again. But until the last few months, she had refused to part with her broadcloth blouses and no-nonsense suits. She supposed it was only with the approach of her wedding day – and the proof that another man did truly want her to be his wife – that she had recovered the confidence to dress up again. This minidress was a copy of an Ungaro original she had fancied in last month's American *Vogue*. When she had pointed it out to Leila, her friend had insisted on spiriting her off to her favourite dressmaker who had run up a copy on the spot. Anne smiled down at this proof that she was almost out of the tunnel now. After so many years in the dark, it felt good to be almost out in the light.

She yawned, gave her hair another shake, and looked at her watch. It was past two in the morning. Camilla's hairdresser would be here at eight. She smiled to herself. Tomorrow she was actually going to be a bride! 'I never imagined a wedding would be so much work. Daddy was right. We should have eloped to Cyprus.'

But Charles didn't seem to be listening. 'Anne,' he said, in an eerie voice that sounded like someone else's, 'we've got to talk.'

She kicked off her tight new shoes and wiggled her toes. At least, she thought with relief, flat shoes were back in fashion. Now that she had decided to be a bit fashionable, she would have hated to wear those excruciating pointy-toed spikes she remembered from the bad old days. As though they were already an old married couple, she was too busy sorting out her own thoughts to have paid attention to what he had just said. Her mind was a tangle of small worries. Would the baker bring the cake on time? Had anyone thought to lay in a king-size supply of sodas for the Muslim guests? Fatima's whole tribe loved Fanta. First thing in the morning, she would have to call the caterer and make sure they brought several more cases of the orange soda. And had they miscalculated and failed to order enough ice? It was amazing how even her small and intimate wedding had got out of hand. Instead of thirty people here in the parlour, there would be two hundred under a marquee out in the garden. She longed to be up in bed, stretched out full length, so she could shut down her brain and try to get some sleep. 'Look, honey, let's just call it a night.' He must be just as tired as she was. His apartment wasn't far away, but he still had to drive home.

'No,' he repeated, even more firmly, and far more

unhappily, 'I think we should talk tonight.'

'Can't whatever it is wait?' Again she yawned without looking at him. She repeated a cliché. 'After tomorrow, we'll have our whole lifetimes together to talk.'

'I don't think we should get married until we've talked.'

Something in his voice made her glance up, and she caught a look she had never before seen on his face. 'Okay. Sure.' Her eyebrows arched, and she frowned as she tried to figure out what was up. 'I suppose I could do with a nightcap.'

Anne poured out a wide snifter of Rémy Martin for him and Cointreau on the rocks for herself – and then followed him out to where he sat, silent and brooding, in a deck chair on the balcony.

She stood waiting for him to tell her what was making him look so desperate.

When still he said nothing, she sipped at her drink. From here the sea was so close she could smell its salt and hear its surf. Again, as always out on the balcony late at night, the atmosphere of Beirut crept up and seduced her.

She stood at the railing and felt the breeze lift her hair off her shoulders. She had always loved coming out here at this time of night, when the teasing part of the city that never slept flirted and winked all around her. On the other side of that darkened window over there, behind every drawn curtain in that high-rise apartment building just here, even in the dusky shadows of the balcony on the far side of the garden, skin burned against skin. The night was caressive. For the soul of Beirut had always been, was, and always would be an Arab town; and, like everything else that was Arab, it was not always what it seemed. At high noon, when the sun beat down on the honking traffic on al-Hamra, Beirut was like any other Western city: hustling for bucks, its eye for the main chance, buying and selling with the greedy panache of the City or the Bourse. But that Western gloss was only a skin-deep, lacquered shell. When the sun went down, Beirut – like Cairo, Baghdad, Damascus and Fez – let the veils fall. Flesh undulated. Eyes flashed. Nobody got a good night's sleep, which was – Anne smiled to herself – why the birth rate was so high and afternoon naps were so much a part of the daily round.

When Charles still remained silent, Anne shut her eyes. She almost fancied, when she concentrated hard like this, that she could hear the city laughing. She sighed, and listened for a moment to a few bars of recorded music that drifted on the wind from an open window – it was Camilla's mother singing a blithe little love song, one of her greatest hits. How she loved the zesty rhythms of this irrepressible city.

She opened her eyes and looked up and away, towards the looming mountains that at night were as black as the sky, except for the lights of the villas and villages that twinkled like stars, way up in the heavens, almost to Paradise. Tonight the orange sickle of a new crescent moon lay low over the sea.

Again Anne sighed. This night was so achingly perfect that she wished she could be mistaken. On such a night – with that moon, those stars, this sea – on the night before what was supposed to be her wedding day, nothing bad was about to happen. Charles was certainly not about to call off the wedding. No, not after his own family had come halfway round the world to witness it. But stranger things had happened, and they had happened to her.

She sat down on the sun-lounge next to the wall. 'Out with it,' she said finally.

When, instead of answering her, he merely stared at the black water lapping on to the deserted beach, she gave him a few more minutes before prodding him again. 'Something's wrong. Aren't you going to tell me what it is?'

Miserably he shook his head. 'Actually, I don't want to tell you at all.' He darted a haunted look her way. 'I think I should tell you, and I will tell you. It's the honourable thing to do.' He hung his head. 'But I don't want to. Believe me, I wish it weren't true.'

Oh God, she thought, oh God. *I knew it. I knew it would happen again, and it is. Dear God, it is.*

She drained her glass and, without another word, she went back to the living room and returned with the bottles. As though they were drinking weak beer rather than strong liqueurs, she topped their glasses up to the rim. And this time she didn't even bother with her ice.

Anne sat on the balcony beside her fiancé, and they drank in silence as they stared at the sea. For now she was in no more of a hurry than he was to get down to the matter at hand. She was certain that lightning was about to strike twice. Once again she was going to be told that the man she thought she was about to marry was already married. Perhaps he, too, even had three children. Would his wife be an American, she dully wondered, someone he had left behind in some upstate New York hamlet? Or would she be Lebanese, someone he had been forced into marrying after some meaningless indiscretion? Anne supposed it hardly mattered. But she was thunderstruck that the one thing that had most terrified her – since Mike, after Mike – had in fact been visited upon her again. She had always feared – no, somewhere in her gut she had always *known* – that she was doomed to go through it all again. How could she have let herself trust Charles?

She drained her glass, prayed for courage, and braced herself for what would surely come next. But her courage failed her. She put her head down in her hands and rocked back and forth in despair. She couldn't endure it again. This time, when she broke apart, she would be broken for good.

His voice came from so deep down inside him that

it sounded like a growl. 'I am a homosexual,' he said baldly.

She raised her head, looked at him blankly, blinked, and then looked away in confusion.

'I mean,' he went on haltingly to explain, as he turned his glass round and round in his sweaty palms, 'what we call a bisexual. Until now . . . I have . . . had . . . relationships with men as well as women.'

'A homosexual,' she repeated, as her mind very slowly began to grasp what it was that he had just said. He was not married. Not married! What had happened before was not, after all, happening again. He was not Mike. He was Charles, and what he had wanted to tell her on the eve of their wedding was that he was a homosexual. *Was that all?* The thought was so strong, and came from so deep within her, that for a moment she thought she must have said it out loud.

But she hadn't. He was still gripping his glass and lurching on with his confession. 'I wasn't going to tell you. When I met you, and then we started seeing each other, and we got on so well, I hoped I was over that other thing.' He faltered and then went on, pronouncing every word as slowly as though he were translating from his native language into a far less familiar tongue. 'Because of you, Anne . . . oh, Anne, I thought I'd change, that you'd never have to find out.' His voice broke. 'But I had to tell you. I don't know, maybe I'll never change. I don't know . . . But I couldn't go through with it and marry you, without your knowing. I had to give you a chance to . . . back out.'

When she looked closely at him, she saw that the hands that held his untouched drink were trembling. Beads of sweat lay like teardrops on his skin. A wave of tenderness for this man swept over her. What must it have cost him to tell her this tonight? She came closer to loving him, here and now, than she had ever come before. Of course she could never marry him now. No woman would choose the lifetime of heartaches that would come from marrying a self-admitted homosexual. The little she knew about men like *that* came from her abnormal psychology textbooks. From time to time, too, she had heard certain things hinted about particularly elegant oldish men or especially amoral young ones. But she had never dreamed that a fine, upright man like Charles belonged to that shadowy world of whispers and off-colour innuendoes.

And yet, Anne thought, as she watched his face crumple with anguish, it was a pity that all this had turned out as it had. In time, it was possible that she might even have been able to love a man like Charles more selflessly and truly than she had loved a brute like Mike. She and Charles, after all, were two of a kind. She had suffered, and evidently so had he. Why did everyone, especially the good and giving souls of this world, have to suffer so? She was accustomed to feeling sorry for her patients and even sorrier for herself, but she was not accustomed to feeling sorriest of all for a man. Men were supposed to be strong, virile and powerful. They were not supposed to have tears in their eyes, as Charles did now.

As her own eyes misted over with affection for Charles, she realized with a start that she was not altogether repelled by this turn of affairs. In way she even liked it. *This one wouldn't hurt me.* It dawned on her, as clearly as if a klieg light had just illuminated not only this darkish night but her own long years of depression, that – since Mike – she had been terrified of men. She wondered not only how such a fundamental truth could have eluded her but also why she was finding his confession so liberating. Perhaps, she decided, it was not possible simultaneously to feel both pity and fear for the same person.

She had an impulse to take poor Charles in her arms and comfort this wonderful man who might be even weaker than she was herself. She had known for years that they liked to listen to the same Charlie Parker records, laugh at the same Lenny Bruce jokes, and read the same Albert Camus novels. But now it seemed that what they really had in common was that Charles was as damaged by life as she was. It was a shame she couldn't go ahead and marry him tomorrow. In time she might even let down her guard and allow herself to trust him. Even though he was a man, he probably would never be able to love her to pieces, as Mike had.

His shoulders were shaking as he wept. She herself, she thought, cried just as Charles did, with her head in her hands, but proudly, in absolute silence. Anne took a deep breath. Could it be that the two of them belonged together after all? Just because Charles was a homosexual didn't mean she couldn't marry him. They would simply have a different sort of marriage – not necessarily better or worse, just different – from other couples of their acquaintance.

Anne looked out to the dark horizon where black sea met black sky. Even her closest friends might be shocked if they found out not only that he was a homosexual but also that she had knowingly settled for such a bad marital bargain. But who were they to talk? Leila's father had all but sold her off to the highest bidder. Camilla had married her Prince Charming but lived to regret it. Of them all, only Fatima – the one they had pitied for being forced into an arranged marriage with her cousin – had achieved a loving union with a good man. Maybe she and Charles, too, could end up being happy together. Or perhaps not.

Along with a sigh, Anne suppressed a shudder at the thought that if they went ahead and got married, he might still hanker after men. What would she do if he left her for another man? No, she couldn't betray herself with this doomed marriage. Or could she?

Charles straightened up, wiped his eyes on the cuffs of his shirt, and hazarded a look at her. 'Say something,' he pleaded. 'Or maybe you think there's nothing to say.' When she remained silent, he thought she had given him an answer of sorts. 'Shall I go?'

She made her decision, tore her eyes away from the sea, and smiled as she shook her head at Charles. They had talked enough. What she was about to try to do would transcend words.

For a long hypnotic moment, she let the fact that she was smiling sink in. Then she beckoned to him with her finger.

'Come here,' she said softly.

When still he didn't move, she reached over and took his hand and pulled him down beside her on the lounge. His passive body was a dead weight in her arms.

'Trust me,' she whispered as she kissed him on the lips.

He groaned and raised his arms as if to push her away. But then, as her gentle kiss continued, he gingerly put his hands on her back. A moment later he stretched out his fingers and began to stroke her hair and – finally, tentatively – he started to kiss her back. In the six years of their courtship, they must have exchanged hundreds of kisses: friendly pecks on the cheek, exuberant kisses on the lips, even passionate open mouth gropings that had left marks on their necks. But this time on the balcony sun-lounge, with both their eyes wide open, was the first truly intimate touch they had ever shared. Shyly they kissed. Delicately they held one another. Once or twice he broke away and opened his mouth to speak. But each time she covered his lips with her own and kissed him so long and hard that he seemed to forget his equivocations. By the time she had wriggled out of her dress and his hands were on her bare skin, they both understood it was now or never.

Yet he was still nervous, and so he shut his eyes as she set about finishing her seduction. It was over eight years since her last time with Mike, but she would never forget his burning lessons in how to arouse a man. As she kissed him and stroked him, his very passivity gave her the confidence to continue. Like a chant inside her, she kept reminding herself that he was not Mike, he was Charles. This one could never hurt her as the other one had. They made love as carefully as if each of them were spun of glass.

Afterwards, he began to cry again as they clung together, naked on the sun-lounge. 'It's going to be all right,' she crooned, although she, too, had tears in her eyes. She didn't love Charles as she had loved Mike, but she liked him far more. And it had been better with him than she had thought it would be. She had not expected to be so moved by his touch. It had been so long since she had been with a man that she had almost forgotten how it felt – so thrilling, so right, so powerful, so vulnerable, all of that, all at once – to have a man inside her. And yet, even as they quivered in each other's arms, there remained a remoteness to their intimacy. He wasn't her first choice, and she wasn't his. They could be close, but not so close as to be alone together on the edge of the precipice.

The moon was gone, the stars were fading, and the sky had begun dimly to catch the light that was rising from the east. In a little while their wedding day would be dawning. Loudspeakers spat out buzzing static, and then from every other street corner the recorded voices of the muezzins began their calls to prayer. '*Allahu akbar*, God is great!' Beirut turned over, rubbed its eyes, and began to wake. 'You'll see,' she repeated, 'it's going to be all right.'

He sighed, moved closer in her arms, and after a while – just when she was almost asleep – he whispered in her ear, 'Thanks.'

She kept her eyes shut. 'Welcome,' she mumbled.

But he was wide awake and wanted to talk. 'Anne? Wake up. We should talk, Anne.'

She yawned. 'Why?'

'To decide things.'

She was waking up now. 'We did already.' Lazily she reached over, touched his cheek, and smiled. 'Has anyone ever told you that you talk too much?'

'So you mean that's it?' He laughed. 'That this is it?'

She stirred in his arms and stretched. 'Of course.' As she twisted her wrist so she could see her watch, her eyes flew wide open. 'It's almost six.' She sprang up and reached for her clothes. 'The maid will be here any minute. Then the caterers, the hairdresser – God, I'm surprised Aunt Bert's not down already!' She threw him his trousers. 'Get dressed.'

But still he had to ask it outright. 'So we're getting married after all?'

She shrugged on her dress and zipped it up without having to ask him for help. 'If you want.'

He threw his arms around her. 'I do,' he said. 'Oh yes, I do.'

After that, the wedding itself was an anticlimax.

Everything was exactly as it was supposed to be. The sun shone bright, and a spring breeze swept in from the sea so it wasn't too hot. Anne looked radiant as she and her father walked out to where the minister waited in the rose bower at the end of the manicured garden on the Rue Bliss. As she passed family and friends, there were murmurs here and there about how lovely she looked in Camilla's borrowed veil, about how glad they were that she'd finally got over that other matter, about how her demure white shantung dress – even up close – looked like a Dior original. Fatima, Camilla and Leila each managed to catch her eye as she swept past them on the way to the rose bower. Camilla wept, Fatima sighed, and even Leila had to brush away tears. The vows took only a few minutes, but it was more than an hour before all the guests passed down the receiving line to wish Anne and Charles a lifetime of happiness. Then champagne toasts were drunk to the happy couple's health. The photographer snapped pictures of the bride and groom, the families, the friends. The children grew restless and began shrieking as they ran around the garden. Anne cut the cake. Waiters passed the tea sandwiches. There was plenty of Fanta and ice.

On the surface everything was exactly as it was supposed to be at Anne's wedding.

Chapter 15

Two years later, on what she was to regard as one of the worst days of her life, Anne had to struggle to keep from breaking down in the taxi on the short ride home from work to the apartment she and Charles shared in fashionable Ras Beirut. The radio blared out one of Nirvana's happy-go-lucky hit tunes, horns hooted in every clogged lane of the downtown traffic jam, and boys leapfrogged from car to car selling newspapers, boxes of tissues and pretty strings of fragrant jasmine flowers.

Silent and still amidst so much noisy movement, Anne concentrated all her life-force on simply keeping her emotions under control. I will not cry here, she repeated over and over to herself like a mantra. I can let go at home, when Charles is there to comfort me. Her marriage had its ups and downs, like everyone else's. But always her husband was the most caring of companions. She could count on Charles to be as consoling as her dearest women friends when she broke the bad news to him as soon as she got home. He would, she suspected, be as devastated as she was; for he, too, had dearly wanted children. Mostly, she thought, it wasn't so much sexual desire as making a baby that was uppermost in his mind on those midnight occasions when he crossed the distance between their twin beds.

In the front seat the driver's three-year-old daughter blissfully licked a lollipop as she chattered to her Baba. Most of all Anne had wanted a sugar-and-spice little girl to dress up in frilly dresses, to help with her homework, and to protect and cherish all the days of her life.

Anne's eyes blurred with tears. The doctors had confirmed her fears that she had never ovulated, and that she would never be able to have a baby. But when she had rung Charles's office after finishing with the doctor, his secretary had informed her that he had gone home early. Anne had cancelled the remainder of her afternoon appointments and fled out of her office and into a taxi. In five minutes, ten minutes at most, she promised herself, I will lock the door behind me and throw myself in Charles's arms. Then, and only then, would she let herself weep the dry tears of a barren woman.

She paid the driver, crept through the lobby, and leaned against the wall of the lift as she ascended to the sixth floor. Almost there, she told herself as she inserted her key into the lock and slipped inside.

'Charles!' Anne let out a deep sighing breath and threw her attaché case down on the beige suede living room sofa her husband had ordered from Milan the year after the wedding. His taste was as trendy and true as a decorator's, and their apartment was an icy gallery of chrome, glass and leather designer chic. She would have preferred a homelier nest to come home to each night, but she regarded this touch-me-not décor as only one of the more superficial compromises of her married life. Yet she had made this cold bed, and she did her best to lie on it without regrets. As she knew only too well, there were worse men than Charles in this world. She was glad to have him to come home to today.

'Honey? Where are you?' A fervent disciple of Scandinavian open plan design, Charles had had the builders knock out the dividing walls between the sitting room, dining room and kitchen. Since she couldn't see him anywhere here, she assumed he was either out on the balcony or in one of the bedrooms in the back of the apartment.

'Charles?' The balcony overlooking the bay was empty but for two deck chairs and two half-full glasses sweating on an Italianate table. Even though the sun was still beating down, the ice in the gin and tonics was unmelted. He, and someone else, must have been out here just moments ago.

Anne frowned. The last thing she felt capable of now was putting on a happy face for one of the multitude of Charles's friends. He knew everyone in Beirut and kept up such a frantic social pace that he seemed to see each of his friends every overbooked week. But she would have stayed at work if she had known he had brought someone here this afternoon.

Absently she straightened Charles's navy-blue blazer on the back of his chair. Then she stared at an identical blazer on the other chair. No, she thought, oh no. It can't be. Not today, of all days. *Another man*. She considered tiptoeing out of the apartment to give Charles and his companion time to say goodbye and cover their tracks.

But this time it was too late to shut her eyes and run away from the truth about what sort of marriage she had.

Charles was rushing down the hallway with his arms open wide. 'Darling!' Usually so impeccable in his appearance, he had failed to button his shirt where he had hastily tucked it into his trousers. 'I didn't expect you home for hours.'

Anne stood in the centre of the living room and looked past her husband down the hallway. Easy, she told herself. This might not be what you think, what you have in fact been half-expecting to find every time you've come upon Charles since you married him. There surely must be an innocent explanation for what your husband and his male visitor have just been doing in the back of the apartment. In a second one of his elderly colleagues – perhaps a Classics professor or a fellow board member from one of Charles's pet charities – will flush the toilet and poke his head out of the bathroom. Yet she was suspicious enough to stay rooted where she could see anyone coming out of the bathroom.

When Charles tried to take her in his arms and lead her back into the sitting room, she brushed him aside. 'Who's here with you?'

'No one.' He smiled as he elegantly hid a yawn with one of his manicured hands. 'I was just having a little nap.'

'Were you?' They would have to face this issue sometime, and wearily she supposed it might as well be now. She was surprised at how jealous she felt. 'Who with?' She had not expected him to lie even when she had more or less caught him in the act. But with all the practice he must get, Charles would have to be a skilled liar. Dully she wondered whether he had continued to go with his men for the whole two years of their marriage or if he had been faithful to her for even a little while. She supposed he could have had flings every time he had gone gadding off on those 'academic research trips' of his throughout the Middle East, Europe and America. Charles went away far more often than any other professor she knew on the faculty.

Yet there was still the tiniest chance that she was wrong. To make sure, she started down the hallway but stopped when she saw the bathroom door and the guest bedroom door wide open. Yes, the owner of the other navy-blue blazer was in the master bedroom.

She returned to the sitting room and slumped down on the sofa. '*I know*, Charles. And now you know that I know.' She could not bear to be more explicit. Even now, she thought, when probably she should be screaming out her hurt and rage, their relationship was so restrained that the most important thing seemed to be to remain civilized. 'I'm afraid we're going to have to talk about this.'

Intently he studied her face. 'Right.' He tried to smile. 'But first a drink, I think. Yes, a nice gin and tonic.'

'We could finish the two out on the balcony.' She raised her head and just managed to look at him. For a second her control slipped. 'In my own bedroom, Charles. *How could you?*'

He had the grace to wince. 'I'm sorry. You must know how very sorry I am.' He bit his lip. 'I had hoped you would never have to know. I've tried to be discreet. I hardly ever bring anyone here. And I can promise you this. I never will again. Bring anyone here, that is.'

She hid her head in her hands. Evidently he had brought his men into her bedroom before, and the most he seemed willing to promise her was that from now on he would meet his lovers elsewhere. She cried without making a sound.

But by the time Charles returned with the drinks, she had wiped her eyes and composed herself. He, too, had pulled himself together and was very nearly back to his usual ebullient self when he presented her with one of his perfect gin and tonics. As though this were not a home but a cocktail lounge, he kept the tall glasses in the freezer so they would always be frosted. The gin was always coolly stored in the fridge, too. Even for this fraught conversation, he had cut the lime in a tulip shape and run it first over the rim of the glass before resting it atop the ice.

Their marriage, Anne reflected with growing resentment, was as artful as Charles's iced drinks. She drank deeply. 'So. Are you going to introduce me to your friend?'

'I think not. There's no sense in making things more difficult than they already are for the two of us. And for him as well.'

She took another drink and swallowed hard. 'Tell me. Is it someone I know?'

'Do you really want to know, Anne?'

She shut her eyes. 'I guess not.' When she opened her eyes, they were full of tears. 'I didn't need this today, of all days.'

Sensing a possible change of subject that might let him off the hook, he was instantly the soul of brotherly concern. 'Why, has something happened?' He leaned forward, all sympathy. 'But of course, you came home early. Something's gone wrong, hasn't it?'

She let out a deep sigh. There didn't seem to be much more, after all, to say about herself, Charles, and whoever was hiding in the bedroom. 'I went back to the doctor today. He says I'll never be able to have a baby.'

'My poor darling.' Charles moved over beside her on the sofa and tried to take her in his arms. But when she recoiled, he contented himself with consoling words. 'Maybe he's wrong. Get a second opinion. Or go back to the States. See specialists in New York and Boston. They can do so much about fertility these days. Maybe—'

She shook her head. 'I saw the reports. There's no way I can ever ovulate. If one of my patients had my insides, I'd say to her exactly what the doctor said to me. No, this is it. No children.'

'I'm so sorry, Anne. So very sorry.'

'Me, too.' But she couldn't stand any more now about Charles, his boyfriend or her infertility. She collected her attaché case and got to her feet. 'I'm going over to my parents' for the night. And I think – as planned – that I'll go down to Fatima's tomorrow.'

'So you'll be back the day after tomorrow?'

He was, she realized, asking about more than her weekend plans. She was ashamed of herself as she shrugged. 'Probably.'

'I'm glad, Anne. So glad. I do love you, you know. In my way.'

'I know.' She had at least to make one thing clear. 'But look . . . why don't you move into the other bedroom before I get back?'

'Whatever you want.'

'No. Not what I want. But what I suppose I'll settle for.' She managed to get out of the door without bursting into tears.

The next morning Anne's battered old '52 Mercedes sedan jerked and jumped from rut to rut on the narrow dirt road that snaked back from the coast towards Fatima's village in the Lebanese foothills. She was used to navigating this twisting trail that passed for a road, and so, as expertly as a lorry driver on the long haul from Turkey to the Gulf, at the last second she repeatedly swerved away from the worst of the deep trenches left by the winter rains. Some patches were so washed out and riddled with gullies that she cut off the beaten path and jiggled the car through stony pastures until she could pick up the precarious road again. Still, on a track like this, the odds were inevitably against her. She veered hard to the left to avoid one pit but then thudded in and bumped out of another hole she hadn't been able to see until she was inside it.

She swore as she ricocheted up and smashed her head on the roof. In all the years she had been driving down to Fatima's village, the government had never once done a thing to maintain this road. Beirut was laced with palm-fringed boulevards, but the south had to make do with glorified donkey tracks. Beirut businessmen zoomed at eighty miles an hour up to their mountaintop summer villas in flashy imported sports cars, but down here in the south the only vehicle – besides an armoured tank – with a suspension system sturdy enough to grind over these hills was a heavy metal museum piece like this eighteen-year-old Mercedes.

She rubbed the crown of her head and wondered anew how it could be that, no matter which fatcat politicians won the elections, the rich central government in Beirut so consistently neglected the poverty-stricken backwaters of the country. Year by year in Lebanon, the gap between rich and poor grew dangerously wider. Life in cosmopolitan Beirut careered along at a frantic twentieth-century pace, while only a few hours' drive away life was still stalled in Biblical times. The past ten years had made a boom town of Beirut. Some of the prosperity came from the oil business, for the two chief Gulf pipelines terminated in the Lebanese ports of Sidon and Tripoli. The port of Beirut, too, had capitalized on its new strategic importance since the closure of the Suez Canal to international shipping after the '67 war. A *laissez-faire* government attitude, Swiss-style secrecy regulations and the collapse of Nasser's Cairo as a Middle Eastern financial centre had all, in addition, resulted in Beirut becoming an international banking centre. In 1951 there had been only five banks; fifteen years later there were ninety-three. Property speculation had made millionaires of many, and they were able to keep that wealth to themselves – or squirrel it away abroad for safekeeping – because income taxes were not only pitched very low but also inefficiently collected. Businesses evaded three-quarters of their tax bills, and the Beirut professional class boasted that they paid only ten per cent of what they owed. Yet they bought air-conditioned limousines and elaborate stereo systems for a song, for the government was in the pocket of the commercial interests and so refused to impose tariffs which would have encouraged the development of a domestic industrial base. Instead of taxing luxury goods, the government raised the price of salt, tobacco and fuel. Few were rich, but many were poor. Four per cent of the population disposed of a third of the gross national income. Even if the politicians cared only for their greedy self-interest, surely, Anne thought, they must begin to worry sometime about what would happen once the oppressed finally awoke and began fighting for their piece of the pie. Years ago, in the wake of the 1958 civil war, the general then serving as president had issued a dire warning: 'If the rich continue to maintain their privileges at everyone's expense this way, there will be a social revolution in Lebanon.' But the Beirut power élite – Christian and Muslim alike – had so far remained blind to what was happening all around them.

As Anne navigated a bend, the glare of the morning sun was so strong that she lost sight of the road for a moment. But she held tight to the steering wheel and soldiered on. She was heading due east now, and the sun would be in her eyes for the rest of the way.

When the road evened out a little, she groped on the seat beside her for her sunglasses. Beirut's heedless politicians, she thought grimly, weren't so much in need of putting on shades as of flinging off their rose-coloured glasses and – before it was too late – taking a hard look at the realities in front of their beaky Lebanese noses. Yet she had hoped, when the President had appointed Leila's husband to the post of Prime Minister five years ago, that Mustafa was going to be a cut above the rest. Certainly, even though the President held most of the power, Leila's husband had seemed eager to redress ancient wrongs. He had talked in newspaper interviews about social justice, had gone on fact-finding rides to rural areas, and even – on one very well-publicized afternoon – had received a deputation of shabby villagers in his wood-panelled office. He had sounded like John Kennedy as he had promised to get his government moving again. Taxes would be more efficiently collected. The postal service would be reformed, for it was a disgrace that it took ten days for a letter to be delivered from one end of Beirut to another. The trains would be overhauled; although it took only a few hours to drive to Damascus by car, it could take four days to get there by train.

So it was that, early on in his régime, at one of Leila's swanky dinner parties, Anne had earnestly lectured Mustafa and his cronies about the wretched living conditions in the one blighted hamlet she knew well. In Suker, she had said, some families had no running water and half had no indoor bathrooms. There was no doctor or any sort of health services within miles of Fatima's village, and as a result – just to cite one statistic she happened to have compiled herself, since the government didn't bother keeping accurate records of an unimportant place like Suker – infant mortality there was five times higher than in Beirut. Children fortunate enough to grow up, however, had to make do with horizons that were every bit as limited as their parents' had been. The girls remained illiterate, and the boys – since the only school in the village was still a hit-or-miss affair at the mosque – did not fare much better. At best, at home, the only work that would be open to them was eking out a back-breaking subsistence as glorified serfs for the landowners who lived the high life in Beirut. But Suker's depleted land wasn't rich enough to support families with eight, ten or even fifteen children. Many sons were sent off to scour Beirut for paying jobs, and others were shipped further afield to lonely exile in Africa, Asia, Australia and the Americas. If it weren't for the remittances they sent home, God only knew how miserable villages like Suker could survive. From generation to generation, the Shia of the south and the Bekaa, the Sunni of the Akkar, and the Druze of the Shouf were doomed to repeat these same cycles of despair. Anne had looked fixedly at every one of the politicians dining at the Prime Minister's table. How, she had demanded, can you allow these injustices to continue?

The road surface was surer but steeper now as it began to wind steadily uphill from the coast. Anne took one hand off the steering wheel and rummaged in a sack for some dates. She didn't want to eat too much, for Fatima would be offended if she didn't tuck into an enormous meal as soon as she arrived. There was sure to be *tabouli*, *kibbe*, fresh bread and those fabulous black *zeitoun* picked from the olive trees just outside the back door.

As she munched on a handful of dates, she recalled the upshot of her soapbox speech at Leila's dinner party. Only a day or two later, one of Mustafa's oily young assistants had bustled into the hospital to ask her advice on what might be done to help those hapless villagers. Anne had promptly sat him down in her consulting room and, after dutifully listening to him complain about lower back pain and a gassy stomach – for budding Lebanese politicians shared the Arab hypochondria and couldn't resist the opportunity for free medical advice – she had once again cited the conditions in Suker as an example of how bad life could be in the neglected villages. The assistant had made copious notes, smiled encouragingly, and promised that something would soon be done to correct this dire situation. Shortly after that, Anne had gone off to America with Charles for a long holiday, and many months passed before Fatima filled her in on the upshot of the Prime Minister's grand promises. That August the surveyors came to Suker, mysteriously measuring this and that, refusing to tell anybody anything, and consequently giving rise to waves of alarming rumours about the imminent destruction of the entire village. Then in October, a parade of bulldozers arrived to dig a series of deep yawning pits on the outer fringes of the village. But still no one bothered to tell the residents of Suker what was the central government's plan. Meanwhile, the winter rains came, and soon the pitted sites overflowed into muddy ponds. When the construction crews arrived the next spring, the sites weren't good for anything but watering holes. Consultants were called in from Beirut to assess the situation. After much head-scratching and drinking of tea, it was finally decided that the bulldozers would have to be summoned again. Eventually, after more delays, new sites were laid out. But by then the builders had moved on to far more lucrative projects back in Beirut, where a massive land and construction boom was in full swing. It wasn't until a full year after Anne had spoken up at Leila's dinner party that two huge concrete blockhouses that were supposed to serve as schools for boys and girls were finally erected in Fatima's village. The government didn't allocate funds for books, desks or teachers' salaries. But as soon as the walls were up and the roof was raised, the Prime Minister's office did send a photographer down from Beirut to record the existence of government schools in Suker. More to the point, sharp colour copies of those photographs were promptly hand-delivered to Anne by the same unctuous young man who had come to see her the year before. As she later confided to Fatima when the two of them talked all this over, what really disgusted her about this incident was what it showed not only of government inertia but also of corruption. *Wasta*, the Arabic word for personal influence in high places, still reigned supreme in Lebanon. Suker had been given its concrete shells of schools not because the politicians believed it was their responsibility to serve the people but because Anne was a friend of the Prime Minister's wife. And her larger point – that Suker was only one of many blighted villages that needed schools, hospitals and every other basic social service – had fallen on deaf ears.

Without warning, the road suddenly dipped and spun round so sharply that Anne almost lost control of the car as she struggled to keep it from skidding off the rim of the precipice. She didn't remember that bend being so fierce. Last week's rains had left the road more precarious than ever. She held on for dear life to this warhorse of a Mercedes and kept going. After she had all but ruined their Ford Cortina on this very road last year, Charles had bought her this cheap old clunker just to use on her monthly trips down to the village. In Lebanon, where wing-and-a-prayer mechanics could keep almost anything on the road, even a rickety and rusty old Mercedes never lost its resale value. Up in the north near Camilla's château, she had once seen a vintage Mercedes taking hairpin mountain bends as if it had come off the assembly line a week ago instead of thirty years before.

Anne gunned the engine and held on tight as she raced up one of the steepest hills in the south. The car slowed from third to second, and then, still far from the crest, she had to shift it down into first. The car faltered as it crept uphill, and then the motor stalled. She tweaked on the emergency brake and revved it again, only to plunge down suddenly into a ditch. Impotently she rocked the car back and forth, trying to get enough play to surge out of the gully and up to the top of the hill. She kept pumping down hard on the gas, willing the car to get back on the track. But when, instead, she stalled the engine again and then flooded it, she had to face the fact that she wasn't going anywhere just yet. She switched off the ignition and settled back to wait for another car to come along and help her out.

In a rut, she thought disgustedly to herself as she assessed her situation. Yes, that's exactly the trouble: I am stuck in a very deep rut. Usually she kept herself so busy, what with her exhausting shifts at the hospital, her demanding private practice in her smart suite of offices overlooking the sea, and her hectic social whirl of family and friends and colleagues, that there was never time just to sit and think and feel. But on this deserted dirt road, there was no alternative. It was so unnervingly quiet here in this wilderness. The only sound was that of bird song, and for a moment she distracted herself by concentrating on the exact timbre and pitch of the twittering. When, eventually, even the bird flew away, she was bereft in the empty silence. She was empty inside, too, she thought, with her empty heart and now the confirmation that she could never have anything but an empty womb.

Anne leaned her head against the steering wheel and started to weep for everything that was wrong in her world. Was she never to have anything that truly mattered in life but work? Self-pitying tears spilled down her cheeks as she gave way to the feelings about Charles which she had dammed up inside her since yesterday. He had deceived her, betrayed her, hurt her more than she had thought he could. Yet how was it, she wondered, that even now she wanted to hang on to this shell of a marriage? Because, she answered herself, I'm still broken up inside.

She rocked back and forth in despair, butting her head gently against the steering wheel. She wished to God she had never seduced Charles on her parents' balcony, much less married him. Looking back on everything that had been said and done between them the night before the wedding, she could not understand how she had gone ahead and made the mistake of marrying him. She had been in such a muddle that night, worrying about small things, forgetting the big ones, and mixing up what had happened with Mike with what was happening with Charles. It was as much her fault as his that they were stuck in a relationship weakened by the most intimate of compromises. At least Charles had been honest with her. With Mike, however, she had been the blameless victim betrayed and deceived with lie upon lie.

Her face crumpled as she began to cry harder, remembering what it had been like truly to love and to lose. That old festering ache had never quite gone away and she supposed it never altogether would; she doubted whether she could ever bear to give him up entirely. But over the years, even if she had never made her peace with it, she had grown accustomed to every familiar nuance of that disaster: the exact expression on his face when he had asked her to marry him, the specific words his wife had spoken to her on the telephone, the precise shading of his lying grey eyes when he insisted he wasn't married even after she had proof that he was. When she looked back on all that – and she still did, often, for feeding on that pain was a way of keeping their passion ever green – sometimes she even took a sort of perverse pleasure in reliving her own romantic tragedy. In a way, for her, Mike – sometimes hero, often demon – had become more of a myth than a man. But now she had to live with the fresh heartache of her infertility. Everything about her life was barren.

Anne straightened up, dabbed at her eyes with a tissue, and tried not to feel so sorry for herself. Everyone, in one way or another, had a hard life. Hers had its ups as well as its downs, and no one she knew – except perhaps dear Fatima, content with what Anne hadn't thought she wanted – was very happy.

Yet still Anne had to struggle against her tears. In a day or two maybe she would succeed in coming to terms with her pain. But now all she wanted was a soft shoulder to cry on and then maybe a nice hot glass of tea. Instead of breaking down on this isolated mountain road, she longed to be pouring out her troubled heart to Fatima. Her first impulse yesterday at the doctor's and then after that scene with Charles had been to flee south and confide all to the friend who had never failed her. Men came and went in one's life, but it was the women who endured.

She blew her nose and wiped away the residue of what she wished could have been the last tears she would ever shed. She had never understood why women like Camilla seemed to enjoy having what they would call 'a good cry'. She preferred holding her sadness inside. Even when she wept where none could see her weakness, she felt, when it was over, not relieved but diminished.

For something to do, she ate the last few shrivelled dates at the bottom of her bag and busily set about the modest business of transforming herself for what she hoped would be her imminent arrival in Suker. The village was less than ten miles away. Usually she didn't whip on her headscarf until she was approaching the last bend. But it wouldn't hurt if she looked the part of the virtuous woman in distress when a car or truck rattled down this road and happened upon her.

Anne reached in the back seat for her overnight bag and then rooted inside for her trousers, hairbrush and the big white polyester scarf she always took care to pack for her visits to Fatima. She had grown accustomed, over the years, to donning the veil when she came down to Suker. Now that she was more or less used to putting on a scarf before she arrived there, it would have felt strange if one day she had walked through the village bareheaded. Still, she thought as she wiped the sweat from her forehead, the scarf would be oppressively hot today. It was a muggy April afternoon, and it had been a stifling two-hour drive down from Beirut. Her hair was already plastered up on the back of her head in a bun, but she brushed wayward strands back off her face and secured them in place with hairpins. Where she was going, it made everything so much easier if she simply bowed to local custom and concealed every wayward lock of hair. Not that anyone, of course, had put any pressure on her to masquerade as a good village woman. She – and they – were very clear about the fact that she was a foreign doctor. But she had found that it helped, when she was trying to get the women to tell her the truth about their ailments, if she looked more like their sisters and cousins than a rich foreigner who had come down from Beirut for the day. The men, too, treated her with more respect when she was covered up like their mothers, wives and daughters.

Yet as she folded the cheap white square into a triangle, she flinched just a little. When she had first come back from Boston, she had rather liked looking as miserable as she felt. It had been almost satisfying, in those seasons of depression, to don this scarf and feel ugly inside and out. But as she picked it up now, she reflected that she no longer took masochistic pleasure in making the worst of herself. Gradually over the years, she had recovered most of her old persona. These days, in her smart tailored wardrobe, at least superficially she looked and acted much as she had before she had met Mike. The older she got, the more convinced she became that basically people didn't change much over the years. Fatima, Camilla and Leila were essentially the same now that they were turning thirty as they had been as teenagers. That thought comforted her.

She tried not to mind when she put on the scarf, tied it tight under her chin, and pulled it down low over her forehead as the village women did. Yet she minded. She cringed as she looked at herself in the car mirror. No woman – herself included – looked her best in these awful polyester squares that hugged the face like ghostly hoods. She was subdued as she slipped on trousers under her cotton minidress.

A moment later, however, hearing a horn hoot behind her, then a chorus of shouts, and finally a sickening grate of brakes too hastily applied, she was glad she would be seen as a respectable woman.

'*El-hakima!*' A familiar smiling face peered in at her window and then screeched back to his brothers in the car that yes, they were right, it was the doctor come back to them again. '*Ahlen was ahlen!*'

Anne climbed out of the Mercedes, grinned at the young man who was – like every other of the three hundred or so Suker villagers – one of Fatima's distant cousins, and began to exchange the ritual Arab courtesies about her health, his health, their families' health, and so on and so forth. By then his three brothers were upon them, and there was another more detailed round of smiles and welcoming questions. Anne had helped two of their wives give birth to healthy sons, and she had been treating their father's rheumatism for years. The babies were fine, the father was limping along, and the youngest brother's wife was pregnant again. Finally, then, they turned to the matter at hand, that *el-Hakima* needed a push so she could be up and on her way to Suker.

Before she could even slide back in the driver's seat, the men were grappling with the rear end of the car and had it out of the ditch. She got in, gunned the engine, tooted the horn, and – after promising that yes, she would be round to see their wives in the morning – she waved and was off.

She grew ever more elated as she took the final turns of her journey at madcap speed. The mountainous passes that lay between Suker and the coast were behind her now, and she was in a land of green rolling foothills that undulated gently like a grassy sea. Wild flowers – violets, hollyhocks and hibiscus – rippled to the horizon. She raised clouds of dust and tooted her horn from an excess of optimism as she rocketed through every comatose village along the way. Women looked up from their work and waved good-naturedly, shepherds shaded their eyes against the sun and then shouted greetings, and packs of small boys laughed and gave chase like dogs. *El-Hakima* was no stranger to these parts.

Always, Anne reflected, as she executed a final set of corkscrew turns amongst the craggy olive groves, her spirits soared when she neared Fatima's home. Even though Suker looked old and worn, with its dusty road that wound round and about its musty shopfronts, its sunbleached mosque that had never been grand enough to rate even a spindly minaret, and its crumbling flat-roofed houses that hadn't been repainted in years, still to her it had a serene beauty. She loved this dear sleepy village and its gentle caring people. She was not, however, so carried away by peasant romanticism that she saw Suker as an unblemished paradise. Often, when she found herself comparing Suker's quiet pleasures favourably to the frenzy of Beirut, she took care to remind herself that this world, too, had its dark side. This village and every other backwater like it was rife with ignorance and superstition. Suker was a closed society, its rules of conduct were carved in stone, and it could be mercilessly cruel to those who refused to conform. Bloodfeuds here could pass from one cursed generation to another. Even in this day and age, brothers had been known to slit sisters' throats for the unforgivable crime of sullying family honour. A woman could die for an unchaperoned ride with a stranger in a car, a stolen kiss in the fields, or even a wayward word to a non-family man by the village well. Such violent enforcing of the old taboos didn't occur often, but it happened none the less. Even so, what redeemed this village – and what in fact made it for Anne the happiest spot on earth – was that, for anyone accepted as one of them, being here was like plunging into a warm buoyant bath. Life in Suker lacked all the amenities, except love.

She sounded the horn as she pulled up in front of Fatima's, and at once the door flew open and children tumbled out, shouting that auntie finally had come again. Boys came running from their play in the fields, and girls with their infant brothers and sisters in their arms rushed down to greet her. Anne was engulfed in a wriggling pack of children. Fatima had nine in her own brood now, and there were a boisterous fifteen or twenty more belonging to Ali's brothers who now lived with them here under the same crowded roof.

Anne hugged and kissed and petted and patted this new generation of Zainabs and Zahras, Alis and Abbases. In the back of her mind, all the way down from Beirut, she had been worried that it might depress her to be surrounded by what the doctors had told her she could never have. Since she was a little girl, she had blithely assumed that when she grew up she would marry the man she loved, have his children, and live happily ever after. Because she had taken this prospect of domestic contentment so much for granted, she had channelled her energies into the more immediate satisfactions of work. How, she thought with a trace of bitterness as she held Fatima's children in her arms, was she to have known that everything except the sterile comfort of professional success was going to elude her? First she had lost the man she had loved, and now came the news that she wasn't ever to have children. She wished she could halt her life somehow, and go back and change it into something other than what it now was.

Oh God, Anne thought, as she clutched another woman's children close to her, I wanted this so much, and I'm not going to have it, ever.

In a panic, then, she looked towards Fatima who stood nursing her latest baby in the doorway of her house. But how could fecund Fatima, who had brought nine children into the world, understand how she felt knowing that she couldn't produce even one? Yet as their eyes met, Anne could feel her tears welling up again. Of course Fatima understood. She was a woman; women understood.

Anne sighed from deep inside. She had taken pride in how well she had handled the doctors' diagnosis. Until her breakdown back on the mountain road, she had not even wept. Yet here and now, with the fruits of Fatima's fertility all around her, the import of what had happened shook her. *No babies! No children, ever!* For years, every time she had seen that first tell-tale spot of menstrual blood, this monthly proof of her empty womb had left her, for one unguarded instant, altogether desolate. How could she reconcile herself to the knowledge that this loss was permanent, that she was never going to experience the wonder of creating a child inside herself? She was never going to get over this grief, either. First Mike, and now this.

And yet, standing in the bright sun of Suker, with her arms full of children whom she loved almost as if they had been her own, she was as soothed as if salve had been stroked on to an open wound. These were not her own babies, and the fact that there never would be babies of her own would always hurt. But as these children twined around her like vines, the simple truth occurred to her that perhaps the best and most nurturing aspects of motherhood were not based on possession. Even though she would never be able to call a child *my* son or *my* daughter, still she could love, guide and protect other women's children. She would have to learn to treasure whatever maternal satisfactions were thrown her way. She could still breathe in their soft yeasty baby smells, still take delight in their dancing-eyed innocence, still sometimes even be in the right place at the right time and so kiss away their when they puckered up and cried. She did not have to renounce all that was maternal in herself. Yet Anne felt achingly vulnerable as she picked up her friend's littlest ones and whirled them around in her arms.

By the time she made her way up the hill to the front door, Fatima had put down her baby and was waiting for her with open arms. They embraced, rocked back and forth, and both talked at once as, with their arms still intertwined, they and the children retreated into the shady recesses of the house. Fatima's oldest girl made the tea, the other girls stood on tiptoe and reached up to the shelves for glasses, one of the boys fetched Anne's bags from her car, and a flock of other boys ran off to alert the rest of the village that the doctor had come down from Beirut. In a moment more children spread newspapers over the frayed Persian rug on the floor, Fatima's two sisters-in-law produced the great platters of food that always seemed to be ready in the kitchen for instant consumption, and Anne was sitting on a pillow on the floor being plied with lentil soup, *kibbe*, rice, *tabouli*, other salads and condiments, and feather-light fresh bread. Neighbours flocked in, tea was poured, excited children jigged in and out of the door. There were more welcoming shrieks and kisses and hugs when Fatima's mother and sisters arrived. The floor was tightly packed with women and children who all talked, laughed, and ate with great gusto. Anne passed round boxes of sugared candies as she listened to the chronicle of who was newly pregnant, who was about to get married, which child was at the top of his or her class at the new government schools, and what was the news in the latest letters from long-lost uncles and cousins halfway around the world. At that point, Fatima's mother broke into loud lamenting sobs as she beat her breast and wept on one of her daughters' shoulders. Fatima's father had died in Africa the year before, and the framed photograph of him in the place of honour on the whitewashed wall just under the Holy Koran had been draped in black sheeting. A few of the women broke into sociable tears to keep Fatima's mother company, and others recounted what a good man he had been, how pious, how generous, what a good husband and father.

Anne sucked a sweet and pretended to listen as the litany of Fatima's father's goodness continued on and on. She had long ago learned the Arab knack of sitting for hours on the floor, daydreaming with an agreeable look on her face, while somebody talked for an astonishing length of time about matters that didn't much interest her. She looked around the floor at Fatima's womenfolk, identically hooded in their white polyester scarves, who also seemed to be paying scant attention to whatever was being repeated about Fatima's father. For all of them, Anne just as much as the others, it was enough just to be squeezed in this hot dense room, fat thighs snug against bulging buttocks, and be lulled into a pleasantly passive daze of sweet security.

Her gaze travelled round the house that Ali had built with his own hands. It was remarkable, she thought, how Fatima's extended family of six adults and thirty children managed to live in such evident harmony in this buzzing hive. In the beginning this bedroom and a small kitchen and hole-in-the-floor *hàmman* out in the garden had been all there was to it. But over the years he had tacked on one room here and another there, as the household had doubled and then tripled. After Fatima's pregnancies had become a yearly occurrence, Ali had expanded the kitchen and bathroom and tacked on a boys' bedroom and a girls' bedroom where the children slept on bedrolls wedged wall to wall on the floor. Eventually, then, when Ali's work at the mosque and Fatima's teaching of the village girls became too much for them, his two brothers and their wives had come to help out. The brothers had built two more small bedrooms for themselves. Centred on the stony pathway connecting these webs of rooms were the two squat watertanks where one and all bent to drink and fill their jugs. Finally, then, just a few years ago, after Ali had been appointed chief *shaykh* for this and surrounding mosques, he had built a separate vaulted room where he could receive a constant flow of male guests. All the rooms, including this one which served as Ali's and Fatima's bedroom by night and as the women's reception room by day, were scant of furniture and adornment. A small black and white television and a large shortwave radio were ensconced in a place of honour next to the big double featherbed. Dishes and jars of provisions were lined up on shelves which had been hammered into the walls. Besides shrine-sized photographs of members of the family, the only decorations were garish coloured postcards of famous Iraqi Shia mosques in Kerbala and Najaf. A cradle hung from the ceiling like a baby hammock, and in it rocked Fatima's newest infant. On the rare moments when this room was empty, it was a gloomy cave lit only by the single bare electric light bulb that dangled from the ceiling. But when, as now, it was chockablock with chattering women, no place could have been jollier.

Yet even so, the heat and the droning women's voices began to put Anne to sleep. She jerked fully awake every time the door banged open with nagging children wanting this or that. The heat, the crying babies, and the sheer glandular excess of all these women and their raggle-taggle children began to get on her nerves. She felt as cranky as a colicky baby. Why had she ever come here, of all places, today? Her hostile eyes followed the mothers who lumbered to their feet and went slavishly off to obey each insistent child's summons. A parade of young mothers traipsed out to the back bedrooms to change wet diapers. Here, there, everywhere, women sat as content as milkcows with nursing infants suckling at their breasts. For a second, Anne longed to bolt out of the door and escape the cloying maternity of this room. As though she were being attacked, she wanted to cry out that there was more to life than babies and husbands. She was a doctor; she helped people; even though she could never have a baby, there was purpose to her life. She longed to be back in the operating room in Beirut or even shopping for expensive clothes with Camilla or being witty at one of Leila's dinner parties. The longer she sat here, the worse she felt. She was revolted at how these women were enslaved by their biology. Surely her lot was better than theirs. If she had it all to do over again – and if this time she could choose her fate – she would never let herself be reduced only to a womb, milky breasts, and a head covered for life in white polyester. And yet, as she sat barren among so much fertility, some reactionary voice deep inside her kept insisting that she would have been happier – not necessarily more productive or more independent, but *happier* – with what they had. Was this wistful impulse to cast off her education, culture and values the weakest – or the strongest – part of herself?

Yet even as she tormented herself with such doubts, Anne still sat amongst the women like a good guest, smiling when the others smiled, frowning when the others frowned.

But she must have dozed off, for it felt like months later when she woke to hear Fatima saying that they had tired *el-Hakima* out with all their nattering. Some of the children had already curled up in their mothers' ample laps for their afternoon naps, and others had begun to whine that they wanted to go home. As the women began making their farewells, Fatima parcelled her children out among the relatives so she could have a heart-to-heart with her friend.

Anne changed into a long-sleeved patterned nightgown, settled back down on the floor on a nest of cushions, and stifled a contented yawn. Most of the time, down here, the women ran hither and yon about the house and garden in their nightdresses. The men, too, delighted in lounging about much of the time in their striped pyjamas. The whole village always looked as if it was either just about to go to bed or had just reluctantly risen. Life, here, was a wink away from a dream.

When finally the last of her family had left the room, Fatima poured two more glasses of tea and settled down on the floor beside her friend. 'Now,' she said, abandoning Arabic for the first time since Anne's arrival, 'we talk in English, no?' She sipped her tea and studied her friend's grave, pale face. 'I must practise my English more now, I forget it sometimes, it is full of rust. Even in the school, when I teach the girls, something – no, *sometimes* – I cannot remember the word I look for.' She smiled gently. 'Now, I think we get down to why you are here. Your eyes, they are so sad, almost like when you first come back from America. So tell me what is wrong.'

'Everything, everything . . .' Anne could hold back her tears no longer. It felt good when Fatima held her in her motherly arms, and so she let go and wept in great wrenching childish sobs. She clung to her friend and felt reassured when Fatima patted her back and murmured to her in Arabic that, God willing, everything was going to turn out all right. After a while, then, Anne sat up, sniffled, and wiped her eyes on the sleeve of her nightdress. She took a tentative sip of tea, and finally blurted out exactly what was wrong: she still felt bad about Mike, she wished she hadn't married Charles, and now – she broke down again – the doctors had said she could never have children. Anne hadn't planned to confess anything more than that to Fatima. But once the truth had begun spurting out of her, she didn't seem able to staunch the flow. She avoided Fatima's eyes as she confided that she had known Charles was a homosexual when she married him, and that she had caught him in the apartment with another man yesterday.

Fatima sipped her tea and chose, just then, to ignore Anne's more sensational revelation. 'And you believe this doctor?'

Grimly Anne nodded. 'I saw the reports. My tubes, the uterus, it's all wrong.' But there was no point in launching into a detailed medical analysis which Fatima would not understand. 'Look, I'm a doctor. I know what's up. I can't get pregnant.'

'I would not be so sure.' Fatima smiled mysteriously. 'There are many examples in the Holy Koran of women who have babies long after everyone said it was not possible. If it is God's will that you have a baby, then you will have one. I will pray that it is so.'

'You do that.' Anne reached for her tea and did her best to hide her impatience. In most matters Fatima was a wise and reasonable woman. But sometimes when she indulged in religious mumbo-jumbo, Anne wondered how it was she considered Fatima her best friend. The silence between them lengthened, until finally Anne broke the ice. 'So . . . about Charles . . . what do you think?'

Fatima shrugged her shoulders. 'My world and your world are very different. What could never happen here, happens there.' She shook her head. Her English grew increasingly fluid the longer she talked. 'I am very sorry that Allah has given you this to bear, too.' Yet, lest what she had said be construed as blasphemy against God's wonderful will, she quickly amended this. 'But, this life is after all only a test. Maybe, for you, to suffer so much in this life is a blessing.'

'Really? A blessing?' Anne's eyes were bitter. 'I come all the way down here to see you, and all you can say to me is that it's a blessing that I can't get anything I truly want? First that business with *him* back in Boston, then Charles being as he is, and finally no babies. If you think all that is a blessing, what would a curse be like?'

'I admit', Fatima said with a ghost of a smile, 'that you have a point.'

Anne smiled, too, and threw her arm around her friend. 'Oh, hell, I can't be mad at you, too.' It was enough, for this moment, just to lean on Fatima. 'I just feel so bad,' she said finally, in an almost inaudible voice, from deep inside. 'So bad.'

'I know,' Fatima said, as she inclined her own head, so that she, too, was leaning on her friend. 'I know.' They rested like that for a long moment until Fatima began probing about Charles. 'So, your husband, what is it like with . . . you and him . . . you know . . . with him as he is? A man like that!'

'You know Charles.' She turned defensive. Now that she had let Fatima in on her secret, she almost wished she hadn't. He was her husband, and he deserved her loyalty. 'You always said you liked him. Everyone likes Charles. He's a very nice man. Sensitive. Caring. Fun to be with.' She hesitated a delicate moment and then went on. 'As for what happens when we're alone together, what can I say? It's not like it was with Mike. But it's okay. Sometimes it's even more than okay.' Again she paused, and when she continued her voice rasped with emotion. 'I don't really think I could stand being with another man who made me feel like Mike did.' She pulled herself together so her voice should not show its raggedy edge. 'Charles is always *nice* to me. Even yesterday, he was *nice*. I like that. He respects me, you know? Maybe he doesn't love me like I thought Mike did, but sometimes he makes me feel . . . cherished. Yes, that's it, cherished. And I like that. Really I do. Maybe that's not much, but most of the time it's enough for me.'

'Ah,' Fatima said. Sometimes, she thought, when she

was with Anne, her friend said or did something that struck such a deeply responsive chord inside her that, then and there, she could feel their friendship growing deeper, stronger and more satisfying. As happens sometimes in the best of complementary friendships, she was as much refreshed by the ways her friend differed from her as she was by the ways in which at heart they were the same. 'Ah yes, I understand.'

As shyly, then, as though she were offering her friend the prettiest flower that bloomed in her garden, Fatima began to talk about the reality of her own marriage. 'Cherish, yes, I know that word. I know that feeling. Men, they are so different from us. So hard sometimes, in their hearts as well as their heads. They are weak, too, in ways that we are so strong. When I talk to you and my mother and my sisters, sometimes I feel so much closer to all of you than I ever do when I try to make Ali understand something that is important to me.' Fatima laughed a high-pitched girl's laugh. 'But that Ali, even though he makes me so angry sometimes, how that man can make me feel! Still, now, after nine children!' Her eyes were shining. 'I was thinking of this the other day, when I was with my sister Zainab. You know Zainab, how she is always singing, like a beautiful bird. That is why I call her *Bilbul*, you know, in English I think it means "the nightingale". We were at her house, and she was singing to us a very beautiful old song. And some of it was very high, you know, almost so high that her voice could not reach it. But she did. She sang one note that was so high and pure, so perfect really, and I thought to myself, yes, that is my Ali. That note sounds like my Ali is.'

'Oh, Fatima, so it's still like that for you?'

'It is, Allah be praised.' Fatima took Anne's hand in hers. 'And I pray that someday it will be like that for you, too. So beautiful, like that for you, too.'

Much later that night, long after everyone had risen

from their naps, and the family had come together for a welcoming feast, and most of the women had filed back to Fatima's front room to visit *el-Hakima* once again, what Fatima had said about Zainab's singing still stuck in Anne's mind. When she begged Fatima's sister to sing her a song, a flattered Zainab was only too happy to oblige.

Anne sat in the crowded room listening to what Fatima had said was the sound of her love. Zainab's voice soared nightingale high, its pitch perfect, its sound so piercingly sweet and rife with love, that Anne wanted to cry for the lack of a love like that in her life.

And yet the sound comforted her. To know there was love that felt like Zainab's song gave Anne hope. All could never be lost in a world that could be as perfectly pitched as that. The pure sweet notes lingered in her heart as she lay down on a bedroll on the hard stone floor and slept that night as soundly as a baby.

Chapter 16

Doubtfully Leila held up the jeans she had just bought, after much hesitation, that very afternoon. How could she, who had been born to wrap herself in the most sensuous silks and sumptuous satins, ever be at home in this coarse working-man's denim? Still, she reminded herself, this green and verdant spring of 1971 was a time of Palestinian hope, change and commitment. Just six months ago, when King Hussein had so viciously turned on the Palestinian commandos in the 'Black September' massacre in Jordan, it had seemed that any chance of a successful revolution had been prematurely aborted. But now that the Resistance had re-established its headquarters here in Lebanon, Beirut had rallied to the cause. The vibrant signs that the Palestinians had come of age were everywhere. The newspapers were splashed with thrilling headlines about the heroic struggle being waged day by day just south of the border. The refugee camps seethed with rumours of great victories that were just around the corner. Down every boulevard café and on every street corner swaggered Palestinian fighters with their Kalashnikovs. The Palestinian flag waved proudly from lamp-posts in the Fakhani quarter and even in Ras Beirut. Wallspace everywhere – on luxury apartment blocks, outside cinemas and shops, in the teeming slums – was spray-painted with Palestinian slogans or plastered with the pictures of Palestinian *fedayeen* martyrs. Now more than ever, Leila was proud to hold her head high and proclaim that she was *Filisteeni*, a member of that once despised but now respected brotherhood. And so, she told herself, in ways great and small, she, too, had to learn to bite the bullet and bend her will to a higher cause. If the wild flowers of Palestinian youth were willing to be plucked off, one by one, to give their life's blood in guerrilla raids against the Zionists, surely she could – at least for tonight – put away her Chanel, Dior and Balenciaga gowns.

Still, she frowned at the jeans. Although trousers were in fashion these days, and even Saint Laurent espoused the 'ethnic' peasant look, she had never – ever! – gone out in public in clothes like these. And yet it was very possible that, with the right accessories and great splashes of make-up, in a smutty sort of way these jeans could look smashing. There was no reason that the coming revolution shouldn't be ushered in with a smattering of her famous style. She intended to cause a minor sensation – and set a new fashion – when she showed up wearing them at tonight's unity meeting at the Shatilla camp. She would arrive even later than everyone else, perhaps when Hussein was on the rostrum haranguing the crowd about the necessity of armed struggle and wars of national liberation. The thought of him looking her over, and perhaps in a subtle, socialist way even salivating over her in her sexy tight jeans, banished her doubts. She wanted him to look at her in *that way* again, remember what they once had been to one another, and wish – a little, as she did now, as her marriage bored her more and more – that they had made their lives together. The man she had married was the Prime Minister of Lebanon, but the man she still loved was the great red hope of the Palestinian revolution. She would wear these bloody dungarees.

She eased the narrow, unyielding fabric up her calves as carefully as though they were ten-denier stockings. *Y'Allah*, these jeans were tight. Today in the boutique it had taken her and the shop assistant ten minutes of artful pushing and tugging to squeeze her into them. When she couldn't wriggle them any further up her thighs, she followed the advice of the shopgirl and threw herself down on her bed. Yes, now when she thrust her legs up in the air so her weight was entirely off them, she was able to work the jeans inch by inch over her hips. Gingerly, then, and hardly bending her knees, she crept to her feet and took a deep breath as she set about the tricky business of forcing up the zipper. She sucked in her stomach, heaved on the two edges, and after a few tries was able to coax the zipper up tooth by painful tooth. Quickly, before the zipper could whiz back down, she snapped the clasp shut. She remembered what the shop assistant had said, that until the jeans had a chance to settle over her like a second skin, she should keep her breaths shallow so the denim wouldn't split.

As stiffly as a saddle-sore cowboy, she wobbled over to her wardrobe and reached inside for the olive drab 'fatigues' shirt she had bought from a barrow in a side street just off the Bourg. This bit of US Army surplus had been ripped at the pocket, soiled under the arms, and wrinkled into a ball. But, nevertheless, it had been the smallest size in the lot and she had thought it would do once her maid had washed, pressed, and mended it back into shape. As she slipped it on and looked at her reflection in the mirror, she decided that her new taste for army surplus was as unerring as it had always been for couture. With the green, red and black Palestinian badges sewn on the sleeves just below the epaulettes, the shirt didn't look bad at all. Soon everyone who was anyone among the society women in the Palestinian Resistance would be rooting through market stalls looking for shirts just like this. Jauntily she flipped her collar up around the neck, left the top three buttons open so she showed a hint of cleavage, and then took the two front ends of the shirt and tied them very tight just above her waist so that a good inch of her tanned midriff was showing. She turned sideways in order to admire her slim silhouette. Thirty-four years old, and not an ounce of fat on her. She was, as she was fond of saying now, 'fighting fit', and ready for the revolution. Yet she narrowed her eyes in the mirror as she considered whether the effect was too much. No, she decided finally, not by half.

She rooted in a drawer for a red silk scarf and knotted it at her neck, but then she untied it and threw it back in her drawer. People would get the wrong idea if she showed up in Communist red. Hussein's politics were not her politics. She wanted him, but on her own terms and in her own way. She wasn't turning herself inside out for him, or any man.

Leila took a deep breath, and when her jeans didn't pop open, she decided she could risk sitting down and pulling on her boots. This week, when she had decided to change her image, she had toyed briefly with the idea of wearing authentic combat boots, the lace-up ones with the thick cut-out rubber soles suitable for wading through the mud. But really, those crude soliders' boots were too mannish, and it wasn't as though she needed them just yet to march over the border and storm the Zionist citadels. For now, her revolutionary activity centered only on fashionable dinner parties, star-studded rallies, and very occasional lightning visits in and out of the depressing squalor of the refugee camps. Her particular role, as she saw it, was to win the hearts and minds not only of the Palestinian masses but of journalists, diplomats and opinion leaders among the Lebanese and the foreign community here in Beirut. And so, when she had spotted these divine but absolutely impractical white suede stiletto-heeled boots in one of her favourite shop windows, she had rationalized their purchase on the grounds that her role didn't necessarily preclude a little glamour. She was Leila Shahine, not some common little nobody from the camps. Lovingly she caressed the costly suede. The Italians, she thought as she slid on the boots, always had been and always would be darlings with leather.

She was finishing her make-up as her husband came into the bedroom. She smiled at her reflection as admiringly as if she were wearing the latest Saint Laurent creation. 'How do I look?'

Without even bothering to give her what had become over the years his customary hangdog gaze of hopeless adoration, Mustafa wearily wondered how many times, in the ten bittersweet years since they had been married, she had asked him that same rhetorical question. Not, he reflected with pained hindsight, that she had ever paid much heed to his answer. In their first years together, however, she had at least shown some semblance of what any reasonable Lebanese man would have considered a proper wifely attitude of respect.

But now, Mustafa thought as he rubbed his tired eyes and sat down on the edge of the bed, his headstrong wife did exactly as she pleased. Sometimes, when he stepped back and considered what their marriage had become, he wondered precisely when it was that the balance of power had so irrevocably shifted between the two of them. In the beginning he had thought himself the masterful male and she the pliant young female, but perhaps that had never been more than a polite social fiction. He reminded himself now, as he often had to when he was with his wife, that he was the Prime Minister of Lebanon. He was powerful, rich, and a force to be reckoned with in his country. Yet even so, now, as always when they were alone, Mustafa knew that next to her he was as soft and bland as tapioca pudding. He took what comfort he could from his suspicion that theirs was not the only marriage in which, the longer they were together, the more dominant the wife became. Yet he loved her, how he loved her! She was so very beautiful, with those lion eyes of hers, and that snaky body which eluded him every time he thought he was about to possess it. The more miserable she made him, the more desperately, obsessively – and yes, sometimes impotently – he loved her. At times he thought their trouble might be rooted in the simple fact that she was so much younger than he, and therefore had the vigour to keep dancing a few teasing steps ahead of him. But at other times he admitted to a more ancient male-to-female fear, that she was stronger, brighter, better in every important way. How was he to have known that she would end up being as she was? He had thought this late-in-life marriage might help keep him young at heart, not consign him to the grave. Yet he supposed that the two of them could not continue like this for ever. Sooner or later, even though the prospect was more than a little terrifying, he would have to take her in hand.

But not tonight, he told himself dully as he stretched out on the bed. Surely he wouldn't have to tangle with her tonight, not after that latest round of savage bickering about the Palestinians at the Cabinet meeting. *Ya Rab*, oh Lord, his fearsome wife and her demanding people were difficult! Mustafa believed in the rightness of their cause, he was pledged in personal and political terms to work for their goals, and it could at times even bring tears to his eyes when he remembered the trials and tribulations which their long-suffering people had undergone. Two years ago, when the Palestinian issue had first come to the boil here, he had even resigned his post for a while as a gesture of solidarity with them. But, dear God, the Palestinians were difficult to live with, in his own country and – especially – in his own bedroom.

He sank his head down on the pillow as he remembered how again today the Christians and the Muslims had been at each other's throats over the festering issue of whether the upsurge of Palestinian power in the Lebanon should or could be curbed. The President's Christian supporters had repeated their charges that the interlopers were flouting Lebanese sovereignty and threatened that, if the Palestinians wouldn't lay down their arms voluntarily, the Christians would force them to do so. Mustafa and the rest of the Muslims – including Kemal Jumblatt, the charismatic leftist leader of the Druze mountain men – had taken the opposite view that the Palestinians after all were their brothers and their friends and must under no circumstances be treated as shabbily here as they had been last autumn in Jordan. The Christians had always resented and despised the 140,000 Palestinian refugees who had flooded north into Lebanon after the 1948 birth of the Israeli state. They had sequestered them in seventeen bleak camps scattered across the country, systematically excluded them from the best jobs, and denied them Lebanese citizenship. But after two more waves of Palestinian refugees had coursed into Lebanon – after the 1967 war and then the civil war in Jordan just last year – the Christians had begun to fear that the 350,000 mostly Sunni Muslim Palestinians would upset the religious balance of power in Lebanon and ultimately take over the country. What had especially inflamed the dominant Maronite Christians was that this new generation of Palestinians were armed with Kalashnikovs and dangerous with revolutionary rhetoric. For this was the era of deadly commando raids in Israeli territory. Palestinian *fedayeen* had dug themselves into southern Lebanon where they had become a law to themselves. Two years ago matters had come to a head when the Christians had goaded the Lebanese army into trying to subdue the Palestinian commandos. Sunni Muslim Lebanese had promptly taken to the streets to demonstrate in favour of the Palestinians, and there had been street-fighting in Beirut and Tripoli between the Lebanese army and the *fedayeen*. For the six months in which Mustafa had resigned in protest, the Lebanese government had been paralysed. Then, in November 1969, the Beirut government had finally caved in and signed an agreement in Cairo which virtually ceded the Palestinians a state-within-a-state. The Cairo Accords assured any Palestinian the right to bear arms for the Resistance and gave them control of their refugee camps and military bases in what had been dubbed 'Fatahland' in the Arquob sector of southern Lebanon. Yet now more than ever, the Christians feared and detested the Palestinians. Every Christian warlord had begun recruiting his own private militia dedicated to taming the Palestinians. Each Cabinet meeting ended in a shouting match. At the height of today's session, a trigger-happy Christian minister had even pulled out his pistol and begun shooting up the Bohemian crystal chandelier that hung over the Cabinet table.

Mustafa shut his eyes and massaged his head where it throbbed at his temples. Time was, he thought, when his wife used to do this for him. But now all she was interested in was gadding here and there, making a name for herself doing Allah only knew what.

His head throbbed with worry. Where, he wondered despairingly, was all this going to lead? The Lebanon was a house built on sand, and month by month its security was slowly but surely being eroded. Until the Palestinians had arrived here *en masse*, Lebanon's Christians and Muslims had with difficulty managed to maintain the delicate subtleties of their political balancing act. But now there was talk of civil war between the Christians and the Muslims or – as the Muslims were beginning to characterize it – between the reactionaries and the progressives. Meanwhile, as though all that weren't enough to make any Lebanese patriot sick at heart, Lebanon's powerful neighbours to the east and south were burning on very short fuses. From time to time Syria imperiously summoned every Lebanese leader to Damascus for private talks about the necessity of curbing the more radical elements in the Palestinian Resistance. Clearly, Damascus didn't want a revolutionary Palestinian-oriented government challenging its own hegemony from Beirut. As for Israel, Mustafa had seen the secret warnings sent through third parties to the Lebanese government. If the guerrilla raids continued unabated across the Lebanese border, Israel would step up its already frequent bombing attacks of suspected Palestinian bases in south Lebanon, the Bekaa Valley, and even in Beirut itself. More than two years ago, the Israelis had landed a helicopter full of their soldiers at Beirut airport and systematically blown up thirteen Middle East Airlines civilian planes. The warning could not have been more explicit. If Lebanon didn't curb its Palestinians, the Israelis would surge north and do it themselves. For a long while, too, Mustafa had feared that the expansionist Zionists longed to seize the fertile Litani river basin. Once the Israelis crossed the border, they might never depart.

Mustafa sighed and reached out blindly to his bedside table for the packet of stomach tablets he always kept there. He ground the antacids between his false teeth. He would never admit it aloud, and above all never say anything as heretical as this in front of the hard-line Christians, but he was beginning to fear it might have been a fatal error to welcome the Palestinian refugees and fighters in here after their bloody expulsion from Jordan. Nothing could excuse King Hussein's action in allowing his ferocious Arab Legionnaires to massacre the cream of Palestinian youth. But now that the Palestinians had set up their headquarters in Beirut, Mustafa saw King Hussein's mortal blunder in a slightly different light. Here in Lebanon now, as before in Jordan, the Palestinians were not only provoking deadly Israeli raids against the civilian population but also destabilizing their host country. They were forming a country within a country, their arrogant young soldiers were a menace to public safety, and they administered their refugee camps and military bases as independently as if they were living in the Republic of Palestine. In his own country, as in his own marriage, Palestinians could be the most difficult of bedfellows. Life was arduous, and he was old. He would be sixty-six next summer. His father had died when he was only sixty-two. He would have to take care and not worry so much about everything.

But just before Mustafa shut his eyes and got on with his nap, he made the mistake of glancing over at Leila. His eyes shot open, as he tried to take in the sight. 'What's *that* you're wearing?'

'Fatigues,' she said absently, as though to one of the babbling children. All she needed to complete her new look, she thought as she remained transfixed by her reflection in the mirror, was a Kalashnikov slung over her shoulder. She had picked one up last week in the Borj al-Barajneh camp and been surprised not only at how light it felt in her hands but how *right*. Maybe she would ask the *fedayeen* to show her how to use it.

She had gone shooting once or twice at house parties back in England and duck hunting down south in the Lebanese hill country, and she had liked the killing. Perhaps she would decide to hell with everything – husband, children and her bourgeois comforts here in Beirut – and bulldoze her way into one of the commando units that had begun to accept girl soldiers. Even though she might be a little older than the other women recruits, she was certain she could prove herself to be the best of the lot. Before long she would be leading a brave band of comrades over the border, would execute a daring raid that would live for ever in the hearts of her people, and of course survive to tell the tale around the campfires herself. Even though she wasn't sure she wanted him anymore, she was delighted at the thought of how mad Hussein would be for her if she became one of the heroines of the Palestinian revolution.

'Ah, fatigues, yes, I see,' he said, although he didn't. To Mustafa, fashion was just the most expensive of the female mysteries. But leave it to Leila, he thought with a touch of his old possessive pride, always to be the first with the latest thing. In a week or two all the rest of her friends, when they were sitting around the house killing time, with nothing much to do but paint their fingernails, would be dressed as she was now. Still, he thought as he yawned and shut his eyes, it was a bizarre new style, and not pretty. In the old days women had looked like women should, covered up in long decent dresses. His mother had never been a fashion plate, but she had always dressed with dignity. After his father died, she had worn a sombre black dress and black shawl over her hair for the rest of her life. Why would a lady want to look like a soldier?

He was about to turn over and surrender to sleep, when a disturbing possibility occurred to him. No, he assured himself with his eyes still tightly shut, of course not. It was well after nine o'clock. She hadn't mentioned any social engagement to him. Surely she was in for the night. On second thoughts, remembering what one of his aides had told him about an important unity meeting of all the Palestinian groups tonight at one of the refugee camps, he sat up and examined her clothing more closely. She wouldn't dare to go outside dressed as she was. And certainly she wouldn't go into one of the *camps* with those tight pants and her blouse unbuttoned and hitched up as if she were a prostitute. 'Leila?' Even to him, his voice sounded old and querulous. He tried, but failed, to be more manly. 'You aren't going out tonight, are you, Leila?'

She pretended not to hear him, as she bent over, with concentration, in front of the mirror and brushed out her hair, and then, like a belly dancer in a cabaret, tossed it vigorously back and forth.

Inwardly, as he watched the hypnotic flow of her fiery auburn hair, Mustafa groaned. Why couldn't she be the wife of his dreams – playful, submissive, childlike everywhere but in his bed? Leila was not a bit like his first wife. For a moment Mustafa longed for that kindly, conventional woman whom he had married in his youth and buried in his middle age. Compared to Leila, dependable old Hoda had never caused him a moment's trouble. But – Allah help him! – he loved Leila so much more. Yet he had known she would be a handful when he married her. His friends had repeatedly warned him that her father had spoiled her. Nonetheless, Mustafa thought, though she may well have been destined to lead him a merry pace in any case, he blamed the coming of the Palestinian Resistance for the deterioration of his marriage. She had begun to spin out of his control only after her pretty head had been turned by all this revolutionary nonsense that was now so much the rage. It wasn't her fault, really. She was still just an impressionable girl. Before matters had gone so far awry, he should have taken the time to instruct her about her more important priorities as his wife. Yet, even though he was exhausted, this time he could not shut his eyes and pretend nothing was wrong. What happened behind their closed bedroom door was one thing, but what transpired in public was another matter entirely. He could end up being the laughing-stock of all Beirut if she went out looking like a cross between a streetwalker and a commando. 'Leila. Answer me. *Are* you planning on going out tonight, like *that*?'

She concentrated on brushing her hair as she chose to answer only part of his question. 'Really, darling, you have the worst memory. Why, my father's only a few years older than you, and *his* mind is as sharp as a tack.' She smiled a sly smile, as her husband's face, reflected in the mirror, revealed that her barb had hit home. As always, however, she took care not to go too far with her taunts. Even though she was discontented with this marriage, the two of them still shared a life that many would envy. He was the Prime Minister, and she delighted in the perquisites of his office. Moreover, he was the husband and she the wife. Unless and until she decided it was expedient to change their legal relationship, she had to appear to respect some of his wishes. She tried to sound the soul of reasonableness as she purred on. 'I know I must have told you, there's another political meeting tonight. Baba's in town – I told you that, too, but you never listen to a thing I say – and I promised him I'd be there.' Charmingly, she shrugged her shoulders. 'You know how my father is. This is a command performance, really. He'd be livid if I changed my mind at the last minute and stayed home. Actually, you might even say it's a family thing tonight. Baba and Ramsey are picking us up any minute.' She looked down at her jewel-encrusted Rolex watch. 'In fact, they're late.'

'What meeting? And where?' His stomach hurt, but he would not give her the satisfaction of watching him pop another handful of antacids into his mouth. He so longed to lie back down and pull the covers over his head, yet he knew that this time he had to stand his ground. 'And who's *us?* I'm tired. I've been in political meetings all day long. I'm not going out tonight to another one.'

'You?' The hand holding her brush faltered and, for one unguarded moment, her contempt showed. It was on the tip of her tongue to tell him not only that he wasn't invited to tonight's meeting but that he was a whiny old fool who was always too tired for whatever she required. Why had she saddled herself with Mustafa, when she could have had everything that was dear in life with Hussein? Marrying the wrong man – even if he was the Prime Minister – was the worst mistake of her life. She would have liked to tell him so, here and now, without mincing words. But, as always between the two of them, most of what was important was left unsaid. Unjust as it was, men still held the reins of power. A woman could never risk telling a man what she really thought of him, except when the masquerade was finally over and she could fire the bare-faced truth at him as her parting shot. She forced a sweetish smile to her lying lips. 'You *look* tired. Poor dear Moo-Moo!' If she had been closer to the bed, she would have leaned over and chucked him on the chin as she used the pet name he loved. Did he have any idea, she wondered, how she hated that silly nickname? Their relationship was a sick joke. She was married to a fat, paunchy cow of a man who liked to be called Moo-Moo. But her face, nonetheless, was a mask of concern. 'You look so tired, darling. But you'll feel better in the morning if you stay home and rest.'

He was only slightly mollified. Even if she called him Moo-Moo until the cows came home, he could not let her go out in that outrageous costume. He tried to plump himself up by pretending that she was one of his underlings in the office. His voice hardened with authority. 'You're going to one of the camps, aren't you? You actually think you're going out to one of your political meetings in the camps, dressed like *this?*'

Despite her best intentions, her patience was ebbing. She shrugged, and her mouth widened into a sulky pout. 'What's it to you?'

'You're my wife. I have a right to know.'

She was not quite up to disputing either of those claims just yet. Yet defiantly she strode over to her dressing table and slung her shoulder bag over her arm as menacingly as if it were a machine-gun.

Just then there was a knock at the door, and a moment later Miriam stuck her dark head inside her parents' bedroom. 'Ummie?' The nine-year-old stood in the hallway patiently holding her sweater and her little girl's miniature purse. 'Are you ready to go out now, Ummie? Hamid, Farid and everyone else are downstairs waiting. Grandfather's here with Uncle Ramsey and Aunt Aisha.'

'What! The children! My sons! You think you're taking my sons without asking my permission?' But even as Mustafa was scrambling to his feet, Leila was already halfway out of the door. 'Well, I forbid it,' he shouted, as she slammed the door behind her. 'I absolutely forbid it.' Mustafa's voice fell to an impotent whisper. 'No wife of mine will go out of my house looking like that.' As he listened to the authoritative click of her high heels marching down the hallway, the Prime Minister sank back down on the bed and held his head in his hands.

He would have taken heart, however, or at least learned another abject lesson in how to handle his temperamental wife, if he had witnessed what happened when Leila's father, brother and sister-in-law caught sight of her coming downstairs. Kemal and Ramsey frowned at her open neck, bare midriff and tight jeans. But they waited until they had greeted her properly with kisses, hugs and the usual gushing inquiries about everyone's health before they went about transforming her appearance.

'You'll catch your death of cold tonight with your blouse like that,' Kemal scolded. He reached over and buttoned his daughter's shirt primly up to her chin. 'There, that's better. Can't have my little flower getting ill.' He ran the tip of one of his manicured fingernails over the Palestinian patches sewn on to her sleeves. 'A very nice touch indeed.'

'But what about this?' Ramsey said, pointing to her bare midriff. 'I must admit, *habibi*, that you look quite fetching in this costume. Ravishing, in fact. It would be quite the thing for the beach, or perhaps when it's just family at home. But in the camps?' He rolled his eyes. 'If you don't mind my suggesting it, this marvellous shirt of yours and those . . . snug . . . trousers might be just a bit . . . *excessive*.'

'You think so?' Leila looked down uncertainly at her shirt and jeans. 'I rather liked it myself.' But then she smiled at the two men who – when all was said and done – she loved best in the world. 'Over the top, is it?' She turned to Aisha. 'What do *you* think?'

Her sister-in-law wisely shrugged. Always she took care to stay on Leila's good side.

Almost meekly Leila untied the long shirt-tails, so that the oversized fatigues fell nearly down to her knees. She walked over to the mirror in the foyer. Her reflection was no longer so very sexy. 'I don't know,' she hedged. 'I think it needs a belt. Perhaps a bandolier full of cartridges. Or maybe I should put a tight tee-shirt under it and wear the shirt open, like a jacket. It's a bit grim the way it is.'

'Oh no, Mama, you look beautiful,' her eldest son Hamid volunteered.

'Mama's always beautiful,' Farid added.

'You look like a real girl soldier,' Mimi said.

'I do?' Leila looked hard at herself in the mirror. 'Maybe I'd better change my clothes.'

'*Habibi*, it's late.' Kemal consulted his watch. 'We have no time.'

'After all, Leila, this isn't a fashion show,' Ramsey said gently. 'It's a political meeting. What's important isn't how you look but what we all do.'

'Palestine!' Mimi said. 'We want to fight for Palestine!' As Leila put her arm around her favourite, the little girl burst out with a most ungirlish war whoop. 'Can I have a uniform, Mama? I want to look like a soldier, too. I want to fight for Palestine!'

'Girls can't fight,' Hamid said.

'Boys fight,' Farid added. 'Girls stay home.'

'Girls can fight too!' Mimi was about to burst into angry tears. 'Can't we, Mama?'

'Everyone can fight for Palestine,' Kemal said judiciously. It saddened him that, with the rise of the militant Palestinian Resistance since the '67 war, the leadership of his own ageing generation had gone into eclipse. Yet he, too, had always loved his country. And he, too, had always done his best to serve it. 'Each of us in our own way must fight for Palestine.'

'I want to look like a soldier, too,' Hamid shouted.

'And me!' Farid answered.

'Can we, Mama?' Mimi's eyes were pleading.

'All right, all right!' Nothing would do but for Leila to promise to have soldier's uniforms made for her daughter and her sons. Yet she refused to set foot outside the door with this shirt so unflatteringly loose. She dashed upstairs to her empty bedroom, grabbed a wide belt, and tucked her shirt closer to her body.

Then as the three generations of Shahines, amid much merriment, were trooping out of the door towards the limousine that waited to take them down the mountain to the refugee camp, Leila thought of her husband seething upstairs in his bedroom. For a passing second she entertained a generous impulse to run upstairs again and assure him that she wasn't, after all, going into Shatilla in such a provocative outfit. But then she shrugged and slid into the back seat. Let the old fool worry, she thought. Let the fat old fool worry.

Hussein was standing on a chair at the front of the packed, smoke-filled school room when the Shahines noisily filed in to take their places among the other Palestinians assembled for the meeting. The leftists in the hall exchanged cynical whispers, nudges and wary looks as these representatives of the *grande bourgeoisie* began to make their way through the crowd. Unity might be the goal of tonight's meeting, but the eddies and whirls of the class struggle could not so easily be set aside. Yet even though the Marxists of the United Front and the other radical splinter groups were hardly willing to welcome the capitalist Shahines with open arms, others from the mainstream Fatah wing fell on them with lip-smacking kisses, hugs and more kisses. Since the Palestinian Resistance had burst on the scene after the '67 war, the Shahines had helped to fund the more conservative elements in the Palestinian Liberation Organization. Kemal was accordingly embraced not only by some of the most influential members of the top leadership but by fawning professors, lawyers and paunchy businessmen in tight-fitting suits. At the same time Ramsey was hugged tight and swept off in another direction by the smart younger generation who had taken their higher degrees in America, England and France. Leila, meanwhile, even as she graciously inclined her fiery mane of hair to acknowledge the greetings of this journalist and that politician, managed to keep an aloof distance from the perspiring mass. She exchanged some intriguing whispers with the editor of *an-Nahar*, the most influential Beirut daily newspaper. Perhaps, he suggested, they could have lunch next week to discuss her coming on board as a columnist. Tuesday at the Saint Georges, she readily agreed, for she had been angling for just such an offer for months. As she insinuated herself deeper into the crowd, Leila flashed a conspiratorial smile when she spotted any of the other women who stuck out in this mostly masculine throng. Some were society matrons she knew from a lifetime of Beirut receptions, and others were boyish girls dressed in soldiering fatigues. She reflected that one of the unexpected dividends of her activities on the trendy fringes of the Resistance brotherhood was how much closer she had begun to feel to other Palestinian women. Even though she didn't feel, at least yet, that they all quite blended together in a happy sisterhood, she had begun to perceive them less as competitive rivals for male attention. She exchanged a word with this one, a wink with that one, and was pleased when – just as she had expected – two of them asked her where she had bought that wonderful shirt. At last she came to a halt near the front, where Hussein could not fail to see her, and made what she thought was a pretty picture standing with her daughter and sons snug in the circle of her arms.

'Diplomacy has failed,' Hussein was saying now, as he and those he spoke for in the Marxist United Front had said time and again. 'We cannot persist in the historical error of believing that the corrupt and degenerate Arab régimes will win back our country for us, either by force of arms or at the negotiating table. They will sell us out if we let them. They failed us in '48, '56 and '67, and they will fail us again unless we take control of our own destinies.' He hammered his fist against his thigh. 'Palestine is ours, not theirs! *Ours* to redeem with *our* blood! As we know now, comrades, armed struggle is our only answer!' First there were answering cheers, and then the hall erupted into rhythmic clapping and stomping as Hussein's followers tried to stampede the meeting into unanimous approval of their radical agenda.

Leila stood silent amid the uproar, staring up at Hussein repeating in public what he had said to her privately in London years ago. The years had marked him little. Haranguing the crowd, dressed as if for combat in his flak jacket and battle fatigues with his neck muffled in a chequered black-and-white *kuffiyeh* scarf, he seemed younger than when she had first known him back in London. Even then his longish crewcut had been prematurely grey and his sagging face had been slashed with careworn lines. Yet now that he was truly middle-aged – in London he had been older than the other students, and so she calculated that by now he must be well into his forties – in a way he looked younger than he had a decade ago. Obviously, she thought, he was thriving in this revolutionary climate. As he exhorted his people to fight to the death for what was right, his charisma, in a woman, would have been called beauty. Perhaps it was true what they said, she mused, that when you're young you have the face you were born with, but when you're old you have the face you deserve.

The speeches wound on and on. After a while, it was someone else's turn to climb up on the chair and repeat the stirring slogans denouncing Zionism and exalting Palestinian nationalism. Representatives of Fatah, Saqia, the Democratic Front, the United Command, the Arab Liberation Front, and a dizzying array of other ephemeral groups said their set pieces. The guerrilla raids across the border into occupied Palestine were applauded, criticized, and then again heaped with fervent praise. This one shouted that he wanted wars of national liberation all over the Middle East, and that one's voice fell almost to a whisper as he hesitantly implied that he wanted peace at almost any price. None of them agreed about anything except the fundamental fact that each of them was dedicated to winning back his lost country. Finally the PLO chairman made his way to the front of the room and gamely set about the seemingly hopeless task of reconciling the apparently irreconcilable differences espoused in this hall tonight.

As Yasser Arafat talked and cajoled and did his best to convince, Leila's children grew restless and whined that they were tired and wanted to go to bed. It was almost midnight. She was just beginning to wonder when her father and brother would be ready to give them a lift back home, when she felt a tap on the miniature Palestinian flag her maid had sewn on her shoulder.

'Let's get out of here,' Hussein said brusquely, without allowing himself the merest courtesy or the trace of a smile.

She tried not to smile, either, although she was jubilant at the thought that he had been unable to keep away. Always in her heart she had believed she could have him back whenever she wanted, and it was gratifying that she had been right all this time. Of course she had kept tabs on his rise to prominence in the Arab Nationalist Movement and then his founding of the United Front. She had followed his wanderings from Gaza to Amman and finally back here to Beirut. Until now they had always been scrupulously polite to one another, but – since London – he had not so much as touched her with the tip of his little finger. She fancied her shoulder burned under the Palestinian emblem, where his hand had briefly rested. She arched one carefully plucked eyebrow his way. 'You must be joking.'

'I never joke.' He smiled. 'Except to my comrades.' His smile widened. 'Should I be joking with you, now?'

He stared pointedly down at her army shirt and jeans. 'You dress like us tonight. Why?'

She shrugged and was about to say something flirtatious, but the silly words stuck in her throat. How was it possible, she wondered, that she had forgotten not only how Hussein was but how he always made her feel? Now, as before, though he was rude, rough and insolent, he was the most exciting man she had ever met. Still the old electricity flowed between them. Standing here beside him in this hot and crowded hall, she was acutely conscious of exactly how many inches separated his head from hers, his chest from hers, his thighs from hers. She hugged her children closer to her, as though to remind herself that she was a mother and a married woman. 'I just wanted to, that's all.' She smiled, sheepishly this time, as for once she blurted out the truth. 'I suppose I wanted to do something for the revolution.'

'So! Finally! You want to join the revolution, and you show it by straightaway marching out to buy the right clothes! Ha!' But his laughter died as he bent his head closer to hers. 'If that is what you want – really! – then come with me tonight. I will show you something, Leila Shahine, that is closer to the bleeding heart of our revolution than the boutiques on al-Hamra.'

'You mock me,' she said. She had a vague sense of *déja vu*, and then remembered his provoking similar words from her the night they'd met in that Mayfair art gallery. Then, as now, he had both repelled and attracted her.

'No, Leila.' There was, now, a tenderness to his smile. 'Come. I will show you something tonight you will never forget.'

'Sorry, but the children are tired.'

'These are yours?' When she nodded, he smiled down at them. 'They are very welcome to join us. It will be good for them to see this, too.'

'Can we, Mama, can we?' Daredevil Mimi was up for an adventure. Her tiredness forgotten, she wriggled like a puppy.

'Yes, please!' The boys caught their sister's enthusiasm. 'Please let's go, Mama!'

Leila looked around the crowded hall, but could spot none of the men of her family. 'I can't just go off without telling my father or brother.'

'I'll see that you get home. And one of my men will tell your brother you're in good hands.'

For another reluctant moment Leila pretended to be undecided. But already she had made the reckless decision to give in, just this once, to her impulse to follow this wild man wherever he led. Finally she nodded, seemingly only to please the children. 'All right, children, you win. But only for a little while. It's past your bedtimes already.' Outside, a United Front soldier in combat fatigues and a *kuffiyeh* wrapped around his head waited in the driver's seat of a battered old red Volkswagen. He flashed Leila a shy smile, offered her one of his Marlboros, and lit it with a flourish. Hussein climbed in the front, and Leila and the children wedged into the seat behind them.

As the driver whisked them off to the main checkpoint at the entrance to the refugee camp and tooted his horn at his comrades standing guard with their machine-guns at the ready, the children bounced and shouted and laughed with near-hysterical excitement. Everyone in Beirut knew that Hussein Ibrahim was a dangerous man. He was the bold leader of the most audacious of the guerrilla groups launching raids across the border into Palestine. To be racing off with him into the black night was an adventure that would be the envy of all their friends at school.

They had left Shatilla behind and were up and away from the seafront into the teeming Muslim quarters, when Hussein turned around and started quizzing the children. How old were they, what class were they in at school, and – this he asked with as much interest as if Miriam, Hamid and Farid were visiting United Nations officials – when they grew up what were they going to do to recover Palestine? He stroked his chin as he listened gravely to their childish answers, and then he smiled and said that, yes, he wholeheartedly agreed, every Palestinian had to fight to the death for honour and freedom. His eyes met Leila's. 'You must be very proud of them,' he said. After he had turned round and told the driver where to proceed in the labyrinthine alleyways of Fakhani, he said so softly that afterwards she wondered if she had only imagined it – or if, perhaps, she was reading his mind – 'I regret not having children. Always, always I regret that.'

Leila studied the back of his neck, sunburned, she supposed, from long hours out in the field training his men. Back in grey London, sapped by all those dreary hours indoors with his books and his politicking, he had been a pale shadow of the tanned and vital man he now was in Beirut's bright revolutionary sun. What would Hussein be like in bed? Until now, she had always been faithful to Mustafa. But what would Hussein be like in bed?

She inhaled, held the smoke inside for a long while in the hope that it would calm her, and then exhaled with something like a sigh. As far as she knew, he did not have a woman just now. She had heard, a few years back, that he had married a Syrian girl who was not only a Communist but a remote family connection, and that the marriage had been both short-lived and barren. He was free, now . . .

She worried the filter tip of her cigarette until it was wet and ragged, and then in disgust she threw it out of the window. If she had been brave enough, back in London, to make this other choice, she wondered what their children – his and hers – would have been like. To her, this night which had seemed so bright with erotic promise suddenly weighed heavy with regrets. She, who seldom wept, had to fight to keep back the tears. Why was she allowing herself to play with fire? She had been a fool not to realize that she would have to pay a high price for trying to recapture what she had forfeited many years ago. It would have been better never again to flirt with him, and all he represented. If all she wanted was a meaningless affair to liberate herself from her troubled marriage, she should never have turned to Hussein. She felt as vulnerable near him now as when she had been a young virgin. It was strange, this burning vulnerability, how she liked and hated it at once.

Finally the driver lurched to a stop in a back alley and waited in the Volkswagen as the rest of them ducked behind Hussein into the darkened doorway of a run-down block of flats above a confectioner's shop. The lift was broken, and so they trooped up the stairs, punching on the timed light switches at each landing. As they mounted to the fourth floor, they could hear raised men's voices, a woman's answering laughter and the happy clip-clop of Arabic music. A party, Leila thought with disappointment. Hussein had lured her away with the promise of something unforgettable tonight, but instead all this was going to be was a radical party in a slummy flat. As finally he knocked at a door, the lights went off again and they were plunged in darkness. A lock clicked, and the door opened a crack. '*Mein?*' The barrel of a gun pointed their way. 'Who?'

Hussein grunted an answer, and at once the door shot open and they all were swept inside a noisy, crowded flat. Heavily armed young men stepped from the wary shadows and respectfully bent to touch their lips to Hussein's hand. But instead he laughed and embraced them one by one. There were kisses all round, slaps on the back, more hugs and kisses.

While Hussein was swamped in these greetings, Leila

kept her arms protectively around her squirming children as she tried to figure out why Hussein had made such a point of bringing her here. Except for the proliferation of military uniforms and guns, this could have been a student party anywhere in Beirut. Young people in the olive drab fatigues favoured by the United Front stood in earnest packs chain-smoking cigarettes in the hallway, swigging Pepsis out on the balcony, and eating honeycakes in the main salon. The setting, too, seemed quite ordinary. At first glance there was nothing unusual in the threadbare furniture and the framed quotation from the Koran on the wall; clearly, this was a predominantly Muslim gathering in an apartment borrowed for the night from a lower middle-class family. Yes, she could see the cheap souvenirs from Cairo and Damascus and the photographs of generations of babies, children and brides clustered on every spare table, on the mantelpiece, over the television. The gathering seemed sedate and, at least socially, conservative. No one appeared to be drinking anything stronger than orange juice, and the men outnumbered the women by ten to one. Although this was revolutionary Beirut, it was nonetheless a Muslim gathering in a Muslim quarter of the city. It was long past midnight, and even a young woman who had found it easy to learn to fire a machine-gun with deadly accuracy might find it impossible to persuade her family to let her stay out so late without a chaperone.

Leila's eyes raked the crowd. Surely, she thought, she must be missing something. Something extraordinary must be afoot here tonight. Yet, hard as she looked, all she could see was a mediocre flat crowded with mediocre people.

Out of the corner of her eye, she could see Hussein still at the vortex of a swirl of his comrades. She lit another cigarette and longed for a whisky. She was a nervous alien in this den of radicals, and she wished she hadn't come. His world had never been her world, and it never could be. She had been mad to follow him here tonight. Impatiently she tapped her foot as she flicked her ash on to the worn wooden floor. She wondered how long she would have to stay before she could politely make her farewells. The next time she fancied some extramarital excitement, she would go after the tennis pro at the club.

In the dim light a vaguely familiar figure in olive drab was heading their way with his arms full of Pepsis. He seemed much younger than the others, but he, too, had a Kalashnikov slung over his shoulder.

'Welcome to the United Front,' he said as he handed them each a Cola.

'Tomas! What are you doing here!' Miriam's eyes were adoring as she drank in the uniform, the gun and the warrior stance of Camilla's son. 'You didn't tell me about this. I saw you just the other day down by the pool at the Saint Georges, and you didn't tell me a thing.'

'Security,' he whispered earnestly, as though the CIA or Mossad were within earshot. He was only twelve years old and short for his age, but under Mimi's admiring gaze he seemed to grow not only more manly, but older and taller. He leaned forward conspiratorially as, without further prompting, he poured out his heart. 'I've just joined up, but you might say this has been in the wind for a long time – all my life, really. I always knew I was different from my family. From grandfather. From my father, especially.' Tomas's eyes shaded darker. 'They are fascists, my family.' He paused and then went on. 'It started for me after I went to a few rallies at AUB with some of the older boys. Then after school I began going to a Marxist study group. And at last they began to invite me to other meetings down in the camps.' Tomas took a swaggering sip of his Pepsi and wiped his mouth with the back of his hand. 'They told me I couldn't join up yet, that I was . . . well . . . too *young*. But then I went to talk to Hussein.' His eyes glowed with hero worship as he gestured towards his leader. 'He is so busy, you know, so important, but he made time to talk to me. And he listened, you know, he really listened. My father has never listened to me like that.' Tomas smiled dreamily. 'He told me I was a born comrade. A born comrade! He said I can't have my military training yet, not for three more years. But I can come to all the meetings, and wear the uniform, and help out where I'm needed. And sometimes, like tonight, someone lets me carry his gun.' Tomas had directed most of this monologue to Miriam, but all of a sudden he seemed to remember that Leila was one of his mother's best friends. His bravado collapsed, and anxiously he turned to her. 'You won't tell my mother, will you?'

Leila gave him a severe look but, considering where they were and that his comrades were armed and evidently dangerous, she resisted the temptation to lecture him as if he were her own wayward son. 'Your mother would not be happy about this,' she contented herself with saying. She could just imagine the fuss Camilla would make if she saw her beloved firstborn toting a gun in a nest of Palestinian Communists. As for Pierre . . . Leila sincerely hoped that Tomas's right-wing father never found out about this leftist escapade. For it was clear to her that Tomas must only be going through a rebellious phase. He belonged among these radicals even less than she did, for he came from conservative Maronite Christian stock. 'And what about your father? From what I've heard, Pierre and your grandfather are doing everything they can to have your comrades here driven out of this country.'

'My family are reactionaries.' Tomas fingered the butt of his borrowed machine-gun. 'And enemies of the people.'

'Oh, Tomas!' Mimi was spellbound. 'You're so brave.'

Leila sighed, looked away into the other room, and

felt old. As she stared into space, she tried to remember what it had been like long ago when she had looked at Hussein just like that back in London. Of course the two of them had been older than Tomas and Miriam, and more guarded in their ways with one another. But even so, it was always the same between a man and a woman. It had not been very much different between herself and Hussein just an hour ago back in Shatilla. Or did she remember it wrong? Maybe, after all, even when she had been young, she had never had the courage to follow her instincts and give Hussein a look like the one she had just seen on Mimi's face. Well, it was too late to start now. She had missed her chance, and now it was another generation's turn. With an effort she pulled herself out of her reverie and back to the matter in hand. Touching as it doubtless was, this impossible infatuation between Tomas and Miriam would have to be nipped in the bud. Mustafa was not about to give his only daughter to the Communist son of a Christian fascist. From now on she would have to take care that the two of them weren't thrown together so much.

Her frown cut deeper as she suddenly focused on the tableau at which she had been unconsciously staring for the last few moments in the main salon. Three solemn young men were enthroned like princes in the place of honour on the sitting room sofa, while other youths buzzed around doing their bidding. She watched one soldier bringing them fresh Pepsis, another fussing over them as he lit their cigarettes, yet a third taking their group picture as respectfully as though they were film stars.

Leila examined the trio of young men more carefully. Like many others at this party, they were at the most in their early twenties. One was tall with tar-black hair, fiercely arresting angry eyes and a lean Bedouin eagle face. The second was dark-complexioned, stout, and by nature so jolly that it seemed an effort for him to keep a straight face. The third, who appeared to be even younger than the others, was slightly built with longish brown hair and a sad waif's face. Each was wearing United Front olive drab, with black-and-white *kuffiyehs* like Hussein's wrapped around their necks. As self-consciously as if they were the bridegrooms at a triple wedding reception, they sat erect on their sofa.

Tomas followed her stare and smiled reverently. 'They go tomorrow night.' His voice was as hushed as if he were talking of something sacred.

Before he could say more, Hussein was upon them with a squadron of his men. He greeted Tomas as though there were no age or rank difference between them, and then swept Leila and her children into the main salon where the three young men held court on the sofa. 'Meet Ahmed. Adil. And Waleed. This is their party. Their going-away party. Tomorrow they're going home.'

The three young Palestinians looked up at their leader and, for the first time since Leila had been watching them, a radiance transformed their faces and they smiled. Their comrades took this as a signal to cheer, shout, and stamp their feet in unison.

Leila bit her lip to stop it from trembling. Allah help them, for this was a commando suicide squad. These three were going over the border into Israel tomorrow, and the odds were that none of them would come back.

As instinctively as she would have looked away from a man beating a donkey or a lunatic ranting in an alleyway, Leila averted her eyes from this tragedy-in-the-making. It wasn't that she shrank in horror from the mayhem these commandos were bent on wreaking south of the border. She was a Palestinian, and – as she always said at dinner parties – she believed her people had to fight to regain their lost land. To her, these youths were not terrorists. They were, rather, soldiers waging a guerrilla war against the Zionist enemy. She would never shed tears for the Israelis. As in any war, it was up to the enemy to bury and mourn their own dead. But she was touched by the fate of these ill-starred soldiers. It was one thing to applaud the theory of armed struggle at a rally, another matter entirely to look into the eyes of young men who were surely going to die before they had ever really lived.

She could not help herself, however, an instant later, from staring back in fascination at these boys who were so eager to die. She did not regard herself as an especially maternal woman. When her children had been babies, she had hired others to get up in the middle of the night to feed them and calm their infant fears. Yet these three on the sofa – even the fierce one, Ahmed – had something of the scared little boy about them. Men, she thought, even or perhaps *especially* macho men with their big guns and their bigger boasts, could be so achingly vulnerable. She had a motherly impulse to sweep these doomed lads into her arms and hold them tight and not let them go until they promised her they would choose to live instead of die. They are too young, she thought, to waste themselves like this. They aren't old enough to understand that life is about holding on, striving always for more, and then in the end achieving the crowning satisfaction of winning against the odds. Never, even in the darkest moments of despair after she had renounced Hussein, had she considered suicide. Nor had she ever believed in anything deeply enough to want to die for it. Yet now, coming face to face with those who lived and died by a different creed, she felt slightly ashamed of herself. She reminded herself, however, that she was a survivor, a winner, a Shahine. She was bloody well not going to let the fanatics here in this room make her feel guilty. Even so she could not stop a sense of shame creeping over her again in the presence of those who not only held stronger beliefs than she but were also willing to sacrifice their lives for their convictions. Despite herself, she was moved by these three young men. For as they sat on the worn sofa, there was about them already the glamour of death. She feared that their dark little boys' eyes would haunt her.

Hussein had been watching her face closely, and now he bent over and whispered in her ear. 'So what do you think, comrade?'

But before she could answer, her youngest son piped up with a question that came in a lull in the cheering, so that everyone heard him. 'Where are they going, Mama? To Israel to live?'

'No!' Miriam's little girl's face was as grim as any warrior's as she corrected her brother. 'They go to Palestine to die.'

'Ah,' Hussein said, and for a second Leila was jealous of the look in his eyes as he beamed at her daughter. But then, as another emotion coursed through her, her throat felt so tight that she wasn't sure she would be able to talk. 'She could have been ours,' she said to him so low that no one else could hear.

'She *is* ours,' Hussein answered.

Leila searched his face, but she could see no tenderness for her there.

His eyes, as he said more, were as hard as his words. 'She is mine as well as yours. She is Palestinian, one of our youth, and part of our struggle.'

Leila felt a sudden chill of foreboding. She looked on in a kind of horror, then, as Hussein stepped forward and untied the *kuffiyeh* from around Ahmed's neck and draped it around Miriam's. 'For our little sister,' he said. As though this were some ancient religious initiation, Hussein proceeded to take the scarves from his other two doomed soldiers and tie them like yokes around the necks of Leila's sons. 'And for our small brothers.' For one breathless moment, Leila's thrilled children stood erect, as though they had been anointed into some mystical brotherhood.

But then Leila sprang forward, swept all three into her arms, and backed away from this entire demented throng. For a moment, Hussein had almost won her over. For a second, when she was still choked with pity for those boys who were about to die, she might even have been on the verge of joining forces with him. But that was before he had turned his seduction from her to her children. By leaps and bounds, he had once again gone too far. She would not put up with this madness for another moment. These were her sons and her daughter. *Hers!* Before anyone could speak another word, she dragged her children up and away, slamming the door hard behind her.

It was only when she was halfway home, and the children were sprawled fast asleep all around her, that she understood why Hussein had taken her to that party. Tonight, she sensed, he had again put her to one of life's crucial tests. Had she passed or failed?

Almost of its own volition, Leila's hand stole over and tenderly stroked the rough cotton of the *kuffiyeh* which Miriam still had wrapped around her neck. Another regret, she thought, to add to all the others. But no matter how much she wanted Hussein – and to herself she admitted now that she wanted him dearly, that she had never stopped wanting him – she could still not wholeheartedly sacrifice either herself or her children to his cause. The same forces which had pulled the two of them apart a decade ago still kept them apart now, and perhaps would do so for ever. For nothing ever changes, she thought sadly, least of all ourselves.

She leaned her head against the back of the seat of the Volkswagen and felt desolate.

Chapter 17

The first time that Israeli bombs began to fall on Fatima's village, it was late morning, the busiest time of the day in Suker, and her family were scattered hither and yon.

Later, as often after a calamity, everyone would remember exactly what they had been doing when the nightmare began.

Ali and his eldest son Muhammad were in the mosque sitting crosslegged with some visiting *shaykhs* from the Bekaa Valley. Toddling along in the background was his youngest son. One of the older boys was lying under the chassis of a neighbour's broken-down Chevrolet trying to repair a faulty gear box. Another was out in the fields helping the uncles plant the tobacco and prune the olive trees. Another son was struggling over his maths at school. An older brother was walking back and forth along the main Sidon road with his French grammar open in his hands, studying the conjugation of irregular verbs for the baccalaureate examinations he soon hoped to be able to pass. The eldest girl was sitting at home crosslegged on the kitchen floor chopping a bundle of parsley to be made into *tabouli* and, at the same time, keeping a sharp eye on her little sister who was playing with empty cotton reels in a corner. Another girl was out by the water tank helping her aunts with the laundry. The daughter whose turn it was to learn to read and write was in their mother's class in the girls' school, valiantly chorusing every syllable of the long '*Yasin*' *surah* of the Holy Koran at the top of her lungs. Fatima herself stood at the front of the crowded room, pacing back and forth, nodding encouragement to this one, correcting that one with a smile and an admonition to try harder.

Meanwhile, the three silver Phantom jet bombers with the blue and white Israeli markings were streaking over the border on what they considered a retaliatory mission. Two days ago, Palestinian commandos had planted a bomb in a crowded cinema in Jerusalem, and the day before that an explosion had rocked a kibbutz in the Galilee. After intense interrogation of three captured Arab saboteurs, Israeli military intelligence had announced that the guerrillas had infiltrated from Lebanon.

In later years, the shell-shocked Shia villagers of south Lebanon would learn to listen intently to radio bulletins about Zionist casualties incurred by *fedayeen* activity in Israel. They even became sophisticated enough to sift through the minefields of conflicting information broadcast on disparate radio channels in Cairo, London and Tel Aviv. For though in their hearts they might want to credit the wildly exaggerated propaganda claims of the radical Arab stations, and though in their minds they might actually believe the dispassionate accounts of what the neutral BBC said was happening on the West Bank, in fact the most cautious villagers would learn to act on what they heard beamed over the airwaves of the Israeli radio stations. No sooner had they heard a Tel Aviv broadcaster claiming that kibbutzim were being shelled by Arab mortars or that an explosion had taken Jewish lives in a crowded market, than those with faint hearts and full tanks of petrol in their cars would pack up their women and children and zoom north to the safety of their relatives in Beirut.

But in these early days of 1973, the deadly cycle of Palestinian attacks and the eye-for-an-eye vengeance wreaked by Israeli bombing raids over this part of south Lebanon was still a relatively new phenomenon, and so this one caught the villagers of Suker unawares.

The Israeli jets met no resistance as they crossed into Lebanese airspace and coursed northwards. The

Lebanese army was a national joke, and the Palestinian forces deployed near the border had no air force of their own. The planes banked in a wide arc over the stony Lebanese foothills which Palestinian guerrilla forces had managed to honeycomb in the past few years with training camps, supply centres and military encampments. As US satellite photographs supplied to the Israelis clearly indicated, one Arab force was burrowed in two miles south-west of Suker, and another detachment was bivouacked a good six miles due east.

Intent on finishing their tasks before it was time for the noon prayers and then lunch, few of the unsuspecting Suker villagers paid any attention to the low droning rumble that was about to rain death from the sky.

But then Hassan, Fatima's scholar son who dreamed of someday being a teacher like his adored mother, looked up from his French grammar as he heard a sound like the clogged backfiring of a car, only louder, coming from not very far away. As he stood unshielded along the Sidon road, he shaded his eyes with his hands and looked south-west, where plumes of black smoke rose from the far side of the olive groves. He threw down his book and started running down the middle of the road towards the fields where his brother and uncles were ploughing. Ahead he saw first the deadly wink of silver in the sky and then the black turdlike objects that fell from them achingly fast. The ground shook, and he screamed and ran faster towards the smoke and the fire. So intent was he on getting to his brother that he did not hear another plane thundering overhead. Before his eyes the road ahead exploded in a horrible blinding whoosh. Too late, he threw his arms up to protect his face as he was blown off his feet. He landed head first in a rocky ditch, where mercifully he lost consciousness.

The jets by then were flying low directly over the village, en route from their first Palestinian target south-west of Suker to the second guerrilla site to the east. Yet the flight crew swooped lower still and let the bombs fall thickly in the buzzing hive of the village.

The roar of the exploding bombs cut through the morning calm. The Hajji's house from the lane from the mosque suddenly disappeared in a puff of smoke, the petrol station was a ball of fire, and the empty shed where the women squatted at dawn every morning to bake their bread caved in upon itself. One bomb scored a direct hit on the feed store chockablock with farmers from the surrounding hills buying their spring seed. But by luck another missile just missed the government school. From one end of the village to the other, walls fell in and cars burned. Fire licked at flat roofs.

But then, as suddenly as it had begun, only a fatal moment or so later it ended. The jets screamed as they peeled out, banked hard to the right, and then headed over to where the Palestinian military forces were encamped.

Suker lay smoking in the blazing sun. But still, even though the jets were gone, the madness wasn't over. Before the stunned village could begin to recover, it was rocked by an even more spectacular series of explosions. The fires which still burned unabated tripped off a succession of delayed chain reaction blasts in the underground storage tanks at the petrol station. The earth vibrated, and every building that was left standing was shaken to its foundations. All over the village great heaving clouds of noxious smoke at first obscured the damage. Most of the bombs had fallen on the cluster of shops and houses at the heart of the village, where the two main roads converged at the mosque. Yet – in what the devout were later to claim was a miracle – even though one of the cars parked just outside had been reduced to a burned out hulk, the mosque itself stood untouched.

Cautiously then, in the calm after the fire and thunder, Ali and Muhammad were two of the first to stagger out of doors. The father and son coughed and held their hands up to their faces as they leaned against one another for support. With the acrid smoke and the choking dust, they could hardly see a foot in front of them. But they could hear the unforgettable sounds of the wounded village. Men trapped under collapsed walls screamed in pain. Terrified children, unhurt but traumatized, shrieked for their mothers. Old people wailed in a quavering panic that was enough to break even a warrior's heart. And, over and above all else, the high-pitched keening of the women began from everywhere at once. That eerie echo, more animal than human, seemed the sound of the ravaged soul of the village itself. In a matter of minutes, Suker had been reduced to a sob.

Then the dust cleared, doors creaked open, and the village's paralysis came to an end as everyone who could manage it crept or crawled outside to search in a mounting frenzy for missing children, fathers, aunts.

All was confusion on the fringes of the village in the government school, where the students had been cowering on the floor since the first explosions. In the beginning, between the howling children inside and the detonating bombs outside, Fatima wasn't sure if the school had been hit. When finally the raid ended, she did her best to calm her hysterical little girls as she herded them together. She was in an agony of dread as she counted heads: sixteen, eighteen – yes, thank God! – twenty-three. After fiercely hugging each one, she heaved a sigh of relief that all her charges – including her daughter Elham – were safe. But by then, too, the boys were streaming out of their adjacent school. For a moment Fatima the teacher forgot all about her pupils, as Fatima the mother raced over to make sure her son Ahmed was unhurt. She kissed the boy and held him tight, and then belatedly she rejoiced with the headmaster that none of their children had been injured. Mustering their students, they walked a few paces out to the fields where, not more than fifty yards from the school, a bomb had scorched the ground and left an olive grove in smoking ruins. Fervently they thanked God that they and their schools had been spared, and led their students in a recitation of the *Fatiha* prayer. Then Fatima and the headmaster ordered the children to run straight home so their anxious families would know they were safe.

Finally, Fatima thought, she could turn to the concerns of her own family. With Ahmed and Elham, she formed a flying wedge as they pounded down the road towards the village. But the slim children outpaced their plump mother. By the time she rounded the final bend in the road before they came upon their house, Fatima's breath was ragged and her chest hurt. Yet when she saw her house still standing on the crest of the hill and heard her children shouting the news that everyone there was unhurt, she whispered a quick prayer of thanksgiving. She forgot all about how tired she was and, propelled by a second wind, she puffed up the hill and burst into her kitchen.

Two more of her girls – her eldest daughter Zainab and the youngest one, Amina – lay sobbing in terror on the kitchen floor while Elham tried to console them. Fatima knelt down, embraced little Amina, and soothed her with crooning noises. The door banged open, and Salma came in with three of her aunts and a flock of cousins. There were more kisses and tears all round, as the women clung to one another. In their panic, no one was exactly sure what had happened, or why. Wild rumours that had sprung up at the first falling of a bomb were repeated, and embroidered, and then repeated again in their enlarged versions. The mosque lay in ruins. All the olive trees had gone up in smoke.

The Israeli army approached, and for a certainty soon they would rape all the women, murder all the children, and cut the hearts out of all the men. In Fatima's kitchen, the terrified women clutched at one another and wept. A very pregnant cousin curled up in a ball and babbled incoherent prayers for Allah to spare them. One of the aunts could not stop shouting at the top of her lungs that the village was burning, that she didn't know where her husband and sons were, and that the village was burning.

In this chaos, even while she was rocking Ali's aged sister in her arms as tenderly as if the distraught spinster had been a newborn infant, Fatima's mind clicked on like a calculator. Thank God, that's five of mine safe: all four of the girls – one back at the school and three more here, and the one boy who had been at the school. But where – and how – were her five other sons? And what of Ali? He had surely been in the mosque, and they said the mosque had been destroyed. She had to go and see for herself what had become of her husband and her sons.

But before she could set about that urgent business, she had to sort out the pandemonium in her own kitchen. As soon as her sister-in-law's weeping and wailing began to subside, Fatima took the rest of the women in hand. She was after all the *shaykh*'s wife, and so she lectured the others in her best schoolmarm voice.

Enough rumours, she said sternly, and no more tears. Had they forgotten who they were and what they were about? They were Shia! '*Shia!*' She said it as if it were a battle cry. They were followers of Imam Ali, who thirteen centuries ago, with his blessed wife Fatima, the favourite daughter of the Prophet Muhammad himself, had set a glorious example of how to transcend their lives of poverty and suffering with grace. Their son Hussein, too, had fashioned his life and especially his heroic death into a perfectly pitched song of blood and honour. Had they forgotten, Fatima asked, how bravely and proudly on the plain of Kerbala Hussein had died for what was right? As one, the women raised their right hands and brought them down hard on their left breasts. 'Hussein,' they chorused as they beat their breasts. '*Ya*, Hussein!' They kept up that sombre beat – fist against skin, fist against skin – as Fatima reminded them how after Kerbala Hussein's suffering sister Zainab had kept the faith alive. 'Zainab!' the women cried as they sat on the kitchen floor beating their breasts and remembering how she had set them such a womanly example. '*Ya*, Zainab!'

Fatima let them carry on towards catharsis, shouting out their martyrs' names, striking their chests harder and faster, until their cries reached a peak. Then, in the exhausted silence that followed, she judged that the time was right to channel their religious fervour into the strength needed to cope with today's fresh calamity. 'We must be strong for Imam Hussein. We are Shia women! We must be strong like his mother Fatima and his sister Zainab.'

'Yes!' the women shouted. 'Yes!'

When Fatima suggested they begin cooking a hot meal for whoever in the village would want it, the women forgot their despair and got to work. Finally satisfied that all was in order in her own house, Fatima and her eldest daughter Zainab struck out for the centre of the village to find out what had become of the rest of her brood.

As she and Zainab made their grim way through the smoky haze towards the mosque, fires burned and debris smouldered. They rushed past the bakery shed that lay in ruins. It was a blessing, the mother and daughter agreed as they tried to savour this small victory in the face of so much horror, that none of the women had been working inside when the bomb fell. Fatima looked back over her shoulder and shuddered at the destruction of the site where she had squatted baking bread for so many dawns of her life. Was Ali's mosque reduced to a hole in the ground like this bakery?

When she and Zainab reached a screeching clutch of mourning women who had gathered outside the mound of rubble that had been the Hajji's house, decency required that they spare a few moments for kind words and sad shakings of the head. The Hajji's wife lay inside, and her sister too, and no one knew how many of her children.

This first whiff of death made Fatima break into a run. She and Zainab streaked past the petrol station, where flames still flickered with a sickly orange glow. Finally they caught sight of the mosque. The walls still stood. The roof was intact. Fatima put her hands up to her face and burst into tears. *El-hamdulillah*, her Ali might be safe!

Today was no exception to the rule that always, when there was something to mourn or celebrate, the villagers flocked to the dusty parking lot in front of the mosque. Dazed old men in tattered clothes milled vaguely about, asking why the Israelis had bombed their defenceless village. Like frightened children, they whined that Allah had forsaken them.

Meanwhile, as Fatima searched in vain for her missing husband and sons, she spotted one of Ali's brothers helping a screaming boy into the back seat of an old Ford. Two old men and four children lay groaning on the seats. Some were bleeding profusely, and others lay terrifyingly still. Sitting half in and half out of the car, with their buttocks resting on the rolled-down windows, were weeping sons and fathers who insisted on accompanying their loved ones to the hospital in Sidon. There was no doctor in Suker, and not even a nurse. The driver gunned the engine, and the car took off on its hour-long dash for medical attention. So much suffering, Fatima thought, so much pain. As though he could feel her despair, Abbas turned, put his arm around her, and led her to the feed store where he had last seen his brother heading the rescue team.

At first she could not spot Ali amid the throng of forty or fifty sweating men who were frantically pawing at the loose ground as they tried to clear away the charred boards and broken building blocks.

'Can you still hear them trapped inside?' Abbas's eyes were haunted. 'They were screaming, before. God help them. They are buried alive.'

Fatima licked her dry lips. 'And my husband? He is safe?' When Abbas nodded and tightened his hold around her shoulders, she took courage and went on. 'And my sons?'

'Muhammad's over there with Ali.' As Abbas pointed, suddenly Fatima was able to pick out her husband and son. 'I think one of the little ones was with them, too.'

At that, a small soot-stained boy hurled himself at his mother's skirts. With a whoop, she scooped Hussein up in her arms and covered his dirty face with kisses. That's two more safe, she thought. And three more to find. Even though the excited child begged to be allowed to stay and help his father, she sent him home with Zainab.

Ali was scrabbling in the dirt like a dog digging for a buried bone, when she came near enough to call out his name. At the sound of her voice he turned, and his eyes were great dark pools of gladness. He reached out with his soiled hands and stroked the hem of her skirt. 'So Allah has spared you.'

'Yes.' She touched the tip of her index finger to his cheek. But with half the village looking on, this was neither the time nor the place for tenderness between a husband and wife. Tonight, when it was just the two of them alone in bed, she would lay in the circle of his arms and feel safe from the madness of the world. But quickly now she assured him all the girls were at home, along with two of their brothers. Muhammad, of course, was right here, too, digging deeply into the wreckage of the feed store. As she watched, she heard her son call out that he'd found someone. At once a knot of men tore at the earth. A bare foot emerged from the wreckage, then a leg, finally an inert body. Fatima's stomach churned as she watched the men standing disconsolately over the corpse. Where were her sons Muhssin, Hassan and Ibrahim?

Ali used the sleeve of his brown mullah's robe to wipe the sweat off his face as he tried to recall what his sons had said they were going to do that morning. He thought Muhssin had gone off to help in the fields, and he seemed to recollect Ibrahim saying he was going to use his precocious mechanical skills on a neighbour's car. Yes, now he remembered, he had seen Ibrahim going over to Abu Jaleel's house to get his old Chevrolet going. As for Hassan . . . Ali shrugged. Who ever knew where dreamy Hassan was off to with his books? The last time he had seen him this morning, Hassan had been searching for a quiet place to study his French.

As worry creased his face, Ali seemed about to bolt off with Fatima to hunt for their sons. But then he looked over his shoulder at the ruins of the feed store. Without him urging them on, too many of the villagers had stopped digging for their neighbours and instead had lit up cigarettes as they passively bemoaned the sufferings of this life. Yet many men – some said twenty or even thirty farmers from the surrounding hills and valleys – were trapped under the debris. If any of them were to be rescued before they stopped breathing, every minute counted. Ali sighed as his eyes met Fatima's in a kind of apology. 'I am needed more here,' he said. But he called over to Muhammad to help his mother search for the other boys.

Tall for his twelve years, Muhammad usually never let anyone forget not only that he was his father's eldest son but also that he was almost a man in his own right. Yet when he caught sight of his mother safe and sound, for a moment he was as boyish as his little brother Hussein. He hurled himself into her arms, kissed her exuberantly on her cheeks, forehead, eyes, even her chin, and then stroked her hair as though every strand were a sacred relic. But then, as his father sombrely charged him with finding his three missing brothers, Muhammad seemed to grow more manly before their eyes. 'We'll go to Abu Jaleel's first,' he said importantly as he put his arm around his mother. When out of the corner of his eye he saw the men recovering another body, he rushed her away from the carnage at the feed store.

On the way to Abu Jaleel's, they passed knots of shrieking women who were tearing their robes and raking their faces with their fingernails as they mourned sons, husbands and fathers who were dead or dying. Houses were flattened, and grass fires burned in the charred fields. Muhammad tightened his hold on his mother. 'God willing, they'll all be fine. *Inshallah*, my brothers will be safe.'

But they knew their luck had run out as they approached Abu Jaleel's. His old stone house still stood without any apparent damage, but out in the road a crowd had gathered around his rusty old jalopy. They rushed up and elbowed their way into the front ranks of the crowd. Then Fatima caught her breath, screamed, and collapsed into Muhammad's arms.

Ibrahim lay trapped beneath the car. His legs were pinned under the chassis, which had come crashing down on his thighs. Abu Jaleel's car had not been damaged, but not more than thirty feet away there was a deep yawning cavity in the road where a bomb had fallen. The impact of the explosion had dislodged the car from its jack and sent it crashing down on

Ibrahim. He was still conscious as he lay whimpering on the ground.

'My boy,' Fatima screeched. 'My son! My Ibrahim!' She lunged forward and, if Muhammad hadn't held her locked tightly in the grip of his arms, she might have thrown herself at what she could see of her son. The women in the crowd pushed and jostled their way over and clustered around Fatima, patting her back, telling her not to worry, that Ibrahim was in God's hands. '*Allah karim*,' they chorused: God was generous, and so surely He would spare this boy who had never done any wrong to anyone.

Meanwhile, Abu Jaleel and a team of burly men debated whether it was best to pick the car up from the back or the front, and then whether they should try to slide or lift the boy on to the makeshift stretcher they had fashioned by throwing a mattress atop a ladder. Without a doctor to advise them, they worried that they might do the lad more harm than good by moving him the wrong way. For five minutes, ten minutes, even longer, they dithered.

Finally they decided to lift the entire car up at once. Accordingly they deployed around the front and back bumpers, and they heaved up together at a signal from Abu Jaleel. Inch by careful inch, they raised the car off the boy's crushed legs. Yet Ibrahim screamed an animal screech of pain when at last he was free of the heavy metal weight of the chassis. Only a moment later, however, another team of men had deftly eased him off the ground and on to the stretcher.

Fatima could no longer be restrained. 'My son!' She threw herself at the stretcher. 'Ibrahim!'

He was in shock and in so much pain that he was barely conscious, but his eyelids flickered. 'Ummie! Oh, Ummie!' Ibrahim for all his ten years liked to style himself a man, but now he cried in his mother's arms like a baby. 'It hurts, Ummie!'

There were frantic blasts from the horn of a pick-up truck that was to take Ibrahim to the hospital in Sidon. Gently the men lifted the stretcher on to the flatbed of the truck. Fatima hooked her foot on the bumper, but her brother-in-law restrained her. 'I'll go. You stay here.' Before she could protest, her eldest son had leaped on to the truck. The last thing Fatima saw, as the pick-up headed down the bumpy dirt road, was Muhammad tenderly cradling his brother in his arms as he tried to cushion him from every jolt in the broken road.

Tears streamed down Fatima's face, as she walked with the uncertain gait of an old woman towards the fields where Muhssin had been ploughing with his uncles. As she stumbled along, she fought her mounting despair. She reminded herself that she was more fortunate than her neighbours whose sons and daughters had been killed. How could she complain about only one son being struck down before he was even old enough to grow a beard? But then, as she remembered how Ibrahim's face had been contorted by pain, she broke into fresh tears. It had seemed to her that his legs were ruined. She was sick with fear that they would cut off his legs in Sidon.

Yet onward she plodded, searching for Muhssin and Hassan. She was still a long way from the fields, and weeping as she walked blindly near the centre of the road, so that the driver of the approaching car had to step sharply on his brakes to avoid running her down. He hooted his horn and was just about to shout at her, when instead he called out her name. She glanced up and recognized two of Ali's brothers in the front seat. Then she caught sight of a figure in the back. 'Muhssin! My son! Oh, thank God, thank God you're safe!' Again there was an emotional reunion as the boy leaped from the car. The mother and son embraced and kissed, and again embraced.

Yet even as the boy clung to her, he evaded his

mother's eyes. When finally she could get a good look at his face, she saw that Muhssin had been weeping. No, she thought, oh no, no, no . . . First Ibrahim, and now Hassan. 'What's wrong? It's your brother, isn't it? Something's happened to Hassan. Tell me!'

When her son looked away and remained mute, her eyes slid to a still form propped up in the back seat of the car next to the window. As she let go of Muhssin and crept closer, she knew with a sickening sense of inevitability that it had to be Hassan who lay there like a dead weight. Yes, she stared down into his dear face. 'Is he dead?' she whispered.

'Be calm, Fatima, be strong,' Ali's brother Hussein cautioned. 'He's alive, don't worry. *Inshallah*, I think he will live.'

'We were out in the fields when the planes came,' Ali's other brother Hamid said. 'We saw them coming and, *el-hamdulillah*, we had time to hide in the olive groves. But we could see the smoke in the village. We were so afraid for you all, that everyone was dead. Are they, Fatima? Is the family safe?' It seemed that Hamid, who was usually a man of few words, could now not stop talking. 'We ran out to where we had left the car. All we could think of was that we had to get home and see to our families. But then, in a ditch near the car, we saw Hassan. There was no blood. There wasn't a mark on him.'

'He was conscious before, and he was talking.' Hussein was doing his best to be reassuring. 'He's just . . . asleep now. But before, he could talk all right. You know Hassan, how he talks and talks.'

'Asleep?' Fatima wanted to believe them, but as she looked from one to the other, she was aware that they were keeping something crucial from her. 'Tell me the truth.'

Ali's brothers exchanged helpless looks, and finally Hussein broke the news. 'It's his eyes.'

'He started to weep,' Hamid admitted. 'And he kept asking us why it was dark outside if it was still morning.'

Fatima sank down on her knees and then all but collapsed into the dust of the road. Her Hassan was blind! She buried her face in her hands and rocked back and forth as she howled for her sons. For Ibrahim who couldn't walk and for Hassan who couldn't see.

'Don't cry, Ummie, don't cry.' Muhssin put his arms around his mother's heaving shoulders.

After a long moment, Ali's brothers gently urged Fatima to get in the car and come back with them to the village. It was almost time for the noon prayers. They would perform their ablutions, Hussein added, and pray together behind their brother Shaykh Ali. Then, *inshallah*, Hamid promised, this afternoon they would all take Hassan to the doctor in Sidon.

The soothing sound of the muezzin's prayer call drifted over on the wind from the mosque in Suker. Fatima let out a deep sigh. Ali's brothers were right. She was no use to anyone crying in the dust. She would let them take her home. Just now she needed to pray. She would wash her hands and face and feet, and then put on a clean robe and headscarf and unroll her prayer mat. If God were merciful, when she prostrated herself full-length in the *sejda* bow, He would give her the grace to go on.

Early the next morning, as Fatima watched her husband don his best brown wool robe and wrap his head fastidiously in a spotless white turban of the finest Egyptian cotton, she knew without having to be told where he had decided to go.

For Ali, who was always quiet and thoughtful, had been even quieter and more thoughtful last night when they had sat, just the two of them, outside in the bleak moonlight fretting about what could be done to save their vulnerable village from the possibility of another devastating Israeli raid. By the time they had dug out the wounded and buried the dead, everyone in Suker had finally been forced to accept the brutal truth about the attack. Accordingly, after yesterday's mass funerals, the surviving men of the village had gathered together on the scorched grass outside the coffee-house to decide what must be done. With Palestinian guerrilla forces dug in nearby for what they said was the duration of their anti-Zionist struggle, the villagers feared that it wouldn't be long before the Israeli bombers would be back. For hours then, the men had sat smoking their *nargilehs* as they argued about how to save their families. The fiercest among them, who had been listening to passionate speeches by Imam Musa Sadr in Sidon and Nabatiya, had wanted to take up arms and defend their village against any and all attackers. But their more passive and peaceable neighbours had said simply that they were going to pack up and move in with their relatives in Beirut. When Fatima had asked Ali which side he had taken, he told her he had merely counselled them to remain calm and do nothing yet except pray for Allah's guidance and protection.

It wasn't until later, when he and Fatima were curled up together in bed, that Ali had hinted at what he thought was an alternative course of action. In the name of God, he had told her, someone would have to go and ask the Palestinians to decamp from the vicinity of the village. Surely, he had added more hesitantly, their brothers the Palestinians would have to take pity on the plight of the defenceless villagers. But Ali's voice had lacked certainty. When the Resistance had dug in here several years ago, the Shia had welcomed them as warriors fighting for Islam and Arab honour. But in the last nervous year or so, relations between the fighters and the peasant farmers had become so strained that the villagers sometimes regarded the Palestinians as no more than an army of occupation. There had been disputes about orchards ruined by careless target practice, complaints about the effrontery of PLO military checkpoints on remote rural roads, and – most unforgivable of all – allegations that the commandos had been molesting Shia girls.

Even when Ali had sighed and turned over, still Fatima had sensed – though he lay as rigid as a man in a coma – that all that anxious night he had remained as sleepless as she. Just before dawn, when the muezzin woke the village with his plaintive call that prayer was better than sleep, she had been relieved to leave yesterday's disasters behind and rise to a new day.

As Ali continued to fuss with his turban, Fatima went out to the kitchen to begin preparing her husband's favourite breakfast. Usually she set out for the school so early that she left preparation of the morning meal to one of her sisters-in-law, but because of yesterday's calamity the school was closed until further notice. With seventeen villagers killed in the bombing raid and scores more seriously injured, every family either lay prostrate in a state of heavy mourning or was frantically hying back and forth to the hospital in Sidon.

She arranged the dishes on a tin tray: creamy *lebnah* cheese churned by her own sister, black olives picked out in the groves by her own sons, slightly stale bread baked yesterday morning by her own daughters. Since the bakery shed had been bombed to smithereens, the village made do this morning with yesterday's bread.

As she fussed with the food, she tried not to dwell on thoughts of her two maimed sons. Yet she couldn't stop looking out of the kitchen window at poor sightless Hassan, who sat unmoving on a chair she had set out for him in the midst of the olive groves. Yesterday, in Sidon, the doctors had been so busy with the critically wounded that they had spared only a cursory glance for a boy who could not see. When Fatima was at her wits' end, Ali's brother had finally got through to Anne on the telephone. She couldn't be sure until she examined Hassan, but it sounded to her as though he had sustained a concussion. As soon as they could bring the boy up to Beirut, she would arrange a series of tests and treatment that might help him regain his sight.

Fatima sighed as she fiddled with her husband's breakfast dishes on the tray. Hassan's plight was dire enough, but Fatima didn't think she could cry any more for Ibrahim. In one hysterical hour yesterday at the hospital, she had cried a full lifetime of tears. Yet, as her thoughts trailed back to that son who would never again be whole, she bent her head and her shoulders shook. *They had cut off both his legs above the knee.* Silently she cried in her kitchen, trying – but failing – to take comfort from the doctor's prediction that Ibrahim could live to a ripe old age. Was a long life, in Ibrahim's condition, a blessing or a curse? He was still only a child.

She wiped away her tears, held her head high, and tried to trust in God's mercy as she carried Ali's breakfast tray into the front room where he sat waiting crosslegged on the floor. Her husband had enough on his plate this morning without having to see her weeping in despair. She took heart, too, from his promise that they would visit the Sidon hospital together later today. Right after breakfast she would get to work preparing the foods Ibrahim loved best: kebabs, and rice with nuts and raisins, and maybe some carrot *halwah*. Later in the week she would take him some *kunnifeh* pastry. Ibrahim had always had such a sweet tooth. Ibrahim had always been such a sweet boy. She hoped, too, that after breakfast Ali might make time to talk to her awhile about Ibrahim and Hassan. She could almost feel his arm sliding around her and patting her shoulders as he said wise and comforting words about the boys' chances for a decent life. It always calmed her just to be near him.

But despite her best intentions, her eyes brimmed with tears as she gave Ali's pot of tea an extra stir and tried to smile as she set down the tray before him.

His hand covered hers on the teapot handle. 'Courage,' he said as he saw two forlorn tears slide down her cheeks. But before he could say more, three of his brothers trooped in the door.

Fatima scurried out to the kitchen, brewed a fatter pot of tea, set out more cheese and bread on a larger tray, and piled apples up on a plate. As she slipped in and out, bringing more food from the kitchen, she heard her husband and his brothers arguing. Hamid and Hussein were shouting, and Abbas was muttering curses about sons of dogs. But Ali's persuasive voice soothed them until finally the brothers were nodding in reluctant agreement. Just as she was bringing them a fresh pot of tea, they rose as one and made for the door. Ali's eyes met hers. For an instant, in that silent communication that can sometimes pass between a man and a woman, they seemed to draw strength from each other. Then he merely nodded and said he would be home in time for the noon prayers. After lunch, *inshallah*, he would take her to Sidon to visit their son. She stood in the doorway waving goodbye as Ali and his brothers piled into Hamid's rickety old Mercedes. Then she sighed and went out to Hassan in the olive grove.

As the old car lurched up the road towards the main Palestinian encampment, the brothers chain-smoked in gloomy silence. Abbas was fiercely independent by nature, and so had no wish to ask the Palestinians – or anyone else – for anything at any time. Hussein, too, who had been down to Tyre the week before to hear Imam Musa Sadr urging his Shia to take up arms in their own defence, had argued passionately that it was a fool's errand trying to persuade the *fedayeen* to move their camp to a less populated area. Although in the end they had all agreed to stand united behind Shaykh Ali, they remained pessimistic about the outcome of their mission. Once or twice Abbas tried to crack jokes to lighten their mood, but he gave up when nobody laughed. As they approached the entrance to the camp, Palestinian guerrillas waved them down with the barrels of their Kalashnikovs. Instead of braking, Hamid gunned his engine and growled that he had half a mind to drive straight through them. But Ali silenced him with a gesture, and at the checkpoint he courteously explained to the guard that they were a deputation from one of the local villages and had come to see the commander.

At first it seemed that their mission might go well. The guard peered into the car, asked to see their Lebanese identity cards, and then good-humouredly waved them through to the dusty centre of the camp where he said they would find the major. But when they alighted by a ramshackle wooden shack that flew the Palestinian flag, two beefy soldiers with two even bigger guns stopped them in their tracks. Again the brothers showed their papers and explained their purpose, but the Palestinians ordered the Shias back into their car. As one ran off to find an officer to deal with this intrusion, the other stood guard with his submachine-gun aimed at Ali's head. Cautiously the brothers peered out at what they could see of the military camp. Apart from the major's headquarters, it consisted mostly of tents and concrete bunkers set deep into the ground. Here and there a charred tent leaned crazily on broken poles, and the blackened ground was pockmarked by craters. But compared to their devastated village, the military encampment had barely been touched by the Israeli raid.

The brothers sweltered in the Mercedes where it was parked in the sun. It was so hot that their clothes stuck to the plastic-covered seats. They waited twenty minutes, half an hour, nearly an hour. Still the commando silently glowered at them from behind the sights of his gun. Even though they were only six miles from the village where they had been born and raised, it was clear that they had blundered on to foreign – and perhaps hostile – territory.

Finally a plump and balding young lieutenant in a freshly pressed uniform sauntered up, dismissed the soldier with an imperious wave of his hand, and then leaned down on the open car window. Politely he shook hands with Shaykh Ali and nodded pleasantly to the others. His face was wreathed in a welcoming smile as he offered them fresh cigarettes and then asked to what he owed the honour of this visit. Pacified by the officer's courtesies, Ali explained that they were from the neighbouring village of Suker. They had come to speak to the commander because their homes had been heavily damaged in yesterday's bombing raid.

'I see.' The officer was no longer smiling. 'That will be difficult.' He sighed, as if with regret, and explained that the major was not available this morning. A mini-bus full of journalists from England, France and West Germany had just arrived on a fact-finding tour, and the commander was showing them the piles of rubble left from yesterday's Israeli raid, wounded *fedayeen* lying in the camp hospital, and new recruits training on the latest generation of Soviet weapons. It would be so much more convenient if Shaykh Ali and his brothers could come back tomorrow or after tomorrow. But then the lieutenant struck his head as though he had just remembered more meetings, manoeuvres and press briefings. No, he added, this week, next week, the timing hardly mattered. The commander was always busy. Smoothly the young officer smiled. 'But I am his *aide de camp*. I will be happy to pass on your compliments to the major.'

Shaykh Ali did not smile back. 'We will wait for

him.' He nodded majestically, precisely as back in Iran he had seen the ayatollahs dismiss their underlings. In regal silence he puffed on his cigarette.

The lieutenant shrugged and strode off, and once again an armed soldier stood guard over them. The brothers broiled in the sun as another half hour passed. When there was still no sign of the major, Ali wiped the sweat off his forehead with his handkerchief and anxiously checked his watch. The time for the midday prayers was upon them. Yet instead of lining up at the water taps to perform the necessary ablutions before *salah*, the soldiers were emerging from a sprawling tent with their lunch trays. Most of these soldiers would call themselves Muslims, yet none of them were performing the obligatory prayers.

Impervious to the loaded gun pointed at his beturbaned head, Ali flung open the car door and haughtily informed the guard that he and his brothers must wash and then pray. Without waiting for the bemused guard's permission, Ali led his brothers to the nearest water tap. Yet even as they performed their ablutions, the gulf widened between the Shia Muslim brothers and the Sunni Muslim Palestinians. As Abbas bent over at the tap, Hamid was incensed to see two soldiers laughing and pointing at the dirty soles of his brother's bare feet. In most crucial theological matters, Shia and Sunni practices were identical. But they differed in niggling details such as whether it was necessary to wash the entire foot before prayer as the Sunnis did or simply to wet the tops of the foot like the Shias. Hamid bristled and might have come to blows with the mocking Palestinians if Ali hadn't urgently restrained him: 'Remember why we're here.' Yet the *shaykh*, too, was tight-lipped as they laid their prayer mats on the ground, turned towards Mecca, and began the bows and salaams of the prayer.

Afterwards, when the guard herded them back into their car, the brothers were not only irritated at how they were being treated but hungry and thirsty besides. Abbas began to insist that they should go home, and Hamid threatened to show the Palestinians whose country they were in after all.

'Patience, all of you.' After prayer, as always, Ali had regained his serenity. But he was beginning to wish he had come alone on this diplomatic mission. 'And when we see the commander, let me do the talking.' He smiled. 'You'll see, the Palestinians are our brothers. They will listen, and then, *inshallah*, they will help us.'

Coaxed back into their lifelong habit of resignation, the brothers dozed fitfully in the heat. Finally, a simmering two hours after they had first entered the camp, the lieutenant bustled up to announce that they were in luck. The journalists had finally left, and the major had found time from his busy schedule to meet them.

They were ushered inside the wooden building where a haggard middle-aged man sat in rumpled camouflage uniform in front of a map labelled 'Palestine' tacked on to the wall. One chair was drawn up before the rough wooden table that served as the commander's desk, and the *aide de camp* ran off and quickly returned with three more. A boy brought coffee.

Hands were shaken all around, and the visitors planted themselves in the chairs. Cigarettes were lit, coffee was sipped, smiles were forced. Ali cleared his throat. 'We are from the village of Suker.'

'A pretty place,' the major said, 'very like my own village in Palestine.' He sat up straighter, and his eyes began to shine as he reminisced about the mosque, the pastures, and the simple stone houses of the home which he hadn't seen for twenty-five years.

Ali listened politely to this nostalgic recitation for some minutes, and then he spoke his piece. 'My village is not so pretty now. Yesterday in Suker seventeen of our men, women and children were killed by the bombs. Many more are in hospital.'

'They are monsters, the Israelis!' The major shook his fist at the sky. 'We will avenge this! We fight not only for ourselves but for you!'

The *shaykh* nodded. 'And for Allah,' he added softly. Ali invoked the Palestinian issue closest to his own heart. 'I will rejoice when you recover Jerusalem.'

'Ah, yes, Jerusalem!' The major's eyes misted over. 'My mother was born there. Would that my sons and the sons of my sons could be born in Jerusalem!'

'God willing,' Shaykh Ali said like a benediction. But he had not waited in the sun in the heat of the day merely to trade sentimental longings for Jerusalem. 'In my village, they are afraid that the Israelis will come again.'

The major's face clouded over, and he rose as though this interview were at an end.

But the *shaykh* persisted. 'In my village, they say the Israelis will come again and again, so long as your camp is so close to us.'

The major consulted his watch, snapped his fingers at his *aide de camp*, and frowned at the *shaykh*. 'The fortunes of war,' he shrugged. 'What can we do?'

Ali told him, and precisely. 'You can go away and leave us in peace.'

To the major, those were fighting words. 'There can be no peace anywhere in the Middle East', he snapped, 'until Palestine is ours once again.'

'But there was peace here until you came.' As his comment provoked a torrent of hot accusatory words from both the major and his brothers, Ali held up his hand to silence them all. He shook his head, more in sadness than in anger, at the major. 'We welcomed you as our brothers. We felt sorry for you, losing your homes and your country. It was a great wrong, what the Israelis did. And because you are Muslims and Arabs, we took you into our houses and did not deny you whatever you asked. And now is this how you repay us? Must even our women and children die for your cause?'

The major sank back in his chair and put his head in his hands in an attitude of despair. When he looked up again at Ali, his eyes were limpid with apology. 'You have my sympathy,' he said. 'I know how it is in the villages after the bombers come. It was the same in Jordan. When the children die, that is the worst. I wish . . .' His voice trailed off, and he did not say what it was that he wished. Instead his voice hardened. 'But you must not forget that we are at war with the Zionist oppressors. That means all of us, not just my men here in this camp but all the Arabs, and that includes you and your whole village. We must strike at them from here, there, everywhere. This is, I can assure you, only the beginning.'

'No.' Shaykh Ali's quiet voice was insistent. 'This must be the end. You cannot stay here for ever. We cannot let our families be killed.'

'We didn't bomb your village, the Israelis did. Your fight is with them, not with us.'

'Our fight is with whoever hurts us.'

The major spread his empty hands out on the table. 'Understand me, please. I am a reasonable man. I have a family of my own in Beirut. Of course a man wants to protect his family. But it's not just my family and your family that matter here. We – none of us – are as important as Palestine.'

He wet his lips with his tongue and seemed about to launch into a rhetorical tirade when he paused, sized Ali up, and reconsidered. When he spoke again, for the first time in this interview he seemed to be saying what was really on his mind. 'You must understand why the Israelis are doing this. You think they bombed your village by mistake? Ha!' The major spat in contempt.

'No! They bombed your village and others like it to make you turn against us and drive us away. They want the Lebanese army to come down here and do their dirty work for them.'

As he saw the disbelief on the faces of the *shaykh* and his brothers, the major elaborated. 'I tell you the truth. If you do not believe me, think back to what happened in Jordan in 1970. You remember Black September? I will never forget it! We had our bases there, just across the river from Palestine. Again and again the Israelis crossed over not only to attack our camps but to level whole villages. Just as you are doing here now with me, those villagers began to ask why the Jordanian government could not protect its own people. King Hussein, then, had a choice. He could have sent his Arab Legionnaires against the Israeli enemy or turned them against the *fedayeen*. Of course you know what happened. The Jordanian army fought us, and killed us, and so we came here.'

Ali's lips narrowed to a thin line. 'The Lebanese army, I think, is not so strong as King Hussein's Legionnaires.'

The major shrugged. 'That is not my problem.'

'There are those in my village who say that if our own government does not or will not defend us, then we must learn to defend ourselves.'

'Good, good.' The Palestinian commander smiled benignly. 'Join us, all of you. We will be happy to welcome our Lebanese brothers into our revolutionary struggle. We will train you, arm you, and let you fight shoulder to shoulder beside us.'

It was Ali's turn for an inscrutable smile. 'That was not my meaning.'

'I ask you, please, Shaykh Ali, to remember who are truly your friends. And who your sworn enemies.'

The *shaykh* and the major stared into one another's eyes. There was sympathy in that look, and – despite their differences – a growing understanding that each was gripped by forces beyond his control.

'And so you refuse my request.' Ali's voice was almost a whisper. 'You will not move your camp away from my village.'

'I cannot.' The major shook his head for emphasis. 'We are here to stay. We have bunkers, gun emplacements, and if and when the Soviets and Syrians give us better armaments, we will be able to shell the Galilee from these hills. Besides, what would be the point of just moving our base ten miles to the east or thirty miles to the west? We might spare Suker further attacks, but we would be putting other villages at the same risk. No, I have sat here and heard you out. But I can do nothing about your problem. Believe me, I am very sorry. I wish it could be different.'

'So do I.' Shaykh Ali stood and put out his hand to the major. Warmly they clasped hands. '*Inshallah*, one day it will not be necessary to fight like this.'

'God willing,' the major agreed. 'One day, when Palestine is ours again, all of us can live in peace.'

On that optimistic note, Shaykh Ali and his brothers filed out of the command post and climbed back in the steaming Mercedes. They were halfway home before Hamid broke the silence. 'So now what?'

It wasn't until a fortnight later, when they heard on the BBC World Service that Palestinian commandos had again struck at an Israeli kibbutz, that Ali looked up at the clear blue sky and then anxiously south to the border before he was finally goaded into answering Hamid's question. 'We must pick up the gun,' he told his brothers, 'and learn to defend ourselves.'

Before the bombers could come again, he made certain that Fatima and the rest of the women and children in the family were squeezed into his and his brothers' cars and well on their way to the safety of the cousins' homes in Beirut. Grimly, then, Shaykh Ali called together the men of the village and urged them to take the defiant example of the long-ago-martyred Imam Hussein as their example. They, like Hussein, had to prepare themselves to fight for what they knew was right. Imam Musa Sadr was right when he urged his Shia to bear arms in their own defence. 'They cannot', he had said in a speech in Tyre, 'humiliate Imam Hussein's people who would have been proud to stand with him thirteen hundred years ago at Kerbala. It is our duty to form a Lebanese resistance before we're expelled from our land. Anyone who doesn't know how to handle a weapon is straying from the teaching of our Imams Ali and Hussein.'

That night, as he and a caravan of Suker villagers once again rode back down that bumpy dirt road to the Palestinian camp, Ali was aware it might take longer to decide whom they were fighting than to complete their military training. But in the meantime, it was enough to pick up the gun and begin the struggle.

Chapter 18

Again, Camilla thought wearily, in this October of 1973, the armies were on the march.

She sighed over the tedious needlepoint that the years had taught her to love to hate. As a way of passing the time she had started this ambitious 'Lady and the Unicorn' tapestry what seemed like a century ago in Paris, when she was pregnant with Tomas.

From where she sat with the women in the main salon of the Château Croisé, she looked over at her eldest son, who at nearly fifteen was so grown up that he huddled with the men in their war councils. Her doting mother's eye drank in every detail of her favourite son: the sharp-witted look on his brooding face, the stylish cut of the expensive clothes she always made sure he wore when he was at the château, how he sat almost at military attention as he listened to the latest radio news. Pierre liked to roar out that Tomas was a chip off the old block, but to Camilla's way of thinking Tomas was finer in every way than his father had ever been. Her son was more handsome, far more astute and sensitive, and – most telling of all – he was the soul of integrity.

Camilla let her eyes trail reluctantly from the son to the father. It wasn't even lunchtime, and she herself hadn't touched a drop as yet today, but already her husband was as drunk as a lord. As she gave him a scornful glance, the kindest thought she could muster was that Pierre was not ageing well. His florid face was bloated from too much drink and too many late nights with his floozies. To disguise his thinning hair, he had painstakingly combed the remaining strands over the bald patches on his pate and then all but glued them into place with – she suspected – stolen squirts of her own hair spray. Over the years, too, he had been steadily putting on weight, so that his thighs were now as fat as ham haunches and his bulging belly flopped over his belt. Worst of all, however, was that Pierre had the dead-eyed look of a man who was not only utterly estranged from his feelings but who had also grown accustomed to never having to have a thought of his own. How could she ever have loved and married a man who was not only coarse and vulgar but weak and really rather stupid?

She bent over her tapestry and stitched faster and more angrily as she admitted to herself that, instead of mellowing their marriage, the years had merely exposed it for the sham that it was. Of course the two of them still tried to masquerade in public as a happy couple. When they and their families deemed it necessary to be seen together at this or that social event, they obediently smiled and postured and did their best to appear to enjoy each other's company. But except for an occasional drunkenly sentimental night when the years fell away and they were able briefly to rekindle the passion that had once burnt between them, they were content to live quite separate emotional and erotic lives. The older Camilla got, the more bitterly she wondered why so many women made so much fuss over men and love. From time to time she still consoled herself discreetly with an occasional lover, but usually she found shopping and warm baths more satisfying. As she had tipsily confided to Leila last month at one of their giggly girltalk lunches at the Saint Georges, a bath was superior to a man any day. With a bath, all you had to do was fill the tub with hot scented water and take off your clothes and give yourself over to a sensuously enveloping experience. When you had had enough, you simply pulled the plug and walked away from it. You never had to flatter the bathtub, or tell it how good and sexy it was, and lie about how much better it was than any other bath you had ever had.

Again she sighed under her breath as she worked at her embroidery. She would have finished this two- by three-foot tapestry years ago if she had kept doggedly at it. But, as always, the small stitches of life bored her, and she had often put it aside for as long as a year. Last week, from a growing sense of desperation, she had picked it up again after Shaykh Georges had forbidden her to go anywhere near Beirut until this latest war emergency was over. Like it or not, she was going to be cooped up here in her in-laws' mountain citadel for the duration. As she sewed she had, however, been keeping absent-minded tabs on the progress of the fighting. Unlike the lightning Six Day War back in 1967, this one was grinding on into its third bloody week. She had been as dumbfounded as everyone else at the astonishing news that the Egyptian army had managed to cross the Suez Canal. And she, too, had hardly been able to believe the evidence of her eyes when she had seen the film of captured Israeli soldiers parading with bowed heads on Arab television. Lately, however, it seemed that the tide had turned in favour of the Israelis. So long as the fighting did not touch her own life, Camilla was mostly indifferent as to who won and who lost. Yet the way the war was going, she might just make it down to Beirut this weekend after all.

This depressing scene of waiting out a losing war was so anxiously familiar that, as Camilla stitched on, her mind wandered back in time and she endured small jagged nightmare flashes of *déjà vu*. So many wars in her own lifetime, she thought, *too many*. As a little girl she remembered the bombardment of Beirut, her mother's panic, and the food shortages as the Free French fought the Vichy for control of the Levant. No sooner was the Second World War over than the Arabs and the Jews – both of them, to Camilla's mind, equally tiresome – threw themselves into their cursed wars in '48, '56, '67, and now again in '73. Sometimes the fighting even touched Beirut, which was a little too close to home for Camilla. Last May Israeli commandos had landed in the heart of the Lebanese capital and assassinated three PLO leaders in their beds. Afterwards, the city had been in turmoil for weeks, as the Palestinians and their left-wing Muslim friends had assailed the government for standing by and letting the Israelis do as they liked in Beirut. At one point the Lebanese army had actually shelled Palestinian positions in the Sabra and Borj al-Barajneh refugee camps.

Camilla plied her needle in and out, in and out, begrudging every stitch. By rights, she mused, she should have been born in a more diverting era, perhaps back in France at the idyllic time of the Sun King, when she liked to think that a beautiful woman would never have been forced to sit in a corner straining her come-hither eyes with needle and canvas. She could have dressed in fabulous gold-threaded gowns and magnificent white powdered wigs – she frowned over her needlepoint, for she was a bit sketchy in her historical details – and ridden in coaches and – *bien sûr!* – been one of the king's mistresses.

But then, as she worked hard to recover the ghost of a memory, shallow lines suddenly wrinkled her usually exquisitely smooth forehead. In an old château along the Loire in which she had been a house guest on her last holiday in France, damp stone walls had been warmed by gigantic tapestries that were not so very different from the one she had been working on for the past fifteen years. In French museums, too, she had looked down her turned-up nose at painstakingly elaborate embroideries which were said to have been stitched by this fabled queen and that notorious duchess. Could it be that, always and everywhere, while the men strutted in the limelight, even the richest women from the best families had been stuck back in corners wasting their time and talents on idiotic frippery like this needlework? Why had women always tolerated this sorry state of affairs? More to the point, why did she put up with it herself?

This germ of a revolutionary thought so distressed her that for one distracted moment her eyes wandered away from the canvas in her lap. She swore as she pricked her finger with the needle. Hastily, she sucked her finger before a drop of blood could sully the purity of the white unicorn that had taken her four years, on and off, to complete. As she stared down at the figure of the unicorn, she fancied that the mythical beast – surely a male, by the smug look of him – laughed back in her face. As savagely as if it were a spear, she stuck her needle into the unicorn's flank and tossed her handiwork aside.

Camilla leaned back in her easy chair and, defying not only Pierre but also his tyrant of a father who hated to see her or any of the other women smoking, she lit up a cigarette. Over the past few years she had been having a devil of a time keeping her weight down, but it was easier not to nibble on fattening foods when she smoked. Still, she fancied that, unlike her dissolute husband, she had not yet lost her looks. She could squeeze into an American size ten straight skirt, and there wasn't a wrinkle on her face or a sag on her body. In this sleek taupe-coloured Missoni sweater dress she had bought last month at L'Aiglon, she fancied she didn't look a day over twenty.

She narrowed her eyes as she looked across the room to where her menfolk sat listening to the war reports with exactly the same rapt attention that they paid to their favourite team's soccer matches. Again she wished that she hadn't been born here in the Middle East in this lifetime of endless wars. Yet she couldn't help counting her blessings. At least she belonged to the region's most privileged class and lived in its most sophisticated country. Her lot could have been far worse – if she had, for instance, had the bad luck to have been born a Palestinian living in a leaky tent in one of those squalid refugee camps that seemed to have sprung up on every bare patch of ground from one end of the country to the other. Or she could have been a Shia like poor, plump, pathetic Fatima. The last time Camilla had been down in Beirut, she had just settled in at Anne's for a good gossip, when who should waddle in but long-lost Fatima with the most appalling tale of woe. One of her boys was blind, another had lost both his legs, and the Israeli bombing raids in the south had forced them to spend most months squatting as refugees in Beirut's blighted southern suburbs. She and that squalling litter of children were squeezed like tiny smoked fishes into a tin shack with no running water or electricity.

Quickly Camilla turned her mind away from Fatima's wretched plight. She had her own problems. Even when she did her best to be as bright and perky as everyone always seemed to expect her to be, she was discontented with her lot in life. She blew pretty smoke rings in the air. Once, she had thought there would be so much more to life than all *this*.

Sourly she looked around the salon at the expensive knick-knacks and gew-gaws of her world. She had always taken pleasure in being surrounded by exquisitely pricey *objets d'art*, and she still did. In these last years she had made good taste her religion and shopping a devotional practice. Like a white hunter who loves to sit around an African campfire swapping tales of the morning when he felled a charging buffalo and the night when a black mamba almost slithered into his sleeping bag, she fondly remembered the afternoon she had spotted a tarnished but priceless antique silver samovar on a dusty shelf in an Amsterdam antique shop and how she had subsequently bought it the next day for a fraction of its worth.

Yet even so, she glared at that same well-polished samovar which now sat in a place of honour on a genuine Louis Seize table she had picked up for a song at a house sale in Rouen. She was beginning to come round to the heretical opinion that, in the end, none of these *things* mattered as much as she had thought. More disheartening still, she wondered if there was any essential difference between herself and a decoratively ornamental Fabergé egg. Wasn't she simply just another of the Nazrani family's expensive possessions, fetchingly displayed in the latest couture? No one took her – or what she thought of as her work – seriously. But who could blame *them*, she thought with a degree of honesty that was rare for her, when *she* had never taken *herself* seriously? She had been no more able to follow her dream of becoming a real artist than she had been to finish this tapestry. Still, from time to time, almost despite herself, she had been so inspired that she had managed to draw or paint something splendid, such as long ago when she had sketched her babies in watercolours and just last winter when she had presented Shaykh Georges with a lifelike portrait of himself in oils. Here and now, however, Camilla had to admit that, in terms of her life as well as her art, she had never been more than a dilettante. One year she dabbled in portraiture, the next year she toyed with opening an art deco gallery, another year she played with the idea of designing clothes. But none of her projects ever came to anything, and perhaps they never would. She was getting old. She would be thirty-seven in January. It was probably too late for her to try to do something exceptional with her life. Yet she was so sick of getting up each morning and going through the motions of another disappointing day. But what could she do, after all, to make her fate any different? *This* was the way it was for almost everyone. She supposed there were worse things than simply being bored. Yet she felt very sorry for herself as she stubbed out her cigarette and went back to her needlework.

But it was only a restless moment later when once again she lifted her gaze from the unfinished tapestry back to Tomas. Motherhood, she suddenly decided, provided the axes on which her life revolved. Being her son's mother and her mother's daughter had mattered far more to her than being her husband's wife. Her relationship with Tomas had moved her more than anything else she had ever experienced. Her two younger sons were nice little chaps, but her heart belonged to Tomas. Her eldest son had always been at the top of his class at school. Everyone always commented on his manners, his charm and his sterling character. He didn't even smoke cigarettes, let alone – like most of the other rich boys in his school – indulge in hashish or whisky. Last summer, at one of his cousin's weddings, he had even refused to partake of the champagne toasts.

It occurred to her, however, watching the histrionic

play of emotions on her son's open face as he listened to what must be bad news from the war front, that Tomas might after all have a flaw. *He could turn into a fanatic*, she thought in a moment of visionary clarity that Madame Kismet might have envied, *and cause us terrible heartache*. Was it natural, after all, for a teenage boy to turn down a glass of champagne? Tomas had caused a minor scandal at that wedding when he had proclaimed, in stentorian tones, that champagne was a 'bourgeois corruption'. For once, even though she would never have admitted it out loud, she had agreed with her husband. It was true, darling Tomas *had* slipped far too much under the influence of what Pierre called 'those dirty little Communists' who were, as he colourfully put it, 'multiplying like cockroaches' down in Beirut. Despite her husband's efforts to nip these radical leanings in the bud, she suspected that Tomas still managed to run around Beirut not only with the Reds but also – yes, she had to admit it, even though she adored Leila and always would – with that dreadfully assertive new breed of wild-eyed Palestinians with their body odours and their uncouth manners and those guns they were always waving around in the air. Leila was always trying to make saints of them in that column of hers in *an-Nahar*, but those PLO terrorists were devils.

Camilla tried to be serene and concentrate on her needlework. Now, as always, she did her best never to worry about anything. As Mama always blithely said, worry made wrinkles, and wrinkles gave away a woman's age. She might have misgivings about her son's absurd leftist flirtation, but she didn't see any reason to panic about it. She hoped that if she paid it no heed, it – like so many of the unpleasant wrinkles of life – would simply go away. Just last month, when Tomas had sat her down and ardently tried to convert her to his complicated dialectical beliefs, she had been moved by this same impulse and had prettily put her hands over her ears and simply refused to listen.

She darted another quick look at her son. As she always said to Pierre and her father-in-law when she was sticking up for her son, Tomas was simply *très jeune* and *trop idéaliste*. She was sure he would outgrow this outlandish leftist phase as soon as Pierre enrolled him in the militia the family had recently formed for its defence. These days every faction – the Druze, the Nasserists and the major Christian clans – each had their own private army. Just last month in Beirut, Camilla had watched the 'Phalange' militia goose-stepping in military formation near the Corniche. Strutting about in uniforms was the latest rage. Tomas was simply caught up in the mood of the moment. The boy was hot-blooded, that was all, and infatuated with the Kalashnikov glamour of the Palestinian Resistance. But in the end, Tomas would never turn against his family and Christian values. Just to be on the safe side, however, she intended to seal his future by marrying him off as soon as she decently could to some luscious Christian beauty queen – perhaps someone like that red-haired charmer from Ashrafiya who had been named 'Miss Lebanese Apple' last year. Still, even though she was certain that all this would turn out well in the end, she thanked her lucky stars that Pierre and his father had not got wind of Tomas's puppy-love infatuation with Leila's daughter. Miriam was a splendid girl, but *both* families would agree that such a match would have been made neither in a Christian nor a Muslim heaven. Already she had her calculating eyes wide open every time an eligible mademoiselle home on holiday from her French convent school made an appearance at a charity ball or under the striped umbrellas of one of the predominantly Christian beaches at Dabarja in Jounieh.

Camilla smiled a slow, contented smile as she worked the fiddly petals of a blue flower that fell almost under the hooves of the unicorn. She would insist that they hold Tomas's wedding here, in that enchanted chapel where she herself had married Pierre. It would happen in the spring, when the hills were aflame with wild flowers. She would fly in a chef from France to make all sorts of exotic concoctions, and she would ask Mama to coax her jet-set friends to fly over for the occasion. Afterwards, everyone would tell her that never in the Republic of Lebanon had there been such a fantastic wedding. Yet she frowned as the memory of her own nuptials, which she mostly succeeded in repressing, came flooding back. The blood, *Yaadra*, O Holy Virgin, the blood . . .

She felt a terrible premonition and looked back up in alarm at Tomas, whom she had already been carrying in her womb on that day of days. But no, her boy still sat there safe and sound, hunched up close to the radio. Surreptitiously she crossed herself to ward off any evil spirits that she might unwittingly have conjured up by harking back to the curse of that old fortune-teller in the Crescent cabaret. Immediately, then, she was ashamed of this evidence of her lingering superstition. She wasn't some gullible peasant who believed in love charms and curses that could be passed on from one generation to the next. At that thought, she shuddered. The gypsy had foreseen so much blood in hers and Lebanon's future. Were all of them – and all they held dear – at risk?

The radio blared with a sudden burst of martial music, and for once Camilla was as eager as the men as she leaned forward to catch the latest news bulletin. Desperately she wanted to be reassured that all was still right in her world.

The announcer's voice rose an octave higher than usual as he proclaimed in shrill Arabic that today the Palestine war had come home to Lebanon. This morning three strategically placed bombs had exploded underwater, off the Lebanese coast, damaging the cable that linked Beirut to Marseilles. Since then all communications between Lebanon and the West had been severed.

Even as the broadcaster continued, saying that afternoon editions of Beirut newspapers were debating whether this sabotage was the work of Israeli frogmen or of Arab radicals protesting Lebanon's non-involvement in the current war, Shaykh Georges was on his feet and dialling the operator to confirm the news. He rasped into the mouthpiece that he wanted to place a person-to-person call to France, and only a second later he flung the telephone back on to its cradle in disgust. 'We are cut off,' he snarled as he began to pace back and forth. 'I can't get Paris! *Intolérable!* They go too far!'

He might have said more if Pierre hadn't flicked on the television set and the announcer dropped a second bombshell. Only moments ago in Beirut, a detachment of Lebanese army troops had sealed off an entire section of the central Hamra district after gunmen had seized control of the Bank of America.

'*Nam!*' Tomas yelled out in triumph. 'Yes!'

Camilla dropped her needlework, turned pale, and ran over to her son's side. If Tomas triggered another ferocious political row with his father and grandfather, she wanted to be there to intercede on his behalf. She put a warning hand on her son's shoulder. But Tomas, who was as avid as the rest of them for more details of the incident, merely leaned forward and turned off the radio so they could hear what was being said on the television news.

The crisis, the announcer said, had broken less than an hour ago when five gunmen from a group calling itself the Arab Communist Organization had slipped into the bank, taken an undetermined number of bank employees and customers hostage, and then demanded a ten million dollar ransom for the Arab war effort.

Motorists and pedestrians were warned to avoid Hamra Street, which was sealed off by government soldiers until further notice.

'Communist scum!' Pierre's face had turned redder. 'I'd teach them a thing or two if I could get my hands on them.'

'Before long, you may.' Again Shaykh Georges stormed over to the telephone, and this time he dialled a number in the Presidential Palace. But the lines were all engaged, and so once more he threw the phone back on its cradle.

Camilla dug her fingers deep into her son's shoulder. 'Sssh,' she cooed, just as she used to do when keeping him quiet as a baby.

All his neck muscles were tensed for a fight, and his mouth was set in a grim line, but Tomas kept silent as he listened to the sketchy details on the television.

This was, the announcer reminded his audience, not the first that had been heard of this radical splinter group. First last spring and then repeatedly last summer, the Arab Communist Organization had robbed other Lebanese banks to raise money for their causes. This same group had made headlines earlier this year by staging an attack on a Beirut supermarket.

As they watched, the announcer was handed a sheet of paper with another bulletin. He stared into the camera as he read it out like an ultimatum.

The government had just refused to negotiate with the gunmen. It was believed that at any time the troops could be ordered to storm the bank.

'Kill the devils.' Shaykh Georges struck his fists one on top of the other. 'Make an example. Let them know we won't tolerate this sort of terrorism in our country.'

'It's the Palestinians again who are behind this.' Pierre poured himself more whisky from the bottle by his side and took a deep gulp. 'They're all Communists anyway. This was a good country – a wonderful country! The best country in the world! – until we made the mistake of letting in the Palestinians. They're the reason for all our problems. We gave them an inch, and they took a mile. And still they're not content! They'll take everything we have here unless we finally stand up and defend what's ours! Mark my words, there will be no peace in the Lebanon until we root out the last of them!' He ground his foot into the Persian carpet. 'We will crush them! If it's necessary, we'll chuck them in the sea. They'll pollute it, but that's too bad.'

Tomas leaped to his feet, and his eyes blazed as he stared down in hatred at his father.

But Camilla stepped between them. 'Tomas! Please don't say anything. Please! For me!'

He stared into his mother's eyes for a long moment, and then his eyes fell. Without another word, he turned on his heel and stormed out of the salon. He slammed the door behind him, and a moment later they heard the whoosh of his sports car pulling out of the driveway.

The sudden silence in the main salon of the Château Croisé was shattered by the martial music blaring on the television.

Four months later, Tomas and Miriam shivered as the cold February wind cut through them on their early morning picketing shift. More to warm themselves than to dramatize their cause, they shuffled back and forth in an elongated circle with their comrades outside the spare parts factory in the blighted southern suburbs of Beirut. Tomas and Miriam were still too young to undergo military training for a United Front guerrilla unit, but they were old enough to stand up and be counted on the picket line. This strike, like so many that had been called in the months of unrest that had wracked Lebanon since last autumn's Middle East war, was a combined 'National Front' action of the Palestinians, the Communists, the Druze Progressive Socialist Party, and the rest of the country's leftist factions.

When Miriam coughed, Tomas took off his jacket and – despite her protests – wrapped it around her shoulders. 'You should have done as I said, Mimi, and stayed home today.'

'It's not so cold, really.' Yet as she smiled up at him, she snuggled down inside his jacket, grateful not only for its warmth but because it was something of *his* next to her. 'I can stand it if you can.'

He shook his head and looked anxiously across the street, where the lorries of the government soldiers who had arrived during the night were drawn up in formation. So far, as they drank their tea and ate their breakfasts, the troops had done nothing more alarming than slouch sullenly against parked cars and direct fierce looks at the picketers. But they looked so big, with their guns. And there were so many of them. Why, Tomas wondered, had the government sent so many soldiers for such a little strike? These past tumultuous months had made him a seasoned picketer, and he fancied there was trouble in the air this morning. Here, at this obscure Beirut factory, the government might finally mean to teach the left a violent lesson. 'Last night, at Headquarters, I heard Hussein Ibrahim saying there might be trouble here today. It would have been better if you, and all the rest of the women, had stayed at home.'

'It's our struggle as much as yours.' She adored Tomas and meant to marry him as soon as she was old enough. But she was not about to tolerate his treating her in the reactionary and patronizing way in which men – especially Arab men – had always treated their women. Their revolutionary generation was going to make everything different, even – or perhaps especially – the relationships between men and women. She and Tomas, as committed Marxists and as members of the Palestinian United Front, had been over this same ground many times. But if she had to remind him once again what the new order they were working for meant in personal as well as political terms, then she gladly would. 'Here, comrade.' She shrugged out of his jacket and handed it back to him. 'Look to yourself. Don't do me any favours.'

He was as hot-tempered as she was, and he opened his mouth to retort that it might be dangerous to be on this particular picket line on this particular morning, and that he loved her and wanted her to be safe, that was all. But instead he meekly put his jacket back on and bit his tongue. Like it or not, he had learned the hard way that he had to bear this sort of political rebuke stoically. He had been criticized before at cadre meetings, not only by Miriam but also by some of the other women, for slipping back into the sexist patterns by which their fathers had always oppressed their mothers. Even though, in his young man's romantic heart, he still believed that it wasn't bad to want to protect the girl he still possessively regarded as *his*, he now knew that he was supposed to keep all such Neanderthal yearnings to himself.

Yet Miriam was still righteously angry. Without another word to him, she went over to another of the strikers and insisted that she be allowed to carry one of the heavier placards. She waved it energetically in the air as she marched ahead of him on the picket line.

Gloomily he trudged behind her, aware that it would probably be most of the morning before this particular storm of hers passed and she forgave him. By then she would doubtless be all worked up about some snippet of news someone had heard on the radio or some outrageous comment someone else had made at a political rally. She would forget their squabble and go rummaging in the sack of food she had brought from home. Sunnily she would offer him an orange or a pitta bread sandwich, and he would fall in love with her all over again.

But until then, he blew his own hot breath on his freezing fingers as he marked time on the picket line. Idly he wondered, as he circled aimlessly behind the other comrades, how many political and industrial actions he had taken part in since he stormed out of the Château Croisé during the October War. Remembering that day, he could almost hear the news bulletin on the television about the seizure of the Bank of America. He recalled, too, the bloody dénouement the next day, when government troops stormed the bank and martyred two of the comrades.

Tomas shivered and again looked across the street at the troops who – it now seemed to him – were spoiling for a fight. Yes, he was sure of it, he could almost smell the blood in the air. Once begun, would there ever be an end to this violence that was rending his country asunder? He had just celebrated his fifteenth birthday, yet sometimes he felt so old and jaded, so used up. What must it be like to be really old like his mother or father or even his grandfather? Unbidden, Tomas recalled the last time he had seen them all together, that day at the château. If his mother hadn't stepped between them, he would finally have taken a punch at his father. *That bastard*, Tomas thought. He couldn't remember when he hadn't hated his father. Though one of the counsellors at school had once suggested that something must have gone wrong between the two of them when he was quite young, Tomas had thought long and hard about that, but he hadn't been able to remember anything specific, only that his father had always mistreated his mother. She was so beautiful, and sweet, and he had known even when he was a little boy that she was utterly unable to take care of herself. Always Tomas had yearned to be the big man who could protect her. He still did. He supposed that longing was sexist, too, but he didn't care.

He thrust his clenched fists into the pockets of his

jacket and willed himself to think of something – anything! – other than his wretched father. He hadn't been back home since that day when he had stormed out. At first, amid the confusion that had reigned because of the '73 war, he had got away with staying in a comrade's seedy apartment down by the port. But then, when the war finally ended and his school reopened, Miriam had talked her parents into letting him stay in one of their spare rooms. It was nice, being so close to Miriam all the time. Of course he had never done anything racier than slip his tongue inside her mouth, and he didn't intend to, not until they were older anyway. Still, he was able to be with her now most of the time, instead of having to make do with an occasional trip to one of the cinemas on al-Hamra. It was gratifying, too, to live under a roof where everyone believed in the inevitable triumph of the Palestinian cause. Back at the château, every time politics came up, he either had to lie or endure another shouting match with his father. But since Aunt Leila herself was active in the Resistance, she all but gave them a wink and a nod every time they went off on another United Front mission. Yet Aunt Leila and his own mother were old college friends, and so as soon as he had arrived on her doorstep Miriam's mother had rung up the Château Croisé to announce where he was. Tomas hated how his mother cried every time she came down to Beirut to plead with him to come back home. But apparently Shaykh Georges had talked all this over with Leila's husband at the Kit Kat Club, and it had been agreed that he could finish up the school year staying with Miriam's family. After that, he gathered from something he had overheard Aunt Leila saying, his family had plans to ship him off to some fancy fascist school in Switzerland.

Over my dead body, Tomas thought defiantly as he walked round and round in that weary picket line slouch he had perfected in the past months of nearly constant political agitation and industrial action. This was his school now, not some Swiss bourgeois playground, but here, on the front lines in the revolutionary situation that was Beirut. Because of all the unrest in the city since the October War, his school had recently been shut more than it had been open. For, as soon as the fighting on the battlefields had stopped, Beirut's radicals had taken up the struggle with a vengeance. In meetings and fevered parades, in every smoky café on al-Hamra, in fancy salons within sight of the Corniche and in crowded tenements and teeming refugee camps, the left had rallied to the Palestinian cause. Tomas especially liked to take Miriam to the Horseshoe café, where all the famous artists and writers sat sipping their La Ziza or Falcon beer. When he was by himself, he headed for the Wimpy bar where the fellows from school hung out, whistling at pretty girls and talking of revolution. For even though turncoat Arabs in Cairo or Amman might be willing to betray their principles for the sacks of American gold that it was said that Henry Kissinger was throwing hither and yon, here in Beirut the Rejectionist Front reigned supreme. There would be no negotiations with the Zionist state, and no peace either. 'Revolution Till Victory!' That sacred principle, Tomas thought grimly, was worth more than the price of any individual life, his and Miriam's included. After a *fedayeen* raid into occupied Palestine, when chilling posters of the martyred comrades were plastered overnight on shop windows and on walls in all the radical Beirut neighbourhoods, he and Miriam would sometimes wonder aloud if and when it would be their turn to die for the cause. *Fedayeen* were worshipped like rock stars. For Beirut's younger generation, death had taken on a glamour of its own. Those who had met, touched, and perhaps loved one of the fallen comrades would reverently repeat his remembered words as though the most commonplace remark was a truth echoing from beyond the grave. Just the other night, when he and Miriam were sitting out by her swimming pool in the moonlight, he had been inspired to say to her that everyone died, and that was that; but to die for what was right was beautiful, like a poem or a flower. She had sighed then, and creeping closer to him on the chaise longue, instead of kissing him had told him what was written in the Koran about the end of each man's days. When every one of us is born, she whispered, Allah marks down in the Great Book of Life the day and even the time when we must die, and nothing that we can do can ever hurry or delay that fated deadline. The only choice we have, she murmured, is how to die, and for what . . . As they gazed up at the crescent moon, they had admitted to one another that they longed – a little – for the immortality of a sweet death.

Yes, it was wonderful, Tomas thought as he walked behind his girl on the picket line, how they agreed on everything that mattered. Shoulder to shoulder, identically clad in their khaki soldier's shirts and imported American blue jeans, they had marched in demonstrations and chanted at rallies. In December, though neither of them was old enough to go to university yet, they had both been thrilled to join a radical student strike at the American University of Beirut to protest at Kissinger's first 'shuttle diplomacy' visit to the Middle East. Afterwards, across the street from the campus, just as though they were real AUB students, they had eaten hamburgers at the famous Uncle Sam's and then held hands and whispered sweet nothings in each other's ears. They had loved feeling that they were in the eye of the tornado, and so just before Christmas when students up in Tripoli had called a strike to protest at the high cost of living, they had been two of the first to sign up for shifts on the picket line.

Remembering how that strike had drawn blood, Tomas surreptitiously looked back across the street at the government troops. It had been tense like this, too, up at Tripoli, just before all hell had broken loose. But on that other picket line they hadn't faced soldiers armed as if for battle. In Tripoli, it had only been the tame Lebanese police who had stood between them and victory. Yet when the policemen had charged that picket line in Tripoli, three students had been seriously injured and one policeman killed by a stray bullet that had been fired from heaven knew whose gun. In the bitter aftermath of that violent strike, Tomas and Miriam had waded deeper into radical action. They had flung themselves from one end of the country to the other, joining student demonstrations wherever the grapevine said they were about to be called. By the New Year, the two of them had been exhausted. But gamely, because they believed in the class struggle and the importance of supporting classic trade union industrial action, they had gone back on the picket line here in Beirut when firemen and night watchmen had staged a three-week strike for money and better working conditions. No sooner was that dispute settled than students and workers had called strikes in Beirut, Sidon and Tyre over the rising cost of living.

Tomas reflected, as he greeted a fresh batch of his friends and comrades who had just arrived to swell their growing ranks on the picket line, that he and Miriam had rallied to so many causes in the past few months that he couldn't have said, this morning at the spare parts factory, what were the particular issues of this one. Purely and simply, whenever and wherever a strike was called, they answered. All that mattered was solidarity, commitment and brotherhood. The radical strategy was to use a range of international and domestic issues – everything from a US-sponsored Middle East peace plan to tuition fees at Lebanese universities – to keep the pot boiling. Here in Beirut especially, everyone was braced for more political fireworks. The trade union federation was threatening to call a general strike over straight economic issues, and student groups were organizing another round of demonstrations to protest against the continuing spectre of Kissinger's shuttle diplomacy. In such times, when the cafés were full of intoxicating talk of revolution, it was heady to be fiercely young and passionately sure of the rightness of the cause. But just last night, hanging around down at Headquarters, Tomas had heard Hussein Ibrahim cautioning the comrades not to be overconfident and never to underestimate the enemy. They were living in a pregnant revolutionary situation, Hussein had reminded them, and the forces of history would ensure that they would win. But they could not expect the ruling class to give up without a fight. Soon, Hussein had warned, it was going to come down to a shooting war between 'them' and 'us'.

Yet he wished, as he heard the approaching rumble of another convoy of military lorries, that Miriam hadn't insisted on joining him on the picket line this morning. Instead of blurting out that he wanted her to go home because he feared for her safety, he should have been cunning and dreamed up some pretext to send her back to her family's villa in the hills. He could have said he needed some political pamphlets he had left behind.

His face creased like that of a man as old as his grandfather as he watched more troops being unloaded across the street. By rights the two of them should call it a day now and go home. Their shift was almost over. They had been on duty for five hours, and no one would fault them for letting the other brothers and sisters carry on the struggle. Yet he knew very well that she would never consent to leave just as everything was hotting up here on the picket line. Perhaps, he thought with growing desperation, what he should have done to get Miriam away from here was to whisper ever so seductively in her ear, just as though guns were some secret love talk of their own, that she should go fetch them their treasure. He was certain she would have gone home for the Kalashnikov he kept oiled and loaded under his bed. She loved it, fondled it, and had confided that she even dreamed about it as much as he did. For, sick and tired of hearing that he wasn't old enough yet to take up arms for the cause, he had last month given up hounding the United Front to issue him a gun of his own. Instead, he had used some of the spending money his indulgent mother still slipped him on the side to buy this gun that he had longed for just as, not so long ago, he had lusted after a toy truck or a cowboy hat. Although he knew that the going rate for a used Kalashnikov on the thriving Beirut black market was a thousand Lebanese pounds – or about one hundred and twenty pounds sterling, because he was so young they had skinned him and made him pay fifteen hundred lira. Yet he couldn't complain. That gun was a bargain at any price. When he held it in his hands, he felt like a real man. His Kalashnikov was so light, so pretty really, and as lithe as a woman. On weekends, he and Miriam drove up in the mountains and, just as they had once played hide and seek in the rocks, they now fired off giddy rounds and pretended they were *fedayeen* about to liberate Palestine. They weren't the only ones to use deserted eyries as shooting galleries. These days, since virtually all the splintered factions in the country had formed their own private armies, it was hard to find a quiet spot for a peaceable picnic without hearing the delicate rat-tat-tat of machine-gun fire and the clumsy boom-boom of heavier mortars. His mother had told him that his two younger brothers, who were not quite fourteen, already had their own American M-16s. After he had left home, his father had begun teaching them to be crack shots in the family militia.

Tomas took off his jacket and threw it over a pile of leaflets on the pavement. It was well past noon. In the past few moments, now that the sun was finally out, even the political temperature seemed to have risen. The pavement was packed with seasoned demonstrators chanting slogans at the top of their lungs. Across the street, where not long ago the men in uniform had propped their guns up against car bumpers as they yawned and sipped their tea, the soldiers had their guns at the ready with their fingers only centimetres away from the firing pins. Worse, just as it had been in Tripoli right before the police had charged the picket line, the soldiers were drawn up smartly in military ranks. Any second now, a full-scale confrontation could break out. Tensely the strikers and the soldiers stared across the narrow gulf of the empty street.

Miriam, who all this while had been proudly carrying her placard, finally passed it on to the fellow next to her. She flexed and rubbed her sore fingers as she looked anxiously across the street at the ferocious line of soldiers. When she turned her head to dart one questioning glance over her shoulder at Tomas, for once her bravado failed and she looked very vulnerable and as scared as any other twelve-year-old girl would be. Promptly Tomas stepped forward and put his arm around her, relieved that finally their little tiff had been forgotten and forgiven. Without feeling obliged to say one reconciling word to each other, they once again marched in step together.

Then suddenly, it seemed at exactly the same moment, the chanting rose to a fever pitch and the line of soldiers surged forward into the street. There were screams on the picket line, and some of the strikers picked up stones and flung them at the soldiers. At once all was chaos on the narrow pavement as everyone tried to run, some towards the soldiers, others away from them.

In the pandemonium, everything was such a blur that later, when Miriam tried to reconstruct every significant second of what had happened, she could only recall at first the noise, the shoving, the panic, and Tomas's arms around her. They clung to each other in the maelstrom, and Tomas was shouting words she could not quite make out when, oddly, over and above all the other nightmare sounds, she swore later that she distinctly heard the deadly hard click of metal.

Tomas must have heard it, too, she decided later. Or maybe it was just that he had guessed what was about to happen from the glint of the sun hitting the aimed barrels of the gun.

For Miriam, in the next few anguished moments time slowed and almost stopped. She seemed to step back and become more of an observer than a participant, for later she was able to recall everything that happened as a separate and discrete set of actions. First she saw the most excruciatingly frightened look in Tomas's eyes. Then he seemed to master his fear since, at the last possible instant, just before the fusillade hit the exposed flank of the picket line, it was Miriam's safety that concerned him. In a reflex as quick and true as when his father had shielded his mother at the altar on their wedding day, Tomas tried to knock her out of the line of fire. 'No!' she screeched, resisting him as he bore down on her. She was still trying to wriggle away when she heard the crack of shots as all at once, in response to a shouted command, the soldiers fired at the strikers. Tomas cried out, and she felt his body spurt even closer against hers. She screamed as he shuddered on top of her, and even as she stared into his eyes and called out his name, she saw his eyes change – she was never to forget how they faded from pain to terror to nothing . . .

Miriam swooned and blacked out before she hit the pavement. Finally Tomas fell on top of her, a dead weight.

Her mother was bending over her in the hospital room when Miriam came to, it seemed like a lifetime later, although it was scarcely two hours.

'Mimi! Oh, thank God, Mimi!' Leila swept her daughter into her arms, while beside her Mustafa shut his eyes in relief and breathed a little prayer of thanksgiving. 'When Anne called, she told us', Leila rattled on, 'that she thought you only had a slight concussion but apart from that, *you* were all right, even though . . .' Hastily Leila once again hugged the girl as she veered away from the dangerous completion of that sentence. 'Then, when we rushed down here and finally found you in that awful ward with all those others, my God, *habibi*, we thought the worst! Mustafa had to call the hospital director to get you a private room. Imagine! The director himself! Even Anne couldn't help us. They nearly ran out of beds, with so many . . .' Leila reached over and smoothed her daughter's hair back from her face. 'You had blood all over you. If they'd told me, I would have brought down something else for you to change into.' Nervously she pulled the sheet up higher and tucked it securely under her chin, like a napkin. 'You had blood all over you!'

Miriam stared up at her mother, and as the memory of what had happened washed over her, tears welled into her eyes. *His blood. That must have been his blood. His.* She looked down in horror at herself. Yes, she could see it clearly under the fold of sheeting. She was still wearing the clothes she had on in the demonstration. Under the fresh white sheet his blood was on her blue shirt. Miriam shut her eyes so she wouldn't have to see his blood spilled on her. She forced the only word that counted out of her lips. 'Tomas?' When no one answered, her eyes shot open. She stared up at her mother. 'Tell me.'

'Not now, *habibi*.' Leila looked to her husband for support, but Mustafa failed her once again by weakly glancing away. He was as helpless in the family as he had been in the government. 'We'll talk later, once we get you home and get you out of those clothes, and after you've had a nice long rest. That's what Anne said to do. She was here. She had a look at you herself. And she said that as soon as you came to, we should take you home and make certain you rest.'

But Miriam was her mother's daughter and would not be deterred. Steadily her black eyes stared into her mother's. 'He's dead, isn't he?'

Leila hesitated but then she nodded her head and once again took Miriam into her arms and held her tight. They remained like that for only a moment, however, before Miriam pulled away. She bit her lip but did not cry. 'Let's go home now, Ummie.'

So it was that not long after, Miriam haltingly walked in her bloodstained shirt and jeans between her parents down a corridor of the American University Hospital. When the girl slipped on the slick tiles, Leila and Mustafa steadied her.

As they approached the main doors, they could hear heartrending sobs coming from someone in a wheelchair. They drew more tightly together and averted their eyes from the sight of such unashamed suffering. They themselves would never break down and carry on so in public. Uncontrollable grief like that of the pitiful woman in the wheelchair belonged at home behind closed doors and within the snug arms of the family, not here, where strangers could intrude. But as they knew from other visits to sick aunts and recovering cousins here in this hospital there were often pathetic old widow women from the villages breaking down like this where everyone could see them. They were almost upon the source of the commotion when suddenly they realized who it was.

A hysterically weeping Camilla screamed and moaned in the wheelchair, while Pierre hovered helplessly above her and Anne crouched in front of her trying to calm her down.

Leila gaped at her old friend. Over the years she must have seen Camilla cry hundreds of times, but never had she seen her like this. If it weren't for Pierre, and Camilla's long fall of platinum hair, and that three-piece brown knit Yves Saint Laurent suit of hers, Leila might not even have recognized her. Her face was bloated and red, her black eyeliner was smeared all over her eyesockets, and her mascara had run down her cheeks. But it was the eyes themselves that were horrifying. Wide open and staring unfocused at the blank wall above Anne's face, they oozed like a mortal wound that would never heal. Leila let go of her daughter and took a step towards her friend. 'Camilla. Oh God, Camilla . . .'

The head jerked up, and the Medusa eyes flashed. 'You!' Camilla was screaming. '*You!*' She half rose in a lunge from the wheelchair. 'You said you'd take care of him, that you'd treat him like your own son. You! It's your fault!'

'Now, Camilla . . .' Anne stroked her arm and tried to restrain her. 'I still think', she said in an undertone to Pierre, 'that you should have let me give her a sedative. It was too much for her, seeing him like . . .' Distractedly she stroked Camilla's hair. She was accustomed to assuaging the grief of strangers but now that she needed to comfort someone she had been close to for most of her life, she could not find the right words. 'It's all right, honey. It's going to be all right.'

'I'm so sorry.' Leila helplessly looked down at her friend. 'We all are. Mustafa and Mimi. Mimi . . .' Leila gave her daughter a stricken look, afraid that the girl, too, would break down. 'Mustafa, why don't you take her home now? I'll stay here with Camilla a little, but you take Mimi home.'

'I don't need you, or your kind!' Until now Camilla's voice had been high and shrill, but now it was pitched low with hate. '*Palestinians!* It's your fault, all of you!'

Leila froze just as she was about to bend and try to hug Camilla. 'You are overwrought.'

'You and your kind, you killed my son, just as if you'd pulled the trigger.'

Leila recoiled. 'Careful,' she warned her old friend.

But there was no stopping Camilla. For the past sixteen years of her marriage, she had heard her husband and father talking their brand of politics. Now their hate spewed out of her. 'You came here, and we let you in, treated you like our family. And now look what's happened! Scum! If you weren't here, none of this would have happened. Palestinians!' Camilla spat in Leila's face.

'You go too far.' Leila drew back her hand and might have hit Camilla if Anne hadn't intervened.

'Leila! Can't you see she's hysterical?' Anne urgently gestured to Mustafa. 'Get her home, will you please?' She put her arm around Miriam and ushered the three of them out of the door.

When she turned back, Camilla was doubled up in the wheelchair, muttering over and over like a madwoman as she wept. 'Dead! My son is dead! Tomas is dead!'

Anne stared down at her broken friend. What next? Where would it end? She very much feared that, here in Beirut, all of them were living on the rim of a smoking volcano.

Chapter 19

Six months into the civil war, at one of Leila's crowded salons, Anne smiled coolly and pretended she was protected by a plastic bubble so that no one could see her, touch her, or hurt her as she wafted through the overheated throng. She regretted coming to this Saturday night soirée, but it would have been harder to say 'no' to Leila than it had been to brave the firefights and roadblocks of Beirut's warring streets.

And so here she was, she thought, alone in a crowd yet again, smiling remotely at this one and that one as she searched for an out of the way corner where she could pull herself together and not be expected to say anything witty or charming or politically astute to anyone about anything for at least ten minutes.

It had been terrible in the operating room tonight – a far cry from the incidents that had led to the death of Tomas a year and a half before. After months of on-and-off fighting punctuated by ceasefires, appeals for calm, and optimistic predictions that the 'incidents' were all over now, the civil war had come back to Beirut with a vengeance. Last month, September 1975, the militant Christian Phalange militia had set up its big guns near the souks by Martyrs' Square and systematically destroyed Beirut's oldest commercial landmarks. Then, in the intense fighting of the last few days, militant Muslim militias had launched their own offensive in the fashionable downtown Kantari quarter. Every night ferocious fighting had raged for control of some of the city's highest vantage points in what was being called 'the battle of the hotels'. In the process Beirut's most luxurious landmarks – from the Saint Georges Hotel to the Phoenicia – were being destroyed. For weeks now, the American University Hospital had been flooded with the wounded. All those dying young men . . .

Anne shook her head. She needed time to collect herself before she could put on her party face and be sociable tonight. She would run screaming into the night if somebody's aunt badgered her to forget all her other patients and devote herself entirely to the care of a wounded Muslim warrior who had been rushed to the hospital just this afternoon or – worse, far worse – if some bloated hypochondriac of a politician backed her into a corner and tried to bully her into giving him free advice about the delicate state of his digestion. In happier days, in the perpetual party that used to be Beirut, she had been adept at fending off professional inquiries with a quip or a laugh. Everybody who was anybody had always tried to use her to jockey his relatives into the hospital's best rooms or simply to sound her out about whatever ailed him and his wife and all his family including the dogs and the cats. Now, even with the war on, almost everyone she knew still couldn't resist the opportunity to chat up a doctor for free. But tonight, after being pressed into doing a double shift in the operating room, she was too tired for that game, or any other game either. These days – with all the wounded, the dead and the dying – she was always so tired. And thirsty, too.

A grinning white-jacketed Sudanese waiter all but tap-danced towards her carrying aloft a silver tray that tinkled enticingly with iced drinks. Anne caught his eye, inclined her head, and when he jigged closer she prudently took not one but two gin and tonics. She wished she had a third hand so she could help herself to three. Since the civil war had ignited last spring, she thought, they were all becoming alcoholics. If the bombs didn't get them, the gin would.

'Anne! Darling!' From out of nowhere Leila hit her like a hundred-and-six-millimetre cannon. They kissed, hugged, kissed again, and then stood back and looked each other over as though they hadn't been together for ages instead of only the day before yesterday.

'You look terrific,' Anne assured her as fervently as if she truly meant it. But these days she thought that Leila, who used to have such good understated British taste, looked like a terrorist in drag. How, Anne wondered, could she continue to dress up in those tight jeans and army shirts, and at the same time incongruously wrap a sultan's ransom in gold around her neck and wrists? But at least, Anne noticed with relief, she had left off her cartridge belt tonight as well as those impossible lace-up combat boots. Leila's shapely aristocratic feet, with the toenails lacquered to a glossy Chinese dragon red, were back where they belonged, tottering in her sleek hundred-dollar Charles Jourdan high-heeled sandals. Still, Anne had to admit as she glanced back up at her friend's radiant face, Leila did in a way look terrific. Like so many others here at this party, the fevered war activity seemed to agree with her. She still wrote her thrice-weekly political column for *an-Nahar*, and in addition she was one of the leading social and intellectual lights of Yasser Arafat's moderate Fatah wing of the PLO. But instead of looking exhausted, she seemed younger and sexier, as though she enjoyed dancing to these dangerous new rhythms. I wish I could be more like you, Anne thought wistfully, so *alive*, like you.

'This must be the new dress! Silk, isn't it?' Leila pinched the sleeve of Anne's ivory-coloured shirtwaist which, although bought only last week during one of the ceasefires, was just as dated and matronly as all the other vaguely surgical clothes she always wore. 'But no, I forgot how you Americans love your natural fibres. Last month's American *Vogue* said that very thing. Cotton is in! Cheap *chic*! And, who knows, maybe you're right. My maid is always making a mess of my silks!' As Leila brightly chattered on in that incessant womanly nattering she reserved for only her very best friends, she could not resist reaching out again and flipping Anne's collar up to a more dashing angle and opening the top two buttons in a sort of impromptu *décolleté*. 'Yes, that's better, much better.' Not content with reshaping the lines of Anne's dress, Leila proceeded to pluck at the severe bun on the top of her head so that soft tendrils of hair curled like a frame around her face. 'You have such pretty hair. So glossy. I would kill for hair like that. And you have such a pretty face, darling, when you smile.'

Anne obediently smiled on cue. She had long ago

given up minding how Leila alternately tried to entice, flatter, bully, and shame her into that slickly fashionable world where image was character. Leila meant well. In a moment, as always, Anne knew her friend would abandon this doomed crusade of hers and relax back into their old camaraderie.

She watched in fascination as Leila fished what appeared to be a hand-rolled cigarette out of her pocket along with a pack of kitchen matches. In the old days, Leila was never without her Craven As, her gold-plated Dunhill lighter and her ebony cigarette holder. Still, even in these war-torn and revolutionary times, she couldn't believe that Leila would dare to smoke what appeared to be a hashish cigarette in front of all these people. Mustafa was no longer Prime Minister in the much-lampooned new 'National Salvation' government that the watchdog Syrians had forced Lebanon into accepting after hostilities had begun earlier this year. But he was still very much in the public eye for his outspoken advocacy of his wife's Palestinian cause. Anne had been appalled at the virulence of the attacks on him in the Maronite Christian press. She had heard, too, that the Syrians were out to get him because of his opposition to their plans to make Lebanon into little more than a province of Syria. With so much attention still focused on her husband, it was foolhardy for Leila to court more public censure. Hashish was certainly just as sedating as alcohol, and undoubtedly the best crop in the world was grown here in the Bekaa Valley. Yet even in these troubled times, with the civilization they had known collapsing all around them, the poppy usually remained a secret and forbidden pleasure.

Leila stuck the cigarette between her highly glossed scarlet lips and noisily lit it with a sulphurous flash of a match. 'So tell me, did you ring Camilla as I asked you to?'

Anne nodded and sniffed suspiciously at the smoke.

But no, all she could smell was nicotine. Sensation-seeking Leila was only taking pains to make it look as though she were smoking hashish in public. This was probably some perverse new fashion she was trying to set. 'She sounded okay. But she's still not herself.' She sipped at her drink, reluctant to discuss her failed efforts as peacemaker. 'I told her you asked about her.'

Leila waited, but when Anne said nothing more, she ecstatically shut her heavy-lidded eyes as she inhaled. 'And?'

'And nothing.' Anne shrugged and wished she could think of how to say this tactfully. 'Perhaps you shouldn't push it with her just yet. Maybe she just needs more time before she stops blaming you. It's less than two years since Tomas died.'

Leila pointed to the far wall. In this unpredictable civil war, the front line could suddenly shift overnight to anyone's front lawn. Already the virtually indiscriminate shelling had shattered the front windows of the former Prime Minister's residence not once but twice. Moreover, even in this exclusive neighbourhood, as soon as there was a lull in the fighting, gun-toting looters had been known to pull up in lorries and ransack the villas for all they were worth. And so, when Mustafa had made her take down and pack away for safekeeping his collection of priceless old masters and Impressionist paintings, Leila had made a virtue of necessity. Her salon walls were now covered with an assortment of exquisitely framed 'martyrs' ' posters of those who had died on the Muslim side in the fighting. In pride of place among them was a crude black and white poster, tastefully matted in buff grey, which glorified the life and death of Camilla's son. 'I thought he belonged up there with the others,' Leila said huskily, 'even though he fell before the war really began. But he was committed to the Palestinian struggle. He was a true progressive. All of us loved him as if he really was one of our own.'

Anne didn't think Camilla would much like Leila making folk art of her son's death, and she didn't think she liked it either. Without comment she stared from the blurry black and white photograph of Tomas's young face to the bright red, black and green Palestinian flag which was now artfully draped over the mantelpiece where the Manet water lilies used to hang. 'What do you hear from Miriam?'

'Not much. Every Friday I call her at her school, all the way to Switzerland person-to-person at peak rates, and most of the time she refuses to talk to me. I give up with that girl.' But Leila's mouth was set in such a stubborn line that it was obvious that she would never give up with Miriam, or with anything else that counted. 'She still wants to come home. And I still won't let her, not with all this fighting. One day the schools are opened, the next day they're closed. It's impossible to get an education here. For once, I had to agree with my husband. She's better off where she is, out of trouble. Mimi's still a child, and these days Beirut's no place for children.'

Anne looked back at the martyrs' gallery. Most of those boys, whose families couldn't afford to ship them off to Switzerland for safekeeping, weren't much older than Miriam. She herself wasn't even middle-aged, but many of those she vainly tried to save on the operating table were young enough to be her sons. She sighed under her breath and wished the world were different. 'Camilla said almost exactly the same thing. She's sent her other two boys off to school in France, you know. And it's not just the kids. She was telling me everyone she knew was either leaving the country or moving to . . . safer areas.'

'Safer?' Leila frowned.

'Yes, safer,' Anne continued as she warmed to her subject. 'It's not just a matter of those who are going to Paris for a while, or Cyprus, or even taking a villa for the rest of the year on the lake near Geneva. Some are just moving from one Beirut neighbourhood to another, depending on whether they're Christian or Muslim, and whose soldiers have control of their quarter. She says there's hardly a Muslim left in Ashrafiya. As soon as they pack up their suitcases and are out the door, the militiamen come in and take the best of what's left: furniture, rugs, silverware, you name it. And right after them come the squatters.'

'I know,' Leila said. 'I've heard. One of Mustafa's own cousins who has lived all her life in a Christian neighbourhood ran for her life after the Phalange came gunning for Muslims in her block of flats. She stayed with us for a while, until an aunt took her in. The poor old thing was terrified. Those Christians are devils!'

'They say the same about the Muslims.'

'So they do. And I should have said they were bloody *lying* devils!' Leila was not about to admit that both sides shared equal guilt for the dislocations and devastations of this war.

There was nothing to be gained, Anne decided, by playing devil's advocate here in Leila's house among Leila's partisans. 'Still,' she said, 'I was surprised when Camilla told me who had left already.'

'Who?' For a moment, as she listened to Anne's recital of the names of the departed Christians who had been friends for all their lives, Leila seemed to forget about politics, the Palestinian cause, and the grievances of the civil war. The sudden regret in her eyes betrayed that she missed not only Camilla but all her old Christian friends and the cosmopolitan life they had shared in a Lebanon that she was beginning to fear might be gone for ever. Moodily she sucked on her cigarette until she had convinced herself once again that the progressive causes of this war were worth the cost of it. 'Cowards!' Leila made that contemptuous Arab gesture with her lips that mimed the act of spitting. 'That just proves we're winning. Good riddance, I say!'

'That's a tough judgement, Leila. Very tough.' There was an edge to Anne's voice. 'What about your own father? Do you think he's a coward for living in London instead of here?' She shook her head. 'I can't blame any of them for leaving. Take my mother, for instance. You know she's always hated it here even when times were good. So now she doesn't let Dad alone, night and day, nagging him to take her away. She's even threatening to leave him flat and go live with her sister in Boston. But nothing – not Mother crying or a car bomb going off right in our street – seems to shake my Dad. He's like you. He can't imagine living anywhere else but here.'

'You've got it wrong, darling. *I* can, and do, imagine living in another place. Palestine!' Leila's glittering eyes were fierce. 'And I will, you mark my words. Lebanon's only the prelude. Palestine's the real drama.'

The tragedy you mean, Anne thought sadly. How could Leila, and all those who espoused her cause with such passion, fail to see reality as it was? Israel was there to stay. Palestine no longer existed except as a memory that had begun to assume mythic proportions. Failing to accept this brutal reality would just mean generation after generation of martyrs' posters, enough to paper the walls of every heartsick Palestinian in aggrieved exile all over the world. But she had learned to keep all such pessimistic heresies to herself. She was, after all, a Jew on her father's side. Always, especially with Leila, she had to tread carefully when the subject of Israel was raised. If, somewhere inside, she nursed divided loyalties, she was not about to admit that even to herself.

'And we *will* win,' Leila was saying as though she could read Anne's mind. 'We're winning here, and it's just a matter of time before we win in Palestine as well.'

Anne nodded as though she agreed. She knew what

was happening in the war just as well as Leila did, and to her mind the militias had been battering one another to a draw. Christian and Muslim extremists had been sporadically fighting one another since 1969. But the hostilities had escalated into a sustained war last spring, first growing out of the government's violent response to a Muslim fishermen's strike in Sidon and then culminating in the massacre of twenty-seven Palestinians who were travelling through a Christian neighbourhood of Beirut on a bus. Since then coalitions of Christians and their Muslim enemies had been fighting here and there. But it was only last month, when the Christians had destroyed the Beirut souks, that Lebanon itself had begun to self-destruct. But there was no point, Anne thought, in dwelling upon every bloody step of the war. She tried always to remain on the neutral cusp between Muslim and Christian. Her job, as she saw it, was to mend all the broken bodies. So it was that once again she diplomatically tried to change the subject. 'Camilla didn't come right out and say it, but I got the impression that she's thinking about leaving Lebanon, too. I'm sure you've heard that her mother's already in Paris. Nirvana's supposed to be opening a very swish supper club and disco. *Le dernier cri!* Camilla didn't sound a bit happy, missing all that *chi-chi* stuff, stuck up instead in the Château Croisé for the duration. You know what she always thought about Pierre's family. And now she says that sometimes she can hear the shelling all the way up there on her mountaintop.'

'So? Why should Camilla be immune? We can hear the guns here, too.' Leila pointed with the burning tip of her hand-rolled cigarette at the sandbags piled up in front of the sliding doors that led to the balcony overlooking the city. 'Those aren't exactly there for decoration.' But then Leila seemed to lose her bluster as she mused softer thoughts aloud. 'Camilla baling out? No, that will be the day. She is *Lebanese*. She belongs *here.*' She shook her head. 'And what do you hear from Fatima?'

'Very little. She's still down in her village.' At the first outbreak of serious fighting in Beirut, Ali had carted all his family back to the comparatively peaceful south. He and his two eldest sons had been trained to fight in a unit of the new Shia 'Amal' militia, and so were sometimes away on duty in Sidon or Tyre. When the fighting came too close or when the Israelis sent their fighter-bombers out on a raid, Ali simply took a few days off from the war to nip home, pack his family up again, and shuttle them back to a relative's apartment in Beirut. It was a crazy war, with part-time soldiers slipping home for their mothers' *tabouli* at the weekend. 'The last I heard, Hassan's treatment was working. He's got some of his sight back already, and I think he'll be all right in the end. But there's not much that I, or anyone else, can do for Ibrahim. It's heartbreaking to see that boy just sitting in a chair all day long, looking into space, thinking about God knows what. This war is madness. Madness!'

Leila hated to hear such talk. 'It's depressing what those Israelis did to that boy of hers,' she agreed. 'But then, everything about Fatima always was depressing. I never did understand what you saw in her.' Already, however, Leila's quick mind was racing off to happier channels. Her eyes were ashine as she leaned over and whispered in Anne's ear. 'Stick around later tonight. Don't tell *anyone*. But I have it on the best authority that we may have a visitor.'

Anne's interest quickened. 'Arafat?' Love him or hate him, the ubiquitous yet elusive PLO chairman was Muslim Beirut's most sought-after celebrity. No one could quite understand how he had managed to remain alive with both the Israelis and the Christian forces repeatedly doing their best to annihilate him. His sheer survival skills had enveloped him in a glamour not so different from that of a film star. No wonder, Anne thought, that Leila was so sparky tonight. Arafat's presence would assure that tomorrow morning, on countless telephone lines stretching from one Beirut penthouse to another, the ins and outs of this party – who had been invited, and who had not – would distract everyone who was anyone in Beirut's Muslim communities. It made for a change from the body counts announced on the radio.

'Can't say!' But just then an armed squad of young Palestinian fighters tramped in the door, and Leila was off in a flash to hear the latest news from the Beirut front lines.

Anne watched Leila back on the prowl. She might be abrasive, but she was a survivor. No one could keep her, or her irrepressible Palestinians, down for long. But then, having lost sight of Leila, Anne gratefully made for an empty corner with as much relief as if it were her bed and she was finally crawling in and pulling the covers over her head. She calculated how long it would be before she could slip out of the door and make her way home. She wouldn't mind staying if Arafat was sure to put in an appearance, but she didn't fancy hanging around until dawn if the rumours were wrong and he didn't turn up after all.

She took a deep gulp of her drink. If she had been alone, she might have downed the whole glass at once, like an undergraduate chug-a-lugging a beer. Her mind wandered back to the time and the place she secretly thought of as her own personal golden year, Eden before the Fall. Back in Boston Mike had sometimes made her chug those wretched beers.

She took another, deeper pull on her drink. This isn't weak Cambridge beer, she reminded herself, this is strong Beirut gin and tonic. She wished she could convince herself that she preferred life as it was now rather than as it once had been.

Anne stared off into space, wondering where he was now and what he was doing. Long ago she had heard that he – and *they* – were living in Buffalo. But it had been many years since she had heard anything else about him. His children must all be out of school now. If she had continued seeing him after *all that*, maybe eventually he would have decided to get a divorce. Perhaps, when his children were in college, the two of them might finally have gotten married. Anne sighed. Years ago her friends had shamed her into giving up talking about him, but she had never stopped wondering.

Leila was in the centre of her room, clapping her hands for attention, announcing that the progressive Muslim forces had seized control of Beirut's tallest building, the Murr Tower, and were about to dislodge the Christians from the Holiday Inn. As everyone cheered and champagne corks were popped, Leila raised a bubbling glass to toast the fighters who were leading her cause onward and upward.

Anne lifted her drink on high with the others, but she drank not to war but to friendship. She could hardly remember a time when Leila hadn't breathed fire, energy and laughter into her life. Funny, how so much of her emotional continuity came not from men but from women, not from love but from friendship. Maybe, she thought, she should switch things around and begin a new erotic life centred on women. She and Charles could be the new liberated married couple, her with a woman on the side and him with his men. But no, that wasn't to her taste.

'So at last we meet again.'

Oh, hell, Anne thought as she looked into the soulful eyes of the Iraqi journalist-cum-poet she had briefly taken as her lover a year ago. She regretted the episode and had been relieved when she had heard an apparently mistaken rumour that he had gone back to Baghdad. 'Hello, Jaleel.' Politely she held out her hand for him to shake.

'I remember a time – such a wonderful time! – when you gave me more than your hand.' He bent and kissed the tips of her fingers. 'Your skin is delicious.' He insinuated his voice lower. 'I long to taste it all again. *All of it*.'

Anne, too, was filled with longing, but what she yearned to do was run to the kitchen and rinse off those fingers he had sullied with his spittle. Instead, she made do with fishing for the wedge of lemon in her drink and then sourly sucking it dry, her eyes flickering over Jaleel as though she were seeing him for the first time. He was one of those skinny rooster Arabs with a concave chest and spindly legs. He was such a parody of a nickelodeon Arab – swarthy like Rudolph Valentino, but without that make-believe *shaykh*'s seething sex appeal – that she nearly giggled out loud. But she remembered how touchy he was and didn't want to risk offending him in public, so she quickly brought her glass back to her lips and all but gargled on her gin and tonic. Obviously Jaleel had either been watching too many melodramatic Egyptian love stories on the television or writing too many purple poems of his own. How could she ever have fancied him? The only thing he had to recommend him was his liquid eyes and a tongue that never stopped. She blushed slightly at the memory.

As she put the lemon back to her lips, she remembered Jaleel's punishing habit of gulping gin straight from the bottle and then biting down on a lemon. When she had tried it that way once, and asked him how he could stand it, he had replied that he didn't like it either. Alcohol was forbidden by the Koran, he had mournfully explained, and yet he was too weak to resist it. The mouthful of lemon was his foretaste of hell after heaven. Considering the implications of all that, she supposed she shouldn't have been surprised that he had been a guilty lover, too, rolling right off her and into his clothes and out of the door. She hadn't missed him at all when she had stopped seeing him, and it had been a long while before she had considered taking on a replacement.

But now as always, she tried not to give away her feelings. Her smile was as icy as her gin and tonic. 'So what's new with you?' she said, as though he were truly a friend and not merely a discarded mistake of a lover.

Without further prompting he lit another cigarette and chatted, at great and pompous length, about all that was new in his world, Lebanon's and the Arab world at large.

It was inevitable, he opined, that in time the progressive Muslim forces would triumph over the fascist Christians and then sweep south in triumph to liberate Palestine from the Zionist oppressors. He delivered this improbable Iraqi Baathist party line with a straight face. But then, having appeased his own personal gods and covered himself in case anyone was eavesdropping or recording his conversation, he moved to a more realistic yet in its way far more chilling appraisal of current events. His voice dropped so low that Anne could hardly hear him as he whispered that a friend of a friend had seen a map of Lebanon tacked to the wall of the French embassy with the country divided into four sectors: a big one for Israel, a bigger one for Syria, and two small states for – respectively – the Muslims and the Maronites. And yet, Jaleel said triumphantly, the Lebanese Muslims and their Palestinian allies had nothing to worry about. The great Arab nation was committed heart and soul not only to the Palestinian cause but to a more equitable Muslim sharing of the power in Lebanon itself. Let the Christians take even one step too far – with his stubby nicotine-stained index finger he drew an imaginary line just in front of Anne's nose – and Arab armour, artillery and air force divisions would come to the aid of their brethren.

Spare me your talk of good brotherhood, Anne

thought with that weary new cynicism with which she was learning to regard all such messianic prognostications of a new era of peace and understanding for Lebanon. She drank the dregs of her drink. She no longer had much trust in the good will of the Muslims, the Christians, the Syrians, the Israelis, or in human nature itself.

But Jaleel was so wrapped up in his own monologue that he hardly noticed either her scepticism or her silence. How was it, she wondered, that so many men – not just Arab men, but most men – thought it was their God-given right to talk endlessly about themselves and their opinions without ever asking what a woman thought, felt or wanted?

As she looked stolidly over his head, waiting for him to wind down and go away, he continued his verbal pirouettes. She gathered that the gossip about his leaving Beirut had not been far wrong, except that his newspaper was fielding him over to Damascus instead of recalling him back to Baghdad. Already, he sighed, he was depressed by the prospect of leaving swinging Beirut for the dour Syrian capital. Even with this messy war on, he rhapsodized, Beirut was 'the sun, the moon, and the stars' of the Arab firmament.

She was beginning to despair that she would be stuck with such witless hyperbole for the rest of the evening when, to her relief, Jaleel spotted an oily businessman who was said to be distantly connected by marriage to the Saudi royal family. Without further ado, the Iraqi clicked his heels together, brushed her fingers again with his lips, and promised he would ring her soon and they would have a quiet drink or two before he was up and away to Damascus. Seconds later he was fawning on the businessman. He was kissing his bearded cheeks, he had his arm around him, he was trying to lead him off into a corner to transact some discreet non-journalistic business.

Anne waved her free hand in the air to dissipate not only the fumes from Jaleel's cigarette smoke but also the reek of the heavy musk-oil scent he apparently bathed in before every social engagement. Since Mike, she hadn't thought highly of men. Charles, of course, she put in a category all his own. He was, at least, always good company. But the thing that she both liked most about him and at the same time could not forgive was that he wasn't manly. She had enough chummy girlfriends in her life; she didn't need another for a husband. Except for dear harmless Charles, however, she had come to believe that men tended to be destructive blunderers who weren't worth all the trouble they caused. Looking around at the unsatisfactory couplings of her colleagues and friends only confirmed her opinion that she was better off keeping her emotional distance from all of them. Yet occasionally, in the sensually arid years of her marriage to Charles, she had followed Camilla and Leila's worldly advice and discreetly let go – at least physically – with the occasional lover. Besides the impossible Jaleel, there had been a cold fish of a British diplomat, a soppy Egyptian dentist, a flashy-eyed Greek restaurateur, and a pleasant but boring Armenian antiques dealer. Sometimes she thought how ironic it was that back in the strait-laced 'fifties she had agonized over sleeping with Mike, whom she had loved; and yet now in these liberated 'seventies she blithely jumped into bed with these strangers, whom she didn't even like. Mike, she reflected, as she continued to suck thoughtfully on her bitter lemon, seemed to have soured her on men for life.

Anne watched the ice melt down and then disappear in her gin and tonic. She couldn't and wouldn't kid herself. She would never forget the taste of what she had so briefly feasted on with Mike. What had happened with him had been the central event of her life. She was thirty-eight years old, and from the relatively safe distance of sixteen years she could now look back on all *that* without bursting into tears. But she had never gotten over the waste of it. Maybe, she thought, I haven't ever gotten over it at all. And maybe I never will.

She sipped the dregs slowly as, from her spy patch in the corner, she observed women batting their eyelashes, men hotly glancing back, unmarried couples standing so tantalizingly close to one another that it was obvious they were sleeping together on the sly. How did they have the heart to keep doing it? So far as she could see, love never worked out long for anyone. How, then, could most of her friends keep throwing themselves into the fray? Women like Camilla were always sneaking off to their holiday hideaways with those one-night stands whose names they could hardly remember when later they gushed about them on the telephone.

'Where's that handsome husband of yours?'

Anne whirled around at the sound of that familiar voice she had not heard for months. 'Ramsey!' They kissed, laughed, and hugged. Leila's brother had been wheedling money for the Palestinian war chest from emirs, *shaykhs* and bankers up and down the Gulf. 'God, I've missed you!' Anne beamed at Ramsey, her living link to what she had once had with Mike. They had drawn even closer in these past years than when they had been young and she had been foolish back in Boston.

'Whatever *are* you doing,' he scolded, 'stuck off in this corner with an empty glass?' He beckoned to the Sudanese waiter and presented her with a fresh gin and tonic. 'Now,' he said, as he settled her in an empty easy chair and elegantly perched himself on its upholstered arm, 'tell me every single thing that's happened to you since this jolly little war of ours got underway.'

'Well . . .' What was there to say? She'd spent the first horrid months of this jolly little war pulling sheets over the faces of teenage boys. But she supposed Ramsey was simply still trying to be what he imagined was very British, facing this gory civil war with a stiff upper lip. 'I've been working.'

'You're always working. Always have been. Always will be.' He leaned confidentially closer to her. 'I mean, what's really been happening? With Charles, for instance. Where is the dear boy tonight?'

'Your guess is as good as mine.' She had no secrets from Ramsey. Long ago she had confided in him the sort of marriage she had. 'Lately he's been away even more than before, if you can imagine that. I know AUB's shut down most of the time, but *other* professors – my father, for instance – are still here. But Charles is hardly ever home.' The alcohol was finally loosening her tongue, and her voice rose with resentment. 'He's my husband, but you'd never know it. I can never – *ever!* – count on that man. I mean, Ramsey, tonight I was *afraid* to drive all the way up here on my own. Because of the casualties from the fighting in Kantari, I had to stay at the hospital late and I missed a ride up here with everyone else who was coming. So there I was, on the road from Beirut, frantically listening to the radio to hear if they were broadcasting warnings about any particular danger spots. Of course I didn't know which militias had put up roadblocks tonight, and where they'd be. They're calling them "flying roadblocks" now. A few militiamen block the road with their cars, demand everyone's identity cards, and sometimes randomly kill anyone from the other side. There were eight roadblocks tonight between here and the hospital. I suppose I was lucky that I didn't have to cross over from what everyone is beginning to call East to West Beirut. And, granted, I'm fortunate that I have a Red Crescent medical logo painted on the side of my station wagon, and mostly I get waved through everybody's checkpoints.' She shuddered. 'But you never know when you're going to run into a wild-eyed, hopped up psychopath with some grudge or other to pay back, and a Kalashnikov or an M-16 to do it with.' Her eyes were haunted. 'So many of them wear those black hoods now, so no one will recognize their faces later. They're so sinister-looking! And you hear such awful stories . . .' She shivered, and then she felt like bursting into tears. 'Let's not talk about this anymore.'

'What a time you've had of it, darling!' He put his arm protectively around her. 'I didn't realize it was as bad as that here. But look, I'm sure you can stay right here tonight. Or, if you prefer, I'll have some of our boys escort you home.' He snapped his fingers. 'No – damn it! – I'll have a squad of them assigned to you as your personal bodyguards. They'll take you to work and then stand guard at your front door.'

'No, no, no bodyguards.' Ramsey had been away from Beirut for too many momentous months. She was safer alone in her Red Crescent wagon than with a provocative pair of Palestinian Fatah militiamen riding shotgun as she tried to smash through Christian roadblocks. 'But maybe I *will* sleep here tonight, if Leila doesn't mind.' Day or night, passing through the checkpoints was dangerous. But at least in the mornings the militiamen were less likely to be high on hashish or drunk on whisky. Fretfully she regressed to the subject of Charles. 'I don't want a couple of armed bodyguards to look out for me. I need a proper husband.' She didn't try to keep the bitterness from creeping into her voice. 'I suppose Charles has someone new.'

'*Here?* In Beirut?' Usually Ramsey's chat was as light and sweet as meringue, but now his face was grim. He wasn't nearly as concerned with Charles's lovers as with his movements to and from the warring camps. 'Where's he been buggering off to lately? Here on the front lines, or back home to the States? Off to Europe? Or just over in Cyprus?'

'Ask him yourself. *If* he ever gives you the chance.'

For a moment Ramsey stared thoughtfully into space. Should he warn her that almost everyone who counted in the radical Muslim camp thought her husband was a CIA agent? That had been the rumour for years. But until this time of paranoia and bloodshed had begun, such a suspicion had not been a life or death offence. It still wasn't. But he – and others – liked to keep tabs on what Charles and the CIA were up to. He decided however that Anne was better off not knowing what they suspected about her husband. If the worse came to the worst someday, it was safer for Anne to be able to claim in all honesty that she had never had even a hint of her husband's spying. 'Poor you!' But he decided the two of them should change the subject. These days it was prudent to watch what one said, even in Leila's house. Tomorrow or the day after, when he was certain no one was in earshot, he would have a more intimate heart-to-heart with Anne about her marriage. 'But enough of this gloom and doom.'

His animated face shone like neon as he looked around at former prime ministers rubbing shoulders with Druze chieftains and young off-duty Muslim fighters. His sister's salon had always drawn the *crème de la crème* of Beirut society, but nowadays that meant a different guest list from those customary before the war. Since the fighting had sundered this city and this country into right-wing Christian and leftist Muslim factions, in place of a single high society in Beirut there now were two armed camps. Powerful and well-connected old Christian friends would no longer dream of risking their lives by crossing enemy lines to socialize at such a Muslim citadel. Instead, Leila had garnered the leading lights of Lebanon's new Muslim power élite.

Those who caught Ramsey's eye first, as he surveyed the scene, were the colourful, and astonishingly numerous, Palestinians. He was accustomed to seeing greying business executives like his father here in this salon, men who had, since the loss of Palestine in 1948, taken an influential role in Lebanon's bustling commercial life. But now a vibrant younger generation – armed, and a bit dangerous-looking in their military uniforms – had become the new Palestinian vanguard. Though for the most part in this war Yasser Arafat had held his troops back from the fighting, the well-armed and seasoned Palestinian fighters were nonetheless the trump card in the Muslim hand. The crowd respectfully parted to give way to mainstream PLO officers striding about in Fatah fatigues. Lurking on the shadowy fringes of the party were others flashing the insignia of the United Front or one of the many leftist splinter militias from the Rejection Front, which refused all negotiations with Israel. Here and there a trendy young militiaman was dragged along by his proud mother or father who all but posed him with his status-symbol Kalashnikov, much as when he was a younger and smaller boy he had been trotted out at grown-up parties to recite an old Arab poem or a verse from the Koran. And everywhere were Palestinians who simply wore the trademark black or red chequered *kuffiyehs* dashingly wrapped around their necks much as old Etonians sport the beloved school tie. It was gratifying, Ramsey mused, to see his own generation taking charge and taking over. Maybe what they said in the camps was right after all: today Beirut, tomorrow Jerusalem.

His whisky tasted as sweet as honey as he looked around at the other guests whom his sister considered important enough now to invite to her home. It was no surprise that, besides the Palestinians, there were the contingents of the old Sunni notables from the best Levantine families. Politicians, landowners, warlord *zaims* and millionaire businessmen clustered in exclusive little knots. And slightly apart from the rest, he could see cliques of white-turbaned Druze *shaykhs* keeping careful watch on the proceedings. In this quicksand of shifting Lebanese alliances, the Druze were some of the staunchest supporters of the Muslim progressive cause. But Lebanese politics were treacherous, and the Druze–Muslim alliance might turn out to be less eternal than everyone made it out to be.

A smattering of Shia Muslims were here as well, mostly bankers, merchants and absentee landowners from the south and the Bekaa who had functioned as country cousins of the Beirut Sunni ruling élite for generations. Missing tonight, however, were representatives of the Imam Musa Sadr's Shia 'Movement of the Dispossessed'. For the past few years this Iranian-born religious leader had been galvanizing the power of the south, the Bekaa and the southern suburbs of Beirut into fighting for their economic and political rights. Just this past summer, the imam had even sanctioned the organization of the Shia's own Amal militia. Ramsey made a mental note to advise Leila that it might be prudent to court these newly militant Shias.

But she had, he noted, invited most of the Arab diplomatic community. The Libyans, the Iraqi and the Syrian ambassadors mistrustfully eyed each other from opposite corners of the salon. The Kuwaiti *chargé d'affaires* chatted amiably with a Gulf *emir*. Three Algerian diplomats drank champagne with a Russian.

Ramsey couldn't help smiling as he observed a bold contingent of Western strangers who were doing their frantic best to insinuate themselves into the ebb and flow of the most exclusive conversations. Before the war had begun, most of the Western news media had anchored their Middle East bureaux in cosmopolitan Beirut. Seasoned Arabist reporters, editors and correspondents had long been a mainstay of the social scene. But now that Lebanon had been transformed into a war zone, packs of journalists who were very different from the old Beirut 'hands' had arrived in droves. The television stars, in particular, looked as if they had answered a Hollywood casting call *circa* 1944. Only romantic newsmen who had grown up on a steady diet of Humphrey Bogart and Clark Gable movies would have turned up at a formal party in the Beirut hills dressed in crumpled battledress or beige linen safari suits. All that some of them lacked were press cards stuck into the hatbands of their fedoras. Still, Ramsey found their eager-beaver adrenalin infectious.

'This scene is really quite something,' he enthused. 'Beirut's incredible these days!'

Anne followed Ramsey's gaze and tried to see this gathering as he must. The mood, as so often was the case these days, was electric. *La crème* of zesty Beirut had taken to these first months of war with as much gusto as if it were a sort of spectacularly violent football match between the Muslim and Christian teams. Some of them, Levantine to the core, had even been resourceful or cynical enough to turn a profit on it by blackmarketing scarce goods, arranging discreet arms deals, and speculating on the rise and fall of the Lebanese pound in the international money markets. The oil pipeline to Tripoli had been cut, and on some days there was no more petrol to be found in Beirut at any price. Bread was now rationed to a kilo per person per day, and every morning there were new shortages of vital commodities. Yet this privileged crowd had remained untouched by the real blood-and-guts hardships of the war. The closest most of them had come to its violence was the occasional bomb explosion in a shop a safe distance down the street or the rumour that somebody's cousin had been roughed up or perhaps kidnapped for a few hours at a Christian roadblock. The wartime air of danger, however, seemed to act like an aphrodisiac. The men seemed more virile and the women more desirable. Anne could feel the party pulsating with sexual tension. Compared to elsewhere in the socially conservative Middle East, Beirut had always been free and easy in its morals. But before the war, even the most torrid extra-marital love affairs here had been conducted with the utmost discretion. It seemed to her, however, as she watched married women all but throwing themselves at young Palestinian fighters, that now not only the old inhibitions but also the foundations of the entire society were beginning to collapse.

Anne stifled a weary sigh. As usual, here she was, standing aloof and critical of the irrepressible tidal wave of life which swirled all around her. She envied the capacity others seemed to have to cast their doubts and fears aside and live their lives to the full. She even wished she could catch their war fever. But, since Mike, she had remained as pessimistic about life as she was about men.

Yet Anne suspected, as she resolutely put her own troubles aside, that the war must be taking a terrible toll on all of them. As the men anxiously darted from one group to another, there was a hyperactive quality to the way they smoked, laughed, and flirted. The ladies still piled on the make-up and dutifully dressed up in the latest Dior and Saint Laurent, but Anne could detect hard new lines of worry etched around their tight-lipped mouths. Perhaps they were all getting used to sleeping through middle-of-the-night firefights underneath their bedroom windows and had toughened up enough now to laugh at rather sadistic jokes. But, still, it blighted the soul to be afraid so much of the time. She felt it, and so must they. It was simply the Arab way to be better actors and actresses than she could ever be. At home they might weep, gnash their teeth, and tear their hair like characters in a cheap melodrama. But out in public they made a show of pretending that all was well in a world that they wanted to believe was governed by a compassionate and merciful God.

Just then there were cries on the far side of the room,

and Anne and Ramsey froze with the others as in the sudden silence they heard the familiar boom-boom of the big guns. Another night of destruction had begun. '*Shouf!* Look!' A woman's shrill shouts came from the balcony. 'Come, it's safe! Come and see!' Without further ado *shaykhs* and soldiers hurried out to watch the latest bombardment.

Ramsey managed to snatch fresh drinks before he and Anne joined the stampede on to the balcony with its panorama of the city and the port. Leila had even thoughtfully laid out a stock of binoculars and set up a telescope so her guests could enjoy a better view.

As she stood packed in with the others, staring down at vulnerable Beirut splayed out before them, Anne remembered when she had last stood just *here* at this railing, in the sweet innocence of only last summer. She must have come up for one of Mustafa's casual American-style barbecues around the swimming pool, for she recalled that she had still been wearing a robe over her bikini at sunset when she and Leila had escaped out here from the crowd and settled down in deck chairs to enjoy the view and the cool mountain air. The two of them had whiled away a few bittersweet hours talking intimately about men and lamenting that neither of them had really gotten her heart's desire. Night had fallen, and still they had talked on, when – to their intense pleasure – dainty bursts of fireworks had exploded over the bay to celebrate somebody's birthday or perhaps the arrival of a visiting Saudi prince. Here and now, watching the city suffer below them, as she recalled how she and Leila had savoured the sight of darkness falling that night on one of the loveliest cities in the world, Anne wondered if another more permanent darkness was falling, perhaps for ever, on the Beirut she had loved as dearly as a daughter loves a father.

Yet she stood in a huddle with the other guests, unable to resist joining in when they let out breathless sighs as the bombs burst below them. The terrible destruction was perversely fascinating to behold. The Holiday Inn was burning, and so was the Saint Georges. The souks were on fire, and so was the port as the Christians sent their missiles from east to west, and the Muslims boomed back their salvoes a moment later. Some of Leila's guests couldn't hold back stricken moans as they watched the boulevards and avenues where they had lived all their lives go up in smoke. Others took to cheering when a Muslim barrage from Chiyah battered a Christian enclave in Ain Rummaneh. In the uncertain light Anne studied the wolfish faces of those who rooted for the Muslim militias, and she was sick at heart at the new savagery she saw in their eyes. Some couldn't have been twenty yet, and already this war had infected them with the most depraved sort of bloodlust. She had seen this same face of evil in the Christian quarters, too, and she shuddered to think how this was all going to end.

As the bombardment increased in ferocity, there was, however, such an awesome glory to the spectacle that even Anne, who knew better, tried to shut her mind and heart to the knowledge that those deadly fireworks were raining death on the teeming neighbourhoods. Red streaks arced over the city, up, up, almost to the stars, and then trailed down to burst into explosions of red, yellow and orange. Coloured flares outshone even the stars. Anne stared at the glowing harvest moon. Already she had noticed that the heaviest cycles of fighting took place when the moon was full. Tonight only the restless black sea lay dark and quiet. The fires that raged in Kantari and the Bourg so lit the city that its uprooted heart seemed to glow, and burn, and quiver. Beirut, as it writhed beneath them, had never looked more beautiful, nor more doomed.

'It's a tragedy,' someone beside Anne mused in a heavy New York accent as the shelling slowed and then seemed to stop. 'A goddamn tragedy.' His deep voice had that naked timbre people use when they don't realize that they're talking not to themselves but out loud. 'This country's killing itself.' As the balcony crowd turned away from Beirut's agony and began drifting back to the salon, the voice continued. 'That's suicide down there. The death of a country.'

Yes, Anne thought, that's it exactly. When she turned to see who had put her feelings into words, and she saw him for the first time, she experienced the most extraordinary sensation that – even then, despite the grimness of the setting – made her want to laugh out loud at herself. She was reminded of once, when she was visiting a cousin up in Maine, and she had been watching television with a golden retriever puppy curled up beside her. Suddenly a single shot had been fired on the programme, and the dog had jumped up and pointed. She had looked up, then, in wonder at the triumph of instinct, for that puppy had never gone out duck shooting. Just so, the first time she saw Sam, she all but pointed. After all these years alone, finally there he was. *And she knew it.* She had thought she had lost the ability to fall in love, but instead that capacity had only been lying dormant all these lonely years. Finally, she knew, here he was.

She was so awash in this sensation that all that registered about his appearance was that he was wearing a natty blue blazer and had dark hair, darker eyes, and a large frame. Suddenly she heard him calling out Ramsey's name.

'Good Lord! Sam Berman!' The two men were bear-hugging like old mates. 'When did you get here?'

Anne stood to one side, listening intently, as Ramsey slapped his friend on the back. Sam, it seemed, had arrived the week before. From the sound of it, he was an American television journalist and knew Ramsey from New York. She gathered that one of Ramsey's buddies at Harvard had dated Sam's younger sister. They had all gone sailing together off Martha's Vineyard. Sam was a Harvard man, too, and they had seen one another last autumn at the Yale game. This year, Sam reported, their team had a new quarterback who was going to knock the socks off the Yalies. This quick little trip down memory lane took only a moment, for Ramsey was eager to introduce his old friends.

'Sam, old man, you must meet Anne Jenkins, who is indisputably, except for my wife and sister of course, the greatest lady in Beirut.' Ramsey's Arab hyperbole soared higher. 'Anne also happens to be the best doctor in the country. With things as they are here now, she could end up saving both our lives, so you'd better be nice to her.'

'I intend to.' Sam smiled.

Ramsey had to dash off to greet someone else, but Anne and Sam stood raptly on the balcony.

Sam had, she noticed, one of those wide-open endearing American smiles. He seemed as likeable and as eager to please as a great floppy dog. Surely, she thought, someone with a smile like that would never hurt her? She risked a little smile herself.

'I saw you before, inside,' he said. 'I thought you were American.'

'Yes.' She couldn't think of another thing to say.

'You look Jewish,' he bluntly continued. 'Like me. But then I thought, no, what would an American Jewish princess be doing here in the middle of this war when she could be home shopping at Bloomingdale's.'

Anne laughed. It seemed natural to tell him something she seldom blurted out to strangers here. 'My father's a Jew. But my mother's a WASP.'

'Aha! Do I sense an identity crisis? A Jewish doctor who chooses to patch up the Muslim and Christian wounded. Is that your story, Anne Jenkins?'

She merely smiled.

He lowered his voice. 'You think it's safe for you to stay here? I mean, being a Jew?'

'It's as safe for me as for anyone else.' She bristled, as she always did when this subject came up. 'As you may or may not know, the PLO itself has taken on the task of protecting Beirut's Jewish community. In case . . . anything happens.'

'The PLO's learned a bit about public relations in the last couple of years.'

'Are you always so cynical?'

'I'm not cynical at all. I'm a romantic. Are you?'

She looked away, back at the bombs falling on Beirut. But it didn't seem to matter whether she talked or not, or what she said, as the two of them made their way back to the salon.

Later, when she tried to remember what they had said to one another that first night, she couldn't recall his words but only her own feelings. The chemistry of once again being around a man like him intoxicated her. As she looked up at Sam, she was dazzled by how much he reminded her of Mike. Besides the physical resemblance, Sam was brash in that same nervy American way . . . It was both terrible and wonderful that this one was so like the other. One second she felt exhilarated, the next moment devastated by feelings she had thought long buried. Careful, she warned herself, this one could hurt. She didn't want to love him, or anyone else either. Dimly she understood that, for her, love and pain were inextricably intertwined.

As they talked, Anne grew paler and paler.

Yet sometime just before dawn, when the servants began to lay out the breakfast buffet and Sam's driver came in to chauffeur him back to the Commodore Hotel, hope conquered fear and she hesitated only a second before she told him her telephone number. He wrote it down, she remembered, on the inside of a matchbook cover from the Four Seasons restaurant in New York City.

Before he left and she went up to one of Leila's

bedrooms to snatch a few hours of sleep, he mixed them orange juice and champagne cocktails, and they wandered back out on to the balcony to watch the sun rise. Apart from a few sullen greyish plumes of smoke rising ecumenically from both the east and west sections of the city, Beirut lay peaceful and golden.

In the first hopeful light of day, they toasted the city, and new beginnings.

Without warning, at the first streaks of dawn light, just as Fatima's village was rising to perform the morning prayers, the Israeli bombers struck.

As they roared over the border into troubled Lebanon, Fatima was stifling a yawn at her prayer mat. With Ali off fighting, she had to be both father and mother to her children. There were food shortages, rumours of approaching Christian militiamen, and those grim Israeli jets that buzzed overhead from time to time as a warning. This morning she was still half asleep. Her infant daughter was sick, and she had been up most of the night keeping vigil until the baby's fever broke. But now she stood facing Mecca with her arms raised in supplication. '*Allah hummagfirlana warhamna wa aafina wa affo anna fiddunya wal aakhirah, innaka ala kulle shaiyin qadeer.*' She recited the dear old words that were as much a part of her as her arms, her legs, her eyes. 'Oh God, forgive us and be merciful to us and give us Thy protection. Forgive us in this world and in the next world. Undoubtedly Thou art the Master of everything.' She bowed from the waist with her hands on her knees, praising the goodness of God.

As she prayed, at first faintly, Suker heard the chilling sound of planes.

The women whose turn it was to bake the bread let the dough drop down in the dirt. This was a squadron of bombers, not a single jet breaking the sound barrier. Children who were old enough to have learned to be afraid ran and hid under their parents' beds. 'Phantom come,' they whimpered. The men who had chosen to sit this civil war out and plough their fields and pick their olives clambered to their feet and ran outside to scan the sky. They couldn't see anything yet, but they cocked their ears and listened to that distant rumble that, once heard, could never be forgotten. Four times before they had heard that sickening sound of approaching fighter-bombers. The first time, when the Israelis had left part of the village in ruins, two of Fatima's sons had been maimed. The second and third times the planes had merely passed overhead on the way to Palestinian bases and training camps secreted in the rolling Lebanese hills. Unsure of what was fated this time, the villagers stared up in horror at the sky as finally they glimpsed the silver warplanes heading their way. For the most part, since the Lebanese civil war had begun, the border with Israel had been quiet. But last week, as Yasser Arafat's mainstream Palestinian militia continued to sit out the Lebanese war, a commando unit had struck out on its own inside Israel. Inevitably, now, this was Israel's answer.

The deadly drone that was almost but not quite like thunder grew louder, and then louder still.

Wrapped up in the web of her worship, Fatima only dimly heard the approach of the jets. She threw herself down prostrate on her ornate cotton mat, into the heart of the prayer. Her forehead was pressed on the smooth round stone that her husband had brought her from the faraway Shia Muslim shrine of Kerbala in Iraq. '*Subhana rabbiyal aala wa behamdehi*,' she whispered as the squadron of fighter-bombers thundered overhead. 'Our most high Allah is free from all blemishes and we glorify and praise Him.'

As the bombs began to fall and her children started

to scream, Fatima sat back on her haunches for one dazed instant. Dear God, she prayed silently to herself. Not now. Not again. Not with Ali gone away to fight again. Dear God, save my children.

A second later Fatima left her prayer and lunged to her feet so that she herself could do her best to save her children. She scooped Amina up in her arms. One of her boys was crying as he clung to her skirt. Already the older girls were in a panic, screeching at their sisters and brothers to go outside and take cover in the makeshift bomb shelter their father had dug in the far side of the hill out by the garden. 'Run!' they screamed. 'Quick!' The sleepy children tripped over the long legs of their pyjamas and nightgowns as they stumbled towards the door.

Fatima stood blocking the doorway as she looked up in the sky. Before she led her children across through the open field to the garden, she had to make sure the way was clear. Through the smoke and fire, she counted three, four, five silver planes banking, strafing, bombing, mostly in the centre of the village. Women were shrieking, and as the bombs struck, the earth lurched. 'Ummie! Ummie!' her children cried as they fought to get nearer to her, to touch her arm or even tug at her skirt. 'I'm afraid, Ummie!'

When she was sure that none of the planes were directly overhead or heading their way, Fatima shouted: 'Now!' She and the children ran in a terrified flock across an open field and through the garden. She was panting as she flung open the wooden door to the bomb shelter. She shoved the other little ones inside.

'Don't cry,' she pleaded. 'Please stop crying.'

But as the children continued to sob and howl, frantically she counted heads. Only five were here. Six were missing! With an effort she pulled herself together. Allah, in His mercy, never gave anyone a burden that was too heavy for him or her to carry.

Now, as always, God would help her be strong. As her panic finally subsided, she remembered that her two oldest boys were off with their father fighting in an Amal militia unit along the coast. Just at that moment, two more of her boys who had been sleeping up on the roof in their striped pyjamas tumbled into the shelter. 'I saw them come, Ummie!' one of them yelled excitedly. His brother mimed a soldier shooting an anti-aircraft gun. 'Next time I will kill them!' Fiercely she hugged them to her.

Finally, as Fatima nerved herself to look around the crowded shelter to see which of her brood were missing, her mind shuddered to the conclusion she had been half-aware of all this time. Hassan and Ibrahim were not there! She hadn't seen the two of them since she got up that morning. Since Anne had sent Ibrahim that wheelchair, Hassan and his brother had become more inseparable than ever. Often these days they were up and out before the muezzin cried the prayer call. Ibrahim joked that he was Hassan's eyes, and Hassan always responded on cue that he was Ibrahim's legs. From morning to night, the brothers haunted the village. Hassan would wheel Ibrahim down to the mosque at prayer time and along the lanes to the fields when it was planting time. Sometimes they rested outside the village shops, and at other times went visiting at the homes of cousins not only in this village but in hills and valleys miles away. But where had they been when the bombing raid had begun?

Fatima put Zainab in charge of the other children and ordered all of them to stay put while she went to search for their two missing brothers. 'Pray for us,' she told them. As she cautiously prised open the door to the bomb shelter, Zainab and the others were chorusing the opening chapter of the Koran.

Her lips, too, moved in that prayer which is most beloved by all Muslims as she wrapped her black *abaya* cloak as tightly as she could around her trembling body. She felt safer inside its dark cocoon but wished to God its cover could make her truly invisible. Her heart was beating too fast as she huddled just outside the bomb shelter. From her vantage point here on the hill, she stared at the falling bombs, the fires and the acrid smoke that were devastating the village. Still the bombs were raining down from the silver planes. Faintly, on the black wind, she heard screams. The planes whined to and fro. The fires were burning brighter. There was an evil beauty to the horror. She was mesmerized by so much destruction of what she held most dear. It was such a long raid for such a small village, she thought dully, much longer than the last attack.

That thought snapped her back to reality and galvanized her will to save her sons. She picked up the hem of her skirt so she could run without tripping, and all but flew back up to her house. She slammed the door, called their names, even climbed up on the roof to make sure they weren't huddled there. Like Lot's wife under edict from the Almighty, she averted her eyes from the sight of Suker burning. Later there would be time to mourn, to wail, to avenge. Now there was only time to run and rescue. A second later she was pounding down the main road into the village. 'Hassan! Ibrahim!' She saw dark forms huddled outside ruined houses, but the only sight that could have stopped her was the unmistakable profile of one boy pushing another in a wheelchair.

In the sky the warplanes banked nearer. Fatima threw her hands over her head and cringed but kept running. Help me, Allah, she implored as she prayed out loud; please help me find my boys. It was at that precise moment that she saw them. Ahead, on the road, out of the inferno of smoke and fire at the centre of the village, Hassan pushed Ibrahim in his wheelchair. The road was rutted, and Hassan staggered as he pushed his heavy load up the hill.

'My sons!' Fatima opened her arms and ran faster. 'Oh, my sons!'

It seemed that they heard her, for she saw Ibrahim pointing at her and heard Hassan calling her name. 'Mother! We're coming, Mother!'

But just then one of the planes turned and dipped lower and began to follow the roadway. The bombs fell in a neat line, like seeds in a ploughed furrow.

'No!' she screamed. 'Get down! Hassan! Take cover! Ibrahim!'

But it was as though Hassan had suddenly turned deaf instead of blind. As the plane whined directly overhead, he waved at her and pushed his brother faster. Both boys had their mouths open and were calling out to her as, to her everlasting horror, she saw a bomb fall just in their path. She screamed as it exploded into a whoosh of fire and then, as the aeroplane roared towards where she stood shrieking in her black robe, instinct took over and she threw herself into the ditch on the side of the road. When she landed, she rolled over and over down the hill, until she finally came to rest against the gnarled trunk of an olive tree. She lay aching on a bed of sharp rocks. Her arms hurt, and her skin was torn and bleeding from her fall.

By the time she recovered enough to crawl to her knees, the road crackled with orange fire and steamed with grey smoke. 'Hassan . . . Oh, Hassan,' she whispered. 'And Ibrahim, my Ibrahim.'

She thought that nothing worse could happen, and in that supposition she was right. But still, on this interminable black dawn, she had to endure one final blow.

She knelt in the olive grove with her robe in tatters around her and looked up to the crest of the hill where the house that her husband had built her had stood for all the happy and fruitful years of their marriage. She had given birth to eleven children within those walls and under that roof. She thanked God that none of them were inside as she watched a bomb score a direct hit upon her home.

Fatima knelt for a long while and watched her past burn.

Then she wiped her tears, leaned against the tree, and supported herself with her bruised arms as she crept to her feet. She longed to curl up in a ball under this tree and wrap her cloak around her and simply cry until she could cry no more. But she had to be strong for her children. Take it slowly, she told herself, step by tiny step. First the living, and then the dead.

She tried to make some sort of plan as she wobbled up the hill towards her burning house. She could not bear to watch the flames turn everything to cinders, and so she looked instead at the hellish devastation of the village. Smoke lay sadder and heavier over these ravaged hills than spring fog had ever done. She couldn't tell if the mosque still stood, but the fields and the orchards were ablaze. Yet surely some of her family – her mother, her sisters and brothers, and Ali's family, too – had come through this raid unscathed. She would soothe the children, feed them at one of the relative's, and assure them that in the end Allah's compassion would deliver them from this evil. She would get one of the brothers, then, and together they would wash what was left of the bodies of Hassan and Ibrahim.

Fatima squinted up at the mid-morning sun. Before the sun set on this terrible day, she would have to bury her boys. Oh God, she thought in despair, I can't do it alone. Ali, where are you, my husband, when I need you?

She sighed and squared her shoulders and once again wiped away her tears. There was no time for weakness and self-pity. Everyone was alone. Each was born alone, and each died alone. She could depend only on herself, and on Allah. Oh God, she prayed, give me strength. Make me as strong as I need to be. Two were dead, but nine more lived.

She looked back up to the crest of the hill where her house still burned. It would not burn for ever. As soon as the fire died down, they would pick through the embers to see if anything – photographs, children's toys, cooking utensils – could be salvaged. She would pack up whatever was left and load the children into the back of Ali's brother's pick-up truck. She loved Suker with the same steady passion as she loved her husband and her children. But the war was destroying, perhaps for ever, the traditional rhythms of village life.

She turned her back on the past and looked north, to the future, in Beirut.

'Joe?' Anne's mother called out querulously to her husband. 'Where are you, Joe?'

God only knew, Martha thought as she held out her hand in front of her to feel the way down the hallway towards her husband's study, why the electricity was off this time. It could be that today's fighting had either come too near the power plant or that some of the crucial cables had been severed by a bomb or mortar attack. Or it could simply be the power company capriciously shutting off electricity from this neighbourhood or that to conserve limited resources.

She swore when she stumbled against the edge of a table and scraped her shin. As she rubbed it, she admitted to herself that she could hardly blame the power company for selective electricity cuts. In the spiralling chaos of Beirut, no one bothered to send – much less pay – their bills. It was a mystery to Martha how the telephones mostly worked and the shops remained stocked with any food at all. This winter, as the scale and ferocity of the fighting had escalated, half the population of Beirut had fled their homes. So many people she knew had left Lebanon that she was surprised when she saw crowds gathered on the street after a car bomb had exploded or a sniper had struck. Since early last month, there had been three terrible massacres of civilians in the Beirut area. On 6 December, a day that the Muslims had begun calling 'Black Saturday', between two hundred and four hundred Muslims had been slaughtered in a day-long pogrom in the predominantly Christian neighbourhoods of Beirut. On 18 January, then, the Maronite Phalange militia had attacked the impoverished area of Karantina near the port of Beirut and killed as many as a thousand Muslims. What particularly inflamed Lebanese Muslims about Karantina were the grisly television reports from the scene showing Christian militiamen dousing the body of a dead girl with champagne, executing men lined up at a wall, and dragging a corpse tied to a car through the street. Two days later, Muslim militiamen had taken their revenge on the Christian town of Damour, twelve miles south of Beirut. Between a hundred and fifty and five hundred people – no one ever knew exactly how many died in these cases – were murdered, and the town was sacked. When Martha took the time to sit down and think about this – and mostly, from the time she rose in the morning until she tried to sleep at night, that's what she did, obsessively and constantly chewing this one question over – she could not understand how anyone in his or her right mind could choose to remain in this war-torn city.

As she inched along in the dark, her foot caught under the edge of a rug and she almost fell. For a moment the little emotional balance she had left slipped, and tears stung her eyes. Beirut was a madhouse, and those who were still here were all raving lunatics. She wished Ben had a real home instead of those Marine camps where he was always stationed. She and her son could have lived together in a pretty cottage in California or even

Vermont. Martha sighed. She supposed she should be grateful that the Vietnam War was over and her son assigned to peacetime duty in South Carolina. Besides, she could always go live with her sister. She longed to be back in Boston, where she would be safe. Her bedroom at Bert's on Brattle Street was as green as a tart Granny Smith apple. It was such a pretty room, and such a safe one. She imagined herself pulling back the freshly pressed white sheets and climbing into the snug sanctuary of that bed. Boston wasn't crawling with gangs of crazed youths with submachine-guns. In Boston, Bert's house never shook to its foundations with falling shells.

She continued creeping down the hallway towards her husband. Surely Joe would give in and take her home. She was afraid to go by herself. That airport was a death trap. To get there, a traveller had first to hazard flying roadblocks where the militiamen had been known to murder people simply because they didn't like their looks. Even once a person had made it to the airport, however, there was no guarantee that he would be able to leave. Just this month, in mid-January 1976, the airport had been closed for a week. The port was just as chancy. It used to be that those who wanted to leave could simply catch the ferry to Cyprus. But she had heard that sometimes even the boats were shelled from the shore. In her estimation the land route, too, was out of the question. She shuddered to think of the dangers of the road over the mountains to Damascus. Anyone rash enough to try to drive to the Syrian border would have to brave scores of checkpoints manned by Muslims, Christians and – she heard tell – by bandits, renegades and deserters from all the armies. The front lines shifted back and forth, and no one could predict who would be holding which turn of the road on any given morning or night. Some of those who went made it to Syria, and some were never heard of again. In this war, there were no safe conducts for anyone.

Fresh tears spilled down her cheeks. 'Are you there, Joe?' From the doorway she could see him sitting at his desk. Dusk was falling, and he was working serenely on a manuscript by the light of an old kerosene lamp. For a second she hated her husband. How could he be so insensitive to her fear and her pain, working on that musty book of his while she crept along like a pathetic little mouse from room to room?

'Ah, Martha, there you are.' Benignly he glanced up from his work and smiled at her. 'Almost ready?'

'Ready?' She wiped her eyes on the sleeve of her dress and stared incredulously at him. All day long the shelling had continued unabated. Even now, she could hear the rattle of automatic gunfire, and from not very far away. 'You're not still thinking of going out?'

'Sure am. Anne's expecting us. Charles is away again. Up in Tripoli this time, she says.' His attention wandered back to the passage in the manuscript he had wanted to clean up before he went out for the evening. He could not resist adding one more comma to a clause, but then reluctantly he capped his fountain pen. It would have to wait until tomorrow. 'I don't like it one bit, how Charles leaves her alone, with all the fighting in the city. I know I sound old-fashioned, but it seems to me a husband should look after his wife.'

If he had happened to glance up just then, Joe would have been shocked at the naked hatred on his own wife's face. But even as he continued to grumble about Anne's husband, his eyes were still locked with regret on his manuscript. 'Sometimes I wish I hadn't pushed her into marrying Charles. A marriage like *that*, with him as he *is*, after all . . .' He didn't complete his sentence. A lifetime of living with Martha had taught him not to blurt out all his thoughts. He and she had never even admitted to each other that they suspected their son-in-law was a homosexual, or a bisexual, or whatever fancy term they had these days for what Charles was. From time to time they worried out loud about how unhappy Anne seemed to be, yet they had never dared to break their unspoken taboos and speculate about the reasons why. Tonight, Joe decided, was not the time to open such a closed subject. 'Anne called again a little while ago, you know, to say that that fellow she keeps talking about will be there tonight. That journalist from CBS. Or is it NBC?'

When she didn't answer him, Joe for the first time looked up at his wife. In the uncertain light he couldn't see the shine of her tears, but he did take in the blank look on her face. Once again he had put his foot in his mouth. He tended to forget that it was a sore point with his wife that Anne confided more in him than in her. Obviously she had not told her mother about this journalist. 'I don't know much more about him than you do, really.' He gave her what he liked to think was a disarming smile. 'I think she said she met him last fall at one of Leila's parties.' To himself he kept his suspicions that Anne might be falling in love with this fellow. 'They're good friends,' he said loyally. He didn't know if she was actually having an affair with Sam or not, but he might be able to tell once he saw the two of them together. He didn't approve of anyone cheating on the marriage vows. But to his mind, she had been forced to put up with far too much from Charles. If divorcing him and marrying Sam would make her happy, then so be it. A whole rampaging battalion of enemy militiamen couldn't keep him from looking this guy over tonight.

He neatly restacked the manuscript pages in their proper order and weighted them down with a shapely red rock he had picked up on his first trip to Petra. He consulted his watch. 'Time to go.'

'No. I'm not going anywhere tonight.' She stood blocking the doorway with her arms folded stubbornly to her chest. 'And neither are you.'

'Now, Martha, not again . . .' Why wouldn't she

understand that even in a war zone life had to carry on? Everyone was afraid when the street-fighting came too close or when the neighbourhood was being shelled by heavy mortars. But his wife only made it worse by cowering at home as she did. If he let her have her way, neither of them would ever venture outside the villa. Moreover, at the first light rat-tat of machine-gun fire or the first heavy crump of a cannon, she scurried down to the makeshift bomb shelter she had set up in the basement. He knew she must die a thousand deaths sitting in the dark in that stale cellar air. 'You know I wouldn't go out, either, unless I thought it was safe. But I heard on the radio that another cease-fire was supposed to be on for tonight at nine o'clock. It's just past that now, and Anne's is only a couple of blocks away. It's perfectly safe for us to walk over there tonight.'

'Perfectly safe? *Perfectly safe?* Nothing is perfectly safe here!' She burst into tears. 'I can't stand it anymore, Joe. As soon as the airport opens up again, we've got to get out.'

He got up, took her in his arms, and patted her back as if she were a squalling infant. He talked to her as if she were a baby, too. 'Now, Martha, you have to try to be reasonable. We've been over this before. You know how it is with my work. I can't go, at least not yet. Just as soon as I can, though, I promise you I will. For a long holiday, anyway.' But as he stared into space over his wife's head, he admitted to himself that it wasn't really his work that was keeping him here. Even though it broke his heart to see the city and country he loved destroying itself all around him, nonetheless he still couldn't bear to leave it. No matter what the risks, he was rooted here for ever. The war had only made him love this threatened city more dearly. Partly he was inspired by the bravery and generosity of the Lebanese who never lost their ability to laugh off despair with a good meal and even better conversation. They were a gallant people, and lovable. He had spent the best years of his life here in this vibrant city by the sea, and he was a steadfast lover of places as well as people. So it was that, just as he had lived here in ease and pleasure during Beirut's glory years, he was dedicated to staying on now to keep faith with his friends in their time of trouble. Yet obviously his wife didn't share the same loyalties. 'But there's no reason why you have to stay here. Bert keeps asking you. So maybe you should go.'

'Not without you!' She trembled in his arms. 'I can't leave you here.'

'So we'll stay then.' Nearly every week they had this same conversation, and always with the same result. But now that they had each recited their parts, he was impatient to get to Anne's. He kissed his wife's forehead and released her. 'You'll see, the worst of the fighting is over, at least here in the city. Everyone says that from here on in, it'll all be up north in the mountains. And it can't go on for much longer. Everyone says it'll be all over soon.' He smiled down at his life's partner. 'Now . . . let's go see what that daughter of ours has up her sleeve.'

'And what about the snipers? The maid said this morning that there's a sniper in the neighbourhood.' Even in the light of the kerosene lamp, she was chalky with fear. 'You can't still expect to go out?'

'Certainly I can.' He snapped his fingers. 'You know you can't pay any attention to anything Samira says. One day she's screeching about snipers up on the rooftops, and the next thing you know she's repeating a rumour that the Israelis have a plan to invade Lebanon and encircle Beirut.' He laughed as though something so preposterous was funny. When she didn't even smile back at him, he changed his tactics and tried to placate her. 'But if you want to stay home, I'll understand. Have a hot bath – if there's water – and turn in early. You'll feel better in the morning.'

Miserably she wrung her hands together. 'I don't want to stay here by myself. I'm afraid here alone. What if someone breaks in? You know, they've been doing that lately. All those thugs have guns now, they say they're militiamen, but they're just common criminals. They break into houses and steal everything. No. I won't stay here alone.'

'Then that settles it.' He put his arm around her. 'Let's get going.'

She let out a great hopeless sigh but was too dispirited to struggle as he led her towards the door.

When they stepped outside, it seemed that Joe's wishful thinking about the cease-fire had come true. Beirut was as hushed and as still as a sleeping village in the small hours of the morning. For a sorcerous moment it was almost possible to block out the fact that it was only nine o'clock at night and that behind every dark window a watchful family sat wondering how long this latest respite from madness would last.

'See,' he said. 'Nothing to worry about.'

It was one of those magical Mediterranean evenings that used to coax one and all out of doors to promenade down by the sea. But tonight few stalked the silent streets. The electricity was still off, and the streetlamps were dark. But the luminous full moon shone so brightly that the two of them cast their own shadows. It was so quiet that they could hear the faint sound of breakers cresting on the far side of the Corniche. Even though it was January, the breeze that swept in from the sea was caressive.

'It's just like it used to be.' He took her hand as shyly as though they were young lovers strolling in the moonlight. 'Remember how it was when we first came out here? I forget sometimes, now, but tonight it seems just like yesterday. How young we were! And how the city was then!' Fondly he smiled down at her. 'Of course, as I recall, you had trouble adjusting to the climate. The food. And the people.'

'I never adjusted to any of it.' Her fingers dug into the palm of his hand, hard. Nervously she looked around her. 'If you ask me, it's too quiet tonight.'

'Nonsense,' he assured her, a little too heartily. For it seemed to him, too, as they hurried on their way, that the streets were indeed ominously quiet. It wasn't right that they appeared to be the only ones out around here. He wished it were a dark and rainy night, not bright like this. There was nowhere to hide on these sullen streets. Martha was right. They should have stayed home. But they were halfway to Anne's now. It could be as dangerous to turn back as it was to continue. Nevertheless, he walked even faster. At the crossroads they could either duck through back streets and be at their destination in five minutes or take another ten minutes to circle around on the main boulevards. There was no way of guessing which was the safer route. 'So which shall it be,' he tried to joke. 'The long or the short of it?' But he was horrified to hear himself whispering.

Martha gnawed her lip, and her eyes welled with tears. She cast a longing look back down the street towards their villa. 'Joe, I really think . . .' She was whispering, too.

Before she could say more, he turned off the main road on to the shortcut. She forgot whatever it was she was thinking and simply clung to him for dear life. They tiptoed inside a deep canyon of a street between fashionable high-rise apartment buildings.

Then, all of a sudden, the silence was shattered by the revving of an engine. Joe flattened Martha against a wall. A heartbeat later, a dirty white Toyota shot out of an alley. Its gears ground desperately from first to second to third to fourth as the car sliced down the narrow street at top speed with its lights turned off. The driver was hunched so low over the wheel that only the top of his head was visible as the car careered towards the corner. A gunman sat hanging out of the back window with a Kalashnikov brandished in his hand. He shot a defiant round into the air.

But then as abruptly as the car had appeared, it was gone. Again the street lay silent in the moonlight. But the phantom car had left the atmosphere charged. The air was thick with tension.

'Oh, my God,' Martha moaned. She hid her head against her husband's chest. 'Oh, my God, my God, my God.'

'It's okay, it's all right.' He stroked her hair. 'Now, c'mon. Courage, darling. We're almost there.'

Arm in arm they skulked from wall to wall. It seemed to take forever to walk five steps, ten feet, twenty yards. But finally the two of them stood at the end of the street. They had to cross to the other side before they could dash down the pavement towards the safety of Anne's building. Joe took her hand in his as they prepared to make a run for it.

High above them, meanwhile, the sniper in the black hood waited. He had been haunting the neighbourhood every night this week, moving from rooftop to rooftop, sometimes a different perch every few hours to ward off the boredom. But tonight was quieter than usual. Until that car had twitched his frayed nerves, he had been nodding off over his gun. But now he guarded his crossroads with his finger on the firing pin. When finally he saw something move far below him, eagerly he pulled the trigger. He shot once, twice, a full round.

Joe took the first shot in his chest. The second one shattered his skull. He fell in a heap before the rest of the shots rang harmlessly over Martha's shoulder. 'Joe! Joe!' For one anguished moment she stood shrieking in the centre of the street. But then, just before the sniper let loose with a second volley, she ran down the sidewalk screaming – almost – loud enough to wake the dead.

'I told you, and that's final!' Mustafa, who rarely raised his voice to anyone about anything, was shouting desperately at Leila a month or so later in their palatial villa in the hills overlooking the Lebanese capital. This was a matter of his family's life or death, and he had already tried – to no avail – to reason with her. 'You and the boys will be on the first flight out tomorrow!'

'And *I* told *you*', she screeched back with her hands planted stubbornly on her hips, 'that we're not going anywhere!' They had had this argument scores of times before, and she assumed that they would have it hundreds of times more. But no matter what he said or did, she wasn't budging from Beirut. He could shout from morning to night about her responsibilities as a wife and mother. The one shining fact, however, which transcended all else was that she was a Palestinian. Her work and her heart were here. Twenty-seven years ago her family in Haifa and hundreds of thousands of other panic-stricken families all over Palestine had made the mistake of fleeing the advancing Israeli army. She did not intend to repeat that error now, in Lebanon, when once again her people were fighting for their lives. She would stay to enjoy the fruits of the struggle. For this time, in early March 1976, the Palestinians and their Muslim allies were winning. The Christian forces had been beaten back in Beirut. The PLO was even marching on the Maronite strongholds in the mountains.

'You're my wife! You'll do as I say!'

'I never have before.' She let her contempt for this tired old mistake of a husband show. She had always been more than his match, and these days she didn't care who knew it. 'Why should I start now?'

'You will!' He towered over her, his eyes locked on to hers.

'I won't!' Years ago she had discarded the last veil of pretence at being a submissive Muslim wife. Fiercely she stared him down.

Mustafa's eyes fell first. 'Unnatural woman,' he muttered to himself as he turned his back on her. 'I never should have married her.'

As he paced uncertainly back and forth in the enemy territory of his wife's bedroom, he noticed how she had tried symbolically to eradicate his presence by changing it all around since he had last been here. The bed was on the opposite side of the room, her dressing table was over by the window, and that brocade chaise longue of hers was resettled in a corner. She had even removed his photographs from a nest of framed family portraits on her bedside table. He ached at this proof that he no longer had an honoured place here in her boudoir. It was still a burning humiliation for him that she hadn't let him pass over her locked threshold for more than two months. He had given into her demand for separate sleeping arrangements only after she had threatened to take the children and move into an apartment of her own down in embattled Beirut. He knew she would have done it, too, although ferocious street-fighting had engulfed even the most fashionable neighbourhoods since the civil war had begun nearly a year ago. I should divorce her, he thought. But he could neither give her up nor cease protecting her from the madness that was pressing in all around them. He despised himself, however, for submitting to the indignity of knocking on her door and pleading to be allowed to come in and talk just this once. He used to be Prime Minister, and he still was one of the leading Sunni Muslim politicians of his country. It was shameful that he had been reduced to begging his wife for a moment of her time. *Binti kelb*, he thought. The

Arabic epithet was similar to the English one. Leila was 'the daughter of a dog'. Whatever language you said it in, she was a bitch.

Out of the corner of his eye he stole a glance at her still standing with her hands on her hips and her eyes aflame. Impossible as she was, Leila was magnificent at moments like this. Even though she always had been and always would be too much for him, still she stirred him. But he hadn't been able to cope with her when he was middle-aged, so what chance did he have now that he was old? Yet he reminded himself that nothing – not his damaged ego, not his shattered marriage – mattered as much as the mortal urgency of getting his wife and sons out of Lebanon. He had been discreetly warned last night by an old friend that the Syrians were out to get him for his opposition to their brokering of a Lebanese peace plan. Alarmed at the possibilities of either a partition of Lebanon into two states or the total triumph of the radical Muslim forces, Syria had been threatening to intervene in the war unless both sides accepted a Damascus compromise. Yet Mustafa had been outspoken in his opposition to the Syrian commands, and so he was taking the threat seriously. An assassin could strike down anyone at any time. No one was immune from danger now. Not Leila, not his children, not himself. Accordingly, he was determined to fly his family out of danger as soon as possible. The airport was open today and would probably remain open tomorrow. But, with the escalation of heavy fighting, Allah only knew how long it would remain so. He would say or do whatever was necessary to get her and the boys on a plane tomorrow. He had even considered, but then discarded, the possibility of drugging Leila and having her carried on board. If he sent her off against her will, he wouldn't put it past her to parachute back into Beirut.

So it was that he turned back to her and tried

sweet reason. 'Leila, darling, think of the children. *El-hamdulillah*, Miriam's safe enough in Switzerland. But I can't have my sons staying here with all this fighting. We used not to have so much to worry about, up here in the hills. But you're always down at PLO headquarters, and so you know as well as I do that there isn't anywhere in this country that's safe anymore.'

She lit a cigarette and tapped her foot impatiently, but she did not tell him to shut up and get out.

Encouraged, he took a deep breath and, as though he were making a political speech, he focused all his persuasive powers on his wife. 'Leila, it's not just the real battles we have to worry about. There's the shelling, the kidnappings, the snipers, the car bombs, the letter bombs, and the militiamen who kill at whim anytime they want to at the checkpoints. We and everyone else who remains here are caught in a death trap.' He liked the phrase, and so he repeated it. 'A death trap!'

She blew smoke rings and regarded him coolly and said nothing.

He smiled in anticipation of what had to be the triumph of his eloquence. 'No one will blame you for leaving now. Half the city's gone, you know that.' He managed to force out a little laugh. 'So why don't you hop off to London and pay a nice long visit to your father? You always loved London. And Paris. Yes! From there you could fly over to Paris whenever you wanted. I've heard that Camilla's going there to join her mother. You girls could have a high old time in Paris.'

The smoke hissed out from behind her clenched teeth. 'Don't you ever listen to me?' Now she wasn't so much angry as exasperated with him. 'Camilla and I had a falling out after her son died. We haven't spoken for two years. I've told you that before. But you never remember anything I say. You never listen. I don't know why I bother talking to you at all.'

As though she hadn't spoken, he smoothly continued

on. 'It's almost spring, you know, the best season in England. Think of the shopping. The shows. And those funny red buses. You always said you liked those funny red buses.'

Leila stubbed out her half-smoked cigarette in a crystal ashtray. 'My people are fighting for their lives here, and you dare to talk to me about what I presume are double-decker buses?' She was beyond anger now. 'After all these years, you understand nothing about me.'

He seemed not to have heard her. 'So be a good girl, now, darling, and do as I say.'

'Good girl?' She threw back her head and laughed, but mockingly. 'I was never what you call a *good girl*. And now I'm not a girl at all. Take a good look at me, Mustafa. I'm thirty-nine years old. A woman, Mustafa, not a girl. I'm a Palestinian woman and proud of it.'

His temper snapped. He hated it when she laughed at him that way. 'But you have to go! For God's sake, woman, use your head! It's too dangerous here!' He pointed at the windows with their splendid view of battered Beirut. Even as he spoke, plumes of smoke rose from the burning neighbourhoods. There might not be rhyme or reason to the fighting, but it did have its rhythms. All night long the shells fell and the machine-guns rattled. And then all day long the survivors did what they could to put out the fires and clear the rubble in preparation for the next round of fighting. 'Look at it! This is no place for women and children.'

'I am a Palestinian woman. I can take care of myself *and* my sons.'

'You think so?' For once, she had goaded him into rounding on her and saying what he really thought. 'What makes you think you're any better, any stronger, and any safer than anyone else? This is a civil war, and people are dying everywhere. Your precious Palestinians as well as my very own dear Lebanese. Tell me, please, just exactly what you would have done if you and the boys had been caught in Karantina in January?'

'I would have fought,' she said, with her eyes blazing. 'I can fight. I can handle a gun.'

'You would have died, you mean,' he said. 'You know what happened there as well, or better, than I do.'

'Our house is not Karantina.'

'You're wrong, Leila. We're all under attack. Any of us can be struck down at any moment.' He turned away from her and bit his lip to stop it from trembling. 'Sometimes, at night, when I hear the guns, I weep for my country.'

'So? I've cried for my country, too. For Palestine. We've been crying for what we lost for most of my life. So what is it to me that you should finally shed a few tears here in the "Switzerland of the Middle East"?' Her anger so consumed her that she no longer cared what she said. 'Lebanon is not my problem. Palestine is my problem.' She snapped her fingers. 'This for your Lebanon.'

Mustafa was so provoked that he raised his hand to strike her. But as he caught sight of himself in the wardrobe mirror – red-faced, menacing and almost totally out of control – he was so appalled at the image that he sank down on the bed and covered his face with his hands. 'All we ever do these days is fight,' he said wearily.

But she was fully roused now and not inclined to give him quarter. 'Why should your people and your country be immune from our struggle? When we had to leave Palestine, yes, you took us in. I was luckier than most, because I was rich. I was a Shahine, and so everyone treated me as though I were – almost – as good as the rest of you.' She spat out the Palestinian party line as if it were a religious catechism. 'But you kept most of my people in squalid refugee camps, used us as slave labour, treated us not like your brothers and sisters but like animals that were here merely to do your bidding. You Lebanese are now only reaping what you sowed.'

He hardly seemed to hear her. Beads of perspiration were forming on his purpling face. He clutched his chest. 'My heart.'

Old habits die hard. Despite everything, she was his wife and he was her husband. She looked hard at this man she had married long ago. He seemed sick now, and old. She didn't like him very much and loved him even less, but nonetheless she sat down automatically on the bed beside him. She put her arm around him and patted him on his shoulder. 'There, there . . .'

They sat in this attitude of reconciliation for what felt to them both like a long while. But then Leila angled her wrist so she could see her watch, and she swore. She was expected down at PLO headquarters shortly for an interview for tomorrow's newspaper column, and she knew that Mustafa, too, had an important appointment in town. Her car had been sprayed by machine-gun fire at a Christian roadblock last week, and it was still in the garage being repaired. She had planned on driving into Beirut this morning with her husband. But it was late, and she hadn't even begun to get dressed. He would have to leave before she was ready. Maybe the PLO Command would dispatch a militiaman to drive her to Fakhani. She sprang to her feet, anxious now to get on with today's pressing matters. 'It's nearly ten o'clock. Aren't you supposed to be down meeting the Syrian Foreign Minister by now?'

'Yes.' Mustafa braced himself to get up and go. As usual, there would be hell to pay if he kept the overbearing Syrians waiting once again. He and a few of his cronies had been summoned this morning for what promised to be yet another patronizing take-it-or-leave-it lecture about what the Damascus régime thought must be done in Lebanon's time of trouble. The Syrians demanded this, and the Syrians demanded that. He wouldn't be surprised this morning if the Syrian Foreign Minister demanded that each of them in turn bend down and tie his shoelaces. He was sick and tired of all this outside interference in Lebanese affairs. The bad neighbour Syrians and Israelis made the most mischief. But the Great Powers seemed just as bent on keeping the pot boiling. In the good old days before this ghastly war, Lebanon's Muslims and Christians had taken pride in how they had got along together. Of course there had always been problems between the rival communities, but Western academics used to write learned treatises on how Lebanon was a model – and fairly stable – liberal democratic state. Mustafa liked to believe that his countrymen would still have been able to work out their problems if only the rest of the world had been content to leave his tortured country alone. Not only Israel and Syria but Iraq, Libya, America, France, the Soviet Union and a hodge-podge of other meddling nations shipped arms and the latest military tools of destruction to their favourite Lebanese factions. The Christians were being armed by the Israelis and the Americans; the Muslims were being armed by the Libyans, the Iraqis and the Soviets. Alliances could and did change overnight. Betrayals were a brother-against-brother commonplace. These days, even though it defied most conventional logic, he suspected that the Syrians were all but in bed with the Christians. He didn't trust anyone anymore, but most especially he didn't trust the Syrians. Get a Syrian drunk on arak, and as likely as not he would admit that he still considered Lebanon a lost province of Greater Syria. It was only in 1920 that the French Mandate had sundered Lebanon from Syria.

Mustafa heaved a sigh that seemed to begin in his toes and travel up through his gut and finally out at his lips. He didn't relish the prospect of dancing to the

Syrians' tune this morning. But even more than that, he hated to leave until he had won his wife's agreement to this one crucial matter. His eyes were pleading. 'One last time, Leila. Please take the boys and go to London.' He hesitated and then decided to tell her. 'I've been warned that the Syrians may take action against me. Maybe the rumours are true, and maybe not. But to be on the safe side, I want you and the boys away for a while. I promise, I'll send for you just as soon as everything gets better here. Who knows? Maybe it'll only be for a few weeks.'

She shook her head. 'Not for a few weeks. Not for even a day. Not for you *or* the Syrians. The struggle is here. And so am I.'

He dragged himself to his feet. At her bedroom door, he turned. 'We'll talk about this again.'

'No we won't. Ever again.'

They stared into one another's eyes, and then quietly he left.

It couldn't have been more than ten minutes later that it happened.

Leila's two little boys were out splashing in the swimming pool. The maid was running her bath water and pressing her military shirt. And Leila herself was out on the balcony, drinking a coffee as she surveyed the wreckage of Beirut and wondering if – after all – she shouldn't heed her husband's warnings and go off to London for a little while.

The short, sharp explosion came from not far enough away.

Leila turned away from Beirut and stared down in horror at what was left of her husband's car burning like a torch in the driveway. The explosion had shredded the car into tons of shrapnel. She could see blood sprayed on the wall of the house, and part of a leg was lying in the rosebushes. 'Allah!' She swooned and might have fallen if she hadn't gripped the balustrade. The flames burned high. 'Oh, Mustafa . . .' As if caught in a dream, she seemed powerless to move as she watched the servants run out and begin pouring water on the fire to stop it from catching the front door of the villa. She closed her eyes, but still she could see the car burning. Her voice screamed inside her head. He was dead, surely, in *that*. The chauffeur and his bodyguard, too. They must have died instantly in the explosion. The fire hadn't killed them. They couldn't have been burned alive. They hadn't suffered, really.

The car burned and burned. The petrol tank must have been full. She dully registered that fact, and then another. If they hadn't had that argument in her bedroom, she would have been sitting beside him in that back seat which was now one crackling tongue of fire. She, too, would have been dead now, in *that*.

A part of her brain kept clicking on of its own volition. The bomb could have been meant for her as much as for Mustafa. They both had so many enemies. Here and now in Beirut, everyone had too many enemies. Her mind reeled off a ready list of them, and she felt sick.

Leila leaned over and vomited over the balcony rail. And still her mind clicked on and on. She supposed someone must have booby-trapped the car during the night. It could have been anyone. The enemy Christians, of course, were the most obvious possibility, but the question was *which* of the many Christian factions would have done it. Or it could have been the Syrians, yes, they had hated Mustafa and had struck like this before. And he had just said the Syrians were out to get him. On the other hand, it could have been the work of the CIA or the KGB. Or even the Palestinians. Leila's head started to throb at the thought that one of the many warring Palestinian factions might have assassinated her husband. Then, finally, just when she feared she might be sick again, she thought of the Israelis. Eagerly she embraced the conclusion that her husband's death was a Zionist plot. She wanted to believe that the Israelis had sneaked up here and planted that car bomb during the night. It was easiest to blame the Israelis for this, and for everything else that was wrong in this mad world.

Yet as Leila stood on the balcony watching that deadly fire cremate her husband, she brushed away her tears and hardly cared who had done this deed. She hadn't loved her husband much – if at all. But they had been married for fifteen years, and he was the father of her children. Though a weak man, he had been an honourable one.

She sank down on the padded seat of a sunbed, put her head in her hands, and wept. She cried for Mustafa, for Lebanon, for Palestine, and for herself. She wept as though her heart was breaking from the losses she had had to endure.

When finally she could cry no more, she wiped her eyes and looked back at the driveway.

Still the car burned.

On the late morning of her first day off in more than a fortnight, Anne opened all her kitchen cupboards and surveyed the meagre contents. Sam would be here for lunch in less than an hour, and there wasn't much to offer him. With the sudden midwinter shortages of fresh vegetables and meat, all she had to choose from was the inevitable pasta and aged tins of this and that.

Yet she couldn't help smiling as she picked out a can of tuna, another of tomatoes, and the box of spaghetti noodles. Sam seemed so besotted with her that she doubted if he would even notice what she served him on his plate. But this would be the first time she had cooked for him, and she would have liked to impress him with her womanly ways in the kitchen.

As she opened tins, heated up a frying pan, and minced her last two withered onions, Anne remembered going through these same domestic motions that seemed like a lifetime ago, back in Boston, when flavouring Mike's spaghetti sauce had seemed like a recipe for marital bliss. Just so, once again, she felt as giddy and hopeful as a girl.

In search of some upbeat music to cook by, she turned on the radio and twirled the dial. But each of the stations in turn was blaring strident political harangues. Not today, she thought, as she clicked it off and determinedly hummed herself a snatch of a happy tune. Just this once she wanted to try to block out everything that was wrong in her world. She would try to forget the war, her grisly work in the hospital, her sterile marriage, even her aching grief for her dead father.

Yet instead of concentrating on souping up her sauce with a bit of cheese she had found at the back of the fridge, she stared off into space. Should she, or should she not, sleep with Sam this afternoon? Charles was away on some shadowy errand in Libya, she didn't have to be at work until tomorrow afternoon, and Sam had just assured her on the telephone that he wouldn't have to file anything for the nightly news on a slow Beirut news day like today. Usually the two of them were so busy, respectively covering the war and patching up its casualties, that all they could manage to snatch was a stolen hour or two for a quick drink at the Commodore bar or an impromptu meal at one of the restaurants which still bravely remained open. But now they had the afternoon, the evening, and all night long.

Anne spooned in the contents of a tin of tomato paste to thicken the sauce. It wasn't that she shrank from betraying Charles. She was as fond of her husband as she was of Fatima, Leila and Camilla. Fonder, sometimes.

But she hadn't slept with Charles for years and years – not since she had caught him with his boyfriend here in this very apartment – and she hadn't been especially choosy about whom she had shared her bed with since then either. If anybody but Sam had been courting her as he had been these past three months, she would long ago have taken him as her lover. Her feelings for Sam, however, cut so deep that she was frightened of letting him come all the way inside her. Or maybe, she thought, it wasn't so much Sam as the emotions he called up that made her feel so vulnerable. She hadn't wanted to love anyone again as she once loved Mike. Sometimes, since she had met Sam, it had made her sick at her stomach to think of taking the risk of going through all *that* again. Yet Sam wasn't Mike, she reminded herself. Despite her fears, she hadn't been able to stop drawing closer and closer to this man whom she supposed she must be beginning to love.

She smiled beatifically as she shook spices absently into her sauce. It was wonderful to feel so happy when she was near him. Every time she caught sight of him, she could feel the strained muscles of her face relax as though they were melting. Sam was just so much fun to be with; she had not realized until she had found him how accustomed she had become to a grey life of duty and depression. It felt so good to share belly laughs with Sam. As for those steamy looks he gave her . . . again Anne smiled.

But as she filled a pan with cold salted water for the pasta, her forehead creased with worry. She couldn't keep Sam dangling on a string for ever. Soon – perhaps even today – she would either have to let go with him or simply let him go. He had made it abundantly clear, with those clutches of passionate goodnight kisses and the way he always caressed her with his dark eyes, that he would not remain content for ever with a platonic friendship. After she had haltingly told him how Mike had blighted her life, he had taken great pains to assure her that he was indeed divorced. She had been grateful to him for even producing his passport which testified that he did not have a wife. Any other man, she suspected, might simply have laughed off her fears instead of providing documentary proof that he was not going to deceive her. Yet still she wasn't sure if she was ready to trust him with her body, much less her heart. Love scared her so, and she feared that it always would. Nevertheless, she had listened carefully to everything Sam had confided about himself: his childhood – rather like her own father's – as the son of a working-class New York Jewish garment-worker, his golden youth on scholarship at Yale, his meteoric broadcasting career that had been launched in a backwoods Texas station and gone into orbit when he reported on the Vietnam war, his early marriage to his high school sweetheart, his amicable divorce a decade later after they had produced two daughters. The girls lived on Long Island with their mother, who had remarried a doctor in Great Neck. When Sam was in the States, he got to see them as often as he liked. He had explained all this, he had gently said, so that later on – if everything turned out as he hoped – she wouldn't be faced with any surprises. Although the evident seriousness of his intentions frightened her, she thought that Sam was the soul of sincerity. Yet sometimes she had caught herself wishing Aunt Bert was here to hire another private investigator to make sure he was on the level. One of the most destructive aspects of living in the emotional aftermath of Mike was that she never altogether trusted her own judgement about men.

The sauce was as ready as it was ever going to be. The table was set. All she had to do once Sam arrived was to turn on the fire under the pasta pot. She was just heading down the hallway for a quick shower before changing into something pretty, when she heard a knock on the door. If that was Sam, instead of being his customary half hour late, he was ten minutes early.

'Anne! It's me! The buzzer downstairs doesn't work, the elevator's broken, and I had to walk all the way up here. C'mon! I need an oxygen mask, so open up!'

She grinned and went for the door. Sam had already seen her at her worst, coming through the doors of the operating theatre after eighteen bloody hours with battle casualties. He surely wouldn't mind her dirty jeans and yesterday's shirt.

She threw open the door, and he smiled exuberantly as he crushed her in his arms and kissed her smack on the mouth. 'That's for openers,' he promised when they pulled apart.

She darted away towards the kitchen, smoothing down her hair and trying to master her rising panic. Sam was so wonderfully – terrifyingly! – male. 'So what's the news?' she said brightly, hoping she could distract him into giving her a complicated appraisal of the root causes of the Lebanese civil war or perhaps the rise of Zionism in nineteenth-century Europe.

But Sam was right behind her, with his hands encircling her waist. 'I've finally got you to myself up here, that's the news.' He nuzzled her neck.

'The wine,' she said desperately, reaching blindly for the nearest bottle in the rack. She tried to ignore the sensation of his lips at the curve of her neck. 'The bottle.' She could not stop the way her body arched as his breath sighed into her ear. But her mind kept clicking on, refusing to surrender to the senses. 'Open the bottle, Sam.'

'To hell with the bottle.'

They were face to face now, and he was kissing her slow and deep on the mouth.

'Don't rush me,' she pleaded when she found her breath.

'Now or never,' he insisted.

Her hand groped for the radio. 'The war,' she gasped. A blast of Phalange propaganda would dampen the ardour of the most rampant would-be lover.

'Forget the war,' Sam murmured as he kissed her even slower and deeper.

But just then – from not far away – there were booming explosions, the heavy crump of mortars, and instants later the nervous rat-tatting of automatic gunfire.

Sam and Anne went rigid and then dropped to the floor when they heard the familiar tinkling shatter of glass on the balcony.

Next to her on the floor, Sam gave her a comradely hug. 'Okay. Call off your men. I'll behave.' Despite the increasing decibel level of the firing outside, Anne laughed.

But as she watched Sam slither on his belly across the living room towards the balcony, she called out, 'Careful. There could be snipers on the building across the street.' Since her father's death, the snipers had scared her more than anything. To lose Sam to one, too, would be more than she could bear.

Crouching down, he peeked through the cracks of the bamboo curtain screening the balcony. Then he whistled. 'That's some firefight out there. It looks like another round in the battle of Kantari has just begun.' He dropped back on all fours and scuttled over to the telephone. 'New York's going to want a feed today after all.' But the phone was dead. 'Damn!' Again he crept back to the balcony and studied what he could see of the fighting. 'No,' he said aloud, but as though he were speaking to himself. 'I could never make it out of the neighbourhood.' He shrugged. 'Can't win them all. But I guess my camera crew will get some of this on their own.' He turned back to Anne. 'Looks like we're trapped here, honey. We may be in for a long siege.'

Whatever she might have said was silenced by another

fusillade, then by far the biggest explosion so far. Anne lay flat with her head covered by her arms as the building shook. She called out to Sam. 'The hallway! Get away from the windows!' After she crawled out of the kitchen and into the corridor, she huddled there praying the walls would hold. But then a ferocious bombardment drowned out all thought.

But not all feeling. Sam was suddenly in her arms, ravenously kissing her lips, and she wasn't resisting as they lay on the beige shag rug making urgent love, as if their lives depended upon it.

A long while after, during a lull in the fighting, she lay supremely happy in his arms.

Later they were to call the fiery forty-five hours they spent in that hallway their 'honeymoon'.

'Camilla? Camilla!' A few weeks later Pierre's voice, on the other end of the telephone, was high-pitched with panic. 'Are you all right?'

'Of course I'm all right.' She frowned at the telephone. She had no time, this morning, for the incessant demands of her husband and his family. She had said goodbye and good riddance to the entire detestable clan yesterday up at the château. But it was just like Pierre to hang on and keep pestering her right up to the last moment when she climbed on to that blessed Middle East Airlines jet. She smiled as she imagined how she would breathe a sigh of relief as she strapped herself into her seat and finally left the night and day terrors of Lebanon behind. There was a lull in the fighting, just now, in Beirut. She and her sons were wait-listed on tomorrow's flight to Paris and had a confirmed booking for the day after tomorrow.

With satisfaction she surveyed the open suitcases. Finally she was going! Still, she was having a devil of a time deciding what to pack and what to leave behind for Beirut's discriminating looters and thieves. She had bought so much over the years! She hardly remembered most of the things the maids had discovered in the back of her closets. Sometimes she wished she could buy cheap paper clothes that she could throw away once the novelty wore off. For even though most of these clothes had cost hundreds – if not thousands – of dollars, she still as good as threw them away as soon as everyone who mattered had seen them. The jewellery, however, was a different proposition. Of course she would take the costly pieces and leave the paste behind. But the fakes were so authentic-looking that she wasted time poring over them trying to decide if they were worth thousands of pounds or only a few piastres. And she still had to sort through a lifetime's sentimental bits and pieces – everything from photographs and letters to matchbook covers and hotel keys from long-forgotten lovers' trysts. Even if the airline allowed her to pay extra for overweight baggage, with the emergency conditions at the airport she couldn't possibly take as much as she wanted and needed to begin a new life in France. Much of her precious baggage allowance was taken up not only by the clothes, books and mementos of her teenage sons but also by her favourite selection of hand-dyed batik cottons that she hoped to sell to a Parisian designer. It would kill her to leave any of her exquisite batiks behind. In these last isolated months up at the château, she had shut out the warring world by slaving at these vibrant colours and intricate patterns. She was thrilled that, for the first time in her life, she had finally succeeded in accomplishing something other than seducing some simple-minded man into worshipping her.

'What is it, Pierre?' As she eyed the stack of batiks piled up on her dresser, she made a snap decision to leave most of her clothes behind but to take all the batiks with her. What did she care, after all, for last year's designer *ensembles*? Too many of them were in mourning black, anyway, in honour of her son. But she didn't have to robe herself in the colour of grief to remember the loss of her beloved child.

'Guy! Emile! Are my sons all right?'

Something in his voice scared her. She forgot all about her packing as she gripped the telephone so hard that her knuckles went white. A shudder vibrated all the way through her as she relived picking up another telephone and hearing that Tomas was in hospital. She could still see that sterile white corridor, and Anne coming towards her with that stricken look on her face. Tomas!

'Camilla? Are you there? The boys? Are they okay?'

'Guy and Emile are fine.' But her voice, now, was as tense as his.

'Thank God!'

There was a long pause, and for a moment she thought her husband was going to ring off. A wave of panic struck her. 'Something's happened at the château, hasn't it? What's happened? Tell me!'

Instead, he asked her another terse question. 'Has the post arrived yet this morning?'

'You must be joking.' She let out a peal of nervous laughter. 'This is Beirut, *chéri*. There is no post anymore. Also no rubbish collection, police protection, or traffic lights that still work.'

'Listen carefully. Put down the phone, go downstairs, and make sure that no one has hand-delivered a letter or parcel this morning. If there's anything there, don't touch it. Don't even let any of the servants touch it. Now! Do it now!'

'*Ya Mar Sharbel!* Oh, Saint Sharbel!' Instead of doing as he asked, she merely sank down on the bed. 'A letter bomb?'

'Camilla! Do as I say! I don't want another one going off!'

If there was a letter bomb on the table in the

foyer, she most certainly wasn't going anywhere near it. 'Rose!' When the maid answered her call, she told her to check downstairs to make sure no mail or parcels had been delivered. If she found anything there, she was not to touch it. And under no circumstances was she to bring it upstairs to her bedroom. As Camilla waited, she insisted once again that Pierre tell her what had happened at the château.

'Two packages came this morning, one addressed to me, another to father.' He spoke slowly and distinctly, as though every word came from the vocabulary of a foreign language that he had only just begun to study. 'We were out when they arrived. But mother was here.' His voice quavered and then broke. 'She opened father's. God knows why. She never opens his mail.'

Camilla could hear him sobbing. 'Is she . . .?'

He was crying harder now, and she couldn't understand his answer. As she questioned him again, the maid came back to report that no one had delivered anything this morning. Camilla breathed easier. 'What happened to your mother?'

'Her face and her hands . . .' Again he sobbed incoherently.

From a word or two she could make out here and there, Camilla surmised that her mother-in-law had been rushed down to the hospital in Tripoli. She was alive but badly burned about her face and chest. Even more ghastly, from what she could gather, was that the force of the explosion had blown off the old woman's hands. Camilla had never made peace with her mother-in-law. Year after year, in matters trivial and large, the two of them had fought a guerrilla war in the salons and kitchens of the Château Croisé. But even in her most vengeful moments, Camilla had never wished anything as grisly as this on Pierre's mother.

As she made soothing noises to comfort her husband, Camilla indulged in Lebanon's most popular new guessing game of wondering who had done the dirty deed this time. She had never been politically astute, but she had learned enough in these past years to be able to point the finger of blame as quickly and accurately as anyone else. Like all of Lebanon's powerful warlord *zaims*, her arrogant father-in-law had a legion of powerful enemies capable of sending letter bombs to the Nazrani ancestral home. Shaykh Georges, over the years, had antagonized not only rival Christian warlords but the Muslim notables and of course the Palestinians. Camilla doubted, however, if the booby-trapped packages were the work of the *shaykh*'s Muslim enemies. Of all the Christian leaders, her father-in-law was the most amenable to compromise with the Druze, the Muslims and the Palestinians. Besides, one of the most chilling features of this brother-against-brother civil war was that too many of the worst atrocities could be traced to internecine betrayals. These days when a Palestinian was murdered, the street wisdom had it that the most likely assassin was either the Israelis or a rival Palestinian.

Camilla only half listened to Pierre babbling on between sobs about finding his mother in a pool of blood in the front hall. She suspected that the letter bombs were instigated – although perhaps not directly sent – by one of Shaykh Georges's blood-feuding Christian warlords. But if a Christian foe had been acting alone, he would most probably simply have sent carloads of militiamen to gun down the Nazranis in cold blood. The Lebanese warlords were as trigger-happy – and crude – as New York Mafia. Letter bombs, however, were a subtlety much favoured by both the Israelis and the Syrians. Still a Christian warlord could have talked either one of them into lending a few of their lethal letter bombs.

Her head thudded with suspects, motives, plots. Beirut's rumour mill whispered that some Christian leaders, had even begun meeting secretly with the

Israelis to cut backstreet deals about arms shipments. As part of this 'supping with the devil', the Zionists were supposedly being promised free rein in southern Lebanon. If that were true, the Israelis might just sweeten the pot by lending a few sophisticated letter bombs to eliminate the troublesome Nazranis.

'Pierre!' When it came down to it, she still cared about her husband. 'You've got to get out of here!' In Lebanon, at the present time, almost anyone was capable of killing anyone else for any one of a number of bloodthirsty political, personal or family reasons. 'Leave with me and the boys! We can get a seat, I know it. We'll bribe anyone and everyone and get you on that plane with us. You can't stay here!'

But he didn't seem to have heard her. 'I have to go down to Tripoli now. Father took her down to the hospital. I would have gone, too, but I had to detonate it out in the fields.' Before she could say more, he hung up.

For a long while she sat trembling on her bed, her packing forgotten. When the telephone sounded again, she snatched it up at the first ring.

'Madame Camilla Nazrani?'

The voice was coarse and grating. Now what, she thought. 'Yes.'

'I call from the bank.'

He sounded more like a thug than a bank manager. M. Blanchard had always spoken in beautiful Parisian French, not in broken English taught in some inferior village school. 'What do you want?'

'More what you want. We have bank.'

'Which bank?'

'Your bank with safe deposit. Banque Nationale de Paris Intercontinentale,' he said, butchering what should have been the lilting French syllables. 'Your name on list.'

Her safety deposit box! The one with the deeds to

the apartment in Paris, the shares of blue chip stocks and bonds, and her best pieces of jewellery. Some of her mega-karat diamond-encrusted pendants and flashy emerald and sapphire rings were sentimental favourites, and she would never be able to replace the fine antique filigree pieces she had been collecting for most of her adult life. She, like so many of her friends, had taken out a safety deposit box at the beginning of the war, when the deteriorating security situation in Beirut had made it unwise to keep her treasures in the wall safe she had installed in the bedroom of their Beirut townhouse. She had postponed going down to the bank to reclaim her valuables until the very last minute, which she supposed in any case had to be this afternoon.

'You come, today, to get?'

'Where is Monsieur Blanchard? I always speak to Monsieur Blanchard.'

'He no here. We here now.'

She could almost hear him smiling. She gulped hard. She had heard that militiamen from both sides had been looting not only the Beirut banks but the port. In the past few weeks the Lebanese army, which until now had remained neutral in the civil war, had split into a Muslim and a Christian wing. Troops were no longer guarding the banks and the port, and so the militias had pulled up their lorries and plundered whatever they could find. At the port, the Phalange were letting anyone who paid them ten thousand Lebanese pounds cart off up to three and a half tons of goods from the warehouses. But she had heard that the Muslim militias had mostly taken control of the banks. 'You are Christian? I mean, you are a militiaman from one of the Christian forces?'

'Ha-ha! What else? You think Palestinians take our banks? Never! We *Maruns*. Like you. That is why I call. Your name on list. I know the name. Nazrani good name. You rich. You take care of us. And we take care of you.'

I bet you will, she thought. Still, she had to get the documents and jewellery. But even before she had heard this very bad news that her bank was under the control of what was referred to euphemistically these days as 'armed elements', she had dreaded venturing out on the streets. The snipers were everywhere. The front lines ebbed and flowed from neighbourhood to neighbourhood. Random mortars could fall anywhere at anytime. Maybe she should simply write off the contents of her safety deposit box.

How could mere money weigh against her own life?

Yet, she thought, as greed warred with cowardice inside her, it was quite a lot of money. Really a lot. The value of the shares alone was enough to support her in style for the rest of her life. Mama had always counselled her that a wise woman made a man pay for it whenever she could, and in the main Camilla was only too glad that she had followed her mother's sage advice. She had been squirrelling away a tidy little fortune of her own since she had married into the Nazranis. Every time Shaykh Georges had exuberantly presented her with a handsome present of jewellery, cash or stocks, she had tucked the gift away in her safety deposit box. Every time Pierre had come sniffing around asking forgiveness for another of his scandalous escapades, she had let it be known that a spectacular gift would incline her towards tolerance. It had only been a few years ago now that she had followed another bit of her mother's practical advice and secretly invested some of her slush fund in real estate. Camilla had never regretted buying that *très chic* two million franc bolt-hole near the Bois de Boulogne. Knowing that it was ready and waiting for her in Paris – Mama was ensconced there already, with a young French racing car driver as her live-in lover – made it easier to leave the life she had known and loved so in Lebanon. Yet she wasn't certain if it was absolutely crucial to take those documents with her to

Paris. It would be horrible if she went through hell to get them and then discovered she didn't need them to safeguard her property and shares after all. She was in such a dither that she couldn't think straight. Whom could she call to ask?

Camilla knitted her brows as she quickly ran down a mental list of her most financially astute friends. But the Christians among them had left the country already, and she wasn't on speaking terms anymore with the Muslims. This time she would have to make the decision entirely on her own, and carry it through alone as well. She tried to convince herself, as her greed began to triumph over fear, that there couldn't be all that much risk if the bank was under control of the Christian militias. And she mustn't forget that in Paris she would need those documents to set herself up in the style to which she was accustomed. Why should she leave Beirut as a penniless refugee? She was a saint – well, almost, anyway, if she discounted those discreet little affairs of hers – for putting up with Pierre and his wretched family. She deserved the best in life, and come what may, she was going to do her best to make sure that she continued to get it. She couldn't let a little bit of danger ruin her future.

'Madame? Madame? I busy man.'

Camilla thought fast. There was also some cash and several smallish gold bars in the safe deposit box. Militiamen being what they were – even the ones who called themselves Christian – she knew the odds were against her returning home with wads of banknotes and a bag of gold and jewellery. Even if they didn't rob her outright, they would expect lavish *baksheesh* bribes for escorting her there and getting her back in one piece. But what were a few thousand Lebanese pounds and a bit of gold next to the value of her documents in that safety deposit box? 'Okay. I'll come now.'

'Wait. We send men in car for you. Streets bad today.'

Before she could protest that she would bring her own bodyguards, the caller had hung up. She was in a panic and sweating with fear, but nevertheless she was – as always – concerned that she should be dressed right for the occasion. Her hands were shaking as she changed out of her hip-skimming Ungaro tube dress and into the most unremarkable clothes she owned, the black Kenzo trousers and long-sleeved tee-shirt that she had no intention of taking to Paris. She unclipped her earrings, unclasped her gold necklace and bracelet, slipped the rings from her fingers, and twisted her jewel-studded Piaget watch off her wrist. For once she didn't want to look rich, or important, or worth kidnapping for a Nazrani-sized ransom. She didn't want to look pretty, either. It would be tempting fate to get herself all tarted up for an assignation with some lawless pack of oversexed soldiers.

She pulled her mane of long blonde hair back in a pony tail and used expensive cleansers to remove the cosmetics she had so carefully applied to her face not more than an hour ago. She worried about rape. But even with all the atrocities of this war, here in the Middle East men at least still paid lip service to the ideal that the honour of women was sacred. Except in some of the worst massacres when troops had run amok and all but cannibalized their victims, rape remained a rare occurrence in Lebanon. Yet just for this afternoon, she would gladly have transformed herself into a toothless old crone.

She crossed herself for luck, murmured a quick 'Hail Mary' under her breath, and tucked a large plastic carrier bag into one of her trouser pockets. She was waiting downstairs when she heard a hammy fist knocking hard. She opened the door to a yellow-haired giant of a Phalangist militiaman who held his M-16 assault rifle in a firing position pointed straight at her.

'*La Dame aux Camélias?*' He laughed as though

pleased at his operatic reference. '*Je suis Jacques.*'

She was too terrified to do more than nod and follow him outside. But she was relieved he spoke in nicely accented French. She felt better, too, that this one at least seemed to have a bit of culture. That lout on the telephone had sounded as though he couldn't even read a newspaper, much less be on speaking terms with the play that had become *La Traviata*. She wanted to believe that an opera buff would never rape her or rob her or gun her down in some back street. She was heartened, too, by the oversized wooden cross that he – like so many of the Christian Phalangist militiamen – wore on a thickish gold chain around his neck. We're on the same side, she reminded herself. I have nothing to fear from this man. Nervously she repeated it again: I have nothing to fear from this man.

Camilla was not so reassured, however, by his partner at the wheel of the battered old black Cadillac. Raoul was a sleek rodent of a man with gleaming rat's eyes. He looked her up and down and grunted as his eyes returned to her breasts. Sharply she regretted answering the door to this pair. But Jacques's gun was still on her and so she climbed in the back seat.

No one said a word as Raoul turned the car around, gunned the engine, and then raced down the deserted street. As neighbourhoods flashed by, Camilla could hear the church bells sounding their warning tocsins. Here she glimpsed a gunman crouching in a corner, there the rubble of a building testified to a recent mortar attack, everywhere entrances were barricaded with sandbags and drained oil drums that had been weighted down with sand. All the shops were shuttered, and some had locked iron grilles pulled across their entrances. Buildings were gutted by fire, stone walls had collapsed on to pavements, and the street was rutted with shellholes. Peering out of the back window, Camilla realized just how long it had been since she had dared to venture out on these warring streets. Until travelling down from the château yesterday, she had spent the war tucked away in her in-laws' mountain fortress. The devastation wreaked on what had been Beirut's best neighbourhoods shocked her. Thank God, she thought, that she was leaving tomorrow. Think of Paris, she told herself. The Seine. The smart shops. The delicious snobberies. *The security*. If God were good to her, tomorrow she would be in Paris.

But today she was still in Beirut.

When, out of nowhere, their careering Cadillac was suddenly fired upon, Jacques screamed for her to get down on the floor. She threw herself full-length on the grimy mats. Raoul forced the car to pick up even more speed. She heard the frightful boom-boom of returning fire coming from just inches away on the front seat and then Jacques and Raoul laughing like madmen. Camilla all but burrowed into the chassis of the car as she prayed fervently for deliverance. Her heart and soul flamed with self-serving devotion to Jesus, Mary, and each and every one of the saints. If He let her survive this, she would never miss Sunday Mass again. She would go to Holy Communion every week, she would never so much as look at another man who wasn't her husband, and she would give a great chunk of money to one of the Maronite monasteries up in the mountains. Yet still the gunfire continued.

The firing stopped just a moment before Raoul jammed on the brakes and the Cadillac screeched to a standstill. '*Sortez!*' Jacques ordered. '*Vite!*'

Camilla moaned as she crept to her knees. That sudden, jarring halt had nearly wedged her under the front seat, and her hip and arm hurt. She tried to do as she was told.

But she wasn't fast enough for Jacques, who was holding open her door. '*Vite! Vite!* There may be snipers!'

She sprang out of the car and instinctively doubled over like a combat veteran as she ran as fast as she could towards the door through which Raoul had disappeared. Jacques was right behind her. Inside, she looked around in sudden, sinking dread. This wasn't the Banque Nationale de Paris Intercontinentale. This was a looted, war-torn office building that she had never seen before. Blackened and bullet-pocked stacks of desks, tables and chairs were piled at every door and window as cover for militiamen firing out at the street. The floor was littered with grimy papers dumped from overturned filing cabinets. Everywhere, militiamen's looted booty – from cigarettes and whisky to cameras and cassette recorders – was stacked in cartons ready to be hauled away during the next truce.

Camilla panted against a wall like a cornered animal and shut her eyes tight. She was as good as dead.

She must have been mad to risk her life for a mere boxful of riches. How could she ever have put herself in the hands of these cut-throats? Maybe they weren't even from one of the Christian militias. They could be Palestinians dressed up in Phalange uniforms. Well, they could do whatever they wanted with her now. First these fiends would rape her, and then they would kill her. Fervently she crossed herself and began reciting out loud an achingly sincere 'Act of Contrition'.

To her surprise, both Jacques and Raoul grinned approvingly and, when she came to the end of the prayer, they joined in with a hearty 'Amen'. Tentatively she smiled. Maybe they were Christians after all.

'Follow me,' Jacques said.

But she didn't move. 'You were supposed to take me to my bank. I'm not going anywhere unless you tell me why you've brought me here instead.'

'You will do as we tell you.' Again Raoul leered at her breasts. 'You will do anything – and everything – we tell you to do.'

She shrank from him. When Jacques turned and haughtily strode away without another word, she either had to follow him or stay behind with the menacing Raoul. Meekly she sprinted after Jacques into the interior of the building. At the end of a long corridor, he turned right. Ahead, a man-sized passageway had been blown into the wall backing on to another building in the next street. Jacques hunched through the hole, and she followed with a glad heart. Since the nearby streets were honeycombed with Muslim militiamen, she reasoned that the Phalange must have blasted a new route that would not expose them to enemy fire. In this way, passing through four more buildings, they steadily threaded nearer to the bank.

Finally, as they approached another dynamited portal, Jacques cautioned her to halt. Gunfire sounded close at hand. 'Ahead is the lobby of your bank.' He looked hurt that she should have doubted he would escort her where he said he would. 'We must take care. The big windows are gone, and they shoot when they see us move. We must crawl.'

'I'm not going in there.' Camilla's ponytail bobbed vigorously as she shook her head. 'Take me home.'

Jacques's smile was no longer so charming. 'If you want to go home, my friend here will drive you.'

'At your service, madame.' Again Raoul leered.

She moistened her dry lips with her tongue, and then she shrugged. '*Eh bien*, Jacques. We crawl.'

In an agony of terror, she watched him drop on all fours and then flatten himself out even more as he slithered across the wide marble lobby of the French bank. She held her hands over her ears as she heard the deadly rattle of machine-gun fire. But Jacques made it to the other side and stood triumphantly beckoning to her.

'Go, now.' Raoul put his hands on her backside.

Camilla knelt down. Before venturing to make a

move, she crossed herself yet again and wished that instead of leading her life of ease and decadence she had entered a Carmelite convent and dedicated herself to selfless devotion to God. If she were a Carmelite nun, Jacques wouldn't be making her crawl across this marble shooting gallery and Raoul wouldn't be feeling her up on the sly. But she wasn't a nun. She was a rich man's wife, and she was about to die!

As the impulse overtook her to run away as fast as she could in the opposite direction, she sternly mastered her panic. Remember, she told herself, that you're Camilla Nazrani and you can do this or anything else you set your mind to. From some previously untapped source inside her, she found the strength this time to be brave. Think of the stocks and bonds, she told herself. And the title to the Paris apartment, the gold bars, the jewellery.

She was off and running on all fours, crawling on her belly across the lobby. Bullets whined above her. Thank God, she thought, as she scuttled faster, for all those diet foods and those missed breakfasts and lunches. She had always been vain about her figure, but she had never thought her silhouette could be a matter of life and death. Yet the lobby was even wider than it had looked, and the fire was heavier now. The gunmen aimed lower, and she shuddered as the bullets raked the floor just inches from her head. Frantically she clawed her way across the exposed area.

Camilla was so traumatized that she didn't realize it when she had passed out of the firing line. She continued crawling on her belly down another corridor, following the heavy tread of Jacques's dusty brown boots until he came to a staircase and gruffly told her to stand up. Instead, she lay where she was and hid her face in her crossed arms and cried.

'Who is that?'

She heard more heavy footsteps and then a new

voice – this one in cultured but rather supercilious French – floating somewhere above her.

'The Nazrani woman,' Jacques answered.

The voice grunted, and then a boot lightly kicked out at her arm. 'Up, now.'

That was too much. She reared up and all but spat at the soldier who had presumed to nudge her with his filthy steel-tipped boot. 'If my husband were here, he would kill you for that!'

Raoul smiled insinuatingly. 'But he is not here. We are here now.' He reached down and grabbed her by her ponytail, and his comrades laughed and closed in as though for a new sport.

'*Arrête!*' An officer with a clipboard in hand raced down the hallway towards them. 'Leave the lady alone!' He barked his orders with the imperial certainty of not only rank but inherited class.

Camilla scrambled to her feet and, as she dusted off the knees of her trousers, from under her lowered lids she examined this newcomer who seemed to be assuming the role of her protector. He was slim, handsome and attired in an immaculate tailored uniform. He looked vaguely familiar, too. Even though he couldn't be more than twenty-one years old and was far too young for her, she did what came naturally and batted her eyelashes at him.

His eyes flashed, and then he leaned over and kissed her hand. '*Enchanté*,' he murmured, as though they had just been introduced at a dinner-dance at the Sporting Club. He clicked his heels together. 'Lieutenant Jean-Paul Boustani at your service.' He smiled adoringly. 'And you must be Madame Nazrani.'

Automatically she simpered back that yes she was and that she, too, was enchanted to meet the lieutenant.

'But I think I have had the pleasure of making your acquaintance before, at my cousin's wedding. Simone

Iskander? In Jounieh? Just before this unfortunate war of ours began.'

'But of course! Darling Simone!' Rapturously she smiled at Jean-Paul.

But this is mad, she thought to herself, as she and the lieutenant rattled on with bright cocktail party chat about everyone they knew in common. We can't be chattering away like this after I have just made myself a living target in a shooting gallery and this wolfish pack of soldiers have been about to tear me to pieces. Yet, as those militiamen stood glumly listening to their betters, Camilla and Jean-Paul nattered on. The lieutenant, she thought, was really very charming. He had gone to the right schools, joined the right clubs, was doubtless destined to marry into exactly the right family. How splendid it was, just as the deathly darkness of this barbaric new Beirut had been about to close in on her, to encounter this young man who personified the bright and sunny Lebanon she knew and loved. Maybe all was not lost after all. Perhaps after this war ended there was hope for her country *bokra, bad bokra*, tomorrow or after tomorrow.

The lieutenant seemed inclined to stand and talk for most of the afternoon. But when the gunfire in the lobby rose to a new pitch, he looked pained. '*Hélas!* Back to business!' He scanned the long list on his clipboard until he found Camilla's name. 'Number 4721, eh?' When she nodded, his voice hardened as he addressed the soldier who had kicked her. 'Bashir! Take the lady down to the vault. When she's finished, escort her back to me.' He wagged his finger playfully at Camilla. 'Now, be a good girl down there. Your box only!' He laughed. But when he turned back to Bashir, his lip curled. 'She will tell me how you act. Remember! She is a lady! Treat her like your own mother!'

Bashir's eyes simmered with resentment, but he nodded and tucked a pistol into his pocket as he set off towards the stairway.

Camilla blew the lieutenant one of her flashiest kisses as she all but skipped after the soldier.

But her high spirits sank as she stumbled on a step leading into the vaults. The electricity was off, and it got darker and darker as she descended into the basement. Ahead, Bashir struck a match and pulled a candle from his pocket to light the way.

Camilla squeezed through the hole that had been blasted through the steel door to the bank safe. Inside the crypt, even in this uncertain light, she could see that militiamen had used everything but their teeth to get the boxes open. Some of the doors to the safety deposit boxes had been sawn off, and others had been burned open with acid. The floor was piled with hatchets and crowbars that had been used to smash and prise open the drawers. But when Camilla fitted her key into the lock, it wouldn't budge. The dynamite charge that had opened a passage to the vaults must have jammed all the boxes.

'Wait. We fix.' Bashir put his fingers to his mouth and whistled, and at once a militiaman with a blowtorch came running.

Another one I'll have to pay off, Camilla thought as he lowered a welder's mask over his greedy eyes and set about his fiery task. But when he finished, still the drawer wouldn't open. Undaunted, he rooted through the piles of metal on the floor until he found a steel rod with a hook on the end. He fastened it to Camilla's box, motioned for Bashir to give him a hand, and both of them heaved until finally the drawer slid open.

The militiamen hovered like vultures as she stood in the candlelight pawing through her life's treasures. She took the carrier bag from her pocket and dumped in the deeds and documents that would guarantee her security for the rest of her life. She reached deeper into the drawer and came out with a lumpy velvet pouch. The militiamen sighed and drew closer as she peeked inside at the glitter of her jewels. She would have liked to have poured them out to make sure everything was here, but wisely she tucked the pouch into her plastic sack. As she did so, she saw the gleam of the militiamen's eyes and teeth. That's what animal greed looks like, she thought. I'm the gazelle, and they're the stalking lions. Under her breath she murmured an exultant little prayer of thanksgiving to the Virgin for stationing that dear lieutenant at the top of the stairs. Without his looming presence, these two salivating militiamen would be about to slit her throat. She angled her candle to see what was left in the box, and then executed a quick little sidestep so the militiamen's view would be blocked by her body. She emptied the gold bars and banknotes into her bag. '*Fini!*' she announced as she turned back to the boys.

The one who had come running with the blowtorch held out his hand. 'Please, madame.' Yet his bold eyes glittered more like a thief's than a beggar's.

'But of course.' She fished in her bag and came out with a wad of Lebanese banknotes.

'No dollars?' The militiaman looked doubtfully at his country's currency. Even he knew that the value of Lebanese lira lessened daily on the international money markets. 'No gold?' He moistened his lips with his tongue as he stared at her bulging plastic sack. 'You have jewellery. I know that.' He lunged for the bag. 'Let me see.'

'No!' This time Bashir outranked the other, and he was as contemptuously commanding as Jean-Paul had been with him. For good measure, he pulled his pistol from his pocket and cocked it as he waved the militiaman away. Bashir kept it trained on him as he motioned to Camilla to get going. She scooted for the door.

Upstairs, she was all smiles as she sidled up to Jean-Paul and the waiting militiamen.

'No problem? My men behaved?' The lieutenant gestured at the sack. 'And was everything there?'

'Thanks to you.' She executed a graceful curtsey.

He beckoned to her to follow him as he walked out of earshot of his soldiers. 'I apologize for my men. They are good boys, most of them. Or they *were* good boys, back in their villages, when they were with their families. But the war! Even the good boys are now like animals!' He shook his head. 'So much blood, it makes them crazy. And so much hate! They are like wolves in the wild now. Always shooting, fighting, stealing. They drink so much whisky and smoke so much hashish that they are like crazy men. Sometimes I think – Christian, Muslim, what's the difference? We are all killers now.' His eyes were wet with sudden tears. 'Where will it all end? What will become of our country, and of us?'

Camilla sighed and shook her head as though she shared his tearful concern. But even as she willed a few artful tears to well up in her pretty eyes, she was impatient to go home and finish packing and get out. The old Lebanon was dead, and she was not about to wait around hopefully for a resurrection that might never come. Jean-Paul was an honourable gentleman and he had done her a gallant turn, but to her way of thinking he was a sentimental young fool. Moreover, she suspected that before very long one of his renegade soldiers would shoot him in the back. Even as she dabbed at her eyes, she looked towards the bank lobby.

'You must go,' he said regretfully. He called together Bashir, Jacques and Raoul. '*Attendez!*' He issued commands that were more threats than orders. 'Madame Nazrani is not only a Maronite Christian but a lady who is under my direct protection. Anyone who so much as touches a hair on her head, or takes anything from her sack, will answer to me!' He looked each of his men in the eye. 'And if anything should happen to her between here and her home, I personally will make sure that all three of you never live to see your villages again. *Comprenez-vous?*'

As his men looked down at their feet and grunted that they had understood, the lieutenant turned to Camilla and whispered as he discreetly rubbed his thumb together with his index finger. 'May I suggest a little *baksheesh?*' He rolled his eyes. 'These three are not angels, eh?'

'*Bien sûr!*' She reached in her plastic sack and came up with the three small gold bars. She presented them with a Lady Bountiful disdain to the soldiers, who immediately pocketed them. Finally she turned to Jean-Paul. 'And for you, monsieur? No, sorry, lieutenant! Perhaps a little piece of jewellery to remember me by?'

'Tch!' Of course a man of his class and culture waved away any suggestion of a bribe. 'I would not dream of accepting a gift for doing my duty.' He smiled. 'And a very pleasant duty it was!' His smile widened. 'But you can promise me a dance.'

'*Mais oui!* Or perhaps a meal. Grilled fish at Ajami's, as soon as the war is over?'

'Ah, but that is impossible.' He looked as though he were about to weep again. 'Don't you know, Ajami's has been destroyed! There's nothing left of it. But I hear the owner will open again, with one for the Muslims in West Beirut and another for us in the East.'

'So it is a date, then, yes? The Christian branch of Ajami's?'

'Yes!' Again he leaned over and kissed her hand, and this time his lips lingered on her flesh. '*Au revoir, madame.*'

'*Au revoir!*' She blew him another kiss as she pranced, with her white plastic carrier bag of treasure, after the two militiamen towards the bank lobby where the shooting never stopped.

Leila looked languorously up into the black glittering eyes of her young man of the moment as he moved in and out of her, in and out, deep and slow. It was very hot, and their naked flesh was still slick with sweat from earlier feverish assaults. The sun was already rising over the sea, but this one showed all the signs of being able to keep it up until breakfast. What the young ones lacked in finesse, they more than compensated for in fervour. This latest in her ardent series of Palestinian fighters, for instance, couldn't be more than seventeen or eighteen even though he had told her he was twenty-six.

While her body rose and fell deliciously, her mind tried to remember what she had been doing when she was his age. Studying hard, she supposed, and giggling over coffee and cakes with her girlfriends, and probably dreaming of eternal love. But what had she known about anything at seventeen? She had been naive then, and too full of silly dreams. It was better to be as she was now. Eternal love? Ha!

Leila's eyes stung with bitter tears, and she missed a beat of the boy's rhythm as her thoughts turned to Hussein. Once he had vowed to love her for ever, but now he treated her with contempt. She concentrated all her formidable will on blinking away her sudden tears. She had better things to do than cry.

As she writhed a little away from the boy so he would have to work harder to get what he wanted, she wondered what his name was. He must have told her before they climbed into his Land Rover and headed up the perilous road to her villa in the Aley hills. But she had been paying more attention to the way his tight pants caressed his round buttocks than to whatever he had said his name was. She never could remember any of their names. Three months ago, when she had begun taking her young lovers after that terrible morning when Mustafa had died, she had solved this somewhat embarrassing problem by simply calling each of them *habibi*: 'dear'. She had never called Mustafa that. Yet, now that he was gone, he was dearer to her than she had realized when he was alive.

This particular *habibi*'s tar eyes widened, and he clenched his teeth and came after her. Oh yes, she thought, as he pinned her wrists down against the pillow. She liked it when they got a little bit rough. They seemed to like it, too.

That's better, she thought, as he burrowed deeper, harder, wilder. The way she liked it. What did she care anymore about eternal love now that she had discovered eternal lust? It was better with strangers. One time only and no repeats, that was her policy since Mustafa had died and left her alone. There were thousands of boys with guns stalking the streets, and in a way she longed to open her legs to all of them. The guns – God! – she loved them. She couldn't get enough of these violent boys with their big guns. When last night's meeting in the Shatilla camp finally broke up after midnight, this one's smouldering eyes had already been hot when he had volunteered to drive her home. She supposed that he must have heard the rumours about her. But she hadn't cared. Insolently looking him over, her eyes had lingered on his crotch. She liked being bold. She enjoyed flaunting the last vestiges of the old conventions. As self-righteous leaders like Hussein were always saying, Beirut existed in a revolutionary situation. By her behaviour, then, she was merely helping history along by rewriting the reactionary old rules.

She moaned with pleasure as he held her down and moved inside her. More, she wanted more. Nothing was enough anymore. Since Mustafa had died, all the old rights and wrongs no longer seemed to matter. Staying alive was not only the main thing but the only thing. If people talked about her behind her back, as she'd heard they did now, she didn't care. She was Leila Shahine, and she would do whatever she wanted. When Ramsey had taken her aside and asked her how she could degrade herself like this, she had even told her darling brother to mind his own business. She loved Ramsey more than she loved anyone else on earth, but she wasn't about to let even him tell her what to do.

Leila slithered her pelvis a teasing centimetre away so that the boy almost slipped out of her. Maddened, he lunged down hard and fast, and still deeper, all the way in, and then further, so it hurt. 'Yes!' she cried. Always, now, in Beirut, she simmered and burned and longed for hot sex just like this. One of the dirty little secrets of this war and all wars was that the bloodlust spilled over into bed. Danger, whether it came from revving an engine and crashing through a roadblock with guns ablaze or – like now – from skating close to the edge and crossing the threshold from pleasure into pain, was an addictive taste. For more than a year now, as this civil war had ground on and on, Lebanon had shuddered and moaned in an orgasm of frenzied violence.

'More,' she panted. 'Harder!' He gave her what she wanted in a fury. He pounded into her until her body convulsed out of control. As he felt her let go, he held on tight and finally came himself. They shuddered and lay still as dimly they heard the mortars falling on the city. They lay replete, listening to the sound of war.

Leila had just reached past the Kalashnikov he had leaned against the bed and was groping for her cigarettes on the nightstand, when another sound, this one far closer than the big guns down in the city, shattered her mood. The telephone rang a second time.

The boy's stubby peasant fingers caught at her arm. 'Don't answer it, woman. Light me a cigarette.' When she still reached for the cradle, he hauled back his hand as though he were about to hit her.

But she was tired of his sexual games. This boy was not the master, and she was not the slave. Before he could lash out at her, she jerked herself out of his reach. 'Don't you dare touch me.' Now that she'd got what she wanted from him, he was only a used-up piece of male rubbish. She had once heard that a particularly poisonous female spider – a tarantula? a black widow? – stung its males to death just after mating. She remembered, too, a learned lecture back in Cambridge about ancient matriarchies where the queen's consort-for-a-year was sacrificially murdered at every harvest. Now she not only understood but relished such behaviour. Disdainfully she turned her naked back to the boy as she picked up the telephone.

'Leila! Ramsey's missing!'

Her sister-in-law's hysterical voice shouted so loudly in Arabic that Leila had to hold the receiver away from her ear. She concentrated on pulling her wits together as she stared in shock at the telephone.

'He's gone! They've kidnapped him! We'll never see him again! I know they've killed him!'

'Slow down, Aisha, and calm down. I can hardly understand you.' But Leila's face had blanched white with fear. She had heard every word her sister-in-law had screeched. 'Now tell me exactly what happened.'

As she waited for Aisha to stop crying and start explaining, Leila reached over for the crumpled sheet and wrapped it modestly round her body. With her beloved brother evidently at risk, she was suddenly ashamed of what she had just done with this boy on this bed. She stole a glance over and saw that he was sulking like a spoiled child.

Haltingly Aisha began to recite what she knew about Ramsey's disappearance. Last night he had set out for the Museum Crossing around midnight to try to negotiate an extension of yesterday's truce with the Christian forces. 'He should never have gone,' Aisha wailed. 'I know they've killed him!' Ramsey had been wedged in the back seat of his Mercedes with an armed bodyguard on either side of him and another riding shotgun in the front. 'He had a white flag on the front of the car. They knew he was coming! They had promised him a safe conduct! But they are devils, those Christians! Honour means nothing to them!' Aisha burst into a storm of weeping.

Leila shook a cigarette from her pack, and her hand trembled as she lit it. She smoked in silence as once again she waited until her sister-in-law could go on.

It happened, Aisha finally said, just after Ramsey's car had crossed over the 'Green Line' that separated the Muslim area of West Beirut from the Christian enclave in the East. A truce was supposedly in force, but behind their barricades the Palestinian fighters had heard gunfire coming directly from the street where the Mercedes had just disappeared. Since a new round of fighting had obviously begun, they had pounded their cannons into the Christian lines. A few minutes later, when the enemy was no longer returning their fire, the Palestinians had surged into the Christian sector to try to rescue Ramsey and his escort. Not more than a thousand yards over the Green Line, however, they had found the ambushed Mercedes with its doors wide open and its motor still running. The driver and two of the bodyguards had lain dead, and the other had been gravely wounded. But there had been no trace of Ramsey.

'They've kidnapped him!' Once again, Aisha was shrieking. 'They're torturing him! He could be dead by now! My Ramsey!'

Even as she made soothing noises to try to calm her sister-in-law, Leila for a moment couldn't bear to face this terrible news. Instead she found herself focusing on the inconsequential Palestinian boy in her bed. She heard him padding off to the bathroom and an instant later the sound of the shower. She supposed that, like most of the young Muslims she took to her bed, the boy must be mumbling purification prayers in her bathroom. However else they differed, the lads all followed the Muslim religious injunction to wash after sex. Absently she wondered if this one would be praying next. Often her boys went very pious just after they had been very sexy. And yet, for once, she could understand that impulse.

As she lit a second cigarette from the stub of her first she, too, longed to purify herself and then pray hard and long for her brother's safety.

Instead, as Aisha continued to babble on about what a good man Ramsey was – how kind, how handsome, how generous – Leila mastered her rising panic and cold-bloodedly assessed her brother's chances of survival. Ever since this war had begun, both sides had indulged in kidnapping with a vengeance. Sometimes the victims were returned unharmed after a few hours or a few days, but sometimes they were never heard from again. Now, more than a year after this internecine war had begun, at least ten thousand Lebanese from virtually every sector of the population were still missing and presumed dead. Even so, Ramsey might be one of the lucky ones. Sometimes the kidnappers' motives were merely mercenary, and their prisoners were released as soon as the ransoms were paid. Leila prayed that this was the case with her brother. Everyone in Lebanon knew Ramsey Shahine, and his kidnappers could expect a prince's ransom for his release. And yet, as a realist, Leila had to admit that, considering Ramsey's ties with the Palestinian cause, he had probably been seized more for his politics than his wealth. The Christians might have lured him into a parley on their territory while all the time plotting to abduct him. Anything, now, in Lebanon, was possible. But Leila liked to think that even in this brutish new Lebanon, where honour had become an archaic memory, the Christian *zaims* would still have observed the safe conduct they had guaranteed her brother. But if his seizure had not been ordered by one of the Christian chieftains, Ramsey was in even greater jeopardy. By now, almost everyone in Lebanon had lost a loved one to this cursed war. Bloodlust ran high: an eye for an eye, a life for a life. If Ramsey had been kidnapped by a renegade band of Christian militiamen bent on avenging a brother's death, by now he could indeed be dead.

'Dead!' Aisha was sobbing as she echoed Leila's thoughts. 'What if he's dead! What if they've tortured him? You've heard the stories. You know .what they do!'

Leila resolutely refused to think of that. She would go mad if she did. Instead, she must keep a firm grip on herself for Ramsey. Leila was so accustomed to being the strong one that it never occurred to her to break down and sob and wail as women were expected to do at times like this. Even as she tried to comfort her sister-in-law with sentiments that were far more hopeful than she felt, Leila's mind was working in overdrive. What should she do first to try to save her brother?

By the time the boy came out of the bathroom and began saying his ritual prayers, Leila had bid goodbye to Aisha and thrown on beige trousers and a white blouse. Usually she wore black, but she wasn't courting disaster by wearing any shade of mourning today. Already she had called the editor of *an-Nahar* at home to ask him to use his *wasta* to find out who had kidnapped Ramsey, and she was in the middle of dialling another number. Anne had always adored Ramsey, and Anne's husband was CIA. If anyone could get Ramsey out of the clutches of the Christian militias, it was the Americans – who had, after all, been arming their Christian vassals since long before the war had begun. She and Charles were old pals. Mustafa, as well, had got on famously with Anne's husband. Leila longed, as the telephone rang unanswered, for her husband still to be here at her side. Mustafa would have known exactly whom to call and what to do. But her husband was dead. She was on her own now. Leila reminded herself, firmly, that she was Leila Shahine and a power of her own in Lebanon. She would, and could, rise to this occasion.

But no one answered at Anne's apartment. Leila remembered, finally, that Anne spent most of her time in her parents' old villa since her father had been killed and her mother had returned to America. With all the refugees flooding into Beirut and squatting under every empty roof, property owners had to occupy their houses or lose them.

She looked up Anne's parents' number and dialled it. But a Lebanese woman said Anne wasn't there.

Leila was at a loss until she recognized that sickeningly sweet voice. 'Is that you, Fatima? It's me! Leila!' Her own screeching Arabic was every bit as hysterical as her sister-in-law's had been. Leila lowered her voice and remembered her manners. She hadn't talked directly to Fatima for years, although Anne had kept her posted on all the boring details of the Shia woman's life. As the precious minutes ticked by, she controlled her impatience and politely asked and answered the ritual questions about health and happiness which Arabs consider a social necessity even at times like this. Meanwhile, she could hear the sounds of a whole tribe of children in the background. It was just after dawn, so obviously they had all spent the night there. She couldn't resist blurting out a question. 'But what are you all doing at Anne's?'

'We live here now.' Fatima let out a sigh of satisfaction at this solitary stroke of good luck. 'But you must come and visit us, really.' Fatima settled down in an easy chair, in anticipation of a nice talk with her long-lost friend. She liked the novelty of chatting on the telephone. Back in Suker, the only telephone had been in Ali's office down in the mosque. Here in Beirut, however, even when it was unsafe to go out, the rich people conducted their social lives by telephone. But Fatima was a novice at this new conversational art, and so she didn't understand that even in Beirut no one rang up at dawn just to gossip. 'You have not, I think, even seen all my children.' By habit her right hand stole up and beat her breast as Fatima mourned the two sons who now lay buried in her village. 'You know we had to leave Suker? After the Israelis came again with their bombs?' Steadily she beat her breast. 'I lost my Hassan and my Ibrahim. My boys! The house, too! First we were at Ali's uncles' in Chiyah and then on the beach at Ouzai in one of the cabanas. But *el-hamdulillah*, Anne insisted we come here to live. You know Anne. She is a saint, that one.'

'Yes.' Even now, at the height of her worry about Ramsey, Leila felt a twinge of jealousy. No one had ever called her a saint. And she didn't like *her* Anne being so intimate with a poor clinging vine like Fatima. Yet this was neither the time nor the place for such petty rivalries. 'Look, Fatima, something terrible has happened. It's my brother Ramsey!' Her voice had skittered into a screech as she said his name, and so she paused until she had mastered herself again. 'He was kidnapped', she went on, speaking slowly and almost calmly, 'just over the Green Line last night. I've got to talk to Anne. Is she at work?'

'Allah protect him!' Fatima rocked back and forth in her seat as she beat her breast harder. 'That poor boy. He was always so good, your brother. I remember—'

'Fatima!' Leila didn't care if she was screaming. 'Where is Anne?'

'She asked me not to tell anyone.'

'Tell me the bloody number! This is urgent!'

'You are right.' Leila could hear her turning the pages of what she assumed must be an address book, and then she read out a number. 'A man may answer,' Fatima said primly. 'That Sam.' Her voice was disapproving.

Leila's eyebrows shot up. 'Well, well.' Fatima was full of surprises this morning. At any other time, Leila would have settled down to pump her dry about Anne's secret love affair. But instead she merely made polite farewells and rang off.

Out of the corner of her eye, she saw that the Palestinian boy had finished his prayers and was smoking a cigarette. As soon as she had finished these phone calls, she would need someone to drive her into the bleeding heart of the city. 'You!' she commanded as she carelessly threw him his loaded Kalashnikov. 'Go and wait for me in the car.'

But the boy didn't budge. 'You should pray for your brother,' he said earnestly. 'He is a good man. Everyone knows Ramsey Shahine. Everyone likes him. I, Muhammad, prayed for his safety.'

Despite herself, Leila was touched. She felt far more tenderness for him now than when, a moment ago, they had shared the closest of physical intimacies. 'Thank you, Muhammad.' She reached over and ran a motherly hand through his dark curly hair. 'Now, why don't you be a good boy and go and ask the cook to give you some breakfast?' She smiled at him for the first time since they'd met. 'I'll be out in the car in a minute.'

When he'd gone, she dialled Sam's number. It was answered on the first ring. 'Berman here,' an American voice snapped, as though he were sitting at his desk in the newsroom rather than lolling in bed with a married woman.

'This is an emergency call,' Leila said, just as crisply. 'For Anne.' But a second later, when her friend came on the line, Leila couldn't resist teasing her. 'Aha! So I've tracked you down!' She managed a dry laugh. 'How long has this been going on?'

'Leila?' Anne's voice was deep with sleep or with lovemaking. But then she came to a little. It was six o'clock in the morning, and Leila obviously wasn't calling just to chat. 'What's wrong?'

Leila didn't mince words as she told her. Anne interrupted her from time to time with a terse question. When Leila had come to the end of her story, Anne simply asked how she could help.

'I need someone who has pull with the Christians.' Delicately she hesitated. 'I don't know how things are with you and Charles these days . . .'

'We've separated.' Anne's voice was matter-of-fact. 'Things are a bit tense. But I think we're still friends. He's living in our old apartment, and I've moved to Rue Bliss with Fatima and the kids. I'm here a lot, too.'

'I see.' Leila lit another cigarette and plunged on. 'I wouldn't ask this if Ramsey weren't in danger. But . . . Anne, as we all know, the word is that Charles is the CIA head of station. If anyone can get Ramsey out alive, it's the CIA.'

'Charles? CIA?' Anne laughed, and Leila heard a rich masculine laugh joining in. 'But you must be joking.'

'No joke.' Leila inhaled, exhaled, and thought hard. How could Anne be in the dark about her own husband's work? Of course she had to know about it. *Everyone* knew that Charles was not only a homosexual but also a spy. But maybe she had taken some solemn CIA wives' vow always to protect her husband. Yes, that must be it. She would have to talk to Charles directly. 'Anne! You've got to tell me how I can talk to Charles.'

But Anne didn't know where he was. 'He's always away. That was one of our problems. One of many.' Anne thought a moment, and then she had a brainstorm.

'What about Camilla? Her father-in-law has more clout than Charles.'

'Camilla! Of course! She won't talk to me, but she'd do anything for you.' Leila frowned. 'But I heard she'd left. That she's in Paris with her mother.'

'Yes, but we still talk on the telephone all the time.'

'So you'll call her? You'll call her for me?'

'Of course I will. Right away. It's still the middle of the night in Paris, and God knows who's in bed with her, but Ramsey's more important than Camilla's beauty sleep.' Anne's voice was as embracing as a hug. 'And Leila? You know we'll all be doing everything we can. I'll get hold of Charles, too, even though I think this CIA stuff is preposterous. And I'm sure you'll have everyone in the PLO moving heaven and earth.'

Outside in the driveway, Muhammad was tooting the horn. 'Anne! I've got to go!'

'So do I.' Anne's voice caught. 'Ramsey was wonderful in Boston, you know. He was like a brother to me.'

'He *was* your brother.' Leila could feel tears welling up in her eyes again, but this time she didn't hold them back. 'I mean, he *is* your brother. He's all right, I know he is.'

'*Inshallah*,' Anne said, 'God willing.'

The dusty black Chevrolet with the cardboard sign marked 'Press' taped across the windscreen wound its way through Beirut's ruined back streets as slowly as though it were part of a cortège. Mercifully, this morning's announced cease-fire was still holding. But it was almost dusk – shooting time in Beirut – and the peace could be breached at any moment by a bored sniper, a drunken gunman with a loaded M-16, or a platoon of militiamen out to settle a grudge.

In the front, Sam's cameraman fretted that it was safer to flash through these sullen streets at top speed.

But in the back, Sam ordered the driver to keep it slow and easy so as not to draw fire. He took Anne's hand and held it tight. Next to him, she was pale and silent. If what they suspected was true, this grisly next hour would try all her strength.

Anne let her hand rest limp in his. 'Oh God,' she prayed to herself as she stared unseeing at the bombed and burned out wrecks of what had once been the bustling souks, 'let that ambulance driver be wrong. Please God, don't let it be Ramsey.'

She shut her eyes and leaned her head back against the seat. For the past three days, they had all been searching frenziedly for some clue about what had happened after the Mercedes had been ambushed. Everyone who was anyone had been telephoned, visited, bribed, threatened. Muslim politicians and military leaders from the Sunnis, the Druze and the Shias had gathered their men together and ordered them to bring back news of the young Shahine. Leila's father had flown in from London and offered a hundred thousand pounds – in British sterling – for his son's return. From Paris, Camilla had cajoled her father-in-law into personally ringing the other Christian *zaims* for information about Ramsey's disappearance. Charles, too, even though he had brushed aside Leila's insinuation that he was CIA, had gone to the American embassy and asked the ambassador to do whatever he could to help find the missing Palestinian. When all else had seemed to fail, a wild-eyed squad of Hussein Ibrahim's commandos had even crossed into the Christian sector and kidnapped ten young men whom they were offering to exchange for Ramsey Shahine. But until this morning, they hadn't heard so much as a whisper about what had happened to Leila's brother.

Anne chewed her bottom lip. This morning had started off like most others. She had been on duty in the emergency room at the hospital when one of the Red Crescent ambulances had screeched in with a fresh load of wounded from last night's shelling. An old Armenian woman who had been burned almost beyond recognition had been dead on arrival. Her little grandson had been trapped under the debris of their collapsing house, and Anne had amputated his right leg above the knee. A very pregnant Greek Orthodox woman had gone into premature labour and lost her baby in the operating room. A young militiaman had sustained a superficial gunshot wound in his leg. Afterwards, she had just come in from the operating room and had been sitting in the doctors' lounge drinking tea and trying to think of whom else she could ring about Ramsey, when one of the Red Crescent ambulance drivers had hesitantly approached her. She had known little bandy-legged Marcel for years. Even before the war, he had been regarded as a character. Marcel had never been anything but an ambulance driver, and yet he had always regarded everyone he brought in as his own patients. Often, after unloading a van of the wounded as he had this morning, he would bustle in later for a consultation about their progress. Anne, like the other medical staff, tried to humour him when she could. Marcel was as sweet as honey-drenched Lebanese pastry.

Anne sighed in the back seat next to Sam. She ran her free hand through her hair in despair. Why her? Why hadn't Marcel gone to PLO headquarters with his suspicions?

Again she sighed. What did it matter why?

She glanced out of the window to get her bearings. They were past the souks and not far from their destination. Since so many of the roads were impassable, they had been forced to skirt around to the Bourg and then double back to Kantari. If she couldn't bear even to remember what Marcel had said, she certainly wouldn't be able to do what she'd have to do once they got out of the car. She took a deep breath and recalled exactly what the ambulance driver had said.

Marcel had wrung his hands and explained that he, along with almost everyone else in Beirut, had heard they were searching for Ramsey Shahine. He himself had once met Ramsey personally, at his cousin's funeral in Ashrafiya, years before this war had made that Christian neighbourhood a no-man's-land for Muslims. That same cousin, Marcel had added, had died last summer in the fighting for the grand hotels down by the Corniche. His cousin had only been twenty-six and had left five young ones. It was a shame, this war, Marcel had said. It wasn't only someone important like Ramsey Shahine who paid the ultimate price. So many had died. Too many.

Anne had stared hard at Marcel. No, she had thought, oh no. But then she had pulled out a chair and asked him to sit down at her table. She had sipped her tea and braced herself for bad news.

But before he had given it to her, the ambulance driver had gone out of his way to explain that even though he was a Christian, he had no quarrel with the Muslims. His job was to bring all the wounded in, and that's exactly what he did. East Beirut or West Beirut, Christian or Muslim, it made no difference to him. He was a professional. He took pride in his work.

Anne had poured him a cup of tea and watched him light a cigarette. Finally, then, Marcel had come to the point.

Because of the latest truce, it had been relatively quiet this morning as he had been making his rounds. And so, after he had brought in that one load of wounded to the hospital, he had been able to take his time driving out again towards East Beirut. If the fighting had been fierce, he might have taken the speedy flyover to his destination. But instead he had wound along the deserted beachfront that lay underneath it.

Anne remembered how Marcel had shuddered and stopped, then. 'Go on,' she had prompted him. She had poured him more tea and waited.

There is a place, under the Charles Helou Bridge, he had finally said, one of the most terrible places in this city of terrible places, where he could always collect the dying and the dead. When he wasn't on call, he had explained, he steeled his nerves and either went to this accursed beach under the motorway where both Christians and Muslims dumped their murder victims or to another ravine under a bridge near Jounieh that served the same grisly purpose. It's not right, he had said to Anne, just to let those poor souls rot in the sun or be washed out to sea. Christian or Muslim, everyone deserved a decent burial. He considered it his Christian duty to collect the dead as well as the dying. When he had the time – like today – he picked up the bodies and delivered them to the morgue. And sometimes, too, in this human rubbish dump, he found someone who was not quite dead yet. Sometimes the assassins had botched up their work and he was able to take the wounded into the hospital. But this morning, when he'd got there, all six of the bodies lying in the sand – five men and an oldish woman – had seemed very dead. Some of the men had been mutilated. One of them had looked like Ramsey Shahine.

Marcel had burst into tears then. He was sorry, so sorry, to be bringing this terrible news. He couldn't stand so much death. Night and day, nothing but the dead and the dying. He loved Lebanon. His country had been the most beautiful in the world, and the happiest, but all that was over now. He wished he could go away from Beirut and never come back. He would take his sainted wife and his nine wonderful children and go away if he could – to America or Australia, where he had cousins. But it was only the rich who could afford to get themselves and their families out of here.

The poor – Christian or Muslim, what did it matter? – had to stay and suffer.

Anne had longed to put her head in her hands and weep along with Marcel. The ambulance driver had been right. There had been too much suffering here for any family or country to endure. But even though Anne had known that she couldn't do anything to save this blighted nation, she had decided that at least she could help this one frightened family. Marcel had been brave and even noble, and – if he was right about Ramsey – she intended to suggest to Leila's father that he give him at least part of the reward he had offered for his son's return. Perhaps Marcel and his loved ones could leave Beirut for a better life somewhere else after all. Yet there in the doctors' lounge, Anne had merely patted Marcel's hand as she gently prodded him for any more information he might have forgotten.

The ambulance driver had wiped his eyes and apologized for not bringing back those bodies. But just as he had been about to load them up, he had heard a big car or lorry stop overhead on the motorway. He had jumped back in his ambulance and driven away as fast as he could, for he had been afraid that whoever was about to heave more bodies down on to the beach might decide to use him for target practice as well. But if the doctor wanted to see for herself, he would take her. His ambulance was waiting outside. They could go at once.

She had told Marcel she was still on duty at the hospital and couldn't leave until she was off shift, which wasn't a lie. But as soon as he had gone, she had rung Sam and asked him to take her down to that beach after she had finished her work.

Anne looked over, and Sam reassuringly patted her hand. She couldn't have come here without him. Today, for once, she had no doubts about having him by her side.

Her thoughts drifted away from their terrible mission, and what awaited them when they alighted from this car. Don't think about that, she told herself. Instead she tried to focus on Sam. She was surprised at how she had turned to him today without hesitation. Even after they had become lovers, she had tried not to be dependent upon him. Although she had separated from Charles and moved into her parents' villa with Fatima and the children, she hadn't altogether been able to shake off her misgivings. Sometimes she spent weeks by Sam's side and in his bed, and sometimes she refused to see him at all.

And yet today, after Marcel had told her his tale, she had instantly called Sam. If the ambulance driver was right, and Ramsey was lying dead on that beach, she had wanted to have no one but Sam with her when she went out to identify him. On the telephone he had known, straightaway, exactly where Marcel had meant. The Lebanese, he had heard, had taken to calling it 'the haunted beach'. As soon as she had finished her shift, then, he had come over with his driver and his cameraman. Whether Ramsey's body was there or not, Sam intended to shoot part of tomorrow's film footage there. He hadn't wanted Anne to come along on such a grisly errand, but she had insisted. Every day of this war, she had worked in this hospital. She had seen everything. She could take seeing this, too, even if it were Ramsey, who was like a brother to her.

'This is it.' The cameraman leaped out of the car as soon as it stopped in the soft wet sand. He stalked the spot, looking for the best camera angles, judging the light, seeing nothing but potential footage.

Anne and Sam meanwhile remained sitting in the back seat.

'You don't have to go through with this, you know,' he told her. 'I've known Ramsey for years. If he's here, I can make a positive identification.' When she still shook her head, Sam offered a compromise. 'Look, I'll check it out first. Maybe it's a false alarm. You may not even need to get out of the car.'

Weakly she nodded. Now that she was here, her bravado had faded. She hadn't even dared to glance out yet at what might be on the sand, but she could hear the buzzing of the flies and could smell the corrupted flesh that had drawn them to this haunted place. She sat in the car, staring ahead and thanking God for Sam, when a moment later he came back and grimly leaned on her open window. 'Bad news, I'm afraid.' But before he would let her get out, he unfolded a blanket he had brought for this purpose. 'Just a minute. There's no point in your seeing . . .' He was gone again without finishing what he had been about to say.

A moment later, he was back. The heat and the stench made her so dizzy that he had to support her as she got out of the car.

Anne sank up to her ankles in the damp sand as she stared at the heaps of bodies rotting in the sun. The place was just as Marcel had described it, only there were more than six bodies here now – there were ten, eleven, even more . . . Her gorge rose, but she swallowed hard to keep it down. Marcel had been right, this was the most terrible place in all of terrible Beirut. For Anne had seen the dead and the dying lying in pools of blood after a firefight. She had watched crushed women and children being dug out of buildings which had collapsed upon them during a bombardment. She had witnessed her own father lying on the street outside her apartment building after that sniper had shot him in cold blood. But nothing so captured the horror of this war as this hellish strip of beach where the remains of what had been human beings had been thrown away like so much rubbish. The bodies lay twisted as they had fallen. She looked up at the highway flyover a good hundred feet above them. Just as Marcel had said, the bodies must have been dumped here from the overpass at low tide this morning when the beach was deep and dry. But the tide was coming in now. In an hour or so, these bodies would be washed out to sea. Neither Christians nor Muslims wanted the stench and pollution of rotting bodies left on their streets. The answer was this beach of horrors.

Sam pulled a handkerchief out of his pocket and gave it to her. She held it to her nose and mouth so she wouldn't gag.

'You don't have to look at all of them, Anne. Please, it's not necessary.' He guided her to the body he had covered with his blanket and called the driver over. 'Here, this one, I think.'

She stood in the circle of Sam's arm as the driver bent down and gently pulled back the blanket just far enough so that she could see the face.

Anne glanced down, blinked, and stared hard. She had thought she would know Ramsey anywhere at anytime, but she hardly recognized what the killers had left of Leila's brother. Yet even with that cross carved on his forehead, and those marks . . . yes.

She nodded, and then she shut her eyes. Obviously they had taken their time killing him. Judging from the condition of his body, he hadn't been dead all that long. They must have been torturing him for three days.

She opened her eyes and looked over at the nearest corpse. That one had been carved up, too. She started to shake, uncontrollably. She supposed they must have done the same to Ramsey.

Anne hid her face in Sam's chest and cried, and cried, and cried. Ramsey had been such a good man, so bright, so caring, so decent in every way. She remembered him back in Boston, squiring her here and there, always dapper, always smiling. She recalled most of all how he had stood up to Mike the night her world had crumbled. He had only come up to Mike's shoulder, but that night he had stood tall and invincible. And she had never forgotten. Not just for her but for everyone, Ramsey had always managed to be there when he was needed. More than anyone Anne had ever met, Ramsey had inspired great devotion. For a long while now, people had been saying that someday he might even end up being the first Prime Minister of the Republic of Palestine. Even the hard-hearted who thought Palestine a lost cause had looked to a young man like Ramsey to help build a new Lebanon once this ghastly war was over, *if* it was ever over. And now, for him to die like this!

She allowed Sam to tuck her back in the car. She sat there, still crying, as the driver loaded Ramsey's remains into the boot along with as many other bodies as would fit.

She wiped her eyes, then, and watched dully as the cameraman shot today's sensational footage of death in Beirut. What, she wondered, did all those people out there who didn't know and love Lebanon think when they saw carnage like this on their television news every night? Did they understand that each of these victims had lives as precious as the viewing audience back in America, England, France or Sweden? Most viewers, she thought, would just pop open another tin of beer and – as they zapped the channels looking for something less depressing to watch – might mutter an aside about how those Arabs were all animals. The more sensitive souls might be moved to ring the station and complain about such disturbing footage being shown during the dinner hour. But hardly anyone would try to understand what this war was about and why it continued.

Anne shook her head. The longer it wore on, the more cynical she got. More than thirty-five thousand Lebanese from a population of three million had died already. Yet no one – certainly neither the arms merchants nor the world's political power brokers – seemed willing or able to stop it. Arms dealers in America, Europe and the Soviet Union kept selling their mortars and their machine-guns and their rocket-propelled grenades to all the Lebanese factions. And in this war, as in so many other proxy wars fought in devastated nations all over the Third World, the Americans and the Soviets pursued their own national interests as though all that was at stake were geopolitics and world markets. The Lebanese starring role in this tragedy was merely to do what they did best, to keep on dying.

Anne listened as Sam did a standup report for the waiting world on this haunted beach in this haunted country.

Chapter 20

In her dream, Anne was running through hell.

Everywhere bodies burned. She retched from the smell of roasting flesh. But then she looked over her shoulder and saw the hooded men with guns coming after her, and so she started running again.

As though this were real and not a dream, Anne wondered, as she ran for her life, whether her hunters were Christians or Muslims. Mostly, these days, it was the Christian Phalange militia who wore those frightening black masks covering all but their eyes. But in the jungle that Lebanon had become, what was to stop the Muslims from putting on those same black masks and blaming the Christians for their dirty deeds? Anyone was capable of killing anyone now, for anything or even for nothing. If they caught her, they would kill her for sure.

Anne ran faster. Her ragged breath knifed through her chest. She didn't want to die, not now that she had Sam.

She came to a curious wide river, it was dark and

sluggish and not like water at all. She leaned over and dipped in her fingers and then brought them up to her lips. She shuddered and looked in horror at this river of blood. But the men were gaining on her, and so she waded into the river. It ran deep. When she could no longer touch the bottom, she shut her eyes and submerged herself in the blood and swam. Against her skin, it felt sticky and clung to her, dragging her down. But she struggled and swam harder, until suddenly she opened her eyes and was on the far bank. She crawled ashore and looked down at herself, covered in blood. Flies suddenly were upon her, buzzing like bombers about to decimate a village. Behind her she heard splashes and saw her pursuers crossing the river.

Again she ran. All around her she could hear the howls of the damned. Help me, they shrieked. Oh, please! But she turned a deaf ear to all their cries until she stumbled over a small smoking body. Anne looked down when the thing groaned. It was a child, a little girl. Oddly, she looked first like Fatima, then like Leila, then like Camilla, and finally just like herself. 'Help me,' the child pleaded.

But Anne's pursuers were so close now that she could hear the men panting, heavily, like animals. In their hands now, instead of guns, they carried axes. The blades gleamed in the flickering light of the fires that burned everywhere.

'Please help me,' the girl begged. But when Anne darted a look down again, she saw that the child's charred face was so deformed by burns that all that marked her as human were her dark suffering eyes. Fire still raced down her arms and legs. Anne could not pass by this poor tormented child. She could hear her pursuers almost upon her, but still she bent down and rolled the girl gently on the ground to snuff out the flames.

She picked her up in her arms, then, and turned to face the masked men who surely were about to kill her. They dripped with blood from the river, and as they closed in a pack all around her they raised their axes . . .

Anne sat straight up in bed and screamed as the phone rang.

Beside her, Sam reached for the telephone, muttered something into it, and then turned and put his arm around her and told her everything was all right, she had just had a bad dream, he was here and everything was all right. 'It's New York,' he explained. 'They say they've been trying to get a line through all night. I have to take it now.'

He turned back to the telephone, lit a cigarette, and seemed suddenly wide awake as his forehead wrinkled with concentration. He whistled. 'You're sure?'

She looked at the digital clock. It was only four, and she wasn't due at the hospital until eight. But it was a hot June night, sticky, like the river of blood in her dream. Stop it, Anne told herself. She padded out to the kitchen and brewed them two black coffees. After a nightmare like that, she wasn't going to risk going back to sleep. Sam was still on the telephone when she came back, and so she gave him his coffee and reached past him for the pack of Marlboros. She, who had always loathed cigarettes, had taken up smoking in the carnage of last winter, when life had become so cheap that it seemed impossible any of them would live long enough to die of lung cancer or heart disease. It was a filthy habit, but sometimes – like right now – it calmed her. She smoked in silence as Sam listened to his producer in New York.

'Okay,' he said finally. 'I'll get right on it.'

He hung up the phone and stubbed out his cigarette. Then he spat out his bulletin to her as authoritatively as though he were talking straight to camera. 'Just after midnight tonight, the Syrians rolled across the border. They've sent fifteen thousand combat troops, armed with the latest Soviet weaponry.' He paused for dramatic effect. 'The Syrians fighting on the side of the Christians.'

'The Christians?' She crinkled up her nose in disbelief. 'But the Syrians are Muslims. They're always saying how much they *love* the Palestinians. And, even if you don't believe all that rot about Arab brotherhood, you can't deny that the Syrians *hate* the Israelis. Think about it, Sam. You know yourself, the Christians are getting most of their arms from the Israelis now.' Knowingly she shook her head. 'No, sorry, darling. This time New York's off its trolley. The Syrians can't switch sides and be fighting with their enemies.'

'Like hell they can't.' He flicked his lighter at the tip of a fresh cigarette. 'But wait. It gets worse. If this were anywhere but the Middle East, I wouldn't believe this myself.' He inhaled down to his toes. 'But today's *New York Times* attributes this to their best sources in Jerusalem, and, believe me, honey, the *Times* practically sits in the Israeli Cabinet. They say the Syrians and the Israelis got together and agreed that, since neither of them wanted to see a radical Palestinian government in power in Beirut, they would make damn sure the Christians won this war. They struck a Red Line agreement to divide up what used to be the sovereign republic of Lebanon. The Israelis get the south. The Syrians get the Bekaa Valley. The Christians get the north and their heartland in the mountains.'

'And Beirut?'

He shrugged. 'The devil gets Beirut.'

Anne stared blankly into space. Everyone knew that the Muslim alliance had the Christians on the run. In another few months, the Christians would have had to sue for peace. Moderate Muslim politicians had already agreed on minimum reforms: a redistribution of power and wealth to reflect the majority Muslim population, new legislation to end discrimination by religion, and a reconstruction policy that would strive to equalize opportunities in blighted villages like Fatima's. There were, however, fanatics in the Muslim and Palestinian camps, just as there were among the Christians. Some of the Muslim radicals would settle for nothing less than a socialist régime in Beirut. But after the horrors of this war, Anne thought most of the Muslim leaders would have been content with an armistice that merely redressed their long-time political and economic dominance by the Christians. More than anything, the great mass of Lebanon's Muslims and Christians were traders who itched to get back to work. Without the meddling of outsiders, the Lebanese might have been able to sell one another some sort of working compromise. But now, only God knew what was going to happen.

Sam's eyes met hers. 'This is the beginning of the end, you know. Lebanon will be as good as partitioned. It's all over now.'

'Is it?' Anne's eyes were haunted. She knew the Lebanese better than he did. She had spent all her life among these people. Even though she loved them and their doomed country, she understood that blood feuds, here, could go on for ever.

She remembered that river of blood in her dream, and she shivered. But then, from an impulse for life over death, she turned to Sam and gave him that certain look. He switched off the light, and urgently they came together.

Six months later, Leila was out on the balcony of her cousin Mona's apartment in a slinky gold lamé Saint Laurent dress, trying her vampy best to charm the pants off a Syrian military chieftain who was one of the *de facto* dictators of occupied Lebanon.

'Ohhh Farouk,' she breathed, hating herself only a little as she sidled up close to him. Inside, laughing voices and the clink of cutlery on china reassured her that the others were still lingering over dinner. Mona had promised to do her best to keep everyone else away from the balcony for the half hour Leila calculated she needed to get him to ask her to marry him. She had been working on the Syrian for nearly two months, and clearly tonight was the night to close the deal. Yet her heart wasn't in it. These days, now that she had lost not only Ramsey but her father, her heart hadn't been in much of anything. Only weeks after her brother's death, her father had suffered a fatal heart attack in London. Yet she reminded herself that life limped along. If she was to get the security and power that she craved, she had to go through with this moonlit seduction.

Yet, even as she was pointing up at the starry Beirut December night, her thoughts drifted longingly back to other nights when Ramsey and hope had still been alive. The heavens, then, had been bright with Palestinian tracers, bombs and mortars. Those good old days were gone. Last month, after they occupied Beirut, the heavy-handed Syrians had declared the civil war over. Nineteen Arab League states – all except Iraq and Libya – had sanctioned Syria's invasion of Lebanon and called upon the PLO to observe the peace. At least for now, the Palestinian cause was in eclipse. Leila grasped the bitter fact that she must not only adjust to the new realities but also try to exploit them as best she could. Accordingly, tonight, she was prepared to play the part she had written for herself. This daring little dress with its provocative cutouts almost down to the waist in the back would make Farouk grunt with desire.

But even as she leaned a tantalizing centimetre closer to him on the wrought-iron balustrade, she doubted once again if she could act out her scenario. When she had been tarting herself up tonight, she had almost lost her nerve. Instead of marrying this Syrian, she had considered leaving Beirut, going into exile in London, and supporting the Palestinian revolution with lavish donations and an occasional splashy fund-raising event. No one had asked her to marry again for the cause. But she had shrugged off her misgivings and resolved to do what she had decided must be done. Just as, before, she had helped Palestinian interests by being the wife of the Prime Minister, so now it couldn't hurt for her to be the wife of the Syrian military chief. And yet, when she had stood back this evening and coldly appraised her image in the bedroom mirror, she had worried that she might not be able to pull off this particular seduction. Ten years ago she could have snapped her fingers and got any man she wanted. But she feared she looked hard now, and old. With a growing feeling of desperation, she had gazed in the mirror and ticked off her good points. She was still as slim as a fashion model. Even when she turned for a side view, her figure was faultless. She had dashed out just yesterday for another red henna rinse on her hair, and her dress was a Paris inspiration. But she was thirty-nine years old, and sometimes – in unkind glaring light – she looked it. Perhaps Farouk liked sweet young things rather than bitter oldish ones. Her eyes, especially, were not what they used to be. No matter how much eyeliner she used, no matter how many coats of mascara, no matter how artfully she layered on her eyeshadow, she couldn't change the grief that stared out from them. No, her heart wasn't in tonight's dirty work. Since the deaths of Ramsey, her father, and even poor old Mustafa, her heart had remained buried in the graves of her men. She hadn't been able to whip up her old enthusiasm for anything these last months, least of all for men. Often Hussein had come over and sat beside her and listened quietly as she poured out her hate and her pain, and – a little – it had been almost like having Ramsey back when she had Hussein to lean on like a brother. Sometimes she had yearned for him to stop being so fraternal and at least put his arm around her, but always he had kept his distance. Yet she hadn't wanted to share her bed with anyone since her brother had died as he had. Hate, she had learned, could be as all-enveloping as love. Savouries could ruin the appetite for sweets.

As she smiled up at the Syrian, Leila vowed fiercely to herself that all was still not lost. We'll win – *and I'll win*. We'll regain Palestine someday, and then we'll get even with all the scum who betrayed us. You, Farouk, in particular, will pay a very personal price for the role you played in all this, and very soon.

Demurely, as if overcome by virginal modesty, she lowered her lashes. But her downcast eyes glared at his crotch. She knew how to get even with Farouk. Ramsey's killers had castrated him before they killed him! Her tongue could cut like a knife.

With an effort, she mastered herself so that her eyes would be veiled and she would give away none of her thoughts to this Syrian enemy. Yet she couldn't help again chewing over her grudge. If the treacherous Syrians hadn't intervened on the side of the Christians last June, the Muslim alliance would by now have accomplished a Lebanese revolution. That victory, then, would surely have served as a catalyst for an invigorated Palestinian army to sweep south to liberate Palestine from Zionist bondage. Instead, thirty thousand Syrian 'peacekeeping' troops had swarmed all over Lebanon and imposed a sullen truce that not only perpetuated Christian power but allowed them to launch a vicious final assault on the Palestinians. Last summer, with the Syrians tying down the Muslim forces, the Christians had laid siege to the Palestinian refugee camp of Tel Zataar outside Beirut. After nearly eight weeks of heavy shelling, the Christians had finally overrun the camp. Accounts of what exactly had happened differed, but all agreed that the worst massacre of the civil war had then occurred. One thousand or more Palestinians had been slaughtered. Leila blamed the atrocity on the Syrians as much as the Christians. Farouk deserved the retribution she intended to wreak upon him. She could almost smell the sweet scent of revenge in the air. And so she resolved to get on with her degrading task.

She simpered girlishly. When she had first met this beefy Syrian bully, she'd known at a glance that the way to bewitch him – fast – was to pull in her claws and coo and giggle like a defenceless little woman who needed a nice fat tyrant's shoulder to lean upon. 'In England, they say that if you wish on the first star you see, then perhaps you'll get what you want.' She batted her eyelashes. 'Let's wish upon a star.'

Instead of looking up at the sky, he gazed raptly down at her face. His hand gripped her bare shoulder. 'You're so beautiful.'

'Naughty boy!' She slapped his hammy fingers. But even as she snaked just out of his reach, her sloe eyes teased him to come closer. 'Now, Farouk, none of that. Remember, you're a married man! You have a wife and children back in Damascus.'

He gritted his teeth. He hated it when this exciting woman reminded him of that dull other life. Just as everyone always said back in Damascus, these Beirut women were she-devils! As always when he was this intoxicatingly close to her, he felt befuddled. Did she want him or not? She acted as if she did, and yet she had never even let him kiss her.

'Now, darling, don't be cross with your little Leila.' She pretended she was kittenish Camilla and pouted so that her lips made a kissable *moue*. 'Look at those stars. You must look up at them, and make a wish.' She laughed. 'You can wish, can't you? What is it that you want, Farouk? *Tell me!*'

'I want you.' His voice was hoarse as he lunged closer and clamped his arm around her shoulder.

She endured his touch. She knew she had to time this

just right if she was to get him to ask her to marry him. Most of gossipy Beirut must know she had slept with a battalion of *fedayeen* after Mustafa was killed last year. She would be surprised if he hadn't heard rumours about her reputation already. She supposed he was simply so besotted with her that he had paid no attention to the gossip.

Clumsily he pulled her towards him and crushed her to his chest. He groaned as his full lips touched hers. She was as practised at love as she was at deceit, and so artfully she kissed him back. Their kiss went on and on. Just as he was about to thrust his tongue inside her mouth, she broke away slightly. 'Divorce her,' she whispered. 'Marry me.'

'No,' he moaned. 'Oh, no.'

She kissed him again, more teasingly, and then her voice cracked like a whip. 'It's her or me. Which is it?'

Dumbly he stared down at her cleavage, and he could not stop himself from reaching for her again. 'You. Yes, yes, I want to marry you.'

She pressed her advantage. 'When?'

He was altogether lost now. 'Whenever you want.'

'Then we'll do it next Thursday,' she said as briskly as if she were at her desk writing down times in her appointment book. 'That gives you a few days to go to the mosque and sign the divorce papers.' When Farouk opened his mouth to protest at such scandalous haste, she covered his lips with her own so he couldn't say no. 'We'll be together Thursday night,' she murmured. 'Thursday night, Farouk.'

As she leaned back on the balustrade and deigned to let him fondle her breasts, she smiled triumphantly.

She still had that same triumphant smile on her lips less than a week later, the night after they had signed their marriage contract. But this time she wasn't pretending. She lay naked on her bed and mocked Farouk for not being able to make love to her. She locked her hands behind her head and spread her legs. 'Don't you want it?' she purred. 'I thought you wanted it.'

He sat limp and ashamed next to her. His chalky Syrian body trembled. This had never happened to him before. With his dumpy middle-aged former wife and with the prostitutes he had habitually visited in Damascus, this had never before been a problem. He couldn't understand it. Since he had asked Leila to marry him last week, she had kept him in a state of almost constant sexual excitement. He had been so frantic with anticipation to have her that he hadn't been capable of rational thought. He had refused to listen when his friends had tried to talk him out of this match. He had accused them all of spreading lies about the woman he adored. Now he wished he had heeded their warnings and broken away before Leila enslaved him. For he was in bondage to her now. Even though he couldn't take her, he wanted her more and more.

'Farouk . . .' Her voice was soft and inviting. He watched as she aroused herself with her hand. 'I'm ready, Farouk. Now come on, *try*. You must try, even if you can't anymore.' Her hips undulated like a cabaret dancer's. 'If you can't do it, I'll find someone else who can. A real man. Maybe one of your own men. Maybe lots of your own men.'

He looked down, but still there was nothing.

Farouk put his head in his hands. As he cried, he heard her laugh.

Cautiously Camilla poked her pretty little head around the corner of the Middle East Airlines door and looked down at the Beirut tarmac.

A Syrian soldier stood at the foot of the flight steps with his machine-gun cocked and aimed at each disembarking passenger.

Camilla shrieked, burst into tears, and retreated back

into the womb of the plane. 'Don't go out there,' she screamed at her mother who was still beside their first-class seats. 'They're crazy here! All of them!'

'Madame, please,' pleaded a stewardess who was trying to guide her back towards the door.

Nirvana had come running at Camilla's first scream. And now, as the other passengers continued filing out of the door, she, too, tried to reason with her daughter. 'Come on. Take it easy, *bébé*. Don't make another problem.'

But Camilla fended her off as she cowered in the galley. 'You lied,' she accused her mother. In the homesick year that they had languished together in Camilla's apartment in the Bois de Boulogne, they had taken out their anxieties upon each other. Neither had been at her best in exile. There had been squabbles over who owed what on their jointly billed couture accounts, skirmishes about who had hurt whose feelings on endless shopping trips up and down both banks of the Seine, and – above all – furious arguments about whose fault it was that they had banished themselves from Beirut. Out of boredom, they had even briefly competed for the favours of a twenty-year-old Italian art student. It had been little consolation when he had left them both for a girl his own age. On the aircraft today, ever since they had strapped themselves into their seats, they had been arguing with each other. 'You and Pierre both told me it was safe. But you lied! Both of you! I can't count on you any more than I can count on him.'

Camilla's eyes were round with fear. *Yaadra*, she prayed frantically, O Virgin Mary, please protect me from these lunatics. If she got off this plane, they would kill her. Why had she ever allowed herself to be persuaded that the war was over and it was finally safe to return to Lebanon? She should never have listened to her husband on the telephone or to all the news reports on the television. It would never be safe here again.

'You are making a scene, *bébé*.'

'So? I am my mother's daughter.' Stubbornly Camilla crossed her arms on her chest. 'You do cabarets. I do aeroplanes.'

'Get off this plane this minute.' Nirvana pinched the tiny bit of fat on her daughter's newly flabby upper arm. 'Pierre's out there waiting for you.' She glanced around at the queue of passengers who were pretending not to watch and listen. 'You're making a fool of yourself.'

Camilla almost spat back at her. 'As I said, I am my mother's daughter.'

'*Eh bien*, do as you like. You always do, anyway. You are *impossible!*' For all she cared, her daughter could take up permanent residence on this plane. But she herself would take her chances in Lebanon – with some nice juicy Lebanese fruitseller, or a filthy rich banker, maybe even a virile young soldier eager to burn up his excess energy in the bedroom instead of on the battlefield. Lebanese men were the best in the world! Nirvana all but ran for the door.

As she fought her impulse to stick out her tongue at her mother, Camilla ignored the twittering stewardesses who were pouring her champagne and getting her aspirin and telling her not to worry, that was only a Syrian security guard positioned down there for her own safety. She resolved to herself again that she wasn't going to get off this aeroplane. She would sit back down in her seat and wait until it took off again and whisked her back to *la belle France*.

When the flight attendants had their backs turned, Camilla sailed up the aisle and buckled herself back in her window seat. She heard one of those uniformed busybodies complaining about her in the galley and saw another one talking on the telephone. But a moment later she decided to be gracious when a stewardess presented her with a glass of the bubbly. She needed a drink. She emptied the glass at a gulp, demanded another, and disregarded the safety regulations by lighting a cigarette. There, that was better, she told herself as the flight attendant came back and left her the whole bottle. By now she had recovered enough to give the label a snobbish squint: Tattinger. Not bad, she thought. With a drink in one hand and a cigarette in the other, she settled down to wait as long as she had to for take-off.

A glass later, she opened her handbag and peered in a gold-plated mirror and dabbed at her make-up so it wouldn't look as if she had just indulged in a flood of tears. One never knew, perhaps some wonderful man would sit beside her for the flight back to Paris. She could do with a delicious new *divertissement*, someone Lebanese for a change. She was sick to death of those snooty Frenchmen who didn't appreciate her as much as they should. Who were they to imply that she was too fat? Women – real women – were supposed to have breasts and buttocks. Although she didn't look it, she was nearly forty, and she deserved an occasional splurge at those yummy *pâtisseries*. She was tired, too, of how conceited those skinny Frenchmen were, always looking in mirrors and rabbiting on about themselves. Yes, men were far more trouble than they were worth. And yet she couldn't bear the thought of giving up the selfish little darlings. Life without men – even disappointing and boring men – would not be much of a life at all. Without men, what would be the point of scouring the boutiques every day, scooting off to Switzerland for those cellulite treatments, and acquiring a lifetime of artful feminine wiles? Sunbeds! Pedicures! Legwax! There would be no point in climbing out of bed in the morning, much less falling into bed at night, without men. Always she believed the next one would be the man who made life worth living. Yet sometimes even she wearied of the hunt and the chase. Last year for a season in Paris, she had given men up and dedicated herself to painting and dipping her batiks. She had been triumphant when she had sold a batch to an *avant-garde* designer who had built his spring line around them. But even when love was bad and work was good, for her the phantom of love was still more enticing than the reality of work. She could hardly go to bed with her tie-dyed fabrics. She wanted, needed, *had* to have a man.

She lit another cigarette and took a swig of champagne. She supposed she should have hung up when Pierre had rung her in Paris and begged her to come home and give him another chance. He had vowed he still loved her. He had reformed, he said. He never touched a drop of whisky anymore, he had given up hashish as well, and he never gambled or chased after other women. From now on he wanted to devote himself to his wife and his children. They could even have another baby to make up for . . . the other.

Camilla stubbed out one cigarette and immediately lit up another. But her hand was shaking, and she spilled ashes on her smart new navy Ungaro blazer. It was three years now since Tomas had died. She had thought she would never again consider bringing another child into this terrible world. But Pierre's offer of another baby had tipped the balance and tempted her back to where she was now, strapped into this seat on a Beirut runway. She still didn't believe that another child could replace Tomas. No one, ever – not a new baby, not even Guy and Emile safely tucked away in boarding school in France – could fill the void he had left inside her. And yet, a little, she longed for another child to fill at least her empty womb, while that was still a biological possibility. A baby would be soft and tiny and needy. It would love her for ever and never fail her . . . She fancied a girl this time. She might call her Julia – her jewel, her hope, a girl who would never fight and lose as the other one had, and die such a violent death.

Camilla sighed and smoked and drank. She had thought she would never come back again, yet here she was. But thank the Holy Virgin she had come to her senses just in time! She would be back in Paris by this evening. And yet she couldn't help wondering what the old homeland was like these days. After she had sat in her seat for five minutes, ten minutes, half an hour, she couldn't resist peeking out of the window.

In wide-eyed horror, she gaped at the devastated airport. The runway was so scarred, with so many craters and heaps of uncleared rubble, that she was surprised the pilot had been able to land. Tanks stood guard on the tarmac. The burned out hulk of an aeroplane leaned precariously on one wheel beside an empty hangar. Some of the terminal's windows were still boarded up, and the building itself was so blackened and battered from the year and a half of war that it seemed the fighting could have been raging here only an hour ago.

Camilla burst into tears again. As she cried, she pretended all this was simply a nightmare, and that any moment now she would wake up between her starched white sheets in her canopied bed in the Bois de Boulogne. Think of France, she told herself as she shut her eyes. But instead of delectable images of the Champs Elysées and boutiques and fashion shows, what came to mind instead was rainy drizzle and a cold people and herself always a barely tolerated outsider. She didn't belong in France; she belonged here. Or maybe, since that horrible war had destroyed not only her home but her people, she didn't belong anywhere anymore.

Again she risked a look out of the window, and again

she shuddered and wept. She would have thought they could have cleaned it up a little by now. It was February 1977, and the fighting had been over for months. Pierre had promised her that everything was just about back to normal, but Pierre had lied. He probably hadn't changed one whit, either. He was probably just as dissolute as he had always been.

She heard a commotion out on the runway and caught her breath as she looked out again. Pierre was standing in the back of a jeep headed towards the stairway to the plane. Her meddling mother must have given the game away once again. And yet, Camilla's heart thudded as she stared at the husband she hadn't seen in nearly a year. Pierre had shed not only pounds but, it seemed, years. For a moment, as she gazed at him, she remembered their gilded youth. Crazily, part of a line from the Mass came to her: 'the joy of my youth'.

Masterfully her husband strode out of the jeep, curtly barked an order to the soldier still stationed by the plane, and then stood by waiting until the gunman shrugged and trudged away towards the terminal. Impatiently Pierre took the aircraft steps two at a time.

As usual, Camilla gave herself no time to think this over, or to think at all. Impulsively she snapped open her seat belt, fluffed up her hair with her hands, and threw her new black sable coat over her shoulders.

'Pierre!' She held out her arms as he ran to her. He hugged her and held her, and kissed her, and murmured extravagant endearments into her ear.

When together they descended the staircase to the Beirut tarmac, Camilla was laughing and crying all at once. She was so happy to be home – finally home, where she belonged, in Beirut with Pierre – that she felt like kissing the battle-torn runway.

Six months later Anne and Fatima sat with Leila in her mountain villa in Aley, nervously smoking their cigarettes as they waited to see whether Camilla would make their reunion complete. Ever since their Christian friend had returned to Beirut, Anne and Fatima had been exerting their considerable diplomatic skills to engineer this encounter. But since Tomas had died, she had steadfastly refused to talk to Leila, much less come to drink tea at her home. All summer long, however, Anne had lectured Camilla that if the armies could stop fighting, surely she and Leila could do the same. Here and now in Lebanon, Fatima had always chimed in on cue, it was a time of reconciliation. At first Camilla had said no, and then she had wavered, and finally she had seemed to be persuaded. But it was past five o'clock, and the invitation had been for four.

'She's decided not to come after all,' Anne fretted. 'Or maybe Pierre talked her out of it. You know how the Nazranis are. To hear them talk, you'd never know the war was over.' At a dinner party up at the château just last week, she herself had heard Pierre say that the only good Palestinian was a dead Palestinian. She averted her eyes from Leila's. 'Or maybe we made a mistake having this *here*.' But the builders, Anne reflected, were at her apartment repairing bomb damage on the balcony and refitting all the shattered windows. With all the hammering and sawing and reconstructing that was going on these days, she had waited months for the workmen to come to redecorate. She hadn't wanted to risk telling them to go away and come back another time.

Anne stared above Leila's fireplace, where during the civil war the Palestinian flag had occupied the place of honour. Now the Manet water-lilies were back dominating the room. There were so many changes now in Lebanon. The Syrians had imposed their peace nearly a year ago, and in some ways the country was beginning to recover. But the war had taken a savage toll. Between thirty and fifty thousand people had been killed, a hundred thousand had been wounded, and the sectarian strife had forced six hundred thousand to abandon their homes. All public services – from schools and hospitals to roads and utilities – were devastated. The damage was estimated at two and a half billion dollars. Yet even now, some Lebanese were managing to turn a profit. Property values in Beirut had doubled in the past year. But one worrying fact – to Anne, at least – was that the rich Lebanese had still not learned how dangerous it could be to flaunt great wealth in the face of abject poverty. An Arab company was planning to construct a seventeen-million-dollar leisure complex along the Beirut coast. 'Summerland' would boast nightclubs, swimming pools, tennis courts and saunas. But on the beach next to it, penniless refugees would be camping in makeshift huts.

Anne sighed and came back to the pettier worry of the matter at hand. They couldn't have had this get-together at Anne's childhood home on the Rue Bliss, not with Fatima and her lively brood still there while Ali was building them another house back in Suker. Leila had suggested Sultan Ibrahim's fish restaurant, but Anne had been afraid Camilla might throw a scene in a public place. The only alternative had been for Camilla to come up here to Leila's.

At least, Anne was happy to see, Leila had taken down those martyr posters that had once adorned her parlour walls. Camilla might well have become hysterical if she had seen Tomas's face displayed like that. And yet, Anne worried, maybe it would be better after all if Camilla didn't come here today. Perhaps they were trying to push her too hard and too soon. As a doctor, she understood that, instead of healing, some wounds turned septic. Perhaps Camilla and Leila weren't yet ready to kiss and make up.

'Maybe we should call it a day. I don't think she's coming.'

'No, she is late, that is all. You forget. She is pregnant.' Fatima smiled serenely. She, too, was once again expecting another child. 'She was maybe just sitting at home, dreaming, and forgot the time. We must be patient. *Inshallah*, she will come.'

'She'll come, all right.' Leila wished she hadn't allowed Anne and Fatima to talk her into this humiliating gesture. Wasn't it enough that her side had lost the war? The least Camilla could have done was to make the first move towards suing for their own personal peace. It wasn't her fault that Camilla's son had been gunned down in that labour dispute. The order for the army to shoot had come straight from the office of the Christian President. 'She won't miss this opportunity for a grand performance. You both know how melodramatic she's always been. Just like her mother! She'll cry and carry on as though she was the only one who lost anything in the war.'

They all smoked in silence as their thoughts turned to the losses each of them had suffered: Leila a not-much-loved husband and an adored brother and father, Fatima two crippled sons and the home her husband had built for her with his own hands, Anne a beloved father and . . .

'Camilla's always been fragile,' Anne said, falling back into her old peacemaker role. She was not about to admit even to her bosom pals that she, too, was feeling very wobbly now that Sam was gone.

Anxiously Anne lit another cigarette and pushed her hair unbecomingly back behind her ears. Since Sam had been reassigned to London at the end of the war, she had grown careless about her appearance again. She had lost twenty pounds, and her clothes hung on her in all the wrong places. But six months ago, when Sam had delivered his ultimatum just before he had left

Beirut, she had simply lost her appetite. She would lose him for ever, he had said, unless she divorced Charles and became his wife. But when it had come down to a permanent commitment, Anne had vacillated, and procrastinated, and made every excuse but the true one. She was afraid to trust another man as she had once trusted Mike. She had hummed and hawed until even Sam had lost patience. They had fought, and made up, and fought again on the eve of his departure for London. They still talked on the telephone almost every day, and Sam had backed down on his all-or-nothing demand. Yet she had been so wrung out that, when Charles had called her a short time later and suggested they have a drink and talk things over, she had been open to reconciliation with her estranged husband. Perhaps, she had decided, her shell of a marriage with Charles suited her. It might be best to keep Sam at arm's length. They could conduct a civilized love affair, take sensuous holidays together, and yet she wouldn't have to risk her equilibrium for Sam. With a gigantic sigh of relief, then, she had settled back into that comfortable old arrangement with Charles. Yet at night, when she lay alone – for she and Charles had separate bedrooms – and couldn't sleep for the remembering, she sometimes rang Sam and admitted that maybe the two of them belonged together after all.

The doorbell sounded, and a moment later they heard Camilla's tinkling laugh in the foyer.

The Filipino houseboy who had long served Farouk in Damascus, and whom the Syrian had insisted on installing here in Beirut, stood ceremoniously in the doorway. 'Madame Nazrani,' he announced.

Camilla waddled in, in all her expectant glory. Just as soon as the doctors had confirmed her condition, she had put aside her mourning blacks and burst out into pregnant splendour. Today she was all abloom in Saint Laurent's 'rich peasant' look: a flouncy purple skirt, a gold lurex blouse, a turquoise beaded turban, and gold hoop earrings that Madame Kismet might have envied. Her smile was as wide as her stomach.

'Anne! Fatima!' She held out her arms and blew rapturous kisses at the two with whom she was on speaking terms. Anne hugged her, and they kissed cheeks twice, twice again, and many more times. Fatima, too, rushed over and their protruding bellies got in the way as they hugged, kissed and cooed.

Dramatically, then, Camilla allowed her baby blue eyes to come to rest on the other one. She blanched as though shocked to find Leila sitting in her own salon. Then she held her hand up to her heart as though she had palpitations, and finally froze in an attitude of indecision.

'Oh, bloody hell,' Leila muttered. But then she couldn't help laughing affectionately at the sheer excess of her old friend's performance. Whatever else Camilla was and wasn't, she was good company and as effervescent as champagne. In those innocent bygone times when their children had been toddlers and Beirut had been like Paradise, the two of them used to laugh until they had to wipe the tears from their eyes as they lolled around their swimming pools. In these last troubled years, she had missed Camilla's infectiously giddy laughter. She couldn't roll the years back and recapture youth for herself and peace for this country, but she could take a small healing step towards reconciliation with Camilla.

Leila smiled uncertainly as tentatively she got to her feet. Anne had told her how Camilla had persuaded old man Nazrani to try to help when Ramsey had first been reported missing. But even though Leila thought that she should reach out her hand and at least thank Camilla for that, other – darker – memories came flooding back: the massacres at Karantina and Tel Zataar, Christians flaying Muslims alive, Camilla herself calling the Palestinians 'scum' on the day Tomas died. Leila's smile hardened. Nothing was the same as it had been, not between herself and Camilla, and not between the Muslims and Christians of Lebanon. Some grudges never could, or should, be forgiven. She and her people had lost this vicious war to Camilla and her kind, and Leila had always been a poor loser.

Nevertheless, Camilla had already launched into what appeared to be the next well-rehearsed scene in her dramatic reunion. 'Ah, Leila, my Leila . . .' Since this new baby had made her so pregnant with hope, she couldn't remain angry with anyone anymore. Tears stood in her eyes, for she had never lost the gift of crying prettily. 'It's been so long!' She swept forward until the two of them were eyelash to eyelash. Leila had predicted that she would claim the role as chief mourner of the Lebanese civil war, but instead Camilla surprised her with a burst of passionate generosity. 'Tomas! Ramsey! Anne's father! Fatima's sons! We've lost them all! It's enough, I say, eh?' She threw herself upon Leila. As if of their own volition, the Palestinian's arms closed around her old Christian friend. By now, Camilla was sobbing heavily. 'When Tomas died, I wanted to die, too. It wasn't your fault, but I blamed you.' Camilla sniffled. 'I was so sorry about Ramsey. So very sorry.'

'And Tomas,' Leila said softly, from the heart. She was surprised that she was so moved by Camilla and her tears. Her own eyes stung. 'We all loved that boy, too, you know.' Her voice caught. 'I kept thinking, it could have been my Mimi who died.'

'Remember, when they were babies, how they played together? They were so sweet, like angels. I loved my son more than anything in this world.' Camilla's shoulders shook. 'Oh, I miss him!'

'There, there,' Leila said as she patted the other woman's babysoft back. 'Don't cry.' But Leila's eyes, too, were brimming. Over Camilla's head, she saw that Anne and Fatima were also wiping away tears. She was touched at how much this reconciliation meant to them all. Because they sometimes fell out of touch with one another for years at a time, Leila had assumed the men in her life mattered more than her old women friends. The four of them weren't even related by blood, and were all so very different in temperament, values and background. Yet it came to her now that they had forged a bond in their youth that would last all their lives. What they had together transcended politics, war and grief.

Still, Leila was – as usual – a little ashamed of her own emotions, and so she was the first to break away and wipe her eyes. 'Now, let's have a nice cup of tea,' she said, in the exact incantation she remembered fine English ladies uttering when they deemed it prudent to sweep overwhelming feelings back under cover, where they belonged. She rang for the Filipino to bring them a fresh pot of Earl Grey, and then she busied herself with the paraphernalia of strainers, milk and sugar. Finally she passed around a plate of Lebanese and French pastries. 'Well, here we are,' she said brightly. 'Together again, after all these years. Just look at us.'

Doubtfully the four of them sipped their tea and did just that. For the moment it took to assess the damage, no one spoke. The years had taken their toll on all of them.

Fatima's girlish plumpness had spread into a middle-aged girth that would not melt away after her next baby. Her face had been lengthened by double chins, and her breasts and her belly sagged. If it weren't for that white scarf she still insisted on wearing, and the kindness that continued to shine from her contented face, the others might not have recognized her in a crowd of peasant women.

The changes in Camilla had not been nearly so startling, although even without the distortions of pregnancy, the lines of her figure too had blurred beyond her old hour-glass perfection. If there was the merest hint of dissipation around the eyes and perhaps a hint of desperation in the way she overdressed, still she was as pretty as a slightly faded old movie pin-up.

Anne, however, had once again lost her sparkle. With Sam gone she looked just as drained of all her womanly juices as when she had returned to Beirut after losing the first love of her life. Even though she had retained her dignity, there was a palpable sadness about her.

The years had left Leila looking sharper, more angular, and stripped to the bone. Her cheekbones jutted nervously over her sunken cheeks. She had plucked her eyebrows into such an exaggerated arch that her face seemed perpetually surprised. Her clothing, too – a severe Issey Miyake black jumpsuit – was an exclamation point. Her restless eyes betrayed the nervous strain of living too long with too much anxiety.

Fatima was the first to break the silence with sweet comforting lies. 'You're all so beautiful,' she gushed. Her eyes evaded Anne's and focused instead on Leila and Camilla, who were indeed, after all these years, still as glamorous as film stars. Leila's minimalist black outfit looked shockingly expensive even to Fatima's untutored eye. Everything about Camilla, from her armful of jangling gold bangle bracelets to her tottering high-heeled strap sandals, cried out that here was a frothy creature born not for work but for play. Eagerly Fatima tried to fix in her mind exactly what they were wearing, for when she finally returned to the village her sisters and cousins would badger her for every delicious detail about how the other half looked and acted. 'And none of you have changed at all.' Mentally she asked Allah's forgiveness for this exaggeration of the truth. To her mind, all three of them had aged more than they should. But it was her observation that Western women who drank alcohol and led fast lives ended up old before their time. Childbirth and the constant demands of her family took another sort of honourable physical toll. But not for a minute would she want to change places with her friends here. Even so, she told them what she thought they wanted to hear. 'You all still look as young as when we were at college.'

'You think so?' Camilla was as susceptible as ever to flattery. She couldn't resist taking her mirror out of her handbag and preening at her reflection. 'Hormone shots,' she confided. 'They are *le dernier cri*! Everyone has them now! I have this wonderful old German doctor in Geneva. Dr Schmidt. An old Nazi, everyone says!' Belatedly she remembered that Anne was a Jew, and covered her embarrassment by turning to Leila and breathlessly continuing her chatter. 'You really must have some, darling. They say you'll never get old if you have Dr Schmidt's injections.'

'Really?' Leila was still on her best behaviour, and so tactfully she took care not to let slip what was on the tip of her tongue, that Camilla's tough-hided skin tones were hardly a recommendation of the redoubtable Dr Schmidt. 'But tell me, darling, how was Paris?' Leila wasn't asking an idle question. She had considered exile before, and might do so again. She had heard better reports of expatriate Lebanese life in France than in England.

Camilla said what she always said when anyone in Beirut asked her about her years away in the City of Light. '*Merveilleuse*! I adore Paris!' She gave her beturbaned head a pretty toss. But then she remembered that these were her real friends, not her detestable in-laws or those obnoxious hangers-on at the château. 'Still,' she hedged slightly more honestly, 'it's not home.' She lit a cigarette and admitted to herself that she was so very tired of living so very many lies. The truth burst out of her. 'I hated it there! I couldn't wait to come home!' Inevitably, she burst into tears. 'I was so lonely,' she sobbed, 'and Mama was so horrible. You remember how she always would pick on me.' Camilla's voice trilled high in a merciless imitation of Nirvana. 'You eat too much, *bébé!* You sleep too much, *bébé!* Do *this*, Camilla! Do *that*, Camilla!' Thoughtfully she exhaled. 'My mother, I think, was not so happy in Paris either.' She sighed and gave her shoulders a weary Gallic shrug. 'So when Pierre called and wanted me to come back, both Mama and I did. He promised me things would be different this time. He said he wasn't gambling and had said goodbye to all his girls and wasn't drinking the whisky, either.' She stopped crying just long enough to utter a bitter 'Ha!' 'So I come back, and what do I find? Yes, of course, still the whores and the roulette. If I can't find him at the casino, I know he must be at the racetrack. But now he drinks vodka.'

'*Plus ça change* . . .' Anne did not try to hide her bitterness, for she, too, was tired of putting on a brave front and bottling everything up inside. 'He still calls, you know. *Sam*. From Egypt, the Gulf, and London of course. It kills me sometimes to talk to him. We might be better off just to give up and let it die.' There was a deadness in Anne's eyes. 'He says he's quite famous now, that he made his name in America covering our war. The Christians didn't win the war. The journalists did.' She tried to laugh, but no one else was even smiling. 'I never know whether to talk to him or not. I can be going along okay for days, and all I have to do is hear his voice, and I'm miserable again. I want him – and I don't want him – *so* much, all at once. I wish I could decide what to do.' She sighed. 'I try to blame Sam and Charles, but I'm the real problem.' She lit a cigarette. 'Sam says that, even though I won't marry him, he still wants to be my friend. But why would I want him just as a friend? I *have* lots of friends.' She shook her head. 'Sometimes I doubt if men and women can ever be friends. At least friends like we are.'

Camilla nodded until her hoop earrings jangled. 'Ah,

oui. When it is over with a man, for me, too, *c'est fini. Complètement!* With Pierre it is a little different, because of the children and because of the families. But maybe it was over with us, too, long ago, when I found him in my bed with those wet nurses. In *my* bed!' Still, after all these years, Camilla was indignant. 'Imagine!' She wrinkled her pert upturned nose. 'And the others, *mes petites amourettes*, all those little men who come and go, I never like them, once it is *fini.*' She reconsidered. '*Véritablement*, I don't think I ever really liked any of them. *Jamais.*'

'What is there to like?' Leila's eyes flashed with contempt.

Fatima frowned. She couldn't believe what she was hearing from these liberated women who had always seemed at least the equals of their menfolk. Her worldly friends sounded every bit as disillusioned as the poorest village women who suffered lives of drudgery and broken dreams. Yet she had imagined that these three – with their dazzling lovers, rich husbands and freedom to indulge in romantic love – would have ended up with a better opinion of men. Some of the women back in Suker were just as bitter, and for some of the same reasons. 'In my village the men and the women live in very separate worlds. Do you say, now, that it is the same here?'

'Not separate enough,' Anne said grimly.

'Men.' Leila snarled that one word like a curse. Her bonhomie was wearing thin, and the predator in her couldn't resist turning on Fatima just as she used to. 'But tell us,' she began silkily, 'what about your Ali? How is everything back in the little village love nest?'

Fatima dimpled a smile. 'As always.'

'He never seems to be with you,' Leila pointed out. 'He comes home long enough to get you pregnant again, and then – like most men – he's off again on his important manly business.'

'No, you are wrong. Always he is with me. Inside.' Fatima touched her heart. 'Here.'

'How very sweet,' Leila said. She was about to say more – much more – but she intercepted Anne's warning look. Sullenly she sipped her tea. It wasn't fair that Fatima appeared to be so happy with so little, whereas Leila's own marital relations were a disaster. Mustafa had been a saint compared to Farouk. Any day now, no matter what the personal or political cost, she was going to demand a divorce. Yet she was determined not to ruin this reunion with such dark thoughts. 'To hell with these cakes and tea.' She banged her cup back down on the saucer and shouted to the houseboy to bring them a magnum of champagne and an ice bucket.

'Not so fast.' Greedily Camilla reached for another piece of *baklawa*. She had promised herself that, during the sweet happy months of this pregnancy, she could eat everything she wanted. Afterwards, she would go on a loathsome diet. Just in case the houseboy was about to take the pastries away, however, she scooped a dripping wedge of *kunnifeh* on to her plate.

'Tch!' Leila smacked Camilla's hand. 'Really, darling, you should be more careful.'

Camilla wrinkled up her baby face and looked about to burst into tears again. Instead, as she bit into a forkful of *baklawa*, her good humour returned. 'The Swiss have a fabulous new treatment. Fat section. No, fat *suction*. It is like a Hoover.' She made a slicing motion at her thigh. 'They put in a tube and – whoosh – out comes the fat.'

'And the muscles, too, I've heard.' Anne shook her head. 'Those techniques are dangerous.' Her no-nonsense tone made it clear that this was the doctor talking. 'I would strongly advise you against any such operation.'

As the Filipino arrived with the chilled champagne, the four of them continued with their own separate agendas. Camilla was pouting and devouring her cakes.

Anne was earnestly suggesting that Camilla and Fatima both adopt a sensible diet and regular exercise. Leila was imperiously directing the houseboy to fill everyone's fluted crystal glasses to the brim. And Fatima was insisting on apple juice instead of champagne. 'A toast,' Leila finally said as the Filipino stood at attention by the ice bucket. 'To friendship!'

As they all drank, the talk turned to more mundane matters: when Camilla and Fatima were due, how they could arrange for Anne to deliver both babies, Miriam's school in Switzerland, Guy and Emile's school in France, whether Leila was going to send her boys to school in England, which of their old acquaintances were still living abroad. For not everyone had come home at the end of the war. Some had chosen to stay permanently in Paris, Geneva, Athens, London or New York.

'But don't let's be so depressed, darlings!' Leila had quickly downed three glasses, and already the champagne had gone to her head. Giddily she laughed. 'What's this', she asked Camilla, 'that I hear about your mother and a garage mechanic?'

Camilla sighed. If Leila had heard about Nirvana's latest scandalous affair, the entire country – Muslim and Christian alike – must know about it. 'You know Mama! I swear before the Virgin, she wasn't back home here for a week, before she started up with a new one! He is not even a garage mechanic! He only fills the petrol tanks! And he is only seventeen! Old enough to be her grandson!'

'No!' Anne grinned admiringly. 'Leave it to Nirvana!'

'I heard', Leila said, 'that she spotted him when she was buying petrol in Tripoli. And that every day from then on – until she got him! – she drove all the way up there from Beirut and had him fill up her tank.' She smirked. 'With premium!'

As even Fatima laughed, Camilla pouted. 'My mother is the laughing-stock of the whole country.'

Fatima laid a consoling hand on Camilla's arm. 'But do you not understand how wonderful it is – with everything so bad all around us – to have your mother to make us smile?'

'She's right.' Anne nodded. 'Everyone loves your mother, you know. We all love her music. And we all love *her!* She is so very *Lebanese!*'

'You just try having her for a mother, though,' Camilla answered. But she, too, was smiling.

'That's the spirit!' Leila drained another glass of champagne. 'Laugh! Keep laughing! We're all together! We should be laughing and laughing!' She leaned forward conspiratorially. 'You must have heard the new Syrian jokes!' When no one responded, she launched into her repertoire. 'Did you hear about the new Syrian invention? Waterproof teabags!'

Everyone but the Filipino politely smiled.

'Or', Leila continued, 'the one about the Syrian orphanage which had parents' day?'

'I don't get it,' Camilla said. 'Orphans don't have mothers or fathers.' She stopped short and giggled as belatedly she understood the barbed joke.

Leila took this as encouragement to continue. 'I hear the Syrians have designed a new parachute,' she said. 'It opens on impact.'

'I think maybe that is not so funny,' Fatima said. 'Not so funny and not so smart.'

'Leila!' Cautiously Anne looked around. Since the Syrian occupation, Lebanese freedom of speech had been severely curtailed. These days, it was said, Beirut had become as spy-ridden as Damascus. The Syrian secret police and their paid informers were supposedly everywhere. Even though no one was here but them and the servant, she had heard too many stories lately about what could happen to those who dared to belittle the overbearing Syrians. 'Don't you think you should be more careful what you say?'

'Careful? Me? Not bloody likely.' Merrily – or was it bitterly – Leila laughed. 'I'm not afraid to say what I think.' For good measure, she threw in a final joke. 'I heard about this Syrian saboteur', she said, 'who was told to blow up a colonel's car. But he burnt his lips on the exhaust pipe!'

'I wish you wouldn't say things like that,' Anne said, unhappily.

Fatima, too, looked worried. 'Your husband, I think, would not like that joke.'

'Oh, I get it! Farouk's a Syrian!' But as the import of what Leila had said dawned on her, Camilla covered her mouth with her hand and stopped laughing.

Leila's bravado only increased as she held out her glass to the houseboy and then gulped down the contents. 'You think I'm afraid of that husband of mine, eh? Just because the Syrians have that deadly little habit of permanently shutting up their Lebanese enemies?' She laughed bitterly. 'They killed Mustafa, you know. And they killed Kemal Jumblatt this year, too.'

The other three froze. Although everyone believed the Syrians had been behind the death of the Druze leader, they thought Leila mad to say so in the home of a Syrian general.

But Leila said still more. 'I'll let you girls in on a little secret.' She was drunk enough to be slurring her words. 'That one's never been a real man with me. *Not once!* He tries and he tries and still he can't.' She spat in the air in that age-old gesture of Arab contempt. 'This for the Syrians!'

'Oh, Leila!' Fatima looked stricken. 'I'm so sorry.'

'Me too.' Anne regarded her Palestinian friend with concern. 'So it's that bad between the two of you, is it?'

Leila merely nodded. When the Filipino poured the dregs into her glass, she drained them.

'I will pray for you,' Fatima promised.

'And we'll have lunch,' Camilla said. 'We'll go to Ajami's maybe. Just as before.'

But times had changed. 'Which Ajami's?' Anne asked. 'The one on al-Hamra's too fancy. It's nothing like the old one that used to be down by the port.'

All four of them sighed. No matter how they tried to pretend that everything – including themselves – was the same as it had been before the war, there was no escaping the differences.

Yet some things *were* still the same. Camilla's tinkling laugh was infectious. 'Old, new, what does it matter, so long as we're together! Just the four of us!' She snapped her fingers. 'Men! Who needs them!'

'Aunt Bert – of all people! – sent me a poster from Boston. "A woman needs a man", it says, "like a fish needs a bicycle." ' They all laughed.

But it was only a few minutes later that they made their farewells and began picking up the threads of the lives they lived now.

And it was only a few hours later that the agents of the Deuxième Bureau came to arrest Leila for seditious talk.

She was shocked when they came for her at nightfall. She was outraged when they courteously but firmly insisted that she get into the back seat of their armoured car and drive with them to the prison. She was frightened when they escorted her to a dark little cell and locked her inside. She had never felt so alone and so powerless as in those terrible hours hunched up on that iron bunk.

It was only after they had brought her out for two hours of relentless interrogation, confronting her with the exact jokes she had cracked in her own parlour in front of her three oldest and dearest friends, that Leila came to and began fighting for her own precious survival. The more accusations they hurled upon her, the cooler she became. She admitted to nothing but a sense of humour. She even smiled as she said so.

But back in her cell, where they left her until well after dawn, Leila paced and seethed and planned revenge on the one who had dared do this to her. She was certain her husband must have engineered this sordid charade. Either Farouk had bugged his own drawing room, or he had that houseboy of his spying on his own wife. Even in this paranoid Levantine netherworld, there could be no other possible explanation for her arrest. She had briefly considered – but then quickly rejected – the possibility that one of her old friends had reported her to the secret police. Both Anne and Fatima were incapable of betraying anyone for anything. And if Camilla had still been harbouring resentment about Tomas's death, she would simply have screamed, wept, and perhaps tried to scratch Leila's eyes out. She was neither devious enough nor malicious enough to tattle to the secret police.

No, Leila decided as she paced in the dark, damp cell. *He's* the one who put me here. And he's the one I shall make pay for it.

Leila sat on the edge of the iron bunk and gritted her teeth. If Farouk thought this was going to make her buckle under and become some submissive little mouse of a wife, he was going to discover that he had sadly underestimated his Palestinian partner. His exercise in intimidation was going to backfire. She wasn't going to let him off easily with a painless divorce. The war between them was far from over; it had, indeed, just escalated. Her tactic would be to become more remote and inaccessible than ever. For she knew her enemy. The more she held out, the more he would want her. Perversely, even obsessively, he would love her all the more. She, the eternal woman, would be the eternal victor.

With a bitter sense of anticipation, Leila came out of the prison and went home, with her head held high, to the husband she hated. She would make him pay for her own and Lebanon's growing sense of oppression. If she, too, had to pay a price for all this – if she was to become colder, harder and more bitter – then so be it.

She would turn their marriage into a kind of guerrilla war between conqueror and rebel, man and woman.

Waning

1978-1982

Chapter 21

By the grim look on her husband's momentarily unguarded face, Fatima knew that something had gone wrong the minute he and their two eldest sons came in from the pelting rain and stepped over the threshold of the new home he had built them in the village.

But, as always, as soon as he was back in the bosom of his family, Ali tried to lay aside the troubled outside world and to pretend – if only for a blissful hour – that this womb-like nest of father, mother, sons and daughters was the only place that existed this side of Paradise. The younger children threw themselves upon him before he even had time to take off his heavy brown wool cloak. He picked four-year-old Amina up in his arms and whirled her around as though he were a dervish caught in a heavenly rapture. The little girl squealed and grabbed dizzily at his white turban for balance before the mullah finally put her down and it was the turn of the others for kisses, hugs and the sharing of small children's triumphs. One of the older girls was with her mother in the kitchen, stirring the pots and seasoning the stews, and the others were down on their hands and knees here in the central room laying out last week's newspapers to serve as a makeshift tablecloth for tonight's dinner. One of the older boys was gravely helping their father shed his cloak, and two of the younger ones were approaching with a basin of water and a ewer so he could wash his hands before eating. Another brother brought out the charcoal brazier, and a sister stirred the live coals so their father could warm his chilled hands. Then the father and the children sat expectantly in a circle around the newspapers on the floor and finally the older girls came in carrying big round tin trays full of steaming tureens of rice, meat and vegetables.

'*Bismillah al-raham al-rahim.*' Ali intoned the grace: 'In the name of God the merciful and the compassionate.'

Merrily they began to eat. The brothers teased the sisters about this and that, but gently, as they always did. The girls blushed and lowered their eyes and neatly and swiftly disposed of great quantities of rice, using not only their right hands but pieces of pitta bread as makeshift shovels. The very best morsels of lamb were daintily pressed upon the *paterfamilias* and the older boys. They joked and laughed and ate their fill from the communal bowls.

Fatima, still busy out in the kitchen soaking the pots and cutting up the fruit for dessert, was the last to come in and take her accustomed place on the outskirts of the family circle. She sat down clumsily, for she was pregnant again. But her coming changed the whole pattern of the group. Before, everything had swirled around Ali's magnetic pole. But now two equal fields of gravity held the sphere of the family together.

As she listened to this daughter and laughed with that son, Fatima wondered what was amiss with her husband. He had been out since early morning and hadn't even come home for lunch as he usually did. But Muharram, the Shia month of religious mourning, would begin in a few days, and she had supposed preparations at the mosque must have kept him away from home. Yet covertly, as she picked at her food, she studied the set not only of his face but also of the faces of the two sons who had been with him down in the mosque. Muhammad and Muhssin were subdued and ate only a little of dishes that they would normally have devoured. Something more pressing than the usual village squabbles about who would take which role in the historical sketch that would be part of the coming religious ceremonies was disturbing her husband. She quickly ran over the possibilities in her mind. Ali's father had been ailing for some time, so perhaps he had taken a turn for the worse. It could be, too, that some hitch had developed in their long-standing plans to send Muhammad, their eldest son, to university in Beirut next autumn. Or perhaps there was trouble brewing at the newly reopened girls' school, where she had once again taken up her duties as headmistress.

Just then, as her oldest daughter broke out in a peal of laughter, Fatima was struck by another dire possibility. Ali had been negotiating for the past few months to marry Zainab to his brother Hamid's son Musa. Maybe something had gone wrong with the marriage negotiations.

Fatima lost her appetite. She dearly wanted Zainab to marry Musa for he was religious, good-humoured and generous by nature. More than anything, she wanted to see all her children securely settled in properly arranged marriages. For despite her education and early exposure to the wider world in Beirut, Fatima was now as the other women in the village.

Fatima smiled at her aged mother, who had come back from Beirut to live with them. Long ago Ummie had told her that the older a woman became, the more she believed in the rightness of the ancient ways. In this, as in so many other things, her mother had been right. The more she had aged, the more conservative she had become. Fatima hardly remembered how, once, she had been so full of despair at the prospect of marrying Ali that she had considered running away to Beirut or London or Boston – anywhere where she could have chosen how she would live and whom she would love. And yet, of all of them in the family, she was pushing the hardest for an arranged marriage for her sixteen-year-old daughter. Such a union had made her so happy that she believed it was the answer for every one of her children. If she had needed any more proof of the pitfalls of romantic love, she only had to conjure up the damning words that Anne, Camilla and Leila had spoken at their last tea party. Ever since each of her four daughters had been born, Fatima had been constantly on the alert to match each girl with her most appropriate first or second cousin. She had worked and schemed to bring off this particular match for Zainab ever since she had watched her daughter playing happily with Musa when they both had been toddlers. Since Zainab was mature for her age and had never been inclined to apply herself in the classroom, Fatima saw no reason why the alliance should be postponed any longer. Both young people, so far as Fatima knew, were just as eager for the match to proceed. But maybe Musa's father had had second thoughts?

Fatima was so sure that this must be what was bothering Ali, and so preoccupied with the possible failure of her matchmaking, that weary hours later, after she and her daughters had washed up and all the children had been settled in bed, she was utterly unprepared for the bombshell that her husband dropped when they were finally alone.

They were sitting side by side on the wide creaky bed Ali had bought for them more than a year ago, when he had finished this new house and furnished it with second-hand bits and pieces bought on market days in Tyre and Sidon. She watched in silence as he went through the ritual of rolling them both their nightly cigarettes, then placed hers between her lips and inhaled as he lit it. She breathed in the smoke and, even though she knew that he was about to break some bad news to her, she relaxed for the first time since dinner. Nicotine, she secretly thought, was a gift from Allah.

For a moment, as she shut her eyes with pleasure and inhaled, Ali merely gazed at the woman he loved.

It seemed to him that the two of them were at their most intimate not when they touched under the covers in the dark but at times like this, when they simply rested together in contented harmony. He thanked God, as he did every day, for giving him this woman and this family.

But then Ali sighed under his breath very softly, so she wouldn't hear him. He couldn't put off telling her any longer.

'There was bad news today, on the radio.'

Her eyes flew open. She had not imagined that, once again, in March 1978, the outside world was about to intrude on their placid backwater. Since the Syrians had occupied Lebanon nearly two years ago, the Muslims and Christians had bided their time and endured this imposed stalemate. Yet under the surface the old hatreds had continued to fester not only between Muslim and Christian but between and among rival Muslim and Christian factions. Last year, after the Druze leader Kemal Jumblatt had been assassinated, his grieving militiamen had run amok and killed the first Christian villagers they could find and from time to time since there had been random kidnappings, explosions and gunfights between rival militias. Meanwhile, everyone kept his well-oiled AK-47, M-16 or Kalashnikov handy under the bed. So who had broken the peace this time, she wondered: the rival Christian warlords, the Palestinian guerrillas, the militant Druze, or the foreign mischief-makers from Syria, Israel, the Soviet Union or America? She sucked in hard on her cigarette, this time with more need than pleasure, as she waited to hear the worst.

'There was a *fedayeen* raid today in Israel. The Palestinians say it was their answer to Anwar Sadat going to Jerusalem last November to seek peace.' Wearily Ali shook his head. 'The radio said more than thirty, maybe as many as forty Israelis died. On a bus,

I think. The Palestinians, too, were all killed.' He paused, so the implication of the next bit of news would sink in. 'The radio said they came by boat from our country.'

'No.' She knew just as well as he did that every time there was a *fedayeen* raid inside Israel or a Palestinian attack on Zionist institutions anywhere in the world, Israel retaliated on south Lebanon. 'Please, God, not again.' She prayed silently to herself for a moment, and then she opened her eyes. 'You are telling me that the Israeli planes will come again?'

'You know how they are.' As he looked south to the Israeli border, a scant twelve miles away, Ali's eyes were bitter. Even after the civil war had ended, southern Lebanon had continued to be a troublespot. In the Chatura Agreement which the PLO had signed with the Syrians, the Palestinians had agreed to pull back from their bases near the Israeli border and cease launching raids into the Zionist state. But the marauding Maronite Christian militia of Major Saad Haddad – which was funded and sponsored by the Israelis – had prevented a neutral Lebanese Army peacekeeping force from patrolling the strategic border area. Since then, between the Palestinians and Major Haddad's militia, southern Lebanon had become more of a no-man's-land than ever. 'I am telling you that we must take precautions. At the mosque, today, the men all talked. Some wanted to stay and maybe fight if the Israelis come against us with their troops. Resist, like our hero, dear Imam Hussein, did at Kerbala.' As he invoked the name of that Shia Muslim martyr whose death thirteen centuries ago in Iraq is honoured every year at Muharram, Ali seemed momentarily to take heart. But then his eyes dulled, and he bowed his head in resignation. 'They want to fight, our men, but what can we do against the big planes? Israel is strong, and we are weak. So most of our men decided to take their families back to Beirut. The weather tonight is very bad.

El-hamdulillah, all this rain will keep us safe. But when the sun comes, you know what else will be in the sky! And so, as I said, we must take precautions. Tomorrow you and the children will go up to Beirut. Two of my brothers and all their families are there. You will not be alone.'

She caught the significance of his words. 'And you?'

'I will stay.' Again he held his head high, as a man does when he has decided not to abandon his self-respect. 'This is my home, and I will defend it. If they come, I will fight with my men in the Amal militia.'

'*Mashallah*,' she murmured, invoking God's blessing, as the Shia always do when someone has said or done something especially worthy of praise. For her husband's words thrilled her. She, as much as he, was sick of always running away. She, too, had sometimes gone to the public meetings in Beirut, Nabatiya, Tyre and Sidon and listened to the stirring sermons of Imam Musa Sadr. She, too, had been inspired by his Movement of the Dispossessed. The imam was doing all he could to goad the government into protecting the Shias of the south against the Israelis. She had been so flattered when, on his last tour of the south, the imam had eaten the chicken she had cooked with her own hands for the special lunch given to him at the mosque in Suker. Even the imam said the struggle was as much the women's as the men's. 'Then I will stay, too.' Her jaw set, and her double chins locked with determination. 'I will not go without you. I, too, will fight.'

'You?' Ali made the mistake of laughing. She had never so much as touched his or their sons' guns.

'Yes, me.' Until this moment she had not considered the possibility of taking up arms in the defence of her family or her village. But his laughter had stung. In the nineteen years of their marriage, she had seldom been so angry at her husband.

Ali, the born diplomat, took care to wipe the smile

off his face. 'My dear wife,' he begged, 'be reasonable.'

'My dear husband,' she responded crisply, 'I am reasonable.' She crossed her arms stubbornly over her chest. When she had been a girl of twenty-two and they had first been married, he had been able to talk her into almost anything. But she was forty-one now, and circumstances had often forced her into assuming most of the responsibilities for their sprawling family. This time the matriarch faced out the patriarch. 'I refuse to go to Beirut again. I won't leave you here alone. I'm your wife. My place is with you.'

'Ah, Fatima! That you are. And that you will always be.' He loved the strong woman she had become even more than the submissive girl she had once tried to be. He wished for a moment that it was only he and she against a lesser world. But there were others to think of besides themselves. He could not let his wife's devotion to him put their children at risk. 'But you are a mother, too. You must take the children where they will be safe. Wait at Dr Anne's a few days, a week, maybe a fortnight, until once again you can all come back.'

'Again to Beirut?' As she sighed and shook her head, her anger at Ali drained away. It wasn't his fault that Suker was once more at risk from this deadly cycle of Palestinian and Israeli violence. But she still could not bear to give in and agree to flee to Beirut yet again. Long ago, when she was young, she had been dazzled by the zest and the beauty of Beirut. But there was little to love now in that teeming, sullen capital which nearly a million penniless refugees had strained beyond its capacities. For nearly thirty years the Palestinians had been forced to live there like penned-up animals in their wretched refugee camps, but now their numbers were swollen by hundreds of thousands of Muslim refugees displaced from both Christian-dominated areas of Lebanon and from the southern Shia heartland that lay too close to the Israeli border. When she, the children and other assorted members of her family had first fled to Beirut after the last Israeli bombardment of her village, nineteen of them had been crammed inside one small room with no running water, electricity or sanitation more sophisticated than a hole in the ground. Their standard of living had markedly improved once Anne had invited them to move into her vacant villa on the Rue Bliss. But Fatima was too proud to live on charity, even when it came from her dearest friend. Moreover, something inside her balked at abandoning this second house that Ali had built for her. They had moved back home and settled down into the gently satisfying rhythms of village life only a year ago last autumn, before her son Jaber had been born. Now that Fatima was rooted back at the centre of her universe, she was not going to be forced out again. Her voice was a whisper. 'A woman has honour, too, Ali. I don't want to run away again.' Her words seemed to renew her inner resolve. 'I tell you, this time I won't go.'

And she did not soften that night, even after her husband's most sensuous persuasions.

The next day, as they awoke not to the muezzin's prayer call but to the revving of engines as their cousins and neighbours got an early start on their exodus to Beirut, Ali let the children in on their quandary. The older ones remembered other Israeli raids. But the younger ones had not yet learned to fear the silver planes that came from the south. Keenly their childish treble voices chorused the Palestinian slogans they had learned to shout in Beirut. One by one they vowed that they, too, would stay in the village and fight with their father and their mother. Yet Fatima suspected that fears of another sort were behind her children's bravado. When they thought she wasn't looking, the little ones trembled at the prospect of returning to war-torn Beirut, where they remembered the terrifying boom of the guns. Wide-eyed they watched their two eldest brothers, who had already undergone military training in the Amal militia, making a great show of getting their Kalashnikovs out from under their beds and readying them for combat.

So it was, that first morning after the *fedayeen* attack, that a tight-lipped Ali stopped trying to persuade his family to flee to Beirut and, staring anxiously up at the dark and heavy sky, reflected on his failure to make his family tow the line. So much, he grumbled to himself, for the myth of Arab male supremacy. When it came to the crux, his wife was a mountain that was not going to come to Muhammad. And yet, as he and his two armed sons marched down to the mosque in the rain, he took hope. So long as this murky weather held, there was still time to evacuate his loved ones to safety. Every time he prayed that day, he besought Allah for more merciful rain.

But that night, when he waded his way home through the mud, he faced not domestic bliss but a nervous and divided family. All day long, as always happens in the Middle East when blood is about to be spilled, the rumours had spiralled out of all proportion. The Israelis were said to be approaching by land, by sea, by air. Fatima's mother heard from a neighbour that they had levelled Tyre, captured Sidon, were besieging Beirut. Every time a housewife heard a car backfiring, she assumed it was a mortar attack and broke out in anguished keening. Small boys ran in frantic packs from house to house, spreading the latest alarms and even climbing up tall trees in order to warn their elders of any surprise attack. Even though Fatima and the children tried to be brave, the strain showed. Salma burst into tears when she dropped a tureen of rice on the floor as she was carrying it in from the kitchen. Baby Jaber was colicky and screamed all through dinner. The older boys snapped at one another and glared at their mother, who had absolutely forbidden any of them to run off to join a PLO unit in Tyre. Miserably they avoided one another's eyes as they huddled around the charcoal brazier. Everyone went to bed early and then lay sleepless, wondering if the bombers would wake them in the morning.

As Ali and Fatima sat tensely smoking in bed, he lost patience and ordered her and the children off to Beirut first thing in the morning. But she argued passionately that she could not bear to be made homeless once again. Look what happened to the Palestinians, she pointed out: as a result of fleeing their homes in 1948, they had forfeited perhaps for ever not only their villages but also their country. She reminded him that their family was a perfect indivisible unit sanctioned by God and man, and so together they would all await their fate in Suker. Yet when Ali softened, and turned to persuasion instead of threats, she finally agreed to send some of the children up to Anne's in Beirut tomorrow with one of the neighbours. The baby was still at the breast and would have to stay here with her. Fatima's mother, too, was adamant about staying. But she would send Zainab to mother the little ones over the rough spots.

The second morning after the *fedayeen* attack in Israel, the skies were still beautifully heavy with clouds and a heaven-sent fog. Fatima waved goodbye to four of the children as they set out in a neighbour's overloaded car, and then she commandeered those remaining to make what preparations they could. They carried tins of food, a small kerosene stove, and great jugs of water and sacks of rice out to the bomb shelter at the far end of the garden. They stocked up on candles, took in a transistor radio Ali had brought home from the mosque, and even lugged in shovels in case they had to dig themselves out.

That night she, Ali and the remaining children were giddy with excitement as they sat around on the floor eating dinner. Last night they had been miserable with fear, but tonight this all seemed like a marvellous family adventure. They were beginning to enjoy being brave and fearless and getting ready for an Israeli bombing attack which most of them were beginning to think would never come.

Yet the next morning – overcast again, *el-hamdu-lillah!* – their fears took over. That night, as she and Ali sat moodily smoking in bed, Fatima's determination to stay finally faltered. What, after all, she asked her husband rhetorically, did she think she could do to defend her family and her village from a swooping Israeli attack from the sky?

'Exactly,' Ali fervently assured her. Mentally he thanked God for her change of heart. He had been praying hard that the rainclouds would continue long enough for his wife to come to her senses.

'You think we should go?' Fatima asked him.

Careful, he told himself. Don't push her too hard again. 'I do,' he said cautiously.

'Then I will.' Her voice was very small. 'But, Ali, I want you to come with us, too. I don't want to go alone. Please.'

Usually their love-making was swift, for they knew one another's bodies as well as they knew every crevice and contour of their village and so could pleasure themselves in a few familiar moments. But that night they lay for a long while in one another's arms and made love as tenderly as though for the first time.

Afterwards, Ali repeated once again that, for him, staying in the village was a matter of principle. As much to steady his own nerves as to reassure his wife, he glossed over reality. Most probably, he said, the Israelis would simply do as they had in the past and send a few bombers north to hit the Palestinian refugee camps clustered around Tyre, Sidon and perhaps even Beirut. Despite the alarmist rumours that had been circulating in the village, there was no reason to believe that this time the Israeli response would be anything out of the ordinary. Besides, he concluded, even if the worse came to the worst and the Israeli planes did come, their shelters were well made and provisioned. *Inshallah*, he would survive this attack as he had so many others.

Sated with love as she lay in the circle of his arm, her head cushioned on his chest so she could hear his great heart beating, Fatima was almost reassured that everything was going to turn out for the best.

But when the next morning dawned pink and bronze and frighteningly clear, she was distraught as Ali supervised the loading up of the car and the packing in of the children. He had delegated Muhammad, his eldest son, to drive the family up to Beirut and temporarily take responsibility for their welfare. But he had relented and agreed that his teenage son Muhssin, who had completed his Amal militia training, could remain with him to defend the village. 'Hurry,' Ali urged them as he looked up at the empty sky.

In the end, however, he was the one who delayed their parting. He kissed each of his children, and then couldn't resist making another round and kissing every one of them again. Finally, he held Fatima chastely in his arms. They had said a more intimate farewell an hour before this morning's dawn. Yet now, although he had rarely showed his passion for her in front of the children, he kissed her on her cheeks, her forehead, her eyes, and finally her mouth. 'Go with God,' he whispered, as she climbed into the back seat with Elham, Ahmed and baby Jaber. Muhammad tooted the horn, and Fatima's mother waved and wept in the front seat.

Ali and Muhssin waved and then ran after the Mercedes until it picked up speed and disappeared around the bend on the road towards the sea.

For a while, as the girls wiped their eyes and the boys cracked silly jokes to keep themselves from weeping, the Mercedes made good time. Yet they hadn't gone very far, only over three hills and around a clutch of slithery bends, before Muhammad had to jam on the brakes. Ahead of them the Tyre road was bumper to bumper with a column of fleeing villagers. For three days, the Shia had been packing up and lashing their belongings on to their cars and their trucks as they prepared to trek to what they hoped was safety. Each morning the narrow road had been unequal to the traffic, and this fourth morning after the Palestinian raid was no exception. As they crept along, Fatima fretted that even after they reached Tyre and then turned north on the coastal road, the traffic would be snarled up like this all the way to Beirut. She began to regret that she hadn't set out as soon as the first news of the *fedayeen* raid had been flashed on the radio.

An hour later they were still stalled in place a few miles east of Tyre, on the crest of a hill that overlooked a Palestinian refugee camp on the outskirts of the city, when they heard the deadly buzz they had been listening for in the sky.

'Out!' Fatima ordered. She and the children scrambled from the car. She looked up and saw the Phantoms coming. She counted two, four, seven, maybe more. 'Take cover!' Dumbly her terrified children looked at the low boulders that lay by the road. Nowhere on this barren hill was there a tree, a cave, or any natural or man-made haven. 'Keep down!' she shouted. 'Don't move once they're over us!' In a panic, her children joined the stampede of refugees from the other abandoned cars who were scattering all over the hillside. Elham and Ahmed took their grandmother by the hands and ran for their lives. The smaller ones tried to creep into cracks between the rocks, and the bigger ones flattened themselves behind anything and everything. Some prayed a favourite *surah* from the Koran, and others burst into tears. The older ones put their arms around their younger sisters and brothers. Fatima cowered with her baby, and Jaber must have felt her fear, for he huddled so close to her that it seemed he was struggling to return to her womb.

Overhead the planes whined, then swooped, finally screaming as they flew so low that they would have shaved off treetops if there had been any vegetation on this exposed hill. There was, then, an awful instant of utter silence before the booming explosions began. The ground flashed and trembled. Orange fires whooshed. Black smoke billowed. The noise, the smell, the sight was hellish as still the bombs continued to fall. Some blasted gaping craters in the earth and burst into raging fires upon impact. Others – oddly – seemed to waver before they hit the ground. But then these peculiar 'cluster' bombs burst into hundreds of glittering deadly fragments that sounded like a mini-war of their own as they rained death on every doomed centimetre of a hundred-metre area. There was a moment's respite as two of the bombers finished their run at this hill and continued on to the refugee camp in the valley. But then two more Phantoms screamed low as they loosened another load and as suddenly as it had begun, the bombardment of the smouldering hill was over.

In a daze, Fatima crept to her feet. The smoke was blinding, but all around her she could hear children piteously wailing for their mothers. She and Jaber were unharmed. Yet the hill was a heap of the dead and the wounded. Frantically she ran from body to body, looking for her sons and daughters. 'Muhammad!' she cried out. 'Are you safe? Ummie? Elham? Ahmed?'

Finally she saw Muhammad bending over the shuddering forms of his younger sister and brother. Elham was doubled over in pain and badly burned on her face, arms and legs. Ahmed was moaning as he clutched his right arm, which dangled lifelessly from his shoulder. Even as he tried to calm his screaming brother and sister, Muhammad wept as he stared at the smoking body of his grandmother.

'Ummie!' Fatima screeched. She threw herself down on the ground, and cradled that dear body. But her mother was dead and her sufferings over. 'Ummie,' she whispered.

Fatima forced herself to turn back to her children. Oh God, she prayed, remembering her first sight of Hassan and Ibrahim after the bombers had struck. The girl and boy had to have a doctor's attention, and quickly. She tried to soothe Elham and Ahmed, and then she looked back to the burning wreckage of their car. Even if the Mercedes had been drivable, the road was impassable. They would have to walk to Tyre. She prayed the hospital there would not be hit in the Israeli raid.

The fear she had been repressing ever since she had first heard the planes overwhelmed her. Had the bombers struck in Suker? Were Ali and her son safe? She shaded her eyes with her free hand and anxiously looked east, towards the village.

But then she put that wrenching worry aside. There was no way of turning back. Ali and Muhssin were in God's hands. It was up to her to muster all her reserves to get her two wounded children to hospital and the rest of her brood to a safe haven.

She directed Muhammad to pick up Ahmed while she herself tenderly lifted Elham in her arms. When the girl whimpered, Fatima kissed her at her temples and crooned endearments.

She led her traumatized children down the barren hill towards the burning city.

It wasn't until several harrowing days later, after Elham and Ahmed had been transferred to the American University Hospital in Beirut, that Fatima understood that this deadly air strike had only been the beginning of a massive Israeli incursion into Lebanon. As twenty-five thousand Israeli combat troops seized control of more than four hundred square miles of Lebanese territory, the Israeli navy had bombarded the south Lebanese coast and the Israeli air force had struck at Palestinian refugee camps and suspected PLO military targets. At first communications with the occupied villages of the south had been sealed off. The first inkling of the full extent of the devastation had come from medical rescue teams who estimated that two thousand civilians had been killed and a hundred Lebanese villages attacked by the invading Israeli troops. Twenty-five hundred homes had been completely destroyed in the fighting, and more than five thousand other houses damaged. A quarter of a million people had been made homeless.

Behind those grim statistics lay the greatest tragedy of Fatima's life.

The bad news finally caught up with her indirectly, via a young Swedish ambulance driver who was a friend of Anne's. Before he had driven south on his mercy mission, he had promised Anne that he would try to discover what had happened in Fatima's village. A day later he had telephoned from Tyre with an eyewitness report from one of the few survivors. When the Israeli troops had rolled into Suker, Shaykh Ali and his men had opened fire from concealed positions in the houses, the shops, even the mosque itself. A short battle had ensued. When it was over, all its defenders – including the mullah and his son – had lain dead. In retaliation for that resistance, the Israelis had demolished every building in the village.

That afternoon Anne had gone over to her villa on the Rue Bliss, where Fatima and the children were ensconced. As gently as she could, she had broken the news. She had held her old friend in her arms then, and the two of them had wept.

But then, only a few moments later, Fatima had wiped her eyes and taken her sons and daughters aside, one by one, to tell them that their father and brother had preceded them to Paradise. And then she had busied herself in the kitchen preparing Elham and Ahmed's favourite foods to take them that night in the hospital. The girl was suffering from burns on forty per cent of her body, and Anne had amputated the little boy's right arm. But both children were expected to live.

Following Fatima around the villa that afternoon, Anne had been astonished at the ease with which her friend had appeared to pull herself together. In the hospital she was accustomed to bereaved widows rending their clothes, tearing their hair, and howling like injured animals when she told them that their husbands had died. But aside from that initial storm of weeping, Fatima had tightly contained her grief. Yet when Anne remarked on how brave she was to be able to go on like this, the widow had let the veil slip for just a moment. Her deep-set eyes had been bottomless wells of pain as she simply said, 'I will mourn him for ever.' But then she had squared her shoulders and set about grating a bushel of carrots for Ahmed's favourite *halwah* candy.

Her husband had been dead more than a week before Fatima let on to anyone – and perhaps even to herself – the depth of the despair she was feeling.

It was on the sacred eve of Ashura, the climax of the holy Shia Muslim mourning month of Muharram, when finally she came to grips with her grief.

Late that afternoon, as the Muharram religious frenzies were about to come to a head, she had carefully dressed her children from head to toe in black and set out with them on foot for one of their sect's mosques in Beirut's southern suburbs. On the way she had remembered how eagerly she and Ali had been looking forward to observing Ashura back in their own mosque in their own village. Last year her husband had been called away to Beirut for the holiday, and before that the civil war had kept them from the village during the Shia commemorations. But this Muharram, when they had thought they were going to be all together at home, had turned out to be the worst of their lives.

And yet, as step by step Fatima plodded to the

mosque with her children, she reflected that tonight's grief-stricken service might take on an especially poignant meaning. The month of Muharram, after all, was not a Yuletide season of peace and joy. Instead, Muharram honours a bloody historical and emotional cycle of oppression, rebellion and martyrdom which the Shia consider to be both triumphant and transcendent. For Fatima's people, the holy days which climax at Ashura cut deep enough not only to draw blood but also to soar into a kind of healing ecstasy. For this commemoration of the death of the most beloved Shia heroes is the heart and soul of the schism which divides the minority Shia from the majority of Sunni Muslims. Long ago on the Iraqi battlefield of Kerbala, a Sunni general wiped out rebellious Shia descendants of the Prophet. This Muharram, Fatima's family, along with many hundreds of thousands of Lebanon's bereaved and homeless Shiite Muslims, would be mourning for the present as well as the past.

The street outside the mosque was a dark and sombre stream of the devout. The women were shrouded in their black *abayas* and the men were dressed in their black shirts and black trousers. Fatima sent her older boys off with Muhammad to the men's section in the front of the mosque, and she filed in the women's entrance with her daughters and the youngest children. Always this shabby mosque was devoid of furnishings or icons, but tonight the bare walls were grimly draped with black banners exhorting the faithful to remember how Imam Hussein had died for everything that was right in this world and the next. It was early, but already the mosque was filling up. There were no chairs, only thick Persian carpets where the religious sat crosslegged listening to the mullahs. Fatima offered a small prayer of thanksgiving when she spotted an empty corner at the side. The service would go on for hours, but she would be one of the lucky ones who could lean her weary back against a wall. With a sigh she settled her brood around her and took out her prayer beads as she waited for the service.

After a long while the speeches began. Mullah after mullah preached about the meaning of the Ashura commemoration. Parallels were drawn between the sufferings of the early Muslims on the battleground of Kerbala in Iraq and that of contemporary Muslims in the Shia villages of southern Lebanon. From time to time, as the sermons wound on and on, the men would interrupt to voice their praise of Allah in hoarse rhythmic chants. Fatima's younger children stretched out all around her and slept with their heads as close as they could get to her lap. Muffled inside the ample folds of her *abaya*, Fatima, too, dozed off as the holy men made their abstruse theological points but she snapped to attention when she heard the familiar voice of Imam Musa Sadr. She tried to catch a glimpse of him through the thick black velvet curtain that chastely separated the brothers from the sisters, but of course she could not see the revered Shia leader who was speaking at the front of the mosque. But she could hear his passionate words. The Shia, he said, had not died in vain either at Kerbala long ago or just this week in south Lebanon. She was thrilled when he mentioned her own Ali's name. 'The fighting mullah of Suker', the imam said, was only the latest in a long line of Shia martyrs. Under her black robe, Fatima glowed. The imam said Ali was a martyr!

Finally then, as the dimming of the electric lights signalled that the soul of the service was about to begin, there was a stir of anticipation in every corner of the mosque. An elderly *shaykh* who was renowned for the emotive quality of his voice climbed up into a black-draped chair which had been erected at the front. He cleared his throat and launched into a heart-rending retelling of the death of the Imam Hussein and his followers at Kerbala thirteen centuries ago.

Every man, every woman, even every child in that mosque knew every detail of how their beloved hero had suffered and died. They did not have to be reminded that Imam Hussein was the Prophet's grandson and by rights should have reigned in Mecca as Islam's Caliph rather than dying for his faith on a dusty and distant Iraqi battlefield. Then, as now, the Shia believed, the good and the holy were robbed of what should rightly be theirs. As the old *shaykh* repeated the saga, they listened with the same rapt wonder as when their mothers and fathers had first engraved this story upon their hearts. For the Shia, no event in the yearly religious calendar is as emotional as this Ashura tale of the epic hero who is slain in the prime of his life for a gloriously lost cause. For them, the wrong rankles as though it had happened only the day before yesterday.

This year, as every year, in the dark mosque the weeping began. Fatima and the other women gathered the loose folds of their black robes around themselves so that even their faces were hidden inside the tents of their *abayas*. The men, too, seemed to shrink inside themselves, and they hid their heads in their hands as they wept not only for Imam Hussein but also for themselves. As the *shaykh* recounted the story, old widows keened and young widows wailed. Grown men sobbed.

Hidden in her robe, Fatima finally lost her composure and broke down completely. Even as a child, she had always wept on Ashura for Imam Hussein. So now, too, she abandoned her inhibitions and surrendered to a paroxysm of grief. She wept until she thought her heart would surely break, and then wept again. She cried for the love of her life. She cried for the husband who had been her life's companion and her best friend. She cried for the father of her children. She was still crying when the mosque lights came back on and the service moved into its next ecstatic and cathartic stage of the *taazia*.

On the other side of the black velvet curtain, the men leapt to their feet and formed a tight circle. Inside it, a band of young mourners stood grimly clapping their hands and then beating their chests as another *shaykh* cried out another version of the death of Imam Hussein. But this time the story sounded less like a dirge than a battle cry. As the men in the circle picked up the rhythm with their clapping hands, the young men in the centre began striking their chests harder and harder, and then their heads. As they beat themselves, they began to shuffle and then leap in a frenzy of dancing grief. Sometimes in some places, the *taazia* dancers lash their bare chests with heavy chains and have even been known to use knives on their bare heads. But this time, this year, here in the southern suburbs of West Beirut, the celebrants merely smacked their chests with their fists. Flesh hit flesh in a muffled sound. Thump! Thump! Hussein! Hussein!

In the back, the women formed their own circle, clapping hard, keeping time with the sombre beat of the *shaykh*. Fatima stood between her daughters Zainab and Salma. As the rhythm speeded up, all the women and girls clapped faster. Some screamed as the story and the clapping gathered in a crescendo.

Time and again the circles formed, reformed and collapsed as the *shaykh* retold the tales of the deaths of Imam Hussein's companions, son, and the rest of his family and friends. As each hero died, the hysteria in the mosque increased. The clapping grew more heated. The beat became ferocious. At its climax the *shaykh* howled long and hard for the death of Imam Hussein himself. The very walls of the mosque reverberated with the beat of the mourning. 'Hussein!' they shouted in unison. '*Ya*, Hussein! O Hussein! Hussein!'

Finally the men and the women formed a last grouping as the *shaykh* recounted the dénouement of the story. For after the men were put to the sword in battle, the women were rounded up for an arduous long march to Damascus. Yet, as the Shia tell it, in this temporary defeat lay the seeds of a more lasting victory. The hero of Kerbala was the dead martyr Hussein, but its heroine was the living zealot Zainab. Instead of bowing her head and surrendering to humiliating defeat, Hussein's sister fiercely shouted the message of Kerbala from one end of the Islamic world to the other. Resistance! Death rather than surrender! Fight the oppressors!

Fatima beat her breast as the *shaykh* chanted out the 'Zainab' part of the *taazia*, which the Shia women take as their particular inspiration. Her daughters stood beside her, and facing her on the far side of the circle were her cousins. All of them had suffered much the same as Zainab. And so, as the women listened to the story of their heroine, they took her trials and tribulations and eventual triumphs as their own. As the *shaykh* retold how an exhausted Zainab marched along to Damascus, how she would walk, and fall, and crawl to her feet and walk again – 'See Zainab,' he shouted. 'She walks and she falls!' – the Shia women of the Lebanon recalled their flight from their villages. They screamed out, yes, that Zainab fell but she rose and she triumphed.

Fatima and the women beat their breasts harder and faster. Some lurched forward to the centre of the circle and began to dance in ecstatic jerking movements, up and down, back and forth. Others began slapping their faces with the flat palms of their hands, so that they blushed red and glowed as if on fire.

Fatima felt a flush coming over her, and she was hardly aware what she was doing as she glided into the centre of the heaving circle. She struck her face and shouted with the other women as a frenzy swept over her. For a moment she forgot all about Ali and the shattering of her life. For a second all that there was in this world and the next was the ecstasy of Kerbala. As the dancing grew more heated, the women reached up and pulled their scarves from their heads so that just this once their dark hair fell free down their backs. 'Zainab!' they screamed. '*Ya*, Zainab! O Zainab!'

With a final cathartic scream from the *shaykh*, the beat suddenly stopped and the mosque dissolved into silence.

Fatima lay in a heap on the Persian carpets, purged, at least for this instant, of her grief.

She lay motionless, with her eyes tight shut, as if in a coma. Yet she was conscious, and her mind was clearer and her heart less sore than at any time since she had heard of Ali's death. A moment ago, when she had danced into the centre of the circle, she had briefly felt herself in a world whose boundaries stretched further than temporal emotions. And in that transcendent instant, one clear and shining insight had come to her. The love she had lavished on her man she must now offer to her God.

A peaceful smile curved her lips as she lay on the worn carpets of the mosque. It was to Allah now that she would turn for comfort.

Her hand crept out and touched her stomach. If the baby inside was a boy, she would call him Ali.

As Anne let herself in at the front door, the villa on the Rue Bliss buzzed with activity. Doors slammed. Feet sounded on stairs. Excited children's voices rang out from upstairs, downstairs, outside in the garden. She set her suitcase down in the hallway, called out that she was here, and then stood back and opened her arms to whichever of Fatima's sons and daughters got to her first.

'Auntie Anne!'

She laughed as she was engulfed by the children whom she liked to think of as almost her own. She kissed them, hugged them, and assured them that no, there were no problems, she had just come early to help with the final packing before she picked Elham and Ahmed up at the hospital and drove out to the airport.

Zainab scurried off to the kitchen to make tea, Salma ran back upstairs to oversee the packing, and Muhammad paced importantly out to the driveway to make sure yet again that the car was ready for its glamorous run to the airport.

Meanwhile, six-year-old Hussein was tugging at her skirt and pouting. 'I want to come, Auntie Anne.'

'Me, too.' His adoring little sister Amina always agreed with everything he said.

'Maybe next time,' Anne promised gravely. 'But I can't take all of you with me today.'

'You like Elham and Ahmed better than us,' Hussein accused her. Of all the children, he had taken the deaths of his father and older brother Muhssin the hardest. These days, he needed constant reassurance.

'Yes, better,' Amina echoed.

In answer, Anne sank down on a sofa in the sitting room and put Hussein on one knee and Amina on the other. 'You know I love all of you,' she began, 'from Muhammad right down to Jaber. There's nothing I'd like better than to take all of you with me today on the plane to New York.'

'Good,' Hussein said. 'Then I will come.'

'Me, too,' Amina added.

'Not this time,' Anne continued more firmly. 'This isn't a holiday. I'm taking your brother and sister to special doctors there. So Ahmed can get fitted for a sort of arm that will be almost as good as his real arm. And so the doctors can try to make Elham pretty again.'

'Isn't Elham pretty anymore?' For once, Amina had an original question.

Anne bit her lip and lied. 'Oh, yes.' She had refused to let Fatima's children see their badly scarred sister until the specialists in New York had a chance to do what they could with skin grafts to reconstruct her face, arms and legs. 'But she'll be even prettier when we come back from New York.'

'Prettier than me?' Amina persisted.

'Nobody's prettier than you,' Hussein said, as a ray of his old sunny self managed to shine through once again.

Shyly the brother and sister smiled at one another and then, seeming to forget all about their demand to be taken to New York, they ran out to play in the garden.

'I worry about that boy,' Fatima said. 'He says when he grows up he wants to get a big gun and kill all the Israelis who murdered his father and his brothers.' In the shadow of the hallway, she was almost invisible in her black dress and black headscarf.

'He's only a little boy,' Anne assured her and moved over so her friend could sit down beside her. In a week or so, Fatima would be going into labour. 'He will grow out of it.'

'Or into it.' Fatima sighed. For her, one of the heaviest burdens since Ali had died three months ago was playing both mother and father to her brood. What would she say and do, she wondered, if one day not far distant Hussein came home with a Kalashnikov instead of his school books? The civil war had been officially over for two years, but still the fragile Lebanese peace was too often shattered by random violence. She did not dare to return to Suker. A few weeks after their invasion, the Israelis had bowed to a United Nations resolution and pulled back most of their forces from Lebanon. A UN force had taken up position in southern Lebanon, but there was sporadic fighting in what the Israelis called their 'security zone' between the UN troops and the

Maronite Christian militia of the Israeli-backed Major Haddad. But there was scattered fighting, too, in Beirut. Sometimes, when she saw her children off to school in the morning, she worried about whether they would all return unharmed for lunch. But there was no point, she reminded herself firmly, in getting obsessional about the fate of her country or her sons. The future was in God's hands. As always, that sentiment comforted her. The lines etched so deeply into her forehead smoothed out, and her face relaxed into its usual curves of plump serenity. When Zainab brought in the tea, Fatima spooned sugar into Anne's glass and sweetly changed the subject. 'So today you return to your country. You must be very happy.'

'I suppose.' Anne blew on her tea to cool it. 'It will be great to get up to Boston and see Mother and Aunt Bert. They're quite a pair, those two. My mother sounds happier now than she ever did when she was here. I know she misses Dad, but I'm sure she doesn't miss Beirut.'

She evaded Fatima's knowing eyes and hoped that was all she would be required to say about her expectations of America. She certainly didn't intend to tell her that she planned to see Sam in New York. Fatima was hardly likely to be sympathetic to an adulterous love affair. Since her husband's death, she had burrowed even deeper into the strict codes of her religion. Fatima was not quite so understanding of others' weaknesses as she used to be.

Guiltily Anne studied her fingernails. Being with Fatima could be like sitting down with your conscience and having it talk back. Her on-off affair with Sam was most definitely 'on' again. Over the past months she had confided each and every detail of her resurrected romance to Leila and Camilla. But she had never so much as admitted to Fatima that she still talked to him on the telephone almost every day. She had also neglected to mention that they had met for a stolen weekend in Paris, that they had slipped off to a week in Greece, and that before he had been called back to the network's headquarters in New York she had stayed with him when she had attended a medical conference in London. Yet, even so, as though Fatima were some primitive, black-shrouded Great Goddess to whom she could never lie, Anne suddenly couldn't help blurting out the truth. 'I'm going to see *him* there.' She paused. 'Sam.'

'I see.' Fatima pursed her lips and sipped her tea. 'Why?'

'Why? What do you mean, "why"?' As she glared at Fatima, suddenly an unbridgeable gap loomed between the two old friends. Maybe, Anne thought resentfully, it had been easier for Fatima – with that perfect marriage and all those wonderful children – to be sanctimonious about what was right and wrong. But what did Fatima know about loneliness and loss? Anne was ashamed an instant later, when she lowered her eyes from the widow in black. Of course, now, she and Fatima were more than equal in loss. 'I suppose I must still love him,' she admitted.

'Oh.' Fatima thought that over, and evidently, from the sternness in her voice when she continued, she remained unmoved. 'But what is all this? You said to me – again and again – that it was finished with him. *Khelas*, you said, *fini*. You said Charles was the man for you. You said you wanted to be a good wife.'

'You forget', Anne heatedly replied, 'that Charles is hardly a good husband.' These days the two of them hardly spoke. He had fallen in love with a Maronite Christian soldier, and – for the first time in their married life – Charles was openly flaunting his affair with a Phalange militiaman in Beirut's restaurants, cocktail lounges and nightclubs. Either he was so in love with the fellow that he couldn't help showing it, or else he was finally getting back at his wife for living with Sam during the civil war. Anne wished, now, that she had kept her mouth shut in front of Fatima. She had known exactly how her hyper-religious friend would react to her intending to see Sam in New York. So why, then, just before she was about to get on a plane and fly off to join her lover, had she found confiding in Fatima irresistible?

I suppose, Anne admitted to herself as she nervously picked the discreet pearl-coloured varnish off the nail of her index finger, that I must want her to talk me out of it. And I guess I believe, in a way, that it might be better if she did.

But instead Fatima was shaking her head in exasperation. 'I do not understand what is wrong with your men in the West. They have travelled, I think, too far from what we call in Islam "the straight path". Some of them like your Charles want men more than women. I try and try to understand this, but I cannot. Your Charles is such a kind man. So sensitive. So sweet, really. But it is wrong what he does with men. Wrong before God and wrong to you, his wife.' Fatima's eyes flashed with righteous anger. 'And then some of your men, like that one in Boston who hurt you so, are even worse. Men like that are bad enough to kill even the best woman's heart. No, soul. Maybe both. I do not know how you women can endure it.' She smiled. 'I thank God for the life I have had, and the man that Allah gave me.' Yet Fatima did not believe that two wrongs could ever make a right. Adultery was a sin, and so she was not about to send Anne off to Sam with her blessing. 'It would be different if you and Charles got a divorce. Then you could marry your Sam.'

'Just because you had a happy marriage doesn't mean everyone else does. I'm not sure I want to marry Sam. Or anyone else.'

Moodily Anne stared at the dregs at the bottom

of her glass of tea. So long as she was with Sam, she felt secure, happy, and sure that she wanted him to be her partner. He was everything she had ever wanted a man to be – kind, sensitive, and stimulating both in bed and when they were talking and laughing over a cup of coffee. Yet still, when they were apart for only a few hours, her old doubts set in.

Anne gnawed her lower lip. She couldn't string this ambivalent situation out for ever. Sooner or later Sam would stick to his resolve either to marry her or forget her. Already he was pressuring her to leave Beirut and take up a residency in a New York hospital. You're a Jew and an American, he always told her, and sooner or later that will put you at risk in the continuing anarchy of Beirut. But then, the last time they had talked this over, Sam had been struck by a brainwave. Why not try, he had suggested, to set up a special medical unit in New York to deal with the continuing problems of Lebanese children injured in the fighting? Like so much else that revolved around Sam, she had found that idea very tempting. She intended to talk to some of the New York hospitals this week to see if the idea was workable. And yet part of her still resisted it, and him.

When the phone rang, for a second Anne almost expected it to be Sam. He must have telepathically read her thoughts, and was about to give her the ultimatum she dreaded.

After answering the caller in Arabic, however, Fatima switched over to her fluent but heavily accented French. She held her hand over the receiver and whispered that it was Camilla's mother. 'She is very difficult to understand, no?'

Anne rolled her eyes. 'Drunk, most likely.' Everyone in Beirut knew that Nirvana was far too fond of the grape. But a moment later, when she could see by the look on Fatima's face that something was very wrong, she regretted her offhand remark. She listened to Fatima exclaiming over and over how terrible that was and how sorry she was and how she would pray for the family, and then she passed over the telephone.

'Anne! Anne! Help! My *bébé*!' Nirvana babbled in a hysterical patois of broken French, fractured English and babyish Arabic. Anne could make out the words *'mort'*, *'désastre'*, and then incomprehensible references to *kelb*: 'a dog', and guns, and – very clearly then – the fact that her daughter was arriving back from France this afternoon. Camilla was due back at the airport within the hour.

Anne begged her in English, French and Arabic to slow down and tell her exactly who was dead and how it had happened.

'Dead! All dead! So many! Too many! Everyone at the château is dead!' Once again Nirvana reverted to a tearful gibberish. But she pulled herself together then and continued on with her tale. 'Pierre! They say Pierre is dead!' A wrenching sob burst from Nirvana. 'And Julia! The little one! They killed her, too! Just a baby, and they killed her, too.'

'The baby, too, oh God!' Anne stared wordlessly at Fatima. If they had been living anywhere else in the world, they would have found such news impossible to believe. But after the carnage everyone had lived through in the past years in Beirut, they at once accepted this latest outrage as not only possible but brutally real. Still, Anne thought, even in Lebanon, what sort of monsters could murder a toddler? She answered her own question as she remembered the Palestinian children slaughtered when Christian militiamen had swarmed over the Tel Zaatar refugee camp, the Christian children massacred by the Muslims in the village of Damour, and the Shia Muslim children killed by the Israeli bombing in the south. Except for Fatima's children, however, she hadn't known any of those other young victims. But she herself had presided in the delivery room when Julia was born eighteen months ago.

Anne bit her lip at the thought of how this would affect Camilla. Ever since her daughter had been born, Camilla had centred her whole life around the little girl. She doted on her, went everywhere with her, and even maintained that the birth of *'mon petit bijou'* had resurrected her failing marriage. And now, at one murderous blow, Camilla had lost her. Anne was aghast at how this might unbalance Camilla's fragile hold on stability. 'Who do they think did it?'

'Those filthy militiamen!' Anne held the telephone away from her ear as Nirvana let loose a screeching torrent of gutter abuse at the Nazrani clan's enemies. Then, more calmly, Nirvana went on, 'You know how always they fight, the *zaims*. Like at my baby's wedding. You remember, eh? How could you forget! And now, still, it is the same. *Toujours*, in Lebanon, it is the same. Always the guns and the blood! They fight for the money and they fight for the power and they fight for the hashish.' Nirvana paused to light a cigarette. 'They came in the night like the cowards they are. There was a big battle. First at the gate. Then in the house. Pierre died with his gun in his hand. His father was very proud of that. Shaykh Georges told me, "He died with his gun." Cowboys. All our men are cowboys. The men of Marlboro!' But then Nirvana's indignation subsided, and she collapsed once again into a shower of fresh tears. 'They think little Julia was killed by a grenade. A grenade! Pierre's sister Marie died, too. And his mother, that poor sick woman. The servants *aussi*. The maid. The chauffeur. Thirty, maybe forty of them are dead. Even, they killed the dog. Even Julia's little pet Tutu.' Noisily Nirvana blew her nose. 'Old man Nazrani telephoned me with the news. He was in Tripoli last night. When Shaykh Georges came home today, he found them. You can imagine how it is with him . . .'

Grimly Anne nodded. By now Pierre's father would be sharpening the knives. By nightfall he would be sending his private army out to slit the throats of every relation of the assassins, however remote. He would commandeer Syrian tanks and destroy every enemy village and town. He would buy Israeli Phantom jets and annihilate every hill and valley that had ever been known to shelter them. And so, she thought dully, on and on the Lebanese cycle of violence would continue.

But then, as Nirvana continued ranting on about the vengeance Shaykh Georges was going to wreak, Anne's thoughts turned back from the political to the personal. 'And Camilla? Does she know yet?'

'No one but us knows. It is not yet even on the radio.' Nirvana paused significantly. 'I do not think I can tell her myself. I am prostrate with grief.' Again she resumed her weeping. '*Ma petite* Julia! My jewel!' She howled into the telephone.

Except for Nirvana's cries, there was a silence as Anne considered the obvious. Someone would have to break the news to Camilla, and wearily she supposed she was the prime candidate. Not again, she thought. It was only three months ago that she had told Fatima about her husband and son's deaths. Fatima had been stoic about the bad hand fate had dealt her. But Camilla . . . Anne considered wriggling out of the intolerable task. After all, anyone would consider having to take Fatima's wounded children to the hospital in New York a valid enough excuse. Fatima's children – not to mention the impatiently waiting Sam – would be disappointed if she delayed her flight to America for a few days. And yet how could she turn away from Camilla in her hour of need?

While Nirvana continued sobbing, Anne made an effort to remember exactly what Camilla had told her a fortnight ago before she dashed off to France. There had been some problem she had to attend to personally at the French boarding school where her sons were enrolled. Originally Pierre and Julia had been going to go with her and make a family reunion out of it. But then Pierre had begged off after a spate of gunfights had broken out in the north between the Christian militiamen fighting for dominance in post-war Lebanon. And then, at the last moment, the little girl had come down with a severe head cold. Anne herself had advised Camilla not to take Julia on the plane. If it hadn't been for the child's sniffles, Anne thought with horror, Julia would still be alive today. But then the American shuddered as another thought struck her. If Camilla had returned home even a day earlier, then she, too, would have died in the Château Croisé this morning. Anne stifled a sigh and said what Nirvana was so obviously waiting to hear. 'Look, would you like me to meet Camilla at the airport?'

'You?' Nirvana gasped as if this possibility had never occurred to her. 'Ah, Anne, *chérie*, you—'

Anne cut off the rush of endearments. 'When is her plane due?'

'Two o'clock. Air France Flight 326,' Nirvana replied, almost crisply. She blew her nose again. '*Quelle tragédie*,' she said. Then, in a low tone of voice, as though she were talking to herself, 'The old *shaykh* is a widower now. Hmmm . . . I always . . .' She did not complete her sentence. But just as it seemed she was about to ring off, she got in one final request. 'And Anne? You will take my *bébé* up to the château?'

'All the way up to the château?' Anne was incredulous. 'Today?'

'Shaykh Georges is sending a car down to the airport for her. He insisted. You know Shaykh Georges. He is so hard to resist! And he wants all of them together. I will come for the funeral, *bien sûr!* But as for today, I told him maybe you would drive up with Camilla. He was very happy to hear that. He said it was good to have a doctor come.'

Anne's lips thinned in annoyance. Manipulated again, she thought helplessly to herself. She would have liked Camilla's mother better if she had asked her straight out to do what she wanted her to do. Yet she had more important matters on her mind now than the failures of Nirvana's character and she was grateful, after she had finally put down the phone, when Fatima insisted on accompanying her to the airport.

When they got there, one of the Nazrani cousins was already having Anne paged on the intercom. He escorted them to a Mercedes limousine parked outside the terminal, and they were immediately whisked out on to the tarmac where the Air France jumbo was taxiing to a standstill. A slim and radiant Camilla all but danced off the aeroplane wearing skintight leather jeans by Rafael, an oyster-coloured Krizia silk blouse, and sexy high-heeled Charles Jourdan suede boots. Behind her a steward carried gaily wrapped parcels and a pink panda bear that was almost as tall as he was. Anne and Fatima scrambled out of the limousine and stood waiting for Camilla to see them.

'*Chéries!* What a wonderful surprise!' Camilla threw herself in the arms of her friends and exuberantly kissed them again and again. 'But where is Leila?' Before they could answer, she burbled on. 'But I forget, she is in Moscow, poor thing, so cold there, such a pity that nasty husband of hers was posted so far from us!' She threw her arms around the shoulders of her friends. 'I rang her from Paris, you know.' Conspiratorially Camilla lowered her voice. 'I think she wants a divorce.' Gaily she laughed. 'Maybe then she will come home to us, eh?' She hadn't noticed the Nazrani chauffeur or car, and so she started to walk towards the terminal with her friends. '*Ah, l'enchantement de Paris!* I went to some of the best collections. But, my dears, you would not believe how the Italians have taken over everything. Milan—'

'Camilla.' Anne stood rooted to the tarmac. 'Listen to us, Camilla. There's something we have to tell you.'

'In the car,' Fatima added. 'Come and sit with us for a moment in the car.'

'Car?' Camilla turned and saw Pierre's cousin and a new chauffeur standing by the Nazrani limousine. 'Pierre? Is Pierre here, too?' She laughed her tinkling little girl's laugh. 'What a surprise! You *all* came to meet me. And Julia? Did he bring the baby?' Without waiting for their answer, she ran back to the empty limousine. She was frowning when Anne and Fatima caught up with her. 'What's wrong? Why isn't Pierre here? And the baby? Why does everyone look so sad?'

Anne preferred to break the news away from the prying eyes of the disembarking passengers and airline crew. 'Let's get in the car,' she said gently.

As soon as the chauffeur shut the doors, he gunned the engine and roared off. At the edge of the tarmac, two more Nazrani vehicles waited. One Range Rover full of armed men coursed in front of the Mercedes, and its twin covered the rear. The convey streaked through the city and then turned north on the route to the château.

Meanwhile, in the back seat at first Camilla listened quietly as Anne said she had some bad news to tell her. Something had happened at the Château Croisé this morning. That was why they were all going up to the château together now.

Camilla's high spirits evaporated. Anxiously she looked at their armed escort. Guns bristled from the open windows of the military vehicles to their front and rear. 'Shaykh Georges,' she guessed. 'Someone has finally gone and killed old Shaykh Georges.'

Anne shook her head. 'Not Shaykh Georges.' She decided to lead up to the worst of it. 'But there was shooting at the château this morning.'

'There is always shooting at the château.' Camilla tried to smile. 'Pierre and his father, always they shoot. I would not be surprised if already they are teaching little Julia how to shoot a little gun.' As she spoke, her eyes searched the faces of Anne and Fatima for clues of what was to come. Her voice faltered. 'So many guns. Too many guns.' She shut her eyes as if to garner her strength. 'Who was it?'

Anne shrugged and wet her tongue with her lips. 'It was bad, Camilla. *Very* bad.'

'You must be strong,' Fatima warned her. 'Remember, God does not give any of us a burden that is too difficult for us to carry.' She put her hand over Camilla's. 'I have always believed that you are very strong, you know.'

'Tell me,' Camilla said as she looked from Anne to Fatima. 'It was my Pierre, *n'est-ce pas?*'

Anne nodded. 'Courage, *chérie*.' She waited for Camilla to start crying, but strangely she did not seem to react at all. Instead she sat staring straight ahead with a blank look on her face.

Anne took a deep breath. 'There's more, Camilla.'

'Pierre's sister Marie,' Fatima told her. 'And his mother.'

Camilla didn't even blink.

'Many of the servants,' Anne continued. 'The maid. The chauffeur. Even the dog.'

'And more than thirty of the men.' Fatima met Anne's eyes. One of them would have to deliver the *coup de grâce*.

'Little Julia, too.' Anne's voice was a whisper.

Silently Camilla slumped forward and covered her face with her hands. Her shoulders shook as she cried without making a sound. Anne and Fatima sat with their arms tight around her, making crooning noises, begging her not to despair.

It was a long while later, and they were already up

in the mountains on the final approach to the Château Croisé, before finally Camilla sat up straight and wiped her eyes. Her face had crumpled into a mask of wrinkles, and when she spoke, her grating voice was deeply pitched with bitterness. 'We will be avenged,' she said. Fiercely she clenched her fists. 'They will pay for this. We will kill them all.'

'Don't talk like that,' Anne said, more sharply than she intended. She had expected Camilla to scream her grief to the heavens, not spit out this deadly bloodlust. Anne shivered in the back seat of the Mercedes. She had known Camilla for most of her life, but now she wondered if she had ever known her at all.

'Pray to God,' Fatima urged her. She patted Camilla's hand consolingly. 'He helped me when my Ali died.'

'You pray,' Camilla said stonily. She brushed off Fatima's hand. 'We Nazranis will help ourselves.'

And that was all she would say the rest of the way up to the château.

Anne and Fatima stayed on to give what comfort they could in the three trying days that led up to the mass funeral for Pierre, Julia, Marie, and the other victims of the massacre.

Anne suggested that she give herself time to allow things to heal. You're in shock, she said. Do yourself a favour and don't make any sweeping decisions before you have a chance to pull yourself together. Maybe you should get some productive work, say, with children orphaned by the fighting. Or perhaps – here Anne betrayed her Americanism – you should consider some counselling. She gave her the name of one of the psychiatrists in West Beirut who specialized in treating those traumatized by the Lebanese violence.

When all that advice apparently fell on deaf ears, Fatima tried a different tack. 'I remember how I felt when I heard about Ali,' she told Camilla. 'I just wanted to die. "*Tuqbirni,*" I said to my Muhammad, "bury me." If it weren't for my children and – most of all – for Allah and His mercy, I think I really might have died from grief. But Allah helped me. And what saved me can save you. Pray for strength, and God will answer you.'

Yet Camilla did not act as though she had even heard Anne and Fatima. Best friends though they were, they still could not reach her. Her face remained frozen in a mask of despair. But the day before the funeral she unbent just long enough to tell them she had decided to leave Lebanon as soon as she could. She would return to Mother France to make a new life for herself away from the butchery of this savage land where even an innocent eighteen-month-old baby wasn't safe. She was very rich, she reminded them. She made a strangled throaty sound that wasn't quite a laugh as she said that perhaps money couldn't buy happiness, but it could buy tranquillizers and thrills.

And yet Anne and Fatima noticed that even as Camilla determined to go into exile, she was still as set on revenge as every other member of the clan. In this one bloodthirsty matter, she was heart and soul a Nazrani. She spent long hours sitting like a statue beside Shaykh Georges in the parlour, as his armed men came from all the villages of north Lebanon to pay their final respects to the fallen son of their chieftain. She spoke only when spoken to, and looked like an avenging angel rather than a bereaved widow and mother. For she, like all the family, made a fetish of dressing in light-coloured pastels. Up here in these ancient mountains where vendettas went on for centuries, it was a Nazrani tradition that the bereaved family never donned the black shrouds of mourning until the deaths they grieved for were altogether avenged. So long as those responsible for the massacre still lived and breathed, the Nazranis would dress in pinks, yellows and blues.

Camilla was in bridal white for the funeral. She

sat straight and tall in the front pew of the church between her mother and father-in-law, and she did not even seem to notice Nirvana flirting outrageously with Shaykh Georges. Contrary to the expectations of all who knew her, Camilla did not shed a single tear. But her eyes never left the one small cedar coffin among the many big ones before the altar.

At the back of the chapel, Anne and Fatima tried to keep a watchful eye on their friend. It had been twenty years since the two of them had sat, just so in this church, waiting for Camilla to walk down this aisle and marry her Pierre. As they remembered so well, the rival warlords had left their bloody mark on that day, too. Now, twenty years later, the sanctuary that had run with blood on Camilla's wedding day was lined from one end to the other with coffins.

Anne and Fatima sat side by side, fanning themselves with their hands in the torrid June heat as slowly the dignitaries began to arrive. Everyone who was anyone in the Lebanese Christian community had trekked up to the Château Croisé for this service. The Maronite Patriarch officiated. The French ambassador was here, as was the papal nuncio and the brother of the President of Syria. There were nearly enough delegates to hold a session of the Chamber of Deputies. When the church was full, the mourners spilled out to the street. Villagers from all over the north stood roasting in the sun. They had brought their wives, and they had brought their children. Thousands of boys and girls wore white tee-shirts decorated with the face of Pierre.

But in the sweltering church the spirit of the day was Nazrani – not divine – vengeance.

Successive preachers praised Pierre, denounced his murderers, and condemned this ruthless killing of innocent women and children. Finally a cleric took the pulpit to pronounce not a benediction but a curse. 'All those who profaned Croisé will be killed,' he said, 'and their descendants for generations, until not a single man or woman remains.'

Outside in the sun, the peasant women let fly their mourning shrieks. The keening continued on and on from the mountaintop that glowered over all Lebanon.

On a cold afternoon in Moscow, the following winter, Leila yawned as she stretched out voluptuously on the settee. Any minute now Hussein would ring from the lobby of her and Farouk's apartment building. She liked waiting for a man when she was smouldering, like this, every pore of her open and ready. She had begun primping hours ago: washing her hair, waxing her legs, painting her fingernails and toenails, soaking in a perfumed bath. Anticipation only sharpened the appetite. She lowered her already low-cut black silk *crêpe de Chine* Karl Lagerfeld blouson and angled herself so that a few more enticing inches of thigh were visible through the side slit in the slinky black skirt. The parlour was overheated, and so was she.

Her lips curved in a sultry siren's smile. She intended to seduce Hussein Ibrahim this afternoon on this couch. The two of them had flirted and fought and flirted again for the past twenty years. Enough was enough. Or rather, enough was not enough. It was bizarre that she had slept with virtually every man she had ever fancied except this one who mattered far more than all the others. And so she had decided on impulse, as soon as she spotted Hussein two nights ago at a reception at the Algerian embassy, that what she must have was that luscious fling at last.

Again she yawned. Life on ice in boring Moscow left her cold. There was nothing to do here except guzzle second-class champagne and chew first-class caviar with the same dour herd of people at dull diplomatic parties. There was nothing to buy in the shops; nowhere – not to mention no one – to meet for gossipy lunches. And perhaps most depressing of all for someone born and bred on the shores of the Mediterranean, there was absolutely no sun for months at a time. It drove her mad, too, that when she suddenly felt an irresistible urge to ring Beirut, London or Paris, she sometimes couldn't even get an outside line. Moscow was so primitive.

She flicked her wrist to read the face of her diamond-studded Rolex watch. As usual, Hussein was late. But at least this time he had a good excuse. When she had invited him over for tea, he had warned her that he might arrive late enough for cocktails. He had explained that he was in Moscow for less than a week, and that he had come armed with a shopping list of military *matériel* he wanted for his Palestinian militiamen. He would be coming to see her directly from a meeting with Soviet military and diplomatic mandarins. It was possible that their wranglings over guns, rocket-propelled grenade launchers, and anti-ballistic missiles would take most of the afternoon.

She lit a cigarette and tried not to fume as she waited. Hussein was here for the cause, just as – in a way – she liked to think she was. When she looked back on that dark day two years ago when she had married the viperous Farouk, she had been able to justify the deplorable act only by styling herself as a Palestinian fifth column inside the Syrian inner sanctums; and in the early days when Farouk had still doted upon her back in Beirut she had in fact been able to do her bit for the revolution. A casual word here and a subtle hint there, and Farouk had seemed willing to shut his eyes to Palestinian machinations in the Bekaa, the south, and in Sidon and Tyre. But ever since he had sent his flunkies to arrest her for sedition, she had failed to exert much political leverage either with her husband or his Syrian masters. She supposed she should have insisted on divorcing him as soon as he was recalled to Damascus and then posted to Moscow as head of the Syrian military mission. How she longed to be back where the action was, in Beirut! Of course she kept avid tabs on everything that transpired there. She had been dismayed when, in the late summer of 1978, the charismatic Shia leader Imam Musa Sadr had gone missing and was presumed dead in Libya. Once again the assassins had cut down one of Lebanon's most promising leaders. She was further depressed, too, last September, when the traitor Anwar Sadat had signed his separate peace with the Israelis at Camp David. And she had taken little joy in last summer's violent fighting between the Christian militias and the Syrian army of occupation in Lebanon. She had sat here in this sitting room watching the Russian television news of Syrian guns shelling the East Beirut quarter of Ashrafiya. She had cried as she watched Beirut burn once again. The Syrians were devils!

Leila again looked at her watch, and drummed a manicured fingernail against the ugly green velvet arm of the plush sofa. This apartment, like everything else in Russia, was furnished in the worst possible taste. Devilishly, then, she considered whether she should taunt the impotent Farouk tonight with the news that she had taken Hussein as her lover. As enticing as that thought was, she hastily decided she had better not. It was one thing to throw the occasional elevator boy or chauffeur up in the red face of her cuckolded husband. But she did not want to risk putting Hussein's arms procurement in jeopardy. Syria was a Soviet client state, and Farouk had the ear of the top men in the Kremlin. In a fit of jealous pique, her husband might sabotage Hussein's well-laid plans to outfit his Marxist-oriented United Front with the latest in Soviet military hardware.

She had just told the maid to forget the tea and instead bring in an iced bottle of champagne, when at last the downstairs buzzer sounded.

Again she arranged the folds of her clothing in delicious disarray and then fluffed up her mane of hennaed hair one last time. Her sloe eyes were predatory as she watched Hussein come towards her from the hallway. He was as boyish-looking but as badly dressed as ever, in those horrid olive drab military fatigues he had insisted on wearing since the heyday of the *fedayeen* movement a good decade ago. And yet, she thought with envy, the years had been kind to him. As in so much else that was unfair about the sexes, men had been dealt the luckier hand when it came to ageing. Except for his brushcut hair that was silver now instead of black, those nests of crinkly wrinkles around his eyes and mouth, and a further squaring off of his always square torso, he looked much the same as he had when she had met him in that art gallery in London long ago.

'Hussein! *Habibi!*' Graciously she held out her hand for him to kiss.

He cocked an eyebrow at her *en déshabillé*, and did not try to hide an amused smile as he brushed past her extended hand. Instead of sinking down beside her on the sofa, he chose an easy chair that was just beyond her reach.

Leila kept smiling, albeit between slightly clenched teeth. Obviously he was still as rude as when they had first met. Most probably he considered kissing a lady's hand too bourgeois an act for a dedicated Communist like himself. Well, later she would make jolly sure he kissed her feet along with any other parts of her anatomy she wished. Yet for now, she would have to grin and bear his bad manners. She reminded herself that she had invited him up here to make love, not to fight. It wasn't as if they were *married*.

As Arabs always do upon meeting, they used the ritual questions about her health, his health, and the health of their families to size each other up. But she was vexed that his eyes did not wander down the length of her body, which she had taken such care to display. He was as courteous, and detached, as an Englishman exchanging pleasantries with another Englishman in a Belgravia club.

The maid arrived with the champagne. 'None for me,' Hussein said. 'I have to go back to the Ministry. I'm afraid I can't stay long.'

'You poor dear,' Leila cooed, as though she cared about anything other than how this altered programme would affect her next move. She would have to work fast. 'Can't you just have one tiny glass? For your little Leila?' But even she was revolted by hearing herself resort to babytalk. No man was worth acting like a witless girl-child. Briskly her own strong persona asserted itself. 'Do have some. It's French. None of that Russian swill.'

'Same old Leila.' Fondly he smiled as he lit a Cuban cheroot. 'No champagne. But perhaps a drop of vodka.' He spoke clearly and distinctly, and as he looked around the sitting room he wondered where the listening devices were hidden. 'The vodka here is excellent. Like so much else in Mother Russia.'

'Vodka! Of course!' She wasn't feigning delight as she clapped her hand for the maid. Vodka was much more potent than champagne. She poured enough in his glass to make him forget about guns and any arms other than her own.

As she leaned forward to clink her champagne goblet against his glass of vodka, her bodice fell open even further. 'To us,' she breathed.

'Yes,' he answered, his eyes determinedly locked north of her chin. 'And to all the Palestinian brothers and sisters. And to the revolution.'

'Of course,' she agreed rather too quickly and a touch sullenly. 'To the revolution.' But for the first time she admitted to herself that this assignation might not turn out as she had planned. It would take more than an ocean of vodka to melt the ice water in this one's veins. And yet Hussein was only a man like all the others; he could be had. When she settled back on the cushions of the settee, she took care that her breasts remained tantalizingly on view. She even leaned slightly forward, so her cleavage was more pronounced. 'So,' she silkily continued, 'tell me how your mission is going. I am all ears.'

'I didn't think it was your ears you wanted me to notice,' he answered.

'Indeed.' She felt like buttoning her blouson up to her chin. But even though she kept herself defiantly open almost to the nipples, she was finding it harder to hide her irritation. She drained her champagne, poured herself another glass, and drank it down as thirstily as though it were the blood of this man who dared to mock her and her body. Sourly she wished it were possible to throw Hussein down on the carpet and rape him. Inside she raged at the injustice of biology: they can force us, but we can't force them. Yet she still wanted to have her way with him, and so with an iron effort of will she managed to keep her voice as effervescent as champagne. 'So! You didn't answer my question, you bad darling.' But her playful laugh fell flat. Before he had arrived, she had convinced herself not only that he would want her but also that nothing much was at stake, but as she looked him in the eyes now, she admitted to herself that she truly wanted him not only to touch her but to love her as he once had. She couldn't keep the urgency of her longing from creeping into her voice. 'Are you getting what you came here for? What you – and I – really want?'

'Do we want the same things, Leila? Did we ever?' He stubbed out his cheroot and ran his hands through his crewcut hair. '*Kefir*, enough. The answer is no.'

'Answer?' Although she was an eyelash away from tears, she managed to smile coyly. If she denied that he had just spurned her, then maybe it had never happened. 'What exactly was the question?'

His eyes met hers. 'Let's just say that I am not prepared to deliver what you want.'

'Oh? What is it that I want?' Her voice quavered high and shrill. Hussein had dared to reject her as if she was some comradely resolution put forth by the United Front's executive committee. Yet she was a woman, and she had opened herself up to this man. She deserved better than a chairman's curt dismissal of an unwanted manifesto. Her eyes fell, and she fought off the angry tears. Don't let him see you cry, she told herself. Don't break down in front of him. *Not one tear!* And yet, at this moment of rejection, she was more vulnerable than she had ever been before in her life. For it came to her, suddenly, that she loved Hussein, that she had always loved him, that she always would love him. That home truth burned in her gut like a phosphorus bomb that sizzled organs, flesh, muscle, and then burned on inside her as in a corpse in a mortuary. If this was what love felt like, why did everyone want it so? In her beseeching eyes, as she lifted her head and looked at the man she loved, was a new desperation. 'Why don't you kiss me?'

He leaned forward and brushed his cold lips lightly against her hot ones.

Part of her wanted to strike him, but instead – to her horror – she heard herself begging. 'Why don't you give me a nice kiss?'

'That was a nice kiss.' And again he barely touched her lips with his own. 'No more.' He set his glass down on a table. 'I think it's time I left.'

But she was angry now, as the full impact of what was happening smote her. *'Ibn kelb,'* she swore, 'you son of a dog.'

'Don't push me,' he warned, 'or you might hear more than you bargained for.'

'Don't you threaten me.' She hissed an extremely vulgar Arab curse.

'Okay.' His quick temper, too, snapped. 'You asked for it, and so you'll get it.' He paced back and forth in front of her as though she were some raw recruit he had just enlisted in one of his military units. 'You invite me up here, you dress and display yourself like a prostitute, and you expect me to fall upon you like a capitalist swine with an empty mind and unzipped trousers. But I am not that sort of man. I never was, and I never will be. *Faama?* You understand?'

In shock she stared at him as he paused to pour himself another hefty measure of vodka. He tossed it back in one gulp, and his voice softened when he continued on.

'Once I loved you, yes. When you were young – when we were young – I loved you as much as it is possible for any man to love a woman. You were something to behold then, Leila. So lovely in mind, body and spirit. So full of fire! So rich in promise! So *Palestinian*.'

His voice hardened. 'But you are lovely no more.' Mercilessly his eyes swept over her. 'Now you are a rich man's toy. What makes you any different from a prostitute who walks the streets? You waste your life on silly people and silly things. And yet, for a while, you had even me fooled. There was a time, back in Beirut, when I believed it was still possible that the girl I loved might mature into a woman who could be my comrade and partner for life. That night when I took you and your children to say goodbye to my warriors, I hoped – no, *dreamed!* – that you would commit to the revolution. But you only played at revolution when it suited you. When it was easy. When it was the latest thing and everyone was doing it. But, of course, how could you be any different? You are a Shahine. A bourgeois.' Again he spat out that word which epitomized everything he loathed. 'A bourgeois! Long ago your father was right. I am not your sort. And you are not mine.'

He stood squarely in front of her. 'You might have played the whore with your husbands and the Palestinian revolution. But I will not let you play the whore with me. I tell you again,' he continued almost tenderly, 'I loved you when you were young.' His voice flicked as savagely as a whip. 'But not for all the gold in America would I sleep with you now.'

'Get out!' she shrieked. In a fury she threw a heavy crystal ashtray at him and then a delicate porcelain vase. She hated him for not flinching when her missiles hit their mark. 'Get out and don't come back.' She brandished a marble bust of Karl Marx.

'As you like.' Hussein gave her that arrogant smile she was beginning to detest. 'But you think about what I said, eh?' As casually as though they had just ended some polite drawing room conversation, he turned his back and walked out of the door.

She could have killed him, then and there. She longed to flay him alive. Cut out his heart, fry it up with mushrooms and onions, and feed it to the dogs. Instead, she did exactly what every other woman in her circumstances has always done since the beginning of recorded time.

Leila threw herself back down on the sofa and cried her heart out.

Yet afterwards, on ice in cold Moscow, she had more time than she wanted to think over everything Hussein had said.

Chapter 22

Anne was the first of them to feel premonitions of the disaster that was to change all their lives.

On a hot early June night in 1982, she was sitting

in front of the television in Sam's apartment in New York sipping a white wine spritzer as she watched him read the network news straight to camera. She tensed up then, when the chromakey image behind him dissolved from a graphic of the White House to that of an Arab in a *kuffiyeh* headscarf.

In London today outside the Dorchester Hotel, Sam sombrely told the nation, the Israeli ambassador had been shot and seriously wounded. Already in Jerusalem, Israeli hawks were threatening to retaliate against the Palestinian Liberation Organization headquartered in Lebanon.

Oh no, Anne thought. Not again. Please, God, not again.

In Beirut, where she and her children were still living at Anne's villa on the Rue Bliss, Fatima was the next to feel the fear.

Her eldest son Muhammad came racing home from his classes at the Arab university in the late morning, hours earlier than she had expected him. Without a word of explanation, he tore off his civilian clothes and donned his Amal militia uniform. He climbed up on to the bed and took down his Kalashnikov from where it rested on top of a wardrobe where his younger brothers and sisters couldn't accidentally get hold of it. Grimly, then, as he cleaned and oiled it, the man of the family warned his mother to expect the Israeli bombers any time now. As every street-wise Beirut urchin knew, a terrorist attack in London meant a tit-for-tat Israeli reprisal in Lebanon.

At once Fatima sent Zainab to fetch her sisters and brothers from school. Then she dispatched Salma and Amina to the souks to stock up on food, kerosene and other staples, and went out into Anne's garden to make sure that the bomb shelter Charles had prudently erected for them the year before was stocked with candles, bedding and tins of food.

Finally she led her children out into the concrete and breeze-block shelter which was sunk deep into the ground and there she opened her worn copy of the Koran and read for a while to calm all their nerves. She was still reading when, at first distantly, and then dangerously closer, they could hear the explosions.

At three o'clock that afternoon, the first wave of Israeli jets were bombing West Beirut.

In Moscow that night, when finally Leila found out what was happening, she was furious that her husband had kept her in the dark about the escalating Middle East crisis. As it was, she heard about it, not on the censored Moscow television but by chance on the telephone, when idly she rang up Anne in New York. Her American friend wanted to know what was wrong with her telephone. She had been trying to get through to Leila for the past twenty-four hours, ever since the assassination attempt on the Israeli diplomat in London.

'*Aiee!*' Leila's first reaction was to clench her fist in solidarity with whoever had gone hunting for Zionists on the London streets.

But then, as Anne tensely told her that already the Israelis had launched heavy bombing raids on south Lebanon and West Beirut, Leila began to nurse second thoughts about what all this could mean to Lebanon and the Palestinian cause.

She worried long and hard that whole night through, mostly on the international telephone lines. She managed to get through to her daughter and her sons who were with Mustafa's family in Beirut for the summer. Miriam assured her that everyone was safe so far. Hamid, who at nineteen had already completed his military training in a PLO Fatah unit, was reporting for active duty later that night. He was taking his seventeen-year-old brother Farid with him as a volunteer for the expected emergency. All Palestinian units were being rushed to the southern border in case the Israelis attacked on the ground.

Next Leila rang her brothers in Kuwait and Jordan, and her sisters in Egypt and Saudi Arabia. When she couldn't think of any more members of her family to call, but still couldn't bear to stop talking, she dialled a number just outside Geneva.

It took Camilla a long while to come to the telephone.

Leila assumed, from the volume of the music and laughter in the background, that her friend must be having another of her marathon parties. Since she had married an ultra-rich expatriate Lebanese banker the year before, Camilla had sunk deeper and deeper into hedonism. As soon as Maurice had taken a villa for the summer along the frightfully expensive shores of Lac Leman, the international Arab glitterati had promptly moved in as more or less permanent house guests.

A manservant finally announced that the lady of the house was about to come to the phone.

But instead of Camilla, another trilling voice came gushing through. '*C'est moi!* Nirvana! Is that you, Leila, *chérie? Ça va?*'

Leila hid her impatience with a sigh. But then she exchanged the inevitable bubbling pleasantries with the effervescent Nirvana before once again asking to speak to Camilla.

Instead Nirvana said she was handing the telephone to 'my dear darling *shaykh*'.

Leila's eyebrows shot up as she heard Shaykh Georges's gravelly rasp. Had Nirvana taken up with Pierre's father? Apparently so.

'What's the news?' Shaykh Georges was never one for pleasantries. 'You have news from Lebanon?'

'It's another war. The Israelis have bombed Beirut and the south. Everyone says they're about to invade us.'

'*Ya Mar Sharbel!*' Shakyh Georges dropped the phone. But Leila could hear him shouting at Nirvana. 'I must get home! The Israelis are coming! It's war! Another war!'

After another long pause, Camilla finally came to the phone. But her slurred voice was heavy – Leila guessed – not only with alcohol but drugs. Yet she tried to make her friend understand the urgency of the news for all those they held dear. 'The Israelis have bombed Beirut. They may invade. It means another war. Another Lebanese war.'

But Camilla just laughed. 'What else is new?' Again she laughed. Arab gunmen, she said, were always shooting at the moon, or Israelis, or each other. And the Israelis were always sending their bombers north over Lebanon. Leila should calm down. Have a drink. Relax. 'I think Moscow makes you a little bit crazy. You must be calm. Like me. Always now I am calm.' Camilla's laughter verged on hysteria, and her speech, as she gabbled on at lightning speed, was as giddy as cocaine could make it. '*Certainement*, you need a holiday, yes? *Ah, oui.* You must come down next weekend. Genève, *chérie*, is fabulous this time of year. Everyone will be here. Michel and Marie, and Rafael and—'

Leila quietly put the receiver back on the cradle.

By early the next afternoon, however, even Camilla, as she lay listlessly in her bed nursing a hangover, was glued to the Middle East news bulletins on the radio. For at eleven o'clock on the morning of 6 June 1982, the massive Israeli invasion of Lebanon had begun.

As Israeli armour and artillery swept north over the border in what Jerusalem called Operation Peace for

Galilee, Fatima was the only one of the foursome who was still in the Lebanon. Yet, like moths to the flame, the others were about to be drawn back to that doomed city and country that they all still called home. The same irresistible instinct that draws sons and daughters to the deathbed of a beloved mother began to draw first Leila, then Anne, and finally Camilla home to their dying Beirut.

Like a caged panther in her slick black Claude Montana trouser suit, Leila stalked the telex room of the Syrian embassy in Moscow waiting to pounce on the latest news from the Lebanese war. The bulletins from the front lines were grim. Israel had announced to the world that its only intention was to establish a twenty-five-mile *cordon sanitaire* in south Lebanon, so that Palestinian artillery could no longer reach Israeli settlements in the Galilee. Yet, having achieved that goal in the first hours of fighting, the Israelis still coursed northward, on a direct trajectory for Beirut.

Leila chain-smoked and studied a map tacked to the wall as she pored over the dispatches. Her sons were fighting at the front. Were Hamid and Farid still alive? Even though the Syrian reports praised the Palestinians for fighting bravely and well, the Israeli juggernaut was rolling inexorably over them. Grisly hand-to-hand fighting was still going on for strategic Beaufort Castle near the Litani river, but it seemed that in the end superior Israeli firepower would assure that they took the old Crusader fort. They had seized PLO strongholds in Tyre and wrested control of the Palestinian *fedayeen* heartland between the Litani and Zahrani rivers. Every time the Israelis had run into entrenched Arab resistance along the Mediterranean coast, they had either bombed those positions off the map or simply leapfrogged over them with helicopters or around them with amphibious landings. Again and again the refugee camps along the coast had been pounded by waves of Israeli bombers. Inland, meanwhile, armoured units had been grinding north through the Druze citadels in the mountains of the Shouf. Still further east in the Bekaa Valley, the Israeli air force had been decimating Syrian missile emplacements.

Leila looked from the map of Lebanon to the map of the Arab world tacked on the opposite wall. Where, she wondered, from the deep well of her Palestinian bitterness, were the other Arab states while all this was going on? Arabs were forever writing poems about Palestine being their palpitating heart. But at this hour of desperate need, only Syria had come to their aid. Yet Leila narrowed her eyes as she studied the dispatches more closely. Long ago she had learned to trust no one. To her, it seemed as though even Syria was holding back its big guns. Had Damascus made some secret deal with the Israelis and the Christians to carve up Lebanon?

Leila breathed smoke through her nostrils like a dragon. But then she put that particular suspicion aside and focused on her searing assumption that this time the Israelis were gunning for Beirut. In a day or two – three at the most – the Zionists would be at the capital. The only question in Leila's mind was whether they intended to annihilate the Palestinian presence once they got there. Ever since the right-wing government of Menachem Begin had come to power in Israel a year ago, the hottest rumour among informed Arab sources had been that the Israelis were waiting for any pretext to invade Lebanon and install a militant Christian puppet government in Beirut. Soon after that – or so speculation had it – the Israelis would make sure not only that the Palestinians were expelled once and for all from Lebanon but also that the newly friendly Beirut régime would conclude a peace treaty with the Zionist state. Israeli Defence Minister Ariel Sharon had reputedly come to East Beirut the previous January to coordinate the planned Israeli invasion with his Christian allies. Since then, PLO Chairman Yasser Arafat had warned reporters where and when the Zionists would be coming, Christian leaders had dropped broad hints to the Beirut press about the Israeli invasion, and the US State Department had cautioned a prominent Druze leader to expect a ground attack by Sharon's troops. From the winter into the spring, tensions along the Lebanese border had steadily increased as the Israelis and the Palestinians accused each other of cease-fire violations.

As she heard another message rattling in, Leila raced back to the telex. She let out a whoop when she read it. President Assad was recalling her husband Farouk to Damascus tomorrow for urgent meetings.

Her mouth hardened with determination to be on the same plane as her husband. Damascus was only a few hours' drive from Beirut. Her eyes shone at the possibility that she could be in Beirut by tomorrow. Ever since Anne had alerted her to the mounting crisis, Leila had longed to be back where the action was. Come hell, high water, or an Israeli invasion, she was going to return to her home away from home. Beirut wasn't Palestine, but to her it was almost as dear. If this was to be her people's last stand, she would rise or fall as one of them. In these last anxious hours, she had finally been seduced by the heady romance of revolution. For her it was no longer enough to sit on the sidelines. Her hands itched for her very own Kalashnikov. She had lived on ice in Moscow for too long. Now, she wanted fire.

And yet, as she read the rest of the message, Leila's exhilaration faded. It was bad news that Israeli warplanes had utterly destroyed the Soviet-supplied ground-to-air missiles which the Syrians had installed along the Beirut–Damascus road. But it was disastrous that the Israelis had also shot down more than eighty Syrian warplanes, a quarter of the Syrian air force. No wonder, she thought, that Assad wanted her husband on the first plane back to Damascus. Either Farouk was going to be the scapegoat for having supplied his country with inferior Soviet weaponry, or they would be priming him to return to Moscow immediately to resupply all that had been lost.

Leila ripped the message off the machine and, before the astonished clerk could stop her, she raced off with it to Farouk's office. She swept past his secretary and barged in without so much as knocking on the door. As she threw the telex down on his desk, Farouk was staring moodily into space. 'Assad wants you home,' she told him. Noisily she tapped one of the toes of her high-heeled shoes on the marble floor as she waited for him to read and digest the message. When finally he frowned and reached for the telephone, she moved it sweetly just beyond his reach. 'Take me, too,' she ordered.

'You?' Farouk's scowl deepened. 'Impossible.'

She would have done almost anything at that moment to be a free woman with her passport in her handbag and a ticket in her pocket. But she was an Arab wife, and her husband kept her passport locked up in his office safe. For all she knew, she wouldn't be able to get an exit visa from Moscow or a seat on a plane to Damascus without her lord and master's permission.

She swallowed her anger and pride. 'Please let me come.'

He leaned back in his swivel chair. He relished having *her* beg for *his* favours for a change. 'Why should I do that – or anything – for you?'

'Because it is right. Because I am needed.' With her crown of flame-coloured hair, and – especially – with the passion that fired her inside, Leila was magnificent. 'Because I am Palestinian.'

He blinked, and his eyes fell as though he had been staring straight into the noon sun for too long. Although at moments he hated his wife perhaps as passionately as he loved her, this time she had his sympathy and understanding. It was from a vain attempt to spare her feelings that he had tried to hold back the bad news from the Middle East as long as he could. Inwardly Farouk sighed. He supposed – this time, as always – he would give in and take her back to Damascus with him. He never ceased hoping that a miracle might happen and that finally she would respond to him as a good wife should. 'Well,' he said reluctantly, 'perhaps . . .' He looked past her out of the window at the dull early summer morning. 'We are so far from home here. And with the war . . .'

As he ran his hands in despair through his thinning hair, for a moment he worried more about his work than his marriage. There would be hell to pay when he landed in Damascus. But he had done his best to prise the latest generation of arms out of the Soviets. It wasn't his fault that they had given Syria outmoded ten-year-old equipment and that the Americans had supplied the Israelis with advanced firepower and weapons systems that were ten years ahead of the best Moscow had to offer.

Leila's impatient toe-tapping brought him back to the equally fraught present. In her way, his wife was harder to stand up to than Assad would be. He might as well give in before she started screeching here in his office and shamed him in front of his staff.

Wearily he buried his head in his hands. 'All right,' he finally conceded. 'You can come with me to Damascus. But no further. I warn you, no wife of mine will go to Beirut. Not now, not with the bloodbath . . .' He stopped in mid-sentence, before he voiced his fears about what would happen once the Israelis besieged Beirut. For Leila had not seen the secret decoded cable his aide had handed him first thing this morning. Syria was about to sign a cease-fire with the Israelis. Now no one, and nothing, could save Beirut from being encircled.

But as he looked up, expecting to have her pounce on him for his indiscretion, he exhaled a sigh of relief. He needn't have worried about giving anything away to his wife. At his first murmur of assent, Leila had raced from the room to go home and pack.

That same afternoon, as the yellow taxi coursed over the Triboro Bridge on the way to JKF Airport, Sam was making a final effort to talk Anne out of returning to Beirut.

'Look, honey.' He beamed his most earnest anchorman look at her. 'It's crazy to go there now. I told you, I talked to our correspondent in Tel Aviv this afternoon. This time the Israelis are going all the way to Beirut. The airport's still open, but it won't be long before the Israelis seal the city off from the outside world. What's about to happen to West Beirut is going to make the Lebanese civil war look like a tea party.'

'So everyone says.' She glared at Sam as though her lover had suddenly been metamorphosed into Ariel Sharon. 'How can the Israelis even think of *doing* that? The *Israelis*, of all people!' Even though she continued to wear her father's ethnic and religious background lightly on her shoulders, usually it was a secret source of pride to her. She had always admired Jewish ethical values, and she liked to think that her brains and compassion came from the Jewish side of her family. Yet, just as in the past she had felt vaguely apologetic every time Israeli warplanes had bombed south Lebanon, now – even though she had nothing whatsoever to do with this war and would have stopped it single-handedly if she could – she was haunted by a feeling of guilt for this invasion. 'My God, Sam, there's a half million civilians in West Beirut. Women. Children. Old people. Normal people, Sam. Families. Just like here in New York. Or in Tel Aviv. But to hear the Israelis talk, everyone in Beirut is a terrorist.'

'You got it.' He pressed home what he thought was the most telling point for his argument. 'Whether you like it or not, honey, they're going to bomb Beirut off the map. There's a half million sitting ducks in that city. Which is all the more reason not to make it a half million and one. I don't want you to be one of the statistics.'

'It's my work, Sam,' she said quietly. 'You're a journalist. You've worked in war zones. In Beirut, even. You should understand how it is with me. I'm a doctor. My place is there.'

'You *want* to go,' he accused her. 'What are you, some kind of danger junkie?'

She grinned and neatly defused the situation. 'Takes one to know one.'

He didn't mean to laugh, but he did. He put his arm around her shoulders and gave her a comradely squeeze. Again she had reinforced his conviction that she was the right woman for him. And yet, even though he knew it was hopeless to try to dissuade her from getting on that plane, he still wasn't ready to concede defeat. If she was his match – and she was – then he was hers. So it was that he narrowed his eyes and tried another tack. 'If you go, you know, I'll try to come, too. Actually, I have already. I put in for special assignment this morning. Made a real pitch to the producers. Sam Berman, our man in Beirut. The anchorman you can trust to tell it like it is.' He laughed. 'This old warhorse may be about to come out of retirement.'

'You'll do nothing of the kind.' Now it was her turn to be protective of her lover.

'It's my work, Anne.' He mimicked her voice in a high falsetto. 'I'm a journalist. My place is there.'

'All right, all right.' Fondly she smiled. At moments like this, it was clear to her that she should divorce Charles and marry Sam. In the past three months that she had been in New York setting up a trauma unit in a West Side hospital, he had almost succeeded in persuading her to start a new life with him here. The sticking point, however, was that she still doubted whether she was capable of making a permanent commitment to anything except her work. It was good with Sam now, but it might not be good with him for ever. A disturbing thought flitted through her mind. Was she running back to Beirut or away from Sam? Later, she told herself; I'll think about that later. For now, she was willing to be conciliatory to the man she was leaving. 'You made your point. I suppose I get a little carried away sometimes.'

'Sometimes? Honey, you've been hanging around with Arabs for most of your life. You and those girlfriends of yours should be awarded Oscars.' But when her smile died and she turned away from him, he could see that he had made a strategic error by reminding her of those she loved in that threatened city.

'Anne, listen to me.' He stopped trying to make light of the situation. 'I know how worried you are about your friends who are stuck there. But I don't want you dying in Beirut because you have either a Florence Nightingale complex or a bad case of misplaced Jewish guilt.' To try to take the sting out of his words, he covered her hands with his. 'Please change your mind and stay here.'

She shook her head. They were on the Long Island Expressway. Kennedy Airport was only a few minutes away. 'Sorry, Sam.'

As he gripped her hand, he was so desperate that he felt like screaming at this impossible woman. Instead, he wheedled like a child who knows he isn't going to get what he wants but can't stop trying. 'Why can't you do something useful in New York? Everyone says that burns unit you're setting up is great. They worked wonders on Fatima's little girl. You can help your Lebanese orphans just as much here as there.'

'Maybe after the war, but not now. Now,' she reminded him gently, 'I'm going to Beirut. I understand your concern. Really I do. But I *have* to go.'

Reluctantly, then, even though he knew she wouldn't like it, he said what he had decided he must. 'Anne, there's something else that's bothering me. The Jewish thing.' Her dark eyes met his dark eyes, and then nervously she looked away. 'You can't go to Beirut this time because you're a Jew.'

'Come off it.' She pulled her hands away from his and recoiled as far away from him as possible beside her window. 'This time you're really off the wall. No, I think I know the Arabs a whole lot better than you do. I've lived there almost all my life, and I've never had any trouble because of *that*. Quite the contrary. If you remember, during the civil war, the PLO actually protected the Jewish population of Beirut. Lebanon is not Nazi Germany.'

'Don't *you* be naive. This Lebanese war is not like the last one. This time it's not the Muslims against the Christians but the Muslims against the Jews.'

'If that's how sophisticated your knowledge of the Middle East is,' she snapped, 'then God help the network news. Listen, and listen carefully. The Israelis launched this war against the Palestinians. The *Israelis*, not the Jews. There is a difference.'

'Yeah, sure.' His eyes were hooded. 'Try telling that to someone like Hitler.'

'Perhaps you've lived in New York too long, Sam. Or perhaps you and I don't have as much in common as I thought. Whether you and the rest of the New York

Jewish community understands this or not, the rest of the world realizes that not all Jews are supporters of the Israeli state.'

'Is that so? Well, I'm afraid what you have to worry about is whether the Arabs of West Beirut continue to make such fine political distinctions once the Israeli bombardment begins.'

'I'll take that risk,' she said briskly, staring straight ahead, wishing they would arrive at the airport before one of them went too far on this loaded issue and said something terrible that could never be forgiven or forgotten.

Instead, after a few miserable moments of silence, he sighed. He, too, did not want to part like this. 'Anne, just be careful.'

From the driver's seat, as he pulled up at the Middle East Airlines gate at the terminal, the cabbie, who was a born New Yorker, could no longer resist voicing his decided opinion. 'Lady, you need your head examined, to go off to that place. You're either very brave or very crazy.'

'She's both,' Sam told him matter-of-factly. He grinned at Anne. 'Which is why I'm going, too.'

'Sam! You're not!'

'Anne! I am!'

As incredulously she laughed, he told her his news in a rush. 'I wasn't going to tell you. I was going to surprise you when I turned up. But what the hell. I guess the cat's out of the bag. The big bosses loved the idea of sending me back. "Dynamite," they said, "dy-na-*mite!*" In a flash they ordered in a new camera crew from London. I wanted to go out with you on tonight's flight, but they're sending me out tomorrow. I'll get in overland from Damascus. Shoot the Israeli side, too. The new promos for my on-the-spot coverage of the story-of-the-year should be all set to fly by the day after tomorrow.'

'I see. But if you're going, too, why did you try to talk me out of it?'

'As I said, honey, Beirut's no tea party. I was worried about you.'

'And now?'

'I'm damn glad you'll be there waiting for me. Someone's got to protect me from all those madmen.'

They were both laughing as they rushed arm in arm through the terminal door for her flight to Beirut.

Before sundown the next night, Leila and Farouk sat side by side, chain-smoking in the executive cabin of the Syrian military transport plane. Leila had the choice window seat and had spent the last anxious hour staring expectantly down at the clouds. Before long they would be landing in Damascus. This time, instead of couture, she was smartly dressed for front-line duty in a grey Norma Kamali tunic and trousers. Her cabin bag was stuffed with jeans, tee-shirts and sandals.

Farouk took a sip of the sixth or seventh whisky he had downed since takeoff, and then his hand stole out and covered hers. Alcohol always made him not only maudlin but amorous. 'It will be good to be home,' he said with a smile. 'And even better to be away from Moscow.'

'My home isn't in Damascus.' She snatched her hand away from his. 'Did you forget? My home is in Palestine.'

Farouk swigged the rest of his whisky and signalled for the steward to bring him another. Sometimes alcohol made him irritable, too. He wasn't up to more of her tiresome carping about lost Palestine. His testy wife, like the rest of her belligerent countrymen, didn't know when to stop gnawing on that whitened old bone. 'You never let anyone forget about your precious Palestine.'

She tore her eyes away from the sublime clouds

to the husband she regarded as ridiculous. She hadn't liked his tone of voice, and today, with the weight of her entire threatened Palestinian world on her shoulders, she was in no mood to put up with anything she didn't like. 'Yes, Farouk, I have said many times that I am Palestinian. And I will continue to say it until you, and those like you, understand exactly what that means. I am Palestinian, and I am going to be with my people in Beirut.' As though she had spoken the last word on the subject, she went back to staring out of the window. Dreamily her gaze softened. Every now and then, even though she knew their flight path wasn't over Lebanon, she fancied she could see Beirut below when the clouds broke.

Meanwhile Farouk seethed and sulked beside her. I knew it, he thought. I've known it all the time. Just as I feared, she intends to barge her way back to Beirut.

He called for another drink, drained it, and ordered yet another. Knowing what he knew, he could not allow her to return to that doomed city. Even though she was hateful and impossible and deserved the worst of all imaginable fates, he couldn't let her go there to die with the rest of them. Very soon, when the Zionist army surrounded the city, the Israeli trap would snap shut. He couldn't let his wife be cornered between the devil and the deep blue sea. Yet he couldn't tell her the reason why, either. Knowing Leila, she would blacken Syria's good Arab name for ever if she had proof of the winks and nods that regularly passed between the Syrians and the Israelis.

As the steward asked them to fasten their seat belts in preparation for landing, Farouk reproached himself for leaving this delicate matter up in the air until they were all but circling Damascus airport. But it was now or never, and so he took a deep breath and repeated what she hadn't waited long enough to hear this morning. 'Listen to me, Leila. I absolutely forbid you to go to Beirut.' When she ignored him and simply went on staring out of the window, he wet his lips with his tongue and tried again. 'No wife of mine will go to Beirut.'

'What did you say?' Her question seemed idle, for she continued staring at the clouds.

He took courage. Perhaps he had overestimated her resolve. Maybe she would be content to stay in Damascus after all. 'No wife of mine will go to Beirut.'

'Good.' Insolently she turned to face him. On her lips was that cold smile he loathed. 'Then divorce me.'

'Now, Leila, *habibi*, please . . .' He wiped the sweat off his forehead. He didn't need this now, not when he had to face that back-stabbing Damascus gang as soon as he landed at the airport. 'We'll talk about this tomorrow.'

'We'll talk about it now.' Matter-of-factly she ignored the flashing sign and lit a cigarette. She had endured more than enough of this man and this marriage. 'There are two important points I want you to understand. First, I am going to Beirut. Second, I want a divorce.'

'I forbid you to go to Beirut.' But he chose to ignore her demand for a divorce. Time and again, they had been over this territory. But he refused to release her from their marriage.

'Forbid? *You?*' She laughed mockingly in his face, and then she played her trump card. 'As soon as I return from Beirut, I will consult the best lawyer in Damascus.' Again she smiled coldly. 'I will sue for divorce on the grounds that our marriage was never consummated.'

Farouk gulped. 'Even *you* would never do that.' Yet he knew she would. This woman was capable of almost anything. Of course she couldn't prove anything, but still she could ruin him. 'I'd be a laughing-stock.'

'*Exactly.*' She ground her cigarette stub out in the ashtray. 'So, whether you like it or not, this is where we say goodbye.'

He maintained a stony silence as the plane descended sharply, bumped down on the runway, and taxied along the tarmac. If this was the way she wanted it, then so be it. She was the worst wife a man could ever be cursed with and the most unnatural woman ever born. She deserved whatever awaited her in Beirut. He – and the world – would be better off without her.

Farouk was so furious that he did not speak another word to Leila as they filed off the aircraft into the terminal and were greeted by dour representatives from the president's office. At once, the officials swept him away to a limousine that was meant to whisk him straight off to high-level talks. By the time he came to his senses, and urgently turned to Leila to explain why he couldn't have her venturing back to Beirut, she was no longer by his side.

He turned and looked for her in the crowd. But he couldn't see her anywhere. By now, he thought, she could be halfway to the Lebanese border. Leave it to Leila to hit the ground running.

He had half a mind to go after her. She wasn't a good wife, but – as he very well knew – a man could love a bad wife with his entire being. It made him sick at heart to think of her trapped like a rat in Beirut. And yet, when an undersecretary plucked at his jacket and a general stepped smartly before him, Farouk allowed himself to be led out of the airport and straight to his meeting.

I've lost her, he thought dully. She – like her people – is lost now. He did not doubt that she would be in Beirut by dawn.

The Syrian cease-fire with the Israelis would be signed tomorrow morning.

That night, at her party, Camilla succeeded at first in rising to the occasion.

She was wearing all her diamonds and her sexy black Saint Laurent strapless top and harem pants. She floated through the throng of guests Maurice had invited over for drinks at their holiday villa artfully nestled along the placid shores of lovely Lac Leman. She kissed this one, hugged that one, kissed another, and twitted yet another for missing last weekend's soirée. Always she loved a good party. The drink, the laughter and the bonhomie for a time drowned out the depression that had settled over her since Julia and Pierre had been murdered. Though tonight she had hardly been able to bring herself to put on her make-up and pile up her hair, now that she was in the thick of the party she laughed and laughed and laughed. From time to time, as she pirouetted through the crowd, she couldn't resist breaking out into a pretty little fancy disco footwork to the beat of John Travolta's 'Saturday Night Fever' which throbbed over the music system. She still insisted on playing this old hit at all her parties. She would never forget the golden days when this record had been so popular. Pierre had still been alive, and Julia had been growing in her womb.

'You look marvellous, darling, simply marvellous,' Maurice whispered in her ear as he refilled her fluted champagne glass. 'See, I told you you'd feel better once everyone arrived.'

For a second, for her, the music stopped as she fixed a cold eye on the husband who never had and never would understand the first thing about her. Maurice was trim, dapper and utterly obtuse. She had been so upset at the latest news from Beirut that she hadn't wanted to have anyone over tonight. It had taken the Israeli army just four days to surge to the gates of Beirut. She did not find this a cause for celebration. In fact, she had worn black tonight as an act of defiance. Above all she hadn't wanted to entertain Maurice's wolfish pack of expatriate Lebanese Maronite friends who supported the Phalange militia from afar. She had known that they – like her husband – would be in exultant mood now that the Israeli army had encircled West Beirut in a 'Ring of Steel' and were demanding the surrender of the besieged Palestinian forces caught inside. She hated hearing about the Christian Lebanese girls who had greeted the conquering Israelis with showers of rosewater, rice and flowers. It made her sick at heart to hear the gossip about the latest round of parties in East Beirut, where the cachet of a hostess was now measured by how many Israeli majors, captains and colonels she had been able to ensnare. Camilla didn't feel like celebrating what, to her, was already a national disgrace and could soon be a personal calamity. Hours on the telephone had confirmed that Anne was back in Lebanon now, and so were Leila, Fatima, Shaykh Georges and many others she cared about far more than Maurice's cronies.

But before she could tell her insensitive booby of a husband exactly what she thought and felt, up sailed a grinning pair of his cousins who kissed him, hugged him, and began mulling over the latest bulletins from the war front.

'The Jews have four hundred tanks and more than a thousand pieces of heavy artillery,' Jean-Marc reported with satisfaction. 'The bay is full of their gunboats, and soon the skies will be full of their planes.'

'This time we've finally got them. We're going to be rid of the Palestinians once and for all.' Claude rubbed his hands together gleefully. 'And I say, don't stop just with the terrorists. Get rid of them all. The women who breed like rabbits. And the children, too, before they can grow up and become terrorists just like their fathers.'

'Lebanon for the Lebanese,' Maurice responded.

While Camilla busied herself with tapping a cigarette out of her case, the three Maronite Christians clicked their glasses together and drank.

'When', Claude asked eagerly, 'do you think the Jews will go in and finish off the job?'

Maurice shrugged. 'That is a matter', he said as he lowered his voice conspiratorially, 'of some delicacy.' His cousins hunched closer to hear what had to be gospel truth. Maurice was well-connected not only with the international banking community but with the American intelligence forces and the Israeli arms merchants who had been selling war *matériel* to the Lebanese Christian forces since the closing months of the civil war. 'I hear, from my best sources, that the siege could go on all summer. For you see, *mes amis*, the Americans are so worried about their Saudi oil supplies that they are keeping the Israelis on a very tight leash. The Americans want a negotiated evacuation, not a bloodbath. There is another problem, too. Maybe a bigger one even than that of the squeamish Americans.' Maurice paused to accept one of Jean-Marc's cigarettes and Claude's lights. 'It's the squeamish Jews.' Maurice let out a bitter little laugh. 'They want us to do their dirty work for them! Imagine! *Incroyable!* Sharon could drive them into the sea any time he wants. But instead – mark my words – he will sit outside the city and hope that our good Christian Lebanese boys will go in and do all the dying for them. The Jews are afraid to try to take West Beirut. They want us to shed Christian blood instead.'

'They are Israelis, not Jews,' Camilla said suddenly, out of the blue. The three men looked at her in amazement, for it had not occurred to them that a pretty party decoration like her could not only talk but think. She rattled on, seemingly unable to stop herself now that she had interrupted the men's political talk. 'My son, my Tomas, my poor lost Tomas, always told me, "Mama, there is a difference. Israel is a country, but the Jews just belong to a religion." ' Uncertainly she smiled. 'He said always to call the Israelis "Zionists". He said the Palestinians never call the Israelis "Jews". So why do you?'

'She's had a drop too much to drink tonight,' Maurice explained to his friends. '*Chérie*, why don't you go and sit down over there with Lulu? You haven't seen her for ages.'

'I do not want to sit down,' Camilla said. 'I want to hear what you say.'

Maurice rolled his eyes. 'As you like. But you'll be bored, darling. You know how talk like this always bores you.' But when his wife still stood listening, he resumed his analysis. 'My view is that the election is more important than the Israeli occupation. I hear', he continued as again his voice dropped to a whisper, 'that the Jews – excuse me, *chérie*, the Israelis – expected to force a *coup d'état* when they reached the Presidential Palace. They wanted Bashir Gemayel to owe the presidency to them. They wanted to make our Lebanon an Israeli puppet state! But Bashir was too smart for them. He said he would wait for our elections at the end of the summer.'

Claude raised his glass. 'To President Bashir!'

As the others drank, Camilla felt as if she was shrivelling up and dying inside. She and Maurice had planned to live their married life in Switzerland and France, not Lebanon. But as expatriates, they were doomed to carry the weight of their native country on their backs wherever they wandered. Even though physically they lived in Europe, in their hearts they had never left the Levant.

'But tell me, Maurice,' Jean-Marc was saying with the air of a man who had dispensed with the trivialities and was finally getting down to the heart of the matter, 'do you really think this war is for the best? For business, I mean? What's going to happen to the Lebanese pound?'

Camilla could no longer endure silently listening to such callous talk. Didn't her husband and his friends care, anymore, that so many of their countrymen were about to be slaughtered in the abattoir of West Beirut?

She slipped away from them and out to the balcony where the air was fresh and free of stench. Over the lake a crescent moon lay curled up at an angle.

Camilla was not a very religious woman, but for once her lips moved in prayer. 'Keep them safe, God. Please keep them all safe.'

On day fourteen of the Israeli siege of West Beirut, late in the morning after two successive days of heavy air and sea bombardment, Leila was hustling between barrages through the rabbit warren of Shatilla refugee camp assessing casualties, listening to complaints, and offering what advice for survival she could to the terrified residents. Shatilla, like the other camps, had started off decades ago as little more than a temporary tent city. The years had turned it into a teeming slum of cement brick houses knitted together by narrow, winding dirt lanes. Most families still didn't have running water, and those with electricity obtained it only by illegally tapping into the power mains. During the bombardments, the Palestinians huddled in the dark and prayed for deliverance. They ventured outside to scavenge for food and water as soon as the barrages stopped.

Just ahead of her, then, in the crumbling concrete and breeze-block shantytown, Leila spotted Hussein coming her way.

She looked to the left and she looked to the right for a bolthole to dive into before he caught sight of her and could hurt her again. But she mastered that craven impulse and stood her ground. She was Leila Shahine, and she wasn't about to run away from anyone. Above all she wasn't about to duck her head and scurry off like a little mouse just to avoid an encounter with Hussein Ibrahim. It was inevitable, after all, she reasoned with herself, that she would have to run into him here sometime. She was working round the clock in the administration of one of West Beirut's main Palestinian refugee camps, and he was one of the major Palestinian leaders. The wonder of it was that she had been locked inside this besieged city for more than two weeks without seeing hide nor hair of him. And yet, even as she braced herself to carry off this meeting with aplomb, she felt so vulnerable inside that she feared she might have to turn and run after all. She wasn't ready to see him now, or perhaps ever.

'*Ya*, Leila!' He was waving and smiling as though a friendly reaction were the most natural one in the world.

Too late, she thought. At that moment she hated him for smiling as though they and their world were not currently being bombed to bits. What did he have to be so cheerful about? But now that he had called out to her, there was nowhere for her to run without losing face.

'I heard you were back! *Marhaba!* Welcome home!'

She nodded and smiled and greeted him as pleasantly – albeit remotely – as if she were still the Prime Minister's wife in the receiving line at a diplomatic reception. They exchanged the usual Arab greetings, lit cigarettes, and traded the latest inside information not only about whether and when the Israelis would try to take West Beirut but also how and where the Palestinian forces might agree to be evacuated. From there, without missing a beat, their conversation moved on to what were becoming the ritual West Beiruti curses of the other Arab states for not coming to the aid of the Palestinians at their hour of need. He told her that American negotiations to evacuate the PLO were stalled on a welter of technicalities: whether they would leave by sea or land, where they would go, whether they would lay down their arms first, and what safeguards would be made for the Palestinian civilian population left behind. She told him about the increasingly desperate conditions in Shatilla: the lack of water, the shortages of fruit and vegetables, the medical supplies which were dwindling to nothing. To hear them talk, it seemed that neither of them remembered their last disastrous rendezvous in Moscow. But all the while those words he had left her with rang through her mind like a curse. *You may have played the whore with the Palestinian revolution, but you're not going to play the whore with me*. It took all her reserves of strength to maintain her composure. Don't let him know how he hurt you, she reminded herself stoutly. Be very distant and professional. Treat him as he treated you. Yet even as she was concentrating on acting out the role she had scripted for herself, inside – at exactly the same time – she wanted both to scratch his eyes out and to throw herself in his arms. Yet she noticed that his arms were crossed on his chest. Here in Beirut, he was hardly reaching out to her either. If that's the way he still wants it, she thought, that's the way it will be.

'I've been looking for you everywhere.' His eyes searched hers.

'Really?' She was as veiled as though she were covered head to toe in black like a religious fanatic. 'I've been right here.'

She didn't say anything more as she thought back over those first hellish days of the siege: the panic in the camps, the deafening pre-dawn noise of the shelling, the shortages of food and fuel, and most of all the fear. She would have liked to have had Hussein with her then. She had thought – or maybe hoped – that after all she had gone through to get here, his might have been the first familiar face to greet her when finally she made it.

In Damascus she had used her Rolex watch to bribe her way on to a military convoy, and then she had talked her way over the border and bluffed her way into West Beirut. But there had been delays – the journey that usually took three hours had expanded to a gruelling fourteen and on the way she had been further depressed to hear there had been heavy fighting in the vicinity of her own villa in the hills overlooking Beirut.

As she stood gravely listening to him assessing the military situation that was now life or death to them all, her mind wandered back to her first anxious hours in the city. The phones hadn't been working, so she hadn't been able to get news about Miriam and her sons. She had trudged for hours around the shuttered streets, unsure where to go and what to do next. As she had hunted unsuccessfully for Miriam among Mustafa's far-flung family, her panic had increased. West Beirut had been electric with tension. The hoarders had all but stripped the shops of their goods. Children ran about like packs of stray dogs. Jeeps and Range Rovers roared down the narrow lanes. In the distance, all the while, the big guns boomed like drums of doom. When she had found herself near the Rue Bliss, she had stopped on impulse at Anne's villa where she had been ecstatically greeted by Fatima and her brood. The telephones had been back in service, and she had finally located her daughter at the home of one of Mustafa's sisters. Miriam reported that both Hamid and Farid had survived the fighting in the south and now were on duty near the Museum Crossing. They would have a family reunion, Miriam promised, the next afternoon. After she had put down the phone, a much-relieved Leila had agreed to spend the night at Fatima's. She had helped the children pile sandbags round the doors and windows, sat crosslegged on the rug for a meal of rice and beans, and then – for the Israelis had cut the electricity off – listened to Fatima read the Koran by candlelight. Why, Leila had wondered hours later, after she and Fatima had sat up far into the night for a heart-to-heart about the losses and triumphs of their lives, had she never before felt so closely bonded to this kind and decent woman? Before Leila had bedded down on the floor of the salon for all the world like a happy peasant, they had called one another 'sister' and meant it. Life under the gun here in Beirut had been studded by many such unexpected moments of human warmth. If any of them got out of this alive, Leila remembered having thought that night with tears in her eyes, they might look back on this siege as their finest hour. When she had reported to PLO headquarters the next morning and been assigned to the staff in Shatilla, she had been proud to don army fatigues and thick-soled combat boots. For once, she had felt utterly at peace with herself.

Yet, Leila reminded herself, all was still not forgiven and forgotten between herself and Hussein. He had behaved like a brute with her in Moscow. Just because they were both now caught in the deadly web of West Beirut, he wasn't going to get round her with a few warm smiles and comradely words.

When he said again that he had gone looking for her as soon as he had heard she was back, she didn't try to keep the bitterness from her voice. 'I haven't been out of this camp for fourteen days. You couldn't have looked for me very hard.'

'I came when I could.' He lit another cigarette. 'We should talk.'

She looked down the alleyway where her work waited. 'Another time perhaps.' She ground out her cigarette with the heel of her military boot, nodded curtly, and was about to hurry away.

'Wait, Leila.' He plucked at the sleeve of her camouflage shirt. 'Please.' They were outside an empty cigarette kiosk, and he motioned for her to follow him inside. 'Please, Leila,' he repeated from the shadows.

She wavered. So far as she was concerned, after Moscow they had nothing to say to one another. But just then the guns opened up again from the air, from the sea, from the hills that brooded over Beirut. The F-16 jets screamed low, the sky was bright with red flares, and a moment later the ground trembled with the impact of exploding bombs. We could die any minute, she thought. They had, perhaps, everything to say to one another. She took cover where he waited in the shop.

'Good.' The sandbags were stacked tight at the open front of the stall and even piled on the floor. It was so dark that he could see only the dim outline of her body. 'Tell me. Why did you come back?'

'I had to.' Her voice was defiant. She didn't owe him any explanations.

He persisted. 'Was it because of what I said in Moscow?'

She concentrated on keeping a tight rein on her emotions. 'You think everything I do is because of you?' But as she lost her battle to control herself, she exploded like a cluster bomb. 'I'm sick of your arrogance. You think you're the only Palestinian who cares about our country? Who's committed to the struggle? Well, for your information, I came back because I had to. Because I'm Palestinian. Because my place is here.'

'Ah!' He sucked in his breath. 'Finally! After twenty-three years, at last you say the magic words.' His voice was very soft. 'Come here.'

'I will not.' But her voice was rough, and her eyes stung with the effort of keeping back her tears. 'I cannot.'

'You're still hurt, eh? Yes, I can hear it. Oh, Leila, don't you understand that there is no more time for our games? We must be good to each other, you and

I. Sometimes it seems three hundred years ago since we were young in London. I tell you now, Leila, that I loved you then. And I love you now. Always I have loved you. Even at your worst – and you are no angel – I could never stop loving you. But never before have I loved you as I do now, in your too big uniform with your dirty hair and your face that is not so young anymore. To me, Leila, you are more beautiful, like this, than when you were a vain and silly girl. Finally, now, here, you are the woman you were born to be. Not only my woman. But *Palestine's* woman.'

Outside the bombardment had increased in ferocity. Rockets whined and burst into flames. There was no escaping the noise and, as the sound of the explosions moved closer, it seemed there was no escaping their reach either. Just outside, a heartbeat away, there was a deadly whistling sound, and she could not help lunging forward into the safety of his arms. They clung to one another as the bombs fell. For a while then, on a stack of sandbags piled inside the cigarette kiosk, the earth seemed to move, and not just from the aftershocks of the falling bombs.

When the big guns fell silent an hour or so later, they emerged from the shop as comrades and lovers. Together they stood in Shatilla, looking with a renewed sense of wonder at the bright sun, the blue sky, the shimmering sea. All around them in the hills that towered over the city, the Israeli sights were trained upon them.

But in this single heady moment, the two of them felt invincible.

'We'll never give in,' Hussein said. 'They had their Masada. Now we have ours.'

Leila shook her fist at the guns. 'You'll have to come in after us,' she taunted the enemy she could not see. 'If you dare.'

'I'll come to you when I can,' he said. 'Tonight

or tomorrow. Just as soon and as often as I can.'

'I'll be there,' she answered.

They parted then, and raced off to do what they could to save their people.

A fortnight later, at the end of the first month of the siege, Fatima and her children anxiously waited in Anne's villa on the Rue Bliss for the signal to break that day's Ramadan fast.

Zainab kept an impatient watch on the fading light at the windows facing the horizon to the west. In these troubled times, with all the smoke, fire, flares, and the waves of Israeli bombers in the West Beirut sky, it could be hard to pick out the blazing noonday sun, much less a discreetly setting one. Her eyes trailed thirstily and hungrily from the sky to the pitcher of water and the dishes of food that were already laid out invitingly on the gigantic tin tray placed in the centre of the room. Just because West Beirut was still under Israeli siege didn't mean that its Muslim inhabitants were released from their religious obligation to abstain from food and drink during daylight hours.

'Can you still see the sun?' Hussein was fasting for the first time this year, and for him the novelty of Ramadan was even more thrilling than the excitements of war. Every morning and every night he fretted lest his mother or sisters had got the time wrong and thus invalidated his fast. 'We can't eat or drink until the sun is down,' he reminded them self-importantly.

'Quiet.' His eldest brother Muhammad, who had become the man of the family after his father's death, looked fierce in his Amal military uniform as he sat on the sofa with a transistor radio in his lap. In Cairo, the official end to every day of Ramadan fasting is still publicly signalled by the firing of a military cannon. But in the ear-splitting night and day bombardment of

Beirut, one symbolic boom would almost certainly be drowned out. So it was that Muhammad was listening for an imam to announce the end of this day's fasting on the radio.

Meanwhile his mother and younger brothers and sisters were strewn all around the room, their eyes locked on the waiting food and their ears attuned for the clerical signal. Some yawned and dozed off in the heavy heat. Others stared into space in a glassy-eyed stupor.

Fatima gazed at their meagre supper. Every other Ramadan, poor as they had been, each night's dinner had been worth the long wait. Always there had been chicken and maybe even a second dish of lamb, salads of every description, lentil stews, freshly baked bread, and the most mouth-watering melons for dessert. But tonight there was only rice and a tahina sesame sauce. As June had bled into July and still the PLO had sat tight and resisted, the Israelis had tightened their blockade of West Beirut. Conditions inside the besieged city had gone from bad to worse. The electricity was off most of the time now, and so was the water. There was no meat in the city, very little fresh produce and absolutely no fuel. Weeks ago they had consumed all the foodstuffs stockpiled in the pantry. Every morning Fatima sent her daughters out to scour the markets for whatever they could find. Today Zainab had queued for bread for three hours, only to be told as she reached the front of the line that she would have to come back and try again tomorrow. Salma had found a Kurdish street vendor selling a few shrivelled vegetables on al-Hamra, but the price he was demanding had been far beyond the family's means. Poor Elham, still self-conscious about her scarred faced despite the best efforts of the New York plastic surgeons, had been able to find only a few battered tins of tahina paste. It's not enough, Fatima thought. The little ones needed milk, and all of them needed protein. She herself had nearly fainted this afternoon when she had made the rounds of the markets scavenging for food. The only times in the past few weeks that the monotony of their rice diet had been relieved was when Anne – with her mysteriously procured bags of fruits and vegetables – had come to spend the night.

For something to do, Fatima sat down on the floor beside the tin tray and carefully spooned tahina sauce over the rice and rhythmically stirred it. These days, besides being worried about the survival of each and every member of her family, she was concerned at how Anne was tottering on the brink of exhaustion. She couldn't continue careering to and fro, without respite, from the American University Hospital to the clinic she was operating out of an old parking garage in Shatilla. Nor, Fatima thought, could she continue vacillating between Charles and Sam. Some nights she spent in her old apartment with Charles, some nights she slept in the Commodore Hotel with Sam, and at other times she either collapsed at Leila's in Shatilla or came here to the Rue Bliss to bed down on the floor. When Fatima tried to lecture her about the morality of all this, Anne would just wearily shrug and say she couldn't think straight anymore about anything except the wounded. And then Anne would shake her head and start telling her the most terrible stories about what the smoking remains of a child looked like after it had been burned to death by a phosphorus bomb or about how many arms and legs she had amputated in the past week from victims of cluster bombs. Fatima, then, would take her old friend in her arms and stroke her hair as though she were her own dear little two-and-a-half-year-old Ali. I will pray for Anne tonight, Fatima resolved.

Just then a blast of static vibrated from the radio. Bored with waiting for the imam to speak, Muhammad was twiddling the dial to catch the latest news from the myriad Lebanese and foreign radio stations that connected West Beirut to the outside world. Reporters for the BBC and the Voice of America agreed that no progress had been made in the stalemate over the evacuation of Palestinian fighters. From Tel Aviv the news was that a hundred thousand anti-war demonstrators had turned out in Israel to protest against the invasion of Lebanon. But a left-wing Lebanese station reported that the Israelis had turned away a Red Cross cargo ship stocked with essential medical supplies. And meanwhile, in Christian East Beirut, an announcer said the roads to the beaches were jammed with holiday-making families.

'*Ibn kelb*.' Under his breath Muhammad cursed those uncaring Christian sons of dogs.

'*Kefir*, Muhammad, enough.' Fatima's eyes flashed at him in rebuke. She wasn't having Ramadan's purity sullied by cursing. Since Ali's death, she had grown more rigid, especially when it came to religion. Her eyes trailed to the bookshelves on the wall where a framed martyr's picture of her dead husband sat beside a colour photograph of Imam Musa Sadr. Since the imam had gone missing in Libya four years ago, Lebanon's Shia had never given up hope that their revered religious leader would someday walk out alive from the African desert. His photograph – and often one of Shaykh Ali, 'the fighting mullah' – was to be found in a place of honour in many Shia homes. Now, as always, the icons calmed Fatima. She reminded herself that this, after all, was no normal Ramadan. The tension was getting the better of them all. She had to referee almost constant fights among the children who, in between cowering in the basement during the bombardments, complained to her that there was nowhere to go and nothing to do. The schools, of course, were closed. Fatima wouldn't allow them to go off and play at any of their friends' houses. Night and day, she caught herself silently counting their dear heads. The waiting was the worst of it. At night she lay awake waiting for the bombs to fall. During daylight she bustled about waiting for their enemies to massacre them all. Never could she shake off the most crushing dread. Yet now she carefully modulated her voice as she smiled at her eldest son. 'I think we should listen to the imam.'

The Arabic chanting that signalled the end of today's fasting was already underway, and the sound of it galvanized Fatima and the children to throw themselves down on the floor around the tray.

'*Bismillah al-raham al-rahim*,' Muhammad intoned, 'in the name of Allah the compassionate and the merciful.'

After first offering the customary prayer before breaking the fast, Fatima and the children tipped the water pitcher and drank with the thirst of a long and dusty day. Greedily then they reached out and rolled balls of rice with their fingers and popped them into their mouths. Gradually, as the food and water soothed them, they began reverting to their own good-humoured selves. The boys turned boisterous, and the girls became giggly. This one teased that one, and suddenly everyone was talking at once.

The peace was shattered by gunfire, it seemed, right outside in the garden. At once the youngest children began screaming and lunged for their mother. Fatima clutched them all to her, babbled endearments, and shrieked at Muhammad to go and see what was happening. As he grabbed his Kalashnikov and strode to the door with two of his teenage brothers in his wake, Salma was shouting that the Israelis must have broken through the Green Line and were going to kill every one of them before morning. Jaber and Ali began to sob.

As still the shooting continued, Fatima wondered frantically whether she should lead the children down to the basement or out to the bomb shelter at the far end of the garden. The last time Anne was here, she had warned that a cluster bomb would turn the shelter into a family tomb, that the basement was a far better place to hide, so long as the villa wasn't hit by one of those imploding bombs that would bring the four stories down on their heads. Fatima supposed the basement was safer than the shelter, and yet she shuddered at the thought of hiding down in the dark. Was it better, she wondered, to be blown to bits in a second or to suffer a lingering death by being buried alive?

But before she could lead the children down to the basement, a smiling Muhammad rushed back inside with his grinning brothers behind him. 'Relax! It's just the *Leilat al-Qadr!* They're just shooting for the "Night of Power"!'

Fatima clutched at her heart, which had been pounding so hard that for a moment she couldn't speak. Even before the siege, Anne had warned that her overweight was putting a strain on her heart. They had joked only last week that the Israelis were perhaps doing her a favour by cutting off West Beirut's food supplies. Yet now, as she panted with the effort of breathing, her heart no longer seemed a laughing matter. Zainab noticed her distress and insisted that she sit down on the sofa. Salma put a cushion behind her head. Muhammad brewed her a cup of tea with his own hands and stood solicitously beside her as she sipped it.

Fatima smiled at her children, who were spread all around her in an anxiously caring circle. God is good to me, she thought. He has taken away some but left me with many. Even at this hour of need during this terrible siege, she was overwhelmed with gratitude to Allah.

'What's the *Leilat al-Qadr*, Ummie?' Three-and-a-half-year-old Jaber had forgotten last year's Ramadan.

'Don't you know *anything?*' Hussein liked nothing better than to lord it over his younger sisters and brothers. But as Jaber screwed up his face to cry, Hussein hastily put his arm around the toddler and explained what tonight's fuss was about. 'This is the holiest night of all Ramadan,' he said in a hushed and respectful voice. 'It's the Night of Power, the time long ago when the Holy Prophet Muhammad was out in the desert and Allah revealed to him the Holy Koran. That's right, Ummie, isn't it?'

'Exactly,' she agreed. 'Your father, if he were alive, could not have explained it better.' She smiled dreamily, as she always did when she spoke about her husband. Not a day passed when she didn't take herself where no one could see her to shed tears for the loss of her husband. And yet, as the weeks and months and years had slid by, she had become accustomed not only to being alone but also to taking deep and abiding comfort from her religion. 'Your father', she continued in that same faraway voice, 'always said that the Night of Power was better than a thousand months and that it was the best and most sacred night of the year. He would always stay up the whole night, praying until dawn.' Her voice faltered. 'He used to say that always there was peace on this night of nights, until dawn, all over the world.' Her voice fell to a whisper. 'Even here.'

Hussein glowed with pleasure at his mother's praise of his religious knowledge. Then, in a rush, he departed from strict theology and was racing ahead with the folktale he had heard not in the mosque but from his brothers and sisters as they had sat outside down in Suker on starlit Ramadan nights. 'At midnight on the *Leilat al-Qadr*, all the angels come down to earth and everything's wonderful. Even the trees bow down to Allah. And if you make a wish at that hour, then it's sure to come true.'

'Really?' Jaber's eyes were wide and trusting. 'At midnight? Is it midnight now?'

'Of course not, silly.' Hussein frowned at his little brother. 'It's only nine o'clock.'

'Then tonight I want to stay up late. Can I stay up late, Ummie? To make a wish?'

She smiled indulgently. 'That depends. But first you have to tell me what you'll be wishing for.'

'Me! Me first!' His sister Amina cut in and answered before he could. 'I'm afraid of all the boom-booms here, Ummie. I want to go to New York with Auntie Anne. Elham and Ahmed say it's very wonderful in New York. No one has Kalashnikovs. And the Israelis don't bomb it, ever.'

'That's true,' Ahmed said. 'I wish I was in New York now.'

'Can't we leave here, Ummie?' Amina repeated. 'Please.'

Fatima bit her lip. 'There's nowhere for us to go, *habibi*.'

But Jaber continued determinedly with his list of wishes. 'I want meat,' he said. 'And chocolate. And watermelons.' He hesitated and then went on in a rush. 'And Amina's right. I want all the guns to stop. I want peace, Ummie.'

'Amen,' she said as she gave both Jaber and Amina a hug.

But by now it was dark outside and time for the evening prayers. 'Ablutions!' Fatima ordered. 'And then tonight I think we will all pray together behind Muhammad.'

As her eldest son proudly squared his shoulders and went off to prepare himself for this special honour by putting on a clean white robe, Fatima for a moment forgot all about the war, and her worries, and her fears. Tonight on the *Leilat al-Qadr* there would be special prayers to be said, and perhaps she would have the children take turns reciting their favourite verses from the Koran.

On this Night of Power, for the first time in many nights, the war no longer was of paramount importance on the Rue Bliss.

As soon as his Lebanese driver had got past the Palestinian checkpoint at the entrance to Shatilla refugee camp, Sam ordered him to stop. He jumped out of the grimy white minibus with its gigantic 'Press' sign in English and Arabic taped to the windscreen and looked ahead. What with the heaps of rubble scattered everywhere and the pitted ditches that were all that was left of the old paved road, the camp's main street had become well nigh impassable.

'Why don't you guys stay here,' Sam ordered. 'I'll be back as soon as I can.' He turned to the photographer and the sound man nursing their equipment in the back. 'See what you can get for colour here. We need something quick and dirty to go with the voice-over about this morning's shelling. There should be plenty of blood and guts here.' He checked his watch. 'We still have nearly three hours before we have to ship today's package to Damascus. If I'm not back in an hour or so, wrap it up without me.'

'Right.' Before Sam could turn the corner and disappear into the devastation of the refugee camp, the cameraman was out of the vehicle and on the prowl for human interest. The soundman trailed behind, checking background levels on his meters.

At first Sam strode off purposefully, in his battle-stained khaki safari suit, for the makeshift operating theatre Anne had set up in an abandoned garage in the heart of the camp. But in the two or three weeks since he had been here, the Israelis had unleashed their three most horrific firestorms on the besieged city, and the refugee camps – or, as the Israelis had taken to calling them, the 'terrorist camps' – had, as usual, taken the brunt of the bombardment. Shatilla lay in ruins. Roofs had caved in, walls had fallen into alleyways, and the way was blocked by debris of every sort. Sam had to zig here and zag there, and still he lost his way twice before he finally spotted Anne's clinic.

Without thinking, he barged past the wounded lying on the floors and the anxious packs of waiting families and into the cramped little room that passed for the operating theatre. He stared, blanched, and turned away as his gorge rose.

Anne and two young Palestinian nurses stood, like butchers in a meat market, over a bloody thing that he presumed must once have been human.

Sam staggered away from Anne and her grisly work. Outside he leaned against a wall and vomited. He had shot enough tragic footage in these primitive camps to withstand almost anything but it overwhelmed him to think that Anne lived amid such carnage day after day. How could she stand it? As a journalist, it was his business to witness everything that happened and then to tell it as it was. All he did was visit tragedy, record it, and then forget it as he moved on to the next sensation. Yet Anne took the responsibility for it upon her shoulders and into her heart. No wonder, he thought, that sometimes in the night he could hear her body shaking with uncontrollable sobs.

He stumbled outside and, as he waited for her to finish her heartbreaking work and join him, he wondered how she would react to the bad news he was bringing her. He supposed he could have let sleeping dogs lie – or perhaps even die – and merely have reported the news to all the world but her. What, after all, did he owe Anne's husband? He had met Charles a frosty time or two, but they were hardly friends. Until now, all Sam had wanted to hear about Charles was that he had filed for divorce. Yet even though he had sometimes wished the fellow dead, he hadn't welcomed the news that Anne's husband had been kidnapped late this morning. Some said he had been accused of being an Israeli spy and taken hostage by the Palestinian United Front. Others said the Shia Amal militia had caught him relaying information to the Israelis and were going to execute him after an impromptu military trial.

Sam lit his fifty-third cigarette of the day, inhaled the burning nicotine as though it were penance instead of pleasure, and thought about the nasty spate of kidnappings that marked the six harrowing weeks of this siege. It was mostly prominent Lebanese who disappeared, never to be heard from again, but very occasionally a foreigner had been victimized. Being taken hostage was just another of West Beirut's hazards, like happening to walk too near a booby-trapped parked car at just the wrong moment or cowering under the wrong windowsill just before a phosphorus bomb fell directly down from the sky. Charles had simply been unlucky. From what Sam had heard about Anne's husband, it was a wonder no one had knocked him off before this.

Anne came through the door with Leila's daughter Miriam, whom she had pressed into service as one of her nurses. 'Get the next one ready, Mimi. I'll only be a minute.' Wearily she peeled off her bloodstained rubber gloves. Her jeans and white surgeon's jacket were so caked with dried blood that they crackled when she walked. 'All right, Sam. What now?'

He was just as blunt. 'Charles has been kidnapped.'

'Kidnapped,' she repeated. But her face remained blank. 'Who has him?'

Sam shrugged. 'Nobody knows for sure. Maybe the United Front. Maybe Amal. It's anybody's guess.' He gave her a cigarette, lit it, and put another fresh one between his own lips. 'They say he's a spy.'

'That old chestnut. He's no more a spy than I am.' Her eyes met Sam's. Just last night, when the two of them had been together in the Commodore bar, one of the newly arrived correspondents from a New York paper had been spreading wild rumours that – as a last desperate act, if the Israelis seemed about to storm West Beirut – the PLO planned to round up all the Jewish press corps and relief workers stuck in the city and kill them for being Zionist spies. Anne had argued passionately with the newcomer that such a thing could never happen here. As she had vowed to Sam when the two of them continued the argument up in his hotel room, she was still willing to stake her life on the certainty that her father's ethnic roots could never put her in jeopardy in West Beirut.

Sam decided to let that particularly touchy issue pass for now. They could deal with only one crisis at a time, and the reality of Charles's kidnapping had to take precedence over the possibility of their own danger. 'They're saying', he told her, 'that he's the one who's been pinpointing Arafat's whereabouts for the Israelis.' At least four times during this siege, Israeli bombers had flattened buildings only moments after the PLO chairman had left them, and on four other occasions they had rocketed a building within twenty-four hours of Arafat's appearance there.

'That would be just like Charles,' Anne mused with a touch of bitterness, 'almost but not quite being able to do what he's supposed to do.' But then she sighed. This was neither the time nor the place to bring up her husband's domestic shortcomings. She reminded herself not only that she had known what she was getting into with Charles before she married him but that she had been the one to seduce him. Their married life, although never radiantly happy, had often been comforting. Whatever else he was, Charles was her friend. She was no more capable of deserting him now than she would have been able to stand back idly and watch Fatima, Leila or Camilla at risk. 'Charles kidnapped. God, what next?' She stared unseeing at the rubble of the camp as her mind raced through her options. 'You say the United Front or Amal might have him,' she repeated, almost to herself, as she considered the best course of action. Then she turned back to Sam. 'Will you help get him out?'

'Me?' He had been watching her face closely, and it seemed to him that she might still love her husband. After being kept on a string by this woman for seven years, was he really ready to lay his life on the line for his rival? Sam shook his head. 'I have work to do, honey. The network's screaming at me for action. Just because your husband – your *estranged* husband – has been picked up as a CIA spy doesn't mean that the whole world stops.' But then, as she merely stared at him and waited, Sam threw his mostly unsmoked cigarette down in the dirt and conquered his jealousy. 'Oh, hell, what am I saying? The boys can handle whatever happens the rest of today without me. Of course I'll help.'

'Good,' Anne said briskly. 'We'll try Leila first.' She had a quick word with Miriam and the other helpers inside the clinic, and then sped off deeper into the camp with Sam at her heels. For ten minutes, half an hour, forty-five minutes, they arrived at Shatilla's pulse points just after Leila had left. But finally they tracked her down at a concrete command bunker that the fighters had dug deep into the ground.

Leila's hair was covered by a sooty scarf, her face was haggard with overwork, her jeans were ripped on the calf, and her outsized military workshirt hung almost down to her knees. But her eyes were brighter than they'd ever been, and she greeted Anne with a hug, and the latest joke which cast wicked aspersions on the manhood of the Israeli army. Shrewdly, then, she studied Anne's anxious face. 'You've heard the news?'

Anne nodded. As usual, the Palestinian tom-toms had been beating with the latest bulletins. 'Yes. Charles. Where is he?'

Leila shrugged her shoulders eloquently. 'Who knows?' She shifted her attention to Sam. When he had needed a certain sort of Palestinian interview or battle footage during these last weeks, Leila had personally made sure that he got precisely what he wanted. Once at the Commodore the three of them had even got drunk together on warm Heineken. The Palestinian doubted, however, whether she would ever consider Sam a friend. Except for Anne, Leila was not enamoured of Americans. She held the United States almost as responsible as Israel for the current slaughter in West Beirut. If the Americans hadn't pumped their billions into the Zionist state for the past thirty-four years, she reasoned that by now the Israelis might have been forced to reach some sort of reasonable accommodation with the Arab world. And yet she had a soft spot for Sam, who seemed after all to make Anne happy. She herself would long ago have cast Charles aside and gone off into the sunset with this journalist. So it was that she bestowed one of her rare smiles upon Sam and was a bit sharpish with Anne. 'But what are you getting involved in all this for? I thought it was all over between you and your husband.'

'It is. Sort of.' Anne squirmed under the scrutiny of her lover and her friend. 'But that's neither here nor there. I still don't want to have to go fetch his body somewhere with a bullet in his brain.' As her eyes met Leila's, Anne didn't have to add the obvious: like Ramsey's.

Leila looked away first. She hadn't needed to be reminded that she still owed Anne – and Sam – for bringing home her brother's mangled corpse. Not only to settle that old debt but also out of simple affection, she had swung into action to get Charles released as soon as she had heard about his kidnapping. Yet she made a show of reluctance. The committed Palestinian in her would have liked to pull the trigger on a known spy like Charles. She supposed, however, that with the end of the siege in sight and the PLO evacuation about to proceed, dispatching a single CIA agent was no longer crucial to her cause. In fact, even though she was loath to admit it, it could be counter-productive now to antagonize the Americans by killing one of their own.

'Okay,' Leila said. 'You may as well know. I called around this afternoon when I first heard the news. I shouldn't have, but I did. All I could find out was that Arafat's people don't have him. So then I asked Hussein to help. At first he didn't even want to listen. He said Charles was guilty as hell and it was high time he paid for it. But because I asked him to, he made some calls. It turns out that Amal has him. The Shia militiamen are holding him over by the Murr Tower.'

Anne's heart sank. Now more than ever, all that mattered here in West Beirut was whom you knew. Her only chance of getting Charles out had been through *wasta* – personal influence – which in this case meant the intercession of a close friend. Because of Leila, she would have had leverage with the PLO and the United Front. Frantically she considered what little pull she had with the Shia militia. Over these past desperate weeks, she supposed she must have treated as many wounded fighters from Amal as from any of the other militias. But she doubted if that professional connection would be enough to guarantee her husband's release.

All this time Leila was waiting for Anne to jump to the obvious conclusion so that she could spring her surprise. Yet time was at a premium. 'If it were me,' she announced, 'I'd go to Fatima. And fast.'

'Fatima?' Anne wrinkled her brow.

'Sometimes, darling, you are very dense.' Leila spread her hands out before her and studied them, as she used to when she was checking to see if her nail varnish needed touching up. But now the lacquer was long gone, and the broken nails even had dirt underneath them.

She smiled at the revolutionary proof of her unkempt fingernails. 'Her husband Ali, as you would surely have remembered by now if you weren't so overworked, was one of the founders and chief martyrs of Amal. You must have seen those photographs of "Shaykh Ali, the fighting mullah" in all the Shia neighbourhoods. Fatima's son Muhammad is with Amal now, too. I have it on the very best authority – my Hussein! – that young Muhammad may be assigned as one of your husband's guards very soon. Hussein says it's chaos over there at that Amal post. And he advises that it might be at its most chaotic when Muhammad is on guard duty at – precisely – five o'clock. But Hussein says to make sure that you don't go in there yourself. The Iranians have been doing all they can to ingratiate themselves with the Shia in Beirut. And you know what the Ayatollah thinks of Americans! But they'll probably do anything for Shaykh Ali's widow.'

'Ah!' Anne hugged Leila. 'I knew you'd help. I knew it.'

'Of course I'd help.' Leila winked over Anne's shoulder at Sam. 'But do yourself a favour, *habibi*, and once that Zionist spy husband of yours disappears back behind enemy lines, divorce him straightaway. Sam, here, won't wait for ever.'

Anne blew Leila a kiss and, as Sam put his arm around her and they rushed out of the Palestinian bunker, they were both laughing as though they didn't have a care in the world.

Yet when they tramped into the Rue Bliss villa and asked Fatima for her help, Charles's peril once again seemed no laughing matter.

Fatima had known nothing about Anne's husband's plight, and her first impulse when they told her was to refuse to get involved. 'I will pray for his safety,' she said. She folded her hands in her ample lap as though that were the end of the matter.

When Anne pleaded for more practical help, Fatima surprised her once again by letting the newly forged steel inside her show. She was no longer a simple village woman who let others do the thinking. To her mind, the crucial issue was whether Charles deserved the rough justice of a firing squad. 'This husband of yours, this man who is not really your man anymore, is it true what they say about him?' She glanced at the shattered glass by the open window and beyond, where every day the sky was dark with Israeli bombs. 'Is he a spy? Does he tell the Israelis where to bomb us?'

'I doubt it.' Anne shrugged. 'I'm not sure, but I doubt it.'

'Then come back and ask me to help you if and when you are sure.' Fatima's white-scarfed head nodded in finality.

'What's gotten into you?' Anne paced back and forth before the one she had always thought of as her best friend. 'I could understand it better if Leila had refused to help. She's so involved in politics, and Charles is accused of trying to get Arafat killed. She, however, came through for me with flying colours. But you! How can you act like this? You've always been so kind and understanding.'

'God willing, I am still kind and understanding.' There was, however, a new fierceness in Fatima's eyes. 'But, you know, even in the Holy Koran it says that we must be strong if we are to do God's work.'

'God's work?' Anne looked at Fatima in disbelief. 'What are you talking about? Or rather,' she added, with a flash of intuition, 'whom have you been listening to?'

Eagerly Fatima leaned forward to tell her friend. 'At the mosque, last week, there was a man from Iran. An imam who knew my Ali when he was there long ago! Imagine that!' For an instant the years dropped away and Fatima's eyes shone like a girl's. She was so lonely without Ali. But even though it was hard to be mother and father to their sprawling family, she had never considered taking another husband. She had always believed that one kind and just man had been more than enough to gladden her life. Yet, lately, under the nearly unbearable strain of the siege, Fatima had felt a bitterness beginning to take hold of her. It had moved her so, then, to hear the imam reminisce about Ali and inspire her with hope for Islamic answers to what she had begun to despair of as Lebanon's insoluble problems. 'He told us about what is happening now in Iran, in the Islamic Republic. He made it sound so beautiful there, so right! He told us about the arms his country has been sending us here in Beirut. And the food. And the medicine. They are the only ones who help us, you know. None of the Arab governments have come to our help. Only Iran is our friend.'

Anne moistened her lips with her tongue. Was it any wonder, she thought, that they were all beginning to crack under the pressures of this horrible siege? She had known Fatima for all her adult life, and could only hope that her old friend would come back to her senses as soon as the siege was over. And yet time was running out for Charles. Instead of trying to talk this Iranian nonsense out of Fatima's head, she simply threw herself down on the floor and reached up and took Fatima's hands in hers. 'Do this for me,' she pleaded. 'Forget everything else but you and me. Help me.'

Fatima stroked Anne's hands. 'I do not understand why you want him to go free,' she said, more to herself than to them. 'But then, I never understood why you married him. And why you stayed married to him. We are so different, you and I.' But then she softened. How could she refuse Anne anything? And what did she know of the dirty political business of men? 'So tell me', she finally said, 'what it is that you want me to do.'

Anne did not wait to be asked twice. 'Come with me to the Murr Tower. Get Muhammad to release Charles.'

'You ask me and my son to betray our people and our cause?'

'I ask you to help me. That's all.'

'Anne, I think you ask too much.' But then, after thinking hard for a moment, Fatima brightened. 'I will consult the Holy Koran as we do back in the village.' As Sam nervously checked the time on his watch, Fatima went off to the kitchen to perform her obligatory ablutions before she was ritually clean enough to touch the sacred tome. Then reverently she took the heavily ornamented, black leather-bound book down from its shelf and held it in her lap. For a moment she shut her eyes and prayed for Allah to guide her to the right decision. Then she opened the Koran at random and, with her eyes still shut, touched her index finger to the page. She bent her head to read whatever *surah* she had come upon. 'Oh, yes,' she said, smiling at Anne. She read the verse aloud: ' "This day shall every soul be rewarded for what it has earned. No injustice shall be done this day, for surely Allah is quick in reckoning. The unjust shall not have any compassionate friend nor any intercessor who should be obeyed." '

Sam knitted his brows. It seemed to him that this colourful little ritual of Fatima's was very like the way a dotty girlfriend of his used to cast pennies for an I Ching verse. In that Chinese book of prophecy, too, he had always thought each ambivalent verse could be interpreted either for or against a proposition. To him, it sounded as though the Koran had just cast its vote for a firing squad.

But Fatima had already decided to help Anne, and so she chose to interpret the words the opposite way. 'I will help,' she said. ' "No injustice shall be done on this day." So in the name of God the merciful and the compassionate, I will help.'

Five minutes later the three of them were hurrying up the street towards the Murr Tower. From the bustle along the crowded pavements, it seemed that the Israeli bombers, tanks and gunboats were taking the afternoon off. On one corner an Armenian vendor was selling watermelons that were apparently worth their weight in gold. At another crossing a queue of boys waited to fill water jugs from an artesian well. Old men stood together trading the latest speculation about when the PLO would leave the city and where they would go.

The front entrance to the Murr Tower was heavily guarded by a contingent of Palestinian, Druze and Shia fighters. 'Wait here,' Fatima ordered. She approached a soldier with the Amal badge stitched to his shirt, gave him fervent Islamic greetings, and explained that she – the widow of 'the fighting mullah, Shaykh Ali' – was looking for her son Muhammad from the village of Suker in the south. The fighter smiled, pointed down the street, and would have escorted her there personally if Fatima hadn't insisted that she could find her way herself. Sam and Anne began to follow her to the Amal post, but once again she cautioned them to wait back at the corner. *'Inshallah,'* she said to Anne, 'I will return with your husband.'

In the fading light Anne and Sam chain-smoked as they kept their eyes trained on the militia's front door. Fatima was gone three minutes, five minutes, an eternity of eight minutes. Finally they saw her white-scarfed head in the doorway. When she sedately sauntered outside a second later, she was not alone. Next to her was a tall, slim man in an Amal military shirt. Most of his face was concealed by a black and white chequered Arab *kuffiyeh* headscarf. But Anne would have known that walk anywhere. 'She did it,' Anne whispered. 'I'm sure that's him.'

If she had been anywhere else but on the streets of West Beirut with armed and desperate men everywhere, Anne would have run down and thrown herself in Charles's arms. Instead, because she couldn't risk attracting attention, she waited silently with Sam. The husband and wife greeted each other as casually as though they were third cousins. The four of them stood together for a moment.

'Exactly what happened in there?' Sam asked Fatima.

She shrugged. 'I went in. They greeted me as though they were expecting me. They all knew who I was, and every one of them had heard of my husband. One of them said it was a great honour to meet the wife of the "fighting mullah". Then they winked and told me where my son was.'

'Winked,' Anne repeated. God bless Leila, she thought.

'My son was sitting in a little room drinking tea and playing cards with Charles. "So finally you come," Muhammad said. Then he took off his own shirt, and told Charles to put it on. He gave him a *kuffiyeh*, too, and had to show him how to fix it. That's all. Muhammad walked us to the door.'

'Everyone smiled and said goodbye to me. The officers, the men, the boy who brings the tea.' Charles shook his head in wonder. 'One minute they're going to kill me, and the next minute they kill me with kindness. I'll never understand the Arabs.'

'No,' Anne agreed. 'You never will.'

'I wish', Sam said, 'that I had my camera crew, and we could do an on-the-spot interview. But I suppose', he added to himself, 'a CIA agent wouldn't go on camera for me anyway.' He looked up and down the street which was crowded with armed men. 'Look, gang, I think it's tempting fate to hang around here.'

All four of them nodded, and then Anne and Charles

set a swift pace. Sam and Fatima fell in behind, just out of earshot.

'I haven't thanked you yet. I don't know how you managed it, Anne, but you saved my life.'

'Thank Leila and Fatima. They're the ones who did all the work.'

'But only because you asked them.' The further they walked from the vicinity of the Murr Tower, the more confidence was returning to Charles's voice. 'They were going to shoot me at sunrise. God, I thought this time my luck had run out.'

Anne was so intent on what she had to ask her husband that she wasn't paying attention to where they were walking. She had assumed they would be heading home to their apartment down by the Corniche, but instead Charles had deftly guided them uphill in the opposite direction, and away from the sea. 'I never did hear', she said, 'exactly how you came to be arrested.'

'Oh,' Charles said airily, 'this morning I was out for a walk, and someone saw me with my little transistor radio – you know, that Walkman you gave me for Christmas – and they assumed I was signalling the Israelis.'

'Yes?' Anne waited for him to assure her that those suspicions were entirely unfounded. But he kept silent as he walked on faster and faster, until the two of them were all but jogging up the street, deeper and deeper into the densely packed slums, closer and closer to the Green Line that separated West Beirut from its Israeli besiegers. Fatima had not been able to keep pace with them, so by now she and Sam were far behind. 'Charles,' Anne finally said, hating to have to ask. 'You can tell me. What about it?'

'What about what?' he hedged. Around them now, in firing range of the Israeli gunners, the blocks of severely damaged flats had long been deserted. No one dared to live here now. Besides the scavenging packs of pariah dogs, the four of them were the only creatures that moved.

'Charles. I've got to know. Were they right? Are you working for the CIA?'

He looked ahead at the trenches, the no-man's-land, and the turrets of the Israeli tanks on the far side of the barricades. Then he shot his wife a brief smile. 'Look, I think this is far enough for you. It's not safe this close to the Green Line. Those snipers are always moving around.'

'Answer me! I'm your wife! I have a right to know.'

'My wife? Come off it, Anne. You haven't been my real wife for years. If ever.' Charles looked over his shoulder at Sam, still dogging their heels. 'You won't miss me. You've still got your anchorman.'

'I'm not talking about Sam, or even about our marriage. I want to know if everyone's right. Are you CIA?'

It was a cold-eyed stranger rather than the man she had been married to for fourteen years who looked her straight in the eye and wouldn't say yes and wouldn't say no.

She stared in the face of another betrayal. Charles had betrayed not only her but also the life they had lived and the friends they had loved for all the years of their married life. 'So you're going over to the other side.'

'Draw your own conclusions.' Charles hesitated and then said more. 'Look, do you want to come with me? The way they've fixed for me to get out is safe enough. We could be in Tel Aviv tonight, Washington tomorrow. I know we haven't had the best of marriages. But it hasn't been the worst, either. I'm sure it would be better between us once we were away from this madhouse.'

Firmly she shook her head. 'If I had wanted to go, I would have left before this. I'm in for the duration. But I think it's about time that we got things sorted out between the two of us, too.' Finally she was able to say what had to be said. 'I want a divorce.'

Absently he nodded. Already his attention had wandered away from her as he concentrated on the dangerous few moments it would take him to pass over to safety. 'I'll call you,' he said, as though he hadn't heard a word she had said. He bent down and kissed her, Arab-style, on both cheeks.

'Judas kisses,' she said.

But before she could say more, her shadowy husband had turned and disappeared inside a darkly crumbling building that leaned sidewise almost over into no-man's-land. She waited a moment for a volley of shots that would mean he hadn't been as smart as he thought he was.

But for once all was quiet along the Green Line.

On the morning of the Palestinian United Front's last day in Beirut, Hussein and Leila were alone in their quarters in the Shatilla camp making their private farewells before he left with his men for South Yemen. All night long they had lain in each other's arms, and come together with tenderness and longing, and then jumped up and cooked rice and beans and talked for hours, and finally tumbled back into bed and come together again with desperate sweetness and a fierce aching need. But now their time together was running out. In a very little while his men would come for him.

There should, she thought urgently, as she raced around compulsively tucking shirts, a clean *kuffiyeh* and favourite books into his suitcase for all the world like a devoted wife, be important things they should be saying to one another on this day of days. Once he had sailed they might not be able to be together for weeks, months, perhaps even a year. He would be with his men in that god-forsaken South Arabian hotspot, and she would be here holding the fort in West Beirut. For at last, in late August, after seventy days of siege and shelling, an agreement for the departure of the thirteen thousand Palestinian fighters had been hammered out between the Israelis and the PLO. Already a detachment of French Foreign Legionnaires had landed at the port as the first wave of an international peacekeeping force which would also include American and Italian troops. Their job, besides overseeing the orderly departure by sea of the Palestinians, was to stay behind in Beirut to protect the remaining thousands of Palestinian civilians in the city which was still encircled by an estimated ninety thousand Israeli troops.

'Cigarettes!' she cried out, almost in a panic. 'Where did you put all those cigarettes?' They had bought ten cartons yesterday on al-Hamra, which had been thronged with Palestinian fighters buying up all the things – from blue jeans to cassette players and whisky – which they feared they wouldn't be able to get in the hole-in-the-corner destinations that had accepted them with such humiliating reluctance. After a summer's frantic negotiations, the commandos were being divided up and shipped off to North and South Yemen, Tunisia, Iraq, Jordan and Syria.

Hussein sat drinking his tea and watching, with some amusement, as she did his packing. She spied the plastic carrier bag of Marlboros and crammed them in his case. 'Stop,' he finally said. 'You are acting like a bourgeois wife.'

'Not so bourgeois any more,' she retorted, looking around the shambles of a room where they had been so much in danger and yet so very happy. 'And not even a wife. Or at least not your wife.' She supposed she would be hearing from Farouk now that the siege was about to be lifted. If he hadn't divorced her yet, she would see that he soon did.

'Marriage is a bourgeois institution,' Hussein informed her, but fondly.

'So you've said.' She grinned. They had grown comfortable enough together to banter about what, only a few months ago, they would both have regarded as irreconcilable differences. 'But what makes you think *I* would want to marry *you* once I do get divorced? I am a free woman.'

'So you are, now,' he agreed. They smiled into each other's eyes. 'But even a free woman can be', he continued, 'freely committed . . . to a free man.'

She sensed negotiations afoot, and so, after giving his shirts a final affectionate pat and shutting the suitcase, she poured herself a cup of tea and sat down with him at the table. 'Okay,' she said. 'I'm listening.'

He laughed but then turned serious. 'You're so different from the way you used to be,' he said. He reached over and ruffled and then stroked her hair. 'Why couldn't you have been like this before? Or why couldn't I have tried harder and been more willing to meet you halfway? We wasted so many years.'

'No regrets,' she said, as she covered his hand with hers and fought back the tears. She could weep later, when he was gone. 'Not this morning. We must look to the future and not to the past.' But as she succeeded in mastering herself, she withdrew her hand briskly and busied herself with the comforting ritual of lighting a cigarette. 'But we digress. A moment ago I thought you were about to – what is it that the Americans say . . . yes, I remember – make me an offer I can't refuse.'

'Is that what I was about to do?'

'I'm sure of it.'

They both threw back their heads and laughed exuberantly.

'Okay,' he said finally, smoothing out the worn oilcloth as though he were about to lay his cards on the table, 'do you want to get married?'

'Joking aside,' she answered, 'are you asking me if I want to get married in general or whether I specifically want to marry you?'

'Whichever.' His eyes narrowed in concentration as he waited for her answer.

She stared into space for a moment and then shrugged her shoulders helplessly. 'I don't know, really. Like so much that I used to be certain about, I really don't know anymore.' She smiled as though one of life's great ironies suddenly struck her as funny. 'It's odd, but now that we're together, married or not married, it makes no difference.' She flicked the ashes of her cigarette on the dirt floor. 'I've had two husbands already, but you're the only man who has ever mattered to me. A legal contract won't change that. Married or not, you are . . .' Her voice faltered and her eyes fell, for she had never thought she could feel – much less talk – like this. 'My . . . mate.'

As he seized both her hands in his, the years dropped away and he was no longer a careworn middle-aged revolutionary but the flashy-eyed Arab lover of their youth. 'And you are mine. For life. And even after that. For ever, Leila. If there is a life after this one, after all, and we are together in Paradise, I will be with you there, too.' But even at this moment of romantic passion, his sense of humour prevailed and again he laughed. 'Who knows? Maybe that's where the Palestinian state will finally be, on the West Bank of Paradise. Allah will give us in the next life what He denied us in this one.' He grasped her hands and held them to his heart, and then took a deep breath and committed himself even further. 'As you know, I do not believe in marriage. But I will marry you if you like.'

'So,' she answered, 'you will join the ranks of the bourgeoisie for me?'

'Why not? You have already joined the revolution for me.'

'Not for you,' she retorted. 'For Palestine.'

'I love you for that answer! Ha!' He slapped her on the back of her wrinkled khaki shirt like the comrade she had almost become: she had still stoutly refused to become an actual Communist. The two of them continued to enjoy the spice of their ideological differences. 'So,' he said with finality, 'when we meet next perhaps we should make all this legal?'

'Perhaps yes, perhaps no. We can decide later. It would be wonderful if we were just any man and any woman, and had all the time in the world . . .' Her face creased with worry. 'But we are not just any man and any woman, are we?' She rubbed her eyes in anguish. Despite a lifetime habit of hiding her deepest feelings, a torrent of anxieties burst out of her. 'All these wars! All this fighting! All this separation! This is the fourth Palestinian exodus! Our people left Palestine in '48, the West Bank in '67, Jordan in '70, and now in '82 you leave Beirut. And tomorrow my sons leave with their Fatah unit. Hamid and Farid will probably end up in Tunisia. And so the diaspora continues. Will it ever end? When and where can the two of us ever be together? I know we've talked about this before, many times, and that you can't give me an answer. But I can't help asking again. How long do you think you'll have to stay in Aden?'

It was his turn to shrug. 'Perhaps a day, perhaps six months, maybe all our lives. I don't know. Maybe we'll go on to Tunis, or Damascus. Or even Iraq or Jordan. In time, I believe, we will come back here and continue fighting our war of national liberation against the Zionists. We leave Beirut only so we can fight another day. And we leave with honour and our guns in our hands!' The fire in his eyes blazed but then smouldered and died down into ashes. 'This going away from you is hard for me, too. To find you and then lose you so soon! I can promise only that, as soon as it is possible for you to be with me, I will send for you. But you know what we decided. For the moment you are needed more here. The men will be gone, and so women like you must be the hearts and minds of our people.'

She sighed her acceptance of what had to be. They had been over this ground before, too. With the Palestinian commandos gone, no one would be left to defend the refugee camps. The fighters were taking their weapons with them, for part of the disengagement agreement had stipulated that there must be no more arms in the camps. Yet she had heard a lot of wild and frightened talk in the past days. Some were afraid that once the PLO left, the Israelis would move into West Beirut, round up all the remaining Palestinian civilians, and deport them to hell if they could. Others worried that Christian militiamen, bound on revenge, would invade the defenceless camps and massacre whoever remained.

Hussein stalked over to the door where he always kept his Kalashnikov at the ready. 'I want to leave this here in your keeping. You know how to use it. I couldn't leave you here without it.'

She bit her lip and tried to hide the sudden fear in her eyes. 'You think it is necessary?'

'I think it is prudent.' He tossed her the machine-gun. 'Hide it. Keep it oiled and loaded.'

Just then, as she took the gun and secreted it in the false bottom of a cupboard, there was an excited rapping on the door. '*Ya*, Hussein! It's time! We're leaving!' For although these were their final moments alone, this was not their final parting. The two of them would go with the rest of their people for a mass farewell at the sports stadium, and then they would parade through the streets of West Beirut towards the port where the boats waited to take the fighters into exile.

'In a moment,' Hussein shouted.

He turned back to Leila and held out his arms. She flew into the safety of their embrace. Wordlessly they held one another for as long as they dared. Then he drew back, kissed her on the lips, on her closed eyelids, at her temples. They were both weeping. 'Come with me,' he said suddenly. 'You still can. Forget what I said before, and come with me. I'll put you on the roster of my fighters. I don't want to leave you here with those wolves all around.'

Gently she shook her head. 'No, no, I cannot.' One of them had to be strong now, and she steeled herself to do her duty. 'How can you ask your own men to go and leave their women and children behind, while you yourself take me? No. I will stay.'

'Until we meet again, then,' he said.

'Yes,' she answered.

'We'll go now.' He stared at her dear face and hungrily kissed her again and again, as though he wanted to devour her and carry her always inside him. 'Oh, God, I love you,' he said, and again he wept as he held her.

'And I love you,' she answered.

'So we will live happily ever after, you and I?'

'Somewhere,' she whispered. 'Someday.'

He took his red and black chequered *kuffiyeh* from his neck and draped it around her hair. 'You have earned this,' he said. 'Wear it for me, for Palestine, and for honour.'

Again there was a frantic hammering at the door. Hussein unlatched it, the two of them put on their flak jackets, and arm in arm they strode out for the port and the future.

By the time they got to the sports stadium, the pandemonium of an hysterical Arab farewell had already swept the thousands of assembled men, women and children away on an emotional tide of laughing, crying, kissing and hugging. For these supercharged families, who were capable of weeping and wailing for days on end when a son went off to study medicine in London for a year, were facing separations that might last for their lifetimes. The old men and the women were sick with fear at what fate might await the fighters who were about to be scattered to the farthest corners of the Arab world. And the fighters were even more apprehensive about how their families would survive the defenceless future in West Beirut. Suitcases were strewn everywhere, along with flowers, guns and colourful banners of every description. Young men kissed their sweethearts, mothers clasped sons to their heaving bosoms, and children were picked up in the arms of their fathers and given years of kisses in a poignant half hour. Hussein and Leila were so busy here and there, assuring this soldier that his girl would get along fine without him, and promising that mother that of course her son would be given enough to eat, that they did not have another second alone until the drivers of the green Lebanese Army trucks began to hoot their horns and fire their guns as a signal that it was time to make for the port.

Hussein was seized by his men and carried on their shoulders to one of the United Front's trucks. Leila stood beside it, holding up her hand to grasp his, fighting back the tears, assuming that this was her last glimpse of him. But instead he gripped her hands hard in his and pulled her up beside him. 'Come, comrade,' he said to her. 'We will share this together.'

Their truck was decked out with scarlet Marxist banners and – incongruously – a green Islamic flag with a Koranic verse stitched upon it in gold script. Someone handed each of them an AK-47 assault rifle, and another fighter seized a silk Palestinian flag and wrapped its green, red, white and black colours around Leila like a skirt. As the truck lurched forward, she brandished the gun above her head and let loose with a triumphant ululation. 'Ayayayayayaya!' Just so, with their heads held high, Leila, Hussein and the fighters began their defiant parade up and down and around and back the streets of West Beirut in a final salute to the people who had stood with them until the end.

The caravan wound slowly through the neighbourhoods, weapons ablaze, as the victorious Arab armies had done thirteen centuries before when they had conquered much of the world for Islam. Women stood on the bombed-out balconies crying, and showering rice, rosewater and flowers down upon them. The fighters flashed them V-signs, and reloaded and fired their guns wildly again and again. Along the route old men pulled pistols from their pockets and shot a few rounds into the air. Women screamed and wept and held up their babies as though for a blessing. The parade wound through the slums and down the Corniche past the devastated luxury hotels and finally – inevitably – to the port where the boats waited for the fighters who had not quite won but had not quite lost this fifth war with the Israelis. 'Beirut will never forget,' promised a hand-lettered sign at the entrance to the port.

Beside the boats, wedged in between the grizzled French Foreign Legionnaires, a delegation of Lebanese Muslim politicians and notables waited in the sweltering heat to bid them a sentimental goodbye. In the troubled thirty-four years since the birth of the Israeli state and the Arab exodus from Palestine, these same politicians had taken turns both loving and hating the Palestinians. Yet now, at the end, they wept to see them go. One of those statesmen caught the mood of the moment. 'My heart bleeds for Beirut,' he said as the tears coursed down his cheeks. 'This was once a beautiful and prosperous town, but now it is a city of ghosts.'

Eager hands seized megaphones to make moving speeches, and their words were cheered and saluted with volleys of gunfire. But then Hussein seized a microphone and delivered a final word.

'Wherever you go,' he shouted, 'tell the other Arabs

of your heroic resistance in Beirut. And then ask them where their MiGs and Mirages were, and ask them why they abandoned us. Tell them you fought the Israeli Army with your Kalashnikovs and RPGs and dynamite sticks.'

His men held their guns aloft and shot off a fusillade that was part anger, part triumph, and all defiance. Hussein held Leila to him one final time. And then the two of them, too, emptied their AK-47s to the heavens.

'What is it that the Jews used to say?' Hussein said to her only a moment before it was time for her to climb down from the truck and for him to go away. 'Next year in Jerusalem!'

She laughed, tossed him her gun, and flashed him V-signs with both her hands.

And then, with a final bravura burst of their own celebratory gunfire, the fighters began to stream into the boats, and off to exile.

From the docks, from the luxury high-rise apartment buildings, from the ravaged refugee camps, those left in the city wiped away their tears. After so much fighting, the suffering people of West Beirut breathed a heartfelt – but premature – sigh of relief.

Two days later Camilla and her husband held on to each other for dear life as they stepped timidly off the ferry from Cyprus on to the Lebanese pier in Jounieh, just twelve miles north but worlds away from that Beirut dock where day by day now the evacuation of the Palestinians continued.

Maurice was the first of the two to recover his nerve. 'Home at last!' he said in wonder as he looked round him at the placid aquamarine bay where lissom Christian girls water-skied in their French-cut bikinis. As always, the red and blue cable-cars of the *téléphérique* yo-yoed up and down the steep inclines by the port. To the south of Beirut, in the war-torn coastal cities of Sidon, Tyre and Damour, scarcely a house was left with all four walls standing. But here in the Christian heartland sienna-coloured villas baked in the Mediterranean sun, while two thousand feet above them, a colossal white statue of Harissa: Our Lady of Lebanon, held up her arms in an endless benediction. Another more worldly sort of icon – the glitzy Casino du Liban – sprawled on another crest of the Jounieh cliffs. 'I've missed it so,' Maurice confided to his wife as they flashed their passports at an official and began to search the crowd for the family chauffeur.

'I, too.' Yet to her this postcard-perfect port was no more home than Geneva had been, or Paris, Gstaad or Cannes. In the four restless years of her discontented exile in Europe's most exclusive cosmopolitan centres and watering-holes, not once had she lost the sense of being an alien in a world that could never be her own. She had flitted here and there, alighting like a gorgeous butterfly on this fragrant site or that. But always she had been aware, with a sense of yearning loss, that she had left her soul behind in Beirut. Even now, as she looked eagerly beyond the southern horizon, she fancied she could hear the sound of gunfire which over the years had become the siren call of home. She cocked her head and concentrated harder. That *was* gunfire. In a panic she dug her fingernails into her husband's hand. 'I thought it was supposed to be safe to come back. That all the fighting was over. But listen.'

Maurice frowned and then asked a militiaman in a Phalange uniform if a new round of fighting had broken out in the few hours since they had left Larnaca.

The soldier grinned and assured them, '*au contraire*', that a new era of peace and prosperity was dawning for their country now that the Palestinians had finally been driven away. 'They are savages.' He spat in contempt. 'Every day they shoot like this before they get on their boats. Yesterday I took my mother down to see it. "Now I can die," she told me, "for at last Lebanon can be clean again." This is a great day for the real Lebanese. At last we get rid of the vermin.'

Camilla paled and held tighter to her husband. She had almost forgotten how hateful all the warring cut-throats in her country could be, and how unforgiving. She might have turned right around and fled away on the ferry, but just then a chauffeur came up and escorted them to the waiting limousine. In the back seat Uncle Paul, the aged patriarch of Maurice's family, waited with sunglasses obscuring most of his wrinkled face and a wool shawl – despite the heat and humidity – wrapped around his thin shoulders. We must hurry, he told them after quickly dispensing with the ritual kisses and the prescribed questions about their health and the hardships of their journey. The voting for a new President of the Republic was supposed to get underway by eleven o'clock in the Chamber of Deputies.

As they sped away, Camilla only half-listened to the self-important political talk of the men. If they could succeed in getting the quorum to open the session, Uncle Paul was saying, they would surely have enough votes to elect Bashir Gemayel. The Sunni Muslim delegates were boycotting the election, but the Druze and the Shia had agreed to bow to the inevitable and come to vote for what everyone fervently hoped was a reunification government. But there had been, he explained delicately, some problems in securing that quorum. One Sunni politician from the Bekaa who had refused to come had been shot and seriously wounded just this morning. The radio was saying that other boycotting politicians had reported being harassed by threatening phone calls. 'We will not forget that you answered the call,' he told Maurice as he gave his hand an approving pat.

'But of course,' Maurice answered, as he bent his head to kiss his uncle's palsied hands in the ancient feudal gesture of obeisance. 'When my country – and you – call, I had no choice but to answer.'

Beside him in the Mercedes, Camilla stifled a snort of derision. Three days ago, after Maurice had received that imperious dead-of-night phone call from his dear Uncle Paul, her husband had paced and shouted and vowed to her that nothing on heaven or earth could entice him back to the slaughterhouse that the Lebanon had become. 'I don't care who is elected president of that god-forsaken country!' he had raged. He had a French passport now as well as Lebanese citizenship, and he wanted to believe that he no longer owed anything to that cursed place where he had been unlucky enough to be born. With a shaking hand he had poured himself glass after glass of Courvoisier brandy as he had racked his brain for a means to avoid answering the family summons. He had considered taking to his bed and paying off doctors to testify that he was too ill to travel. He had even thought of shooting himself in the foot so that no one would expect him to venture home. He had told her that he sorely regretted having let his family talk him into standing for election to the House of Deputies what seemed like an eternity ago, before the civil war, when politics had been a far less dangerous game. But in the end, even for a modern international banker like Maurice, the old ways and the old tribal loyalties had prevailed. The family would never have forgiven him if he had let them down, and – even though he had physically settled in Europe now – an emotional life stranded beyond the only pale that mattered would not have been a life worth living. Sullenly and with trepidation, he had told Camilla to book him a first-class seat to Cyprus. Beirut airport had been closed since the early days of the Israeli invasion, and so the daily ferry from Larnaca had become the Christians' safe passage in and out of their sector of the Lebanon.

Yet now, as Camilla watched him gleefully rubbing his hands together at the thought of imposing a truly Christian government on a Christian Lebanon, it seemed impossible that only a few days ago Maurice had been so loath to return. Still, she had wisely waited until it was time to pack last night to tell him that she had reserved a seat on the flight for herself as well. For Camilla's heart had begun to pound with joy as well as fear when that call had come through from his uncle. At once she had known that she could not resist the opportunity to steal back with him. She and her mother had sat out the awful weeks of the siege in her lakeside villa in Geneva, ruining their manicures by biting their nails as they drank and sighed and followed the ghastly news bulletins. Camilla had wept sometimes as she had watched the technicolour destruction of Beirut on the television each night. As the bombs fell, she had wrinkled her forehead with concentration and tried to pinpoint exactly which landmarks were going up in smoke. She had been so happy there, once, in this city that was being blown to pieces right before her eyes. Anne was still in there somewhere, and so were Leila, Fatima and so many others. Mostly, remembering how terrified she had been there in the dark days of the civil war, she had thanked her lucky stars that she was now far removed from such danger. Yet at the same time she felt rather as if she hadn't shown up for the party of the year. So it was that she had argued long and hard to convince her husband – and her mother, too, who was dead set against this sentimental journey, and who had flatly refused Shaykh Georges's pleas for her to join him at the Château Croisé – that it was safe for her to come back with him. She had missed the war, Camilla had told her husband, but she didn't intend to miss the peace. The siege was over, the Palestinians were leaving, and even Maurice said that soon everything would be exactly as it was supposed to be in their country. Finally, after so many years, the triumph of the Christian forces in Lebanon was complete. She, too, had a right to be there to toast the great victory.

The limousine purred through Phalange checkpoints, where the soldiers smiled and deferentially saluted their own. Near the Chamber of Deputies the streets bristled with tanks and military trucks sporting not only the green cedar-tree insignia of Lebanon but also the blue-and-white Star of David emblem of the Israelis. Camilla stared curiously at this first martial evidence of the occupying force. The Israelis looked more Arab than the Arabs. So many of the Christian Lebanese forces were tall, blond and fair. But the Israelis seemed not so foreign as she had expected, being mostly as short, dark and stocky as all the other Semitic peoples. As their limousine pulled up at the government building, Maurice told her that the chauffeur would take her to the family home in East Beirut. She was to remain indoors, and he would join her there as soon as he could. If all went as they expected today in Parliament, they would have much to celebrate this evening. Chastely he touched her hand in farewell. They were back in Lebanon now, where a husband would be reluctant to kiss his wife on such a state occasion and in front of so many strangers.

There was far less restraint when, after another half hour of passing through the armed camp that East Beirut had become, Camilla arrived at her in-laws' townhouse. Although they had met one another only a few times before at family outings in Monte Carlo and Marbella, Maurice's mother greeted her as though she were her own long-lost daughter. His sisters were just as welcoming, as were the spinster aunts and a smattering of cousins. Of course Camilla was pressed to sit down without delay and eat all the Lebanese delicacies she must have missed so in Switzerland. Food was the last thing on her mind, and her stomach was a tight ball of tension. But Lebanon was after all Lebanon, and so she gave in gracefully and allowed herself to be led into the dining room where the servants had already laid out a feast fit either for a king or his conquering army. As the women of Maurice's family twittered and laughed all around her and filled their own plates to overflowing, Camilla remembered all those news reports she had heard about the food shortages in Beirut, and especially the lack of fruit and vegetables. But she had never seen such gigantic melons, such juicy tomatoes, such plump olives. Had they come from the north, she asked, as she popped a black olive in her mouth and extolled the unparalleled taste of real Lebanese *zeitoun*, or from the Bekaa? No, from Israel, they told her. The Israelis had brought not only tanks and victory in their wake but also tons of fruit and vegetables to their newly-opened Lebanese market. Camilla dropped her voice, then, and asked them what it had been like, *vraiment*, with the Israelis here.

Jeanette, one of Maurice's gigglepuss young cousins, laughed and blushed and said she had danced with a few at parties. She reported that they had scratchy beards, rough manners and roving hands. '*Très viril,*' she added, 'always they bring their guns. They are very like the Palestinians, I think. You know how before, they would always bring their guns even to parties? The Jews are the same.' Jeanette rolled her eyes and giggled again. '*Sauvages!* How delicious!'

'Jeanette! That is quite enough!' But then Maurice's mother couldn't resist reporting that this summer, in East Beirut, a few token Israeli soldiers had been *de rigueur* at every gathering. Everyone who was anyone had collected them like china cups. Some of the Israelis were quite charming in their way, even if few of them spoke passable French.

And what had it been like here during the siege, Camilla asked.

'Aieeeee!' Maurice's dowdy sparrow of a mother held her hands to her ears. 'The noise never stopped. Morning, noon and night, always the noise. Never could we sleep.'

'Imagine what it must have been like for them in West Beirut,' Camilla ventured to say.

Maurice's mother shrugged. 'In '78, when the Syrians shelled us here in Ashrafiya, did the Palestinians and the Muslims cry for us? I do not cry the tears of the crocodile for them. They got just what they deserved.' But then she called for the servant to uncork another bottle of wine. 'Enough of such talk,' she said with an air of finality. 'All the bad times are over now.' She filled all their glasses and raised hers in a toast. 'To our Bashir! And the new Lebanon!'

They had opened another bottle or two and then after toasting the future again and again, Maurice's womenfolk deluged Camilla with questions about the latest fashions. Was it true what they'd read about Italian and Japanese designers taking the lead over the French? They cooed over her short, leggy black Valentino dress and made her parade back and forth in front of them like a mannequin as they studied how those new shoulderpads changed the lines of her dress. An hour passed before Camilla could finally sneak upstairs.

First she made a dutiful call to Shaykh Georges to assure him that Guy and Emile were still safely tucked away in France. Guy, she told him, had gone back to school to study law, and Emile was embarking on a career as a banker, like his stepfather. Shaykh Georges emitted a low growl at this reference to Maurice. He had been against the match and had offered Camilla a million Lebanese pounds to remain single. But this time the *shaykh* contented himself with a few vague curses against her husband's friends before he boyishly began to pepper her with questions about her mother. 'Does she act as if she misses me? Is my photograph still beside her bed?' Then, jealously, 'She hasn't been with anyone else, has she?' As Camilla assured him that her mother was being unusually faithful, it occurred to her – for the first time since her mother had begun sharing the *shaykh*'s bed last year during a visit to Europe – that these two old ones were acting as if they had truly fallen in love. The next thing she knew, her mother would be marrying her father-in-law!

Finally Camilla made the phone calls she had been longing for since she first stepped back on Lebanese soil. In the first days of the siege she had been able to dial directly through to Anne's apartment, but for more than two months now she hadn't been able to get through to the encircled city. She had overheard men on the ferry saying that the phones in West Beirut were all back in order, and that already some of the crossing points had been reopened. But there was no answer at Anne's apartment, and when she dialled Leila's number in Aley the telephone made a whirring noise that meant the number was disconnected.

One of Fatima's daughters, however, answered brightly on the second ring. When her mother came on the line, tears welled up in Camilla's eyes. 'It's me!' she said. 'Camilla! I am here! Yes! In Beirut!'

Fatima seemed her old self as she thanked God and gushed and thanked God again for the safe return of her old friend. Yes, she assured Camilla, Anne and Leila had all survived the siege. Leila had been in Shatilla almost from the beginning, and Anne and Leila's daughter had spent much of the time there as well. It had indeed been terrifying with all the bombing, but *el-hamdulillah* none of her own children had been hurt. Leila's sons had been fighting with the PLO and had been evacuated on one of the troop ships to Tunisia. No, Farid and Hamid hadn't been wounded. Quickly, then, she filled Camilla in on the domestic gossip, how it had turned out that Charles had been a CIA spy, how she herself had helped get his release, how Leila had been reunited with Hussein, and how it seemed that Anne had at last decided to divorce Charles and marry Sam. 'But enough talk,' Fatima had said finally. 'When do we see you?'

'*Tout de suite,*' Camilla grandly answered, without having thought her answer through. 'Why don't all of you come over here tonight for dinner? Or this afternoon, for tea?'

But there was a sudden silence on the other end of the line. 'Come there?' Fatima said finally. 'To the other side?'

Camilla let out one of her tinkling social laughs. 'Haven't you heard? The war's over, *chérie*. That's why we came back. Maurice – my new husband, you have not met him yet, he is a dear, most of the time – he had to vote for the new president. He is there now, at the Chamber of Deputies.'

When she spoke again, Fatima seemed more distant than West Beirut. 'I am afraid that it is not possible for us to come to you.' But then, for old time's sake, she unfroze just a little. 'Perhaps you can come here. Yes. Come tonight. Or now. Yes, now. Do not wait. It is better in the daylight, I think. I will send my boys out to get Anne and Leila, too. We will have a reunion.'

'I don't know,' Camilla said cautiously. Maurice had told her not to go out. And the thought of crossing through the Israeli lines and into the bull's-eye of West Beirut unnerved her. 'I am afraid,' she admitted in that tremulous little girl's voice which she had never quite outgrown.

Fatima made a sympathetic clucking with her tongue. Fear was nothing to be laughed off these days. 'You will be safe here,' she promised. 'Always, in West Beirut, the women are safe. We are good Muslims here, in case you have been away so long that you have forgotten everything that is important about us.'

Camilla frowned. She didn't remember Fatima ever using that hectoring voice before.

But then Fatima seemed to soften into her old sweet self. 'Really, you will be safe. I guarantee it. Look, I will send my son Muhammad to the Sodeco crossing. He told me today it was open, for the first time in two years. You cross there, and he will be waiting with his militiamen. He is a big man in Amal these days, my boy.'

Camilla was not reassured. She had assumed that, with the armed Palestinians going or gone, there were no more wild men with guns in West Beirut. But she had forgotten the Shia, Sunni, Druze, and every other armed splinter group of militiamen. 'I don't know,' she hedged. 'Maurice would be very angry.' But then she realized how weak and dependent she must sound. Her friends had survived the siege of Beirut, yet she was afraid to risk her husband's displeasure. She took a deep breath and decided – just this once – to live dangerously. After all, she was back in reckless Beirut where getting up every morning was a life-or-death adventure. She hadn't had the guts to come back and brave the ordeal of the siege, but at least she could make the gesture of this one daunting crossing to those she still held dear. 'I will come,' she announced.

She went back downstairs, yawned melodramatically, and announced that she was going to retire for a long afternoon nap. But then, after making a great show of going upstairs and shutting tight her bedroom door, she slipped down the back stairs and out of the door. Even though she bribed him with a newly-minted hundred-franc Swiss banknote, she had to argue long and hard before the family chauffeur would agree to shuttle her to the Sodeco crossing. He did so only after she swore to the Virgin that she would never tell anyone who had taken her to the West Beirut frontier.

When they were still half a mile away from the crossing point, the massed Israeli and Phalange military equipment made the street nearly impassable. Tanks glowered everywhere, jeeps were stacked high with fancy electronic equipment, and gigantic armoured personnel carriers were parked on the pavements. Soldiers lounged in the sun or stood guard looking west. Guns were held at the ready.

'You are sure you want to go on?' the chauffeur asked anxiously.

Camilla did not trust herself to speak, so she merely gave her head a regal nod. She could feel the sweat under her armpits and yet, curiously, she felt more alert and alive than ever before in her life, except perhaps for that perilous afternoon at the height of the civil war when she had risked all for the contents of her safety deposit box. Now, as then, the adrenalin pumped through every vein in her body. She could hear her heartbeat thumping.

As they joined the nervous queue at the crossing point, Camilla craned her neck to see what was ahead. Israeli troops were busily dismantling the fortifications that had served to demarcate no-man's-land not only for the two months of this siege but for most of the seven years of intermittent warfare that had preceded it. Bulldozers crashed through the symbol of years of strife. The barricades fell away, and only a mound of red earth now kept the two sides apart. West Beirut finally lay almost open.

'I must leave you here, madame,' the chauffeur said. 'I cannot cross. You must walk to the other side.'

'All by myself?' Camilla had not bargained for this. Throughout her life, she had striven never to do anything alone.

'Do not go, I beg you,' the chauffeur pleaded. He had begun to wish he hadn't even taken her this far. What were a hundred Swiss francs against the forfeit of his life, if anything happened to her? 'Please do not go.'

In answer, she threw open the door and shakily stepped out on to the killing ground. She clutched her identity card in her hand and pretended she was anywhere but here. As airily as though she were approaching the *maître d'hôtel* at a smart restaurant in which she had already booked the best table, she clicked her high heels on the crumbling pavement and marched up to the Lebanese army soldier at the crossing. Wordlessly she held out her card. Briefly he gave her a bored glance, then waved her on. Armed men, not disarming women, were all he was interested in today. Camilla held her head high and imagined that instead of being in this horrifying place she were somewhere wonderful – a stick-thin model wearing the latest Saint Laurent creation entering a Paris catwalk with flashbulbs popping. She faltered once, only a few yards away from the West Beirut checkpoint, when she realized that at this instant both sides must have her in their gunsights.

But she walked on, and just after she had handed over her identity card to the man on the other side, she heard a volley of automatic gunfire behind her. She screamed and felt so dizzy that she thought she might faint when, a second later, there was another fusillade from the East. All around her, on the Muslim side of the earthworks, militiamen were aiming their guns as though a new round of fighting were just about to begin.

But then a Druze militiaman with a transistor radio in his hand ran up to the commanding officer. 'Bashir!' he shouted. 'They have elected Bashir Gemayel as President! They are shooting to celebrate!'

'Hold your fire!' the commander shouted.

Camilla held her hand to her palpitating heart. The Chamber of Deputies, she thought faintly. Maurice's candidate had won. But all that now seemed a universe away.

The soldier with her identity card grinned as he

handed it back to her. 'Welcome to West Beirut,' he said.

'Madame Camilla! Madame Camilla!' A young open-faced fellow in a faded green uniform rushed up to the checkpoint with three others like him in his wake. 'You are Madame Camilla? I am Muhammad, the son of Fatima!'

'I am so happy to see you, Muhammad,' she said, in perhaps the greatest understatement of her life. Weakly she smiled at Fatima's son, whom she hadn't seen since he was a boy. Yet he was a man now, and her guardian angel. Happily she drank in the suddenly reassuring sight of the big black guns which Muhammad and his comrades had slung over their shoulders. 'So happy to see you.'

'Come,' he said. 'Mother said to bring you home right away.' Without further ado, she climbed into their waiting jeep and they were off to the Rue Bliss.

If she had not, with every frayed nerve in her body, been aware that she had just crossed over into the Muslim sector, she would not have believed that this nightmare wasteland was the same Beirut where she had been born and raised and lived out the happiest years of her life. The streets were torn up with bomb craters as big as caves, crumbling hulks were all that was left of once-grand hotels, and the blazing sun sparkled on splinters of glass that lay everywhere like a glittering of fresh snow. She was beyond tears as she drank in the desolation. When she had glimpsed all this on the television, she had refused to believe it could be as bad as it looked. She had assured herself that only a few squalid pockets of the city – the eyesore refugee camps, surely, and perhaps also the miserable slums where the Palestinians had squatted and seethed – had been consumed in the Israeli fire. But the evidence of the saturation bombing was everywhere. Even on what had been the very best streets, there wasn't a wall unscarred by the shelling. The once beautiful city lay in ruins.

Camilla was shaken when Muhammad's driver finally pulled up at the villa. Blankly she looked at the ochre-coloured walls of the old three-storey dwelling where she remembered visiting Anne as a teenager. Part of the stone wall that had enclosed the garden lay on its side like a thousand-year-old ruin. All the windows had been blown out. The walls were riddled with shell-holes. Worst of all, immediately next door, what had been a five-storey apartment house had crumpled in upon itself in a pile of rubble.

'We were lucky, eh?' Muhammad said as he helped her out of the jeep. 'Allah was with us.' He shook his head. 'But our neighbours were not so lucky. Many died. We could hear them calling out to us to come and save them for one night and two days after the house came down. We tried to get to them, but all we had was our hands and two shovels.'

Oh, God, Camilla prayed to herself, under her breath. But then the front door opened, and Fatima came running out in her long black widow's dress. She was fatter than Camilla remembered, and looked far older than she had been the last time they were together. But as the two old friends flew into one another's arms, and rocked back and forth, time stood still and the years fell away. 'You are exactly the same,' Camilla murmured. Fatima's arms were so all-enveloping and motherly that, for the first time since she had set foot back in Lebanon, Camilla felt that at last she had come home.

They had just turned to go inside, and were walking arm in arm towards the house, when Camilla saw the other slim, somewhat sinister figure standing just outside the front door in military fatigues. The sun was in her eyes, and as she frowned and squinted she could not quite place him – or was it her?

Leila stepped out of the shadows and stood unsmiling as she straddled the threshold. She could not have looked more grim if she had been pointing a gun at Camilla's head.

'So it has come to this,' Camilla said, sadly. 'I have known you since we were six years old, and now this is how you greet me?'

'Everything has changed,' Leila said. But some of the deeply etched lines in her face eased, and she looked less fierce than she had a moment ago. 'Why have you come? To gloat at your great victory?'

Camilla looked around at the rubble, the shell-holes, the utter destruction. 'This was no victory for anyone.' Her voice caught. She had been brooding by herself during the siege, and she had come to some conclusions of her own. 'God knows some of our Christian leaders – certainly my husband's friend Bashir – schemed and dreamed to get the Israelis to intervene. But I don't think anyone really thought an invasion would mean all *this*.'

'Eighteen thousand Lebanese and Palestinians were killed this summer,' Leila said. 'And thirty thousand were wounded. More than two million people are homeless now. And the blood for all that is on the hands not only of the Israelis but of the Christians who all but invited them in. Your people did this as surely as if they flew every plane, dropped every bomb, pulled every trigger.'

'Careful, Leila.' Camilla's own quick temper was rising. If Leila wanted a fight, she would give her one. She hadn't scared herself half out of her wits to come here and be insulted by someone she had not altogether forgiven for the death of her son. 'I never held you responsible for every bad thing the Palestinians did. But if you make me answer for the Christians, remember that your hands are bloody, too. You Palestinians are not innocent little lambs, either. Your *fedayeen* terrorized the villages in the south, like poor Fatima's for instance. You brought the civil war upon us all and provoked the Israelis to bomb and invade us, too. You were always willing, all of you, to sacrifice our Lebanon for your precious Palestine. Are you happy, now that we have lost our country just as you lost yours?'

Before Leila could jump at her throat in answer to those fighting words, Fatima threw a heavy arm around the shoulders of both her friends and drew them closer together. *'Kefir,'* she scolded, 'enough. Where is our peacemaker Anne when we need her? The two of you fight like my very small children.' Wanly she smiled. 'Or like the very big politicians and soldiers who run what is left of our country. But you are not the Phalange and the PLO! You are only Camilla and Leila!'

As Leila and Camilla hung their heads, Fatima continued to lecture them. 'I always thought that if we women were running our country, we would do a better job than the men. But now I look at the two of you, making a liar out of me. In the name of God, I ask you both to remember that you are my guests. And my friends. And still, I think, friends to each other. So don't be so silly. Come inside and stop this.' She was bigger than both of them, and swept them with her indoors. 'I think now we will eat bread and salt.' Everywhere in the Arab world, to share bread and salt meant to live in harmony. Fatima looked capable of force-feeding peace to her reluctant guests.

As Leila and Camilla perched uneasily on opposite ends of the sofa, Fatima called for Zainab to bring in the refreshments. 'I am sorry I have so little to offer you,' she said as she poured Camilla a weak cup of tea and offered her a water biscuit smeared with the faintest gloss of honey. 'But Salma was so happy when she found these biscuits this morning in the shop off al-Hamra. Real biscuits! Imagine! They say soon everything will be back in the shops.'

'I was so worried about all of you,' Camilla said. 'I cried, sometimes, watching those terrible pictures on television.'

'We cried, too,' Leila said, biting hard into a biscuit. But she unbent enough to pick up the sugar bowl and pass it more or less civilly to Camilla.

'No, thank you. I am on a diet again.' Camilla smoothed her tight Italian skirt over her newly round thighs. 'I was so nervous, this summer, worrying about you all, that I gained eight kilos.'

'I lost six pounds,' Leila said. 'But I wasn't dieting. There just wasn't anything to eat here.' Yet tentatively she smiled, just a little, at Camilla. 'Except for Fatima here, who never had a girlish figure, we all managed to get ours back this summer. Maybe you should have been here with us.'

'Maybe I was, a little.' Camilla smiled back. 'In my heart.'

Fatima beamed happily at the pair of them. 'Good, good. Better, better. Now you are Leila and Camilla again.' She laughed as she patted her bulging stomach. 'It's true, what Leila says. Always I get bigger. My Muhammad says maybe I have a new baby in here.' Then she sighed. 'I wish it were so. If Ali . . .' She bowed her head, and her shoulders shook.

Camilla had just put her arm consolingly around Fatima when Anne burst into the room. She had evidently come straight over from her surgery, for she was still in her stained white doctor's jacket. 'Is she here? Did she really come?' She caught sight of the friend she hadn't seen for four years. 'Camilla!' The two fell into each other's arms with a whoop of joy, and then stood back surveying one another and saying insincerely how young they both looked.

'This is more like it,' Fatima said. Ever the Arab mother, she proceeded to do her best to make Leila feel guilty. 'I am happy to see that at least Anne knows how to welcome home our Camilla.' She gave the Palestinian a reproving look.

'Oh, all right,' Leila grumbled. But her face was eager as she uncoiled from the sofa and held out her hand to Camilla.

'You silly thing,' Camilla said as instead she swept Leila into her arms. Slowly the Palestinian's arms closed around the Christian. When they pulled apart, both had tears in their eyes.

'That felt good,' Leila said as she bit the lips that had just kissed the one who was – and yet was not – the enemy.

'I hope so,' Camilla answered. 'I risked my life for it.' She rolled her eyes. 'That crossing! *Yaadra!* Mother of God, I was afraid!' She dug in her handbag and produced three small boxes exquisitely wrapped in silver paper. 'It's perfume. *Joy.* I thought I'd try to bring you a little joy here in West Beirut.' Camilla smiled sadly. 'I suppose I should have thought to bring food.'

'No! To bring us joy, yes, that is better than food!' Fatima wiped away a sentimental tear.

'Truly, you have brought us joy,' Anne told her.

'Yes, indeed,' Leila admitted, as Camilla gave them each their fifty-dollars-an-ounce French perfume.

But then Zainab sailed in with a fresh pot of tea in one hand and a transistor radio blaring the latest news in the other.

'Turn it up!' Leila commanded. With that automatic reflex which all West Beirutis had acquired during the siege, when the news was a survival matter, everyone but Camilla immediately fell silent. When she continued, however, to babble on about her fears at the crossing, Leila silenced her with a guillotine look. Tensely they listened to the Christian Phalange station, which was all but delirious with the news that their favourite son Bashir was the newly elected President of the Lebanese

Republic. As the announcer extolled the virtues of the president-elect, even in the studio someone was shooting off a pistol in jubilation.

Leila curled her lip. 'Listen to them. They're like wolves howling.'

'They do not howl alone,' Camilla tartly reminded her. 'The first thing I heard when I landed here today were the guns of your Palestinians leaving.'

'Ah!' Leila's face lit up like neon. 'The day when my Hussein left, I swear before Allah, was one of the most glorious days of my life. All Beirut was with us then! You should have been here, Camilla. And the next day, too, when my sons left. I will never forget those days. Never!'

'It was really something,' Anne agreed. 'So much emotion. Glorious in a way, just as Leila says. Everyone cried. Even Sam. But it was bittersweet, too. Beirut will never be the same. Never!'

'What will happen to all those boys?' Fatima, the eternal mother, worried for the next generation. 'And what will happen to us here without them to defend us?'

'Have you forgotten?' Anne said, more brightly than she felt. But she couldn't bear it if the four of them should get depressed. 'The American Marines and the rest of the French and Italian peacekeeping force arrived at the port today. I called Mother in Boston, and she says my brother Ben is with them. You can just imagine what my mother thinks of *that*. Ben and I *both* back in Beirut! I was going to go down to the port to try to see him today. But I guess I'll have to postpone it until tomorrow.' Anne smiled. 'I'm glad the Marines are here. President Reagan has given his pledge that the civilians of West Beirut will be as safe as they were when the Palestinian fighters were at the barricades.' She nodded her head. 'Safer, probably.'

'So you say.' Gloomily Leila lit a cigarette. The short burst of elation she had felt, remembering the inspiring departure of the *fedayeen*, drained away. She sank back into that pit of depression where she had languished since Hussein had sailed away. When he had been here, Shatilla had been glossed with a romantic sheen that had made even hole-in-the-ground toilets seem a colourful novelty and the stuff of anecdotes that would last a lifetime. But without him, the refugee camp was only crushingly squalid. She was as committed to the Palestinian cause now as when he had been here to share it with her, but she could no longer pretend that living so desperately was any kind of lark. And there was, too, the matter of security. The camps were no longer guarded by their commandos. Massacres had occurred before in Lebanon. As Leila stubbed out her cigarette and lit another, she yearned not only for Hussein but also for the entire departed Palestinian army.

Camilla was meanwhile asking the same question she had put to her in-laws in East Beirut. 'So what was it like here during the siege?'

'You can't imagine,' Anne answered.

'I can try, if you'll tell me,' Camilla said.

'We survived.' Fatima said that proudly, and she, Anne and Leila exchanged a look of solidarity that made Camilla feel envious.

'It must have been horrible,' Camilla said.

'The house shook from the bombs.' Just remembering, Fatima's voice trembled. 'So many days and nights we spent down in the basement in the dark. There was no electricity, no water, and my children cried and cried.'

'The hospital was like hell. More like a slaughterhouse than an operating room. We ran out of everything. Sometimes I had to operate by kerosene light.' Anne shook her head. 'The worst were those who had been hit by phosphorus bombs. They burned and burned, even after they were dead.'

'All my life I will remember every moment of that siege.' Leila spoke in a faraway voice. 'Of everything that has ever happened to me – where I've lived, what I've done, even having my babies and loving Hussein – I am most proud of surviving that siege. If I never do another thing in my life, at least I survived the siege of Beirut. I didn't leave. I stayed!'

Uncertainly Camilla smiled, and then she looked at her watch. It was well past six o'clock. If she were going to cross back to East Beirut before nightfall, she had better begin to make a move. But just as she was about to start saying goodbye, she heard another scrap of radio news on the BBC frequency. Since the election of Bashir Geinayel this afternoon, three East Beirutis had been killed and eleven more wounded by the stray fire of the celebrating Christian militiamen. That compared, the announcer added drily, to six dead and seventeen wounded by the stray fire of the departing Palestinians.

'I think we are all crazy here,' Fatima said. 'All of us! If we are happy or sad, out come the guns.'

'This is Beirut,' Anne said.

'There is no place like it in the world,' Leila added.

'Thanks be to Allah!' Fatima and the rest of them laughed.

'But it wasn't always like this,' Anne said. She got up and went over to a table by the television which was cluttered by a welter of Fatima's framed family photographs. She picked up the one Leila had given them long ago, and she smiled at the image of the four of them dancing in the sunlight down by the sea. 'We were so young and keen then,' she mused. 'And so happy.'

'Those were the days,' Fatima agreed.

'The golden days,' Leila added.

'*Ah, oui.*' On that note, Camilla embraced them

one by one. 'Maybe next time I see you, we will all dance as in the good old days. Maybe then there will be no East and West, and no men with guns at the crossing.'

'Inshallah,' Fatima answered. 'God willing.'

They clung to one another as they parted. Then Muhammad escorted Camilla back to the jeep for the crossing to the other side.

Two weeks later, Anne was making her final rounds in the American University Hospital wards when she heard a gigantic explosion. She stood stock-still. No, she thought, surely not again. The Palestinians were gone, and the war was over. Now, in mid-September, the electricity and the telephones were back on, the civil servants had begun reporting for work, and the newspapers were full of grandiose billion-dollar plans to rebuild a bigger and better Lebanon. An exhausted calm had settled over the city, and just last week – when the American, Italian and French peacekeeping force had left the port – a US marine had held up a hand-lettered sign for the television cameras: 'Mission Accomplished'. And yet now, another explosion.

But she heard nothing else – no whizzing shells, no crumping mortars, no rat-tat-tat of automatic gunfire – and so she continued checking progress reports on clipboards, consulting with nurses, even soothing an irate Armenian businessman who was insisting that his sick mother be moved off the wards and into a private room. Desperately he offered her cash – 'Five hundred American dollars!' he whispered, flashing her a bankroll – and then, when she still refused, he whined that she had to help him, that his second cousin was a laboratory technician in this very hospital and his wife's uncle held a seat in the Chamber of Deputies. Everything, she mused, as she vaguely promised to do what she could for his mother in the morning, seemed almost back to normal in bartering Beirut.

But still she couldn't put that explosion out of her mind. It occurred to her, as she collected her things and prepared to go home, that perhaps she should stay on in case the emergency ward was flooded with a new batch of casualties from some fresh disaster. That sound could have been a car bomb. Scores of passers-by might have been slashed by the flying shrapnel. But no, she decided. That blast had been too big for a car bomb. She remembered, then, that just yesterday, in violation of the agreement hammered out before the departure of the Palestinians, the Israelis had moved their lines six hundred yards closer to West Beirut so they could demine the roads. The Israelis were now smack up against Shatilla. Anne decided that explosion must be the efficient Israelis dynamiting the Palestinian barricades still in place from the siege.

She was turning her key in the lock of her apartment door when she heard the telephone ringing. Sam's voice, on the international line from New York, was so loud that she had to hold the phone back from her ear.

'Anne! Thank God I got you! I called the hospital, and they said you were gone. Then, when I couldn't get you at home, I rang Fatima's. You've got to get out of there, honey!'

She lit a cigarette, sank down on the sofa, and prepared herself for another wrangle about whether or not she would leave Beirut and join him in New York. 'I was going to call you tonight,' she said cautiously. 'You've only been gone three days, but it seems like forever.'

'I shouldn't have let them talk me into leaving. I told them no, you don't know Beirut like I do, it might not be all over yet. That place could still blow sky high, I said, and I was right. But they didn't listen to me. Nobody listens to me. You don't either. But this time you'll have to. Even you have to throw in the towel now.'

'I've told you before, Sam, I'll come to New York as soon as I can. But I can't leave now, not with my patients all but sleeping on the floors in the hospital. The refugee camps are worse. When things are a bit better at this end, I'll take the first flight out. I'll divorce Charles, marry you, and everything will be hunky-dory.' She settled back and tried to change the subject. 'They say, you know, that the airport should be ready to re-open any day now.'

There was silence for a moment on the other end of the line, and then Sam took a deep breath. 'Don't you know what's happened? You're there, right in the middle of it and you don't know?' Without waiting for her answer, he plunged in and told her the news that had been flashed on the teletype a half hour ago. 'An explosion has ripped through the Phalange headquarters in East Beirut. Bashir Gemayel was caught inside. He may be dead.'

'Oh, no.' So that was the sound she had been trying to ignore. Someone had tried and maybe succeeded in assassinating the President-elect, who was the darling of the most ferocious Christian militia. Like every seasoned Beiruti, she could not resist another round of the inevitable guessing game. 'Who did it?'

'Does it matter? You know Beirut. It could be anybody with a grudge and a couple of ounces of *plastique*. Bashir was no altar boy, that's for sure.' As if he were sitting in the studio facing the cameras, Sam launched into an instant rundown of suspects. 'I've been hearing a lot this week about how he has fallen out with the Israelis. They wanted him to sign a full-scale peace treaty with Begin, and he said no, he was nobody's shoeshine boy. Or it could have been one of the other Christian warlords. Then, of course, we have the Syrians. Everyone thinks they killed Kemal

Jumblatt, the Druze leader, and others, too. So there's no reason to think they'd have any qualms about getting rid of Bashir, who's been a thorn in their side for years. Besides all these bloodthirsty possibilities, we have everybody's favourite scapegoat, the CIA or perhaps even the KGB. And finally, last but certainly not least, it could have been the gone-but-not-forgotten Palestinians kissing Beirut a very spectacular goodbye. Take your pick. Personally, I'd say it was probably either the Israelis or one of the rival Christian warlords. But it could have been any of them.' Sam sighed. 'What does it matter, anyway? We'll never know for sure. All that counts is that now, in Beirut, all bets are off. If Bashir dies, for sure there'll be another bloodbath. You've got to get out of there, honey, and get out fast.'

As he rattled on about whether it was best for her to flee on tomorrow morning's ferry to Cyprus or brave the Damascus road to Syria, Anne's mind was racing. Sam was right. No matter what peace agreements had been signed, someone was going to pay dearly for this attack on the President-elect. The Palestinian army was gone now, and so was the international peacekeeping force which had been supposed to protect the civilian population. But the Israelis were still at the gates of West Beirut, and the Phalange militiamen were right behind them. Despite the departure of the PLO fighters, almost everyone in this war-torn city – from the aged owners of cigarette kiosks to boys who were too young to dream of buying condoms – had a gun stashed away somewhere for last-ditch insurance. There would be more fighting, maiming, dying. Dully Anne turned once again to that same old decision she had faced during the year and a half of the civil war, the short weeks of the Israeli incursion in '78, and the long summer of the siege. Should she stay or go? In a few days, the already overburdened hospital would overflow with yet another generation of the wounded. How could she go when she was sure she would be needed here? She had survived all these other Lebanese convulsions, and chances were that she would survive this one. Yet, just now, she felt so depleted that she couldn't bear to go another round on this one with Sam. If she told him the truth, he would bull his way back here to be by her side. It was enough that one of them would remain at risk. For his own good, she would have to lie to him. 'Okay. You win. I'll come home. I'll call you tomorrow or the day after from Damascus or Larnaca.'

But before they could say more, Anne heard a producer in the newsroom bellowing something about cut-ins and deadlines. Sam bid her a hasty goodbye.

That night Anne sat up in bed twiddling the radio dial from one station to another. When she heard the Lebanese national anthem played like a dirge on the airwaves, she knew that Bashir Gemayel – and Lebanon's chance for a peaceful tomorrow – had died in the rubble of Phalange headquarters. She lay sleepless that night.

The next morning when, at first light, the Israelis moved in and occupied West Beirut she was standing on the half-demolished balcony of her apartment. Stay in your homes, they shouted on loudspeakers as they wound their way through the bombed-out streets which had remained beyond their grasp all summer long. The Voice of America reported only scattered fighting between the Israelis and the Muslim militias. The BBC World Service repeated the Israeli claim that they had come in only to preserve the peace. But a Sunni Muslim broadcast warned that the Israelis were about to proceed with a house-by-house disarming of the city. Meanwhile, the Phalange had given itself over to such an orgy of mourning for its fallen leader that their radio station scarcely mentioned the Israeli occupation of the capital.

Anne went off to work. If she pretended nothing

was terribly wrong in Beirut today, perhaps her itching sense of dread would go away. Besides, even on the day that West Beirut finally fell, life went on in the hospital. A fresh batch of wounded were brought in from the morning's fighting. A little boy whose leg had been amputated weeks before was discharged in the care of his doting family. A nurse announced that she was about to marry the owner of a children's clothing shop. And still the Armenian hounded her for the best room for his mother. Before Anne went off duty, she finally gave in and had the old woman moved from the ward to a private room. At least, she thought, in a world that was utterly beyond the grasp of any sane person, she had the power to solve this one small nagging problem.

Then, as though this were any other normal week, she went home and packed a small bag for her regular Thursday overnight visit to Leila in Shatilla. Ever since the siege began, she had worked from dawn to dusk on Fridays with Leila's daughter in the clinic she had helped set up in the Palestinian refugee camp. Tonight, she fervently wanted to believe, would be no different from any other night. She and Beirut, who had survived so much else, would survive this crisis, too.

Yet when she arrived, Miriam was still at the clinic and Leila was utterly engrossed cleaning and loading the Kalashnikov Hussein had left her. Usually the two of them laughed and joked and talked far into the night. But tonight, as Leila grimly packed up her ammunition in two dirty cloth shoulder-bags, they couldn't think of anything much to say to one another. Instead of eating dinner, they drank most of a fifth of Jack Daniels and smoked a packet of Marlboros apiece.

When they finally stretched out on their iron bunks, they were still unaware that before sundown a detachment of Phalange militiamen had broken into this refugee camp and neighbouring Sabra. Bent on avenging the death of their leader, they had begun slaughtering the camp's men, women and children. The Phalange had started on the outskirts and had been methodically working their way towards the centre.

Halfway through the night, with darkness still upon them, Anne suddenly stirred. Half-asleep, she thought she must still be in the grip of a nightmare. She imagined, groggily, that she heard screams and shots. But often, these days, her dreams ran with blood and violence. During the siege she had learned to sleep through even the heaviest bombardments, and so a little yelling and a short fusillade were nothing. She was so tired. She had hardly slept the night before, and the whisky she had drunk just before she turned in last night had made her head feel heavy. She yawned, turned over automatically towards where Sam should be, and even though he wasn't there, tried to sleep again.

A moment later she sat bolt upright in bed as she heard another scream. '*El-rahmia!*' A woman's shrill voice was screeching in Arabic for mercy, and closer than any dream. '*El-najda!* Help!' Though she listened hard, the cry was not repeated.

Anne stared befuddled into the darkness. Where was she, and why was she sweating? The night was hot, and heavy with menace. The bed was hard, narrow, and not her own. Shatilla! She was in the refugee camp. Bashir Gemayel had been murdered, the Israelis had taken West Beirut, and now an Arab woman was shrieking for mercy.

Anne swung out of bed, pulled on her jeans, and wriggled into a tee-shirt. 'Leila! Wake up! Something's happening!'

'*Nam?*' Leila muttered incomprehensibly in Arabic for the length of time it took Anne to slip on her sandals, and then she, too, came to her senses and shot out of bed. By the time Anne flicked on the light, Leila was already reaching for her Kalashnikov.

'Turn off that light, you fool!'

Anne hastily did as she was told. As her eyes got used to the dark, she could make out Leila's slim silhouette in her military fatigues with the gun pointed straight at the door. Leila's eyes, and the trigger of the machine-gun, glittered. 'What do you think's happening?' Anne's voice was a whisper.

'They've come for us.'

Anne moistened her dry lips with her tongue. 'The Israelis?'

'Or their mad dogs, the Phalange.'

'You think they're attacking the camp?'

'I think they're massacring my people.'

'That just can't be.' Though she had spent her lifetime here in Beirut, Anne was still both an American and a Jew. She might not always agree with their policies, but in her heart she believed in her country and her father's people. Before the PLO left, the American negotiators had promised that the civilian population, particularly in the refugee camps, would be protected. A massacre simply could not be happening. The Israelis were in control of West Beirut now. Surely they wouldn't let either their own troops or those of their Christian allies enter this refugee camp and begin a pogrom against the Palestinians. The Israelis were Jews, and civilized people.

'You're wrong, Anne. This is Lebanon. If the Phalange are running amok here in Shatilla, then God help us. Because they'll make us all pay for the death of Bashir. You've heard what the Phalange say. "The only good Palestinian is a dead Palestinian." A massacre *can* happen here. The Christians have done it before, and they can do it again. You remember the hundreds who died during the civil war on Black Saturday here in Beirut and in Karantina. And the thousands who were slaughtered at the Tel Zataar camp.'

As though keeping the record straight still mattered, Anne reminded Leila that the Muslims had conducted their own revenge massacre during the civil war. 'And Damour? The Muslim forces wiped out a whole Christian town there.'

'As I said, this is Lebanon.' Leila's gun moved up and down on her shoulder as she shrugged. 'But tonight, my friend, I am very much afraid that it's the Christians who are out for blood.'

From far away a short burst of automatic gunfire rent the night, followed by high-pitched women's screams, and finally silence.

'You hear? How else do you explain that, eh?' Leila waved the butt of her machine-gun in the direction of the shooting.

'Maybe some militiamen are fighting the Israelis. The airport's not far away. Maybe Amal and the Druze are trying to retake the airport.'

'Brilliant deduction, Anne. Very likely. An Amazon unit of Druze women are taking Beirut airport tonight. That would account for the women's screams. Tomorrow they'll take their pistols and bows and arrows and ride down on horseback to seize Tel Aviv.'

'You don't have to be so sarcastic.' Anne lit a cigarette and passed one to Leila to make peace. 'I heard on the radio this afternoon', she continued, giving voice to the fear inside her, 'that Sharon said there were two thousand terrorists in Sabra, Shatilla and Borj al-Barajneh. The BBC said he wanted to "winkle" them out.'

'Kill us all, he means. Kill every Palestinian man, woman and child.' Leila smoked in silence for a moment. 'Do you have your passport with you?'

'My passport? Yes, of course.' Like everyone else in Lebanon, during the civil war she had got into the habit of always carrying her identification papers in case she was stopped at a roadblock. 'Why do you ask?'

'Because, if I'm right about what's happening out there tonight, that passport may be your only way out of this death trap.' Leila let that possibility sink in for a moment before she asked another question. 'But tell me, in your American passport, does it list your religion?'

'Of course not. America's not like here.' Lebanese identity cards always stated the bearer's religion. 'At home church and state are totally separate.'

'That's too bad. Being able to prove you're an American *and* a Jew might be double indemnity when they finally get around to us.'

'I wish you wouldn't talk like that.' Anne laughed nervously.

Again they heard screams, but this time they went on and on.

'Are you afraid?' Anne's eyes were so accustomed to the dark now that she could see the expressions cross Leila's face.

The Palestinian's eyes widened, and a spasm passed over her features. 'Petrified. Why else would I be standing here talking to you instead of going out there to see what's up?' Leila took her hand away from the trigger. 'And you? Are you afraid?' She brushed her curly hennaed hair away from her eyes. 'To die, I mean?'

'Sure. Especially tonight. When it's so near you can feel it.' Anne shuddered. 'Funny, but it smells like death tonight. I mean, sometimes when I'm with somebody who's about to die, I can smell it on them. There's a dry smell, like the earth, and yet wet, like blood.' Again she shuddered. 'I'm giving myself the willies.'

'Can you smell death on me tonight, Anne?'

'You or me. One of us for sure. Maybe both of us.'

'Allah!' Leila swore under her breath. 'If I die, now, just when I've found him . . .' But then the corners of her mouth curled up in a sort of smile. 'At least I would die happy.' She laughed, but unhappily. 'I've never been very happy, you know. If I had been born an American, I would be considered a total failure. I've never pursued happiness very well.'

'Neither have I.' Anne threw her cigarette down on the floor and ground it out with her sandal. 'I don't want to die tonight, either. I know what you mean about just finding Hussein. It's like that with Sam and me now, too . . . He'll never forgive me if I get killed here. I lied to him, you know. When he called to tell me about Bashir and that explosion, I promised him I'd leave Beirut right away.'

'And now I bet you wish you had.'

'You bet.'

They both laughed.

In the dark, the only movement was the glowing tips of their cigarettes as they smoked in silence.

Shyly, then, Anne brought up something else. 'Do you remember that day long ago when the four of us had our fortunes told at the Crescent?'

'How could I forget? Ha! Remember how scared Camilla was when the hag saw blood in her future? And Fatima hadn't wanted to do it at all, but she believed every word.'

'Madame Kismet warned me about betrayal.' Anne smiled ruefully. 'She wasn't far off on that one. But you know, just the other day, when I was thinking about all that – actually, it was after I found out that Charles was CIA – I tried to remember what she'd seen in your future.'

'Power. Most of all she saw power. I was very pleased about that at the time.' Leila laughed. 'And she saw two or three husbands. Again, spot on. But I don't remember much of the rest of it.' This time there was a touch of hysteria to her laughter. 'I don't recall her saying a word about my being murdered in a refugee camp at the age of forty-five.'

'Leila! That's enough!' Anne looked down at her watch. It was almost four. It would be light soon. 'I should go to the clinic. Mimi's there. I'd like to make sure she's all right.'

'Mimi!' Now that her daughter's name had been spoken aloud, Leila's careful control snapped. 'I wish to God she wasn't stuck in here, too. I should have sent her back to Switzerland. Or England. Or insisted that she be evacuated with Hussein and her brothers. She's only twenty, Anne! *Twenty!*'

'She's a wonderful young woman. My best nurse. You must be very proud of her.'

'I love her more than anything.'

'Yes.' Anne sighed. 'Look, I really think I should go to the clinic. If people are being hurt, that's where I should be.'

Leila was quiet for a second until once again she had mastered her emotions. 'And if there's any fighting, that's where I should be. If what I think is happening out there is happening, it's better to go out and meet it than to cower here waiting for it to come and get me.' She cleared her throat. 'Anne, maybe we should try to stick together for a while. I'll be your armed escort. At least we can go to the clinic together to check on Mimi.' Leila's voice sounded strangled. 'I want to see her, you know?'

'I know.' Anne smiled. 'Lead on, captain!'

Leila put down her Kalashnikov and wordlessly hugged her old friend. 'Courage,' she said. They clung to each other for a moment before Leila hung her ammunition bags from her shoulders and picked up her gun.

Cautiously, Leila opened the door and then looked both ways up the narrow lane that ran outside the ramshackle breeze-block house. She nodded to Anne, and together in the greying light they crept outside. The clinic was near the centre of the camp in an abandoned garage a good half mile from Leila's house. At first, as they skulked along towards their destination, they could see and hear nothing. No one moved in the narrow lanes. But as Leila led the way with her gun in firing position, once or twice they saw anxious faces just behind the shattered windows. When they had progressed a little way, an old man poked out his grizzled head and asked them what was happening. The shooting had woken him, but he could find nothing about it on the radio. He was alone, for his sons – all three of them fighters in Fatah, he said proudly – had left with the PLO. Could he join them, he begged? He had a pistol. He was sorry he had no bullets for it, but at least he had a pistol. When Leila and Anne nodded, he at once came out and tagged along behind them.

They had just turned into a wider lane that traversed the camp, when a teenage girl came running at them full tilt from the outer perimeter of Shatilla. 'Haddad!' she screeched at the top of her lungs. 'And the Phalange!' She was in such a panic that her Arabic sounded like some foreign language. 'Run! Hide! Now! They kill everyone!' When she saw Leila – in uniform, and with a big black gun – she stopped dead in her tracks and began crying for mercy, please not to kill her, she was a good girl and had never hurt anybody, she had always been such a very good girl.

Anne put her arms around her, patted her back, and told her not to worry, Leila was Palestinian, she had nothing to fear here.

When the girl's sobs finally began to subside, Leila stepped in and asked what she had seen.

Instead of answering, she burrowed her head babyishly in Anne's chest.

'You must tell us, *habibi*.' Leila was gently insistent. 'So we can protect you.'

The girl sighed like an old woman, and then she obeyed the woman with the gun. 'We were asleep, so at first we heard nothing. We live on the lane near the shop of Abu Hassan, you know the one, not far from the main way to Sabra? Then my mother shook me, and I sat up, and I heard something terrible. A woman crying. A little boy screaming. And bad noises.'

'Shots?' Leila suggested.

The girl shook her head. 'No. Worse. Hitting sounds. Like when we go to buy meat in the shops and the man is cutting everything up.' Again she began to cry. 'My big brothers are gone, and so is my father. There is only my mother, my aunt, my two sisters, and my small brother Ali. My sister Aisha and I ran outside to see what was the matter, and it was terrible . . .' She hid her face against Anne again.

'Go on,' Leila prodded her. 'We have no time.'

The girl wiped her eyes with her fingers, and she began to tremble. 'They were killing our neighbours. With big knives. And hatchets, like for cutting wood. They were cutting up our neighbours. Um Jaleel, and Hajj Ibrahim and little Farhad.'

'Who?' Leila's voice cracked like a whip. 'You said Haddad's men and Phalange. How do you know?'

The girl shrugged, relieved to be talking of something other than the blood. 'They were big men. Five of them. They spoke in Arabic, but not like us. Three of them talked like people from the south, and the other two like Lebanese from Beirut.'

'So how', Leila relentlessly continued, 'do you know they were Haddad's militia and Phalange?'

'I will tell you. As soon as I saw them and heard them, I did not wait, I turned and ran away. I do not know what happened to my sister. Have you seen her? Aisha? She looks like me, my sister.' The girl broke down again and then blew her nose on the sleeve of her dress. 'I yelled for her to come, and for my mother and everyone else to get out. To run! But when I turned to see if they were with me, I was alone. All around me, the people were screaming and running. Old men were jumping out of the high windows of their houses. Women were trying to climb up walls to get away. I ran and ran and ran. Finally, then, I was so tired that I had to stop. There were not so many people running away there, but there was one woman. She was from the south. Tyre, I think. She told me she had seen the badges on their uniforms and that some of them were Haddad's men and some were Phalange.'

Leila and Anne exchanged worried glances. Major Haddad's Christian militia had roamed at will for the past few years in the 'security zone' the Israelis had set up near the border. Word had it that not only was Haddad in the pay of the Israelis but that his men were bloodthirsty even by Lebanese standards. Leila shook her head. 'That's quite a combination – Haddad and the Phalange.'

'They are killing everyone,' the girl repeated. 'Maybe my mother. My sisters. My brother. My aunt.' Her red face was contorted like a howling infant's. 'Maybe they will kill me, too!'

'No, no, you'll be all right. You can stay with us,' Anne soothed her. 'Come now, stop that crying, we can't stand here for ever.' Now that Leila's chilling prediction of a massacre seemed to be coming true, Anne snapped into her familiar professional emergency mode. There was no more time, now, for morbid talk about death. She had to get to the clinic. 'Let's go.'

Leila ran ahead as the four of them coursed down the lane towards the heart of Shatilla. Others followed behind them, raising the alarm. There was screaming all around them now. Women, old men and children were pouring from their houses, running blindly like rats in a maze.

In the dawn light, they saw the clinic ahead. As though the Red Crescent insignia tacked on the crumbling wall made this makeshift hospital an inviolate sanctuary, people were fighting to get inside.

Miriam was blocking the door. 'One at a time,' she ordered. 'There's room for everyone. But be calm. Come in one at a time.'

'Mimi!' Leila held out her arms. 'Oh, Mimi!'

Anne took her nurse's place at the door, as Leila and Miriam embraced. Leila held tight to her daughter and her Kalashnikov.

'They say the Phalange are killing everyone, Ummie.' Miriam studied her mother's face. 'They say it's as bad as Tel Zataar. They say the soldiers are at the edge of the camp and that they won't let anyone out. They say the Israelis sent up flares during the night so the Phalange could kill us better. Is what they say right, Ummie?'

Leila's eyes widened and then glistened with sudden tears. She had not known it was as bad as that. 'We must be brave, *habibi*.'

The mother and daughter looked into each other's eyes.

'There's no way out then, Ummie?'

'I will see.' Leila had never coddled her daughter, and now was no exception. If death was coming this morning, she would give Miriam time to prepare for it. 'But probably not.'

The girl sighed. 'So all we can do is be brave, then?'

'Yes.' Leila managed to smile. 'You can be brave for me, and I will be brave for you.'

'No,' Miriam answered softly. 'Both of us will be brave for Palestine.'

Leila was crying as again she embraced her daughter. But then she broke away. 'I'll be back,' she promised Anne as she gave the old man and the teenage girl a reassuring pat on the back. Without another word, she turned and ran back with her gun in the direction from which they had just come.

Anne stepped inside the chaos of the clinic. Two

more young Palestinian volunteer nurses and the head Swedish nurse were fighting a losing battle to soothe their patients. Those who could walk or crawl were trying to get out of their beds and escape from the clinic. At the same time, others who had just barged in from outside were trying to sneak into the beds so they could pretend they were patients. Some were screeching tales of horror to their disbelieving neighbours. Haddad's men were lining everyone up against walls and shooting them in their backs. Even dead women were being raped. The Phalange were cutting people up with knives, blowing them to bits with grenades, butchering the dead bodies. They were even killing the cats, dogs, horses and donkeys. An old woman sobbed that she had seen one of Haddad's men cut her infant grandson's throat, and then carve him up into bits like a chicken, and then arrange his dismembered limbs in a circle, or was it a cross? Some of the patients were so afraid that the clinic began to stink of urine and faeces.

For the next two hours Anne was so busy trying to calm the hysteria that she didn't have time to be afraid for herself. She had assumed she would have to cope with the medical emergencies of those injured in the night, but this time there were no wounded. She failed to convince those who had come to her clinic for sanctuary that they would be just as safe somewhere else. Stubbornly they refused to move. When an old man said he had been turned back by a Lebanese soldier at the edge of Shatilla, a fresh wave of tears and lamentations swept the clinic. They were all stuck here. They would all die here. They were all doomed.

By mid-morning they could hear the gunfire coming closer. So many people were packed inside the clinic that Miriam had to turn everyone else away. An old man in a corner chanted verses from the Koran. A young woman beside him nursed her infant daughter. Everyone's eyes were trained on the door.

Leila burst in. Her uniform was torn at the knee, and her left arm was bleeding profusely from a gunshot wound. 'They're coming! They'll be here any minute!' She waved her gun at Anne and her daughter. 'Over here! Quick! Do as I say!'

When the three of them were together by the door, Anne whispered quickly in English. 'How bad is it?'

'Worse than you can imagine. They're killing everyone. They'll kill us, too.'

'Allah protect us!' Miriam's lip trembled.

'But from what they're all saying, this has been going on all night long,' Anne said. 'Surely someone – the Israelis, the Lebanese army, *someone* – will come in and stop it.'

'Not soon enough to save *us*.' Leila looked her old friend in the eye. 'The most we can hope for is to get you out alive.' She looked speculatively around the room. 'And that nurse over there. The fair one. What is she, English?'

'Ingrid's a Swede, Ummie.'

'She looks it.' Leila frowned at her daughter's dark hair and eyes. 'I wish to God I could pass you off as anything but a Palestinian. I'd shoot Ingrid right between the eyes and give you her passport if it would get you out, Mimi. But I'll try to get that Swede out, instead.' Leila looked intently around the clinic until she spotted the old man they had first picked up in the lane outside her house. 'You! Old grandfather! Do you still have your pistol?'

'No bullets,' he reminded her.

'*Malesh*, never mind. Can I borrow it? Please? And quickly! We have no time!'

When he surrendered it to Leila, she handed it over to Anne. 'Hold it as if you know how to use it. And don't tell anyone it isn't loaded.'

'But this is crazy,' Anne protested. 'You can't really tell me that they're about to come in here and kill all these people.'

'That's exactly what's been happening in Sabra and Shatilla since sundown last night.' Leila's voice caught. 'Hundreds, maybe thousands, have been slaughtered.'

Just then the screams outside grew louder, and the door banged open. A big man with a bigger knife stood framed in the doorway. Leila let not only him but three more of his blood-spattered comrades get all the way inside. Then she lunged in front of Anne and screamed an imperative command in English. 'Stop where you are. One more step, and I shoot.'

The four Phalange militiamen stared into the barrel of Leila's Kalashnikov. Two of them were carrying M-16s, and another had a hatchet in his hand. But, after all these hours of killing unarmed civilians, they had entered with their guns on their shoulders instead of in firing positions.

'A real terrorist,' one said as he sized Leila up.

'They're all terrorists,' another corrected him as wolfishly he took in the crowded clinic.

'Step up now, all of you! All four of you away from that door!' Leila motioned them to come closer. Reluctantly they obeyed. 'Are any of you officers?' she demanded imperiously. They remained silent, but a boy with his legs in a cast pointed to the lieutenant's insignia on the tallest one's shoulder. 'You!' Leila ordered. 'Step forward.' When he did, she pointed to Anne. 'You see this doctor? She's an American. And not just any American. Her husband's a CIA agent, and her brother's a US Marine captain. Charles Jenkins is the CIA head of station here in Beirut. Maybe you've heard of him? And her brother is Captain Benjamin Rosen. He was just here in Beirut with the Marines. You may even have met him.' When the lieutenant shook his head, Leila briskly continued. 'You'll hear of them both if you kill this doctor. This lady is very special, you see. She's not only a doctor, an American, and the wife of a CIA agent and the sister of a US Marine. She's also Jewish. Aren't you, Anne?'

Anne nodded. This was no time to quibble about her father being a non-religious Jew, her mother being an Episcopalian, and herself being nothing much more than terrified.

'Show him your passport, Anne.'

When she handed it over, the lieutenant blanched when he saw the dark blue cover with the gold fighting eagle. This one most certainly was not a Palestinian. He did not know whether to believe that story about her being Jewish and having connections with the CIA and the Marines, but he wasn't inclined to take any chances. '*Ahlen was ahlen,*' he said, his Lebanese manners automatically working even in the midst of a massacre. 'You are welcome. But how can someone like *you* be *here*? You should not be here! An American! In Shatilla!'

'Quite right,' Leila agreed. 'Which is where you come into the picture. You are going to escort this American doctor out of this camp. And you will take that Swedish nurse over there with you.'

'Ingrid!' Anne called out to her head nurse. 'Show the lieutenant your passport.'

When she did, he shrugged sullenly.

'Neither of them should be here.'

'I say we kill them all,' one of the militiamen muttered.

'No one will know we did it,' another added. 'What are two more bodies among so many?'

'And don't forget,' the last one chimed in, 'we're bringing in the bulldozers. No one will ever even find their bodies.'

'There will be an international outcry', Leila snapped, 'if these two women are killed. Do you want to risk that?'

The lieutenant briefly thought it over. 'No,' he admitted. He looked at his men for support. 'What do we care about letting two go? Be satisfied with the others.'

'Then,' Leila continued, 'you will take the doctor and nurse out of the camp?'

'Yes,' he finally conceded.

'Just in case you change your mind outside,' Leila continued, 'the doctor here has a pistol. She will keep it trained on you until she and Ingrid are outside the camp. You understand?'

When he nodded, Leila's eyes flicked back to Anne. 'Now, go while you can.'

'And you? And Mimi? I can't leave you here. And all my patients!'

'You have no choice. There are, finally, no more choices.' Leila's eyes were as steady as her trigger finger as she stared grimly at Anne. 'Just do me one final favour. Tell Hussein I died well.'

'Oh, Leila!' Anne gave her old friend a final anguished look. But then she aimed the pistol at the head of the lieutenant and followed him and the Swedish nurse out of the door.

Inside, Leila faced the three remaining militiamen. 'Now you die,' she said as she pulled the firing pin and cut them down in cold blood. But a few moments later there were others behind them, and this time they came in with their guns blazing. Miriam was one of the first to fall. Seconds later, after an especially sharp volley, Leila fell dead on the floor. More militiamen streamed inside. They sprayed the clinic with automatic gunfire until not one person inside was left alive.

And, only a little later, when they saw Leila clad in a Palestinian uniform with a Kalashnikov beside her, five of them raped her dead body.

Epilogue

Anne and the taxi driver peered to the left and peered to the right, looking for what had once been the Crescent cabaret. But even though the driver had been born and raised in Beirut, and Anne had spent almost all her life here, they couldn't get their bearings amidst the rubble. The turquoise sea still beat on the golden rocks, and above them the green mountains arched to the sky. But too many man-made landmarks were gone now. Down here by the seaside in Raouche, as almost everywhere in West Beirut, the damage sustained during the summer's siege had been so heartbreakingly extensive that Anne would not have been surprised if the surf, too, beat red with blood. Once bustling luxury hotels were now grim burned-out hulks. Rubbish blew in the wind. Except for the nervous American, French and Italian peacekeeping troops – who had been ordered back to Beirut as soon as an outraged world learned of the massacres in the refugee camps – the haunted streets seemed a neighbourhood of ghosts.

'It isn't what it used to be,' the driver said as he watched a fat old peasant woman carrying a plastic jug of water on her head back from the sea. Refugees from the south and what was left of the Palestinian camps now squatted inside shuttered cinemas, restaurants, nightclubs, cocktail bars – any shelter that was still left standing. Beirut's once-shimmering Western façade had fallen away, and so much of the city had regressed back in time that on certain streets at certain times 'the Paris of the East' seemed little more than a primitive village. Once, thirteen centuries ago, the thriving metropolis that the Phoenicians, Greeks and Romans had built in Beirut had been destroyed by an earthquake. This second, man-made catastrophe was no less devastating. The driver sighed. 'Tch! I remember . . .' He was too disheartened to compare the present with the past.

'I remember, too,' Anne said. These days, just a week after the massacres in the Sabra and Shatilla refugee camps, she remembered too much. Once she had left Beirut tomorrow for New York, those memories, she thought, were going to be too painful for her ever to bear to come back. 'Perhaps you should stop here,' she suggested. 'I think I can find my way better on foot.'

'Please, no, lady,' the driver said. 'These streets are not safe. I would not let my sister walk them. No, you sit. We will find it together.'

Anne smiled and settled back on the dusty seat. Everything that had been gracious in Beirut was not lost, after all. The ordinary people were as caring and as gallant as ever.

The taxi turned a corner and crawled down a road that had lost its street sign in one or another of the wars. Ahead, squatting patiently on what was left of the kerb, a big woman in an all-enveloping black *abaya* robe fingered her prayer beads.

'Look at that,' the driver said in disgust. 'Shia, I bet! Always before I defended the Shia. They are Muslims just like us, I always said. Even though they were always different and always will be different, they are our brothers and our sisters. But now they are taking over our city. If they have their way, they will make Beirut like Teheran. On my street now they are taking down the martyrs' posters of the Palestinian fighters and putting up big pictures of their Ayatollah. Here! In Beirut! I ask my God when I pray, now, to have mercy on Beirut. But maybe Allah does not hear us anymore. Maybe He never heard us.'

As they passed the peasant woman in black, Anne idly glanced at the small triangle of her face which was all that was left uncovered by her cloak. She looked again incredulously. 'Fatima!' Excitedly she told the driver to stop and reverse.

'You know her?' The driver looked doubtfully back at the obviously rich Western woman who had flagged him down outside the American University Hospital.

'She is my best friend,' Anne said as she gave him a generous tip. 'Or one of them, anyway.'

She bounded out of the taxi, and the two women fell on one another. They held on and rocked back and forth in a loving embrace. In the week since the massacre, they had talked often on the telephone. But until now they had not been able to manage to see each other. This afternoon's reunion with Camilla would, they knew, be the last time they would be together before they went their separate ways.

'Let me look at you,' Anne murmured. She stood back and beamed at that dear face which she might never see again.

'I was waiting and waiting,' Fatima said. 'Muhammad brought me over early, but then he had to leave for another of his meetings at the mosque. I didn't think you were coming. You know, with things as they are now, I thought . . . was afraid . . . something had happened.'

'I just couldn't find the place, that's all. It's so different here now.' Anne looked curiously around the ravaged street where once chauffeurs had double-parked their air-conditioned limousines as they waited for their masters to finish their pleasure-palace diversions. This street used to be lined with bistros, discos and fancy luxury shops. But now every entrance was barricaded with sandbags and barrels piled high to minimize bomb damage. Here and there a building had collapsed upon itself. But soiled laundry flapping on clothes-lines which had been strung up on second-floor balconies was evidence that families had moved in for the duration. Anne frowned at the sadly decrepit building behind them. 'That can't be the Crescent?'

'What's left of it.' The top floors had sustained a direct hit from some barrage or other, but the ground floor still stood solid. Sandbags were piled helter-skelter in front of what had been the plate glass windows. There was no signboard outside it. But from the rickety tables and chairs scattered inside, it seemed the once-glorious Crescent had been pressed into service as a night-time coffee-house for the men who now lived in the neighbourhood.

'I guess it wasn't such a good idea to come back here,' Anne admitted. 'We should have gone to the Rue Bliss. Or even my apartment. But I thought . . . Leila would have liked us to have it here.' She smiled crookedly. It still hurt even to say Leila's name. Nonetheless, before she left Beirut, she had felt compelled to call Fatima and Camilla together for a sort of memorial service for their friend. None of them had had the heart to say goodbye to her in the ghastly mass grave that Shatilla had become. Instead, sentimentally, they had wanted to harken back to the halcyon days. But the Saint Georges Hotel was utterly destroyed now, along with so many of the other haunts of their youth. Remembering those last hours in Shatilla, when she and Leila had recalled Madame Kismet, Anne had suggested they assemble one final time at that cabaret where the gypsy had told their fortunes so long ago.

'*Malesh,*' Fatima assured her. 'Never mind. All that matters is that we are together. This is as good as anywhere else.' She pointed at the tattered reed bag she had left sitting by the kerb. 'I brought my primus stove. And cups. And some carrot *halwah* and *kunnifeh* just for you, Anne. It is so wonderful to be able to buy things in the shops now. And to eat what we want! My children were so hungry!' She smiled. 'So, you will see, we can have our tea inside the old Crescent. Like a picnic. No one will bother us.' Anxiously she turned back and scanned the street. 'But where is Camilla?'

Just then they heard horns blaring, and the first of a cavalcade of three shiny black Mercedes limousines rounded the corner with a whine of brakes. Green, white and red Lebanese cedar-tree flags waved gaily above the polished fenders. The doors of the first car were plastered with poster-sized portraits of Bashir Gemayel, whom the Phalange had all but canonized since his assassination. An instant later, the cars screeched to a halt before them. Doors flew open, and Phalange militiamen jumped out with their guns at the ready. In the back seat of the middle car, Camilla sat resplendent in a flowered black silk Givenchy tea-dress. One militiaman opened the door for her, and another escorted her out with a flourish.

'Chéries!' Rapturously, as the militiamen looked stonily on, Camilla threw herself first in Anne's arms and then in Fatima's. But when her friends didn't embrace her with the same feeling, Camilla drew back. 'What's wrong?'

Anne could not bear to be so near to these Phalange. The last time she had seen men with that insignia on these uniforms was in Shatilla. She had hoped that she would never see their like again. Icily she inclined her head towards the militiamen. 'They're what's wrong. How *could* you bring them here today?'

'Oh, them.' Camilla moved closer and whispered. 'I didn't want to, really. But Maurice insisted. He said no wife of his was coming over here on her own.' After the massacres, in another hastily called election at the Chamber of Deputies, Bashir's brother Amin Gemayel had been elected president. But after enduring so many convulsive shocks, traumatized Beirut was still in a state of high anxiety. So much had happened that it was impossible to believe that the nightmare was finally over. 'He shut me up in the house. When I go out now – *if* I go out – all these go with me.' She shrugged. 'What could I do? I wanted to come. Maurice and I go back to Switzerland next week. I wanted to say *adieu* to you. And to *chère* Leila.' As she looked around at the war-torn street for the first time, she shuddered. 'And to all this.'

'Always you are welcome here.' Fatima resolutely took Camilla by the arm. 'But, come, let us go inside. All the street is watching us.'

As Anne glanced up at the blown-out windows of the buildings flanking the street, she glimpsed dark heads disappearing back into the shadows of their squatters' havens. These battle-hardened Beirutis knew enough to keep their heads down at the arrival of every conquering army, whether it was the Israelis, the Syrians or the Phalange. She wondered if there were still snipers on these streets. Her father had been gunned down only a few blocks away. 'Yes,' she agreed. 'Let's go inside.'

But before Camilla's military escort would allow the women to enter the coffee-house, they first burst in the door and reconnoitred for gunmen. When they were finally satisfied that the wife of the Christian deputy would be safe, they sullenly retreated to the doorway where they kept a watchful vigil on the street with their M-16s in firing position.

'This isn't quite as I imagined it,' Anne apologized as the three of them gingerly stepped inside the coffee-house. She hated having these cut-throats keeping such a sinister watch over what she had hoped would be a fond memorial service. She could never forgive the Phalange for the atrocities at Sabra and Shatilla. She blamed the Israelis, too, for sitting on the sidelines and letting that massacre proceed. She had only been slightly mollified by Israel's appointing of a panel to investigate their country's responsibility for the atrocity. All the fact-finding panels in the world, however, couldn't raise Leila and those hundreds – or perhaps thousands – of victims from their mass graves. So far as Anne was concerned, America, too, shared the bloodguilt for Sabra and Shatilla. Before the Palestinian commandos had departed from the besieged city, the Americans had guaranteed the safety of the civilian population of West Beirut. Yet the US Marines and the other peacekeeping troops had left before the shooting started. When her brother Ben had arrived back in Beirut with the Marines last week, for once the two of them had agreed that it was a national disgrace that American troops had pulled out of Beirut so prematurely. Ben had confided to her that he had argued over the decision with his commanding officers, but had been told that here once again – as in Vietnam, Ben told his sister hotly – the politicians had overruled the military's best judgement. Brother and sister had agreed that, as Americans and as Jews, they could never forgive or forget Sabra and Shatilla.

Camilla was shaking her head as she looked around at what had once been her mother's beautiful cabaret. The jangling amber bead curtains and red plush banquettes were long gone, as were the French bistro tables and the candles flickering under red glass shades. The phosphorescent crescent moon that had glowed in the dark above the womb of a stage where Nirvana had entertained the *beau monde* of Beirut had disappeared. So, too, had the gilded audiences that had once filled the place to standing-room-only on weekend evenings. Now the shabby coffee-house was bare except for scarred tables and a few meagre wooden chairs and benches. Glued up on the walls were those ubiquitous West Beirut 'martyrs' posters' of young Palestinian *fedayeen*. 'Beirut will never surrender!' was spray-painted in Arabic along the wall where the mirrored bar had once nestled. 'Mama will be heartbroken when I tell her what has happened to her club.'

'Hers is not the only heart that is broken,' Anne said as she pulled up a chair and sat down. Camilla wrinkled her nose in dismay as she teetered in her stiletto heels across the rough wooden floor. She opened her Gucci handbag, extracted an embroidered linen handkerchief, and dusted off a chair before lowering herself into it with a sigh.

Fatima, meanwhile, had gone to work lighting her primus stove and boiling up her pot of tea. But as she leaned over to rummage in her bag for the cups, Fatima's robe and scarf slipped. Before she could cover herself again, Anne and Camilla caught a glimpse of her snow-white hair. She – and they – were only forty-five years old.

'Blanc!' Camilla was more aghast at this sign of the passage of time than she had been at the devastation all around them. Her hand crept up to touch her own youthful blonde hair. Her beautician had touched up the roots only yesterday. Yet she was as old as Fatima. If she were to let her hair grow out, would she look like an old woman, too?

'It has been like that since my Ali died,' Fatima confided. 'It happened the night after Anne told me.' She snapped her fingers. 'I went to bed with black hair and woke up with white.' She made a sound almost like a laugh. 'I am lucky, no, that always I wear this scarf? Only my girls – and now, the two of you – know how it is with me.' Again she laughed, but this time with more humour, as she unwrapped her homemade cakes and laid them out on the table. 'Good thing that I never wanted another husband, eh? Even the old Hajj, back in Suker, would not have wanted to marry an old lady like me.'

'Any man would be lucky to have someone like you,' Anne said loyally. She popped a mouth-watering piece of *kunnifeh* into her mouth. Almost everything else had gone sour in Beirut, but Fatima's cakes were as sweet as ever. For the first time since she had arrived this afternoon, she began to feel at home.

Camilla, too, relaxed and slipped back not only into their old sisterly camaraderie but also into her old carping about men. 'You're better off without one,' she told Fatima. 'I should have stopped with Pierre. And even with him, it was good only for a year or two.' She rolled her eyes and took a satisfying bite of carrot *halwah*. 'Men! They are all such bad boys. With their big guns. And their bigger lies.'

But Anne had finally learned to sing a different – and more harmonious – tune. 'They're not *all* bad,' she said, thinking of Sam. 'They're not so very different from us, you know. It's only sometimes that they seem to come from a different planet, that's all.'

'I think I hate them all,' Camilla confided.

Fatima handed them both their tea. 'I cannot say the same. With my Ali, it was always very wonderful. So many happy years we had!' Her round face was wreathed in a smile as she remembered. 'You know,' she continued, 'my mother said something to me once. "You're born alone, and you die alone. Praise Allah for everyone and everything He gives you in between." My mother was a very wise woman. God gave me a good man, many children, and you, my good friends. I cannot complain.'

'I would, if I were you,' Camilla said.

'Yes, you probably would,' Anne agreed. They were all laughing as they used to, when Fatima finally finished making their tea and pulled up a chair for herself.

'It is good to be together again, *n'est-ce pas?*' Camilla said.

'If only . . .' Yet Anne could not bear to mention the name of the one who was missing.

Both Camilla and Fatima reached out and covered her hands with theirs.

'It must have been terrible.' Fatima shook her head. 'So terrible!'

'You were, I think, with her at the end.' Camilla bit her lip. 'Do you want to talk about it?'

'I don't want to think about it, much less talk about it.' Anne's eyes clouded over. 'But, yes, I suppose I must. We are here today for her.' She ran her hands despairingly through her hair. 'She was very brave. *So brave!* But I guess that shouldn't have been a surprise. You know how bold she always was. The first on the dance floor. The first in the swimming pool. The first to let a boy French-kiss her. The first at everything . . .'

'And now,' Fatima finished for her, 'the first of us to die.' She sighed. 'I pray for her every day now. My prayers get longer and longer, I have so many to remember.'

'She saved my life.' In fits and starts, Anne told them about her last hours at Shatilla, and how at the bitter end she had been forced to leave Leila and Miriam. When she and the Swedish nurse had marched out of that clinic with her pistol trained on the Phalange lieutenant, she had known in her gut that Leila and her daughter had died in the long burst of gunfire she heard a few moments later out on the lane. She had feared that she, too, might never make it to the perimeter of the camp. Every step of the way, she had been expecting a bullet in the back or a hatchet in her head. When finally she had stumbled through the main gate and screamed in American-accented English at the Lebanese and Israeli soldiers there to let her and the others out, she had been closer to madness than ever before in her life.

'But maybe she didn't die after all,' Camilla suggested. 'You know Leila, how smart she was . . . is.'

'I went back two days later, when the troops had

finally gone in and stopped the killing. I had almost as much trouble getting inside Shatilla as I had getting out. The Israelis and the Lebanese Army weren't letting anyone in. I suppose they were ashamed, eh? Sam told me on the phone that even the networks could hardly get inside to record what happened there. But I used my medical identification.' Anne shook her head. 'I had to wear a mask over my nose and mouth. The stench from the bodies . . . I don't have to tell you how that was, do I? *Do I?*'

'Not if you don't want to,' Fatima assured her. 'We have all seen the newspapers.' Her lip curled at the Phalange militiamen silhouetted in the doorway. 'They are devils!'

'I haven't seen a newspaper all week,' Camilla admitted. 'Maurice's family won't let anybody bring anything into the house that says one word about what happened in the camps. Maurice say only a few people died there. He says everything the Muslims put on the television about Sabra and Shatilla is lies and Palestinian propaganda.'

'I was there,' Anne said quietly. *'And I know.* Certainly many hundreds of people died in those camps. Perhaps as many as three thousand were actually killed. And Leila was one of them.' She let out a despairing rush of breath. 'I went back to the clinic, you know, that day when I finally got inside Shatilla. Or rather, I went back to the place where the clinic had been. But I couldn't find Leila or anyone else who had died there. Because the Phalange had brought in bulldozers and covered up their dirty work with tons of earth. So I guess in a way she's buried there. In her Shatilla.'

'Poor Leila,' Camilla sighed. 'To die like that. And so young.'

'Not so young,' Fatima corrected her. 'She's *our* age. But her girl was only twenty. Just a little older than my girls. I wept when I heard about Mimi.'

'I called Hussein,' Anne continued. 'As soon as I was sure she was dead, I rang Sam in New York and had his bloodhounds track down Hussein in South Yemen. She had asked me to do that, you know. The last thing she said was for me to call Hussein and to tell him that she had died well.'

'Allah!' Fatima wiped away a tear. 'So that was her last request!'

'So what did Hussein say, exactly?' Camilla's eyes were as wide as a child's listening to a fairy tale by Grimm.

Anne shrugged. 'What does anyone say at a time like that?' She thought for a moment. 'He didn't say anything at first. But then he said that he had known he had lost her as soon as he heard about the massacres. He asked me if she had his gun with her at the end, and he seemed glad when I said that she did.' Anne swallowed hard as she struggled to keep back the tears. 'He started to cry then. Hussein Ibrahim weeping on the phone!' Anne, too, broke down.

While Anne sobbed and Camilla, too, hid her face in her hands and cried, Fatima poured them all more tea. 'I will miss her,' she said when finally the other two sat up and wiped their eyes. 'But I like to think that at the end Leila found a sort of peace. Yet her answers were not always my answers. Always Leila burned so hot about so much! Truly, she was very Palestinian. She had their good points and their bad points, too. For her, maybe it was right to die like that. Maybe, in a way, she died happy.'

'And yet,' Anne said, remembering that hellish morning . . . 'For *her* to die like *that!*'

They all sighed.

'There's one other thing I wanted to tell you about . . . all that.' Anne's voice was thin with emotion. 'Those terrible moments when I walked through Shatilla, I promised myself that if I ever got out of that hellhole alive, I would stop being such a fool and let myself go and love Sam all the way.' Tremulously she smiled. 'Like he deserves. And I guess like *I* deserve, too.' She bit her lip to stop it from trembling. 'When you live through something like that, when you see what I saw, either you give in altogether to despair at how terrible life can be. Or – somehow, against the odds, despite everything! – you dig in and commit yourself to all that's good in this life.' Again – hopefully – she smiled. 'Having lived through the worst that day, I'm damned glad to have the best of life with my Sam now!'

'Ah!' Fatima beamed at Anne. '*Mabruk!* God's blessings upon you!'

'So you're finally marrying Sam,' Camilla said.

'Finally.' Anne nearly blushed. 'We have to wait until I get my divorce from Charles. But then, yes, we'll get married in New York.'

'Maybe you can have a double wedding.' Camilla paused for dramatic effect. 'My mother and Shaykh Georges are getting married!'

Anne and Fatima grinned.

'Her tenth husband – or is it the ninth or the eleventh – who knows?' Camilla wagged her head. 'They're getting married at Christmas. At the Château Croisé. And she is wearing white! Along with the Nazrani veil that *we* all wore.'

'White!' Anne couldn't help laughing.

'I will pray for their happiness,' Fatima promised.

'You do that,' Camilla said. 'I'm sure the two of them are going to need all the help they can get. What a pair!' She giggled, but then she leaned forward to bring up something else that was on her mind. 'Do you remember the last time the four of us were here, in the Crescent? Mama had that gypsy tell our fortunes. How young we were then! How sure of ourselves! We were so certain that everything was always going to turn out right!' Camilla tried to laugh but managed only to smile. 'I still remember how scared I was when Madame Kismet looked into that crystal ball!'

'As I recall,' Anne dryly added, 'you were always scared to death.'

'I still am. I'll be glad to leave Beirut.' Camilla shivered and made the sign of the cross. 'There is something evil here now in this city. Do you feel it?'

'No, but I see it.' Fatima glared at the Phalange. 'At the mosque, now, they talk much about *el-jihad* – the holy war – which good Muslims must wage against the forces of evil in the world. It is so inspiring, what they say now in the mosques. Sometimes learned mullahs come all the way from Iran to talk just to us. They say, too, that there is much evil in Lebanon now. But they say that only an Islamic solution will make my country clean again.'

Camilla recoiled from her old friend. She hated it, these days, when Fatima sounded like a religious fanatic. Her eyes met Anne's, and she was relieved when the American changed the subject.

'Leila and I talked about old Madame Kismet. It was the oddest thing, but the morning of the day she died, out of the blue we both started talking about her telling our fortunes here in the Crescent. We tried to remember exactly what she had said to us. But Leila had forgotten a lot of it. All she could remember was that the gypsy had seen power for her, and two or three husbands.'

'I remember it all.' Camilla cleared her throat and summoned back the past. 'She promised Leila a big life. And then Leila said, you mean a long life. And the gypsy said no, she meant what she said.' Camilla looked tremulously at her friends. 'She was right, you know, Madame Kismet. She promised Anne betrayal. Fatima, love. Leila, power. And me, blood.'

'We all got more blood in our lives than we wanted,' Anne said.

'She saw that, too. Don't you remember how she

saw a cedar tree on a mountain, and how it all turned to blood? Lebanon!' Again Camilla had tears in her eyes. 'It's all over here now, everything!'

'Not everything.' Fatima folded her hands on her ample lap. 'I'm still here, and my children, and two million other people who can't afford to get out.'

'Would you go if you could?' Camilla asked.

Fatima shook her head and then leaned forward to share something that she thought was wonderful, which had occurred to her in the years since her husband had died. 'You remember when Madame Kismet looked into her crystal for me and saw part of a word written? She could make out an "A" and an "L", but then the rest of it was lost in a mist of what she said was "a great love". We all thought she must see my Ali in there.'

'I remember. I was very jealous. *I* wanted a great love.' Camilla sighed. 'I still do.'

'*Inshallah*. But I've been thinking that maybe that great love she saw for me wasn't "Ali" but "Allah". The love of my life is not my man but my God!' Fatima's eyes were ashine. 'I will have my great love not only for all this life but the next life, too, God willing!'

Anne smiled kindly at lonely Fatima. Each, she thought, to her own consolations.

Camilla, however, was passionately continuing on her own train of thought. 'I wonder, if Madame Kismet walked in here this minute with her crystal ball, what would she tell us this time? Will I ever find the right man? Or will I spend the rest of my life just like Mama? I can just see her, ninety-nine years old, with her twentieth husband.' Camilla laughed and then turned thoughtful. 'If we – all of us – had known that what the old gypsy told us was really our future, would we have done anything differently?'

'Everything is written in Allah's Great Book of Life,' Fatima said calmly. 'What will be, will be. *Inshallah*.'

'I have regrets,' Anne said slowly. 'If I had it all to do over again, I could have done without Mike in Boston.' Shyly, then, she reached in her handbag. 'This is for you,' she said, as she handed a document to Fatima. 'It's the deed to the villa on the Rue Bliss. *Beiti beitak*.' She invoked the customary Lebanese greeting of host to guest. 'My house is your house. But for ever, this time. Signed, sealed and delivered.'

'Your house? No, no, I could not accept that. The villa is your home. If you like, my family will live there now, and take care of it for you as long as you want. But always it is yours to come back to, Anne.'

'Ah, Fatima, when I leave tomorrow, I do not think I will ever come back.' She and Sam would live together in New York, where finally she would try to stop running away not only from the man she loved but also from the homeland and the Jewish world she also loved in her way. She would try to keep faith with what had once been the spirit of Beirut by heading that medical trauma unit she had been setting up for Lebanese children hurt in the years of fighting. But for her and those like her, Anne believed that the years in the Beirut sun were finally over. 'The villa – and Beirut, too, I suppose – are yours now.' She had thought long and hard about what to do with her parents' villa. Finally she had concluded that Fatima and her kind were heir to whatever was left now in Lebanon. After all that had happened, the exuberant and enchanting Beirut that she had loved had gone the way of other lost cities which rose and then fell and finally were no more. The old Lebanon was indeed lost, but from its ashes – as has happened many times over in the ancient, much-conquered Mediterranean – a new society would eventually rise again. Anne liked to think that her philosophical father would have seen the seeds of a civilization's regeneration in this act of inheritance.

'You are very generous, Anne. But you always were

generous! May Allah always bless you and keep you!' Fatima kissed Anne's hand. 'I will accept your gift, but only for my children. Zainab will marry her Musa this year, *inshallah*. And it is time for my Muhammad to marry his cousin Sukena. Salma will be ready soon. And somehow I will find a wife for my dear Ahmed with his American doctors' arm and a husband for my darling Elham with her American doctors' face.' Her smile was as contented as ever. 'I am such a lucky woman. To have had my Ali and our children, and now maybe grandchildren, too, very soon. The family goes on and on. I am part of something that will never end. We are a chain that will never be broken.'

Suddenly Anne remembered something. 'Hussein said almost exactly the same thing. After I told *him* about *her*, he said he would go to Tunis to tell Hamid and Farid himself. "Her sons are my sons," he said. "While they live, so does she. The chain is not broken." '

'And ours isn't either,' Camilla said. She stretched out her hands over those of her lifelong friends.

One of the militiamen at the door waved his gun their way. 'It is late,' he announced. 'Soon it is dark, madame. You must go now.'

The three of them looked at one another. They all understood there was a real finality to this parting.

'I can't bear to say goodbye,' Camilla said. 'Will I ever see either of you again? I'll never come back here either, you know. Never again. My world now will be the Riviera and the Alps and the Ile de France. But here in Beirut, there is too much heartache. Too much for me.'

'But we will always be friends,' Anne said.

'For ever,' Fatima agreed.

'*Toujours*,' Camilla promised tearfully.

As they looked at each other, Anne thought to herself that they were not the only Christian, Muslim and Jew in the troubled Middle East who still, after all that had happened to themselves and their world, were able to salvage staunch friendships with those who were supposed to be their mortal enemies. But what was fatal for the Levant, she feared, was that it was only on the personal level that trust and forgiveness were able to transcend hatred and bloodlust. At their wake of a table, they were mourning not only Leila but Beirut and Lebanon itself.

Finally then the three friends stood, kissed and promised to write. Then wiping away their tears, they made their separate ways away from the killing ground, away from the city and the country and the youths that were no more.